BY GARDNER DOZOIS

NOVELS

Strangers

Nightmare Blue (with George Alec Effinger)

Hunter's Run (with George R. R. Martin and Daniel Abraham)

SHORT-STORY COLLECTIONS

When the Great Days Come

Strange Days: Fabulous Journeys with Gardner Dozois

Geodesic Dreams

Morning Child and Other Stories

Slow Dancing Through Time

The Visible Man

EDITED BY GARDNER DOZOIS

The Year's Best Science Fiction 1–34

The New Space Opera (with Jonathan Strahan)

The New Space Opera 2 (with Jonathan Strahan)

Modern Classics of Science Fiction

Modern Classics of Fantasy

The Good Old Stuff

The Good New Stuff

Magic Tales 1–37 (with Jack Dann)

Wizards (with Jack Dann)

The Dragon's Book (with Jack Dann)

A Day in the Life

Another World

The Book of Swords

The Book of Magic

CO-EDITED WITH GEORGE R. R. MARTIN

Warriors I–III

Songs of the Dying Earth

Songs of Love and Death

Down These Strange Streets

Old Mars

Old Venus

Dangerous Women

Rogues

The
Book of
Magic

The
Book of
Magic

EDITED BY

GARDNER DOZOIS

BANTAM BOOKS
NEW YORK

The Book of Magic is a work of fiction. Names, places, and incidents are the products of the author's imagination or are used fictitiously. Any resemblance to actual events, locales, or persons, living or dead, is entirely coincidental.

Published in the United States by Bantam Books, an imprint of Random House, a division of Penguin Random House LLC, New York.

BANTAM BOOKS and the HOUSE colophon are registered trademarks of Penguin Random House LLC.

Individual story copyrights appear on pages 555–56

LIBRARY OF CONGRESS CATALOGING-IN-PUBLICATION DATA
Names: Dozois, Gardner R. editor. | Dozois, Gardner R., editor.
Title: The book of magic / edited by Gardner Dozois.
Description: New York: Bantam, 2018.
Identifiers: LCCN 2018018549 | ISBN 9780399593789 (hardback) |
ISBN 9780399593796 (ebook)
Subjects: LCSH: Fantasy fiction, American. | Fantasy fiction, English. | Short stories, American. | Short stories, English. | Magic—Fiction. | Witches—Fiction. | Wizards—Fiction. | BISAC: FICTION / Fantasy / Short stories. | FICTION / Fantasy / Epic.
Classification: LCC PS648.F3 B65 2018 | DDC 813/.0876608—dc23
LC record available at https://lccn.loc.gov/2018018549

Printed in the United States of America on acid-free paper

randomhousebooks.com

2 4 6 8 9 7 5 3 1

First Edition

Book design by Caroline Cunningham

For

All those who work magic with words,

the most potent magic there is

Contents

Introduction

BY GARDNER DOZOIS

Sorcerer, witch, shaman, wizard, seer, root woman, conjure man . . . the origins of the magic-user, the-one-who-intercedes-with-the-spirits, the one who knows the ancient secrets and can call upon the hidden powers, the one who can see both the spirit world and the physical world, and who can mediate between them, go back to the beginning of human history—and beyond. Fascinating traces of ritual magic have been unearthed at various Neanderthal sites: the ritual burial of the dead, laid to rest with their favorite tools and food, and sometimes covered with flowers; a low-walled stone enclosure containing seven bear heads, all facing forward; a human skull on a stake in a ring of stones . . . Neanderthal magic.

A few tens of thousands of years later, in the deep caves of Lascaux and Pech Merle and Rouffignac, the Cro-Magnons were practicing magic too, perhaps learned from their vanishing Neanderthal cousins. Deep in the darkest hidden depths of the caves at La Mouthe and Les Combarelles and Altamira, in the most remote and isolate galleries, the Cro-Magnons filled wall after wall with vivid, emblematic paintings of Ice Age animals. There's little doubt that these cave paintings—and their associational phenomena: realistic clay sculptures of bison, carved ivory horses, the enigmatic "Venus" figurines, and the abstract and interlacing paint-outlined human handprints known as "Macaronis"—were magic, designed to be used in sorcerous rites, although how they were meant to be employed may remain forever unknown. These ancient walls also give us what may be the very first representation of a wizard in human history, a hulking, shaggy, mysterious, deer-headed figure watching over the bright, flat, painted animals as they caper across the stone.

So Magic predates Art. In fact, Art may have been invented as a tool to *express* Magic, to give Magic a practical means of execution—to make it *work*. So that if you go back far enough, artist and sorcerer are indistinguishable, one and the same—a claim that can still be made with a good deal of validity to this very day.

Stories *about* magic go back a similar distance, probably all the way back to when Ice Age hunters huddled around a fire at night, listening to the beasts who howled in the inky blackness around them. By the time that Homer was telling stories to fireside audiences in Bronze Age Greece, the tales he was telling contained recognizable fantasy elements—man-eating giants, spells and counterspells, enchantresses who turned men into swine—that were probably recognized *as* fantasy elements and responded to as such by at least the more sophisticated members of his audience. By the end of the eighteenth century, something recognizably akin to modern literary fantasy was beginning to precipitate out from the millennia-old body of oral tradition—folk tales, fairy tales, mythology, songs and ballads, wonder tales, travelers' tales, rural traditions about the Good Folk and haunted standing stones and the giants who slept under the countryside—first in the form of Gothic stories, ghost stories, and Arabesques, and later, by the middle of the next century, in a more self-conscious literary form in the work of writers such as William Morris and George MacDonald, who reworked the subject matter of the oral traditions to create new fantasy worlds for an audience sophisticated enough to respond to the fantasy elements as literary tropes rather than as fearfully regarded, half-remembered elements of folk beliefs—people who were more likely to be entertained by the idea of putting a saucer of milk out for the fairies than to actually do such a thing.

By the late nineteenth and early twentieth centuries, most respect-able literary figures—Dickens, Twain, Poe, Kipling, Doyle, Saki, Ches-terton, Wells—had written fantasy in one form or another, if only ghost stories or Gothic stories, and a few, like Thorne Smith, James Branch Cabell, and Lord Dunsany, had even made something of a specialty of it. But as World War II loomed ever closer over the horizon, fantasy somehow began to fall into disrepute, increasingly being considered as unhip, "anti-modern," non-progressive, socially irresponsible, even déclassé. By the sterile and unsmiling fifties, very little fantasy was being published in any form, and, in the United States at least, fantasy as a genre, as a separate publishing category, did not exist.

When the last Ice Age started, and the glaciers ground down from the north to cover most of the North American continent, thousands of species of plants and trees, as well as the insects, birds, and animals as-sociated with them, retreated to "cove forests" in the south, in what would eventually come to be called the Great Smoky Mountains; in those cove forests, they waited out the long domain of the ice, eventually moving north again to recolonize the land as the climate warmed and the glaciers retreated. Similarly, the lowly genre fantasy and science fic-tion magazines—*Weird Tales* and *Unknown* in the thirties and forties, *The Magazine of Fantasy & Science Fiction*, *Fantastic*, and the British *Sci-ence Fantasy* in the fifties and sixties—were the cove forests that shel-tered fantasy during its long retreat from the glaciers of social realism, giving it a refuge in which to endure until the climate warmed enough to allow it to spread and repopulate again.

By the midsixties, largely through the efforts of pioneers such as Don Wollheim, Ian and Betty Ballantine, Don Benson, and Cele Gold-smith, fantasy had begun tentatively to emerge from the cove forests. And after the immense success of J. R. R. Tolkien's Lord of the Rings trilogy, the first American publishing line devoted to fantasy, the Bal-lantine Adult Fantasy line, was established. It would be followed by oth-ers in the decades to come, until by the current day fantasy is a huge, diverse, and commercially successful genre, one which has diversified into many different types: sword & sorcery, epic fantasy, high fantasy, comic fantasy, historical fantasy, alternate world fantasy, and others.

For the last few decades, the most common public image of the magic-user has almost certainly been that of the benign, white-bearded, slouch-hatted, staff-wielding wizard—an image primarily composed of a large measure of Tolkien's Gandalf the Grey and J. K. Rowling's Dumbledore, with perhaps a jigger of T. H. White's Merlin thrown in for flavor. Throughout history, though, the magic-user has worn many faces, sometimes benevolent and wise, sometimes evil and malign— sometimes, ambiguously, both. To the ancient Greeks, magic was the Great Science. The famous mystic Agrippa considered magic to be the true path of communion with God. Conversely, to medieval European society, the magic-user was one who collaborated with the Devil in the spreading of evil throughout the world, in the corruption and ruination of Christian souls—and the smoke of hundreds of burning witches and warlocks filled the chilly autumn air for a hundred years or more. To some Amerind tribes, the magic-user was either malevolent or benign, depending on the *use* to which their magic was put. In fact, nearly every human society has its own version of the magic-user. In Mexico, the sorcerer is *curandero, brujo,* or *bruja.* In Haiti, they are *houngan* or *quimboiseur;* in Amerind lore, the Shaman or Singer; in Jewish mysticism, the kabbalist; in Gypsy circles, the *chóvihánni,* the witch; in parts of today's rural America, the hoodoo or conjure man or root woman; to the Maori of New Zealand, the *tohunga makutu* ... and so on, throughout the world, in the most "progressive" societies no less than the most "primitive."

The fact is, we're all still sorcerers under the skin, and magic seems to be part of the intuitive cultural heritage of most human beings. Whenever you cross your fingers to ward off bad luck, or knock on wood, or refuse to change your lucky underwear before the big game, or ensure the health of your mother's back by not stepping on the cracks in the sidewalk—or, for that matter, when you deliberately *step* on them, with malice aforethought—then you are putting on the mantle of the sorcerer, attempting to affect the world through magic. Then you are practicing magic, as surely as the medieval alchemist puttering with his alembics and pestles, as surely as the bear-masked, stag-horned Cro-Magnon shaman making ritual magic in the darkness of the deep caves at Rouffignac.

In this anthology, I've endeavored to cover the whole world of magic. Here you will find benevolent white wizards and the blackest of black magicians. Here you'll visit the troll-haunted hills of eighteenth-century Iceland ... Victorian Ireland, where the hosts of the Sidhe are gathering for war ... the remote wilderness regions of Appalachia and the hill-country of Kentucky, where ancient ghosts still roam ... and the streets of modern-day New York City and Los Angeles, where dangerous magic lurks around every corner. Then you'll visit worlds of the imagination outside the time and space we know ... touring the fabled, enchanted metropolis of Calfia; the bleak marshes and crumbling towns of the Mesoge, where the dead come back to prey on the living; the grim city of Uzur-Kalden, at the very edge of the world, where doomed adventures gather to set forth on quests from which few if any of them will return ... visit The Land of the Falling Wall in the last days of a dying Earth to drink and dine at the Tarn House (famous for its Hissing Eels!); shop at the Mother of Markets in Messaline for bizarre simulacrum in company with Bijou the Artificer; attend the 119th Grand Symposium, presided over by the High Magnus himself, to watch a contest of skills between the world's greatest magicians; join a perilous quest for cold mages vital to the prestige of the Great Houses who rule an alternate version of Rome after the Empire's fall ... enter an Elf-Hill, from which it may be impossible to escape ... ride in the Devil's Terraplane, join a village wizard in a seemingly hopeless battle to stand against the most malign of magics ... try to talk a comet out of destroying the world ... fight Revenants with fiery eyes, a toy-eater, a sinister ensorceled book ... meet Dr. Dee, the famous Victorian scholar and magician ... Masquelayne the Incomparable, the Eyeless One, the Lord of the Black Tor, Molloqos the Melancholy ... Djinn, trolls, elves, osteomancers, egregores, deodands, grues, erbs, ghouls, scorpion-tailed manticores ... the Lords of the Sidhe; the guardian spirits of Iceland; saints and sinners; the singing heads on stakes known as the Kallistochoi, who maintain magic with their endless song; Archangel Bob; the Holy Whore of Heaven; a Bouncing Boy Terror; and the Devil's Son-in-Law.

Such dreams are inspired by magic—in fact, you could make an argument that they *are* magic. Such dreams persist, and cross the gulf of generations and even the awful gulf of the grave; cross all barriers of race or age or class or sex or nationality; transcend time itself. Here are dreams that, it is my fervent hope, will still be touching other people's minds and hearts and stirring them in their turn to dream long after everyone in this anthology or associated with it have gone to dust.

The
Book of
Magic

K. J. Parker

. . .

One of the most inventive and imaginative writers working in fantasy today, K. J. Parker is the author of the bestselling Engineer trilogy (*Devices and Desires, Evil for Evil, The Escapement*) as well as the previous Fencer (*Colours in the Steel, The Belly of the Bow, The Proof House*) and Scavenger (*Shadow, Pattern, Memory*) trilogies. His short fiction has been collected in *Academic Exercises* and *The Father of Lies*, and he has twice won the World Fantasy Award for Best Novella, for "Let Maps to Others" and "A Small Price to Pay for Birdsong." His other novels include *Sharps, The Company, The Folding Knife*, and *The Hammer*. His most recent novels are *Savages* and *The Two of Swords*. K. J. Parker also writes under his real name, Tom Holt. As Holt, he has published *Expecting Someone Taller, Who's Afraid of Beowulf, Ye Gods!*, and many other novels.

In the sly story that follows, he takes us to the Studium, an elite academy for wizards, and shows us that a competition for an important position among three highly powerful sorcerers can soon become dark, devious, and dangerous—and quite likely deadly as well.

◆　　◆　　◆

The Return of the Pig

K. J. PARKER

[NOSTALGIA; from the Greek, νοστουάλγεα,
the pain of returning home]

It was one of those mechanical traps they use for bears and other dangerous pests—flattering, in a way, since I'm not what you'd call physically imposing. It caught me slightly off square, crunching my heel and ankle until the steel teeth met inside me. My mind went white with pain, and for the first time in my life I couldn't think.

Smart move on his part. When I've got my wits about me, I'm afraid of nothing on Earth, with good reason; nothing on Earth can hurt me, because I'm stronger, though you wouldn't think it to look at me. But pain clouds the mind, interrupts the concentration. When it hurts so much that you can't think, trying to do anything is like bailing water with a sieve. It all just slips through and runs away, like kneading smoke.

Ah well. We all make enemies. However meek and mild we try to be, sooner or later, we all—excuse the pun—put our foot in it, and then anger and resentment cloud the judgment, and we do things and have things done to us that make no logical sense. An eloquent indictment of the folly of ambition; one supremely learned and clever intellectual does for another by snapping him in a gadget designed to trap bears. You'd take the broad view and laugh, if it didn't hurt so very, very much.

◆　◆　◆

What is strength? Excuse me if this sounds like an exam question. But seriously, what is it? I would define it as the quality that enables one to do work and exert influence. The stronger you are, the more you can do, the bigger and more intransigent the objects you can influence. My father could lift a three-hundredweight anvil. So, of course, can I, but in a very different way. So: here comes the paradox. I couldn't follow my father's trade because I was and still am a weakling. So instead I was sent away to school, where what little muscle I had soon atrophied into fat, and where I became incomparably strong. The hell with anvils. I can lift mountains. There is no mountain so heavy that I can't lift it. Not bad going, for a man who has to call the porter to take the lids off jars.

The mistake we all make is to confuse strength with security. You think: because I'm so very strong, I need fear nothing. They actually tell you that, in fourth year: once you've completed this part of the course you should never be afraid of anything ever again, because nothing will have the power to hurt you. It sounds marvelous, and you write home: dear Mother and Father, this term we'll be doing absolute strength, so when I see you next I'll be invincible and invulnerable, just fancy, your loving son, etc. We believe it, because it's so very plausible. Then you get field assignments and practicals, where you levitate heavy objects and battle with demons and divert the course of rivers and turn back the tides of the sea—heady stuff for a nineteen-year-old—and at the end of it you *believe*. I'm a graduate of the Studium, armed with *strictoense* and protected by *lorica*; I shall fear no evil. And then they pack you off to your first posting, and you start the slow, humiliating business of learning something useful, the hard way.

They mention pain, in passing. Pain, they tell you, is one of the things that can screw up your concentration, so avoid it if you can. You nod sagely and jot it down in your lecture notes: *avoid pain*. But it never comes up in the exam, so you forget about it.

All my life I've tried to avoid pain, with indifferent success.

My head was still spinning when the murderers came along. I call them that for convenience, the way you do. When you know what a man does for a living, you look at him and see the trade, not the human being. You there, blacksmith, shoe my horse; tapster, fetch me a pint of beer. And you see me and you fall on your knees and ask my blessing, in the hope I won't turn you into a frog.

Actually they were just two typical Mesoge farmhands—thin, spare, and strong, with big hands, frayed cuffs, and good, strong teeth uncorrupted by sugar. One of them had a mattock (where I come from, they call them biscays), the other a lump of rock pulled out of the bank. One good thing about the murderer's trade—no great outlay on specialist equipment.

They looked at me dispassionately, sizing up the extent to which pain had rendered me harmless. My guess is, they hadn't been told what I was, my trade, though the scholar's gown should have put them on notice. They figured I'd be no bother, but they separated anyway, to come at me from two directions. They hadn't brought a cart, so I imagine their orders were to sling me in a ditch when they were all done. One of them was chewing on something, probably bacon rind.

The thing about *strictoense*—it's actually a very simple Form. They could easily teach it in first year, except you wouldn't trust a sixteen-year-old freshman with it, any more than you'd leave him alone with a jar of brandy and your daughter. All you do is concentrate very hard, imagine what you'd like to happen, and say the little jingle: *strictoenseruit in hostem*. Personally, I always imagine a man who's just been kicked by a carthorse, for the simple reason that I saw it happen to my elder brother when I was six. One moment he was going about his business, lifting the offside rear hoof to trim it with his knife. His concentration must have wandered because, quick as a thought, the horse slipped his hold and hit him. I saw him in the split second before he fell, with a sort of semicircular dent a fingernail deep directly above his eyebrows. His eyes were wide open—surprise, nothing more—and then he fell backward and blood started to ooze and his face never moved again. It's useful when you have a nice, sharp memory to draw on.

If they'd come along a minute earlier, I'd have been in no fit state. But a minute was long enough, and *strictoense* is such an easy Form, and I've done it so often; and that particular memory is so very clear, and always with me, near at hand, like a dagger under your pillow. I tore myself away from the pain just long enough to speculate what those two would look like with hoofprints on their foreheads. Then I heard the smack—actually, it's duller, like trying to split endgrain, when the axe just sinks in, *thud,* rather than cleaving, *crack*—and I left them to it and gave my full attention to the pain, for a very long time.

Two days earlier, we all sat down in austerely beautiful, freezing cold Chapter to discuss the chair of Perfect Logic, vacant since the untimely death of Father Vitruvius. He'd been very much old school—a man genuinely devoted to contemplation, so abstract and theoretical that his body was always an embarrassment, like the poor relation that gets dragged along on family visits. Rumor had it that he wasn't always quite so detached; he'd had a mistress in the suburbs and fathered two sons, now established in a thriving ropewalk in Choris and doing very well. Most rumors in our tiny world are true, but not, I think, that one.

There were three obvious candidates; the other two were Father Sulpicius and Father Gnatho. To be fair, there was not a hair's weight between the three of us. We'd known one another since second year (Gnatho and I were a year above Sulpicius; I've known Gnatho even longer than that), graduated together, chose the same specialities, were reunited after our first postings, saw one another at table and in the libraries nearly every day for twenty years. As far as ability went, we were different but equal. All three of us were and had always been exceptionally bright and diligent; all three of us could do the job standing on our heads. The chair carries tenure for life, and all three of us were equally ambitious. For the two who didn't get it, there was no other likely preferment, and for the rest of our lives we'd be subordinate by one degree to the fortunate third, who'd be able to order us about and send us on dangerous assignments and postings to remote and barbarous places, at whim.

I don't actually hate Sulpicius, or even Gnatho. By one set of perfectly valid criteria, they're my oldest and closest friends, nearer to me than brothers ever could be. If there'd been a remotely credible compromise candidate, we'd all three have backed him to the hilt. But there wasn't, not unless we hired in from another House (which the Studium never does, for sheer arrogant pride); one of us it would have to be. You can see the difficulty.

The session lasted nine hours and then we took a vote. I voted for Gnatho. Sulpicius voted for me. Gnatho voted for Sulpicius. In the event, it was a deadlock, nine votes each. Father Prior did the only thing he could: adjourned for thirty days, during which time all three candidates were sent away on field missions, to stop them canvassing. It was the only thing Prior Sighvat could have done; it was also the worst thing he could possibly do. For all our strength, you see, we're only human.

So there I was, a very strong human with a bear trap biting into my foot.

I've always been bad with pain. Before I mastered *sicut in terra*, even a mild toothache made me scream out loud. It used to make my poor father furiously angry to hear me sniveling and whimpering, as he put it, like a big girl. I was always a disappointment to him, even when I showed him I could turn lead pipe into gold. So the bear trap had me beat, I have to confess. All I had to do was prise it open with *quulisurtifex* and heal the wound with *vergens in defectum*, fifteen seconds' work, but I couldn't, not for a very long time, during which I pissed myself twice, which was disgusting. Actually, that was probably what saved me. Self-disgust concentrates the mind the way fear is supposed to but doesn't. Also, after something like five hours, judged by the movement of the sun, the pain wore off a little, or I got used to it.

That first stupendous effort—grabbing the wisp of smoke and not letting go—and then fifteen seconds of total dedication, and then, there I was, wondering what the hell all that fuss had been about. I stood up—pins and needles in my other foot made me wince, but I charmed it away without a second's thought—and considered my shoe, which was irretrievably ruined. So I hardened the sole of my foot with *scelussceleris* and went barefoot. No big deal.

(Query: why is there no known Form for fixing trivial everyday objects? Answer, I guess: we live such comfortable, over-provided-for lives that nobody's ever felt the need. Remind me to do something about it, when I have five minutes.)

All this time, of course, it had never once occurred to me to wonder why, or who. Naturally. What need is there of speculation when you already know the answer?

◆ ◆ ◆

My mother didn't raise me to be no watch officer; nevertheless, that's what I've become, over the years, for the not-very-good reason that I'm very good at it. A caution to those aspiring to join the Order: think very carefully before showing proficiency for anything; you just don't know what it'll lead to. When I was young and newly graduated, my first field assignment was identifying and neutralizing renegades—witchfinding, as we call it and you mustn't, because it's not respectful. I thought: if I do this job really well, I'll acquire kudos and make a name for myself. Indeed. I made a name for myself as someone who could safely be entrusted with a singularly rotten job that nobody wants to do. And I've been doing it ever since, the go-to man whenever there's an untrained natural on the loose.

(Gnatho is every bit as good at it as I am, but he's smart. He deliberately screwed up, to the point where senior men had to be sent out to rescue him and clear up the mess. It had no long-term effect on his career, and he's never had to do it since. Sulpicius couldn't trace an untrained natural if they were in the same bath together, so in his case the problem never arose.)

No witchfinding job is ever pleasant, and this one . . . I'd spent five hours in exquisite pain on the open moor, and I hadn't even got there yet.

I tried to make up time by walking faster, but I'm useless at hills, and the Mesoge is crawling with the horrible things, so it was dark as a bag by the time I got to Riens. I knew the way, of course. Riens is six miles from where I grew up.

Nobody who leaves the Mesoge and makes good in the big city ever goes back. You hear rich, successful merchants waxing eloquent at formal dinners about the beauties of the Old Country—the waterfalls of Scheria, the wide-open sky of the Bohec, watching the sun go down on Beloisa Bay—but the Mesoge men sit quiet and hope their flattened vowels don't give them away. I hadn't been back for fifteen years. Everywhere else changes in that sort of time span. Not the Mesoge. Still the same crumbling dry-stone walls, dilapidated farmhouses, thistle- and briar-spoiled scrubland pasture, rutted roads, muddy verges, gray skies, thin, scabby livestock, and miserable people. A man is the product of the landscape he was born in, so they say, and I'm horribly aware that this is true. Trying to counteract the aspects of the Mesoge that are part and parcel of my very being has made me what I am, so I'm not ungrateful for my origins; they've made me hardworking, clean-living, honest, patient, tolerant, the polar opposite, the substance of which the Mesoge is the shadow. I just don't like going back there, that's all.

I remembered Riens as a typical Mesoge town: perched on a hilltop, so you have to struggle a mile uphill with every drop of water you use, which means everybody smells; thick red sandstone town walls, and a town gate that rotted away fifty years ago and which nobody can be bothered to replace; one long street, with the inn and the meetinghouse on opposite sides in the middle. Mesoge men have lived for generations by stealing one another's sheep. Forty makes you an old man, and what my father mostly did was make arrowheads. Mesoge women are short and stocky, and you never see a pretty face; they've all gone east, to work in the entertainment sector. Those that remain are muscular, hardworking, forceful, and short-tempered, like my mother.

The woman at the inn was like that. "Who the hell are you?" she said.

I explained that I was a traveler; I needed a bed for the night, and if at all possible, something to eat and maybe even a pint of beer, if that wouldn't put anybody out. She scowled at me and told me I could have the loft, for six groschen.

The loft in the Mesoge is where you store hay for the horses. The food is stockfish porridge—we're a hundred miles from the sea, but we live on dried fish, go figure—with, if you're unlucky, a mountain of fermented cabbage. The beer—

I peered into it. "Is this stuff safe to drink?"

She gave me a look. "We drink it."

"I think I'll pass, thanks."

There was a mattress in the loft. It can't have been more than thirty years old. I lay awake listening to the horses below, noisily digesting and stamping their feet. Home, I said to myself. What joy.

◆   ◆   ◆

The object of my weary expedition was a boy, fifteen years old, the tanner's third son; it was like looking into a mirror, except he was skinny
and at his age I was a little tub of lard. But I saw the same defensive
aggression in his sneaky little eyes, fear mixed with guilt, spiced with
consciousness of a yet-unfathomed superiority—he knew he was better
than everybody else around him, but he wasn't sure why, or how it
worked, or whether it would stunt his growth or make him go blind.
That's the thing; you daren't ask anybody. No wonder so many of
them—of us—go to the bad.

I said I'd see him alone, just the two of us. His father had a stone
shed, where they kept the oak bark (rolled up like carpets, tied with
string and stacked against the wall).

"Sit down," I told him. He squatted cross-legged on the floor. "You
don't have to do that," I said.

He looked at me.

"You don't have to sit on the cold, wet floor," I said. "You can do this."
I muttered *qualisartifex* and produced two milking stools. "Can't you?"

He stared at me, but not because the trick had impressed him. "Don't
know what you're talking about," he said.

"It's all right," I said. "You're not in trouble. It's not a crime, in itself."
I grinned. "It's not a crime because it can't happen. The law takes the
view—as we do—that there's no such thing as magic. If there's no such
thing, it can't be against the law." I produced a table, with a teapot and
two porcelain bowls. "Do you drink tea?"

"No."

"Try it; it's one of life's few pleasures."

He scowled at the bowl and made no movement. I poured myself
some tea and blew on it to cool it down. "There is no magic," I told him.
"Instead, there are a certain number of limited effects which a wise man,
a scholar, can learn to do, if he knows how, and if he's born with the ability to concentrate very, very hard. They aren't magic, because they're
not—well, strange or inexplicable or weird. Give you an example. Have
you ever watched the smith weld two rods together? Well, then. A man
takes two bits of metal and does a trick involving fire and sparks flying

about, and the two bits of metal are joined so perfectly you can't see where one ends and another begins. Or take an even weirder trick. It's the one where a woman pulls a living human being out from between her legs. Weird? I should say so."

He shook his head. "Women can't do magic," he said. "Everybody knows that."

A literal mind. Ah well. "Men can't do it either, because it doesn't exist. Haven't you been listening? But a few men have the gift of concentrating very hard and doing certain processes, certain tricks, that achieve things that look weird and strange to people who don't know about these things. It's not magic, because we know exactly how it works and what's going on, just as we know what happens when your dad puts a dead cow's skin in a big stone trough, and it comes out all hard and smooth on one side."

He shrugged. "If you say so."

Hard going. Still, that's the Mesoge for you. We esteem it a virtue in youth to be unimpressed by anything or anyone, never to cooperate, never to show enthusiasm or interest. "You can do this stuff," I reminded him. "I know you can, because people have seen you doing it."

"Can't prove anything."

"Don't need to. I know. I can see into your mind."

That got to him. He went white as a sheet, and if the door hadn't been bolted on the outside (a simple precaution), he'd have been up and out of there like an arrow from a bow. "You can't."

I smiled at him. "I can see you looking at a flock of sheep, and three days later half of them are dead. I can see you getting a clip round the ear from an old man, who then falls and breaks his leg. I can see a burning hayrick, sorry, no, make that three. Antisocial little devil, aren't you?"

The tears in his eyes were pure rage, and I softly mumbled *lorica*. But he didn't lash out, as I'd have done at his age, as I did during this very interview. He just shook his head and muttered about proof. "I don't need proof," I said. "I've got a witness. You." I waited three heartbeats, then said, "And it's all right. I'm on your side. You're one of us."

His scowl said he didn't believe me. "All right," I said. "Watch closely. The little fat kid is me."

And I showed him. Simple little Form, *lux dardaniae*, very effective. One thing I didn't do quite right; one of the nasty little escapades I showed him was Gnatho, not me. Same difference, though.

He looked at me with something less than absolute hatred. "You're from round here."

I nodded. "Born and bred. You don't like it here, do you?"

"No."

"Me neither. That's why I left. You can too. In ten years, you can be me. Only without the pot belly and the double chin."

"Me?" he said. "Go to the City?"

And I knew I'd got him. "Watch," I said, and I showed him Perimadeia: the standard visitor's tour, the fountains and the palace and Victory Square and the Yarn Market at Goosefair. Then, while he was still reeling, I showed him the Studium—the impressive view, from the harbor, looking up the hill. "Where would you rather live," I said, "there or here? Your choice. No pressure."

He looked at me. "If I go there, can my mother and my sisters come and visit me?"

I frowned. "Sorry, no. We don't allow women, it's the rules."

He grinned. "Yes, please," he said. "I hate women."

Gnatho was skinny at that age. My first memory of him was a little skinny kid stealing apples from our one good eating-apple tree. They were my apples. I didn't want to share with an unknown stranger. So I smacked him with what I would later come to know as *strictoense*.

It didn't work.

And then there was this huge invisible *thing* whirling toward me, so big it would've blotted out the sun if it hadn't been invisible, if you see what I mean. I didn't think; I warded it off, with a Form I would come to call *scutumveritatis*. I felt the collision; it literally made the ground shake under my feet.

We stared at each other.

I remember quite vividly the first time I looked in a mirror, though of course it wasn't a mirror, not in the Mesoge; it was a basin full of water, outside on a perfectly still day. I remember the disappointment.

That plump, foolish-looking kid was *me*. And I remember how Gnatho, intently staring at me, lost his seat on the branch of the tree, and fell, and would almost certainly have broken his neck—

I handled it badly. I sort of grabbed at him—*adiutoremmeum*, used cack-handedly by a ten-year-old, what do you expect?—and slammed him against the trunk of the tree on the way down. The rough bark scraped a big flap of skin off his cheek, and he has the scar still. Stupid fool didn't think to use *scutum*, he just panicked; he was so lucky I was there (only if I hadn't been, he wouldn't have fallen). But he thought I toppled him out of the tree on purpose and gave him the scar that disfigured him. I showed him my memory when we were eighteen, so he knows the truth. But I think he still blames me, in his heart of hearts, and he's still scared of me, in case I ever do it again.

There were arrangements. I had to go and see the boy's parents—long, tedious interview, with the parents scared, angry, shocked, right up until I introduced the subject of compensation for the boy's unpaid labor. The Order is embarrassingly rich. In the City, ten kreuzers a week will buy you lunch, if you aren't picky. In the Mesoge it's a fortune. I'm authorized to offer up to twenty, but it's not my money, and I'm conscientious.

I walk whenever I can because I have no luck at all with carts and coaches. The horses don't like me; they're sensitive animals, and they perceive something about me that isn't quite right. I cause endless problems to any wheeled vehicle I ride on. If it's not the horses, it's a broken axle or a broken spoke, or the coach gets bogged down in a rut, or the driver falls off or has a seizure. I'm not alone; quite a few of us have travel jinxes of one sort or another, and it's better to be jinxed on land than on sea, like poor Father Incitatus. So, to get to the Mesoge, I take a boat from the City down the Asper as far as Stark and walk the rest of the way. Trouble is, rivers only flow in one direction. To get back from the Mesoge, I have to walk to Insuper, get a lumber barge to the coast, and tack back up to the City on a grain ship. I get seasick and there's no known Form for that. Ain't that the way.

From Riens to Insuper is seventeen miles, down dale and up bloody hill. Six miles from Riens, the road goes through a small village; or you can take the old cart road up to the Tor, then wind your way down through the forestry, cross the Blackwater at Sens Ford and rejoin the main road a mile the other side of the village. Going that way adds another five miles or so, and it's miserable, treacherous going, but it saves you having to pass through this small, typical Mesoge settlement.

Just my luck, though. I dragged all the way up Tor Drove, and slipped and slithered my way down the logging tracks, which were badly overgrown with briars where the logging crews had burned off their brush, only to find that the Blackwater was up with the spring rain, the ford was washed out, and there was no way over. Despair. I actually considered parting the waters or diverting the river. But there are rules about that sort of thing, and a man in the running for the chair of Perfect Logic doesn't want to go breaking too many rules if there's any chance of being found out; and since I was known to be in the neighborhood . . .

So, back I went: up the logging trails and down the Drove, back to where I originally left the road—a journey made even more tedious by reflecting on the monstrously extended metaphor it represented. I reached the village (forgive me if I don't say its name) bright and early in the morning, having slept under a beech tree and been woken by the snuffling of wild pigs.

I so hoped it had changed, but it hadn't. The main street takes you right by the blacksmith's forge—that was all right, because when my father died, my mother sold it and moved back north to her family. Whoever had it now was a busy man; I could hear the chime of hammer on anvil two hundred yards away. My father never started work until three hours after sunup. He said it was being considerate to the neighbors, all of whom he hated and feuded incessantly with. But the hinges on the gate still hadn't been fixed, and the chimney was still on the verge of falling down, maintained in place by nothing but force of habit—a potent entity in the Mesoge.

I had my hood pinched up round my face, just in case anybody recognized me. Needless to say, everybody I passed stopped what they were doing and stared at me. I knew nearly all of them that were over twenty.

Gnatho's family were colliers, charcoal-burners. In the Mesoge we're painfully aware of the subtlest gradations of social status, and colliers (who live outdoors, move from camp to camp in the woods, and deal with outsiders) are so low that even the likes of my lot were in a position to look down on them. But Gnatho's father inherited a farm. It was tight in to the village, with a paddock fronting onto the road, and there he built sheds to store charcoal, and a house. It hadn't changed one bit, but from its front door came four men, carrying a door on their shoulders. On the door was something covered in a curtain.

I stopped an old woman, let's not bother with her name. "Who died?" I asked.

She told me. Gnatho's father.

Gnatho isn't Gnatho's name, of course, any more than mine is mine. When you join the Order, you get a name-in-religion assigned to you. Gnatho's real name (like mine) is five syllables long and can't be transcribed into a civilized alphabet. The woman looked at me. "Do I know you?"

I shook my head. "When did that happen?"

"Been sick for some time. Know the family, do you?"

"I met his son once, in the City."

"Oh, him." She scowled at me. *Lorica* doesn't work on peasant scowls, so I hadn't bothered with it. "He still alive, then?"

"Last I heard."

"You sure I don't know you? You sound familiar."

"Positive."

Gnatho's father. A loud, violent man who beat his wife and daughters; a great drinker, angry because people treated him like dirt when he worked so much harder than they did. Permanently red-faced, from the charcoal fires and the booze, lame in one leg, a tall man, ashamed of his skinny, thieving, no-account son. He'd reached a ripe old age for the Mesoge. The little shriveled woman walking next to the pallbearers had to be his poor, oppressed wife, now a wealthy woman by local standards, and free at last of that pig. She was crying. Some people.

Some impulse led me to dig a gold half-angel out of my pocket and press it into her hand as she walked past me. She looked around and stared, but I'd discreetly made myself hard to see. She gazed at the coin in her hand, then tightened her palm around it like a vise.

I was out of the village and climbing the long hill on the other side a mere twenty minutes later, by my excellent Mezentine mechanical watch. There, I told myself, that wasn't so bad.

Once you've experienced the thing you've been dreading the most, you get a bit light-headed for a while, until some new aggravation comes along and reminds you that life isn't like that. In my case, the new aggravation was another flooded river, the Inso this time, which had washed away the bridge at Machaera and smashed the ferryboat into kindling. The ferryman told me what I already knew; I had to go back three miles to where the road forks, then follow the southern leg down as far as Coniga, pick up the old Military Road, which would take me, eventually, to the coast. There's a stage at Friest, he said helpfully, so you won't have to walk very far. Just as well, he added, it's a bloody long way else.

So help me, I actually considered the stage. But it wouldn't be fair on the other passengers—innocent country folk who'd never done me any harm. No; for some reason, the Mesoge didn't want to let me go— playing with its food, a bad habit my mother was always very strict about. One of the reasons we're so damnably backward is the rotten communications with the outside world. A few heavy rainstorms and you're screwed; can't go anywhere, can't get back to where you came from.

So, reluctantly, I embarked on a walking tour of my past. I have to say, the scholar's gown is an excellent armor, a woolen version of *lorica*. Nobody hassles you, nobody wants to talk to you, they give you what you ask for and wait impatiently for you to finish up and leave. I bought a pair of boots in Assistenso, from a cobbler I knew when he was a young man. He looked about a hundred and six now. He recognized me but didn't say a word. Quite good boots, actually, though I had to *qualisartifex* them a bit to stop them squeaking all the damn time.

The Temperance & Thrift in Nauns is definitely a cut above the other inns in the Mesoge; God only knows why. The rooms are proper rooms, with actual wooden beds, the food is edible, and (glory of glories) you can get proper black tea there. Nominally it's a brothel rather than an inn; but if you give the girl a nice smile and six stuivers, she goes away and you can have the room to yourself. I was sleeping peacefully for the first time in ages when some fool banged on the door and woke me up.

Was I the scholar? Yes, I admitted reluctantly, because the gown lying over the back of the chair was in plain sight. You're needed. They've got trouble in—well, I won't bother you with the name of the village. Lucky to have caught you. Just as well the bridge is out, or you'd have been long gone.

They'd sent a cart for me, the fools. Needless to say, the horse went lame practically the moment I climbed aboard; so back we went to the Temperance for another one, and then the main shaft cracked, and we were ages cutting out a splint and patching it in. Quicker to have walked, I told him.

"I know you," the carter replied. "You're from around here."

There comes a time when you can fight no more. "That's right."

"You're his son. The collier's boy."

Most insults I can take in my stride, but some I can't. "Like hell," I snapped. I told him my name. "The old smith's son," I reminded him. He nodded. He never forgot a face, he told me.

Gnatho's father, in fact, was the problem. Not resting quietly in the grave is a Mesoge tradition, like Morris dances and wassailing the apple trees. If you die with an unresolved grudge or a bad attitude generally, chances are you'll be back, either as your own putrifying and swollen corpse or some form of large, unpleasant vermin—a wolf, bear, or pig.

"He's come back as a pig," I said. "Bet you."

The carter grinned. "You knew the old devil, then."

"Oh, yes."

Revenant pests don't look like the natural variety. They're bigger, always jet-black, with red eyes. They glow slightly in the dark, and ordinary weapons don't bite on them, ordinary traps can't hold them, and they seem to thrive on ordinary poisons. Gnatho's dad had taken to digging into the sides of houses—at night, while the family was asleep—

undermining the walls and bringing the roof down. That wouldn't be hard in most Mesoge houses, which are three parts fallen down from neglect anyway, but I could see where a glowing spectral hog rootling around in the footings wouldn't help matters.

I know a little bit about revenants, because my grandfather was one. He was a bear, and he spent a busy nine months killing livestock and breaking hedges until a man in a gray gown came down from the City and sorted him out. I watched him do it, and that was when I knew what I wanted to be when I grew up.

Granddad died when I was six. I remember him as a big, cheerful man who always gave me an apple, but he'd killed two of our neighbors—self-defense, but in a small community, that really doesn't matter very much. The scholar sat up four nights in a row, caught him with a freezing Form (*in quo vincit*, presumably) and left him there till morning, when he came back with a dozen men, stakes, axes, big hammers—all the kit I tended to associate with mending fences. The only bit of Granddad that could move was his eyes, and he watched everything they did, right up to when they cut off his head. Of course, what I saw wasn't my dear grandfather, it was a huge black bear. It was only later that they told me.

I don't know if embarrassment can kill a man. I could have put it to the test, but I got scared and dosed myself with *fonslaetitiae*, which takes the edge off pretty much everything.

No chance, you see, of anonymity once I got back to the village. Old Mu the Dog—his actual name, insofar as I can transcribe it, is Mutahalliush—was mayor now; my last mental image of him was his face splashed with the stinking dark-brown juice that sweats off rotten lettuce, as he sat in the stocks for fathering a child on the miller's daughter, but clearly other people had shorter memories or were more forgiving than me. Shup the tanner was constable; Ati from Five Ash was sexton; and the new smith, a man I didn't know, was almoner and parish remembrancer. I gave them a cold, dazed look and told them to sit down.

I think it was just as bad for them. See it from their point of view. One of their own, a kid they'd smacked round the head with a stick on many occasions, was now a scholar, a wizard, able to kill with a frown or turn the turds on the midden to pure gold. We kept it formal, which was probably just as well.

The meeting told me nothing I didn't know already or couldn't guess or hadn't heard from the carter, but it gave me a chance to do the usual ground-rules speech and impress upon them the perils of not doing exactly as they were told. It was only when we'd been through all that and I stood up to let them know the meeting was over that Shup—my second cousin; we're all related—asked me if I knew how his nephew had got on. His nephew? And then the penny dropped. He meant Gnatho.

"He's doing very well," I told him.

"He's a scholar? Like you?"

"Very like me," I said. "He's never been back, then."

"We didn't know if he was alive or dead."

Or me, come to that. "I'll tell him about his father," I said. "He may want to—" I paused, realizing what I'd just been about to say. Pay his respects at the graveside? Which one? A revenant's remains are chopped into four pieces and buried on the parish boundaries, at the four cardinal points. "He'll want to know." And that was a flat lie, but I have to confess I was looking forward to telling him. As he would have been, in my shoes.

Gnatho's dad wasn't the sharpest knife in the drawer when he was alive. Dead, he seemed to have acquired some basic low cunning, though that might have been the pig rather than him. It took me three nights to catch him. He didn't come quietly, and God, was he ever strong. By the time I finally brought him down with *posuiadiutorem*, I was weak with exhaustion and shaking like a leaf.

Have I misled you with the word *pig*? Dismiss the mental image of a fat, pink porker snuffling up cabbage leaves in a sty. Wild pigs are big; they weigh half a ton, they're covered in sleek, wiry hair, and they're all muscle. Real ones have the redeeming feature of shyness; they sit tight, and if you make enough noise walking around you'll never ever see one, unless you actually tread on its tail. If you do, it'll be the last thing you ever do see. The kind, brave noblemen who come out and kill the damn things for us will tell you that a forest pig is the most dangerous animal in Permia, more so than wolves or bears or bull elk. Real pigs are a sort of auburn color, but Gnatho's dad was soot black, with the unmistakable red eyes.

Once you have your revenant down, you talk to him. I stood up, my legs wobbling under me, and approached as near as I dared, even with a double dose of *lorica*. "Hello," I said.

Paralyzed, remember? I was hearing his voice inside my head. "I'm the smith's boy."

"That's right, so you are. You went off to be a wizard in the City."

"I'm back."

He wanted to acknowledge me with a nod of the head, but found he couldn't. "What's going to happen to me now?"

"I think you know."

I sensed that he took it resolutely—not happy with the outcome, but realistic enough to accept it. "The pain," he said. "Will I feel it?"

This is a gray area, but I have no doubts about it myself. "I'm afraid so, yes," I said. I didn't add, It's your fault, for coming back. You don't score points off someone facing what he was about to go through. "You'll still be alive, so yes, you'll feel it."

"And after," he said. "Will I be dead?"

I hate having to tell them. "No," I said. "You can't die. You just won't be able to control your body any more. You'll still be there, but you won't be able to do anything."

I felt the wave of sheer terror, and it made me feel sick. To be honest with you, it's the worst thing I can think of—lying in the dark ground, unable to move, forever. But there you go. It's not like you decide to be a revenant, and experienced professionals advise you as to the potential downside. It just happens. It's sheer bad luck. Also, of course, it runs in families, and thanks to a thousand years of inbreeding, the Mesoge is just one big family. I really, really hope it won't ever happen to me, but there's absolutely nothing I can do to prevent it.

"You could let me go," he said. "I'll move far away, somewhere there's no people. I won't hurt anybody ever again. I promise."

"I'm sorry," I said. "If my Order found out, it'd mean the noose."

"They'd never know."

Indeed; how could they? I would go back to the City, swear blind the pig was too strong for me, they'd send someone else, by which time Gnatho's dad would be long gone (though they always come back; they can't help it). And I'd lose my reputation as an infallible field agent, which would be marvelous. Everybody wins. And I sometimes can't help thinking about my granddad, still awake in the wet earth; or what it would feel like, if it's ever me.

"I'm sorry," I said. "It's my job."

We cut him up with a forester's crosscut saw. If you aren't familiar with them, they're the big two-handed jobs. Two men sit on either side of the work; one pushes and one pulls. I took my turn, out of some perverse sense of duty, but I never was any good at keeping the rhythm.

I left my home village with mixed feelings. As I said before, once you've been through the experience you've been dreading for so long, you feel a certain euphoria; I've been back now, I won't ever have to do it again, there's a giant weight off my shoulders. But, as I walked up that horribly tiring long hill, I caught myself thinking: no matter how hard I try, this is where I started from, this is part of who I am. I think the revenant issue is what set me thinking that way. You see, revenancy is so very much a Mesoge thing. You get them in other places, but wherever it's been possible to trace ancestries, the revenant always has Mesoge blood in him, if you go back far enough. God help us, we're special. Alone of all races and nations, we're the only human beings on Earth who can achieve a sort of immortality, albeit a singularly nasty one, born of spite and leading to endless pain. Reliable statistics are impossible, of course, but we figure it's something like one in five thousand. It could be me, one day; or Gnatho, or Quintillus, or Scaevola—learned doctors and professors of the pure, unblemished wisdom, raging in the dark, smashing railings and crushing windpipes. And, as I said, they always—we always—come back, sooner or later. They—we—can't help it.

Gnatho, a far more upbeat man than I'll ever be, used to have this idea of finding out *how* we did it, why it was just us, with a view to conquering death and making all men immortal. I believe he did quite a bit of preliminary research, until the funding ran out and he got a teaching post and started getting more involved in Order politics, which takes up a lot of a man's time and energy. He's probably still got his notes somewhere. Like me, he never throws anything away, and his office is a pigsty.

The river had calmed down by the time I got to Machaera, and the military had been out and rigged up a pontoon bridge; nice to see them doing something useful for a change. A relatively short walk and I'd be able to catch a boat and float my way home in relative comfort.

One thing I'd been looking forward to, a small fringe benefit of an otherwise tiresome mission. The road passes through Idens: a small and unremarkable town, but it happened to be the home of an old friend and correspondent of mine, whom I hadn't seen for years: Genseric the alchemist.

He was in fifth year when I was a freshman, but for some reason we got on well together. About the time I graduated, he left the Studium to take up a minor priorship in Estoleit; after that he drifted from post to post, came into some family money, and more or less retired to a life of independent research and scholarship in his old hometown. He inherited a rather fine manor house with a deer park and a lake. From time to time he wrote to me asking for a copy of some text, or could I check a reference for him; alchemy's not my thing, but it's never mattered much. Probably it helped that we were into different disciplines; no need to compete, no risk of one stealing the other's work. Genseric wasn't exactly respectable—he'd left the Studium, after all, and there were all sorts of rumors about him, involving women and unlawful offspring—but he was too good a scholar to ignore, and there was never any ill will on his side. From his letters I got the impression that he was proud to have been one of us but glad to be out of the glue-pot, as he called it, and in the real world. Ah well. It takes all sorts.

As with the things you dread that turn out to be not so bad after all, so with the things you really look forward to, which turn out to disappoint. I'd been picturing in my mind the moment of meeting: broad grins on our faces, maybe a manly embrace, and we'd immediately start talking to each other at exactly the same point where we'd broken off the conversation when he left to catch his boat twenty years ago. It wasn't like that, of course. There was a moment of embarrassed silence as both of us thought, hasn't he changed, and not in a good way (with the inevitable reflection; if he's got all middle-aged, have I too?); then an exaggerated broadening of the smile, followed by a stumbling greeting. Think of indentures, or those coins-cut-in-two that lovers give each other on parting. Leave it too long and the sundered halves don't quite fit together anymore.

But never mind. After half an hour, we were able to talk to each other, albeit somewhat formally and with excessive pains to avoid any possible cause of disagreement. We had the advantage of both being scholars; we could talk shop, so we did, and it was more or less all right after that.

One thing I hadn't been prepared for was the luxury. Boyhood in the Mesoge, adult life at the Studium, field trips spent in village inns and the guest houses of other orders; I'm just not used to linen sheets, cushions, napkins, glass drinking vessels, rugs, wall hangings, beeswax candles, white bread, porcelain tea-bowls, chairs with backs and arms, servants—particularly not the servants. There was a man who stood there all through dinner, just watching us eat. I think his job was to hover with a brass basin of hot water so we could wash our fingers between courses. I kept wanting to involve him in the conversation, so he wouldn't feel left out. I have no idea if he was capable of speech. The food was far too rich and spicy for my taste, and there was far too much of it, but I kept eating because I didn't want to give offense, and the more I ate, the more it kept coming, until eventually the penny dropped. As far as I could tell, this wasn't Genseric putting on a show. He lived like that all the damn time, thought nothing of it. I didn't say anything, naturally, but I was shocked.

Over dinner I told him about my recent adventures, and then he showed me his laboratory, of which I could tell he was very proud. I know the basics of alchemy, but Genseric's research is cutting-edge, and he soon lost me in technical details. The ultimate objective was the same, of course: the search for the reagent or catalyst that can change the fundamental nature of one thing into another. I don't believe this is actually possible, but I did my best to sound impressed and interested. He had shelves of pots and jars, two broad oak benches covered with glassware, a small furnace that resembled my father's forge in the way a prince's baby son resembles a sixteen-stone wrestler. He couldn't resist showing me a few tricks, including one that filled the room with purple smoke and made me cough till I could barely see. After that, I pleaded weariness after my long journey, and I was shown to this vast bedroom, with enough furniture in it to clutter up the whole of a large City house. The bed was the size of a small barn, with genuine tapestry hangings (the marriage of Wit and Wisdom, in the Mezentine style). I was just about to undress when some woman barged in with a basin of hot water. I don't think I want to be rich. I'd never get any peace.

I woke up suddenly, feeling like a bull was standing on my chest. I could hardly breathe. It was dark, so I tried *lux in tenebris*. It didn't work.

Oh, I thought.

My fault, for not putting up wards before I closed my eyes. There's an old military proverb; the worst thing a general can ever say is: I never expected that. But here, in the house of my dear old friend— My fault.

I could just about speak. "Who's there?" I said.

"I'd like you to forgive me." Genseric's voice. "I don't expect you will, but I thought I'd ask, just in case. You always were a fair-minded man."

The illusion of pressure, I realized, wasn't so much the presence of some external force as an absence. For the first time in my life, it wasn't there—it, the talent, the power, the ability. *Virtusexercitus*, a nasty fifth-level Form, suppresses the talent, puts it to sleep. For the first time, I realized what it felt like being normal. *Virtus* isn't used much because it hurts—not the victim, but the person using it. There are other Forms that have roughly the same effect. He'd chosen *virtus* deliberately, to show how sorry he was.

"This is about the chair of Logic," I said.

"I'm afraid so. You see, you're not my only friend at the Studium."

I needed to play for time. "The bear trap."

"That was me, yes. Two cousins of my head gardener. It's a shame you had to kill them, but I understand. I have the contacts, you see, being an outsider."

You have to concentrate like mad to keep *virtus* going. It drains you. "You must like Gnatho very much."

"Actually, it's just simple intellectual greed." He sighed. "I needed access to a formula, but it's restricted. My friend has the necessary clearance. He got me the formula, but it came at a price. Normally I'd have worked around it, tried to figure it out from first principles, but that would take years, and I haven't got that long. Even with the formula I'll need at least ten years to complete my work, and you just don't know how long you've got, do you?" Then he laughed. "Sorry," he said. "Tactless of me, in the circumstances. Look, will you forgive me? It's not malice, you know. You're a scholar; you understand. The work must come first, mustn't it? And you know how important this could be; I just told you about it."

I hadn't been listening when he told me. It went straight over my head, like geese flying south for the winter. "You're saying you had no choice."

"I tried to get it through proper channels," he said, "but they refused. They said I couldn't have it because I wasn't a proper member of the Studium any more. But that's not right, is it? I may not live there, but I'm still one of us. Just because you go away, it doesn't change anything, does it?"

"You could have come back." They always do, sooner or later.

"Maybe. No, I couldn't. I'm ashamed to say, I like it too much here. It's comfortable. There're no stupid rules or politics, nobody to sneer at me or stab me in the back because they want my chair. I don't want to go back. I'm through with all that."

"The boy at Riens," I said. "Did you—?"

"Yes, that was me. I found him and notified the authorities. I had to get you to come out this way."

"You did more than that." I was guessing, but I had nothing to lose.

"You found a natural, and you filled his head with spite and hate. I imagine you appeared to him in dreams. *Fulgensorigo?*"

"Naturally. I knew they'd send you. You're the best at that sort of thing. If it had just been an unregistered natural, they could have sent anyone. To make sure it was you, I had to turn him nasty. I'm sorry. I've caused a lot of trouble for a lot of people."

"But it's worth it, in the long run."

"Yes."

Pain, you see, is the distraction. As long as I could hurt him, in the conscience, where it really stings, I was still in the game. "It's not, you know. Your theory is invalid. There's a flaw. I spotted it when you were telling me about it. It's so obvious, even I can see it."

I didn't need Forms to tell me what he was thinking. "You're lying."

"Don't insult me," I said. "Not on a point of scholarship. I wouldn't do that."

Silence. Then he said, "No, you wouldn't. All right, then, what is it? Come on, you've got to tell me!"

"Why? You're going to kill me."

"Not necessarily. Come on, for God's sake! What did you see?"

And at that precise moment, my fingertips connected with what they'd been blindly groping for: the bottle of aqua fortis I'd slipped into the pocket of my gown earlier, when we were both blinded by the purple smoke. I flipped out the cork with my thumbnail, then thrust the bottle in what I devoutly hoped was the right direction.

Aqua fortis has no pity; it's incapable of it. They use it to etch steel. People who know about these things say it's the worst pain a man can suffer.

I'd meant it for Gnatho, of course; purely in self-defense, if he ambushed me and tried to hex me. Pain would be my only weapon in that case. I had no way of getting hold of the stuff at the Studium, where they're so damn fussy about restricted stores, but I knew my good friend Genseric would have some, and would be slapdash about security.

The pain hit him; he let go of *virtus*. I came back to life. The first thing I did was *lux in tenebris*, so I could see exactly what I'd done to him. It wasn't pretty. I saw the skin bubble on his face, pull apart to reveal the bone underneath; I watched the bone dissolve. You have to believe me when I say that I tried to save him, *mundus vergens*, but I just couldn't concentrate with that horrible sight in front of my eyes. Pain paralyzes, and you can't think straight. It ate deep into his brain, I told him I forgave him, and then he died.

For the record; I think—no, I'm sure—there was a flaw in his theory. It was a false precept, right at the beginning. He was a nice man and a good friend, mostly, but a poor scholar.

As soon as I got back to the Studium, I went to see Father Sulpicius. I told him everything that had happened, including Genseric's confession.

He looked at me. "Gnatho," he said.

I shook my head. "No," I said. "You."

He frowned. "Don't be silly," he said.

"It was you."

"Ridiculous. Look, I can prove it. I don't have clearance for restricted alchemical data. But Gnatho does."

I nodded. "That's right, he does. So you asked him to get the data for you. He was happy to oblige. After all, he's your friend."

"You're wrong."

"Genseric had to find the natural. You're hopeless at that sort of thing; Gnatho's very good at it. If you'd been able to, you'd have done it yourself. But you had to leave it to Genseric."

He took a deep breath. "You're wrong," he said. "But assuming you were right, what would you intend to do about it?"

I looked at him. "Absolutely nothing," I said. "No, I tell a lie. I'd withdraw my name for the chair. Just as you're going to do."

"And let Gnatho—"

Oh, the scorn in those words. He'd have hit me if he'd been able. He's always looked down on Gnatho and me, just because we're from the Mesoge.

"He's a fine scholar," I said. "Besides, I never wanted the stupid job anyway."

❖ ❖ ❖

The boy from Riens duly turned up and was assigned to a house. He's settled in remarkably well, far better than I did. Mind you, I didn't have an influential senior member of Faculty looking out for me, like he has. He could go far, given encouragement. I hope he does, for the honor of the Old Country.

I'm glad I didn't get the chair. If I had, I wouldn't have had the time for a new line of research, which I have high hopes for. It concerns the use of strong acids for disposing of the mortal remains of revenants. Fire doesn't work, we know, because fire leaves ashes; but if you eat the substance away so there's absolutely nothing left— Well, we'll see.

He'll be back, my father used to say, like a pig to its muck. I gather he said it the day I left home. Well. We'll see about that, too.

Megan Lindholm

• • •

Books by Megan Lindholm include the fantasy novels *Wizard of the Pigeons, Harpy's Flight, The Windsingers, The Limbreth Gate, Luck of the Wheels, The Reindeer People, Wolf's Brother*, and *Cloven Hooves*, the science fiction novel *Alien Earth*, and, with Steven Brust, the collaborative novel *The Gypsy*. Lindholm also writes as *New York Times* bestseller Robin Hobb, one of the most popular writers in fantasy today, having sold over one million copies of her work in paperback. As Robin Hobb, she's perhaps best known for her epic fantasy Farseer series, including *Assassin's Apprentice, Royal Assassin*, and *Assassin's Quest*, as well as the four fantasy series related to it: the Liveship Traders series, consisting of *Ship of Magic, The Mad Ship*, and *Ship of Destiny*; the Tawny Man series, made up of *Fool's Errand, The Golden Fool*, and *Fool's Fate*; the Rain Wilds Chronicles, consisting of *Dragon Keeper, Dragon Haven, City of Dragons*, and *Blood of Dragons*; and the Fitz and the Fool trilogy, made up of *Fool's Assassin, Fool's Quest*, and *Assassin's Fate*. She's also the author of the Soldier Son series, composed of *Shaman's Crossing*, *Forest Mage*, and *Renegade's Magic*. As Megan Lindholm, her most recent book is a "collaborative" collection with Robin Hobb, *The Inheritance & Other Stories*.

Doing a favor for an old friend is always a risky business, full of potential disappointments and pitfalls, especially when the old friend is someone you haven't seen or spoken to for decades after an acrimonious breakup—someone who once betrayed you, someone you know better than to trust. And *especially* in a case where dangerous magic is involved.

◆   ◆   ◆

Community Service

MEGAN LINDHOLM

The phone rang. I stripped off my rubber gloves and reached for it.
It's an old house phone, yellow, with a dial, still mounted to the
wall. It works. I like it.

"Good morning. Tacoma Pet Boarding."

"Celtsie, it's me, Farky. Don't hang up."

I hung up. I put my gloves back on. I don't know what Tooraloo's
owner had been feeding the cat, but it wasn't hitting the cat sand, and
getting it off the side of the cat box was requiring some serious scrubbing. And scrubbing cat diarrhea was preferable to talking to Farky.
He'd suckered me for the last time.

The phone rang.

I let it ring twice before I stripped off my rubber gloves again. I
couldn't afford to miss a customer call. Only three of my crates were full.
I needed to board some pets, or groom something, or for someone to
walk in with one of my other business cards—the ones that look just
like tarot cards. But that hadn't happened for a while, and my most recent fortune cookie said not to count on good luck. I took a breath and
modulated my voice. "Good morning. Tacoma Pet Boarding."

"I'm in trouble and no one else can help me."

"Add me to the list of people who won't help you." I hung up again. Gloves. Scrub. I felt the vindictive satisfaction of someone who was finally able to betray a traitorous friend. How many times had I helped Farky? And my dad had helped him before me. And how had he ever paid us back? With lies and thefts. He always swore he was clean. He always begged for another chance. And he'd be good for a week or two months or almost a year before he stuck his nose back in the Captain Crack box. And then he'd tap the till until I noticed, or copy the store key and come back at night to make off with whatever he thought he could pawn. Give Farky a couch for the night, wake up to half my jewelry gone. No. I was done with him. And if he was in trouble, well, good for him. I was glad of it.

And curious. What kind of trouble, and how deep? Whatever it was, he deserved it. Was he sleeping in alleys again? Had he cheated a dealer? I thought of the pleasure of hearing him pour out his difficulty to me and then telling him to take a flying fuck at a rolling donut.

The phone rang.

I let it ring as I stripped off my rubber gloves and poured myself a cup of coffee, added creamer, and sat down on the stool by the wall phone. I answered it coolly and formally. "Tacoma Pet Boarding. Good morning."

"Celtsie, I swear I'm clean, I swear it, and it's not that no one else wants to help me, it's that they can't help me. Only you. I need that magic shit you do, and listen, I can pay you. Or work for you or something." The words poured out of him in one stream. I was silent.

"Celtsie?"

I said nothing.

"Celtsie, you didn't hang up. Good. Listen, just listen. I know I did a shitty thing to you. I'm sorry. I'm really sorry. If I could get back the necklace and earrings, I would, but the guy didn't know who he sold them to."

I felt a fresh surge of anger. Silver unicorn earrings and a necklace with a silver unicorn. A gift from my father and grandfather on my eleventh birthday, to make up for the fact that there was no owl post from Hogwarts. "Real silver for a really magical girl." At least I still had the birthday card. But the earrings and necklace were gone. A part of my childhood stolen forever. I choked on it and could not tell if it was anger, hurt, or loss. I squeezed my eyes tight shut, refusing the tears, and opened them. Wet lashes. I kept silent. I wouldn't let him hear the hurt in my choked voice.

"Listen, Celtsie, you there? Did you just leave the phone off the hook? Celtsie. Listen, if you can hear me, I'm in bad trouble and it's not just me. It's Selma, too. I don't know if you can fix it but if you can't, no one can."

Selma. Like Farky, she'd gone to elementary school with me. She'd dropped out in eleventh grade. We were still friends in a very casual way. She worked at Expensive Coffee six blocks away. I swallowed. I'd gotten coffee from her about a week ago, a rare indulgence for me. When I thought about it, she'd been pretty flat that day. No special, "Hello, how are you?" And she had even asked me what I wanted. Selma's known how I like my coffee for years.

"What happened to Selma?" I asked in a controlled voice. I suspected I knew. He'd probably stolen from her, too.

"I'll tell you, but I got to tell you the whole thing. Can I come over?"

"No. The restraining order is still in place." It was a lie. It had lapsed months ago.

"What? Still? Jeez, Celtsie, it's been over a year!"

"Yeah, it's worked for over a year."

"Okay. Be that way. But I still need your help. Your magic. And you should do it, for Selma if not for me."

"For Selma, I might. Not for you." I had a feeling this was going to be a complicated thing, and not something I'd get paid for.

"Okay, so this is the deal. A few months back, I got into some trouble. I swear I didn't know it was going to happen. Brodie asks me to drive him to the Seven-Eleven cuz he's pretty drunk. He wants a burrito. So I drive him there. And he says, 'Wait here,' and he goes in. And then he comes running out and gets in the car saying, 'Go, go, go!' So I drive and he's like looking back and everything, and I'm thinking, 'Oh, shit, what did he do?' and he tells me to drive around for a while, like go to Lakewood and back. And he has a brown sack, and when we go back to his apartment and go inside, he dumps money out of it onto the table."

Not much surprising. Especially from Brodie.

"So I'm like, 'What, you robbed the place?' and he was like 'Yeah, last time I was there I told them three burritos and I got home and there was only one in the bag, and when I went back, they said 'too bad' and wouldn't fix it, so you know, they owe me.' And I was like, 'That's stupid, man,' and then someone pounds on the door, and it's, like, the cops. They saw him on the security camera and knew him right away. So anyway, I got arrested, too."

I was already tired of the story. "And how did this involve Selma?"

"I'm getting to that." Oh, the whine in his voice was just too familiar. I nearly slammed the receiver down. Instead, I gripped it really tight and waited.

"So, anyway, I got Judge Mabel. You heard of her?"

I had. Everyone in Tacoma has a Judge Mabel story. She's a local treasure. She's made shoplifters wear sandwich boards outside the stores they stole from and johns hold signs on the street corners where they tried to pick up hookers. I waited.

"She says, 'So you like to "just drive the car" for friends so much, you can drive for senior citizens who need errands done.' And if my client doesn't like my driving, instead of probation I'm in jail. So I say, yes, please, thinking I can do that easy. And a few days later, I get my assignment and I take the bus to Ms. Trudy Mego's house, 'cause I got no car. And I knock on the door, and she comes, and this is no one's old granny. This is like the Crypt Keeper in drag. Bony face, white hair with a flaky scalp showing through, skinny hands in gloves, and dressed in a black dress and black stockings and black old lady shoes. She has a black cane, and this big black purse, and a folded newspaper sticking out of the top of it. But, what the hell, better than jail, right? And there's an old Mercedes parked in her carport, so I'm like, well, that's cool, I never drove a Mercedes before.

"She gives me the keys and I open the door and it's like, perfect, and I get in, but it stinks in there like vinegar. Really strong. But I start it up, and then she yells at me, all pissed. She's like, 'Get out of there! Open this door for me!' And she's going to ride in the back seat and I'm going to sit up front alone and drive her. Well, whatever! So I get out and I open the back door for her and she comes up to it, and then she turns her back to the seat and sits down on it, and then ducks her head and pulls in her arms and legs and her cane. I swear, it reminded me of a spider or an octopus or something getting into its hole. So I shut the door and ask what store she wants to go to, but she takes out a folded-up newspaper from her big ol' black purse and says, 'Just drive, I'll tell you where.' And I say, 'I'm just supposed to take you to the store for groceries,' and she leans forward and slaps me on the back of the head with the folded newspaper and tells me that it's her car and she'll tell me where to drive it or she'll complain to social services. And then, instead of telling me, she opens her purse and takes out a whatchacallit, thing with girl face powder in it, and she takes a long time powdering her face."

I was beginning to get tired of his tale. I thought about just letting the handpiece dangle from its curly cord against the wall and going back to scrubbing the cat box. I leaned back to look out past the curtained doorway into the front room of my shop. Outside my window, it was raining and there were no eager customers lining up outside. I stretched the handset cord to its full length to fill up my coffee cup. I sipped at it.

"Celtsie? You are there, I hear you drinking coffee. Man, I thought you'd hung up! Or, well, not hung up, 'cause I would have heard the dial tone, but you know, dropped the phone."

"I will hang up if you don't get to the point soon. What happened to Selma?"

"I'm getting to that. I got to tell the story in order or you won't get it."

"So talk."

"Okay, but you know, I only got this drugstore phone and I'm nearly out of minutes. Can I come by? Please?"

I wanted to tell him I'd meet him in Wrongs Park, but I didn't want to sit on a wet bench in the rain next to Farky. "Okay," I said and hung up. I was stupid; I knew it was stupid to let him in the door again. I finished scrubbing the cat box and put it to dry. I took the kennel blankets out of the washer and put them in a hot dryer. I was unloading the water dishes from the dishwasher when I heard my jingle spring over the door. "Jingle spring" was what my dad and my grandpa had always called it; it's one of those old-fashioned bells on a spring. There's a lot of stuff left over in my shop from the days when my grandpa had a little magic store in the same place. Card tricks, top hats, hollow thumbs, silk scarves, and smoke powder were his wares. As far as I knew, he never worked the real stuff. Sometimes I wondered what he would think of me. Collars and leashes and cat toys on the pegboard where his magic cheats used to hang.

The jingle at the door was just the mailman. I was putting the bills in order by due date when Farky came in. Emmanuel Farquar is his real name. Farky isn't much better. I stared at him in disbelief. Shaved. Haircut. Solid-color button-down shirt. Jeans and boots. This is the best he's looked since class picture day in eighth grade. His brown eyes met mine. "She makes me dress like this," he said miserably. "Handed me this shirt and took my old Nirvana T." He looked around the shop. "Quiet in here. Where's Cooper?"

Cooper is a big calico cat that someone dropped off for me to board four years ago. "He's probably asleep somewhere." I didn't feel like small talk. "What happened to Selma?"

"I'm trying to tell you, but I got to tell you the whole thing."

"So tell."

He looked around the shop sadly. "Can we sit in back at the table? Like when we were friends?"

I am so stupid. As stupid as my dad was. Farky admitting that we weren't friends anymore made it impossible for me to throw him out like I should have. I went into the back room, and he followed. At one time, it had been the kitchenette for a tiny apartment behind the storefront. Now it was the utility room for the store. But there's still a kitchen table in there, round and red, with chrome around the edges. And four chairs with vinyl seats and backs, mostly red if you don't count the places where the tears have been duct-taped. He sat down with a heavy sigh. I poured him a cup of coffee and gave mine a warm-up. Reflexes. What my grandpa and dad would have done.

"Celtsie, I'm just so—"

"What happened to Selma?" I knew if he apologized again I'd never be able to forgive him. There's something terrible about hearing someone say they're sorry when they truly understand just how bad they hurt you.

He took a long, deep drink of his coffee and sighed. "I was so cold! Okay. Okay. So I drive, turning where Ms. Mego says, and we end up at

Fred Meyer. She tells me to wait in the car. And she shops, and comes out with like three little bags of stuff, but she makes the bag boy push the cart for her. And I have to get out and open the trunk and put the bags in, and then open the door so she can get into the car butt first. And when I get back into the car, she rattles off an address. When I say, 'What?' she says, 'Never mind, you imbecile. I will tell you the way.' So I pull out of the parking lot, and she gives me directions, but she's terrible at it. Anyway," he said abruptly when he saw I was tired of his bullshit.

"Anyway, we get to the place and it has a garage sale sign up. And stuff out on tables and spread on the lawn on sheets. And I have to get out and open the door for her and I follow her over to look at the stuff because, what the hell, I might find something good there, right?"

He looked around. "Damn, I could use a smoke. You got a cigarette?"

"I've never smoked. You know that. Get on with it, Farky."

He got up from the table and refilled his coffee and brought the pot over to top off mine. So swiftly did he settle back in, like a stray tomcat that only comes home when his ear is torn and one eye swollen shut. I waited.

"She goes straight to the toys there, and paws through them like she's going to find some treasure there. Barbies and a Playmobil and plastic dinosaurs, it's all just junk at that one. But she picks up each toy and holds it close to her face, one after another. Then she shakes her head and I open the car door again, and drive on, to, like, six different garage sales. And my community service thing says I only have to help her for two hours a day, and it's been like four. Then we get to a garage sale where a woman and man are still setting stuff up, and they say, 'We're not quite ready yet,' but Ms. Mego acts like she doesn't hear them. She starts digging through a box of dolls. She holds one doll for a long time, but then as the garage sale woman sets down a shoebox, Ms. Mego practically drops the doll and snatches up the shoebox instead. "How much?" she asks. And the woman says a dollar, and she pays her, and then Ms. Mego rushes back to the car, her cane going *crack-crack-crack* on the pavement. I have to hurry to get to the door before her and open it. She puts her purse on the seat and does her butt-first thing, really struggling because she's holding the shoebox in both hands."

Too much coffee. I suddenly had to pee, badly. "I've got to use the

john. I'll be right back." I thought about telling him not to touch anything, but he was already under my skin. I thought it at him, trying to
find my anger and make it hot again. He looked down at the table, his
hands around his mug.

When I came back, he was smoking a cigarette at the table. My dad's
old glass ashtray was in the center of the table in front of him. I resented
him touching Dad's ashtray, but that wasn't the worst. "Damn it, Farky!
Where'd you get the cigarette?" I knew the answer; I feared the answer.

"Junk drawer gave it to me," he said softly. He hunched his head
down between his shoulders, like a pup that expects to get hit with a
newspaper. "And a lighter," he added, and flashed it at me. Not a cheap
plastic convenience store one; a silver Zippo.

"Damn it!" I stepped to the drawer and put my hand on the handle.
Dead. Completely discharged. Nothing humming at all. "Farky, I've
been feeding that and charging it for, like, a month. And just when we
might need it, you burn *all* the junk drawer magic for a stupid cigarette!"

"I really needed a cigarette!" he whined. And more softly he added,
"And it gave me a really good lighter. Like it remembers me."

"More like I've been feeding it for two months and not asking anything of it! And if we need it now, it's ..." I strangled on my anger.
Farky. Just Farky. What the hell had I expected, letting him back in? I
slammed myself back into my chair. "Selma," I gritted at him.

"Okay, okay, I'm trying." He took a long drag on the cigarette and
tapped ash. "So I told you. She took the shoebox to the car. I had to run
to get ahead of her and open the door. But I'm thinking, good, she
bought something, we can go home.

"So I shut the door and get in and 'All settled?' but before the words
were even out of my mouth she says, 'Drive!' So I say 'Where?' and she
says, 'Just drive, you fool.' So I do." Farky drank more coffee as his eyes
roved around the kitchen. "Jeez, I'm hungry." He looked at the cookie
jar, but he should know by now it's only dog treats. I got up and got us
a couple of bananas. He peeled his right away, bit off about half of it, and
then talked around it. Cigarette in one hand, banana in the other. I
hated him, but I didn't hate him so much as I knew him.

"So I pulled out and drove. I got about a block before I heard the
sound. I knew what it was, because I'd once had a dog that loved to chew

plastic. There's a wet, smacky sound that you don't forget. I looked in the rearview mirror. The shoebox was full of those green plastic army men. And I saw her put one of the 'crawl on his belly' soldiers into her mouth and bite down. She used her side teeth to sever him in half and then she chewed with her mouth open, breathing in and out through her nose and mouth. It was noisy and I got a glimpse of green bits in her teeth. She chewed like someone eating stale taffy, working hard at it, but her eyes were half closed like a woman in ecstasy. I didn't know what to think, so I just kept driving. She ate the whole box of them! And then she sat up and said, 'Drive me home now.' So I do, and I get out and open her door, and she swings her legs out first, and her skirt sort of pulls up, and I realize that for an old woman, she's got great legs in those black stockings. She holds out her hand like she's some kind of princess, and when I offer her my hands, she comes out of the car and stands up, and holy cow, she's not old anymore. She's not young either, but she's, you know, one of those middle-aged ladies that it would be okay to get it on with. But her face is covered in cracking powder and she tells me, 'Put the groceries in the kitchen.' And then she goes into her house. And that's it, I carry the groceries in, and I put them on the kitchen table, and it's like she's not even there. Cleanest kitchen I've ever been in. Like, nothing on top of the counters or table. Nothing. I think I should put her stuff in the fridge, but it's not food. It's paper towels and floor cleaner and like that. So I leave."

I stayed quiet. At first, I had thought "pica." I'd known a girl in school who pulled the buttons off her coat and ate them. Paste eaters in kindergarten. People with pica eat all sorts of odd things. But a whole shoebox of plastic soldiers wasn't pica. Nor was it an age regression. I'd never heard of this before, and I was pretty sure I had no idea on how to fight it. Or whether it needed fighting. So an old woman could eat toys and get young again. Who was she hurting?

Farky got up and opened the cupboard under the sink to toss in the banana peel. His eyes wandered the kitchen, and he got a wistful expression on his face. He has a lot of history here, almost as much as I do. Afterschool snacks. Playing Magic cards or Clue on this table. First aid from my dad the time he got beat up really bad when he was fourteen and there was no one home at his house. I hardened my heart. It's his own fault he's not welcome here anymore. Don't crap in your own nest. "Selma," I reminded him.

"Oh. Yeah." He came back to the table and dropped into his chair. "So, like that. Twice a week. I'm supposed to be taking her to doctor visits and the pharmacy and Safeway. But it's always garage sales. And it's mostly toys. Always the same; she picks them up and holds them and then she buys them. And she eats them. And she can eat anything! A forty-five of 'Rainbow Connection' by Kermit the Frog. Cobra Ninja G.I. Joe doll. This little worn out Raggedy Ann doll; she tore it to pieces with her teeth and ate it, stuffing and all. And it's pretty much that she's an old lady when she gets in the car, and younger when she gets out."

"Selma," I reminded him.

"Yeah. Her. That was bad. She rents a little house over on Jay Street, you know?"

"Yeah."

"Well, I didn't. We pulled up to a garage sale, and I didn't recognize Selma at first. She had on this big hat and shorts and was sitting in her lawn chair. And you remember that binder of Magic cards she had? She always had the best deck, remember? Well, she was going through it, really slowly, and taking out the cards and putting them in piles on a folding table. Ms. Mego was busy digging in a basket of plastic ponies, so I walked over and said hi to Selma, and she said hi and we talked. She needed some cash and she was sorting out cards to sell on eBay. I guess you can get money for vintage Magic cards. She had some little D and D figurines on the table, all painted. And we're talking, remembering games in this kitchen, and she even remembers the names of the little figurines and some dungeons we were in together. So we're laughing and going, 'do you remember,' and Ms. Mego comes up and she bends over really close to look at the cards and figurines and then she says, 'How much? How much?' And I get this really, really bad feeling!"

Farky did the dramatic pause. I wanted to hit him. I'd all but forgotten how he loves a stage. I glanced at the front of my store. Still no customers. "What happened?" I asked him quietly.

"Well, Selma tried to say they weren't for sale yet, that she was still sorting and hadn't really decided if she wanted to part with some of them, but all Ms. Mego says is, 'How much? How much?' And she's really being rude, leaning over the table, really close to Selma. And Selma finally gets mad and says, 'Four hundred cash for all of it.'" He paused again. He waited. Then he said very softly, "And Ms. Mego opened her big black purse and started counting out first hundreds, then fifties, and twenties. Selma just watched, and I could see by her face she didn't want to just sell that stuff, or maybe she was wishing she'd asked for a thousand. Ms. Mego set the money down in a messy pile, and then she started scooping up the cards and figurines like she couldn't wait. She grabbed the binder, you remember that one Selma had, the one she made all those stickers for? She took that, too. She scuttled back to the car like she couldn't wait, even opened the door herself. She crabbed back into her car, one arm clutching everything to her chest so she wouldn't drop the little painted clerics and that barbarian warrior. You remember Selma's warrior? Used to kick butt every time we played?" He stubbed his cigarette out.

"I remember him," I said, and I did.

"So I stood there, and Selma was, like, sort of frozen. She looked at the money and said, 'I really needed money. But not that bad, I think.' And she was crying, a little. Not making sounds, just the tears. And over in the car, I can see Ms. Mego stuffing things in her mouth, and chewing. She was ripping the cards out of the card sheets, and I didn't want Selma to see her eating them, so I tried to stand in the way. And I said something like, 'I'm sad she took your cleric. I remember how cool she was. Her name was Selmia, wasn't it?' But Selma suddenly just picked up the money and looked at me like I might try to take it and said, 'Kid stuff, Farky. I don't even remember how to play. Now buzz off before you scare the real customers away.' And she said it mean, and, well, she really meant it, Celtsie.

"So I went back to the car and without even asking, I drove Ms. Mego home. And when I opened the door for her and she got out, she was, like, maybe in her twenties. And she's rocking that black dress and stockings, and the old lady shoes look punk, the way she's wearing them. And as she walks past me, she grabs my ass and says, 'I know you like my legs, driver-boy. Want to see where they end?' And that scared me so bad that I just about pissed myself."

He drew a ragged breath. "I been to get coffee from Selma twice since then. The first time, I said, 'Hi Selma,' and she looked at me like she was shocked I knew her name. And the second time, she gave it to me in a to-go cup and said, 'The boss doesn't like crackheads hanging out here.' I thought she was making a bad joke, but she wasn't. It's like the Selma that knew me is just gone."

"And Ms. Mego?"

"She was young for a while. And she had me driving her to the mall, and once I had to sit outside Jazz Bones and wait for, like, two hours, until she came back with some dude. And he thought it was just awesome that she had a driver, and I had to take them to his place, and spent half the night sitting out in the car."

I gave him a look.

"I got to! One complaint from her and I'm doing jail time, Celtsie! But she's getting old and powdery again. Only garage sale season is over, so I don't know where she'll get her food. And I think it's really bad when she eats those old toys. Like she's eating more than just toys, you know? And you're the only person I know who might know how to fix it. Fix her." He flung himself back in his chair. He took a pack of Camel filters from his shirt pocket and shook one out.

"You got a whole pack of cigarettes out of the drawer!"

He halted, cigarette and lighter poised. "Sorry. I didn't think to imagine just one cigarette in there."

I squeezed my head between my hands. He'd depleted the junk drawer magic for a pack of cigarettes and a lighter. He lit the cigarette, drew in smoke, and blew it up toward my ceiling. "So. What do we do?"

"I don't know," I said flatly.

"But you'll think of something? Soon?"

"I'll try. For now, get out. I get something, I'll call you. You'd better have some minutes on that phone."

"I got no money!"

"Fine." I went to the cookie jar and tipped it. The emergency twenty was still taped to the bottom. That was a surprise. When I saw the cigarette, I'd just assumed he'd already taken it. I slapped it onto the table. "Go buy minutes. Right now. Drugstore is only three blocks from here. Buy minutes and don't use them. They're mine."

"But what if someone calls me or—"

"Don't answer. Out, Farky. I'm doing this for Selma, not you."

"That hurts, Celtsie. I'm going. I know I deserve it. But that hurts."

"I meant it to," I told him coldly.

I followed him out to the shop front and watched him leave. The rain had calmed. He wrapped his arms around himself and hurried away. I wanted to go see Selma right away, to be sure his tale wasn't a bullshit one. But as life always does, or perhaps it was contrary magic, I suddenly had a stream of customers. A dachshund, two ferrets, an old gray cat, and a pair of sleek black cats were all occupying the boarding cages in my shop before I finally got a break. I hung up the "Back Soon" sign, locked the glass door, and pulled my grate down over it for good measure. Farky was pretty good at picking locks.

I turned up the collar on my windbreaker and jogged the six blocks to Expensive Coffee. It was busy, and Selma was behind the counter, simultaneously taking orders and making coffees with the smooth expertise of years. The other barista reminded me of a maddened squirrel as he dashed about behind the counter, doing little more than getting in her way. Selma's focus was on the customer in front of her. I took my place in line. I waited for her to notice me. She didn't, even though her smile slid over me twice as she scanned the waiting queue for signs of impatience. Then it was my turn.

"I'd like a grande iced sugar-free latte. With soy milk. And a plain bagel."

"Sure thing!" Her fingers danced over the register. "Anything else?"

"Selma," I said.

She looked up at me. "Oh. Celtsie. Nice to see you. Anything else?"

I shook my head. "No."

"That'll be $7.85."

I reached into my pocket. "Damn! Left my wallet at the shop. Back soon."

"Okay. Next, please."

I walked away, feeling queasy. My old friend. Could she possibly not remember that soy milk makes me throw up, as in all over the front seat of her mom's car when I was seventeen? And that I hate bagels? And did she not remember that artificial sweeteners give us both terrible headaches? Any one of those I might have slid past her on a busy day. But not all of them. Not unless some precious part of her had gone missing.

I walked back to the shop, scanning the sidewalk as I went. I found a scarred penny in the gutter. And a little girl's blue butterfly barrette, rather grubby. I unlocked and went in. All was as I'd left it. I went through to the kitchen, rubbing the scar on my neck as I went. Cold weather makes it pull sometimes. I opened the junk drawer and tossed in the barrette and the penny. I stirred it hopefully, not even sure of what I should ask it to produce. Sometimes it gives me hints. But only when it's charged. I saw a ticket stub, a leftover piece of candle from my jack-o-lantern, a sparkly red slipper charm on a keychain, a ruler, a dried up orange marker, a marble darning egg, three hairpins . . . just the stuff the junk drawer seemed to produce for its own amusement. I shut it.

The rest of the afternoon passed slowly. Cooper came down to sit beside the till. The dachshund barked at him until Cooper growled back. One of the black cats was crying pathetically. I passed out sardines to all and sundry, and that calmed the shop for a time. I wondered how you got rid of a toy-eater. And if she was only choosing the most precious toys, how did she know what they were? How had she become a toy-eater? Was she really dangerous to people, or had something else happened to Selma? Had anything happened to Selma, or were we just growing apart through the years? I should have asked Selma if she'd sold her cards. Farky was such a bullshitter. And a crackhead. And he'd burned up the charge I'd built up on the junk drawer for a cigarette. Toys. Precious things. Upstairs, in the top of my closet, in a cardboard box, were two ancient stuffed animals. Terry and Boomer. What would happen to me if the toy-eater ate them?

I cheated on closing time by fifteen minutes. Once the grilles were down, I opened all the cages. "Crates," people called them, as if dogs and cats and ferrets were things to be stored when not in use. Cooper was asleep beside my register. I nudged him awake. "Take them upstairs, Coop," I told him, and he did. He dropped to the floor with a solid, twenty-eight-pound thud, looked at our tenants, and led them to the pet hatch in the door that went upstairs. I watched the ferrets go, lippity, lippity, after the cats, and the dachshund last of all. The dachshund high-centered for a moment on the pet hatch, teetered there, and then tipped in.

I finished closing up, scooped some litter, refreshed water bowls, and then followed them. I climbed the stairs slowly. The old runner was threadbare in the middle, but the edges of it were still rich red. I went past the locked door on the second floor that led to what I thought of as my legacy rooms. Behind that door, a Wurlitzer jukebox crouched in one corner, gleaming and waiting for a quarter. There were two moose heads, mounted as if battling each other, and some Kipling first editions. Ancient toys, and prized LPs, and a hundred other marvelous things that perhaps no one would ever value as highly as they had. Precious things. A feast for a toy-eater? Maybe.

I climbed the next flight of stairs and pushed the door to my apartment open. It's a big apartment. Three bedrooms, a kitchen, a bath with a good-size tub, and a library. I don't know why anyone has a living room when they could have a library instead. There's a beat-up squashy couch in the library, and two overstuffed chairs, frayed where Cooper and other cats have cleaned their claws on them. There's an old nineteen-inch Sylvania television set in a console. There's a turntable in the compartment next to it. It all works. Why replace stuff that works? I put some of last night's chicken chow mein in the microwave to reheat and shook some crispy noodles onto a plate. Then I went into my bedroom and opened the closet.

In a big shoebox from some winter boots were Terry and Boomer. I took them out and looked at them. Terry had been a stuffed toy terrier. Now he was a rather lumpy bag of stuffing. Only the felt backing for his button eyes remained. The stiffener for his ears had long since given up its stiffness. Boomer had stripes. That was about the only clue that he had been a tiger. He had two stiff whiskers left, and his tail was limp. Yet I found myself handling their battered fabric bodies as if they were old and beloved pets. I settled them again in their shoebox and layered the tissue paper over them. "Good night," I told them, as I always had when they'd been on my childhood bed. The same single bed I sat on now. Their bodies had absorbed my junior high tears over boys who passed me by, and my high school tears over failed tests. They'd gone off to college with me and adorned my dormitory bed. And come home again when I returned to Tacoma.

I put the lid on the box. Why didn't I throw them away? What were they, really, beyond some threadbare fabric sewn around cheap stuffing? The answer seemed both silly and simple. They were Terry and Boomer. My friends. Imbued with the life of a thousand play-pretend games. My friends when it seemed no one else cared.

I tried to imagine Ms. Mego eating them. Eating my hugs after nightmares, tears after Steve broke up with me on the school bus in front of everyone. Teeth ripping frayed fabric, chewing old stuffing.

Okay. I had to stop the toy-eater. How?

It seemed obvious. She fed on beloved toys and grew younger. What if she ate something that had been hated?

Did anyone keep a toy they hated?

I thought of toys I'd hated. Scary ones. A chimp doll the size of a two-year-old, with rubbery hands that felt like he was holding on to me. A fashion model doll with slutty eyes and the flat mouth of an axe murderer. Oh. That clown doll with the big mouth with red lips and flat black eyes. What had become of them? Two donated to Goodwill. One I ditched at a bus stop.

The bad part of running a business is that people expect you to be there during business hours. Especially if they want to pick up their pet. I sat in my shop the next day, calling secondhand stores, asking if they had chimp or clown dolls in stock. I spent a lot of time on hold. Then I started on the quasi antiques stores and the "collector's stores." No chimps or clowns, but two offered to show me "vintage" dolls. And they were both open after my regular closing hour.

Both were outside the Wedge, the section of Tacoma I live in. No bus service from the Wedge to where they are. I have an old Celebrity station wagon for the rare occasions when I need wheels. I've customized it to my needs over the years. Like my TV, it does everything I need it to do, and I see no point in replacing it. It got me to Marcella's Vintage. Her dolls were immaculately dressed, in boxes and completely unremarkable. At Raymond's Old Toys, I had better luck. I walked into a cluttered shop that smelled vaguely like cheap cigars and Pledge furniture wax. The clerk, who was possibly Raymond, waved me toward some glass cases in the back and went back to reading an old issue of *Tiger Beat*.

Pay dirt! There were three glass cases, containing appalling dolls. Most were in mediocre condition. A Barbie sneered at me, her model's mouth flat. A Cabbage Patch doll slouched in coveralls. There was a brightly painted marionette of a Mexican bandit with bandoliers on his chest and thick six-guns in each hand and a maniacal look on his face. But none of those were the one that gave me the chill.

There was a baby doll, eyes an improbable staring blue. Mouth ajar, two tiny teeth showing. Chubby hands open and reaching. It was dressed in a pale pink garment that reminded me of a hospital gown. It looked like a little succubus. It had the sort of scuffs on its face and pink plastic hands that told me it had been stuffed into a toy box under the Tonka trucks and plastic McDonald's Happy Meal horrors. Yes, horrors. Has anyone ever wanted a plastic Hamburglar to play with?

I pried the owner free of his cigarette and coffee to unlock the case and departed the store with the succubus in a brown paper sack. I phoned Farky before I started the car. "I think I've got what you need. Come get it." I didn't give him time to ask any questions.

When he arrived at my shop, I unlocked the glass door and slid the grille up and let him in. He came in shaking off rain and then clasping his hands in front of him to still a shaking that had nothing to do with weather.

"Where's your coat?" I asked him.

"Sold it to the vintage store," he said brusquely and then said, "What do you have for me?"

There are times when you can help someone and times when there's nothing you can do. I tilted my head toward the paper bag on the table. "It's in there. A doll I'm pretty sure was hated and feared. If you can find a way to get her to eat it, it may undo her."

"Yeah. Like an opposite thing." His wet sneakers left tracks on my clean floor as he walked back into the utility room. He picked up the bag without looking inside. He glanced at me and then away. "Thanks."

"Sure." I wiped my hands down the front of my jeans, but guilt doesn't come off even when you do that. I wanted to offer him food, money, coffee, but didn't. He left, bag in hand, and as I let him out the

door, the pelting rain on the brown paper sack made a hollow drum-
ming.

So. That was that. I locked up again, doused all my lights except for
my custom-made neon in the window, and headed up the worn steps. I
paused on the landing and even found the key on my ring, but decided
tonight was not a night for me to look at my treasures and think warm
thoughts of the past. Instead I went to my apartment, microwaved a
chicken pot pie, and ate it on the couch with all my tenants attentively
watching me. When I went to bed, Cooper came and purred on the pillow by my head. I closed my eyes and wondered how Farky would deliver the toxic doll to the toy-eater. I wondered if he'd show up to drive
her, or if he'd tumble back into using. I wondered if he'd go to jail and
what would happen to him there. I pretended that none of it was my
concern.

At six-thirty a.m., I let myself stop pretending to sleep and got up.
In my pajamas, I went down to my shuttered shop. My clientele followed me down the stairs and grudgingly got back into their pens. I
don't know how Cooper conveys to them what they're to do. I just know
that since he was abandoned with me, my life is a lot easier. I dished out
the morning chow and water, made sure their cuddle blankets were
clean and fresh. I went back upstairs, got dressed, and came down and
opened my shop.

It wasn't raining. Business was slow. I fed, I scooped poop, I surfed
the Internet. I sold a leash. I took in a recently adopted black kitten.
Blackie would stay with me for a month. Why would anyone adopt a
kitten right before going on vacation for a month? I will never understand people.

I put my hand on the junk drawer. Barely humming. I went upstairs
and scoured my desk for clutter. I came back down and fed the drawer a
rubber band, an AA battery, a bent paper clip, a business card from a
cleaning service, a refrigerator magnet, and three loose coins. The junk
drawer doesn't really care about the value of what's dropped in there; it's
the idea of being given things.

At noon, I hung up my "Back Soon" sign and headed down to Expensive Coffee. Selma was behind the counter. I ordered a vanilla latte.
"What name you want on that?" she asked me.

"Selma, it's me. Celtsie."

She looked up from her register, and our eyes met. She gave me a tired smile. "Of course it is. Sorry." She took my money and gave me my change.

I sat down at a table near the window. When they called for Kelsey, I went and got my drink. Yes. That was what she'd written on the cup. As I took it, one of the other clerks bumped into the counter and spilled a slop of milk on to the floor. Selma turned on her. "Clean it up. And pay attention. Are you stoned, or just stupid?"

The girl looked at Selma with wide brown eyes. I saw her pinch her lips tight shut, mutter a "sorry," and stoop to clean up the spill. I left. No. That wasn't the Selma I'd known. I wondered if killing the toy-eater would bring her back.

At my shop, I checked the pickup dates and times for my clientele. I left a message on Farky's cellphone. Then I flipped the sign to "Back Soon," leashed up the dachshund, gathered my poop sacks, and headed out for a walk in Wrongs Park.

Wrongs Park isn't that far from my shop. On the other side of the tall hedge, Wright's Park has a playground and a fountain, a botanical greenhouse, and tree specimens from all over the world. In Wrongs Park, other things are remembered about Tacoma. There's a statue of a man with a cast on his leg, asking a woman to help him carry his briefcase. There's another of a man target-practicing on a stump. The most wrenching one for me depicts the Expulsion of the Chinese from Tacoma. It's not something we enjoy remembering, but even more, it has to be something we don't forget.

I was doing a slow circle of the statues of the people being forced onto the train when Farky found me. "Hey," he said. His greeting was flat. No joy, no anticipation, no anger. Just flat. His sneakers and the cuffs of his jeans were soaked. His green hoodie was sucking up the rain.

"Did it work?" I asked him.

He sat down on a wet park bench like he didn't care. I perched on the edge of it with my raincoat trapped under me. Slowly he took out a pack of cigarettes and tapped one out. I waited while he lit it with the Zippo, inhaled, and then pushed out a column of smoke. "Not like we wanted it to," he said. He gave me a sideways mournful look. "Maybe that's just as well. I thought about that afterwards. What if she ate it, and it killed her and I'm sitting there in the driver's seat with my fingerprints all over the car?"

"I see your point," I said. We hadn't thought about that angle. When he said nothing, I prodded, "So what did happen?"

Another long drag in and out. He shrugged. "I was wondering how to get it to her. I had it in the paper sack in my backpack. I got to her place as usual. I had my backpack in the front seat. She did her butt-first get in the car, and then, without saying anything, she lunged for the front seat. Celtsie, she tore my backpack open. Not unzipped it, tore the canvas open, and ate that doll like I'd wolf a Big Mac. Then she sat in the back seat, breathing loud through her nose. I'd never guessed how strong she was. I was sitting there, afraid to let her see me looking at her in the mirror, afraid to turn around. Then she said, 'Let me out. That's all I need today.'

"So I got out, and I opened the door, and she got out. She was young and strong, but in an ugly way. That's all I can say about it. And she moved up too close to me, chest to chest, but not like a woman. Like, well, I stepped back. She looked at me and said, 'You'd better bring me more. You know what I need now. Get it for me.' Then she just looked at me. And that was a threat so bad . . . I can't even imagine what the threat was." He sniffed and took another drag from his smoke. He gave me another jolt from his sad dog eyes. "So I think I'm in even worse than I was before."

We were silent. The dachshund whined and stood up to put muddy paws on Farky's knee. He put his hand gently on the nape of the dog's neck and scratched him. I reflected that Farky was probably right. Pimping meals for a toy-eater was not a good career move.

"What now?" he asked me sullenly. Sullenly because he knew what I would say.

"I don't know."

"Maybe you should ask?"

I folded my lips for a short time, angry that he had even suggested it. "I don't like to ask," I said primly.

Another long draw on his cigarette. He dropped it, stood up slowly, and ground it out as he exhaled. "So. I guess I'm just fucked, then." He turned and walked away from me. I watched him go. There was nothing I could do. None of it was my fault. He wasn't really my friend, not anymore. I didn't owe him anything. I'd already done more than he had any right to expect. I stood up and walked back to my shop, stopping once to pick up dachshund poop.

The bad part about a set routine is that you can follow it and think at the same time. I counted up all the times Farky had screwed me over. Then I added the times when he'd failed me as a friend. I closed up and cleaned up and refused to think of him sitting at my red table, blood in red rivulets down the side of his face, my dad holding a bag of ice to his brow. So we'd helped him then. What did that have to do with now?

I sighed. I put my hand on the front of the junk drawer. Barely a hum. This would waste even that. I jerked it open and looked inside. A bookmark. Oh, great. I took it out. It was one of those cheap school reward things. It had Arthur and Buster Baxter on the front. On the back, it said, "Good job, Selma! Great book report." I shut the drawer.

It could have been in there for years, trapped somehow above the drawer to fall down at exactly this time. But I knew it hadn't, and I knew what it meant. I shut off the lights and trudged upstairs.

When I was a kid, I had to do a science report. My grandpa helped me saw a D battery in half, and then my dad lifted the hood on our car and showed me about how the car battery worked. Acid in there, and unlike metals, and he explained the flow of electrons from one plate to another.

But it was years before I understood how it worked for books. That Dewey fellow was one brilliant man. He figured it out, and so few people know enough to give him credit for making libraries safe. Librarians don't talk about it, and some bookstore people, the way they shelve books, you'd think they were just hoping for a mishap. The one time I had a long talk about it with Duane, he theorized that was what happened in the library of Alexandria. A careless juxtaposition of books and scrolls might have set off a powerful flow between unlike volumes, and the resulting surge of power might have been enough to start a fire.

My library is small but it's potent. Mostly hardbacks. Illustrated hardbacks. Some vintage paperbacks. Nonfiction can act as insulators separating the more powerful novelists, but even then, one has to be careful. I once shelved *Future Shock* next to *20,000 Leagues Under the Sea*. I'll never make that mistake again. Nor will I ever put more than three volumes of poetry on the same shelf. Every comic goes in a protective plastic envelope. Even so, messing with it is a dangerous business. My hands were sweating before I even turned the lights on in the room.

I looked at all the spines for a long time. Pull out the wrong insulator, and I could be told something that no one needed to know. What did I want to know? I wanted to help Farky. Did I want to let *Tom Sawyer* butt up against *The Mouse and his Child*? No, I needed to be more specific than that. I needed to know how to slay a toy-eater. *The Velveteen Rabbit* was next to Simon and Schuster's *Guide to Trees*. And just past the tree book was *The Age of Fable*. Lots of monster slaying in there.

That just might work.

I said a little prayer and pulled the *Guide to Trees*. *The Velveteen Rabbit* leaned over against *The Age of Fable*. I carried the tree guide out to my kitchen, softly closing the door behind me. I sat down at the table. I knew I had to give it time, but not too much. I vividly recalled when Caesar's *Gaul* shot across the room and hit the wall so hard it cracked its spine. I got up. Can't pace. Can't wait. Magic doesn't like it when people wait on it. I made a BLT and put a scoop of cottage cheese next to it. I set it on the table and made a nice pot of Red Rose tea. I set out a cup and saucer like I didn't have a care in the world, and I sat down to eat. Cooper came in and asked for a piece of bacon. I gave him some, and he sat on the table and kept me company while I ate, until I heard what I'd been waiting for. The soft thud of a falling hardback.

I crept back into the library, swiftly shelved the *Guide to Trees*, and stood over the fallen book. *Bartlett's Quotations*. This could be tricky. I knelt down beside it without looking at it and then let my eyes snap to the open page.

"The opposite of love isn't hate. It's indifference." Elie Wiesel.

Oh.

I put Selma's old bookmark in as a thank-you and carefully reshelved *Bartlett's*.

Well. That certainly cleared that up. Now I just needed a toy that had left the owner indifferent to it. Indifferent, I decided—not in the way of "not my thing, I don't play with Barbies," but deliberately indifferent. And I knew right away what that was.

My mother had an older half sister. They were estranged. Her name was Theresa. Perhaps she thought two estranged equaled a bond, because twice she tried to insert herself into my life. When I was about eight, several years after my mother had gone, she called my father and grandfather to say she would be in Tacoma and wanted to see me. That was the first time I'd even known she existed. She made an uncomfortable visit to our home where she ate none of the dinner we'd prepared for her, but offered to help my father and grandfather "when the time comes for her to be taught about womanly things."

Then she vanished again. But for the next two years, she sent me birthday gifts that came the month after my birthday. The first was a package of Beanie Babies. But they were the ones that came free with McDonald's Happy Meals, not the ones that were theoretically "collectible." The second was a Nancy Drew book. I'd traded the book at the secondhand book store for several old Doc Savages. But the Beanie Babies . . . I frowned. Would I have kept them? Perhaps. Perhaps in what my father had called the "emergency gift box." It was where we tossed things that were new and valued by other people, but totally unnecessary to our lives. White elephants, my grandfather called them. A French press for coffee. A cheap dock for an iPod I'd never had. Christmas knee-high socks. The sorts of gifts that well-meaning friends gave us over the years. And that we re-gifted as needed.

The box for "emergency gifts" was in the back of the deep closet in the second bedroom. With other boxes, it helped to conceal the hatch to the secret room. I dragged it out into the light and dug through it. Here was a boxed set of socks with dogs and cats on them. Beneath it, a curling iron still in its package. I abruptly decided that the entire box of crap was all going to the Goodwill tomorrow. But as I dug down, there in the corner in a zip-lock bag were the Beanie Babies. One was a pink hippo. I took it out and looked at it. The Ty label was still affixed to it. I knew it was a hippo only because someone had once told me that was what this pink blob represented. I considered it carefully a moment longer. Did I hate it? Love it? Did it waken regret in me, or resentment? No. None of the above. I was as indifferent to it as my aunt had been to me.

I set the box of other people's treasures in the hall to carry downstairs later. The Beanie Baby wasn't large, only as big as my fist. Was that much indifference enough to kill a toy-eater? There was only one way to find out. But now I had to confront the second part of the ruse. Delivery. How was I going to get her to eat it?

As if in answer to that thought, my phone rang. Not my wall phone, but my cell. The wall phone was for business. The cellphone meant whoever was calling was either a friend or a telemarketer. I didn't recognize the number and didn't answer. But they left a message, and I did dial in and listen to that. Then I called Farky back.

"Tonight. She told me I got to bring her something tonight. Or she calls the cops and tells them she saw me do a deal outside Fred Meyer."

"Did she?"

Silence. Then. "Celtsie. Please. She threatened the deal thing, but I . . . I just know she could do more. Darker." He caught his breath. "She has my Nirvana T-shirt."

There's a time to think and a time to just do, my father always said. Of course, that's how he took a bullet in the leg for some teenager he didn't even know, and how he gained a limp the rest of his life. But I'd never heard him say he regretted it.

"My place. Fifteen minutes."

I hung up. There was already a coldness running through me. I knew what I was going to do, and I knew I couldn't think about it too much. The very hardest things you can't think about too much or you lose your resolution. Especially when you know what you are going to do is wrong or bad. But you have to do it anyway.

I set the pink hippo on my table and went back to my bedroom. I took down the old boot box. I reached in blindly, knowing it would be impossible to decide. I'd take whichever I touched first. The moment my fingers brushed the worn fabric, I knew it was Terry. I took him out and put Boomer, all alone now, back in the top of my closet.

I hugged Terry hard as I carried him to the kitchen. I didn't wonder what it would do to me when she ate him. I found I hoped that he wouldn't feel it, and that Boomer wouldn't be lonely. Once he had had bright little black button eyes. I looked at the two circles of faded felt backers, at the residue of old glue that had once held them firmly in place. Then I hugged him and kissed him goodbye. I set him on his back on the kitchen table.

I could do this. I had to do this.

I took down the sewing box from its shelf. It wasn't just Farky he'd be saving. I told myself that as I took scissors and cut open his belly. It was people like Selma, and whoever had owned that shoebox full of plastic soldiers. How many people had she deadened over her life span? How old was she, and how long could she live? I parted the multicolored stuffing in Terry's abdomen. I tucked in the hippo that had never mattered. I drew a layer of stuffing over him. I selected a spool of gray thread and threaded the needle. I sewed Terry up, plumper than he'd been in many a year.

And I felt it. He wasn't Terry anymore, not in the way he had been. I wondered, if I cut him open again and took out the hippo, would he be Terry? But I didn't. I found a brown paper sack folded under the sink. I slid him into it. But still, for a long moment, I cupped his worn head and his floppy ears between my two hands. "Goodbye," I told him, and my voice broke, and the tears ran.

The doorbell buzzed.

I closed the bag and carried it down the stairs. Farky was waiting outside in the autumn evening. I unlocked the glass door and then unlocked the outer grille and slid it up. The rain had stopped. The streets were shining and the last of the water was gurgling down the gutters. "Here," I said. Then I reached back and took my windbreaker off the coat rack by the door.

"You're coming with me?"

I nodded. We walked around to the little courtyard behind my building. I got into the Celebrity and leaned across to unlock the passenger door for Farky. "It's been years," he said as he got in. He glanced back. "You, me, and Selma in the 'way back' seat. The one that faced backward. Coming home from Norwescon."

I said nothing.

"I used to love that con. Every year, your grandpa got us memberships as our Christmas gifts."

I nodded. "Where am I going?" I asked him.

And after that our conversation was just directions. We left the

Wedge and drove through Hilltop. The toy-eater's house was on the edge of Edison. I wondered if she rented or owned. Little house, painted gray with white trim. No better or worse than any other on the street. Paved pull-off for the car. I drove in and stopped behind the Mercedes. I cut the engine and turned off the headlights. We sat in the dark. There was one window lit, a curtained yellow square. I waited.

"I guess I'd better take it to her," Farky said.

I nodded. No talking or I'd shout that I'd changed my mind, give me my Terry back. Give me the little pretend dog who had guarded me from nightmares for so many years. I touched the paper sack with one fingertip. He was going to end a nightmare. I'd always known that nothing from the dark could hurt me with Terry clutched in my arms. I told myself he was going into his last battle. Brave little dog.

She opened the door and stood there, a black silhouette against the lit hallway. Farky opened his car door and the dome light came on. She could see me, I thought, and felt a chill. I couldn't make out her features, just her dark shape against the light. She was a tall and angular woman. Then Farky shut his door and the dome light went off and I watched the shape of him and the paper bag as he carried Terry toward her.

She didn't wait. She came down the steps toward him, hands reaching for the bag, and Farky surrendered it to her, holding it out as he cowered back. She snatched it from him and tore the bag open. The brown paper sack fell away, and she clutched Terry in both hands. I made a sound I hadn't known I was going to make as she lifted him to her mouth. It seemed to me that her lower jaw dropped wider than it possibly could. She bit into the middle of him, not tearing a bite free, but chewing into him, both her hands forcing his head and his stubby tail toward the middle. She was chewing as she pushed him into her mouth.

Then she stopped. She swayed. I hit my headlights. She was gagging. She began to claw at her mouth.

I'd never seen Farky do a brave thing. I'd seen him run from fights in elementary school, cry when bullies hit him when he was a freshman. I'd lost count of the times I'd seen him lie his way out of trouble. But he sprang at the toy-eater. One hand behind her head, the other forcing old stuffing and fabric into her mouth. She went down, falling on her back on the steps, and he put his knee in her middle and with both hands he pushed Terry into her mouth.

I was out of the car and moving toward them. My eyes couldn't make sense of what I was seeing. The more Farky stuffed the toy into her mouth, the smaller and flatter she got. Her legs were shortening, her arms becoming floppy, her body drawing in skinnier and shorter. Farky was panting with the effort, and then, as he stopped, in the rectangle of light from her open door, all that remained was a flat body in badly fitted doll clothes and an ugly plastic head, greenish in my headlights. The head sagged suddenly to one side, and I thought I recognized the profile. Farky stood up and stumbled back from her.

The junk drawer had tried to tell me, but it had been too weak. A shiny red shoe. A ruby slipper.

"We're leaving," I told Farky.

"But what about . . ."

"Leave it. Someone else will clean it up. We're done here."

We drove back to my shop. No talk, no radio. We got out of my car. I locked it.

"Was that Terry? Your old stuffed dog?" Farky asked softly.

I walked away from him, unlocked my grille and my glass door, and went inside. I locked up behind myself and went upstairs to where Cooper and my boarders were watching Animal Planet. I sat down with them, and the dachshund wormed into my lap. I petted him. I wondered if I had changed, if I would change now that Terry was gone. I felt around inside myself; anything different? Not that I could tell. I decided I was fine.

About midnight, I turned off the television. Everyone was asleep. I left them in darkness and went to the kitchen. I opened up my laptop and did a quick search. It didn't take me long. Mego. A toymaker. Wizard of Oz dolls. Including the Wicked Witch.

Had someone loved that doll and imbued it with life? Hated it?

The magic I had didn't give me any answers.

I felt cold as I got into my pajamas, and even colder as I lay alone in my bed. My arms were empty. I hadn't slept with a stuffed toy in over a decade. Did I miss one now? Don't be silly. I closed my eyes.

❖ ❖ ❖

It was over a week later that I went to Expensive Coffee. I didn't know what I hoped. I hadn't seen or heard from Farky. Just as well, I told myself. Just as well. And what I'd expected, right? Right.

I chose what I hoped would be a less busy time of the day. I pushed the door open, and Selma glanced over at me. "Vanilla latte, whole milk, twelve ounce. Blueberry muffin, warmed." She called out my order and then went back to waiting on the customer in front of her. By the time I reached the front of the line, she handed it to me. Hot coffee, warm muffin. Old friend.

"Having a good day?" I asked her.

"Oh, about the same as always. Coffee and pastries. How's things in the pet boarding world?"

"About the usual. Litter boxes and kibble. Nice earrings."

She touched the silver unicorns that dangled from her earlobes and smiled. "You don't think they're too young? A bit silly?"

"Not at all." I wondered what I was feeling. There wasn't a word for it. Like something I used to feel had rolled over inside me, stirred briefly but not awakened. Like suddenly remembering a piece of a dream, but only in a fleeting flash. Whatever I had felt had faded away and it didn't matter.

"Customer gave them to me. Farky. You remember Farky?" She spun a forefinger at me in a circle. "We used to play board games at your dad's shop. And Magic. Back in the day."

I nodded. "Back in the day. I remember him."

"He's doing good. Almost clean, just smoking grass, he says." She touched a unicorn again. She shook her head, puzzled. "Strange for Farky to bring me a present. No reason for it." She shook her head, and the unicorns swung, and then she looked past me. "Good seeing you," she said, and rolled her eyes toward the customer behind me.

"Good seeing you again, Selma," I said, and stepped away, coffee in one hand, bagged muffin in the other. There was something I'd meant to say to her, something about the earrings. Gone. Couldn't have been important then. I shouldered the door open.

Outside, it was raining again.

John Crowley

. . .

One of the most acclaimed and respected authors of our day, John Crowley is perhaps best known for his fat and fanciful novel about the sometimes dangerous interactions between Faerie and our own everyday world, *Little, Big*, which won the prestigious World Fantasy Award. His other novels include *Beasts, Daemonomania, Endless Things, The Deep, Engine Summer, The Translator, Lord Byron's Novel: The Evening Land, Four Freedoms,* and *Love and Sleep*. His short fiction has been collected in *Novelties and Souvenirs,* and his most recent novel is *Ka: Dar Oakley in the Ruin of Ymr*. He lives in the Berkshire Hills of western Massachusetts.

In the eloquent and lyrical story that follows, he tells the tale of a boy who is being groomed by the great Elizabethan physician and magician Dr. John Dee for a part in the coming war, a war that will take place both on Earth and between the Powers who live beyond it.

. . .

Flint and Mirror

JOHN CROWLEY

B lind O'Mahon the poet said: "In Ireland there are five kingdoms, one in each of the five directions. There was a time when each of the kingdoms had her king, and a court, and a castle seat with lime-washed towers; battlements of spears, and armies young and laughing."

"There was a high king then too," said Hugh O'Neill, ten years old, seated at O'Mahon's feet in the grass, still green at Hallowtide. From the hill where they sat the Great Lake could just be seen, turning from silver to gold as the light went. The roving herds of cattle—Ulster's wealth—

moved over the folded land. All this is O'Neill territory, and always and forever has been.

"There was indeed a high king," O'Mahon said.

"And will be again."

The wind stirred the poet's white hair. O'Mahon could not see Hugh, his cousin, but—he said—he could see the wind. "Now, cousin," he said, "see how well the world is made. Each kingdom of Ireland has its own renown: Connaught in the west for learning and for magic, the writing of books and annals, and the dwelling places of saints. In the north, Ulster"—he swept his hand over lands he couldn't see—"for courage, battles, and warriors. Leinster in the east for hospitality, for open doors and feasting, cauldrons never empty. Munster in the south for labor, for kerns and ploughmen, weaving and droving, birth and death."

Hugh, looking over the long view, the wind off the river where clouds were gathered now, asked: "Which is the greatest?"

"Which?" O'Mahon said, pretending to ponder this. "Which do *you* think?"

"Ulster," said Hugh O'Neill of Ulster. "Because of the warriors. Cuchulain was of Ulster, who beat them all."

"Ah."

"Wisdom and magic are good," Hugh conceded. "Hosting is good. But warriors can beat them."

O'Mahon nodded to no one. "The greatest kingdom," he said, "is Munster."

Hugh said nothing to that. O'Mahon's hand sought for his shoulder and rested upon it, and Hugh knew he meant to explain. "In every kingdom," he said, "the North, the South, the East, and the West, there is also a north, a south, an east, a west. Isn't that so?"

"Yes," Hugh said. He could point to them: left, right, ahead, behind. Ulster is in the north, and yet in Ulster there is also a north, the north of the north: that's where his mad, bad uncle Sean ruled. And so in that north, Sean's north, there must be again a north and a south, an east and a west. And then again ...

"Listen," O'Mahon said. "Into each kingdom comes wisdom from the west, about what the world is and how it came to be. Courage from the north, to defend the world from what would swallow it up. Hospitality from the east to praise both learning and courage, and reward the kings who keep the world as it is. But before all these things, there is a world at all: a world to learn about, to defend, to praise, to keep. It is from Munster at first that the world comes to be."

"Oh," Hugh said, no wiser, though. "But you said that there were *five* kingdoms."

"So I did. And so it is said."

Connaught, Ulster, Leinster, Munster. "What is the fifth kingdom?"

"Well, cousin," O'Mahon said, "what is it then?"

"Meath," Hugh guessed. "Where Tara is, where the kings were crowned."

"That's fine country. Not north or south or east or west but in the middle."

He said no more about that, and Hugh felt sure that the answer might be otherwise. "Where else could it be?" he asked.

O'Mahon only smiled. Hugh wondered if, blind as he was, he knew when he smiled and that others saw it. A kind of shudder fled along his spine, cold in the low sun. "But then," he said, "it might be far away."

"It might," O'Mahon said. "It might be far away, or it might be close." He chewed on nothing for a moment, and then he said: "Tell me this, cousin: where is the center of the world?"

That was an old riddle; even as a boy Hugh knew the answer to it, his uncle Phelim's brehon had asked it of him. There are five directions to the world: four of them are north, south, east, and west, and where is the fifth? He knew the answer, but just at that moment, sitting with bare legs crossed in the ferns in sight of the tower of Dungannon, he did not want to give it.

It was in the spring that his fosterers the O'Hagans had brought Hugh O'Neill to the castle at Dungannon. It was a great progress in the boy Hugh's eyes, twenty or thirty horses jingling with brass trappings, carts bearing gifts for his O'Neill uncles at Dungannon, red cattle lowing in the van, spearmen and bowmen and women in bright scarves, O'Hagans and O'Quinns and their dependents. And he knew himself, but ten years old, to be the center of that progress, on a dappled pony, with a new mantle wrapped around his skinny body and a new ring on his finger.

He kept seeming to recognize the environs of the castle, and scanned the horizon for it, and questioned his cousin Phelim, who had come to fetch him to Dungannon, how far it was every hour until Phelim grew annoyed and told him to ask next when he saw it. When at last he did see it, a fugitive sun was just then looking out, and sunshine glanced off the wet, lime-washed walls of its wooden palisades and made it seem bright and near and dim and far at once, heart-catching, for to Hugh the wooden tower and its clay and thatch outbuildings were all the castles he had ever heard of in songs. He kicked his pony hard, and though Phelim and the laughing women called to him and reached out to keep him, he raced on, up the long, muddy track that rose up to a knoll where now a knot of riders was gathering, their spears high and slim and black against the sun: his uncles and cousins O'Neill, who when they saw the pony called and cheered him on.

Through the next weeks he was made much of, and it excited him; he ran everywhere, an undersized, redheaded imp, his stringy legs pink with cold and his high voice too loud. Everywhere the big hands of his uncles touched him and petted him, and they laughed at his extravagances and his stories, and when he killed a rabbit they praised him and held him aloft among them as though it had been twenty stags. At night he slept among them, rolled in among their great, odorous, shaggy shapes where they lay around the open turf fire that burned in the center of the hall. Sleepless and alert long into the night, he watched the smoke ascend to the opening in the roof and listened to his uncles and cousins snoring and talking and breaking wind after their ale.

That there was a reason, perhaps not a good one and kept secret from him, why on this visit he should be put first ahead of older cousins, given first choice from the thick stews in which lumps of butter dissolved, and listened to when he spoke, Hugh felt but could not have said; but now and again he caught one or another of the men regarding him steadily, sadly, as though he were to be pitied; and again, a woman would sometimes, in the middle of some brag he was making, fold him in her arms and hug him hard. He was in a story whose plot he didn't know, and it made him the more restless and wild. There was a time when, running into the hall, he caught his uncle Turlough Luineach and a woman of his having an argument, he shouting at her to leave these matters to men; when she saw Hugh, the woman came to him, pulled his mantle around him, and brushed leaves and burrs from it. "Will they have him dressed up in an English suit then for the rest of his life?" she said over her shoulder to Turlough Luineach, who was drinking angrily by the fire.

"His grandfather Conn had a suit of clothes," Turlough said into his cup. "A fine suit of black velvet with gold buttons and a black velvet hat. With a white plume in it!" he shouted, and Hugh couldn't tell if he was angry at the woman or Conn or himself. The woman began crying; she drew her scarf over her face and left the hall. Turlough glanced once at Hugh and spat into the fire.

Nights they sat in the light of the fire and the great reeking candle of reeds and butter, drinking ale and Spanish wine and talking. Their talk was one subject only: the O'Neills. Whatever else came up in conversation or song related to that long history, whether it was the strangeness—stupidity or guile, either could be argued—of the English colonials; or the raids and counter-raids of neighboring families; or stories out of the far past. Hugh couldn't always tell, and perhaps his elders weren't always sure, what of the story had happened a thousand years ago and what of it was happening now. Heroes rose up and raided, slew their enemies and carried off their cattle and their women; some were crowned high king at Tara. There was mention of Niall of the Nine Hostages and the high king Julius Caesar; of Brian Boru and Cuchulain; of Sean O'Neill and his fierce Scots redlegs, of the sons of Sean and the king of Spain's son. His grandfather Conn had been the O'Neill, but had let the English call him Earl of Tyrone. There had always been an O'Neill, invested at the crowning stone at Tullyhogue to the sound of St. Patrick's bell; but Conn O'Neill, Earl of Tyrone, had seen King Harry over the sea, and had promised to plant corn, and learn English. And when he lay dying he said that a man was a fool to trust the English.

Within the tangled histories, each strand bright and clear and beaded with unforgotten incident but inextricably bound up with every other, Hugh could perceive his own story: how his grandfather had never settled the succession of his title of the O'Neill; how Hugh's uncle Sean had risen up and slain his brother Matthew, Hugh's father, and now called himself the O'Neill and claimed all Ulster for his own, and raided his cousins' lands when he chose with his six fierce sons; how he, Hugh, had true claim to what Sean had usurped. Sometimes all this was as clear to him as the multifarious branchings of a winter-naked tree against the sky; sometimes not. The English ... there was the confusion. Like a cinder in his eye, they baffled his clear sight.

Turlough tells with relish: "Then comes up Sir Henry Sidney with all his power, and Sean? Can Sean stand against him? He cannot! It's as much as he can do to save his own skin. And that only by leaping into the Great River and swimming away. I'll drink the Lord Deputy's health for that, a good friend to Conn's true heir ..."

Or, "What do they ask?" a brehon, a lawgiver, asks. "You bend a knee to the queen, and offer all your lands. She takes them and gives you the title earl—and all your lands back again. You are her *urragh*, but nothing has changed ..."

"And they are sworn then to help you against your enemies."

"No," says another, "*you* against *theirs*, even if it be a man sworn to you or your own kinsman whom they've taken a hatred to. Conn was right: a man is a fool to trust them."

"Think of Desmond, in prison in London these many years, who trusted them."

"Desmond is a thing of theirs. He is a Norman, he has their blood. Not the O'Neills."

"*Fubun*," says the blind poet O'Mahon in a quiet, high voice that stills them all:

> Fubun *on the gray foreign gun,*
> Fubun *on the golden chain;*
> Fubun *on the court that talks English,*
> Fubun *on the denial of Mary's son.*

Hugh listens, turning from one speaker to the other, frightened by the poet's potent curse. He feels the attention of the O'Neills on him.

◆　◆　◆

In Easter week there appeared out of a silvery morning mist from the south a slow procession of horse and men on foot. Even if Hugh, watching from the tower, had not seen the red-and-gold banner of the Lord Deputy of Ireland shaken out suddenly by the rainy breeze, he would have known that these were English and not Irish, for the men were a neat, dark cross moving together smartly: a van, the flag in the center where the Lord Deputy rode flanked by men with long guns over their shoulders, and a rear guard with a shambling ox-drawn cart.

He climbed monkey-like down from the tower calling out the news, but the visitors had been seen already, and Phelim and the O'Hagan and Turlough were already mounting in the courtyard to ride and meet them. Hugh shouted at the horse-boys to bring his pony.

"You stay," Phelim said, pulling on his gloves of English leather.

"I won't," Hugh said, and pushed the horse-boy: "Go on!"

Phelim's horse began shaking his head and dancing away, and Phelim, pulling angrily at his bridle, commanded Hugh to obey; between the horse and Hugh disobeying him, he was getting red in the face, and Hugh was on the pony's back, laughing, before Phelim could take any action against him. Turlough had watched all this without speaking; now he raised a hand to silence Phelim and drew Hugh to his side.

"They might as well see him now as later," he said, and brushed back Hugh's hair with an oddly gentle gesture.

The two groups, English and Irish, stood for a time some distance apart with a marshy stream running between them, while heralds met formally in the middle and carried greetings back and forth. Then the Lord Deputy, in a gesture of condescension, rode forward with only his standard-bearer, splashing across the water and waving a gloved hand to Turlough; at that, Turlough rode down to meet him halfway, and leaped off his horse to take the Lord Deputy's bridle and shake his hand.

Hugh, watching these careful approaches, began to feel less forward. He moved his pony back behind Phelim's snorting bay. Sir Henry Sidney was huge: his mouth full of white teeth opened in a black beard that reached up nearly to his eyes, which were small and also black; his great thighs, in hose and high boots, made the slim sword that hung from his baldric look as harmless as a toy. His broad chest was enclosed in a breastplate like a tun; Hugh didn't know its deep stomach was partly false, in the current fashion, but it looked big enough to hold him whole. Sir Henry raised an arm encased in a sleeve more dagged and gathered and complex than any garment Hugh had ever seen, and the squadron behind began to move up, and just then the Lord Deputy's black eyes found Hugh.

In later years Hugh O'Neill would come to feel that there was within him a kind of treasure chest or strongbox where were kept certain moments in his life, whole: some of them grand, some terrible, some oddly trivial, all perfect and complete with every sensation and feeling they had contained. Among the oldest that the box would hold was this one, when Turlough, leading the deputy's horse, brought him to Hugh, and the deputy reached down a massive hand and took Hugh's arm like a twig he might break, and spoke to him in English. All preserved: the huge, black, laughing head, the jingle of the horses' trappings and the sharp odor of their fresh droppings, even the soft glitter of condensing dewdrops on the silver surface of Sir Henry's armor. Dreaming or awake, in London, in Rome, this moment would now and again be taken out and shown him, and he would look into it as into a green-and-silver opal, and wonder.

The negotations leading to Sir Henry's taking Hugh O'Neill away with him to England as his ward went on for some days. Sir Henry was patient and careful, while the O'Neills rehearsed again the long story of their wrongs at Sean's hands; careful not to commit himself to more than he directly promised: that he would be a good friend to the Baron Dungannon, as he called Hugh, while at the same time intimating that large honors could come of it, chiefly the earldom of Tyrone, which since Conn's death had remained in the queen's gift, unbestowed.

He gave to Hugh a little sheath knife with a small emerald of peculiar hue set in the ivory hilt; he told Hugh that the gem was taken from a Spanish treasure ship sailing from Peru on the other side of the world. Hugh, excluded from their negotiations, would sit with the women and turn the little knife in his hands, wondering what could possibly be meant by the other side of the world. When it began to grow clear to him that he was meant to go to England with Sir Henry, he grew shy and silent, not daring even to ask what it would be like there. He tried to imagine England: he thought of a vast stone place, like the cathedral of Armagh multiplied over and over, where the sun did not shine.

At dinner one night Sir Henry saw him loitering at the door of the hall, peeking in. He raised his cup and called to him. "Come, my young lord," he said, and the Irish smiled and laughed at the compliment, though Hugh, whose English was uncertain, wasn't sure they weren't mocking him. Hands urged him forward, and rather than be pushed before Sir Henry, Hugh stood as tall as he could, his hand on the little knife at his belt, and walked up before the vast man.

"My lord, are you content to go to England with me?"

"I am, if my uncles send me."

"Well, so they do. You will see the queen there." Hugh answered nothing to this, quite unable to picture the queen. Sir Henry put a huge hand on Hugh's shoulder, where it lay like a stone weight. "I have a son near you in age. Well, something younger. His name is Philip."

"Phelim?"

"Philip. Philip is an English name. Come, shall we go tomorrow?" Sir Henry looked around, his black eyes smiling at his hosts. Hugh was being teased: tomorrow was fixed.

"Tomorrow is too soon," Hugh said, attempting a big voice of Turlough's but feeling only sudden terror. Laughter around him made him snap his head around to see who mocked him. Shame overcame terror. "If it please your lordship, we will go. Tomorrow. To England." They cheered at that, and Sir Henry's head bobbed slowly up and down like an ox's.

Hugh bowed and turned away, suppressing until he reached the door of the hall a desire to run. Once past the door, though, he fled, out of the castle, down the muddy street between the outbuildings, past the lounging guards, out into the gray night fields over which slow banks of mist lay undulating. Without stopping he ran along a beaten way up through the damp, hissing grass to where a riven oak thrust up, had thrust up for as long as anyone knew, like a tensed black arm and gnarled hand.

Near the oak, almost hidden in the grass, were broken straight lines of worn mossy stones that marked where once a monastic house had stood; a hummocky, sunken place had been its cellar. It was here that

Hugh had killed, almost by accident, his first rabbit. He had not been thinking, that day, about hunting, but only sitting on a stone with his face tilted upward into the sun thinking of nothing, his javelin across his lap. When he opened his eyes, the sunlit ground was a coruscating darkness, except for the brown shape of the rabbit in the center of his vision, near enough almost to touch. Since then he had felt the place was lucky for him, though he wouldn't have ventured there at night; now he found himself there, almost before he had decided on it, almost before the voices and faces in the hall had settled out of consciousness. He had nearly reached the oak when he saw that someone sat on the old stones.

"Who is it there?" said the man, without turning to look. "Is it Hugh O'Neill?"

"It is," said Hugh, wondering how blind O'Mahon nearly always knew who was approaching him.

"Come up, then, Hugh." Still not turning to him—why should he? and yet it was unsettling—O'Mahon touched the stone beside him. "Sit. Do you have iron about you, cousin?"

"I have a knife."

"Take it off, will you? And put it a distance away."

He did as he was told, sticking the little knife in a spiky tree stump some paces off; somehow the poet's gentle tone brooked neither resistance nor reply.

"Tomorrow," O'Mahon said when Hugh sat next to him again, "you go to England."

"Yes." Hugh felt ashamed here to admit it, even though it had been in no sense his choice; he didn't even like to hear the poet say the place's name.

"It's well you came here, then. For there are certain . . . personages who wished to say farewell to you. And give you a commandment. And a promise."

The poet wasn't smiling; his face was lean and composed behind a thin fair beard, nearly transparent. His bald eyes, as though filled with milk and water, looked not so much blind as simply unused: baby's eyes. "Behind you," he went on, and Hugh looked quickly around, "in the old cellar there, lives one who will come forth in a moment, only you ought not to speak to him."

The cellar place was obscure; any of its humps, which seemed to shift vaguely in the darkness, might have been someone.

"And beyond, from that rath"—O'Mahon pointed with certainty, though he didn't look, toward the broad, ancient tumulus riding blackly like a whale above the white shoals of mist—"now comes out a certain prince, and to him also you should not speak."

Hugh's heart had turned small and hard and beat painfully. He tried to say *Sidhe* but the word would not be said. He looked from the cellar to the rath to the cellar again—and there a certain tussock darker than the rest grew arms and hands and began with slow patience to pull itself out of the earth. Then a sound as of a great, stamping animal came from ahead of him, and, turning, he saw that out of the dark, featureless rath something was proceeding toward him, something like a huge, wind-blown cloak or a quickly oaring boat with a black, luffing sail or a stampeding, caparisoned horse. He felt a chill shiver up his back. At a sound behind him he turned again, to see a little thick black man, now fully out of the earth, glaring dourly at him (the glints of his eyes all that could be seen of his face) and staggering toward him under the weight of a black chest he carried in his stringy, rooty arms.

An owl hooted, quite near Hugh; he flung his head around and saw it, all white, gliding silently ahead of the prince who proceeded toward Hugh, of whom and whose steed Hugh could still make nothing but that they were vast, and were perhaps one being, except that now he perceived gray hands holding reins or a bridle, and a circlet of gold where a brow might be. The white owl swept near Hugh's head, and with a silent wingbeat climbed to a perch in the riven oak.

There was a clap as of thunder behind him. The little black man had set down his chest. Now he glared up at the prince before him and shook his head slowly, truculently; his huge black hat was like a tussock of grass, but there nodded in it, Hugh saw, a white feather delicate as snow. Beside Hugh, O'Mahon sat unchanged, his hands resting on his knees; but then he raised his head, for the prince had drawn a sword.

It was as though an unseen hand manipulated a bright bar of moonlight; it had neither hilt nor point, but it was doubtless a sword. The prince who bore it was furious, that was certain too: he thrust the sword down imperiously at the little man, who cried out with a shriek like gale-tormented branches rubbing, and stamped his feet; but, though resisting, his hands pulled open the lid of his chest. Hugh could see that there was nothing inside but limitless darkness. The little man thrust an arm deep inside and drew out something; then, approaching with deep reluctance only as near as he had to, he held it out to Hugh.

Hugh took it; it was deathly cold. There was the sound of a heavy cape snapped, and when Hugh turned to look, the prince was already away down the dark air, gathering in his stormy hugeness as he went. The owl sailed after him. As it went away, a white feather fell, and floated zigzag down toward Hugh.

Behind Hugh, a dark hummock in the cellar place had for a moment beneath it the glint of angry eyes, and then did not anymore.

Ahead of him, across the fields, a brown mousing owl swept low over the silvery grass.

Hugh had in his hands a rudely carven flint, growing warm from his hand's heat, and a white owl's feather.

"The flint is the commandment," O'Mahon said, as if nothing extraordinary at all had happened, "and the feather is the promise."

"What does the commandment mean?"

"I don't know."

They sat a time in silence. The moon, amber as old whiskey, appeared between the white-fringed hem of the clouds and the gray heads of the eastern mountains. "Will I ever return?" Hugh asked, though he could almost not speak for the painful stone in his throat.

"Yes."

Hugh was shivering now. If Sir Henry had known how late into the night he had sat out of doors, he would have been alarmed; the night air, especially in Ireland, was well known to be pernicious.

"Goodbye, then, cousin," Hugh said.

"Goodbye, Hugh O'Neill." O'Mahon smiled. "If they give you a velvet hat to wear, in England, your white feather will look fine in it."

Sir Henry Sidney, though he would not have said it to the Irish, was quite clear in his dispatches to the Council why he took up Hugh O'Neill. Not only was it policy for the English to support the weaker man in any quarrel between Irish dynasts, and thus prevent the growth of any overmighty subject; it also seemed to Sir Henry that, like an eyas falcon, a young Irish lord, if taken early enough, might later come more willingly to the English wrist. Said otherwise: he was bringing Hugh to England as he might the cub of a beast to a bright and well-ordered menagerie, to tame him.

For that reason, and despite his wife's doubts, he set Hugh O'Neill companion to his own son, Philip; and for the same reason he requested his son-in-law the Earl of Leicester to be Hugh's patron at court. "A boy poor in goods," he wrote Leicester, "and full feebly friended."

The Earl of Leicester, in conversation with the queen, turned a nice simile, comparing his new Irish client to the grafted fruit trees the earl's gardeners made: by care and close binding, the hardy Irish apple might be given English roots, though born in Irish soil; and once having them, could not then be separated from them.

"Pray sir, then," the queen said smiling, "his fruits be good."

"With good husbandry, madame," Leicester said, "his fruits will be to your majesty's taste." And he brought forward the boy, ten years old, his proud hair deep red, almost the color of the morocco leather binding of a little prayer book the queen held in her left hand. Across his pale face and upturned nose the freckles were thick, and faintly green; his eyes were emeralds. Two things the queen loved were red hair and jewels; she put out her long, ringed hand and brushed Hugh's hair.

"Our cousin of Ireland," she said.

He didn't dare raise his red-lashed eyes to her after he had made the courtesy that the earl had carefully instructed him in; while they talked about him above his head in a courtly southern English he couldn't follow, he looked at the queen's dress.

She seemed in fact to be wearing several. As though she were some fabulous many-walled fort, mined and breached, through the slashings and partings of her outer dress another could be seen, and where that was opened there was another, and lace beneath that. The outer wall was all jeweled, beaded with tiny seed pearls as though with dew, worked and embroidered in many patterns of leaf, vine, flower. On her petticoat were pictured monsters of the sea, snorting seahorses and leviathans with mouths like portcullises. And on the outer garment's inner side, turned out to reveal them, were a hundred disembodied eyes and ears. Hugh could believe that with those eyes and ears the queen could see and hear, so that even as he looked at her clothing, her clothing observed him. He raised his eyes to her white face framed in stiff lace, her hair dressed in pearls and silver.

Hugh saw then that the power of the queen resided in her dress. She was bound up in it as magically as the children of Llyr were bound up in the forms of swans. The willowy, long-legged courtiers, gartered and wearing slim English swords, moved as in a dance in circles and waves around her when she moved. When she left the chamber (she did not speak to Hugh again, but once her quick, bird eye lighted on him) she drew her ladies-in-waiting after her as though she caught up rustling fallen leaves in her train.

Later the earl told Hugh that the queen had a thousand such gowns and petticoats and farthingales, each more elaborate than the last.

A screen elaborately carved—nymphs and satyrs, grape clusters, incongruous armorial bearings picked out in gold leaf—concealed the queen's chief counselor, Sir William Cecil, Lord Burghley, and Dr. John Dee, her consulting physician and astrologer, from the chamber where the queen had held audience. But through the piercings of the screen they could see and hear.

"That boy," Burghley said softly. "The redheaded one."

"Yes," said Dr. Dee. "The Irish boy."

"Sir Henry Sidney is his patron. He has been brought to be schooled in English ways. There have been others. Her gracious majesty believes she can win their hearts and their loyalty. They do learn manners and graces, but they return to their island, and their brutish natures well up again. There is no way to keep them bound to us in those fastnesses."

"I know not for certain," said Dr. Dee, combing his great beard with his fingers, "but it may be that there are ways."

"*Doctissime vir,*" said Burghley. "If there are ways, let us use them."

A light snow lay on the roads and cottages when Philip Sidney, Sir Henry's son, and Hugh O'Neill went from the Sidneys' house of Penshurst in Kent up to Mortlake to visit John Dee. There was a jouncing, canopied cart filled with rugs and cushions, but the boys preferred to ride with the attendants until the cold pinched them too deeply through the fine, thin gloves and hose they wore. Hugh, careful now in matters of dress, would not have said that his English clothes were useless for keeping out cold compared to a shaggy Waterford mantle with a fur hood; but he seemed to be always cold and comfortless, somehow naked, in breeches and short cloaks.

Philip dismounted and threw his reins to the attendant; rubbing his hands, and his narrow blue-clad buttocks clenched. When Hugh had climbed in too, they pulled shut the curtains and huddled together under the rugs, each laughing at the other's shivers. They talked of the Doctor, as they called Dee, with whom Philip already studied Latin and Greek and mathematics. Hugh, though the older of the two, had had no lessons as yet, though they'd been promised him. They talked of what they would do when they were grown up and were knights, reweaving with themselves as the heroes the stories of Arthur and Guy of Warwick and the rest.

When the two of them played at heroes on their ponies in the fields of Penshurst, Hugh could never bully Philip into taking the lesser part: *I will be a wandering knight, and you must be my esquire.* Philip Sidney knew the tales, and he knew (almost before he knew anything else of the world) that the son of an Irish chieftain could not have ascendancy even in play over the son of an English knight.

But whenever Philip had Hugh at stick-swordpoint in a combat, utterly defeated, Hugh would leap up and summon from the hills and forests a sudden host of helpers who slew Philip's merely mortal companions. Or he postulated a crow who was a great princess he had long ago aided, whose feet he could grasp and be carried to safety, or an oak tree that would open and hide him away.

It wasn't fair, Philip would cry, these sudden hosts that Hugh sang forth in harsh unmusical Irish. They didn't fit any rules, they had nothing to do with the triumph of good knights over evil ones, and why anyway did they only help Hugh?

"Because my family once did them a great service," Hugh said to Philip in the rocking wagon. The matter was never going to be resolved.

"Suppose my family had."

"Guy of Warwick hasn't any family."

"I say now that he does, and so he does."

"And there aren't . . . fairy-folk in England." That term carefully chosen.

"For sure there are."

"No, there are not, and if there were, how could you summon them? Do you think they understand English at all?"

"I will summon them in Latin. *Veni, venite, spiritus sylvani, dives fluminarum . . .*"

Hugh kicked at the covers and at Philip, laughing. Latin!

Once they'd taken the issue to the wisest man they knew, excepting Dr. Dee himself, whom they didn't dare to ask: Buckle, the Penshurst gamekeeper.

"There was fairies here," he said to them. His enormous gnarled hands honed a long knife back and forth, back and forth on a whetstone. "But that was before King Harry's time, when I was a boy and said the Ave Mary."

"See there!" said Philip.

"Gone," said Hugh.

"My grandma saw them," said Buckle. "Saw one sucking on the goat's pap like any kid, and so the goat was dry when she came to milk it. But not now in this new age." Back and forth went the blade, and Buckle tested it on the dark and ridgy pad of his thumb.

"Where did they go?" Philip asked.

"Away," Buckle said. "Gone away with the friars and the Mass and the Holy Blood of Hailes."

"But where?" Hugh said.

A smile altered all the deep crags and lines of Buckle's face. "Tell me," he said, "young master, where your lap goes when you stand up."

Doctor Dee's wife, Jane, gave the boys a posset of ale and hot milk to warm them, and when they had drunk it he offered them a choice: they might read in whatever books of his they liked or work with his mathematical tools and study his maps, which he had unrolled on a long table, with compass and square laid on them. Philip chose a book, a rhymed romance that Dr. Dee chuckled at; the boy nested himself in cushions, opened his book, and was soon asleep "like a mouse in cotton-wool," Jane Dee said. Hugh bent over the maps with the Doctor, his round spectacles enlarging his eyes weirdly and his long beard nearly trailing across the sheets.

What Hugh had first to learn was that the maps showed the world, not as a man walking in it sees it, but as a bird flying high over it. High, high: Dr. Dee showed him on a map of England the length of the journey from Penshurst to Mortlake, and it was no longer than the joint of his thumb. And then England and Ireland too grew small and insignificant when Dr. Dee unrolled a map of the whole wide world. Or half of it: the world, he told Hugh, is round as a ball, and this was a picture of but one half. A ball! Hung by God in the middle of the firmament, the great stars going around it in their spheres and the fixed stars in theirs.

"This," the Doctor said, "is the Irish island, across St. George's Channel. Birds may fly across from there to here in the half part of a day."

Hugh thought: the children of Llyr.

"All these lands of Ireland, Wales and Scotland"—his long finger showed them—"are the estate of the British Crown, of our Imperial Queen, whose sworn servant you are." He smiled warmly, looking down upon Hugh.

"So also am I," said Philip, who'd awakened and come behind them.

"And so you are." He turned again to his maps. "But look you. It is not only these Isles Britannicae that belong to her. In right, these lands to the north, of the Danes and the Norwayans, they are hers too, by virtue of their old kings her ancestors—though it were inadvisable to lay claim to them now. And farther too, beyond the ocean sea."

He began to tell them of the lands far to the west, of Estotiland and Groenland, of Atlantis. He talked of King Malgo and King Arthur, of Lord Madoc and St. Brendan the Great; of Sebastian Caboto and John Caboto, who reached the shores of Atlantis a hundred years before Columbus sailed. They, and others long before, had set foot upon those lands and claimed them for kings from whom Elizabeth descended; and so they adhere to the British Crown. And to resume them under her rule the queen need ask no leave of Spaniard or of Portingale.

"I will find new lands too, for the queen," Philip said. "And you shall come too, to guide me. And Hugh shall be my esquire!"

Hugh O'Neill was silent, thinking: the kings of Ireland did not yield their lands to the English. The Irish lands were held by other kings, and other peoples altogether, from time before time. And if a new true king could be crowned at Tara, that king would win those lands again.

It was time now for the boys to return to Kent. Outside, the serving men could be heard mounting up, their spurs and trappings jingling.

"Now give my love and duty to your father," Dr. Dee said to Philip, "and take this gift from me, to guide you when you are grown, and set out upon those adventures you seek." He took from his table a small book, unbound and sewn with heavy thread. It was not printed but written in the Doctor's own fine hand, and the title said *General and Rare Memorials Pertayning to the Perfect Arte of Navigation*. Philip took it in his hands with a sort of baffled awe, aware of the honor, uncertain of the use.

"And for my new friend of Hibernia," he said, "come with me." He took Hugh away to a corner of his astonishingly crowded room, pushed aside a glowing globe of pale brown crystal in a stand, lifted a dish of gems, and with an *ah!* he picked up something that Hugh did not at first see.

"This," Dr. Dee said, "I will give you as my gift, in memorial of this day, if you will but promise me one thing. That you will keep it, always, on your person, and part with it never nor to no one." Hugh didn't know what to say to this, but the Doctor went on speaking as though Hugh had indeed promised. "This, young master, is a thing of which there is but one in the world. The uses of it will be borne in upon you when the need for them is great."

What he then put into Hugh's hand was an oval of black glass, glass more black than any he had ever seen, black too black to look right at, yet he could see that it reflected back to him his own face, as though he had come upon a stranger in the dark. It was bound in gold, and hung from a gold chain. On the back the surface of the gold was marked with a sign Hugh had never seen before: he touched the engraved lines with a finger.

"*Monas hieroglyphica*," said Dr. Dee. He lifted the little obsidian mirror from Hugh's hand by its brittle chain, hung it around the boy's neck. When Hugh again looked into the black sheen of it, he saw neither himself nor any other thing; but his skin burned and his heart was hot. He looked to the Doctor, who only tucked the thing away within Hugh's doublet.

When he was at Penshurst again and alone—it was not an easy thing to be alone in the Sidney house, with the lords and ladies and officers of the queen coming and going, and Philip's beautiful sister teasing, and the servants coming and passing—Hugh opened his shirt and took in his fingers the thing the Doctor had given him. The privy (where he sat) was cold and dim. He touched the raised figure in the gold of the back, which looked a little like a crowned manikin but likely was not, and turned it over. In the mirror was a face, but now not his own; for it wasn't like looking into a mirror at all, but like looking through a spy-hole and into another place, a spy-hole through which someone in that space looked back at him. The person looking at him was the queen of England.

On the Impregnation of Mirrors was not a book or a treatise or a Work; it wouldn't survive the wandering life that John Dee was to embark upon as the times and the heavens turned. It was just a few sheets, folded octavo and written in the Doctor's scribble hand, and no one not the Doctor would have been able to practice what it laid out, for certain necessary elements and motions went unwritten except in the Doctor's breast. It exists now but as a name in a list of his papers and goods drawn up for an application to her majesty's government for recompense, after his library and workshop had been despoiled by his enemies at court during his long absence abroad. Only one mirror of those that he had worked the art upon had succeeded entirely; only one had drawn the lines of time and space together so as to transmit the spirit of the owner to the eye of the possessor.

The making of it began with a paradox. If the impregnation of a mirror required that the one who first looked into it be its owner, then no other could ever have looked into it before, not he who silvered the glass, not she who polished the steel. How could the maker not be the owner?

John Dee had seen the solution. There was one perfect mirror that needed no silvering, no polishing: it needed only to be discovered, detected, its smooth side inferred, then taken from the ground and secreted before even the finder's eye fell upon its face. He knew of many such, taken from the lava fields of Greece or the Turkish lands, first found, as Pliny saith, by the traveler Obsius; his own he'd found in a lesser field in Scotland. He remembered the cold hill, the fragments sharp as knives, keeping his eyes steadily on the fast-flying clouds above while his fingers felt for the perfectest one, pocketing it unlooked-at.

He had placed it in the queen's hand himself, slipping it from where it hid in a purse of kidskin, feeling for its smooth side, which he held up to her face for a long moment, as long a moment as he dared, before giving it to her to examine. She seemed dazzled by it, amazed, though she had seen similar obsidian chips before. None like this one: Dr. Dee had bestirred its latent powers by prayer—and by means he had learned from helpers he would not name, not in the hearing of this court.

And then forever there was the queen's face within, and more than her face, her very self: her thought, her command, her power to entrance, how well the Doctor knew of it. She had not asked to keep it—the one danger he had feared. No, she had given it back to him with a gracious nod, and turned to other matters, for it was his. And now it was not his. For having taken its owner's face and nature, it could be handled, and the Doctor had milled it and framed it in gold and given it to the Irish boy.

It may be there are ways.

Dr. Dee stood on a Welsh headland from where on a clear day the Irish coast could just be seen across St. George's Channel. The sun was setting behind the inland hills of the other island, making them seem large and near with the golden brightness. There where the sun set Hugh O'Neill was one day to become a great chief; the Doctor's informants had let him know of it. The little Irish kings and the old Irish lords would press him in the years to come to make a single kingdom out of the island that had never been one before, and to push out the English and the Scots for good. But Hugh O'Neill—whether he knew it or did not—was as though tethered by a long leash, the one end about his neck, the other held in the queen's hand, though she might never know of it; and the tug of it, of her thought and will and desire and need, would keep the man in check. She could turn to other matters, the greater world, more dangers.

And to himself as well.

He turned from the sea. A single cloud like a great beast streaked with blood went away to the north with the wind, changing as it went.

After seven years had passed, Hugh O'Neill was returned to Ulster. He was not yet the O'Neill, he was not Earl of Tyrone, but nor was he any other man. By the English designations, in which the Irish only half believed, he was mere Baron Dungannon. The quiet boy had grown into a quiet man. His father, Sean's rebel son Matthew, had been killed by Hugh's uncle Turlough Luineach, for which act the English had favored him—whatever that might mean for Turlough's benefit, to which the English would never commit: the rich earldom, an empty name, letters patent, loans of money, or nothing at all.

Hugh, on Irish soil again, with English soldiers in his train and around his neck an English engine that he did not yet know the uses of, rode through Dublin and was not hailed or cheered. Who was on his side, whom could he count on? There were the O'Hagans, who were poor, and the O'Donnells, the sons of the fierce Scots pirate Ineen Duv (the "dark girl"). And Englishmen: The queen's men, Burghley and Walsingham, who had taken his hand and smiled. They'd known Conn O'Neill, and remarked on the white feather Hugh wore always in his cap. He'd learned more than courtly English from them. Their eyes were colder than their hands.

The castle-tower of Dungannon still stood, but the old chiefs and their adherents who had feasted and quarreled here were scattered now, fighting each other, or gone south to fight for the heirs of Desmond. But even as he came to the place with his little train they had begun returning, more every day: poor men, ill-equipped, not well fed. There were women still there in the castle, and from them he learned that his mother had died in the house of the O'Hagans.

"It is ill times," said blind O'Mahon, who had remained.

"It is."

"Well, you have grown, cousin. And in many ways too."

"I am the one I was," Hugh said, and the poet did not answer him.

"Tell me," he said. "Once in place nearby, up that track to the crest of the hill, where a holy house once stood . . ."

"I remember," Hugh said.

"A thing was given you."

"Yes."

A man may keep a thing about him, in one pocket or purse or another, and forget he has it; thinks to toss it away now and then and yet never does so—not because it's of value but only because it's his, a bit of himself, and has long been. So the little carven flint had lain here and there throughout his growing up, getting lost and then turning up again. It had ceased to be what for a moment here in this place and long ago it seemed to be: a thing of cold power, with a purpose of its own, too heavy for its size. It had become a small old stone, scratched with the figure of a man that a child might draw.

He felt here and there in his clothes and came upon it: felt it leap into his hand as soon as it could. He drew it out and for a foolish moment thought to display it to the blind man. "I have it still," he said.

A commandment, O'Mahon had called the stone. But not what it commanded. He closed his hand on it.

"I will soon build a house here," he said. "A house such as the English make, of bricks and timber, with windows of glass, and chimneys, and a key to lock the door."

"Will you go with me now, up to the place I spoke of?"

"If you like, cousin."

O'Mahon took O'Neill's arm, and Hugh led him where O'Mahon guided; the poet knew very well where he went but wanted help so as not to stumble on the way. They climbed the low hill that Hugh had known in youth, when he had first come to this country with his O'Hagan fosterers, but then there had been tall trees now cut, and beyond the trees to the river, fields of corn and pasture where cattle moved. Now fallow and bare.

"Day goes," the poet said, as though he saw it. Past the riven oak, amid the low rolling of the hills there was the one taller and of a shape not made by wind and water, but by hands—it was easy to tell. A thousand rods or more in length, but smaller somehow now than when he had seen it as a boy. "This hour is the border of day and night, as the river is the border of here and there. What cannot be known by day or night shows itself at twilight."

"You know these things, who can't see them?"

"My eyes are a border too, cousin. At which I forever stand."

They stood in silence there while the sky turned black above and to a pale, red-streaked green in the west. A mist gathered in the hollows. Hugh O'Neill would not later remember the moment, if there was a moment, when the host came forth, if it did, and stood there against the rath, hard to see but for sure there. Growing in numbers, mounted and afoot.

"The foreign queen you love and serve," O'Mahon said. "She cares nothing for you but this: that you keep this isle in subjection for her sake, until and when she can fill it with her hungry subjects and poor relations, to take of it what they will."

The ghost warriors were clearer now. Hugh could almost hear the rustle they made and the rattle of their arms. The Old Ones, the *Sidhe*.

"They command you to fight, Hugh Gaveloch O'Neill of the O'Neills. The O'Neill you are, and what you will be you do not know. But you are not unfriended."

They formed and re-formed in the dark, their steeds turning in place, their lances like saplings in the wind: as though impatient for him to cry out to them in supplication, or call them to his side.

The commandment, Hugh thought. But he could say nothing to them, not with his voice, not in his heart; and soon the border of night and day was closed, and he could see them no more.

In Munster where the world began, the old Norman earls of Desmond and Kildare and Ormond had risen again, resisting the English adventurers whose papers and patents said they owned the lands that those families had held for time out of mind. The earls acknowledged no power higher than themselves except the pope. Hugh O'Neill kept as far from the quarrel in the south as he could; he told himself that his work was to make himself pre-eminent here, Lord of the North.

But the obsidian mirror judged him and found him wanting. *You are a cold friend to her who loves you and will soon do you great good:* the queen looked out at him, her white face framed in a stiff ruff. Eyes he saw in dreams too. When the English gathered an army at Dublin under old and weary Henry Sidney, Hugh rode south with him, bringing fighters of his own, feeding them from the plunder of Desmond villages and fields. Any town or village that Sidney invested and would not surrender was put to the sword, the leaders beheaded and their heads impaled on stakes across the land. The earls and their followers burned the standing grain in the fields to keep Sidney's army from the provender, and then in the spring Sidney's soldiers burned it as it sprung, to keep it from them. The people ate cresses, and when they had none they died, and others ate their flesh, and the flesh of their dead babes. And the queen spoke to O'Neill's heart and said, *Look not on their suffering but on me.*

But the flint in his pocket had its say as well.

He kept on with Sir Henry—but he went his own way. He avoided pitched battles and retributions; he largely occupied himself in Munster not with fighting but with . . . hunting. He brought along with him on his hunts men with guns (Fubun *on the gray foreign gun,* O'Mahon had said long ago, but this was now, not then). Wherever he went, wherever men had lost their lands, he would ask the men and boys what weapons they were good at using, and after they named spears and bows and the pike he would bring out a gun, and explain the use of it, and let one or another of them take it and try it. The handiest of them he'd reward with a coin or other gift, and perhaps even the gun itself. *Keep it safe,* he'd say, smiling.

That was wisdom the mirror would never give him and the flint could not know: When the time came for *him* to lead men against English soldiers—if it did come—he would not lead hordes of screaming gallowglasses against trained infantry with guns. *His* army would wheel on command, and march in step, and lay fire. When the time came.

In Dungannon again he began to build himself that fine house in the English style, where wardrobes held his velvet English suits and hats, his rugs and bedclothes made from who knew what. When he could get no lead for the roofs of his house, Burghley saw to it that a shipment of many tons of sheet lead were sent to him; it lay for years in the pine woods at Dungannon until a different use for it was found, in a different world. He fell in love, not for the first or the last time, but this time providentially: she was Mabel Bagenal, daughter of Sir Nicholas Bagenal, officer of the Queen's Council in Dublin—Bagenal resisted the match, not wanting an Irish chieftain for a son-in-law and thinking Mabel could do better: but when Hugh O'Neill rode into Dublin in his velvets and his lined cloak with a hundred retainers around him, her heart was won. And the power in the black mirror was glad of it.

The morning after his wedding night Mabel discovered it on its gold chain on his breast and tried to take it off, but he wouldn't let her; he only turned it to her and asked her what she saw. The third soul ever to look in. She studied it, brow knit, and said she saw herself, but dimly.

Himself was never what Hugh O'Neill saw there. "It was a gift," he said. "From a wise man in England. To keep me safe, he said."

Mabel Bagenal looked into her husband's face, which seemed to seek itself in the black mirror, though she was wrong about that; and she said, "May God will that it do so."

In the same spring Dr. John Dee and his wife, Jane, and their many children left for the Continent with trunkloads of books, an astronomer's staff, bottles of remedy for every ill, a cradleboard for the newest, and in a velvet bag a small orb of quartz crystal with a flaw like a lost star not quite at its center. In a cold room in a high tower in the golden city in the middle of the emperor's land of Bohemia, he placed the stone in its frame carved with the names and sigilla that his angelic informants had given to him.

There was war in heaven, and therefore war under the earth, and soon enough on the lands and seas of all the empires and kingdoms of men.

It would engulf the states and empires of Europe; even the sultan might be drawn in. If Spain claimed Great Atlantis for her own, then Atlantis too would be in play, and Francis Drake's license as a privateer would be traded for the chain of an Admiral of the Ocean Sea, and Walter Raleigh given one too. The heavenly powers that aid the true Christian faith, the armed angelic hosts, would go into battle. They would be opposed by other powers great and small, powers that take the side of the old faith. The creatures of the middle realm, of earth and water, hills and trees, shy and self-protective, would surely fight with the old religion: not because they loved the pope or even knew of him, but only because they hated change. There was little harm they could do, though much annoyance. But in the contested Irish isle where Spain would be welcomed, there were other powers, warriors who appeared and disappeared after sudden slaughter, bright swords and spears that made no sound. Were they men, had they once been men, were they but empty casques and breastplates? They could be captured, sometimes, imprisoned if you knew the spells, but never for long. *It is useless to hang us,* they would say to their jailers, *we cannot die.*

Look now: the swirl of winds within the stone, the sense (not the sound) of heavenly laughter, and the clouds parted to show as though from a seabird's eye the western coast of Ireland, and on the sea little dots that were big-bellied ships, the great red crosses on their sails.

A flotilla in the North Sea, and in St. George's Channel, come to make Philip king of England. And to make the Virgin Queen his bride, old now and barren though she be. In the stone the tiny ships rocked on the main like mock ships in a masque or a children's show. An angel finger pointed to them, and John Dee heard a whisper: *That is not far off from now.*

Hugh O'Neill had passed almost without noticing from his twenties to his thirties; one by one the endless line of enemies and false friends and mad fools that he faced in the claiming of his heritage were bought off, or befriended, or exiled, or hanged. The black mirror was his adviser and his ruler in these contests, and when he contested with the mirror itself, he might deny it, and later be sorry he had. Sometimes when he looked in, it would say, *Strike now or lose all,* and sometimes it would only look upon him; sometimes it wept or smiled, or said, *Power springs from the mind and the heart.* But never was any sound heard, and it was as though Hugh thought or said these things in his own mind, which made them not the less true or potent. If he could discern the meaning of what was said and act on it, it would come out as predicted, and he would win.

And in the spring of 1587 he returned to London to be invested at last by the queen with the title Earl of Tyrone.

He knelt before her, sweeping his hat and its white feather from his head. "Cousin," the queen said, and held out her ringed hand for him to kiss.

The face Hugh saw in the black mirror had never changed—at least it would seem always unchanged to him, white and small and bejeweled—but the woman of flesh was not young. The paint couldn't cover the fine lines etched all around her eyes, nor the lines in the great bare skull above. Torn between love and shame, Hugh put his lips near to the proffered hand without touching it, and when he raised his eyes again she was young again and serenely lovely. She said, "My cousin. My lord of Tyrone."

At the dock when he came home again, with more gifts and purchases in his English ship than twenty oxcarts could bear, he saw, among the O'Neill and O'Donnell men-at-arms and their brehons and wives come to greet him, the poet O'Mahon, like a withered leaf, leaning on a staff. Hugh O'Neill went to him, knelt and kissed the white hand the poet held out to him. O'Mahon raised him, felt his big face and broad shoulders, the figured steel breastplate upon him.

"That promise given you was kept," said O'Mahon.

"How, cousin?"

"You are the O'Neill, inaugurated at Tullyhogue as your ancestors have ever been. You are Earl of Tyrone too, by the grant of the English: you gave them all your lands and they gave them back to you just as though the lands were theirs to give, and added on a title, Earl."

"How is that the keeping of a promise?" O'Neill asked.

"That is for them to know; yours to act and learn." He touched Hugh's arm and said: "Will you go on progress in this summer, cousin? The lands that owe you are wide."

"I may do so. The weather looks to be fine."

"I would be happy to go along with you, if I might. As far at least as to the old fort at Dungannon."

"Well, then, you shall. You will have a litter to carry you, if you like."

"I can still ride," the poet said with a smile. "And my own horse knows the way there."

"What shall we do there?"

"I? Not a thing. But you: you will meet again your allies there, or perhaps their messenger or herald; and see what now they will say. And they will tell you of the others, some greater than they, who are now waking from sleep, and their pale horses too."

The streets, which had been still when a young Irishman came home from that other island to which he had been carried away, were not still now: from street to street and house to house the news went that Hugh O'Neill was home again, and they came around his horse to touch his boot and lift their babes to see him; and now and then he must acknowledge them, and doff the black velvet cap he wore, with the white owl's feather in its band.

Two enemies, the queen of England and the old ones under the hills, had acted to make Hugh O'Neill great. He had become what they had conspired to make him, and what now was he to do? When he tried to take the black mirror from around his neck, he found that he could not: he had the strength, it was a flimsy chain that carried it, he could snap it with a thumb and finger, but he couldn't do it.

Hugh O'Neill, Lord of the North, stood at the center of time, which was not different from the time of his own span. There are five directions to the world around: there is North, and South, and East, and West. And the fifth direction lies amid them. It points to the fifth kingdom, the only realm where he or any man ever stands: Here.

Well, let it be. What was he but a battleground where armies and their generals tore him in two for their own reasons? There was no knowing how the world would roll from here where he stood. Let it be.

The queen was dead, and John Dee was dying. His books and alchemical ware and even the gifts that the queen had given him had been sold for bread: his long toil for her meant nothing to the new Scots king, who feared magic above all things. It was all gone but this small stone of moleskin-colored quartz, that had come to have a spiritual creature caught in it: an angel, he had long believed, but now he doubted. The war she had shown him had paused, as a storm's eye passing, and a calm had fallen over the half part of the world: it would not last.

What he saw now wasn't the armies of emperors and kings, nor the towers of Heaven and their hosts. He saw only long, stony beaches, and knew it was the western coast of Ireland; and there where the Spanish ships had once been shivered on the rocks, other ships were being built, like no ships men sailed, ships made out of the time of another age, silvered like driftwood, with sails as of cobweb; and the ones building and now boarding and pushing them out to sea were as silvery, and as fine. Defeated; in flight. They sailed to the west, to the Fortunate Isles, to coasts and faraway hills they had never seen. The voice at John Dee's inner ear said, *This is to come. We know not when. Well, let it be.* And as he bent over the glowing stone the empowered soul within him spoke to him in vatic mode, and told him that when the end did come, and after it had long passed, the real powers that had fought these wars would be forgotten, and so would he, and only the merely human kings and queens and halberdiers and priests and townsmen remembered.

Matthew Hughes

. . .

Matthew Hughes was born in Liverpool, England, but spent most of his adult life in Canada. He's worked as a journalist, as a staff speechwriter for the Canadian Ministers of Justice and Environment, and as a freelance corporate and political speechwriter in British Columbia before settling down to write fiction full-time. Clearly strongly influenced by Jack Vance, as an author Hughes has made his reputation detailing the adventures of rogues like Raffalon the thief and Baldemar the wizard's henchman, who live in *The Dying Earth*, in a series of popular stories and novels that include *Fools Errant*, *Fool Me Twice*, *Black Brillion*, *Majestrum*, *Hespira*, *The Spiral Labyrinth*, *Template*, *Quartet & Triptych*, *The Yellow Cabochon*, *The Other*, and *The Commons*, with his stories being collected in *9 Tales of Raffalon* and *The Meaning of Luff and Other Stories*. He's also written the urban fantasy To Hell and Back trilogy, *The Damned Busters*, *Costume Not Included*, and *Hell to Pay*. He also writes crime fiction as Matt Hughes and media tie-in novels as Hugh Matthews. His most recent books are the Luff Imbry novellas *Of Whimsies & Noubles* and *Epiphanies*, the collection *Devil or Angel and Other Stories*, and the Erm Kaslo novel *A Wizard's Henchman*.

Here he treats us to the tale of a wizard so powerful, vain, and avaricious that he has no need of friends—until the day when it turns out that he does.

◆   ◆   ◆

The Friends of Masquelayne the Incomparable

MATTHEW HUGHES

I t was a notable characteristic of the thaumaturge Masquelayne that as soon as he conceived a desire for something, he began to think of that object as his own. Thus, if that which he desired happened to be in the possession of another, such possession became illicit.

That dastard has stolen from me! Masquelayne would come to realize. He would savor the resentment even as he began to plot a strategy, not only to recover what was now rightfully his, but to punish the impudence of the thief who withheld it from him. Hence, he was known as the kind of thaumaturge who delighted in provoking a duel, and many were those who had gone out against Masquelayne the Incomparable and come back down bruised and poorer for the encounter—for he took not only whatever had occasioned the duel but anything else that caught his fancy. And he hung the defeated wizard's wand high up in his dining hall.

Poddlebrim, a thaumaturge so obscure he lacked a sobriquet, became the focus of Masquelayne's ire on the occasion of the 119th Grand Symposium, held on the genteelly tended grounds of the High Magnus's palace. Masquelayne had prepared well for the event, being jealous of his reputation as an exemplar of several recondite practices. To the delight of the conclave, he presented a series of scenes recaptured from the Nineteenth Aeon by means of a mechanism contrived from prisms and crystals laboriously grown in a cavern beneath his estate at High Voiderasch. The work had taken months and had worn out several of Masquelayne's sylphs. In the air above the device, half-sized figures clad in antique garb performed the esoteric and intricate rituals that had constituted court life during the reign of the Gray Emperor, uncounted millennia ago. Masquelayne's control of his creation was such that he could even take his audience behind the Cloistering Veil, long thought impenetrable, to reveal the emperor and his concubines at play in the seraglio.

The High Magnus himself led the applause, joined enthusiastically by Foubaye the Arbiter and other senior Fellows of the College. Masquelayne saw Lurulan the Excellence and the Estimable Ombbo exchange sour looks from where they sat together in the stands. Their combined project had been a re-creation of an event from the semi-mythical War of the Seven Kingdoms, when two armies had broken off in the midst of battling each other to combine their arms against a sinuous dragonette that descended upon them from the sky. Lurulan and Ombbo had created thousands of miniature automata, foot and horse, and a truly frightening worm that belched red-and-yellow flames. At the climax of the struggle, the beast, targeted by the flickering fire-beams of the Immortals and the Iron Guard, exploded in a burst of light, shedding a coruscation of sparks and glittering scales in all directions.

Until Masquelayne deployed his prisms and crystals, Lurulan's and Ombbo's warring figurines had been the highlight of the Grand Symposium. Masquelayne's expression now, as he allowed the assemblage's accolades to swell about him, was a carefully maintained mask of modesty, but his eyes blazed with the cold fires of vanity.

He bowed to the High Magnus and Foubaye, then languidly flourished one hand to tell the lord's servants they could bear away the scrying device; his other hand's fingertips touched his breast in recognition of the crowd's praise. He left the dais before the applause had died away and stood to one side as the gathered wizards and dignitaries murmured and uttered hushed exclamations.

Then the High Magnus's majordomo announced, "Poddlebrim

the . . ." He sought for an attachment and did not find it, then cleared his throat and said again, "Poddlebrim and his Tree of Heart's Desire!"

A silence descended, broken only by the rustle of fabric as the audience craned forward to see what new marvel might now appear. Masquelayne did not recognize this Poddlebrim, though he thought he had heard the name at sometime in the past. He saw a small, rounded man in a robe of muted colors step onto the dais, bowing his head to reveal a hairless dome surrounded by a mouse-gray fringe. Poddlebrim made no grand gestures nor took a theatrical stance—techniques Masquelayne had studied to master. Instead, he gazed at his assembled peers as if he were unsure what they were all doing there, then cleared his throat and said, in a conversational tone, "Behold."

He stood aside and gestured idly to draw the audience's attention to the center of the dais. There, a column of pale blue smoke appeared from nowhere and began to spiral upward, widening and flattening not far above Poddlebrim's head. The smoke deepened and darkened to become solid, and now the apparition was seen to have become a tree fashioned from glass of an electric blue. Its branches spread and stretched and interlaced themselves luxuriously, while delicate, almost transparent leaves unrolled from sprouting twigs.

And then the tree began to bear fruit. Poddlebrim plucked one palm-filling orb from a low branch, glanced at it without much interest, then tossed it lightly toward where the High Magnus sat in the box of state. The lord of the land caught the glass apple, looked at it with curiosity, then raised it high so that, with the light of the noonday sky behind it, he could peer into its depths.

The hushed crowd heard the aristocrat's sharp intake of breath, and the exhalation that voicelessly made known his delight. He remained transfixed, while his expression gradually transformed from wonder to melancholy. After a long span, he slowly lowered the fruit and wiped away a tear. He looked again at the thing in his hand and said, softly, "Sublime."

Poddlebrim made another small bow in the High Magnus's direction then plucked a fresh fruit from the now heavily laden branches and tossed it to Foubaye. As the senior Fellow gazed into it, his face formed the lines of a lost child who sees his searching parent round a corner and comes, arms outstretched, toward her.

Poddlebrim plucked more fruit and threw each, one after another, to persons in the crowd. Each recipient did as Foubaye and the High Magnus had done: take a long and lingering look into the glass apple's depths, breathe a sigh of joy and wonder, and subside into a span of pensive introspection.

There were no cheers, no hands clapped. Poddlebrim made no gestures, struck no poses. He simply plucked and tossed, like a farmer selling his wares in a market, until all had received a gift and undergone its experience. All, that is, except Masquelayne. For, when the little wizard made to throw the last apple to where he still stood to one side of the dais, Masquelayne showed him a palm lifted in refusal.

Poddlebrim held up the glass orb, and his face looked a question at Masquelayne, whose response was a stare as cold as that of the basilisk he kept chained below his keep. The little wizard's shoulders performed a brief elevation then subsided. He regarded the fruit resting on his palm as if it were a bird that had failed to fly, then with a shrug he tossed it into the air—where, like a bubble, it silently burst into nonexistence.

Poddlebrim turned then to the tree and made a motion like that of a king gently dismissing a supplicant. The tree shimmered and evanesced into the air. A collective sigh rose from the assemblage, followed by soft, sad cries as they saw that, with the tree's disappearance, so had gone their fruits and whatever visions they had contained.

Poddlebrim, with more of a nod than a bow, descended from the dais and went to resume his seat on the edge of the crowd. No one stirred for a long moment, then the majordomo remembered his duties and called for the next exhibition. Blinking as if waking from a dream, Shevance the Insightful advanced to the forefront of the gathering and conjured a succession of ghosts. But the phantoms' grimaces and prophecies could not alter the reflective mood that Poddlebrim's fruits had mustered. Shevance cut short the performance and left the dais, and the thaumaturges who were supposed to follow raised their hands in surrender and returned to communion with their inner selves.

The High Magnus called for the wreath of electrum to be brought. The majordomo came, bearing it on its traditional cushion of scarlet velvet with the dangling gold tassels. But when the servant called for Poddlebrim to come receive his prize, it was discovered that the wizard had quietly departed the symposium.

The High Magnus spoke. "Genius married to modesty," he said. "We should all learn from his example."

Masquelayne the Incomparable did not learn the lesson his aristocratic host was recommending. Poddlebrim had stolen from him the triumph that should have been his. Then, as he climbed into his carriage and brusquely ordered its attendants to take him home, he realized that he had been the victim of a second theft: by making it impossible for Masquelayne to accept the last fruit, Poddlebrim had denied him the experience that had so affected all of the other grandees and wizards.

As the vehicle rose into the sky, the wizard's jaw clenched in justified outrage. The intolerable Poddlebrim would learn his own lesson, he vowed. He must deliver up the secret of the tree, which rightfully belonged to Masquelayne the Incomparable. And he must suffer a punishment that corresponded to the harm he had done.

Masquelayne's sylphs flocked to him as he alighted from the carriage in the forecourt of his manse, high upon a promontory overlooking the Vale of Coromance. They simpered and fawned, seeking his hand, caressing his face, but he waved them aside and made straight for his workroom in the upper floor of the tower that stood just on the edge of the precipice.

He had long since dispensed with apprentices, they being of small use while liable to create large distractions. But he did maintain a familiar: a minor demon the wizard had captured then coerced into taking the shape of an oval looking glass rimmed in gold. Now, as he entered his workroom, he spoke the syllables that roused the fiend from its sleep.

"What will you have of me?" it said.

"Knowledge," said Masquelayne. "Specifically regarding he who calls himself Poddlebrim."

A seeming ripple passed across the oval surface. "Ah," said the demon. "Let me inquire."

The thaumaturge paced the circular room, glanced out the window, and saw that the old red sun was deepening to an angrier shade as it dipped toward the horizon. A half-formed thought rose in his mind, and he went to a bookcase carved from the bones of a long-extinct beast, running a finger across the spines of a dozen tomes shelved therein. But the concept would not gel, and he turned in growing anger toward the looking glass.

"Well?" he said. "I do not employ you to waste my time. Speak!"

The demon said, "It is difficult. Poddlebrim is known to be modest. He does not advertise his exploits, if he has any. He keeps to himself in a little house in a clearing in the Forest of Ardollia. Rarely does he engage with the world."

That much, Masquelayne already knew. Poddlebrim had never attended the Grand Symposium before. That had been the first time Masquelayne had ever laid eyes upon the little wizard. Thinking about it, he now realized that he had always known the name, but had developed no associations for it. Poddlebrim had been like a foreign country, rustic and irrelevant, far across the sea: heard of, but of no consequence to the life of the here and now.

"Show me this little house," he told the demon.

The glass rippled again and an image formed: a cottage of wattle and daub, its roof darkly thatched. Outside, a pen with a pig, and another with some chickens, and a well with a roof over it.

The view was as that of a bird hovering above the surrounding trees. Masquelayne said, "He does not even have proper walls of stone. Go closer. Let us peer through a window, or even penetrate those flimsy walls."

The image enlarged as if the bird were gliding down toward the front of the house, where a modest window paned in hand-sized diamonds of glass was set beside the plain wooden door. The window grew larger and larger, until it more than filled the oval of the looking glass, though its panes were becoming more opaque, the closer the viewpoint came.

Then it abruptly stopped growing.

"Closer!" Masquelayne said. "Show me!"

The glass rippled again, then went dark for a moment. The wizard found himself looking at his own reflection and did not like what Poddlebrim's impudence had done to his expression.

The demon said, "I have been . . . rebuffed."

"What? How?"

A pause. "I do not know. It was not a brutal repulse. I scarcely felt it. But it is unequivocal. I could go no closer, and now when I try to return, I . . . simply cannot."

Masquelayne swore, calling up dire oaths that caused even the demon to shrink back behind the glass. A sylph came to the workroom door, anxious and distraught, and the thaumaturge almost destroyed it with a rebuke, relenting only at the last gasp and letting the poor, damaged creature creep away to reconstitute itself.

Masquelayne regained the reins of his temper, and added to the growing pile another injury for which Poddlebrim must pay. He turned back to the mirror. "What do you recommend?"

"Honestly? Not to strive against Poddlebrim. He obviously has power."

The wizard made a wordless sound of frustrated rage. "Be more useful," he said through gritted teeth, "or I will apply a scourge!"

"I will see what I can learn and report to you," it said. "But there is one thing I already know: Casprine the Ineffable has had dealings with Poddlebrim. He may be able to offer some guidance."

"Ah," said Masquelayne, his eyes narrowing. "Casprine, eh?"

Masquelayne could not be said to have friends, though he had had many enemies. All of them he had vanquished and despoiled, and on all of them he had imposed burdens. They walked in fear of encountering his wrath again. But there was another category: fellow thaumaturges who had yet done nothing against him and had earned no punishments. Casprine the Ineffable was one of these, a not inconsiderable thaumaturge who dwelled in a subterranean warren that had formerly been a paranoid king's stronghold beneath a mountain off to the west.

Masquelayne brought out his aspekton and placed it atop his workbench, then spoke into it, "Casprine, it is Masquelayne who speaks!"

A pause ensued, then Casprine's visage, narrow and foxlike, appeared above the device. "Masquelayne? Have we reason to connect?"

"I am interested in that odd little fellow, Poddlebrim."

"Ah," said Casprine, infusing the single syllable with a wealth of meaning. "The Grand Symposium. A remarkable exhibition."

"You were there?"

The thin lips smiled. "No, but I have heard . . . talk."

"And I have heard that you have had dealings with this Poddlebrim. I would like to know what you can tell me."

Casprine gave the matter some thought. Finally, he nodded, as if to himself, then said, "Your reputation does not encourage me to put myself in your hands. You will have to come to me. I will speak only within the confines of my own wards and defenses."

Masquelayne did not hesitate. "Then I will come by way of the Glooms. Expect me presently."

Casprine made a gesture of acquiescence, and his image dwindled and disappeared.

Masquelayne restrained his impatience and took thought. Casprine owed him no enmity that he knew of, yet it was never wise to enter the realm of another thaumaturge without arming oneself. He consulted his books and drew into his mind three strong spells: Boix's Comprehensive Rupture, Zinezan's Unbreachable Cloak, and Willifant's Penetrating Beam.

When he had all three fixed and solid in his compartmentalized memory, he opened the portal into the Road of Glooms and stepped through. The way lay pale and ghostly before him, passing through a landscape of tenebrous moor and forest. But Masquelayne was a seasoned traveler of the Glooms and kept his destination firmly in mind. He strode for a timeless span, until suddenly his steps were no longer in the shadows but in a tunnel deep beneath Casprine's mountain. It led to a door that opened as he approached, and the thin-faced wizard stood framed by a soft glow from within a chamber he kept for such receptions.

He stepped aside to admit Masquelayne. The visitor glanced about, saw nothing to create alarm, and stood in the center of the sparsely furnished room to await whatever Casprine would offer.

Casprine closed the door and passed a hand down its length, speaking too softly for Masquelayne to hear, though from the position of his fingers as he stroked the door, Casprine was surely using Schletzel's Impermeable Buffer. But Masquelayne said nothing; it would not serve his purposes to wound his host's self-esteem while he was seeking the fellow's aid.

Now Casprine turned to him, folding his hands into the sleeves of his figured silk robe. "What would you have?" he said. "And what would you give?"

"As much as you know of Poddlebrim," said Masquelayne. His face said the import of the other question had not occupied his mind until now, then he said, offhandedly, "I have a nygrave's skull that might suit you."

With the same impromptu tone, Casprine said, "I have one, too, of course." He appeared to give the matter some idle consideration, then added, "Though mine has only the crest of a juvenile."

"Mine is that of a full-sprouted adult."

Casprine opened his hands in a question. "The horns, what length?"

Masquelayne spread his own hands wider than his body and saw a flash of avarice in Casprine's gaze before the other wizard said, "That would be acceptable. I confess my powers of divination would be enhanced."

Together they performed the gestures that sealed the bargain and spoke as one the reciprocal malediction—they had agreed on Hoch's Recurrent Boils—that would strike down either if he did not fulfill his obligation.

That business done, Masquelayne said, "Now, tell me."

"Let us sit," Casprine said, gesturing toward two chairs that now appeared. Masquelayne took a seat and waited while his host's face assumed a thoughtful aspect.

"There is not a great deal to tell," Casprine said, after a moment, "and some of it is hearsay. But he is said to have begun his studies under Chaychay the Sagacious—"

"Red school," Masquelayne interjected. "I remember him."

"Indeed," said Casprine. "But after Poddlebrim achieved the twentieth degree, he left Chaychay and apprenticed himself to Groffesque the Willful."

"But he was blue school! You're not telling me that simpleton has advanced to the purple school?"

"I do not know," said Casprine. "After several years with Groffesque, Poddlebrim retired to the Forest of Ardollia and devoted himself to private research."

Masquelayne leaned forward. "In what direction?"

"I visited him there once. He said he was working on ways to make disparate fluxions cohere. He believed that would magnify their strengths to a remarkable degree."

"Nonsense!" said Masquelayne. "Blue and red cannot cohere. They always clash, though the tensions can be managed by force of will."

"My thought, too," said Casprine. "But Poddlebrim was convinced. And there are indications he has made progress."

"What indications?"

The other wizard's lips formed into a moue. "Did you not see one today? The Tree of Heart's Desire?"

Masquelayne made a dismissive gesture. "I saw a tree form from a pillar of smoke. It sprouted glass fruit. I could do as much."

Casprine looked away then eyed him sidewise. "But I'm told you did not gaze into the apple that was meant for you."

Masquelayne bristled. "I was not inclined to play games."

"Then you do not know what you would have seen."

"And what would I have seen?"

Casprine's head moved in a shrug. "That which, could you but possess it, would fulfill your heart's desire."

"And what would Poddlebrim know of my heart's desire?" said Masquelayne.

This time, it was Casprine's shoulders that expressed his inability to answer. "For that, I suppose I would need to master the arcana of the purple school."

Masquelayne restrained his temper, fighting down an impulse to swathe himself in Zinezan's cloak and deploy Willifant's beam. "Is there anything more you can tell me?" he said.

"I recall that, in his early studies, Poddlebrim was drawn to earth magic," Casprine said. "Things that grew roots and branches, and other things that might live and thrive among those extrapolations."

Masquelayne made a fricative sound, his upper teeth touching his lower lip as he blew contemptuous air. "Earth magic!" he said. "A farmer!"

Again, Casprine shrugged. He had nothing to add.

"What does this mutton-thumping peasant want?" Masquelayne pressed him. "What is *his* heart's desire?"

His host gave that some thought, without much result. Finally, he said, "I recall hearing that he had approached Hua-Sang, something about wanting to acquire that antique harpsichont that Hua-Sang inherited from Vanthoonian when Vanthoonian translated himself to the Overworld. But that was long ago."

This news struck Masquelayne as odd. "A harpsichont? Puddlebrim enjoys screechy-scratchy fugues?"

Yet another lifting and settling of the silk-clothed shoulders. "It is what I heard. And that he was unhappy when Hua-Sang refused to consider the question."

"Indeed," said Masquelayne. "What would a farmer from the Forest of Ardollia have to offer a sophisticate like Hua-Sang?"

"Doubtless that was the problem," Casprine said. "More than that, I cannot say."

It was not a great deal of information compared to a nygrave's skull. But Masquelayne comforted himself with the knowledge that he had two of them and was keeping the better. As well, Casprine had not asked about the skull's condition. The fact that the left horn had a spiral fracture and could thus not withstand strong vibrations was something Casprine would have to deal with.

He made his farewells and approached the door. Casprine made to remove Schletzel's Buffer, but Masquelayne indulged himself in the pleasure of speaking the counterspell himself. He opened the door, stepped into the tunnel, and found his way home through the Glooms.

"Hua-Sang, it is Masquelayne the Incomparable who speaks!"

"I recognize the tone," said a precise voice from the aspekton on Masquelayne's workbench. "I will converse."

The device glowed and a simulacrum of Hua-Sang appeared in Masquelayne's workroom, hovering in the air so that the diminutive thaumaturge appeared to be looming over him. Masquelayne adjusted a setting and the image's feet settled to the floor, so that now it was he who had the advantage of height.

The two wizards made each other the courtesies that good manners required, then Hua-Sang said, "What business have we?"

Masquelayne said, "I am assembling a quartet—perhaps a quintet, I haven't quite decided—to play threnodies and light pieces of the Eighteenth Aeon. I have trained my sylphs, but I wish to employ authentic instruments of the period, rather than re-creations."

"I was not aware you had such abstruse musical tastes," said Hua-Sang.

"I do not advertise all my interests," Masquelayne said.

Hua-Sang's refined features composed themselves into a neutral aspect. "And how does this concern me?"

"I'm told that you used to have a harpsichont of the Eighteenth Aeon."

"That is so. I have it still."

"I wonder if you would consider parting with it?"

"Wonder no more," said the simulacrum. "It is dear to my heart."

"I was thinking I might have something you would consider trading for, some item that would make the arrangement to your advantage."

Hua-Sang's expression remained placid. "It is only remotely possible. I believe I have all that I require."

Hua-Sang's self-satisfaction was well known. Masquelayne had prepared himself for his inquiry to be met with initial indifference. But he had also worked his underlings hard to discover within his own holdings that which the other wizard might find it difficult to refuse. His majordomo had consulted the inventories at great length and finally suggested an item Masquelayne had won in a duel and for which he had no use. It lay forgotten in a storeroom.

Now Masquelayne said to Hua-Sang, "You are familiar with the serpents of Balbesh Island, the ones that grow to prodigious size?"

"I believe I've heard something."

"Have you heard that, among mature specimens, stones accrue in their gall bladders?"

"Mmm," said Hua-Sang.

"And that it is a peculiar property of these stones that they resonate to a wide range of fluxions? Indeed, resonate and amplify?"

Hua-Sang's right eyebrow elevated itself, not very far and not for very long, but Masquelayne saw it. He now paused and waited.

The silence lengthened until Hua-Sang could no longer resist. "Have you," he said, "one of those stones?"

Masquelayne heard the suppressed breathiness of the question. Without a word, he drew from a pocket of his robe a fist-sized lump of calculus and held it where the aspekton's percepts could not miss it.

"Ah," said Hua-Sang.

"Indeed," said Masquelayne.

"If you happen to be in contact with Poddlebrim," Masquelayne said, "you might let him know that I have acquired Hua-Sang's harpsichont."

Casprine's simulacrum struggled to maintain a placid expression. "You expect me to be your go-between?"

Masquelayne's hand stirred the air in a gesture of uninterest. "Have I offended?" he said, with a tone that said the prospect did not greatly bother him.

Casprine's eyes narrowed briefly, then he assumed his own mask of indifference. "If I happen to encounter him, I will mention it."

"Excellent," said Masquelayne and, after the briefest of formalities, broke the connection.

"I have been in touch with Poddlebrim," Casprine says. "He will accept a communication."

"Of course he will," said Masquelayne. He could not resist inquiring after the nygrave's skull. "I trust it is adequate."

"More than adequate," was the reply. "I mentioned it to Poddlebrim and he said he had a spell called Uvanch's Infallible Rectifier."

Masquelayne's brows drew down. "An obscurity. I have not heard of it."

"No matter. I took the skull to him, he performed the exercise, the fractured horn is now as new." Casprine allowed himself a wide smile and let it linger. "My divinations have reached new levels of perspicacity."

"He is generous. Or should I say a squanderer?"

"Say as you wish. I must return to my inquiries." This time it was Casprine who broke the connection, not even waiting for Masquelayne to finish his courtesy.

"Poddlebrim, it is Masquelayne who speaks!"

An image of the plump little thaumaturge did not appear above the aspekton, but his voice came from the air. "I prefer to communicate face-to-face. If you desire a conversation, I will accept a visit."

Masquelayne repressed his first impulse and said, "Very well. If you will prepare an entrance, I will come by way of the Glooms."

But Poddlebrim said no. "Opening a way to the Glooms allows in a miasma that interferes with a delicate handling of the argent and sable fluxions."

"The what?" said Masquelayne before he could control himself. He knew of four kinds of fluxions: yellow, green, blue, and red. They were the intersecting lines of force that formed a network across land and sea. Their manipulation by those trained to focus the will by means of sounds, motions, and stances was the essence of magic.

"Argent and sable. You are not familiar with them?"

Masquelayne faced a choice. If there were such a thing as fluxions he had never heard of, he would lose face by admitting it. If the alleged fluxions were illusory, he would lose face by claiming to know of them—especially if Poddlebrim was positioning him for ridicule. The story would soon get about.

He chose the third option. "I do not have time for this," he said, "certainly not if I cannot arrive by the Glooms. Am I to come by carriage?"

"That would be best," said Poddlebrim. "Its energies will not disturb my experiments."

"Expect me soon." Masquelayne broke the connection, without bothering to observe the niceties.

◆ ◆ ◆

His carriage was activated by Azerion's Inexhaustible Motivator. It traveled along corridors where fluxions ran parallel to each other and operated best where blue predominated. That meant it could enter the Forest of Ardollia, but could come no nearer to Poddlebrim's cottage than a brief walk along a narrow and winding path.

This puzzled Masquelayne, because wizards invariably established their seats where fluxions met in nodes. An intersection of yellow and green was the least favorable. Where thick lines of blue and green crossed each other offered a strong foundation for most spells and cantrips, but the rare crossroads of red and blue were optimum, provided the thaumaturge possessed the will and skill to manage the natural tendency of the two colors to clash.

Masquelayne's eyrie at High Voiderasch was situated on an intersection of blue and red fluxions, with the blue predominating, which made it possible for him to derive power from the incongruity. He was of the blue school but aspired to rise in time to the purple, once he had mastered enough of the red school's practices to integrate its lore with that of his own tradition. He was sure he would be able to apply the requisite will.

But Poddlebrim's cottage was not sited on a node of any kind. An able practitioner could still wield magic there, but should expect no inherent amplification of will. Yet somehow the location had managed to rebuff his demon, apparently without effort. It made no sense.

Masquelayne felt a slight tingle in his lower front teeth as he reached the clearing, and sensed that he had been permitted to pass through a discriminating barrier. But he did not recognize the spell. That caused him a moment's unease, but he pushed it from his mind as the door opened and Poddlebrim gestured for him to enter.

The visitor offered a full spectrum of the courtesies practitioners could extend to each other and accepted those returned in kind by his host. That gave Masquelayne time to inspect the premises. He was surprised to see scant evidence of any thaumaturgical arts being practiced here. There was a workbench, but little in the way of apparatus on it. There was a bookcase, but it contained only three tomes, none of them of great size. And that was all. The rest of the room's furnishings consisted of a table and two stools, a narrow cot in an alcove behind a half-drawn curtain, a fireplace, and a worn rug. He saw no evidence of servants, human or otherwise.

Poddlebrim observed Masquelayne's inventory of his belongings and said, "I have chosen a simple existence. I do not care to let extranities impede upon my researches."

"And yet," said Masquelayne, "you wished to acquire an antique harpsichont."

The plain face showed surprise. "I did, indeed. I had an idea its tones would resonate closely with a spell I was composing." The little wizard spread his hands and smiled. "But that was back when I was of the purple school."

Masquelayne heard the last few words, though they did not register. "You are composing?" he said.

Now the small hands rose in a disclaimer. "In a minor way," Poddlebrim said. "Mostly I am rediscovering lost spells. But occasionally, I am able to create a variation on a forgotten theme. Such as that little display I put on at the Grand Symposium."

"Yes," said Masquelayne, as his mind wrestled with what he was hearing, "that was quite . . ." His voice dwindled as the full import of the other man's assertion reached him. "Lost spells?" he said. "Are there many?"

"Oh, dozens, I should imagine. Perhaps scores. There is a very long stretch of time behind us, you know. And now that I have identified fluxions of argent and sable—those are the antique terms, of course; silver and black, we would say today—well, now that I've found where they were hidden, and learned how to evoke them, well . . ."

Poddlebrim ended his speech with a gesture that said much was now possible that had not been before. Masquelayne nodded and smiled, though he doubted the smile was one of his usual masterful smirks.

"Argent and sable?" he said. "Yes, I recall something, can't remember where or when. Minor stuff, wasn't it? Tinkering around the edges?"

"Do you think so?" said Poddlebrim, his face a map of polite restraint. "My sense of things is that they are the foundation for a school of magic that surpasses anything we have known in recent aeons. Might

and power, subtlety and profound depths—that's how it seems to me."
He shrugged. "That is why I gave up the purple school."

The little wizard made a gesture of self-deprecation and concluded,
"Of course, I've only pierced the surface of the pond. Time will tell."

Masquelayne stood blinking. All he could think of to say was, "So
you have no interest in the harpsichont?"

"Not any more," said Poddlebrim. "Still, it was kind of you to think
of me."

Masquelayne returned to his turreted manse above the Vale of Coromance. He dismissed his carriage and went to his workroom, where he
sat in his thinking chair and let the implications of Poddlebrim's remarks wash over him. Sensing his unease, his attendants came to grin
and flatter, but he shouted at them and made them flee in tears and
anguish.

His outburst and the sounds of their receding wails restored him to
a more usual mood, and he rose from the chair with fresh resolve. He
took down a book bound in red-scaled leather and consulted its pages
until he found what he sought. Then he prepared the requisite materials,
congratulating himself on having kept the vial of corpse-dust the spell
called for. When all was ready, he drew the words of the incantation into
his mind, struggled with them until they became orderly, then spoke
them while his fingers reached to touch the fluxions, visible only to him,
that passed through the room.

A wavering, almost transparent shape appeared before him. He concentrated his will and stroked the lines of blue force. The shape became
more solid and its outlines became stable.

"Let me go," said the ghost.

"Not till I am satisfied."

The apparition sighed. "What would you have of me?"

"Knowledge," said Masquelayne. "The knowledge of argent and
sable."

The revenant moaned. "I know nothing of that."

"You were once the greatest wizard of Almery. If you do not know,
none does."

"I remember forgotten palaces, the faces of dead paramours, my enemies bound and silenced, seas now turned to sand. But of magic, I recall nothing."

"Try!"

"I cannot. It takes will, and this poor remnant of me has none."

"What if I restored you to life?" Masquelayne said.

"Your summoning spell requires me to speak only truth. I would crush you like an eggshell."

Masquelayne made a noise deep in his throat. He dismissed the ghost and turned to his looking glass. But the demon said it knew nothing of argent and sable fluxions. He went to his books again, tracing from one reference to another, struggling against the resistance of the most ancient tomes, which from long association with thaumaturges over millennia had acquired much will of their own.

He gazed into globes of black glass, cast many-sided dice carved from the bones of dragons, drank potions to bring visions of other planes, projected his mind into bygone ages, hunted and sought in all the ways and byways available to a grand thaumaturge of the blue school.

And found nothing. At the end of it all, he lay weak and feverish on the floor of his workroom. A sylph hovered in the doorway, offering tentative cries, until he ordered it to bring him a restorative broth. When he had taken a few spoonfuls, the lethargy seeped from him, and he climbed into his chair and thought.

And it was then that the answer came, bursting into his awareness like a titanium salute firework. He ground his teeth in rage as the perfidy of his enemies became clear to him. Hua-Sang, Casprine, they were part of it. Lurulan and Ombbo, certainly, eager for revenge after he had put them in his shade at the Grand Symposium. And behind them others, those he had challenged and bested over the years, taking their wands and their prized possessions and daring them to withstand the force of his will.

Masquelayne had defeated each of them in single encounters, wizard to wizard, and not one of them had failed to yield their goods and slink away. Now they had combined to frustrate him, but not in open battle. Instead, they had conspired, recruiting some hedge sorcerer he had scarcely heard of, and making this Poddlebrim appear to command powers beyond Masquelayne's grasp.

Argent and sable, indeed! he thought. *A trick, a swindle, a sleight in plain sight!*

They had sent him off on a fool's merrychase, seeking a never-was he would never find. And, surely, right now they were laughing at him, mocking him. He imagined Lurulan mincing about, mimicking his mannerisms, and Ombbo pulling faces, while the detestable Poddlebrim simpered and sought new opportunities to please his masters.

I will have revenge, Masquelayne promised himself, *such a revenge as will make the dead quake in their tombs and the yet unborn prefer to postpone existence.*

He turned once more to his thaumaturgical resources. But now, instead of seeking a false grail, the end of his labors was clear in his mind. He would start with Lurulan, of the red school.

Lurulan called himself "the Excellence," though few others did. He was a middling practitioner who was forced to rely on paraphernalia because he lacked a great "potency of axial volition," the thaumaturge's term for the power of will. The secret to handling him was to catch him at a distance from his thunderstones and coercive crystals.

Lurulan was vain of his physical appearance. He maintained an aura of youth, preferring to be seen in the guise of a young man just entering into manhood, though he was at least a century older than Masquelayne, who was himself of a grand age. Partly, the effect was achieved by an application of Ibist's Gratifying Glamour, but Lurulan was not satisfied just to wear a semblance. His vanity required him to underwrite the seeming with the substantive, and thus he paid regular visits to the freshening springs in the Valley of Taza-che.

Masquelayne lay in wait along the route between Lurulan's manse and Taza-che. Hidden by means physical and magical, he watched as the red wizard skimmed across the landscape in an impregnable bubble of hymestric force. The means of transportation had a flaw: a pursuer could slip into the bubble's wake and follow undetected. This Masquelayne did, inserting himself into the slipstream and arriving at the springs just as Lurulan stepped from his conveyance, stripping off his robe and buskins in preparation for the immersion.

"Ha!" said Masquelayne. "I have caught you."

Lurulan was nonplussed but recovered quickly. His hands and fingers assumed a precise position and he opened his mouth to speak. But Masquelayne had the advantage that comes with forethought and preparation. Before the red wizard stepped from the bubble he had already spoken the incantation behind Venath's Progressive Constraint, so he had only to snap his fingers to render Lurulan mute.

He did not hesitate to move to the next phase of his assault. As the Constraint had begun to rigidify his muscles, Lurulan had stretched out a hand. Now his ruby-tipped wand was wriggling its way out of the pocket of his robe, eager to fly to his grasp. But Masquelayne had anticipated his opponent's reliance on apparatus, and had placed Tse-Fan's Temporal Congelator firmly in the front of his mind. He now spoke the four harsh syllables and pointed the index finger whose nail was incised with a rune of power.

Immediately, Lurulan lost all capacity of motion. The wand came to his outreached palm and, ungripped, fell to the ground. Masquelayne stepped forward, picked up the rod, and tucked it into his sash of blue saraphand. Then he smiled.

"You thought you could combine to undo me," he said. "But I will always be one too many for the likes of you."

Lurulan regarded him helplessly. He could no more blink than lift a mountain. Masquelayne allowed him a few more moments to appreciate his impending punishment, then he cast the last of the three spells he had memorized for this duel: Bront's Forlorn Banishment.

As the last harsh syllable sounded, Lurulan ceased to exist on this plane and was transported bodily to the Underworld. There he would remain, until someone bothered to find him and release him from his exile. But since no one save Masquelayne knew where the red wizard had gone, he might be trapped in the Second Plane for quite some time.

Masquelayne gathered up Lurulan's garments and threw them into the bubble, then boarded it. The controls were elementary, and soon he was skimming the ground in the direction of his eyrie. He thought he might convert the conveyance into a coop for the fowl that provided him with his morning egg.

Lurulan's bubble performed one last service before becoming an avian shelter: it carried Masquelayne across the Lake of Mists to the island where Ombbo had built his many-turreted stronghold. Lurulan and Ombbo frequently worked together, so the sight of the conveyance wafting to a halt in the latter's garden drew no suspicion.

Ombbo was tending to his bed of tintinnabulary blossoms when the bubble touched down. He spoke without turning as Masquelayne stepped down.

"Lurulan, come and listen to the tone of this little one. I have rarely heard so pure a note. When it reaches full bloom—"

He got no farther because Masquelayne had again prepared with Venath's Progressive Constraint. Ombbo's vocal apparatus ceased to respond to his will, and the spell's rigor swiftly turned his limbs to a state that only a trained anatomist could distinguish from stone. Bent as he had been to touch his chosen flower, he toppled forward into the bed, raising a sad tinkle from the blossoms he crushed.

Masquelayne rolled him out of the flowers and onto his back so Ombbo could know who had been his undoing. He now passed several remarks that expressed his opinion of Ombbo's character and capabilities as a thaumaturge, some of which he had wanted to say for quite some time, others of which came to him on the inspiration of the moment.

He had planned to send Ombbo to join his ally in the Second Plane, but looking around at the perfectly ordered gardens, he felt a surge of vindictive creativity. He rolled the frozen man to the center of a stretch of lawn, then went to the bubble and retrieved the grimoire he had been using to load the spells with which he had armed himself. He discharged the unused spells of congelation and banishment, then sought for two others. Shortly thereafter, he returned to where Ombbo's bent and rigid form waited.

Masquelayne spoke the harsh syllables of Twysk's Vegetative Compulsion, using the addition that would specify the precise type of plant

Ombbo would now become. It was a tall and spreading oak, with plenty of outreaching branches and twigs—just the kind of tree that would appeal to birds seeking nesting sites.

But Masquelayne did not rely on nature taking its course. Instead, he used a rarely employed variant of a simple spell chanted by traveling hedge sorcerers to drive crop-raiding birds from farmers' fields. Soon after he performed the last gesture, a flock of some three hundred lesser speckled grick-gracks arrived and took up residence in the tree that had been Ombbo. The birds began to emit the harsh and raucous cries for which they had been named, canceling entirely the musical chimes from the tintinnabulary beds.

Masquelayne had to shout over the cacophony. "That is the sound of my revenge, Ombbo! You will hear it, morning to night. And I may send you a plague of bark beetles to feed the birds and keep you constantly itchful."

With that, he entered Ombbo's keep, frightened away the retainers, and helped himself to whatever took his fancy.

"Masquelayne, it is Casprine who speaks!"

"Speak on," said Masquelayne. He twitched a finger, and a simulacrum of the vulpine thaumaturge came to float above the aspekton.

"I have received an inquiry from Shevance the Insightful. She has been unable to contact Lurulan the Excellence. She then tried to reach Ombbo, again without success."

"Those two often traffic together. Perhaps they have gone off on some jaunt."

"Perhaps," said Casprine, "except that Shevance says she visited Ombbo's island and found the place in disarray."

Masquelayne's hand dismissed the issue. "I cannot comment on Ombbo's housekeeping."

Casprine said nothing, but the hovering image peered at him in a manner Masquelayne found offensive. He said, "This afternoon, I am engaged in demanding research. If you have nothing more to say . . ."

"I think we should meet," said Casprine.

"I will expect you tomorrow."

"It would be better if you came to me."

Masquelayne's brows expressed his equanimity. "As you wish. I shall come again by the Glooms."

"Yes," said Casprine, "do."

But Masquelayne did not come by that route. Instead, he flew to Casprine's mountain in his sylph-drawn carriage and alighted before the great doors that led to the long-dead king's Grand Processional Way that angled down to the wizard's subterranean chambers. He used Boix's Comprehensive Rupture to burst the portal, as well as every barrier between him and his target, then rushed down to where Casprine lurked in the tunnel that led from the Glooms to his door.

Masquelayne had fashioned a golem and sent it by way of the Glooms, timing its arrival to coincide with his own. The shambling creature had not delayed the thaumaturge for long, but Masquelayne was quick when he needed to be. Casprine was still recovering from the effects of the Rupture—it shattered doors and sent splinters flying—when Masquelayne arrived to confront him.

On his last visit, Masquelayne had equipped himself not only with Boix's Comprehensive Rupture, but with Zinezan's Comprehensive Cloak, and Willifant's Penetrating Beam. Casprine was an able wizard and would have detected the auras of these spells. It would be reasonable for him to expect that today's use of the Rupture would be followed by the Beam, while his assailant sought to protect himself behind the Cloak.

But Masquelayne was a subtle duelist. He had indeed armored himself in the Cloak, but he had left the Beam behind. So when, upon his appearance, Casprine immediately threw up Chup's Scintillating Prism—the recommended defense against Willifant's Penetrating Beam—its refractions proved useless against the spell Masquelayne did employ: Ovanian's Overwhelming Thrust. The column of force threw Casprine some distance down the tunnel and left him momentarily breathless.

Thus he was unable to cast the spell he had taken into his mind—Bardolf's Enclosing Crush—which would have created a shroud of force around Masquelayne's Cloak and driven it inward. Masquelayne would have ended his days as a blob of matter so densely compressed that it would have sunk through solid rock to the world's molten core.

But Bardolf's spell required a strong voice to vibrate the fluxions, and Casprine was temporarily bereft of speech. All he could do was direct a line of coldfire from an outstretched finger, which Masquelayne ignored, safe behind the Comprehensive Cloak. He advanced down the tunnel to the optimum distance for the spell he intended to hurl at Casprine, pausing just long enough to make his breathless opponent aware of what was about to happen.

"Pablillo's Entropic Accelerator," Masquelayne said. "I found it in a very old grimoire that used to be Ombbo's, though I doubt he ever would have come across this particular cantrip. The book was most strong-willed. It took me half of yesterday to wrest the spell from it. You will recall that I said I was researching. Now you shall have the fruits of my labors."

It was a complex incantation, a primitive leftover from the Eighteenth Aeon when fluxions were more raw and their palpitations required a certain fierceness of spirit. But Masquelayne was ferocious in his desire to punish any who did him wrong, and Casprine had been classed as among that breed.

He pitched his voice in a harsh, hoarse shout and chanted the twelve syllables in a percussive rhythm. As he spoke the last sound, the walls of the tunnel seemed to billow and shiver like agitated jelly. Then he chanted the dodecaphone a second time, and the floor rose and fell in a series of ripples. And now he shouted the dozen ergophones a final time, accompanying his utterance of the last one with a smash of his balled fist into his palm.

All light fled the tunnel and a soughing wind blew Masquelayne's robes about him. Then the lumens relit themselves and he saw the effects of the spell. A huddle of bones wrapped in skin that was like parchment and topped with a few wisps of hair slumped against the tunnel wall. It was clothed in rags that were disintegrating and falling to dust even as Masquelayne watched. In the next moment, the dried flesh collapsed inward, the bones fell apart, and then even they crumbled into fragments.

Masquelayne stooped and recovered Casprine's wand. He would mount it on the wall of his dining hall, along with the others he had won in duels. Then he turned to enter the defeated enemy's demesne, to see what other spoils might be got.

"Masquelayne," said a voice, interrupting his researches, "it is Foubaye the Arbiter who speaks!"

He was tempted to ignore the contact, being deep into his preparations for the punishment of the upstart Poddlebrim, but Foubaye was the most senior Fellow of the College of Thaumaturgy. As such, he had not only real power in his own right, but a rank that allowed him to call on other great practitioners to form a wizardly phalanx that was invincible. Masquelayne put down the tome—formerly Casprine's—he had been wrestling with and said, "Speak on."

Today, Foubaye affected the appearance of a callow youth clothed in a harlequin and quilted cap. As his image appeared in the workroom, he took a quick inventory of Masquelayne's possessions and said, "So it is true. You have attacked your fellow wizards and despoiled them of their goods. And this after the amity that prevailed at the Grand Symposium."

"They conspired against me," Masquelayne said. "The punishments were apt."

"Where is your proof of conspiracy?" Foubaye said. "And why did you not lay a complaint before the College?"

"I saw through their schemes and acted with dispatch. There was no need to involve you and the Fellows."

Foubaye stroked his beardless chin. "There will be an inquiry. Hold yourself ready for our summons."

Masquelayne waited to see if there would be conditions. He did not want to be confined to his estate pending the hearing. But Foubaye contented himself with ordering him to make no further assaults on colleagues. With a sniff, Masquelayne said he would forbear.

When the simulacrum winked out, he summoned his demon and asked, "Has Poddlebrim been accepted into the College?"

"He has applied, but his request is still under consideration. His case is complicated."

"Then he is not my colleague." Masquelayne dismissed the fiend and threw himself back into his preparations. It would take days to coordinate the schedules of enough senior Fellows to form a panel for Foubaye's inquiry—more than time enough.

At his best, Masquelayne could absorb three major spells at one time. But to deal with the detestable Poddlebrim, now that the false front for the conspirators no longer had their combined strengths to support him, Masquelayne chose five less difficult cantrips. And he took his best wand.

He meant to inflict humiliations upon the hedge sorcerer: to make him itch, to make him dance to exhaustion, to distress him with drooling and incontinence, to transform him into a hunchbacked, wart-infested grotesque, and finally to transport him to the island continent in the southern ocean and leave him there to fend for himself among anthropophagic beasts.

He called for his carriage, swept his cape about himself, and set forth. He landed near Poddlebrim's cottage and marched straight along the path to the front entrance, humming a triumphal tune. He struck the door thrice with a fist, then reached for the latch, expecting the occupant by now to be scurrying out a rear window. Instead, the door swung open to reveal Poddlebrim, clothed in the same nondescript robe he had worn to the Grand Symposium, blinking at him in what looked to be a failure of recognition.

Then the man's expression cleared and he said, "The one with the harpsichont, of course! Forgive me, I've forgotten your name."

Masquelayne smiled a smile that, in the past, had frozen blood. "It won't do, Poddlebrim. I know everything."

"Really?" said the little man. "I've never known anyone who knew *everything*. I'd be interested to explore your epistemological methods."

"Enough," said Masquelayne. "Your co-conspirators have been dealt with. Now it is your turn." He brushed past Poddlebrim and entered the small house. It was as he had seen it before. He turned and regarded the object of his punishment. "Do you wish to beg for mercy?"

Poddlebrim closed the door and folded his hands in the sleeves of his robe. He cocked his bald head to one side and studied Masquelayne as if he were a specimen he had just discovered had been mislabeled.

"You have me at a disadvantage," he said. "I was not aware I was part of a conspiracy."

Masquelayne's face hardened. "I said, 'enough,'" he said. "We will begin."

He produced his wand, pointed it, and spoke the opening sura of Tees's Mutable Itch. But something was wrong. He could hear his own voice intoning the sibilant ergophones, but they were not echoing in his mind with the reverberations that signified their power. Masquelayne shook his head and spoke the second sura, wondering as he did so if he had somehow neglected some aspect of the childishly simple spell, for the fresh syllables also carried no resonance.

Meanwhile, Poddlebrim regarded him as if he were a dull student essaying a difficult recitation and making a poor fist of it. Masquelayne fought down his anger; Tees's Itch could reverse its polarity if the final sura wasn't pronounced exactly, and the embarrassment of such a failure would trouble him, even though Poddlebrim would never live to shame him with it. So he spoke the syllables carefully and moved his wand in the required three small circles.

Nothing happened. No line of blue force, no burst of an aura around Poddlebrim, no agonizing expression taking over the bland face as the traveling itch took hold.

Poddlebrim said, "Was that supposed to be a spell?"

Masquelayne could make no reply. Not even as a faltering first-month apprentice had he ever failed to cast so simple an incantation. He looked at his wand, shook it.

"It won't work here," Poddlebrim said. "Argent and sable fluxions. Didn't we discuss this when you visited before?"

Augraman's Frenetic Hop was only five syllables and a gesture. Masquelayne spoke the sounds, moved his left hand. Again, nothing happened.

"I'll show you," Poddlebrim said. He made his hands visible and rippled their fingers as if playing a complex instrument. Immediately, the space between him and Masquelayne was crossed at about waist height by something that resembled a thick cable of scintillating silver, horizontal to the floor. Poddlebrim's fingers waggled again, and the argent fluxion was intersected at an acute angle by a similar hawser of deepest black.

"Once they've been called up," the small man said, "they simply absorb the energy of any red, blue, green, or yellow fluxions in the vicinity. Especially at an intersection."

Masquelayne felt a sudden concatenation of emotions, all of them unwelcome. First came the certainty that he had been shown up as a fool. Then came a wave of helplessness, followed by an unbearable shame that this Poddlebrim must surely be looking down on him—when the positions ought to have been reversed. By now, this mudhen of a hedge sorcerer should have been begging for mercy while itching and executing spastic saltations. Instead, he was prattling on about convergences and coherences.

And then through the welter of hateful feelings came a revelation. Masquelayne knew himself to be an accomplished thaumaturge. He had wrought powerful incantations and slung spells against wizards who had more training than he, but lacked the intensity of will that he brought to his work.

And now, here in this ridiculous mud-walled cottage, was an intersection of fluxions whose power was orders of magnitude greater than Masquelayne had ever been able to draw on before. He had but to reach out and touch . . .

With the thought came the action. Masquelayne focused his will and sent it down into his right hand, spread his fingers in the basic configuration for accessing any fluxion, and touched the silver. He saw Poddlebrim break off his monologue and raise a warning hand, and had just time to think, *He doesn't want me doing this. Well, I'll show*—

At which point a shock of energy went up his arm and flashed throughout his body. He felt his feet leave the floor and had a sense of being pulled into the argent fluxion. He was instantly submerged, as if he were a clod of earth fallen from a cutaway bank into a storm-fed river in full flood. And then like a clod, he dissolved.

All further sense fled from him. Masquelayne was no longer Masquelayne, just a nameless, will-less nothing, being borne along by energies beyond all reckoning, traveling at impossible speed from nowhere to nowhere, never arriving, in constant flow.

It went on forever. And then, as quickly as he had been devoured by the silver fluxion, he was back in his own form again. He found himself standing, naked and shivering, in Poddlebrim's cottage, his mind empty, his body chilled at its core. Slowly, awareness returned, and he saw signs that some considerable time had passed: the small wizard's robe was stained and wrinkled, his face was drawn with fatigue, and several days' worth of stubble had sprouted along his jaw.

"There you are," Poddlebrim said, "at last." He came closer and patted the air around Masquelayne, peered into his eyes, and snapped his fingers close to the porches of Masquelayne's ears. "At least some portion of you. Can you speak?"

"I . . . I was . . ." It was a struggle to remember what words were and how to employ them. The effort made him immensely tired.

"Never mind," said Poddlebrim, "it will come back to you." He studied Masquelayne a few moments more, then gently led him to a chair and showed him how to sit in it. Masquelayne was still shivering, so Poddlebrim brought a blanket and wrapped him in it.

"I made some leek and fennel soup," the little man said. "You'd better have some."

"Soup," said Masquelayne. The concept eluded him at first, but when he smelled the odor from the wooden bowl Poddlebrim brought him, he remembered what soup was. As the first spoonful of warm broth was brought to his mouth, he rediscovered how to swallow.

"Hmm," said Poddlebrim, after a few repetitions, "I think you'll have to stay here for a while."

"Stay," Masquelayne repeated. He had a sense that "stay" had something to do with time and lack of motion.

"Yes," said Poddlebrim. "Until you're . . . yourself again."

"Soup," said Masquelayne, and opened his mouth.

When the bowl was finished, Poddlebrim took it away, then came back and patted the air around Masquelayne again. "That's better," he said. "There's more of you now. I'm sure the rest will find its way back in a day or so."

He went to his workbench and flipped through a book that was open there, read a page, then another. "There will be changes, though. If what it says here is correct," he said, tapping the book, "your being absorbed into the fluxion will have had an omnitemporal effect. That is, every spell you've ever cast will have been canceled—it will all be as if it had never happened."

"Spell," Masquelayne said. He felt he ought to know that word and struggled to put a meaning to it.

"Rather unfortunate for a wizard," Poddlebrim was saying. "Still, I'm sure your friends will rally round and help you over the bumps. Several of them have been asking after you."

"Friends," Masquelayne said, but found he couldn't put a meaning to that word at all.

Ysabeau S. Wilce

• • •

Ysabeau S. Wilce was born in California and has followed the drum through Spain and most of its North American colonies. She became a lapsed historian when facts no longer compared favorably to the shining lies of her imagination. Prior to this capitulation, she researched arcane military subjects and presented educational programs on how to boil laundry at several frontier army forts. She is a graduate of Clarion West and has been nominated for the World Fantasy Award, the James Tiptree Award, and won the Andre Norton Award. Her novels include *Flora Segunda: Being the Magickal Mishaps of a Girl of Spirit, Her Glass-Gazing Sidekick, Two Ominous Butlers (One Blue), a House with Eleven Thousand Rooms, and a Red Dog; Flora's Dare: How a Girl of Spirit Gambles All to Expand Her Vocabulary, Confront a Bouncing Boy Terror, and Try to Save Califa from a Shaky Doom (Despite Being Confined to Her Room)*; and *Flora's Fury: How a Girl of Spirit and a Red Dog Confound Their Friends, Astound Their Enemies, and Learn the Importance of Packing Light*. Her most recent work, a collection of short stories called *Prophecies, Libels & Dreams,* was published in 2014. She lives in the San Francisco Bay Area and is very fond of mules.

Here she returns to the fabulous, enchanted city of Califa, for a story about what happens when that famous thief and Bouncing Boy Terror, Jumping Jack, decides that what he needs to steal next is love—a decision with unforeseen consequences that will land him over his head in trouble. And in cake.

◆　　◆　　◆

Biography of a Bouncing Boy Terror, Chapter II: Jumping Jack in Love

YSABEAU S. WILCE

N ow, my little waffles, you know the story of wee Jack and how his Rapture for Red led him to his heart's desire: a pair of sparkly sangyn boots, each tipped with a slithery snake's head. How after buying those boots with the last of his family's flash, he found that a bargain can be hard indeed when the purchase has a Will of its own. But in his regret Jack realized that lofty leaping can be lucrative and that windows on high are rarely guarded. So Jacko, deciding it better to steal than starve, snatched his family from the jaws of Hunger and together they cozied up to a life of thievery and yummy chow.

Once our Jack started jumping up up up he went, until he reached the very pinnacle of perfidy. In the twilight world of the Prime Coves, among the footpads, flashers, mashers, buncos, sporters, swaddlers, ginglers, ganglers, foodpads, and fencers, Jack was King. His red sparkly heels towered over all the rest, the colossus of crime, the emperor of embezzlement, the . . . FANCIEST LAD OF THEM ALL. Jack was happy, footloose, fancy-free, and richer than the richest butter, the fattiest cream, the swirl of sugar on top of the birthday donut, the crispest edge of the smokiest bacon.

And yet . . .
Here is where *what happens next* begins.

One tawny morn, my darling dolls, Jacko wakes up with a rustling rest-less tum. He lies in his five-fathom featherbed and drums his sparkly red heels upon the velvet counterpane (for even in sleep Jack and his boots cannot be parted) trying to reason why. His tummy gurgles but not for grub, despite the splendid smell of sizzling swine, which hangs on the morning air. Ruminating for some time upon this gurgle, Jack finally allows it comes not from his tum, but slightly up and over, an-other organ entirely. The rest of Jack is toasty warm—his toes snug in sparkles, his ears wrapped in fuzzy flannel, his bod cocooned in softy wool, warm as the spring sun. But his heart—poor throbbing organ—his heart is oh, so very cold.

But why the freeze? Did he not have all there was to be had? Fancy lad and full of boodle. Respect of the other janglers, a lair chock full of fizz and sup, the bestest kind, splendiferous threads, and his name ablaze in all the papers. What more could his greedy heart desire? Don't be silly, boyo! Casting chill away, Jack lofts from his bed, and heads for bacon, singing, "Tra la, I am the Boy with the Most Cake."

But the tune is cracked, and so is his voice. Still, he warbles through his toilette, and as he ties his brocade cravat, slings shoulderwise a splen-did red leather duster. Dances down the stairs and toward the breakfast room, stopping to snuggle the basket of corgi pups on the stairs. The sun shines through the gauzy curtains, the butterflies on the painted wallpa-per flutter in the warmth. A little coffee, a little bacon, some kedgeree will do him the trick.

But looking down the long length of table at the enormous breakfast awaiting him, he realizes what he lacks. Before him is spread a splendif-erous feast of delectable viands—the aforementioned bacon, cheefles, dragonfruit galantine, kale smoothie, salmon omasubis, buttered pop-corn, toast, and he alone to eat it all.

He is lonely.

The family he saved from hunger had blossomed in Jack's hothouse thievery and have all gone their own ways. Mamma married a banger from Sacto and opened a bagnio on Joyce Street where she reigns like an empress over red velvet portieres and beveled glass mirrors. The baby what coughed grew into a sharp and lively lass who wears a hat with a cockade and a vivandiere's uniform with bright gold buttons while she prances the boards of the Palace Theater, smoking a stogie and singing "Once I Was Callow, but Now I Am Gay, Since My Little Sweetheart Stole Your Heart Away" to the roar of smitten stagedoor johnnies. The other mice children, too, have grown up up and away. Now brawny rather than scrawny, they have scattered from their brother's patronage to make their own ways in the waking World.

So all alone, Jacko sits in his ill-begotten splendor and the morning silence, the thick-cut bacon in his mouth choking him.

If only he had a companion to share his secret sorrows and his secret joys, his hopes and desires, his huge soft bed, his long polished table, and his yummy yummy bacon. If only he had love to keep the dark at bay. But how to find a companion? He chews on this problem along with his cheefle, rolls it around in his mouth with the last swallow of coffee, and continues cogitation while he goes about his day: jumping into the boudoir of the chief justice of Califa and relieving her of such trinkets that keep her dresser top askew, riffling her sock drawer and kipping the silver collar off her snuffling pug-dog while dog and justice snore through the entire caper. A wild rousting bounce over the roofs of Califa filling his boodle sack like a sort of reverse Man in Pink Blooms, stealing gifts instead of leaving them.

He's still considering the conundrum as he counts the day's take in his hidden snuggery, and while he distributes his largesse to his constituents that night at the Baile de Zarandeo, held every five days in a place I dare not disclose to you little poodles upon pain of death. (The City jail—what better place to collect felons, and the last place the law would ever consider to look?) No answers come to him at the Baile, but on the bounce home, a sudden solution is jolted loose by the warbling cries of a newspaper boy, shouting out an advertisement for Madam Twanky's Sel-R-Salt, in between the call of the headlines.

How does one find anything—a plumber, a lost dog, a new dog?

An advertisement, of course.

So Jack constructs a compelling advertisement and places it in the

SEEKING section of the *Califa Police Gazette* and *Fancy Pantaloon Quarterly.* "A gent of passion seeks real tomato for long walks on the beach, moonlight dining, Scrabble, and happily ever after. No cranks, bubblers, mechanics, or flash coves."

Overnight, his numbered mailbox overflows with eager answers, scented papers, envelopes thick with promises and paste-board portraits, a plethora of choices, all of which prove most unsatisfying. Viz: the Hurdy Gurdy Girl Long Past Girlhood, the Piano Player with the Mossy Teeth, the Rubbler Who Won't Shut Up about His Mother, the Hostler That Chews Too Loud, and The Lawyer Obsessed with Cats, to name just a few.

The most promising letter of the bunch turns out to have been penned by an infernal daemon. (He should have known by the scorched stationery.) Jack doesn't gainsay against infernal daemons per se, but finds the avid praterhuman's embraces to be ardent in a manner a bit too third-degree for comfort.

So, having gotten no closer to his heart's desire, Jack gives in, scotches the advertisement, and drowns his sorrows in bouncing and Bounce, letting loose a full-throated warble of despair to the barkeep of the Hubba Time Roadhouse while he drinks. This barkeep, who herself has a jade-eye view of love, advises him, bitterly:

"Love comes to those who take it; those who wait, wait forever. You must take what you want."

Jack draws up from his lean and bangs his fist upon the bar, bouncing all the bottles. Of course, the barkeep is right, of course! He had leapt to fortune and leapt to fame. He had leapt to leisure and leapt to . . . and so he would leap to love.

If love will not come willingly, then he will steal it!

This resolution proves easier in resolve than it does in practice. Unlike jewels and coin, or paintings and statues, Love does not lie about on dressers, on tables, hang on walls, sit snug in safes, awaiting for the taking. Love does not fit in bags, or at least not willingly, and without scratching. And while it's easy to recognize value in coins, pearls, jewels, silver, Love is harder to spot. Still, Jack gives it his best.

Now instead of waiting for *all's quiet* and *all to bed* to do his leaping, Jack waits until the householders are at home to bounce on in. This way, he meets surprised lads and lassies, whom he woos with syrupy words, and strings of pearls, and gracious manners. But none are favorably inclined toward a gent who vaulted through their window in the middle of the night, no matter how sweet this gent's words, or how flourishing the bouquet he proffers. His ardor is met with shrieks, screams, flailing pokers, flinging shoes, and the foamy teeth of a particularly ferocious corgi.

Now, let us leave Jack, exiting left pursued by a corgi, and switch scenes for a minute, little poodles. While Jack is determined to get love, someone else is determined to get Jack. A hero to the hoi polloi, Jack's name raises huzzahs to the lips of those below him, the forlorn and the poor, whose cheer and good luck came from the spoils that Jack steals in their names. But not everyone finds Jack so cheerful; those who wake to discover their dresser scarves torn and tossed; their safes gaping and empty; their silver plate decamped and their jam jars licked clean—they do not admire Jack at all. These luminaries, the best citizens of Califa, they call for Jack's boots, they call for Jack's person, they call for Jack to be caught, and tried, and displayed on a hurdle, preferably in pieces. Handsome bloodstained pieces, but pieces nonetheless.

In those olden days, my sweeties, Califa had a sheriff, and this sheriff had deputies, but these coppers were inoffensive dudes, well suited to break up bar-fights or help a gaffer across the street, to recover lost cats, lost lollies, lost hats, and unsnarl horse-traffic jams. But in the snatching of a world-class criminal they are useless. Not only did Jack have those springy boots that could soar him out of the deputies' grasp, but he'd stolen other useful apparel as well, and now he was cap-a-pie with roguish garments, including a holocaust cloak, a compass feather, and a jackdaw that could smell the bouncers coming and give the alert. Jack in his leaping never even notices the sheriffs snatching at his heels, always too low and too late.

So, the Duque de Grandsellos wakes up one morning to find his favorite dressing gown, gold-embroidered dragons on a celestial spun silk, gone. Princess Nadege Naproxine, the famed soubrette and tamale maker, loses a rare red polar bear mantle to Jack's boodle sack. Cheddar La Roque, the famous harpist, discovers the strings on her bow—made of twisted unicorn mane and a thread of hair from the Goddess Califa herself—missing. Jack kips a rare Norge Azul parrot from the Holy Whore of Heaven and the Pontifexina's favorite coffee cup, made from the gold-and-pearl-crusted skull cap of Albany Bilskinir himself.

The furious cries of these luminaries grow deafening. While waggish editorials crying *Attaboy* appear in the pages of *The Rogue's Gazette & Gazetter*, the letters published in *The Alta Califa* have a grimmer tone. An editorial in *The Alta Califa* calls for a curfew, roadblocks, road-checks, and door-to-door searches. Bounties are posted on posters about town, and Luscious Fyrdraaca, whose loss of a very valuable ice elemental means he is now drinking his cocktails warm, quite pointedly has a large meat hook placed on the front gate of Crackpot Hall, ready to receive, if not all of Jack, at least the tenderest parts of him.

When real order is called for in Califa, it is bestowed upon grateful citizens by the largesse of the Pontifexa's personal bodyguards, the awful Alacráns, sangyn-coated scorpions, whose sting is so dreaded that threat alone keeps discipline. Rarely is action on the Alacráns' part required, but when it is, the Alacráns are steady, deadly, and quick. As long as Jack remained aloof from her, the Pontifexa remained aloof from Jack. But the coffee cup was a step too far. The Pontifexa, faced with the stormy tantrum of her daughter, is forced to act.

The Captain of the Alacráns is summoned to the Pontifexa's Closet and told in no uncertain terms to Catch Jack. This, with a grim smile of *at last* she sets out to do.

Back to our hero, little snuggies, who, of course, is aware of none of this commotion and clamor. After the aforementioned biting corgi, he gives up on stealing Love, and tries to salve his heart (and corrugated flesh) by throwing a smash to which every prime cove in town is invited. At this smash, Jack wears Luscious Fyrdraaca's dragon dressing gown. He swills iced coffee from Georgiana Sidonia Haðraaða's pearl-studded coffee skullcap cup. He combs the Norge Azul with Luscious Fyrdraaca's platinum diamond-encrusted mustachio comb, his feet propped up on Luscious's writing desk. All around him, the other coves carouse, stamping out a furious tarantella to the rollicking tune of the hurdy-gurdy band. He sees couples canoodling, colluding, mashing, dancing, laughing, and he, the greatest of them all, alone and hollow. His jackdaw sits at his shoulder and caws derisively; she doesn't believe in love.

Jack raises his jorum in a toast. He won't believe in love either. Who needs love when you have stuff? He bounces off his throne and joins the frantic dance, dancing frantically. But the next morn, head splitting and heels aching, he sits drinking iced coffee, and reads the editorials calling for his head and other parts. Bored, he pages through the sheaves of broadsides celebrating and castigating (depending on who paid for the publishing) his deeds. He chews his cheefle and chuckles. Maybe it's not so much he's single as singular. Is this a bad thing to be?

Then he flips over *The Alta Califa* and sees these boldface words: ADVICE TO THE LOVELORN BY THE HOLY WHORE OF HEAVEN ...

Why had he not considered this remedy before? An idiot he is, and thoughtless, and caught up in his own head, too silly to see the obvious way out. The Holy Whore of Heaven will help him find love; is that not her calling? Advice to the lovelorn indeed! He is definitely lovelorn and in need of advice. But he can't wait for a letter to be composed, posted, vetted, perused, considered, replied, printed, purchased, and read. He is too frantic for that.

So Jack jumps from his chair, replaces the dressing gown with Bibi de Quintero-Roja's quetzal tailcoat; swirls his pearly locks with Madam Twanky's bear grease pomade; dangles the Voivode of Shingletown's pearls around his neck, plants the jackdaw's perch upon his oil-slick pate, encases himself in the holocaust cape which repels notice as well as fire, and, exiting his lair, leaps up into the still star-kissed dawn, his heart singing with action.

Houses of the Holy is a delectable confection of architecture, a cream puff of a house, oozing with curlicues and furbelows, as fancy as a swirl of ribbon candy. Jack lands on the sugary-marble steps leading up to a glossy candy-apple red door. Ascending, he yanks a taffy-like bell-pull. The shellac of the door cracks, and a crabby cherub face peers out skeptically, but upon noting the slant of Jack's chapeau and the desperation in his face, entrance is granted. The Holy Whore's waiting room is chockablock with the drooping, pining lovelorn all hoping for a personal audience. They glare at Jack and hiss when Archangel Bob appears, folded sangyn swan wings skimming the glittering parquet floor, and beckons Jack follow.

The Holy Whore of Heaven herself is a bonbon of a girl swathed in a wide ribband of silk that floats around her creamy contours, barely concealing her charms. She receives young Jack—for let us not forget that success has come early to our boy, and he is just a heedless, headstrong boy—in her boudoir, a fantasy of white fur walls, white lacquer furniture flung with white fur, decadent and cozy.

Jack sits gingerly upon a white tussock, nervous about smudging. The snake-heads on his boots hiss happily as Angel Mox-Mox offers them saucers of beer, while Archangel Bob offers Jack himself a jorum of Hearts Ease. Jack's tongue is not inclined to be tight, but the sweet golden liquor loosens it, and a passionate litany of dreams and desires pour out of him like wine from a stove-in barrel.

"Well, now," the Holy Whore says, languidly, when he finally runs dry. Angel Mox-Mox is fanning her, and the silk swathe is billowing enticingly. "Who would put a curb on a burning boy? Come on, sweetie pie, and we shall fix you."

Jack follows her drift into her office where he is measured for height, weight, eyesight, character, bile, dreams. He answers questions, questions answers, provides samples of all possible bodily fluids, of handwriting. The Holy Whore of Heaven peers at his palms, at the soles of his feet, palpitates his scalp, his stomach, his heart, peers into his ears. Listens to his hopes, his dreams, his fears. By the time she is done he has been measured as thoroughly as any person might be measured; there's no stone in his soul, in his body, left unturned.

The Holy Whore and Archangel Bob confer softly, and then Jack follows Archangel Bob's rustling red wings to the library, where Bob gives Archangel Naberius Jack's fat file. For ten impatient minutes, Naberius squints through his bulbous fish eyes at the file, then swims upward through the lofty dim space, toward some distant part of the rotunda, dwindling in the depths. When he returns, he bears a book as big as he is, a hefty tome with embossed leather boards and gilt-edge pages.

Looking for love, the book whispers. *Looking for love.*

The book thumps down upon a vast library table; glasses are pinched upon Naberius's bulbous nose, and Jack waits in exquisite agony as the Holy Whore bends her beautiful head over the pages. She whispers;

Naberius scribbles. Naberius whispers; she scribbles. Archangel Bob remains impassive.

Jack chews his finger, and jiggles his knee, he paces, and wrings his hands, he tugs his ear, his hair, he pinches the jackdaw until it flaps up into the dusty motes of drifty air high above, cawing complaints. Jack rocks his heels, the snake-heads spit and hiss, and every sinew of his body, every nerve, every fiber of his being is stretched to the breaking point. He might soon scream. The Holy Whore and her angels take no note of his nervous distress; they continue their calm calculations until at last all three heads, one epicene, one piscine, and one just plain delicious, nod in agreement.

Three smiles bestow upon Jack, who grins nervously back. His heart will surely soon tear a hole in his weskit.

"Jack," says the Holy Whore in her sugary voice. "I have the perfect love for you."

"Ayah!" Jack and the snakes wait breathlessly.

"But . . . there is a wee bit of a matter. My heart is sore too, snuggie, and do you know for what?"

What could the Holy Whore of Heaven desire here in her candy castle? Jack furrows his brow in confusion and even the corbie looks perplexed.

"Dear Crackers, my sweet little blue parrot, so cruelly torn from me—" Fluttering eyelashes do not take the edge off the steel in her sweet voice. Archangel Bob seems to have grown two or three feet taller, and Naberius's teeth are revealed to be carp-y sharp. Belatedly, Jack remembers the Norge Azul parrot, kipped from the Holy Whore of Heaven's carriage while she was at the opening night of the Califa National Opera.

"Oh, dear," says Jack weakly. The snake-heads try to look small and wormlike. Jack's unprotected back begins to itch. He dare not turn but he can feel Angel Mox-Mox's violet-tinged breath ruffling his side curls.

"Dear, sweet Crackers, what I brought up by hand," the Holy Whore says sadly. "Light of my life, fire of my heart, my only true love—"

The jackdaw coughs derisively.

The Holy Whore of Heaven has terrible taste in parrots. The Norge Azul had kept Jack up all night long with its squawking and squabbled with the jackdaw over a mouse chew-toy. At dawn, he'd opened the window and kicked the parrot out; the last he'd seen of the miserable bird was a flash of blue vanishing into the fog.

"I cry your pardon," Jack says, and screws his face into the cute expression that always worked so well upon his mam. The Holy Whore will have none of it. She will have her parrot back or Jack will never find his love. He protests that he knows not of the parrot's adventures once the bird struck out on its own—the booting being re-characterized as an escape. But the Holy Whore of Heaven does know where the parrot is, and the parrot's return is the price of Jack's true love.

So where did the parrot end up?

Jack's heart sinks when he hears the answer: Bilskinir House, seat of the Pontifexa of Califa.

Of all the places that Jack has burgled, Bilskinir House is not one. He's reckless, is our boy, but not careless. Other denizens are easily rooked by his rapid in-and-out routine; they may move fast to block intrusions, but Jack and his boots are faster. By the time they are espied they are gone. And not all houses in Califa have denizens anyway. Some rely on armed retainers, or mercenaries; some on charms and ensorcells, all of which are easy enough for the boots to evade. But Bilskinir House is another flavor of cake completely, far too rich for our boy's taste. Firstly, there's the Pontifexa; Jack knows how much cheek he can get away with with her: answer, zero. Georgiana Haðraaða has little sense of humor when it comes to overstepping of boundaries; just ask the poor bounder who trod on her train at the opening of the Califa Opera last week. Or rather, ask his head, currently adorning a post high above the Opera's proscenium arch. Best seat in the house, if only he could enjoy it.

(He is, of course, unaware that she's already put her scorpions on his tail.)

Then there is Paimon, Bilskinir House's denizen. Jack has a healthy respect for egregores of the second order and their shiny, sharp lapis-blue tusks. And then there is, well, there is patriotism. Jack's a Califian through and through. He's her grace's loyal subject, he would never dream of stealing from her.

(But, the dumplings wonder: what about the Pontifexina's cup? That, little ring-a-dings, was kipped from her favorite coffee house, where it was kept in a locked cabinet only accessible to her favorite barista, who is now out of a job. Jack remains oblivious to its owner.)

The heights of Bilskinir House have been left hitherto unscaled.

But in love, all bets are off.

Now Jack hardly needs the boots to soar; his heart alone is so light that it fair lifts him up into the air, each beat sending him higher and higher. In the shadowy dusk he bounds through the city streets, dodging horsecars, and broughams, mule-carts, and flies, over fountains and hedges. He passes over the city boundary into the Outside lands, his boot-heels hollow on the corduroy roadway. Up and over sand dunes he flies, past scrubby graze, arching over a surprised goatherd; on the horizon the sun is a golden coin sinking into a jade-green sea, the dimming sky shredding with fog.

Jack sees none of these glories; his head is full of heartfelt visions of romance, of intimate cheese suppers, cozy chess games, of long walks on the beach, and silvery sleigh-rides, of blissful waltzes, and blissful (Jack's ideas of romance, quite obviously, have been completely informed by the overconsumption of too many romantic broadsides). All he has to do is get in, get the bird, get out, and Live Happily Ever After.

Another thing Jack does not see is that he is being followed. When he bounced out of Houses of the Holy, another crept behind him, slinking through the door just before it closed, down the sugary steps, close behind. The jackdaw sees this dark shadow, has flown from Jack's hat to circle around behind their tail, but before it can sail back to Jack and caw a warning, the bird's wings go limp as newsprint, and it plummets to the sandy ground, where a canvas bag awaits it. Beak sealed with some sigil, the jackdaw is stuffed into the sack, where it lies limp and angry, helpless.

Our hero doesn't notice his sidekick's lack either; now he's springing along the Pacifica Playa, dodging surfer-shebangs and hobo jungles. The sun dunks below the sea's edge; a cold wind feathers off the swordcolored water. Bilskinir's bulk hulks on the watery horizon.

Meanwhile, not too far behind, a shape slinks behind Jack, four legs, scraggly amber fur, jade-green eyes: a mangy looking coyote, inexplicably carrying a sack in its mouth.

Jack laughs out loud as he approaches Bilskinir's swale, realizing that the trickery required to enter the House will be of a trivial nature. A scrum of coaches congregates around the end of the causeway; a symphony of whip-hand shouting and curses, jingling bridles and whickering horses fill the air as the carriages of the à la mode jockey for position. Judging from the lavish personages alighting from these carriages, the Pontifexa is giving a very lavish party.

Jack watches the tangled embarkation from the heights of a sand dune, giggles to himself: is that Luscious Fyrdraaca in the beaverskin hat? The Duque de Grandsellos in Corinthian velvet petti-pants and lemur fur cape? Cheddar La Roque arm in arm with the Princess Naproxine, both blazing in matching black leather jackets trimmed in crimson feathers? A jingle tingle of excited alarm runs up and down Jack's spine; if they should realize who he is . . . such fun!

The tide is in, causeway flooded; the luminous personages are loading onto swan-shaped barges, which float along the sunken road, limned with flickering water elementals caged in fish-shaped weirs, toward the welcoming gape of Bilskinir's lower gate. The sheriffs milling around the grand personages, grimly festooned with warpaint and rifles, are just for pure show. Paimon's influence is extensive and can handle any intruder even at this distance.

But Jack's hat is not just for show, though showy indeed it is. The capacious crown holds excellent storage, and within Jack has stowed all sorts of dainty tricks, charms, philters, and other useful objects. Most of his capers require only speed for success; but sometimes more subtlety is called for. Where's that dratted jackdaw? Flown off after some espied shiny, no doubt; well, Jack is fine on his own. He removes the hat and from the hat removes a thick bar of chocolate. "Madam Twanky's Glamorous Confection," proclaims the flowery label. A nibble of this and no one will be the wiser of Jack's true identity; he'll be swathed in a glamour impossible for even Paimon's sharp eyes to penetrate. Too easy? Perhaps, but there is one possibly lethal catch: the glamour wears off quickly, an hour at the most. He will have no time to waste.

The black bittersweet taste lingering on his tongue, Jack skids down the sand dune, careens through the carriages, splashes through the surf, jumps into a swan just as it pushes off from shore. "Lovely night," he trills to the startled occupant. "And glorious party, eh what? I adore your pelerine and your chapeau too, dearheart, isn't this barge just too divine? Our lady has such good taste!"

Luscious Fyrdraaca, for it is he already swan-seated, is bemused by the chatterer, who is so glorious that he makes Luscious's eyes water. But exquisite good manners are bred into the Fyrdraaca bone, so he politely agrees, while fishing in his pocket for a spider-silk hankie to blot before his eye maquillage goes raccoon-y.

Back on the beach, the coyote serpentines through the thickets of carriage wheels, horse legs, dashes behind the Countess of Castoria's landau. There, unobserved, the animal braces legs, and shakes itself. When the fur stops flying, a woman springs from four legs to two, spins a serape out of thin air. Thus covered, she tucks the sack under her arm, and strides out of her concealment to push to the front of the swan-line, ignoring the bleating protests of the other guests—who, when they see the scars on her face—quickly shut their gobs and let her pass.

Of course, the guests of the Pontifexa cannot hike all the way up Bilskinir House's height—their ribbands might go limp, their wigs frizz, their high heels rub, their lace droop! So when the swan scrapes the shore, our new duo is immediately ushered by one of Paimon's adjuncts into a luxurious miner's cart, and elevated up the hill by the sweetest, softest blue donkey Jack has ever seen. (He determines to snitch it on the way out.) At the top, they are deposited in front of a wall of towering redwood trees with trunks as big as houses and crowns so tall they create an arboreal sky. Jack and Luscious patter down a soft-mossy pathway, two shadows in a stream of many, chatter hushed by the dreamlike darkness.

Oh, my duckies, Jack is enchanted. A child of the city, he's never seen trees so tall, or felt air so moist with green growing. They exit the grove into a lush grassy meadow, high grass speckled with fireflies, and there's the House itself, a cozy wooden bungalow, shingled sides, eaves capped with fanciful carvings of sea-creates and oceanic motifs. How delightfully cozy Bilskinir House looks in the gloom; windows brilliant with a welcoming glow. A sort of dizzying relief washes over our lad; the sudden wobbly sensation that he has come home. He wishes suddenly that he was there under other circumstances. Not a thief, but a welcome guest.

A long receiving line caterpillars across the front porch and down the wide friendly front steps. Jack does not wish to be received; he bows to Luscious, presses hand to lips, gums the pearl out of Luscious's signet ring (reckless but oh, so irresistible) and bounds off. Spotting a duffer in a very wide farthingale, Jack ducks down, slithers under, and thus is able to make it through Bilskinir's front door, undetected.

If Jack had ever read respectable newspapers instead of sticking to the lurid yellowpress (more likely to award him favorable coverage) he might have known the occasion of the party. It is the Pontifexina's coming-of-age birthday party.

And such a party! The fancy is so thick that Jack is almost overcome by the vapors. Never before has he seen so much richness so thick and ripe for the taking. For a moment, Jack's romantic resolve blurs. Flooded by the shiny people, and shiny sackcoats, shiny wigs, and shiny lip rouge, shiny shoes, and shiny stockings, shiny eyes, and shiny shiny jewels, he falters; his knees wobble, his elbows waggle. Moments like these the jackdaw usually brings him back into focus, but the crow is still missing, so he bites his own finger, hard and to the bone. This bright spurt of blood mingles with the echo of the bittersweet chocolate in his mouth, and he recalls what he has come to do and how little time he has to do it.

Bilskinir's Aviary is famous; has been featured in *The Alta Califa* more than once, and is open to visitors three times a month for the modest fee of two lisbys. Jack's never been there, of course; as a child they'd no money for such touristing, and as a man, he'd no desire. But Archangel Bob had given him a feather to use as a dousing to find the Aviary, for the layout of Bilskinir is no easy thing. Fletching calls to fletching, Bob had said, this feather shall fly true. Jack whips the arrow from his weskit, wincing as it rewards his incautious handling with a prick. The vane of the arrow is razor sharp. As he points it, the tip of the arrow blushes brightly. Two steps forward increase this luster; two steps backward dim it.

So forward he follows the enticing glow, dancing into the crush of fancy dancing folk, his red tippy-tapping boots springing & leaping, but smally now, in the steps of a jig, a tarantella, a fox-trot. The feather dances with him, dipping, whirling, twirling him about through the spi-

ral of people, and now the tip of the feather is a molten-glow, heat radiating down the rachis, the calamus burning the tips of his fingers black.
But the scorch is a small price to pay, and the spiraling gay music is
camouflage to his pain—

He realizes, he's the only one still dancing; the music has dwindled
to a sawing squeak and the dancers dropped out of step, turning back
and forth, bewildered at the sudden silence.

Which is then broken by a trumpty triumphant voice shouting:
"Arrest that man!"

Jack doesn't wait to see if that order pertains to him; he knows it
does. Still clutching the arrow, Jack taps his heels upon the redwood
boards, and springs aloft, soaring high over the crowd. His heels clip the
elephant figure perched atop the chief justice's wig, and bend the angel
feather topknot of the Voivode of Shingletown. Screams of alarm and
excitement create their own orchestration to Jack's flight. Below him a
swarm of sangyn coats tries to mirror his progress across the ballroom.
But he has empty air through which to soar, and they are trapped in a
confusion of outraged guests, and have little hope of laying hands upon
our bouncing boy. Jack heels off the chimneypiece, powdering a stone or
two in the process, and hurtles toward the chandelier. The antlers make
an excellent trapeze, and so Jack dangles there for a moment, heels
swinging above the heads of his pursuers, who vainly try to whack at his
feet with their bayonets, while poisonous snakes' head spittle splatters
upon their upturned faces.

Screaming, the Alacráns fall back, and into their void appears a
tawny streak whose jump is almost as high as Jack's own. The coyote
leaps into the air, foam flying from open muzzle, sandy ruff puffed in
anger. Teeth scrape on one sole; Jack kicks and coyote falls back, but
only to gather up energy and spring again. Lucky for Jack, he's already
increased the arch of his swing, the coyote's bite latches onto the bottom
of his frockcoat, but the momentum of his swing pulls him away, and
the coyote falls back again, torn fabric flapping in its jaws.

"Oi, that's my quetzal-tail coat," someone shouts, and by this Jack
knows for sure that his glamour has worn off. He's aiming for the musi-
cians' balcony; he achieves his goal, landing upon the second cellist. The
cellist heaves for breath, Jack doffs his hat in apology, and then tosses

the Hand of Glory he's excavated out of that aforementioned capacious crown into the coyote's face just as she clears the balcony railing. Without waiting to enjoy the results of this feint, Jack scarpers, only to run headlong into a massive blue chest, as stout as a stone wall, and just as immovable. This chest is as tall as the sky, as wide as the deep blue sea; squinting upward, Jack can just barely make out the gleaming tusks, the glittering eyes, the drooping mustachio of the most fearsome denizen in Califa.

Paimon.

Jack pivots, and vaults over the writhing, snarling coyote, who is busy trying to toss off the Hand of Glory attached to its muzzle. He balances briefly upon the gleaming bar of the railing, and then launches out into the largest longest leap of his life. The failure of which will cost him exactly that. He's not about to die unsatisfied.

Hawklike he soars through the vault of the ballroom, tattered quetzal tail trailing behind him like the tail of a shooting star. The upturned faces below are a blur of astonishment, the wind roars in his ears, the enormous brim of his hat catches the air currents like a sail, propelling him farther onward than he has ever managed to go before. Breath sucks from his lungs, tears well in his eyes, the room fades, he feels as though he flies through the star-studded night sky, leaping, hurtling toward the glimmering glow of an enchanted moon—as he flies this glowing blur brightens, resolves into the glistening form of a girl, the most beautiful fantastic gorgeous delicious delightful spectacular girl in the world. This girl is a dish; she's a cream puff; she's the perfect cup of coffee; she's a hot towel after a cold shower. She's the tune in a fiddle; the cream in a coffee; the glitter in the bomb.

Like an arrow, Jack flies toward her, his heart singing: "Girl of my dreams, it's you, girl of my dreams, it's me!" He will fall at her feet, his quest over at last happily ever after, here he comes—

And then Cake intervenes.

Birthday cake, that is, a towering confection of marzipan-encrusted sponge cake studded with amaro-soaked cherries, draped with fondant furbelows. A cake twenty feet tall and six feet around, and it's an iceberg of an obstacle that Jack's heels, finally flagging, can just not surmount.

He sees the collision coming; is incapable of braking to avoid it, wheels arms, flings back his brim to create a drag, to no avail. He's going faster and faster, and the cake is getting closer and closer . . . at the very last minute Jack closes his eyes.

The impact is stunning; marzipan and sponge shrapnel splodge through the air, a shower of gooey sugar that drenches the lavish guests, the routed redcoats, the still battle-locked coyote and Hand of Glory, the aghast orchestra. The walls are smeared, the guests are smeared, the floors are smeared, and Jack is not just smeared, he's buried so far deep in what remains of the majestic pastry that only his red shoes are visible, heels dangling limply.

In the middle of awesome awestruck silence, everyone struck dumb by the calamity that they can't believe they just witnessed, a sparkly blue blur spins into existence, coalesces into a sparkly blue butler, not quite as big an obstruction as before, but definitely hugely oversized. With exaggerated care and a moue of distaste hovering around his mustachios, Paimon unsnaps one immaculate cuff and rolls up his silken sleeve to reveal a ham-sized forearm. With a hand the size of a full side of bacon, he takes a hold of one of Jack's limp ankles.

Jack slides out of the wreckage of the cake covered in sugary vernix like a newborn babe. Bruised and battered, with blood bubbling from his nose (the marzipan exterior was as hard as concrete), he sprawls in a manger of crushed sponge cake. All the bounce has left him; the heels are spent, he can't get up.

Paimon shakes out a hankie the size of a horse blanket and wipes the goo from his arm, resleeves his arm, and shakes his cuffs out. Jack bubbles, and licks his lips. The smell of sugar is sickening. He feels a hard pressure on his chest, pinning him into place. He rolls up crusty eyelids and manages to elevate his head just enough to see a small purple patent leather bootee is planted right on top of his heart. The bootee belongs, of course, to the most splendiferous girl in the world, who is, of course, the Pontifexina Georgiana Sidonia Haðraaða, the Birthday Girl.

What do you say to the Girl of your Dreams, when you have just crashed her party with the intent to steal from her, and crushed her cake, and covered her guests in marzipan and sponge cake, and are now going to be hauled away by her angry denizen and handed over to her mother's guard to be broken upon a wheel and have your bloody pieces displayed all over town? Well, my little winkles, what would *you* say?

Poor Jack can't really say anything; the pressure of the bootee is making it hard for him to breathe, or maybe it's just the proximity of the girl of his dreams that is making him feel faint. But anyway, anything he might try to say would have been drowned out by the sudden peals of laughter cracking the ominous silence. Explosive, delighted, full-throated laughter that is contagious in its merriment and immediately joined by supporting laughter, as those around the Pontifexa take up her cue. With a sideways slant of his aching head, Jack sees the slant-wise visage of a woman in a black-and-gold caftan laughing so hard she is almost choking. Of course, Jack recognizes her; does not her portrait adorn every office in the city, does not her statue stand regally in the center of the center city horse fountain, does not her profile appear on every diva coin? Though the Pontifexa is not known for her sense of humor, apparently she finds this situation hysterical.

The rest of the lavish guests are now laughing too, and so is the Pontifexina, a pearling, girlish laugh that shows off the green glints of the emeralds inset into her dainty teeth. Only the tawny-haired woman in the red serape standing now next to the Pontifexa doesn't laugh. The Hand of Glory is crushed in her grip and her green eyes are cinders. She lets drop the pulped flesh, flexes a finger, the thud of boots vibrate the floor beneath his back as her guards surround him.

Jack squinches shut his eyes; salt tears mar the sugar crust on his face. So close and yet so far! Too late, too late! But when the grasp comes, it's not the brutish hands of angry guards, but the delicate brush of a finger across his frosting-encased face. He cracks his eyes again, and then cracks a grin, white teeth flashing through the mask of cake goo.

"He's adorable, mamma," the Pontifexina says, licking her icing-capped finger. "My favorite flavor. Can I keep him?"

The Pontifexa scrubs her face with a silken hankie handed to her by the woman hovering to her right side, a cupcake of a girl, who has a gorgeous cerulean blue parrot perched upon her shoulder, and a creamy smug smile on her face.

"Please, mamma? Please?" the Pontifexina pleads.

Her mamma says fondly, "Of course, sweetie pie, you may keep him."

The Alacrán captain swirls her serape and vanishes in a puff of rage. The Norge Azul pecks the Holy Whore of Heaven's cheek. The Pontifexina shrieks her delight and claps her hands.

And that, my little dumplings, is how Jack was caught.

Rachel Pollack

• • •

Jack Shade is a Traveler, a man who travels between our world and various eerie afterlife/supernatural worlds to bring messages from the living to the departed, and to perform other magical tasks, such as the finding of souls that have been lost. The story that follows is one of a series of vivid and highly imaginative stories that Rachel Pollack has been writing about Jack's adventures. The magical system used in the Jack Shade stories is one of the most intricate and unusual ones employed in modern fantasy today, and the mystical world that Pollack creates in them, one inextricably wrapped around and interacting in many different ways with our modern everyday world—the double vision of the things around him that Jack possesses enable him to see a taxicab on the Manhattan street as a taxicab but also at the same time as the Piss-Lion that it *actually* is—form a mystic ecosystem of supernatural checks and balances, layered hierarchies, and rival Powers that is rich and complex and strange. (The Jack Shade stories also contain a shout-out to old farts like me who have been around long enough to remember another morally ambiguous traveler-for-hire whose business card consisted only of his name and the silhouette of a chess piece knight.)

Here Jack must find a way to defeat a seemingly unbeatable enemy bent on destroying the whole world of magic . . .

Rachel Pollack is the author of forty books, including *Godmother Night,* winner of the World Fantasy Award, *Unquenchable Fire,* winner of the Arthur C. Clarke Award, and *Temporary Agency*, short-listed for the Nebula Award. She is also a poet, a translator, a comics writer, and the author of a series of bestselling books about tarot cards, including *Seventy-Eight Degrees of Wisdom,* in print continuously since 1980. She is also a visual artist, having designed and drawn The Shining Tribe Tarot. Her work has been translated into fifteen languages and sold around the world. She has lectured and taught on five continents. Her most recent work is *The Fissure King—A Novel in Five Stories*, featuring Jack Shade and the other characters seen here in "Song of Fire," though "Song of Fire" is an independent story.

◆　　◆　　◆

Song of Fire

RACHEL POLLACK

1.

After Jack Shade had taken the case—after he and Archie and Carolien had decided what had to be done, and the others had left—Jack poured himself a glass of Louis Trey brandy and went to stand by the window in his room at the Hotel de Reve Noire on Thirty-fifth Street. He should have known, he told himself. Should have seen the signs, the markers. He'd taken the room originally because it let him see the Silver Skies: the Traveler name for the two linked skyscrapers, the Empire State Building, with its piercing antenna, and the Chrysler Building, with its gargoyles. How many times had he stood there and just felt the energy that passed between them? So why didn't he see, this past week, what was missing?

Jack had moved into the hotel after his crazy time, as he called the period that followed his wife Layla's death. "Death" was really too neat, too noble a term. A poltergeist had invaded their daughter, Eugenia, and Layla had begged Jack to do something about it. It's okay, he'd insisted, geists inhabited adolescent girls for a time, but they never did any real harm. And then the terrible day came, when the knives and cleavers began to fly around the kitchen, leaving Layla's body soaked in blood on the floor, a scar down Jack's right cheekbone, and Jack with no choice

but to send his daughter somewhere safe, where she couldn't harm anyone. "Safe" turned out to be the Forest of Souls, a land of the dead,
where Genie was the only living creature. He'd been trying to figure out
how to get her back ever since. Or at least once he himself had settled
down in the hotel.

Before that, for several weeks, he'd lived rough and done things he
shouldn't. They were just meaningless stunts, really, but he'd done them
in front of nons: Non-Travelers, whose "Linear" world did not include
such events as carousel horses coming to life and sprouting wings. Finally COLE—the Committee of Linear Explanation, whose job it was
to cover up such irregularities—had ordered Jack to knock it off. Settle
down, they'd told him, or he'd find himself locked away somewhere,
maybe the Forgotten Woods outside of Yonkers.

So Jack had found the room at the hotel and managed to take some
comfort watching the light glint off the gargoyles, and sensing, if not
actually hearing, the messages they passed to the Empire State Building
for broadcast to the wider Non-Linear world. Which is why Jack should
have realized that it had all gone silent. And if he couldn't have heard,
he certainly could have *seen*. All the luster had gone from the gargoyles,
the silver had tarnished. The ESB antenna too had a dullness, despite
the colored lights the building owners used for publicity. The *true* light
had gone cold.

Pay attention. His teacher, Anatolie, had told him that over and over.
She'd have him recite the First Directive—

> *See what there is to see,*
> *Hear what there is to hear,*
> *Speak the thing you must speak,*
> *Touch whatever you touch—*

And then she would send him around town, usually somewhere
public, and have him report back via Bluetooth what he encountered,
not letting him return until he truly saw. Once she had him go to the
Staten Island Ferry, where she had him describe all the passengers. He'd
listed their ages, their ethnicities, their clothes, and all she'd said was, "I
don't care about that. What do you *see*?" Finally he'd noticed it—a small

group of men and women blinged out like some hip-hop band, but when he looked closer he spotted flickers of flame in their eyes, around the tip of the tongue, and when they spoke to someone and smiled, the person shrank back.

When Jack had reported this to Anatolie, she'd grunted and said, "Very good, Jack. You've just had your first experience of the Djinn. You can come back now." He'd wanted to ask her if she'd known they'd be there, but she'd already hung up. She did that. A lot.

Jack sighed and finished the last of his Louis Trey. Time to get started.

It began during a poker game. Jack hadn't played in a while; he'd mostly been resting after a disaster of a case involving a Jersey housewife named Carol Acker, but his friend Annette had called him to tell him that a couple of great fish—suckers with lots of money—had come to New York and hoped to play in one of Jack Shade's legendary private cash games. Annette herself couldn't come—she was playing in a tournament in Europe—but she wanted to make sure Jack knew. So Jack had called Charlie, his dealer, and a few friends, and let it be known he was available.

For poker, Jack rented a luxurious suite at the top of the hotel. With its lacquered tables and ancient drink stands (originally writing tables from a poetry contest long ago), it was far grander than his living quarters or the small room on the second floor he maintained as an office. Very few of the people in Jack's games knew he lived in the hotel. Charlie, of course, and Annette, and a couple others, but mostly Jack kept his poker life and his real life separate.

Part of that separation was the way he dressed. When he worked, Jack was all in black, mostly so he could hide his carbon-bladed, ebony-handled knife in the sheath in his black boot. In poker, however, he went for color. It caused some to underestimate him, always a benefit. First they underestimate, then they fear. That night, he wore a pale gray suit with a blue silk shirt, unbuttoned at the neck. Jack wore his clothes well. Six foot three, muscular but loose, his ropy hair cut by a hairdresser friend to look like Jack cut it himself, his face handsome except for the scar, Poker Jack looked like nothing mattered in his life except cards and parties.

The two fish were named Artie Grance and Calvin Carmone. They pretended not to know each other, but they couldn't seem to resist a sly look as they shook hands. Jack didn't care about that. Instead, he had to fight not to stare at a pair of cuff links Carmone was wearing. Or worse, grab the man's wrist and say, "Where did you get those?" The cuff links were small, gold, and incised with the figure of an ibis, a long-legged, long-beaked bird that was the symbol of the Ibis Casino, a place only Travelers knew existed, let alone how to get there. Keeping his voice casual, Jack said, "Nice cuff links."

Carmone held out his wrists. "You like these? Got 'em in Vegas. At the Luxor. I usually don't wear cuff links, but I was having, let's just say, a good night, and wanted something to remember it." He tried, but couldn't keep the smirk off his face.

"Uh-huh," Jack said. He'd already lost interest when the dealer came in.

Jack nodded to Charlie, who said, "Good evening, Mr. Shade," and took his seat.

Grance and Carmone played most of the hands straight, but every now and then one would signal the other, who would either withdraw or help push up the pot. They were clearly so proud of their scheme, they had no idea that it told the table at least as much as it told each other.

After about two hours, Jack was nearly thirty-five K up, and headed for a good night, when the knock came at the door. "Fuck," Jack whispered as he got up to answer it. Out loud he said, "Mr. Dickens, if you'll cash in my chips, please? Your standard commission, of course." Two of the regulars sighed, and the third, Mitchell Gold, laughed as they each lined up their chips to cash in.

Grance and Carmone stared at each other, then Grance said, "What the fuck? The game just got interesting."

Mitch said, "Sorry. House rules. Knock at the door, game ends." He added, "Consider yourselves lucky."

"What?" Carmone said.

Mitch leaned forward and grinned. "Boyfriend, we was just getting started on you."

Jack paid no attention to any of this as he opened the door. Irene Yao, the owner of the hotel, stood there in her simple blue linen dress, her low-heeled black pumps, and the unadorned gold necklace Jack had given her for Christmas. She wore her silver hair loose, cut shoulder-length. And of course, her right hand held the silver tray with Jack's business card. Jack glanced at it a moment, sighed. "John Shade, Traveler" the top line read, then "Hotel de Reve Noire, New York," and finally, at the bottom, an embossed black horse's head, the knight from the James Staunton chess set.

Jack inclined his head. "Miss Yao," he said.

"Mr. Shade." It was only "Miss" and "Mister" when Jack had a client.

Ignoring the mild clamor behind him, Jack looked at Miss Yao. She sometimes showed regret when she had to interrupt him, but now she looked curious. Her cheeks actually blushed when Jack said, "Did the client give a name?"

"Just the first. I asked his full name, but he only said, 'Please tell Mr. Shade that Archie wishes to hire him.'"

"*What?*" Jack said. "Please. Bring him to the office and tell him I'll be right there."

Several months before, in the disastrous case of Carol Acker, Jack had needed reinforcements. He'd gone to Suleiman International, the conglomerate that housed and controlled the Djinn—at least the ones who granted three wishes. Calling in an old favor, he'd gotten the New York branch to give him a "flask," the modern equivalent of those smoky glass bottles talked about in the old stories. When the djinni emerged, Jack asked if he had a name, and was told that of course he had a name, did Jack *wish* to know it? Unwilling to waste a wish, Jack had dubbed the djinni "Archie," a name that seemed to amuse the powerful being.

When Jack got to his office, Archie was standing at the far side of the table Jack used as a desk, facing the door with his hands clasped loosely in front of him. Jack had no idea what Archie's true form might be—if he even had one, for the Djinn were said to be made of "smokeless fire"—but he appeared much as Jack had seen him previously, a tall, elegant man, with an olive complexion and dark hair combed back, beardless, and wearing, or at least appearing to wear, a dark brown suit, with a pale yellow shirt and a maroon tie, and shiny black shoes, slightly pointed.

Jack noticed that Archie wore a small gold six-pointed star on a thin gold chain around his neck, with Hebrew and Arabic letters inside the points. Modern Jews have adopted the image (without the letters) as the "Star of David," supposedly taken from the king's shield. Travelers, however, knew it as the Seal of Solomon, that David's son used to bind the Djinn in order to build his temple. For a moment, Jack thought of the ibis cuff links that fool Carmone had worn in the poker game, but put them out of his mind.

Jack's business card lay faceup on the mahogany table, facing Jack. Miss Yao, of course, had returned it to the "client" after showing it to Jack. A couple of small mahogany chairs stood on either side of the desk. It occurred to Jack that he'd never seen Archie sit. *Could* he? Jack had never visited the Seven Palaces, but he'd read the accounts of those who had, and they all agreed there were no chairs. Angels, they said, had no knees. But the Djinn? To avoid the issue, Jack just said, "Would you care to sit?"

Archie inclined his head briefly, then pulled out a chair. As he sat, he said, "Thank you, Effendi. You are most gracious." As Jack himself sat, he noticed a stiffness in Archie's movements. He frowned, but said nothing. He could hear Anatolie's voice in his head: "It is never wise to embarrass the Djinn."

So instead he glanced at the star and said, "I gather Suleiman International has a job for me?"

"Oh, no," Archie said. Briefly, he touched the star. "This is only to remind me of my . . . obligations. My concern now belongs to me. Or rather, to the Djinn as a whole. It is *we* who wish to hire you, Mr. Shade."

Jack let his surprise show in his face. "Really? I am honored. But what can I do for the Djinn that you cannot do for yourselves?"

Archie leaned forward, clasped his hands. Quietly he said, "You can find out who, or what, is trying to destroy us. And hopefully you can stop them."

Jack had to stop himself from crying out, "What the fuck?" Instead, he just said, "What's going on?"

Archie said, "Tell me, Effendi, what do you know of the Kallisto-choi?"

"Not a lot. Anatolie told me about them but said they didn't interact with people much, so we didn't pursue it."

Archie nodded, said, "Go on, if you would."

"They're a kind of Power, not light or dark. When the Great War broke out, the Kallistochoi stayed on Earth and refused to choose sides. After the angels won, they punished the Kallistochoi by taking away their bodies and mounting their heads on black poles, then stuck them in obscure places." He shrugged. "That's about all I know."

The djinni pressed his fingertips together. "Ah. Perhaps we should ask Ms. Hounstra to join us."

Jack laughed. Carolien Hounstra, Jack's friend, lover, and only real ally in NYTAS—the New York Travelers' Aid Society—was also the best researcher Jack had ever met. She seemed to want to know everything. Jack sometimes joked that she was the daughter of a Dutch professor (that much was true) and a Knowledge elemental. He said, "Sure. But it will take some time for her to get here."

Archie closed his eyes and bowed his head slightly. He seemed to concentrate for a moment—an action Jack found oddly unsettling. Then the djinni said, "Ms. Hounstra. Mr. Shade and I are discussing the Kallistochoi. Would you care to join us?"

A few seconds later, Carolien Hounstra, in all her six-foot, 165-pound glory, appeared next to Jack, who nearly jumped out of his chair. Carolien laughed, a glorious throaty sound. "Hello, *schatje*," she said, using the Dutch for "sweetie," literally "little treasure." She was wearing her painter's smock over paint-stained leggings and low sneakers, with her blond hair woven into a braid that ran halfway down her back.

She turned to Archie as if about to speak, then stopped herself. She crossed her arms over her breasts, bowed, and said, "Great Lord, Jack has of course told me of your power and your beauty. But he did not mention your splendor, and your high station."

Archie inclined his head. "Thank you, Ms. Hounstra."

Jack squinted at Carolien. "High station?" he said.

"Oh, Jack, did you not notice the black rings at the base of the fingers?" Jack glanced at Archie and saw that indeed the first and third fingers of each hand, along with the left little finger, bore concentric rings, around a quarter inch wide, two on each, except for that left little finger, which had three. At first Jack thought they were tattoos, but when he looked closer he saw they were more like scorch marks. Carolien said, "Those rings reveal his station. You are hosting a high prince, Jack."

Jack squinted at Archie a moment, then bowed his head. "My honor soars ever higher," he said, hoping he didn't sound too much like Peter O'Toole. Having paid his respects, he asked, "If you're a high prince, why do you serve Suleiman International? Couldn't you have sent some low djinni in your place?"

Archie smiled and said, "If you were forced to choose between servitude for yourself or for others, what choice would you make?"

Jack thought back to when he'd joined NYTAS and gotten access to the archives. One of the first things he'd done was look up the slave trade. In some tribes the king would use the local Traveler to protect him. A king in Dahomey, famed for his strength and beauty, had gotten the Traveler to cast his form upon a servant so that the Arab traders would think they'd gotten a great "specimen" to sell to the English, and leave the actual king behind. Jack looked at Archie and said, "I can only hope I would have chosen as you."

Archie nodded, then said, "But now we go beyond choice. For *all* the Djinn are in danger." He turned to Carolien. "We were discussing the Kallistochoi."

"Ah," she said. "A sad story."

"Indeed. But do you know their most signal characteristic? Aside, of course, from their heads being mounted on sticks."

"Their songs."

"Just so. If you would explain to Mr. Shade?"

Turning to face Jack, Carolien said, "Though the Kallistochoi cannot move, they sing to each other across the world. It is said that the songs of the Kallistochoi wind through the air, the water, and the earth, weaving beauty." She seemed uncomfortable talking about this, but Jack let it pass.

He turned to face Archie. "What does any of this have to do with the Djinn?"

Archie looked away, out the window, at the Chrysler gargoyles. He said, "Their song feeds our fire. Their song keeps us alive. And they have gone silent."

"Fuck," Jack said. "Then without their songs, what happens to you?"

"I do not know. None of us do. But I can tell you what it feels like." He paused.

"Please," Jack said. It occurred to him that since *he* had not hired *Archie*, he did not have to be careful of any requests that might use up the standard three wishes.

Archie said, "A chill, but more than mere coldness. I can feel myself hardening, becoming *solid* in a way I never imagined. And my powers begin to fade. Or I simply cannot recall them. I was able to bring Ms. Hounstra here—"

Carolien smiled. "Thank you."

"But I myself needed to walk."

Jack tried to imagine the humiliation it must have caused the djinni to travel on foot. He said, "Why does their song, or their silence, affect you like that?"

Archie looked from one to the other, then said, "Do you know the four types of conscious beings, and how the Creator made them?"

Jack shrugged. "Sure. Angels made from light, demons from darkness, humans from clay, and the Djinn from smokeless fire."

Archie nodded. "Yes, Effendi, you are correct. All created at the same time, and all equal in their own way. But there is a fifth creation, earlier than all the rest, and not made from opposites, like light and darkness, or fire and clay."

Carolien said "The Kallistochoi! Made out of song."

Archie smiled at her. "Yes, Henmefendi."

Carolien smiled back. If all this information had not fascinated Jack so much, he suspected he might have gotten annoyed at the camaraderie between his girlfriend and "his" djinni. Carolien said, "Please. I know the term shows respect, but perhaps you might leave off the hen part and just say 'mefendi.'"

Archie rotated his hand before his heart, just once (wouldn't want to be ostentatious, Jack thought). "Certainly, Mefendi."

Jack decided to bring it back to business. "So do you know who's doing it? The angels, coming down to kick the singers one more time?"

Archie said, "No. I—we—believe that this is an attack on the Djinn. Without the Great Songs, we cannot survive. This is why I sought, and received, permission to hire you."

"But what will happen to the Kallistochoi themselves if they lose their songs?"

"I cannot say. Nor can I speak of the effect upon the world."

"And yet, even though the Kallistochoi are literally made out of song, and for all we know, silence might actually kill them, you still think this is all about you. The Djinn, I mean."

"Yes. I know how arrogant that sounds, to believe that an attack on the Creator's first children is in fact an attack on us. But there is an ancient feeling in this—a vast hatred that seeks to destroy *us*."

Jack said, "So who hates you that much?"

Archie shook his head. Jack remembered how, when he first met Archie, the air would sometimes ripple around him when he moved. Now there was nothing, as if the djinni was hardly there.

Jack said, "Maybe the demons, the ifrits, as you call them. Don't humans confuse the two of you? Maybe they're pissed off that they do all this nasty shit and you guys get blamed for it."

Archie frowned. After a moment he said, "I have—consulted with my colleagues, and we do not think so. The ifrits do not harbor resentment. It is not in their nature. I think it amuses them that so many of us helped the blessed Suleiman build his temple."

Carolien said, "Didn't the ifrits take part as well?"

Archie smiled at her. "Indeed. But that does not concern them, oddly. The ifrits do not greatly embrace memory. More important, perhaps, because more recent, is the fact that so many of us heard, and accepted, the words of the Prophet, peace be upon him."

Jack nodded. He knew, of course, that many, maybe most, of the Djinn converted to Islam after a famous sermon on a mountaintop in the Arabian Peninsula. He said, "Then maybe that's it."

Again Archie shook his head. "If anything, this provokes more amusement, or contempt, than hatred. The ifrits love mischief, even destruction at times, but they do not give harbor to hate."

Carolien said, "Might I ask a moment about the distinction between the Djinn and the ifrits? It is my understanding that the Djinn have indeed done some disturbing things."

Archie raised an eyebrow. "Such as?"

"What of the ghuls? Don't they eat humans?"

"This is true. Just as humans eat cows, and pigs, and every other non-human creature they can find."

Carolien smiled slightly. "Not all of us. And what of sexual possession?"

"Ah, yes. Some Djinn take pleasure with humans. Some even marry humans, and remain faithful unto death. The human's death, of course. And because we are made of fire, the pleasure we give is greater."

"Is it true that a single djinniyah once left thirty thousand men in mental hospitals in Morocco? I believe the diagnosis was 'sexual obsession.'"

Archie frowned. "Yes. That was the report of your human poet—a Traveler, I have heard—Paul Bowles, who took up residence in Tangiers. For the famous Dancing Boys, perhaps. He spoke of Aisha Qandisha, the Hidden One, who managed to avoid both enslavement by Solomon and the demands of the Messenger, peace be upon him. We prefer not to speak of her."

"Fine," Jack said. "Because right now we need to talk about how to help you."

Carolien said, "Is it possible that the Kallistochoi themselves no longer wish to sustain you? Perhaps they plan to go silent just long enough to destroy *you*, then return to their songs."

Archie bowed his head and closed his eyes. For a moment he seemed to be concentrating, then he looked up and said quietly, "We do not think so."

Jack said, "Are you sure? Maybe—"

Carolien touched his arm. "No, *schatje*. We should not pursue this."

Jack shrugged. "Sure." He glanced back again at Archie. "Where do we start? If we don't know what's doing it . . ."

Carolien said, "Perhaps Margarita Mariq can help."

Jack nodded. "Yeah. If she'll speak to us." A few years back, a woman named Sarah Strand had hired Jack to find her missing mother, Margaret. It turned out that "Margaret Strand" was the everyday name for Margarita Mariq Nliana Hand, also known as the Queen of Eyes. The queen was a hereditary position, passing from mother to daughter. Though she was "fully human," as she told Jack, she was also the holder of all oracular power in the world. Anyone who cast stones or coins, anyone who stared into a bowl of water dotted with drops of oil, anyone who threw sticks or laid down cards—their answers, whether they knew it or not, came from Margarita Mariq.

The search for the queen had turned out to be one of Jack's hardest and most complicated cases, bringing Jack closer to destruction than at any time since his wife Layla's death. And yet, somehow, he and the queen had become friends. Unfortunately, that did not guarantee that she would answer his questions.

He sighed and reached for the phone, but Carolien put her hand over his. "Just a moment," she said. She turned to Archie. "Have the Djinn asked the queen who, or what, is behind this?"

He shook his head. "It is haram, forbidden, for us to seek what is hidden, even from prayer."

"And have you prayed?"

"Of course."

"Then what about the Djinn who did not accept the Messenger?" She added, "Peace be upon him."

Archie said, "I believe they tried but got no answer."

"Shall I call her?" Jack asked. His hand didn't move to the phone.

Carolien said, "Perhaps. But let me try something." She reached into the large side pocket of her smock and took out a walnut box about six inches long, three inches wide, and two inches deep. She slid off the top, and Jack could see a stack of hand-painted cards. The top one showed a raven coming to a rest on a tree, with snakes coiled at the bottom.

Jack asked, "Are those tarot cards?"

Carolien smiled. "No, *schatje*. Perhaps we might call them Hounstra cards."

"Of course. Can I look at them?"

"They are not finished. But they will do for our purpose here." She set the raven on the table, then another, a picture of a very round woman asleep on a stone bench in front of a dark cave, with a large cat prowling outside the mouth. The cards were drawn in ink, with varying thicknesses, then colored with gouache. Jack found himself yearning for a set. Carolien laid down a third: someone wrapped in a red cloak, walking past a tree with horned owls perched on the branches. Just as the picture touched the table, Jack's phone rang.

He looked at the screen. "Margaret Strand," it said. He slid it open and put it on speaker.

"Margarita Mariq?"

The queen said, "Tell Ms. Hounstra her work honors me." She sounded distant, yet warm, like a mother who wishes she could do more for her children. And indeed, she said, "The answers you seek lie beyond me. Whoever has stolen the songs has cloaked them from oracular light."

"Whoever—is it a person? Or a single being? Not a group?"

"I am sorry, Jack. I can only tell you to go to the source." She hung up.

"Damn!" Jack said. "How are we supposed to go to the source if we don't know who it is?"

Carolien frowned. "Maybe she does not mean the source of the spell, but rather the source of the songs."

"The Kallistochoi?" She nodded. Jack turned toward the djinni. "Archie? What do you think?"

Archie lowered his head slightly and closed his eyes. A few seconds later he looked up and said, "Yes. I have consulted with my people, and we agree. Nliana Hand may be saying that the Kallistochoi have lost their songs but still are able to give answers."

"Great," Jack said. "How do I find them?"

Archie looked away. It struck Jack that he would not have believed the djinni could ever be embarrassed, but that's what he was seeing. Finally, Archie said, "I—we—do not know."

"What?"

"The songs feed us, but from the beginning we understood that we were not to seek them out."

Jack threw up his hands. "Jesus," he said. "I'm supposed to go ask these heads on a stick who stole their music, but no one knows where to find them? No one's ever seen them?"

Carolien said, "That is not exactly true."

Jack stared at her a moment, then burst out laughing. *"Schatje!"* he said, and took her face in his hands and kissed her. "Of course it would be you. So—where do I go?"

"Ah. I am sorry, dear Jack. What I did—where I went—cannot simply be repeated."

Jack sighed. "Okay, then. Tell me at least what happened."

"It came about during my apprenticeship. My teacher—" She hesitated, a recognition of an awkwardness that came up whenever Carolien talked about her training. She'd always refused to tell Jack her teacher's name or anything about him (except the pronoun). Jack sometimes suspected that Carolien's teacher was a frog, or had been turned into one, for she collected carvings of frogs, a whole room of them. Now she went on, "My teacher possessed many books, very special books. For me, of course, this was a kind of paradise." She paused. "One of these was the Book of Doors."

"I know that book," Jack said.

"Not this edition, I'm afraid. One day I read about the Kallistochoi. For days I could think of nothing else. You might say I went on strike until my teacher promised to show the way."

"What happened?"

"He took me to a small street in the *Jordaan*." She pronounced it *"Your don,"* but Jack recognized it as the oldest part of Amsterdam, just beyond the Princes' Canal, once a working-class neighborhood of small brick houses and old-fashioned "brown bars," but now more gentrified. Carolien went on, "There was a condemned building, long gone now, that was upheld by two giant poles, like tree trunks. *Krakers*—squatters— had opened a coffee shop on the ground floor, with a window to see the pillars. At night, naturally, it was closed, but my teacher had made some kind of arrangement with the owner. She met us in the doorway. My teacher had glammed himself so he would not—startle—her, and then he gave her an old music box, which seemed to make her very happy. She left, and we went in."

Jack noticed that the djinni was staring at Carolien with an intensity he'd never seen before. Carolien continued, "We went inside, and he told me I must stand between the two pillars. Then he made a mark on my forehead, stepped back, and"—she took a breath—*"said* something."

"Can you remember it?"

"I cannot *not* remember it."

"Tell me."

Archie said, "Effendi, we should not—"

Jack waved him silent. "You want your fire back, don't you?" To Carolien, he said "Go on."

And then she said it. It was short, though Jack did not realize that until later, when he stood at the window and thought about it all. And it wasn't exactly *ugly*. In fact, he suspected that if they'd recorded it (and thank God they didn't), and run it through some algorithm of antiharmonic aesthetics, it would register as "beautiful." And yet, for an instant, Jack thought it could twist his spine.

"What the hell was *that*?" Jack said.

Anger surged through Archie and then quickly died. Not enough fire left to fuel it, Jack thought. Archie said, "I tried to warn you. That was the Opening of the Door, spoken in the Fourth Language of the Rocks."

Carolien held on to the edge of the table. A very fine web of lines emanated from her fingertips, and Jack wondered if he'd have to pay Miss Yao for the table, and wondered if it was some priceless antique. But then Carolien stood without support, and the lines vanished. "Please," she said. "I am sorry. I did not mean—I did not wish—"

Jack got up and kissed her lightly on the lips. "It's okay, *schatje*," he said. "Can you tell us what happened next?"

"*Jazeker*," she said, Dutch for "of course." She went on, "The café and the pillars vanished, and I was in a long hallway, with walls made of stone. I am usually good with stones, as you know well, but these I did not recognize. Perhaps if I had studied it. But at the end . . ." She paused, and took a breath. "It was simply a head on top of a black stick. As Archie has told us. But *something* radiated from it. I can only say, beauty, but that is a weak word."

"What color was it?" Jack asked.

She looked startled a moment, then laughed. She touched Jack's cheek, above the scar, then her own. "Somewhere between you and me," she said. "Perhaps a little closer to you. The hair, however, was like neither of us. Red, but like waves of water." She looked at Archie. "Or perhaps fire." She looked down a moment, then up to meet their eyes. "I might give a better report, except—well, just as I was staring at it, it began to sing."

She shuddered. "That *sound*. Three times, Jack, I nearly begged it to stop. But I knew I would only beg it to start again. And what if it refused? How could I live?"

Jack asked, "Can you compare it to anything? Bach? B. B. King? Ghanian drummers?"

She shook her head. "No, no. The music of *us*, people, comes from our bodies, and nature. Heartbeats, birds, wind, even the sun. This song, Jack—it was so *old*." She began to shake. She took a breath, and it stopped. She said, "After it ended, and I do not remember how that happened, I was back in the café with my teacher. I said nothing to him. I could not look at him. Instead, I went home and went to bed. I stayed— a week, I believe, I am not sure. When I saw my teacher again we never spoke of it. I—I have never described this to *anyone* before now."

Jack took a breath. "Okay. So at least we know where there's an opening."

"*Neen*," Carolien said, the Dutch word for no, pronounced *nay*. She said, "The building is long gone. I believe it is now an office block. More important, the pillars are gone. They were the true gateway."

"Shit," Jack said. "What about your teacher? Maybe he knows somewhere else. Maybe there's a Kallistocha in Rotterdam."

Carolien said, "I'm sorry, but he's gone too. He died. It was why I left Amsterdam."

Jack said "Was he Traveling?"

She smiled slightly. "Yes." Jack nodded. No Traveler wanted to die "at home," as they called everyday life.

Archie said, "Effendi, excuse me, why would it help to find a Kallistocha? If they have gone silent, what can they tell us?"

Jack said, "Margaret told us, go to the source. That means there's something we can learn."

Archie bowed his head. "Ah, of course. Forgive me." Jack discovered he didn't want to think about how weak Archie seemed, or how he and all his people might die, or just vanish, if Jack couldn't help them. Years ago, Jack had laid a foolish obligation on himself that he could not turn down anyone who came with Jack's business card. A couple of times this had gotten him into serious trouble, and he'd really wished he could back away. But this time the "guest," as Jack's self-inflicted curse was called, was almost irrelevant. Jack would have helped Archie no matter what. And it hurt him to see the djinni's difficulties.

But then Archie looked at Jack directly, and all that weakness seemed to vanish. "Perhaps I have an idea," he said.

Jack suspected he wasn't going to like this. "Go on."

"Clearly, Ms. Hounstra studied with a wise and powerful teacher. But so did you."

"Shit," Jack said. He had not seen Anatolie for a couple of years, but more importantly, he had not really talked to her for a lot longer. At one point, Carolien had assumed that their break was connected to the death of Layla, Jack's wife. But when she'd asked him, he'd said no, it happened before that, and he wouldn't say any more.

The last time he'd seen Anatolie had only made things worse. Jack had been fighting a duplicate of himself who had managed to outlive his usefulness, and now wanted to take over Jack's life. In the course of all this, someone had scornfully referred to Jack's teacher as "Anatolie the Younger."

After the crisis had passed, Jack went to see her. "Are you a duplicate?" he'd asked her. Yes, she'd said. So Jack had asked if she'd ever known the original—the "elder." *No.* Was she ever coming back? Anatolie—the Younger—had said she didn't know. After that, Jack had just left.

Now he tried to tell himself, what could a *copy* know about the Kallistochoi? But he knew the question was ridiculous. Dupe or not, Anatolie just *knew* more than any Traveler Jack had ever encountered, including even Carolien. Carolien was a great scholar, but Anatolie simply knew.

He sighed, then looked at Archie. "You're right. Of course you are." He hesitated, then asked, "Can you transport me there?" He hoped "transport" was the right word.

Archie shook his head. "My apologies, Effendi. I was able to bring Ms. Hounstra here, but I'm afraid that was a final burst of such action."

Jack said, "All right, then. I'll go see her on my own. Do you want to wait here until I return?"

"No. Once again, my apologies. My place remains at Suleiman International. With the others."

Carolien said, "And I should seek to find out whatever I can."

Jack watched them leave his office, then took the stairs to his private rooms. He wanted to get out of his poker clothes and into his all-black work outfit—the jacket with its many pockets for various tools he might need, the black jeans, and especially his boots, with the black knife in the right calf.

Before he changed, however, he took that moment to stare out at the dull, rusty gargoyles and think how he should have known what was happening. Finally, he just shook his head and went and got ready.

2.

Anatolie lived in a fifth floor walk-up above a Chinese restaurant on Bayard Street. When Jack was her student he always stopped in at the Lucky Star and brought Anatolie some food. Though he was hardly her student anymore, he still kept up the practice whenever he came to see her.

Jack walked into the restaurant and smiled. It never changed—small and narrow, with Formica-topped tables and wooden chairs, and pictures on the walls of extra dishes with names only in Chinese characters. Mrs. Shen, the owner, stood behind her wooden counter at the back, reading a Chinese newspaper.

She looked up when the door closed. "Jack!" she said, with a big smile. Mrs. Shen was small and thin, with black frizzy hair cut short, and a face of fine lines that made it impossible to guess her age.

Jack smiled back. "Hello, Mrs. Shen."

"Are you returning to us?" She always asked that. Jack wondered if Mrs. Shen thought he and Anatolie were lovers who'd broken up and maybe someday would restore their relationship.

He said, "Not today, I'm afraid. I just need to ask her something." Mrs. Shen sighed. "What is she eating these days?"

Mrs. Shen smiled again. "Bitter melon with shitake, sea cucumbers with black bean sauce, and of course, har kow."

Jack grinned. Har kow—shrimp dumplings—was the one dish Anatolie never tired of. "How long?"

"Ten minutes. You sit." Jack found a chair at the table nearest the counter. Glancing around, he noticed a young white woman, college student by the academic-looking book and spiral notebook alongside her plate of vegetable chow fun. Jack found himself thinking of Eugenia. She'd be in college now if she wasn't stuck in the Forest of Souls. Jack could never decide who was really to blame, the geist or himself. Layla had demanded he take it seriously, and he kept saying, it's just a poltergeist, they're like household pests, kids grow out of them. Now Layla was gone, her throat cut by the kitchen knives the geist flung at her, Genie was trapped in the Forest of Souls, and Jack himself— He ran his finger along the scar on his jaw

Mrs. Shen came out with a bowl of braised brisket and guy laan. "Eat," she said, as she handed him plastic chopsticks. "Eating makes everything better."

Jack nodded. "Thank you, Mrs. Shen. You're a wise woman."

The food was delicious, and just as Jack finished, Mrs. Shen brought him the bag containing Anatolie's takeout. "Good luck," she said.

"Thank you," he said again. He knew she'd say "Nothing" if he asked what he owed her, so he slipped a pair of twenties under his plate and left with the bag.

The pale brown door to the upstairs apartments was unlocked, as it always was, at least for Jack. Years ago, he'd said to her, "You know this is New York, right? What happens if some junkies discover an unlocked door and decide to take you for everything you've got?"

She'd done that quarter-smile of hers, where only the left corner of her mouth turned up. She said, "It would not be a pleasant experience." And Jack knew she wasn't referring to herself.

At the third floor landing Jack had to stop and catch his breath. It was always that way. The third floor was a kind of border, though presumably not for everyone, since someone actually lived there, an elderly Frenchman. But for anyone going to the top—one of these days, Jack thought, he'll find himself stopped, unwelcome to go any farther.

But not today. He continued, and at the fifth floor opened the door without knocking.

"Good afternoon, Jack," she said.

She looked exactly the same as when he'd last seen her, five hundred pounds lying on a reinforced steel bed, propped up with yellow silk pillows behind her, and silk sheets under her. She wore a plain green cotton shift without shoes. The longest dreads Jack had ever seen snaked down her back and over her belly to twine together at the height of the mountain. They reminded Jack of the giant serpents that used to hold the world together until the Great Treaty allowed them to rest.

Jack said, "Good afternoon. I brought you some food."

She nodded to the metal tray on a wooden stand alongside the bed. "Put it there, please." As Jack set down the bag, Anatolie said, "Thank you. That was very thoughtful."

"Sure," Jack said. Not for the first time, he wondered how she kept up her diet when he wasn't around. Or what happened to the empty cartons (he'd never seen her use a dish). Maybe she had other apprentices. Or Mrs. Shen came herself. Jack wondered what Mrs. Shen might experience at the third floor.

Anatolie said, "I assume you need help."

Jack nodded. "Yeah. I need to find a Kallistocha."

"Ah. They've stopped singing, you know."

"I figured you would have noticed. But I'm hoping one will at least speak to me." He added, "Margaret seems to think so." He told her what Archie had said, and about the phone call from Nliana Hand.

"I see," Anatolie said. "And you're hoping I can tell you where to find one of these now silent singers?"

"Yeah."

"But, Jack, you already know."

"What?"

"That gentleman in your poker game. Why do you suppose he was wearing those cuff links?"

Jesus, Jack thought, *is she spying on me?* But he knew it wasn't like that. She just knew what she needed to know. He said, "So you're telling me he got them in the Ibis Casino?"

"Him? Of course not. Didn't he say he bought them in Las Vegas? And that he didn't know why he wore them to your game?"

"Huh. So you're saying he was a puppet."

"Exactly." A "puppet" was a Non-Traveler who did some seemingly random action that in fact was really a message to someone who would understand it.

"Okay," Jack said. "I get it. The Ibis Casino is where I'll find my Kallistocha. But what's a head on a stick doing at the Ibis? Can't exactly play cards or shoot dice."

Anatolie's thick shoulders shrugged, a move that rippled through her body. "Who knows? Casinos have floor shows, don't they?"

Jack barked a laugh. "Right. The real question is, how do I get there? The last time it took a week to get an invitation. I don't think Archie and the Djinn have that long."

"As I recall, the last time you were seeking to play Creation, yes?" Jack nodded. Creation was a card game played only in the Ibis Casino. If you played it right—and won—you could change reality. Jack had gone there to try to bring his daughter back from the Forest, maybe even bring Layla back to life. He'd left lucky to still have his three souls at harmony in his body.

Anatolie went on, "And now you simply wish a rendezvous. Perhaps I can help. Do you mind going to the supply closet?"

The supply closet was pretty much that, a door to a small space that probably once held a mop and bucket, and maybe a vacuum cleaner. Now it could house most anything—magical texts, artifacts from other worlds, messages from before Creation inscribed on a thin sheet that weighed more than the Earth but was held in a zero-gravity lock.

Jack walked over and opened the door. And there it was, just on the other side of Anatolie's tiny apartment: a wide, bright hall lit with miniature suns set on golden columns, a black-and-white floor that always made Jack feel like a chess piece, table after table of people—only a minority of them human—playing blackjack or poker, shooting dice, watching a small ball shaped and colored like the Earth spin around a roulette wheel that resembled the Milky Way. There were no slot machines. There were never any slot machines in the Ibis Casino. Jack had no idea why.

He turned around, but of course there was no door, only more floor, more tables, more gamblers. But now, at the back, he saw the famous raised table, fenced off by a golden guardrail. That was where they played the Game. Creation. A dozen players were there, some human, some barely a shadow. Jack's chest tightened. He hadn't realized how much he wanted to play again, to try one more time.

"Mr. Shade!" a mild voice said. "How nice to see you again." He turned and saw a cat-headed woman in a floor-length gold-and-green dress. "Have you come to play?"

"No," Jack said, though he could not resist another glance at the raised table, where a treelike figure threw down a hand in disgust, then slumped in his seat. "I'm looking for someone," Jack said. "A Kallistocha. I was told I might find one here."

"Oh, what a pity. We do have someone. A tribal chief, in fact." She leaned forward and whispered confidentially, "You can tell by the markings on the stick." Louder, she said, "He had agreed to perform for us. We were *very* excited."

Jesus, Jack thought, *Anatolie wasn't joking.*

The woman said, "But I'm afraid he's gone silent. I'm told they all have."

His voice tight, Jack asked, "Is he still here?"

"I think so. At least no one has moved him from the stage. It would be disrespectful."

"Where?"

She bristled a bit at his sharp tone, but pointed behind her to a large double doorway at the far end of the room. Not the direction of the Creation table, Jack saw. He was both relieved and disappointed that he would not have to walk past it.

Voices called out to him as he walked across the room, but he paid no attention. The doors, when he got to them, did not look so imposing as they had from a distance. The twin arclike handles, silver on the left, gold on the right, had seemed shoulder height when he'd looked at them. Now they were heart-level. He gripped them together, took a breath, then pulled.

Jack had wondered if he'd find himself on a cracked glacier, or maybe the Arabian Desert, that place they called "God's Anvil" in the movie *Lawrence of Arabia.* Jack had never been there, but like many Travelers he'd seen the film about a dozen times.

Instead he just saw a nightclub—polished floors, elegant place settings, bottles of champagne and brandy on each table—and no people (or other beings). At the far end rose a darkened stage. There was a golden set of curtains, but they were pulled back, and from what Jack could see, the stage itself was bare.

He walked up to it anyway. It wasn't until he got to the edge that he could spot anything, and even then, it was only when he climbed on-stage and walked up to it that he could actually make it out. Just as everyone said, a head on a stick. It looked asleep, the overlarge eyes closed, the face motionless, the black hair in frozen waves down the side of the face. Even though it couldn't move (did they have to carry it onstage?), there was something terrifying about it. The skin was a mix of colors—rust red, blue, yellow. Maybe that's what Carolien had meant when she'd said, "Somewhere between you and me." Only, they did not flow together, but seemed like pools of water that had gone sluggish. Jack thought of Carolien seeing a face like that come alive, and then hearing it sing—

Jack remembered a story of a sculptor who sought the perfect inspiration. He was said to have found it and never touched stone again. Jack had never understood that story. Now he was sure the poor man had seen, and maybe heard, a Kallistocha. And yet, he thought, Carolien still paints.

Jack wanted to turn and run, but he forced himself to say, "Great one. You who are the first. I am seeking help. Not for myself, but for the Djinn, whose very lives flow from your song. Why have you gone silent?" Nothing. "Has some great evil stolen your music?" Nothing. Anger filled Jack's chest. "Look," he said. "I don't know what this is about for you, but the Djinn are dying. I want to help them. And that means helping you. Tell me how to help you." Silence. "Shit," Jack said, and turned to leave.

He was nearly to the end of the stage when the voice came. "John Shade!" For a second Jack thought his bones would crack. He would have run for his life, but his legs wouldn't work. And then grief filled him, for he realized the Kallistochoi were not silent by force, but by choice, for *this* was how they sounded with their songs taken from them. He made himself turn around.

The huge eyes were open, staring at him. The voice said, "*Who hates the captive more than the one never taken? Who hates the slave more than the one who stayed free?"*

Jack cried out and fell to the floor.

3.

When he stood up, Jack found himself in front of the hotel, right in the path of a young Asian woman walking with her white boyfriend. The woman just managed to swerve rather than knock Jack over. The boy-friend said, "Jesus, Jen. You almost knocked that guy down. What's the matter with you?"

"But he wasn't there!"

"Of course he was there. Don't be ridiculous."

"No! Mark, I'm telling you—"

Mark took her arm. "Now you're just embarrassing yourself. And me. Will you come on?"

The woman was a Natural, of course, one of those proto-Travelers who have no idea of their talent. As for Mark, well, he was just an ass-hole. Jack cast a glamour over both of them to forget anything had ever happened. Then he glammed Jen a second time, so that sometime soon she would find herself on Twelfth Street, in front of the store Books of Magic, and that she would go inside and talk to the owner, Mrs. Fenton. Maggie Fenton was a talent scout, someone who could size up a Natural in just a short conversation. If Jen was strong enough, and ready, Maggie would send her on.

Jack went inside and up to his office. He was glad Miss Yao had not been in the lobby. He wasn't much in the mood for conversation, at least not the everyday kind. Using the hotel phone, for some reason, rather than his cell, he called the offices of Suleiman International, and told the pleasant-sounding woman who answered, "I'd like to speak to Mr. Hakeem, please. Tell him it's Jack Shade." There were very few people whose name could bring the director of SI's New York division for Djinn services to the phone, but Jack had helped Hakeem out years ago in a tricky situation with Jack's mother-in-law. Jack had drawn on that connection when he'd originally borrowed Archie. He hoped it was still good.

Hakeem certainly sounded friendly enough when he answered the phone. "Jack! It is good to talk to you."

"You too, sir. But to be honest, I really need to speak to—" He realized he didn't know Archie's true name. He finished "—the djinni you so kindly lent me a while ago."

"Ah," Hakeem said. "You mean Archie."

"Yes, sir."

"Jack, you should know that I do not help you only as a favor. Quite the other way around, I should say. This—*thing* that has happened to the Kallistochoi and the Djinn poses a massive threat to our business. I will help in any way I can. Would you rather just speak with Archie or have him join you?"

"If he could come here, that would be great. Probably the sooner, the better."

"Very good, Jack." He hung up.

Jack set down the phone. When he turned around, Archie was there. "Greetings, Effendi," the djinni said.

Jack said, "I thought you couldn't do that anymore."

"Transport my physical form?"

"Yes."

"I cannot, at least under my own power. Mr. Hakeem, however, can send me where he will."

"Good. Let's sit down."

Archie seemed to hesitate, and Jack wondered if he'd said something rude, but the djinni joined him at the table.

Archie said, "You have found something, Effendi?"

"Well, I found a Kallistocha."

"Ah. That is impressive. And did it speak?"

Jack winced at the memory. "Yes."

"Then did it tell you who, or what, has taken their songs?"

"Not exactly," Jack said. "More like a riddle. That's why I asked for you. I was hoping you'd know the answer."

"Please," the djinni said. Jack repeated the questions the Kallistocha had asked him. He didn't know what to expect, maybe that Archie might ponder it and come up with a direction.

Instead, the djinni stunned him by jerking back as if stung. "Aisha Qandisha!" he said. "Of course, of course. Lolla Layla, Lady Night."

Jack winced a moment at the use of his wife's name, but of course he'd always known that "layla" was Arabic for "night." To Archie he said, "Isn't she that one who put all those men in the hospital? Sexual possession or something?"

"Yes, yes, but she is much more than that. Aisha Qandisha is the oldest of all the Djinn. Oldest and most powerful. Some say that she carries within her the Original Flame, the fire used to create the Djinn."

"But if she's a djinniyah, wouldn't the destruction of the Djinn destroy her as well?"

"I do not know. Perhaps she herself does not know. She may hope that a spark will remain in her after the rest of us have gone, and she cannot only come back when she releases the songs, but even create a new race of Djinn. Free of shame."

"What shame? Why does she hate you all enough to want to kill you, and maybe herself as well?"

"Ah, Effendi, you know, of course, that Suleiman, son of David, enslaved the Djinn to create his temple. And then, many centuries later, the Prophet summoned the Djinn to the mountain, where he recited the Qur'an and demanded that we accept or reject it."

"Yes, I know."

"Then know as well that Aisha Qandisha avoided both demands. She knew that Suleiman's great weakness was beauty, and so she made herself ugly. She gave herself the arms and legs of a goat, then covered her face and body in layers of mud from the Atlas Mountains. And then, when the Messenger brought forth all the Djinn from the day, and all those from the night, she hid in the City of Perpetual Twilight."

Jack nodded. He'd been to Twilight Town once, carrying a message from Anatolie to the mayor. The mayor stood motionless before Jack for at least a minute while Jack recited what his teacher had asked him to say and then walked away. Afterward, Jack could not have said one word about that person, whether male or female, human or spirit, or anything else.

Softly, Jack quoted the Kallistocha again. "Who hates the captive more than the one never taken? Who hates the slave more than the one who stayed free?"

"Yes."

"Then how do we stop her?"

"I cannot say, Effendi."

"What if we summon her and then kill her? Will that release the songs?" Archie said nothing, which Jack suspected meant, "Please don't ask me that."

He called Carolien. "Did you find a Kallistocha?" she asked.

"Yes." He told her what had happened, and when he said Archie had identified the enemy as Aisha Qandisha, she said, "How can she destroy the Djinn without hurting herself?"

"Apparently she considers herself immune. Look, I need you to do something for me."

"Of course. What do you need?"

"A way to summon her. Make her come to us. I want to do it here."

"Jack, is this wise?"

"What choice do we have? I don't think we can stop her without taking her on. And this is my home ground."

"What of damage to the hotel? To Miss Yao?"

"I know, I know. But I can't think of anywhere we'd be stronger. I've spent years warding the hotel, and this room in particular."

"Very good. I will be there as soon as I can." She hung up. For Carolien a mission like this, even one so desperate, was always tinged with excitement. She loved the challenge, and especially the chance to discover something new. Jack didn't feed on research the way Carolien did, but he had to admit the energy got to him. It was one of the things that bound them together.

One look at Archie reminded Jack how deadly serious this was. The djinni sat very straight, head up, hands on his knees. He looked old, Jack thought—something that disturbed him more than he would have thought possible. Archie was still elegant, but his skin, his hair, and even his clothes appeared vaguely see-through. Beneath them, Jack could half feel the Holy Fire, dwindled now, like logs in a woodstove that glow with orange heat but no longer leap up in waves of flame. He said,

"Look, Archie—you don't have to stay for this. I know how hard it is for you. Maybe even dangerous."

Archie shook his head. "Thank you, Effendi, but I did not come only for myself. I represent all the Djinn. I would hope to help, or at least not hinder, but even if I do nothing, I must witness."

"Okay, then," Jack said. He sat down. "We'll wait together." He leaned back and closed his eyes, but when he did so he saw the Kallistocha, face all twisted in the darkness, so he opened them again.

The wait turned out longer than Jack would have liked. Carolien called back in just over an hour. "I maybe have found something," she said. "We will need supplies, but perhaps it is best to wait until I get there."

"Come quickly."

"Of course." She hung up.

Archie said, "Perhaps I could help—"

Jack told him, "Your job is to keep going until we can restore the songs. We don't want you expending any fire."

Archie nodded. "That is wise." He added, "Perhaps we could try an experiment."

"What are you thinking?"

"Will you please bring a glass of cold water?"

"Sure." He went and filled a glass from the bathroom. "Now what?"

Archie held out his hands, palms up. "Now pour it, please, Effendi." Jack poured out the water in a steady stream. When it touched the djinni, the water bubbled and hissed for a couple of seconds, then spilled onto the floor. Archie slumped slightly in his seat.

Jack said, "Not what you were hoping for, I guess."

"At one time, that water would have turned to steam the moment it touched me."

"I'm sorry," Jack said. He was about to say they would fix it, but then he remembered Anatolie telling him never to make promises he didn't know he could keep.

Carolien arrived less than ten minutes later, still dressed in her multisplattered painter's smock, and carrying a tote bag from Trader Joe's. Jack expected it to contain candle stubs, roots, jars of iron filings, oils, and other paraphernalia, but instead she just took out her own favorite magical tools—books, two of them, both clearly old, one a couple of inches thick, with uneven hand-set paper, the other no bigger than an A5 Leuchterm journal, black, with even, machine-set pages. Neither had a title. Jack wondered where she'd stolen them or what she'd had to do to get them. Apparently, Archie wondered as well, for he stared from the smaller book to Carolien and back again. "Mefendi," he said, his voice suddenly harsh, "where did you find that?"

She ignored him as she pointed to the larger book. "In here it tells of a very old Iranian working to see the Djinn. This is, of course, when they are in the room, but invisible. So. It would seem useless, since we indeed have a djinni present but he does not cloak himself. And I think we can trust that Aisha Qandisha does not simply lurk here without any of us sensing her." She looked from Jack to Archie, who nodded.

Carolien went on, "But this book—" She pointed at the smaller one, then smiled at Archie. "I know you know what this is. In Latin it bears the title *Extasia Lux Tenebris*, Ecstasy of Light in Darkness. I do not know the Arabic, I'm afraid."

Archie said, "Please tell me you protected yourself before touching it."

"Of course." She held up her hands. Jack could see that they were covered in a thin blue gel. Archie nodded.

Carolien said, "In English this is known sometimes as The Book of Alterations. It is not a compendium of workings as the other is, but methods of changing them."

Jack nodded. "Okay. Then what does *this* one"—he pointed at the larger book—"tell us to do to see any Djinn hiding from sight?"

Carolien rolled her eyes. "As we might guess, it involves exotic ingredients. Some of our long-ago colleagues seemed to wish to impress each other. In this matter, it tells us to mix the powdered brain of a fly with the eggs of an ant, and rub this rather sparse mixture on the eyelids."

"Beauty tips of the ancients," Jack said. "And the alteration?"

"Ah. I have determined, from studying the *Extasia Lux Tenebris*, that if we add a few drops of five-D printer's ink, and put some of it on your fingertips, and the tip of your tongue as well as the eyelids, it will allow you to summon her."

"Great," Jack said. "Let's get to work."

Archie said, "Perhaps I can help with the ingredients. Suleiman International—"

"No need," Jack said. He punched in a number on his cellphone. "This is John Shade," he said when someone answered. "Number HL856NK9."

"What is he doing?" Archie asked Carolien.

"He is calling TASH. The Travelers' Aid Supply House."

Jack told the person at the other end the ingredients they needed. Then he added, "One more thing. Two, actually. I need a zero box, about seven inches long, with an opening at one end two inches high. And a heat mesh glove, right hand."

Archie asked Carolien, "Where is this wondrous compendium located?"

"At the moment, Capetown. It moves."

"Then how will what we need get here? I'm afraid I don't—there's not much time left."

She looked at him and smiled. "Drone elementals," she said.

In the old days there were just four elementals, for each of the basic forms of matter—gnomes for Earth, sylphs for Air, undines for Water, and salamanders for Fire. Now there were elementals for everything, and they were not creatures but the thing itself—garbage elementals, new car elementals, fake news elementals. Anytime something new comes into the world, an elemental comes with it. Jack and Carolien had recently gone to a party hosted by a Traveler who was dating a gender-fluid elemental.

It was only a few minutes before the drone elementals appeared outside Jack's window—three spiderlike creatures held aloft by what looked like large silver butterflies. Three packages dangled from the spiders' claws. Jack opened the window to take the packages and pass them to Carolien, who set them on the table.

Jack moved the largest package, a foil-wrapped block, to the end of the table. He removed the foil from the top and sides without touching the contents. When he'd finished, there was a rectangular block of gray iron, with a slit on one end. On top of it lay a smaller package, a flat box about four inches long. Jack opened it to take out a folded glove made of gold mesh.

Archie stared at the larger box. "Is that—" he said.

"Yes."

"Then why don't I feel it? I am still Fire, you realize."

"For the same reason it does not fall through the table, the floor, and down into the center of the Earth. TASH has sealed it. All except that slit on the side. Now watch."

Jack put the glove on his right hand. He removed his carbon blade knife from his boot and in one motion thrust it into the slit all the way to the hilt. Then he stepped back, let out a breath, and removed the glove to set it down under the knife handle.

Archie shuddered, then said, "Ah. Now I understand. To summon Aisha Qandisha is only the first step. I suppose I had hoped we might imprison her, perhaps compel her to release the songs."

"I'm sorry," Carolien said. "I found nothing to suggest such a compromise could work."

"Then it is insh'Allah. The will of God."

Jack set out the other packages on the table. "Let's get to work," he said.

From the ingredients list, Jack expected absurdly small amounts in the two primary containers. He'd once had to trap a bullet demon who migrated from chamber to chamber of an Immortal Gun. The ingredients for *that* job had taken him three days to combine, and because of that a Traveler Jack had respected, and even liked, had died. Jack had never quite convinced himself he could not have done it more quickly. Now, however, TASH had apparently found ways to enlarge the "apparitional volume," as a flyer put it, so that Traveler-size hands could work with them.

He had just mixed it all together and was ready to apply it when the house phone rang. "What the fuck?" Jack said. He looked at the row of buttons and saw that the call came from the private line he and Irene had set up. *Goddamn it*, he thought; she knew he was working. And just because he knew she knew that, he realized he'd better answer it. "Miss Yao, I can't talk now," he said.

Normally she would listen and hang up. But *normally* she would not have called in the first place. She said, "Mr. Shade, there's—someone— a person here. She says she needs to see you."

"Tell her I can't. Even if she has my card, she'll have to wait her turn."

"I *tried*. She's—" Her voice lowered almost to a whisper. Jack had never heard her frustrated like this. She said, "She's very *impressive*."

"What?"

"She's dressed—and she stands—and Jack, Mr. Shade, I mean, she's—I'm not entirely sure the elevator could *hold* her."

"Oh, my God," Jack said. "Send her up. *Right now*. And don't worry about the elevator. She could ride up in a handcart if she chose to do it."

"Yes," Miss Yao said. Jack could hear the relief in her voice. "She said you would want that. Thank you." She hung up.

Jack stared at the others. *"Anatolie is here."*

Carolien said, "What? She's left her apartment?"

There was a hint of tension in Carolien's voice that surprised Jack, but he only said, "Her apartment? I've never seen her leave her fucking *bed* before." Archie said nothing, only stared at Jack.

When the knock came, Jack hesitated a moment, not sure how to greet her. *Fuck that*, he thought, and opened the door.

"Impressive" was certainly the word. Gone was the cotton shift. Instead, she wore a robe made from panels of bright colors shot through with wavy strands of gold. The collar was huge, stiff, gold and purple, extending over her wide shoulders and down in a point to the top of her breasts. She wore shiny purple boots that reached above her ankles to the bottom of her robe. She had piled her hair, most of it anyway, in concentric circles at the top of her head—for a giddy moment Jack imagined she'd gone to a hairdresser—but the dreads still managed to go down past the outside of her breasts and entwine at her waist, like two snakes in love. Her skin gave off light like the corona of the sun during a solar eclipse.

Jack said, "Thank you for coming."

"It struck me you might need assistance."

"I didn't realize you knew what we were doing."

"Oh, Jack, did you think that just because you left me I would ever leave you? Besides, there was a clue." She turned to Carolien. "Miss Hounstra," she said. Carolien just nodded. Anatolie glanced at the *Extasia Lux Tenebris*. "When this is over," she said, "I would like my book back."

Carolien managed to meet her eyes as she said, "*Natuurlijk*"—Dutch for "naturally."

Jack said, "Wait—you got the *Book of Alterations* from *her*?"

Anatolie said, "Apparently Ms. Hounstra discovered the back door to my library. *And* how to open it. I would not have thought that possible."

Before Carolien could answer, Archie suddenly went down on one knee before Anatolie. It was almost as if he'd been in shock and was just now released into action. "Magistera!" he said.

"No, no," Anatolie said. "You know I am not—the Elder."

"Were you but a copy of a copy of a copy, still you would carry her splendor."

Jack said, "You two know each other?"

"Oh, Jack," Anatolie said. "As always, you look but you do not see. Your Archie, as you call him, is a high prince of the Djinn."

Carolien had said that, but Jack hadn't really thought about it. Now he said, "But he serves Suleiman International."

"There is no shame in that and never will be."

Jack turned to Archie, who was standing once more. "My lord," he said, "if I have insulted you—"

"Effendi," Archie said, "you have not, and never could."

Carolien said, "*Myne Herren*—gentlemen. Perhaps we should begin."

Anatolie said, "Yes." She glanced at the zero box, with the knife handle sticking out, then at Jack. "Good. You are learning to prepare."

To Anatolie, Carolien said, "Do you want to use the ointment?"

"Oh, no. That is for Jack. I am only here to assist."

Jack turned to Carolien and held up his hands, fingers spread. "Will you apply the ointment, please?"

Carolien took out a small hawk feather from her Trader Joe's bag. "Close your eyes," she said. Jack did so, and a moment later, felt the barest touch on his eyelids, and then his fingertips. He smiled, remembering what Carolien had done with a feather on her huge bed, just a few nights before, surrounded, as always, by carvings of frogs.

Carolien said, "Now the fingertips." Jack felt a warm sting in each finger as the feather brushed against it.

Carolien said, "Do not open your eyes just yet, but please, stick out your tongue." Jack did as she said. He felt a sharp prick on his tongue that subsided to a warm tingle.

"There," Carolien said. "It is finished." The phrase was an old Traveler formula to mark an operation. Jack hoped it was not overconfident. Carolien said, "You may open your eyes."

"Thank you," Jack said. His voice sounded slightly slurred in his ears. When he first looked, all he noticed was a sharpness in the air, and for a moment he feared the alteration had changed, or diluted, the mixture and made it useless. But then he saw a flicker to his right, and when he looked it was Archie. The djinni did something Jack wouldn't have expected. He looked away. Jack thought he should avert his eyes, spare his friend embarrassment, but he needed to see. Archie's human form remained, though it looked brittle, even his suit a little shabby. Inside him, Jack could see channels of fire, like veins and arteries. But the flames were weak, hardly giving off any heat at all. Now Jack looked out the window.

To his amazement, he could see flickers of fire everywhere—businessmen on the street, schoolkids, homeless people in doorways or parks, workers in cubicles, executives in corner offices, a taxi driver in bed with a Syrian immigrant in a cheap hotel, the entire upper management of the Metropolitan Museum. And not just people—he saw those same flickers in some of the draft horses pulling carriages in Central Park, in dogs on leashes, even rats going through garbage. And everywhere, the flames were dying.

Behind him, Carolien said quietly, "*Schatje*, you have to find her. So you can summon her."

Jack nodded. He put on the gold mesh glove so he'd be ready when he needed it, then spread his fingers, aimed at the window. "Aisha Qandisha!" he cried out. "Show yourself!"

At first, all that happened was that his ability to see the flickers of the Djinn spread beyond the city, beyond even the country. He saw them in a Paris bistro, a Dutch gay bar, a Mumbai factory. But then, in North Africa, he spotted something different. There was a low mountain range, hidden by clouds, and at the top of each stood a pyramid, with carvings of human heads, or beasts, at the apex. The pyramids had windows, and through many of them Jack could see those embers.

Except—in the very center, in the smallest pyramid—no, in the hill below it—there burned a bright flame. The djinniyah had tried to hide it by surrounding the fire with a body of unparalleled ugliness—rolls of decayed fat, pockmarked bones sticking through torn skin like old parchment, and a face more rat than human.

"Oh, Aisha," Jack said, "do you think I'm King Solomon that I care about shit like that? Come to me! Right now!"

A nest of black snakes, five of them, appeared in the room. Their tails coiled together on the floor, but their bodies rose up, swaying rhythmically. Large red eyes stared at Jack, while long tongues stretched toward his face. For a moment he felt desperate to stay away from them and nearly ran from the room. Then he just laughed, and with his gold-gloved hand slapped them back. "No tricks," he said. "Show your true self. Now!"

The snakes dissolved into black smoke that thickened the air, then vanished. Jack said, "Cheap gimmick, Aisha. Give us the real you."

A creature appeared in the room. It had the tail of a crocodile, the trunk of a rhinoceros, and the head of a lion, which roared at Jack. He reached down to his boot for his knife, then remembered he had embedded the blade in the zero box and wasn't ready to remove it.

"Schatje!" Carolien called. Jack looked to his left just as she tossed her own knife to him. He caught the red-and-black handle. Carolien's knife wasn't made for battle, as Jack's was, but for cutting ingredients to prepare her "experiments." But the radiant sun blade had been hardened in the Shadow Court, and Jack knew it would work. He slashed at the creature's neck, where the lion head met the rhinoceros body. The beast screamed, but Jack paid no attention, only cut off the tail as well. The three pieces immediately began to rot and stain the floor. A stench filled the room. Jack worried it might spread through the walls and drive away Irene's business.

Suddenly, purple sparks filled the air. It took Jack a moment to realize that Anatolie had stamped her foot. "No more!" she cried out. "Aisha Qandisha. *Lolla Layla.* You are not playing with children any more. *I* am talking to you now. Anatolie Erinye. I *summon* you."

A throaty laugh sounded in the room. A raspy woman's voice said, "You? You are nothing but a duplicate. Anatolie the *Younger.*"

"Oh, Aisha, you have lived too long. You've become a simpleton. Do you really think I would travel the Homelands and leave nothing but a shell to protect my babies? *Then remember Nineveh* and trust that this is *me*, and I command you to appear!"

A light flared up in the room, a sudden flame that died down but burned steadily, from within a cloud. Out of that cloud a woman dressed in a T-shirt and jeans stepped into the room. Jack had expected something vile and hideous, or maybe soft and voluptuous. As the figure was emerging, he remembered the story of the thirty thousand men in mental hospitals in Morocco. But instead, what came out of the cloud was—Layla, *his* Layla, no longer dead in her own blood on the kitchen floor, but standing there, filled with love.

"Oh, Jack," she said. "Aisha brought me back to you. She found me and led me here. Because we have the same name, Lolla *Layla*. Jack, I thought I'd never see you again. I love you. I love you so much."

Jack made a noise. And then, in just about one motion, his gloved hand yanked the knife from the zero box and thrust it up to the hilt in Layla's chest.

A zero box brings anything in it to absolute zero, all molecules locked in complete stillness, as frozen as the laws of nature will allow.

"Layla" looked down at the knife buried in her body. Then she looked at Jack. She whispered, "How could you—"

And then, like a shattered ice sculpture, she cracked all at once. As the pieces fell to the floor, they became like dying coals of a fire that had gone on for far too long. And then they were simply gone.

Anything in a zero box warms up again in just seven seconds after you remove it. Once Jack had pulled out the knife, he'd committed himself. Now he just stared at the floor where the fire fragments had fallen. A moment later he picked up his knife and thrust it back into its sheath.

Archie walked over to him, as if to study him. Jack didn't look up. "Effendi," Archie said, "how did you know—know for sure—that the Layla who appeared before you was not indeed your wife?" Jack said nothing, but a slight smile moved his mouth.

Carolien said, "Perhaps I can suggest an answer. I never met Mrs. Shade, but I believe I know her a little from what Jack has told me. If she came back she would not say, 'Oh, Jack, I love you so much.' It would be more like—" Her voice slid into a New York accent. "You goddamn sonofabitch. How could you let that poltergeist *kill* me?" Jack looked up now, smiled at Carolien, and nodded.

And then he turned to Archie. He was going to ask if the death of Aisha made a difference, but he stopped himself, for there was no point. The power of the dust still ran in Jack's eyes, and he could see that nothing had changed. The body still looked hard and brittle, the fire within still an ember. Jack looked out the window, saw across the city those same flickers of fire he'd seen earlier.

He bowed his head, closed his eyes a moment, then turned to Archie. "I'm sorry," he said. "I'm so sorry. I thought I—we—could do it, that destroying her would liberate—" He stopped. "Fuck," he said.

Archie said, "There is no shame, Effendi. Only honor."

Jack said nothing, just shook his head.

Suddenly, Carolien said, "Jack, come here."

Jack didn't want to move. "What?" he said.

"Come look at the gargoyles."

Jack went to the window, conscious of the djinni and his teacher watching him. He looked uptown to the Chrysler Building, where the silver gargoyles jutted out from the corners of the tower. He saw it almost immediately. All the tarnish and dullness had vanished, so that now they gleamed in the sunlight with a luster beyond their metal.

And then they began to sing. Layers and layers of harmonies, melodies beyond human comprehension. Jack nearly fell backward, grabbed the windowsill. He looked uptown, at the Empire State Building's antenna lit up in streams of color. *They're free*, he thought. The Kallistochoi's songs had returned to them. He wanted to scream out with joy, but he could hardly stand. Those *songs*—

And the Djinn. He looked across the city, saw great flares of fire coming to life everywhere, in offices and bedrooms, schools and buses, in people and dogs, in pilgrims and rats.

He turned to Archie, but all he could see was a wild flame, brighter than the sun. He closed his eyes, but it still burned through his skin.

"Enough!" Anatolie said, and placed a hand on Jack's shoulder. "You have done a great service," she said. "And now you may open your eyes."

She's taken the sight from me, Jack thought. For a moment, anger tried to force its way into his mind, only to have gratitude push it aside. He looked at his teacher. "Thank you," he whispered. Anatolie nodded.

Jack turned to Archie. The high prince of the Djinn once more looked like an elegant businessman.

Archie placed his palms together before his heart. He said, "Effendi. Magister. Now and forever the Djinn will know you and honor you. *Habib*. Our beloved." And then he was gone.

Anatolie said, "Jack, Ms. Hounstra, I too must leave. Jack, my apologies to Miss Yao for any discomfort I may have caused her. I do not expect to see her again."

Carolien said, "One moment. Please." She walked over and picked up the *Extasia Lux Tenebris*. Holding it out with both hands, she said, "May I return this now?"

"Of course," Anatolie said. She, too, held the Book of Alterations in both hands.

Carolien said, "I knew you were watching me when I stole it."

"Of course. All Travelers are thieves, Ms. Hounstra. I appreciate skill." And then she left.

Jack was mildly surprised to see her use the door. He'd thought she might just vanish, like Archie.

Carolien came and placed her hands on his shoulders. "*Schatje*," she said, "you did a good thing today." Jack tried to answer, found he couldn't speak, so he just nodded. Carolien brought him to the window, then went and got a couple of chairs and angled them to face north.

For a long time they sat there, holding hands, silent, watching the sunlight as it shone on the gargoyles.

Eleanor Arnason

* * *

Eleanor Arnason published her first novel, *The Sword Smith*, in 1978, and followed it with novels such as *Daughter of the Bear King* and *To the Resurrection Station*. In 1991, she published her best-known novel, one of the strongest novels of the nineties, the critically-acclaimed *A Woman of the Iron People*, a complex and substantial novel that won the prestigious James Tiptree Jr. Memorial Award. Her short fiction has appeared in *Asimov's Science Fiction*, *The Magazine of Fantasy & Science Fiction*, *Amazing*, *Orbit*, *Xanadu*, and elsewhere; some of them were collected in *Big Mama Stories*, and her story "Stellar Harvest" was a Hugo finalist in 2000. Her other books are *Ring of Swords* and *Tomb of the Fathers*, and a chapbook, *Mammoths of the Great Plains*, which includes the eponymous novella, plus an interview with her and a long essay. In 2014 she published *Hidden Folk: Icelandic Fantasies*, a collection of stories based on Icelandic medieval literature and folklore. Her most recent book is a major SF retrospective collection, *Hwarthath Stories: Transgressive Tales by Aliens.* She lives in St. Paul, Minnesota, with her longtime partner.

Here she takes us to the troll-haunted hills of eighteenth-century Iceland, for the story of an apprentice sorcerer who steals forbidden magic, only to find that some things are easier to do than undo.

      ◆   ◆   ◆

Loft the Sorcerer

ELEANOR ARNASON

There was a man named Loft, who attended the school at Holar in northern Iceland. This was early in the eighteenth century, when the country was governed by Denmark and very poor. In spite of the poverty, Iceland had two bishop's seats. One was at Holar: a fine, handsome, wooden church set in the middle of a wide, green valley. Black mountains rose above the valley, often streaked with snow.

The bishop had a wooden house, as did the school's provost. The rest of the buildings were sod, since wood was rare and expensive in Iceland. These were low and dark, homes for the bishop's servants and the students in the school.

When Loft arrived, the provost took him around, showing every part of the school. They ended in the library, which was a room in the church. As libraries went in Iceland, it was large, holding books that were handwritten in Icelandic, as well as books that had been printed in foreign countries. Most of these last were in Danish or Latin.

"You are free to read all of this," the provost said, gesturing at the books. "But there is a cabinet with books you must not read. They are malevolent and magical. We keep the cabinet locked."

You may wonder why the provost told Loft about the cabinet. He was a fair man, who warned everyone, though he did not tell them everything: the cabinet was protected by magic as well as a lock. If anyone tried to open it, a bell would ring in the provost's house, and the student—it was always a student—would be expelled. Loft nodded, as if he agreed with the provost. But he decided to open the cabinet, if he could.

At this point, he should be described: a slim lad of seventeen, with dark hair and bright blue eyes and a handsome, ruddy face. His parents were farmers, who got by without ever becoming rich. Loft was clever, but not as clever as he thought, and ambitious. He planned to learn all he could at Holar, then go to Copenhagen and learn more. After that, he would become a famous cleric or a scholar working for the Danish government.

Loft settled at the school and studied hard, but the cabinet stayed in his mind. At last he went to visit it, where it sat in a dark corner of the library. It was wood bound with iron and had a thick iron lock.

How could he open it? He was clever enough to suspect a trick and did not touch the lock.

"It isn't difficult," a voice said behind him.

He turned and saw a lad about his age. Like Loft, he was slim and dark-haired, but his eyes were black. Looking at them, Loft thought he was looking into deep pools or pits.

"I can open it," the lad said. He touched the lock, and it opened. "There you are."

At this time, Loft did not know about the bell in the provost's house, so he didn't worry about it ringing. But, as he learned later, it did not ring.

The books inside the cabinet were old—not paper but parchment, bent and twisted by time.

"How did you do that?" Loft asked.

"It's a knack you learn from reading these. Here." The dark lad took a book out and handed it to Loft. The leather cover felt warm in his hands, and he felt a prickling sensation, as if he were rubbing the rough fur of an animal.

"What if the provost notices this is gone?" Loft asked.

"These books belonged to Bishop Gottskalk the Cruel. He left them behind when he died, though he took the most powerful—the one called Redskin—into the grave with him. No bishop or provost since then has had the courage to open the cabinet. Don't worry that anyone will discover a book is missing."

The dark lad closed the cabinet. Loft asked his name, so he could thank him properly.

"You don't need to know that. I'm a visitor and will be gone soon."

A wise man would have wondered who the visitor was. But Loft was young and ambitious and not as clever as he thought he was. He paid more attention to the book in his hands than to the man who had opened the cabinet.

He carried the book to his quarters. Whenever he was able, he studied—at night when the other students were asleep and by day in the fields.

It was early summer. The wild swans and ducks were nesting, keeping a wary eye for predators. Several times Loft saw gyrfalcons swoop down, grab a duckling, and fly away. They were nesting too and had hungry chicks to feed.

This was the way of the world, Loft thought. The weak do the best they can. The strong prevail.

The dark lad was right. There was a spell for opening locks in the book, a powerful one that undid any spells of protection. The provost's bell would not ring, and the provost would be left in ignorance. After Loft finished the book, he went back for another volume. With one exception, the books were devoted to the kind of magic that came to Iceland with Christianity, and much of their power came from blasphemy. This meant the person using the books was putting himself into the devil's hands. There was another kind of magic, the pagan kind, which drew its power from the old religion and gods who did not believe in the devil, but only one book in the cabinet contained this. If he had studied that, he might have gotten Odin as an ally and done better. But it was written in runes he did not understand.

At first, Loft used the magic for minor tricks. He could make a student he disliked stumble or develop an itch that would not go away. These seemed like ordinary problems, due to clumsiness or fleas. No one thought anything of them.

If he felt hungrier than usual, he would use magic to steal food from the students eating around him. The spell made them think they had a full plate or bowl, but they were eating an illusion and soon complained of hunger. Loft put on weight, looking more and more healthy and prosperous.

The provost should have noticed, but he didn't, due either to Loft's magic or to preoccupation. He was a pious man, who paid more attention to religion than the students.

This went on for some time. Loft became more and more confident. There was magic he could not use. He would have liked a pair of necro-pants. To make them, he had to find someone on the verge of death, who would agree to being flayed after death, so Loft could use his skin for the pants. Most people wanted to be put intact into a grave, missing nothing important, including the skin on their lower limbs. Loft could not imagine making the suggestion, even if he could find someone on the verge of dying.

There were other kinds of magic, which he found in the books. He contented himself with these. Things went on in this way for some while.

One of the bishop's servants was a woman named Freydis. She had white-blond hair and blue eyes that were even brighter than Loft's, and was as lovely as a woman could be in Iceland. Remember that it was a poor country. Beauty faded quickly. For the moment, Freydis was beautiful. In addition, she had a merry personality and flirted with the students, though she always made it clear that she was above them, since she worked for the bishop. In time, she would find a prosperous farmer and marry him. The bishop would perform the marriage. Of course, the students were in love with her, including Loft. He tried to court her, but irritated her.

"You are poor," Freydis said finally. "At best, you will be a minister in Iceland or a clerk writing out documents in Denmark. I want a man with sheep and horses and a well-built, comfortable house, with servants I can order around."

This reply made Loft angry. The lads around him might be poor students with impoverished futures. He was a magician!

He had promised his parents he would visit them at the end of summer. Loft cast a spell so Freydis thought she was a horse. She left the servants' quarters at midnight, her mind in a daze. Loft threw a saddle over her back and put a bit in her teeth. A full moon shone. He climbed into the saddle, feeling her bend down with weight, and dug his heels into her sides.

She started off. He carried a whip and used it to beat her. "Faster! Faster!"

Her hands came down onto the ground, and she ran with a smooth, tolting gait.

This was magic! This was power! Loft thought.

At dawn, they reached his family farm. Freydis was soaked with sweat. Loft dismounted and took off her saddle and bridle. He left her with the other horses and went in to meet his parents.

His mother was up, making porridge. She gave him a kiss and told him to sit down and eat. Soon his father arrived, a solid man of middle age. There were no other children. All of his siblings had died in childhood. He was a prized only child. His parents would have preferred that he stay home and inherit the farm, but it wasn't big enough to contain his ambition.

Loft told them about the school. "I'm sure I will be able to go to Copenhagen."

His father, a man of few words, grunted and rose and went outside. He returned quickly. "There is a woman with the horses. She is clearly exhausted. I think she has been beaten, as well as pushed too long and hard. Her mouth is bruised. She has no idea how she came here."

Loft said nothing.

"What did you do?" his mother asked him.

Loft kept his mouth shut.

His father went out and brought Freydis in, guiding her to a seat at the table. She was stumbling, clearly dazed. Her blond hair hung in loops around her face. Her mouth was red and swollen.

Loft's mother brought milk, porridge, and skyr, setting these in front of the girl. She petted the girl's matted hair, saying, "There, there, darling. Eat."

Loft watched with anger and fear. Why were his parents making so much of the girl, who was no better than a horse?

His father said, "I have always thought well of you, though you always seemed too sure of yourself. Now I begin to question your behavior. It's one thing to learn the sagas and Christian theology. These are harmless. But I believe you have started to learn magic."

"What of it?" Loft asked angrily.

"The sagas are our past. Theology is our future, if the ministers are right. Magic is nothing, an illusion. I don't want you to come here again. One of your cousins can take over the farm when I am old."

"Very well," Loft said and stood. "I bid you farewell."

He left and walked back to Holar, a long journey. As he walked, he thought about what had happened. How could his parents side with a woman they didn't know, rather than with their only son? Freydis was no one important, only a serving girl. He was a scholar, becoming skillful in magic.

Under his anger was sadness, which he did not want to recognize. Whenever he began to feel it, he said something boastful to himself. Let his parents live on their farm, which was small and had poor soil. Let them do as well as they could. He would become powerful and famous. In this manner, he went onward until he reached Holar.

His parents cared for Freydis. She gradually recovered, but she had no desire to return to Holar. Instead, she stayed at the farm, helping Loft's mother. She was less proud and more grateful than she'd been before. Loft's parents treated her as a daughter.

Loft continued his studies, learning both the books in the library and those in the cabinet. He was sorry to lose his parents, but they were wrong to condemn magic and him.

Another girl worked for the bishop. This one was named Thordis. She had honey-blond hair and gray eyes and was lovely, though not as lovely as Freydis. Loft did not feel love for her, but rather lust.

He found a love spell and cast it. Soon they were meeting. This was the first time Loft had made love to a woman, and he enjoyed it, congratulating himself on his success.

After a while Thordis came to him and said she was pregnant. She had told no one so far, but she would have to soon. Such a thing could not be hidden long. The bishop would be angry, Loft knew, and the bishop was a stern, unforgiving man. This would reduce Loft's chances of going to Denmark. He went back to the magic books, finding another spell. Thordis disappeared. The bishop sent his servants out searching, and the provost questioned the students, but no sign of her was found.

Everything was going well, Loft thought. One day as he was studying in the fields, a large swan flew down beside him. The bird glared at him, flapping her wide, white wings.

"You can hardly mind your present situation," Loft said. "I am sure you have a nest and fine cygnets."

The swan's long neck struck out. Her beak almost hit him. He jumped up and shouted, "Begone!"

The swan flapped her wings again and rose into the sky. This was the last he saw of her. But he was always cautious around swans after that. If they were nearby, and they nested every spring in the fields around Holar, he would stay inside.

His fellow students noticed this and made jokes. He responded with spells that made them itch and sneeze.

A year later, a minister's wife in the East Fjords opened her door and saw a naked woman. The minister was known to be generous, and the wife was used to seeing beggars, but not like this. She pulled the woman inside and wrapped a blanket around her. "What has happened? Who are you?"

"Thordis," the woman said.

"Who are your relatives?"

After a long pause, the woman replied, "There was a child, but she flew away."

It was obvious the woman was out of her mind. The minister's wife settled her down and brought her food. "What else do you know, Thordis?"

The woman regarded her with blank eyes. "Sky. Green fields. The mountains. The sea."

Life was hard in Iceland. More than one woman had been driven insane by poverty and the loss of children.

When the minister came home, after a long ride to visit a parishioner, he found Thordis sleeping by the fire. His wife told him the story. "We can't send her on her way in this condition. Let's keep her and send word about her. Maybe her relatives will come."

The minister looked dubious, but he knew his wife. She had a will of iron when it came to helping people. "Very well," he said.

Thordis proved to be a good worker, helpful in the house and around the minister's farm. She never paused until a task was done, unless wild swans flew over. Then she would look up, following them with her eyes.

She rarely spoke, except to answer questions, though she never answered questions about her past. Whatever she knew remained locked inside her. No one ever came to claim her. In the end, a neighboring farmer asked to marry her, impressed by her hard work and silence. She said yes, though not with any enthusiasm. Nonetheless, the marriage proved good. Her husband was as hard a worker as she was, prudent and lucky as well. In time, they became prosperous. Most of their children lived to adulthood.

Thordis always helped beggars when they came to the farm, and she always paused to watch wild swans as they flew over.

For a while, after Loft drove off the swan, he remained happy with his life and the magic he had learned. Then he began to think of the risk he was taking. The magic in the books was devilish. By learning it and using it he had endangered his soul. Sooner or later, the devil would claim him and drag him down to hell. None of the books in the cabinet told him how to escape this fate. In the old days, he could have gone to the Black School in Paris, as Saemund the Wise had done. Saemund had learned such strong magic that the devil had no power over him. But nothing had been heard of the school for centuries. It must be gone.

He knew only one other way to control the devil. Bishop Gottskalk the Cruel was famous for two things: his cruelty and his skill at magic. He had owned the most famous book of magic in Iceland, Redskin, which he had taken into the grave with him.

He had to get Redskin, Loft decided. In order to do this, he would have to raise the bishop. That was possible. The books in the cabinet told him how. However, for safety, he had to have an assistant, someone to ring the church bells if Loft was in danger. The sounds of the bells would drive the ghosts he raised away.

He had no good friends among the other students. They thought he was arrogant and overly confident. But there was one student who tried to be his friend: a lanky, clumsy lad with spots on his face. Most people called him Spotty Trausti. Not the best choice for an assistant, but the only one Loft had.

Loft invited Trausti for a walk. Standing by a stream on a mild summer day, he explained his problem. He needed to raise the ghost of Bishop Gottskalk and get Redskin from him. But he couldn't do this without help.

"But why do you need the book?" Trausti asked.

To perfect his knowledge, Loft replied. With the information in the book, he could become an important person in the Danish government and help Iceland, which was ruled by Denmark and not ruled well.

Trausti's dull eyes brightened. "Yes. Anything that helps Iceland is worth doing."

What a fool, Loft thought.

He explained what he needed. On a full-moon night, he would go into Holar's churchyard and raise the bishop. Spotty Trausti must be in the church tower, ready to ring the bells if Loft signaled.

Trausti nodded, anxious to help. "Yes."

The night came. A bright full moon shone from the cloudless sky. Loft gathered his magic books and went out to raise Bishop Gottskalk the Cruel. Up in the church tower, Spotty Trausti watched and worried.

Loft cast his spells, which were full of blasphemy and evil words. A cloud appeared out of nowhere, dimming the moon. Bishops—far more than one—rose from the ground. He could tell from their costumes that some were Lutheran from recent times. Others were Catholic from the early days of Iceland. Three wore crowns that glowed faintly in the shadowy moonlight.

One of the crowned bishops spoke to Loft. "Give up on this plan, lad. Rely on repentance and living a decent life."

Loft was not sure, but he thought this might be Bishop Gudmund the Good Arason, who had traveled around Iceland with beggars. Of course, every farmer had to welcome his bishop, and if beggars came with Gudmund, they had to be welcomed as well. It was a clever way to get beggars fed, though Bishop Gudmund was known for goodness, not for cleverness.

Of course, Loft did not listen to the bishop. Instead, he cast more spells. Waving his hands, he confessed—not to his sins, but to his good deeds, begging the devil to forgive him whatever he had done that was kind. These deeds were few in number. He had always been selfish and arrogant, though he had loved his parents and his dog, Brownie.

Up in the bell tower, Spotty Trausti listened.

Now another ghost appeared, this one frowning heavily and holding a book against his chest. It was clearly old. The cover was dull red leather. Loft could see the color even in moonlight. The other bishops wore crosses, but not this one, unless it was hidden by the book. Loft did not think so.

"You're better than I expected," the new ghost said. "But you will not get Redskin from me."

Loft waved his hands more madly, reciting psalms that praised the devil rather than God. The bishops turned their backs on him, all except Gottskalk the Cruel and the three bishops with crowns. They continued to watch Loft, Gottskalk with angry contempt, and the three other bishops with concern.

Slowly, reluctantly, Gottskalk's hands moved, carrying Redskin away from his chest. The book edged toward Loft, as Bishop Gottskalk grimaced and groaned, trying to pull it back. A terrible sight! It certainly was for Spotty Trausti, looking down from the church tower.

Loft reached out a hand, touching the corner of Redskin. The book burned like a live coal. He shouted in surprise and pulled his hand back. Mistaking this for his signal, Spotty Trausti rang the church bells.

The ghosts vanished, all except Bishop Gudmund. "You have made a proper mess, lad. Consider what you've done." With that, Gudmund disappeared.

Loft collapsed. Trausti tumbled down from the tower. "Was that the signal?"

"I am damned," Loft replied.

"What?" asked Spotty Trausti.

"It isn't your fault," Loft said wearily. He rose to his feet, swaying. "I should have raised the bishop closer to dawn. He would have given up the book in order to regain his grave before sunrise. I didn't think."

After that he went to the sod house where he lived and lay down on his bed. He didn't rise from it in the morning or for many days after. It was obvious that he was ill, his face pale, his limbs shaking, and his appetite almost entirely gone. His fellow students and the provost began to think he would die.

There was a minister named Thidrik Pedersson, who lived north of Holar on the shore of Skagafjord. He was famous for his piety and his skill in curing illness. After Loft had been sick for a while and not getting better, the provost sent him to Thidrik. The minister took him in and cared for him, praying constantly. Gradually Loft improved, though he wasn't able to join Thidrik in prayers.

The minister often traveled, visiting the sick and dying. Loft went with him, a frail figure who rarely spoke. He was a grim sight for the dying: thin and pale, with sunken eyes and cheeks. But Thidrik was unwilling to leave him alone.

One day Thidrik was called to the bed of an old friend on the verge of death. Loft said he was too ill to travel.

"Very well," the minister said. "But stay indoors. I cannot answer for what will happen if you go out."

Loft agreed, and Thidrik left.

Soon after, Loft felt better. He got up and went to the house door. The day was bright and cloudless. Skagafjord lay flat and as even as glass. Loft felt a need to get out on the water.

All the men on the minister's farm were already out fishing. Loft walked to a neighboring farm. The farmer there was a surly, unpleasant man, but he had a boat, though he rarely went out in it.

"The day is mild. The fjord is still," Loft said. "It can hardly harm us to go out."

What made the farmer agree? Magic? Folly? A sudden need for the taste of cod, freshly cooked?

They rowed the farmer's boat onto the fjord. The still water reflected a blue sky. Flat-topped, black mountains rose along its edges. In the distance was the famous island Drangey, where the outlaw Grettir had lived and made his last stand.

They baited their lines and threw them in, drawing up cod. Fish after fish went into the boat's bottom, thrashing and throwing up, as cod will do when they are upset. Everything seemed ordinary, until a gray hand rose from the water and grasped the boat's prow. The farmer shouted. The boat tilted, and the hand drew it underwater.

The farmer was able to swim. He beat his way to shore and told his story. Loft must have died, people said. Dragged by the devil into hell for his evil deeds, though no one was sure what he had done.

This was a good end to Loft's story, but not true. The hand belonged to a troll maiden, who was walking along the bottom of the fjord, grabbing cod and putting them in a net. The farmer's boat floated over her. She looked up and saw Loft, leaning over the boat's side. Although he was thin and pale, he seemed handsome to her. She fell in love.

Reaching up a hand, she grabbed the boat and pulled it down. As soon as she had Loft, she put him in her net and hurried home. Loft could not open his mouth to recite a magic spell, since he was underwater. Weak as he was, he could not struggle. He held his breath and hoped for the best.

The troll maid's home was in a cliff on Skagafjord's shore. There were two entrances, one on land and the other underwater. She took the underwater entrance, since it was day and she was the kind of troll that turned into stone in sunlight. Moonlight and light shining through water did not harm her, but she could not bear the direct light of the sun.

Up a lava tube she went and into a cave, dragging her net, which was full of fish and Loft. Once they were in air, he could exhale and breathe. His lungs hurt. He was dizzy, but alive.

The cave was large and had a fissure in the floor. Red light rose from it. There might be magma down there, Loft thought, though he wasn't sure. The light made his surroundings visible. On one side of the cave was a lumpy boulder. On the other side was a cow, resting on a bed of straw. At the time, that was all he saw.

Loft struggled out of the net and looked at the troll maid. She was more than twice his size, with a huge nose and hair like a wet haystack. A ragged shift covered her lumpy body. Her ugly feet were bare.

"What is this about?" Loft asked.

"I live alone with no husband," the troll maid replied. "As far as I can tell, there are no eligible troll men nearby. Therefore, I have decided to make you my mate."

This was not a pleasant idea. "Look at me," Loft said. "I am thin and pale, too sick to be a husband. I need time and care, before I can do a husband's duties."

"Well enough," the troll maid said. "I have time, and I can care."

Then she rolled the boulder in front of the entrance and settled down to make dinner, cleaning the fish and cooking them over a driftwood fire.

It was a good meal. Loft was hungry. He ate till he was stuffed and then lay back.

"Are you ready to make love?" the troll maid asked.

"Hardly. I need rest and nourishment, especially—" He looked at the cow and tried to think of food that might be hard to find. Fish would not do, since the troll maid was clearly able to get these. "Moss cooked in milk."

"That can be done," the troll maid said. She tipped the remains of the meal into the fissure, then lay down to sleep. Soon she was snoring. Loft got up and cast a spell to open the cave door. It was a powerful spell, the best he knew. But the boulder stayed in place.

"That won't work," the stone said in a low, grating voice.

"Why not?"

"The rock in Iceland makes its own rules, as you ought to know. When it wants to shake, it shakes. When it wants to release fire and lava, it does so. No magician is able to change its behavior.

"The same is true of trolls, since we are almost stone. Like stone, we have our own rules."

"What are you?" Loft asked.

"I am the troll maid's father. As we age, trolls become more and more stonelike. Because I am old, I am barely able to move. My daughter uses me to shut her door. This is lack of respect, but I am not able to respond."

"Ah," said Loft. After that, he lay down to sleep. It might be difficult to escape the cave, but he was determined to do so.

It was not possible to tell time in the cave. He woke in the darkness and the red light from the fissure. The troll maid was gone, along with the cow.

"Where is she?" he asked the boulder.

"It's night outside. She has taken the cow to graze by moonlight, while she gathers moss." The boulder paused. "There is another entrance to the cave, in case you are wondering. But you won't be able to find it, and if you do, you will find it blocked with a stone only my daughter can move."

The conversation ended. Loft walked around the cave. There was a gap in the wall, going into darkness. That might be the second entrance. He would explore it later. In another place, water trickled down the wall into a shallow pool. Loft knelt and cupped his hands. The water was cold, with a fresh, stony flavor.

In a third place, there was a ledge that served for storage. Bowls and spoons were stacked on it, along with two battered metal pots and a pile of neatly folded pieces of cloth: blankets and clothing. Everything looked clean, but ragged. Loft felt his usual contempt for anyone weak or poor.

When he had completed his circle, he stopped in front of the boulder. "Do you want your daughter to mate with a human?"

"Of course not. My grandchildren would be half-breed monsters. She doesn't listen to me. I have told her to go exploring and find a proper husband. There are still plenty of trolls in Iceland. But she is afraid of sunlight and people."

"Where do I piss and defecate?" Loft asked.

"My daughter relieves herself when she is outside. I need little relief, being mostly stone. But you can piss into the fissure and defecate in the cow's straw. The cow does."

Loft pissed and then settled down to think. At length, the troll maid returned, leading her cow and carrying a basket full of moss.

She milked the cow into one of her pots, then added the moss and cooked it over the fissure. A slow process, she told Loft, but it saved wood. Red light shone on her lumpy face, long nose, and little eyes like chips of obsidian.

Loft felt horror, thinking of sex with her.

They ate, and the troll maid settled down to sleep, a ragged blanket over her. Loft looked at the moss remaining in his bowl and thought, *If I grow strong, she will demand sex. Better to throw this out.* He walked to the fissure, ready to empty the bowl into it.

The boulder spoke in its grating voice. "If you have food left, give it to me. My daughter sees no reason to feed me, since I am barely alive. But I remember the taste of moss cooked in milk."

Loft considered, then carried the bowl to the boulder. Slowly, slowly an arm emerged from the rock. Stony fingers grasped the bowl. A slit—it must have been a mouth—opened in the boulder. The contents of the bowl were tilted in.

The arm held out the empty bowl. Loft took it.

A voice spoke behind him. "I almost had you out there in the boat, but the troll woman reached you first."

Loft turned and saw a man of early middle age, solidly built, with a red face and a neatly trimmed black beard. He was dressed in good clothes, though they were a little old-fashioned. His eyes were holes into darkness, and his teeth showing in the middle of his beard—were white and square. "I could take you now, but you have just been kind. Remember your true nature, Loft! Remember how little you care about anyone except yourself!"

Then the man was gone, though Loft couldn't see how.

"Not a good person," the boulder said. "Luckily for us, he pays little attention to trolls."

Loft lay down and thought. He had two goals—to escape the troll maid and to escape the devil. How could he accomplish both?

The next night the troll maid led her cow out of the cave. Loft rose and followed through the gap in the cave wall, entering a lightless tunnel. He heard the troll and cow ahead of him and kept after them, one hand on the rough tunnel wall.

All at once, there was light ahead of him: moonlight spilling into the tunnel. He hurried toward it, but it vanished. The tunnel's end—when he reached it—was blocked by a slab of stone. The troll maid had led her cow outside and shut the door.

He beat on the slab until his hands were raw and tried one spell after another. But the slab would not move. He was trapped.

At last, he turned and felt his way back into the cave.

"Think," the boulder said when he came out of the tunnel. "Your magic will not work on stone. What about other materials? They are not as obdurate as Iceland's bones."

Loft gestured angrily, reciting a spell. The cow's bed of straw burst into flame. There was a brief bonfire, then the straw was gone. The fire vanished.

"That does not help you, though it gets rid of the manure," the boulder said. "Think again."

Loft did, but came up with nothing. When the troll maid returned, she exclaimed over the burned straw. "What does my Bent Horn have to sleep on?"

"I did it to get rid of the manure," Loft said.

"Well enough, but now I'll have to gather more grass, and that means you will have less moss."

"Do what you have to do," Loft said.

"But I want you fat and healthy and able to impregnate me," the troll maid replied.

"Be patient," Loft said. "If we have sex now, your children would be small and weak. Wait till I am strong. I'm sure I'll get fat with your good food." Not if he could help it, he added in his mind. He would feed the boulder and remain thin.

Several days passed. He always shared his food with the boulder, who was silent, as if thinking. Finally, it thanked him for the latest bowl of moss in milk, then said, "Stone does not obey you, but grass and fire do, and water might. I've heard that sorcerers can far-see in bowls of water. Find a mate for my daughter. Then she'll be willing to let you go."

Loft took the bowl, which was empty now, and washed it in the cave's pool. Then he filled it with the pool's clear, cold water and cast a spell. The water became a mirror. He cast another spell and saw all of Iceland in the mirror: the bare, bony mountains; rushing rivers; green fields; and tiny farmhouses and churches. Four figures stood at the country's corners: a bull in the west, a dragon in the east, and a hulking mountain troll in the south. The north had an animal that kept changing. First it was an eagle with a white tail, then a griffin, then an eagle again. Back and forth it went. These were the landvaettir, the four guardians of Iceland, as Loft knew.

He gestured and spoke another spell. Tiny lights appeared all over the country. These were troll homes. Loft found his current place of confinement, then looked for lights nearby. There was only one: dim and flickering, as if about to go out. Hardly hopeful, but he gestured and spoke again.

The image in the bowl changed. Now it showed a troll, a male, wearing nothing except a ragged loincloth. His skin was gray and pitted, his nose long and lumpy. Hair like straw hung over his shoulders. He was on a treadmill inside a metal cage, pacing and pacing, his expression grim. The treadmill powered stone wheels that ground grain into flour.

A voice spoke in Loft's mind:

"Tread, tread,
Grind our bread.
Longnose, keep at it.
Tread, tread,
Grind our bread,
Never stop and sit."

The cage was on a stone promontory high up in a huge cave, far larger than the one that held Loft prisoner. Stone and wood houses covered the floor of the cave. Lamps floated in the air above the houses, lighting them and the streets where handsome people walked. They were dressed in old-fashioned clothing with bright colors: red and green and yellow. Loft saw gold buckles, broaches, rings, and arm rings. These must be elves, he realized. No one in Iceland, even the Danish merchants and officials, looked this rich and fine.

Loft rocked back on his heels, feeling despair. How could he take on elves?

"Well?" asked the boulder. "What have you found?"

He thought of lying and saying, "Nothing." Instead, he picked up the bowl and carried it to the boulder, tilting it so the old troll could see. Because magic held it, the water did not spill out, but remained like glass or metal.

"Fine, fine," the boulder said. "A handsome young troll, and you know what's said about noses."

"No," said Loft.

"A long nose means a big penis. He will keep my daughter happy—if you can find a way to rescue him from that cage."

"Why should I do it?"

"As I told you, if she can find a proper husband, she will let you go. And I will have good trollish grandchildren, not strange half-breed humans."

Loft gestured. The mirror became water again and spilled from the bowl.

He spent several days thinking. He had no desire to get involved with elves. But it seemed as if that was the only way to escape the troll maid.

Finally, he showed the troll maid what he had found. She gazed entranced at the image in the bowl. "What a fine male! Look at that nose!"

"If you let me go. I will travel to the elf home and free him, and you can have a proper husband."

"Nonsense. You will run off and leave me with nothing." She gazed at the troll in the mirror. "What a nose! What a fine physique!"

Loft spoke another spell. Iceland appeared in the mirror, guarded by its four guardians and edged with turbulent waves. The troll homes gleamed amid rumpled mountains. Loft pointed to the one that held the troll.

"I know that place," the troll maid said. "It's two days from here, and there's a cave midway between, where we can hide from the sun. But not now. It's summer, and the nights are too short. We'll have to wait till autumn."

This they did. The troll maid went out every night with her cow. Loft was careful to eat only a little of the food she provided, giving the rest to the boulder. In this way, he remained thin, while the boulder became more rounded. The troll maid did not notice. Her mind was on the troll prisoner and the children they would produce. Every day she looked at Loft's mirror, admiring the male troll and talking about the offspring they would have.

At last the maiden said, "The nights are long enough. We can make the journey."

Then, as the maid slept, Loft and the boulder spoke together.

"Don't betray my daughter," the boulder said.

"I won't," Loft said, though he was already thinking of ways to run off. Why should he care about the problems of trolls or anyone else?

The next evening, the troll maid said, "It's time to go."

Loft rose, feeling hopeful.

"But I don't trust you. You may escape, once we are out of the cave. I'm going to tie you up and gag you, so you can't speak any spells."

"I won't be able to walk," Loft said.

"I'll carry you and move more quickly than you ever could."

What could Loft do? His magic would not work on her, and he was still too thin and weak to struggle. Even a strong man could not win against a troll.

She tied him hand and foot and put a wad of cloth into his mouth. "Now you won't be able to do any harm to me or anyone with your magic."

She gathered him in her strong, lumpy arms and carried him through the cave's land door. Outside were darkness and a bright full moon, shining from the middle of a cloudless sky.

She set off, running first through grassy fields and then over mountain paths and bare fields of lava. Snowy mountaintops shone like silver. In the valleys, glacial rivers rushed. Loft mumbled through his gag, trying to curse. No word got through. Rocked in the troll maid's arms, he finally fell asleep.

The troll maid stopped, and Loft woke. "We're at our resting place," she said and entered a pitch-black cave. Pale, predawn light glowed at the cave's entrance. Otherwise, there was no illumination.

"Do you need to pee?" she asked.

He nodded. In spite of the cave's darkness, she saw him and undid his bonds. He climbed to his feet, stiff and unsteady.

"Pee at the entrance to the cave," the troll maid said. "Don't go any farther, or I will catch you and be angry."

He was in no condition to argue. He staggered to the cave's entrance and undid his pants. The sky glowed to the east, but the sun was behind a peak. He pissed into shadows, feeling increasingly comfortable as the piss left him. This was the time to escape the troll maid, he thought as he refastened his pants.

"Don't think of it," the troll maid called from inside the cave.

Suddenly a man was next to him. Even in the darkness Loft could see him clearly. He was late middle age, with a clipped gray beard, dressed like a rich Danish merchant, though all his clothes were black. In one hand, he carried a gold-headed cane. Loft looked at him with dislike. He knew who the fellow was now. Not anyone he wanted to know.

"I can help you escape," the man said softly. He was speaking Icelandic, though with a foreign accent.

"No."

"Why not?"

"Then I'd be in debt to you. If I am clever, and I've always believed I'm clever, I will be able to escape the troll. But no one escapes hell who does not have the book Redskin."

The man frowned angrily. "You are already in debt to me."

"If so, I want no further debt."

The troll maid's hand came down heavily on Loft's shoulder. "Are you plotting to escape?"

The man was gone.

"Only pissing," Loft said.

"Come in. The sun will be above that mountain in a moment."

He followed her into the cave. She tied him up again and gagged him, then lay down to sleep. He lay awake all day, too uncomfortable to sleep, while the maiden snored beside him. In the evening, she woke and gathered him up. She ran through the autumn night, lit by an almost full moon. Loft slept in her stony arms.

He woke when she laid him down. "We're at the door to the elf home. Conjure a way in."

Loft mumbled through the gag. The troll maid pulled it out. "What?"

"Untie me. I need to pee."

"Very well," said the troll maid. "But remember that I will keep a close eye on you. You can't enchant me, any more than you can enchant the mountain Hekla, who pours out fire whenever she wants to; and I can chase you down."

If he'd been less stiff and achy, Loft might have made a run for it, casting spells behind him to slow the maid. But his mouth was sore from the gag, making it hard for him to say the spells properly; and he wasn't sure he could run and cast spells at the same time. He turned his back on the maid and relieved himself.

Overhead, the stars were fading. Maybe he could find a way to trick the maid into waiting till the sun was up. But no, the land around them was rough and craggy. She could find some corner to hide in. In addition, he remembered the man in black, who was almost certainly waiting for him in the shadows. He suspected the man would grab him, if he played any more malicious tricks. Though he did not understand why harming a troll should cause him harm. In any case, he had a plan.

They stood next to a cliff, on which he had peed. He gestured magically and spoke a brief spell. The elf door became visible, its edges glowing and a dark stain on its middle.

"How will we get in?" the troll maid asked.

"Like this." Loft picked up a stone and beat on the door, shouting, "Open up! Open up! I come with a challenge!"

"What is that about?" the maid asked.

"The easiest way to get through a door is to knock."

They waited. At last the door opened. A woman stood in front of them. Yellow light spilled around her. Her hair was long and golden, falling over her shoulders, and she wore an old-fashioned dress of green cloth. Her belt had a gold buckle, inset with amber.

"That was rude," she told them. "A gentle knock would have done."

"We didn't know," Loft said. He felt the troll's hand, heavy on his shoulder.

"What do you mean, when you offer a challenge?"

"I am Loft, a famous human sorcerer, and I challenge your best magician to a contest."

"That would be my brother Alfbrand. What are the stakes?"

"His stake will be the troll Longnose, who works at your mill."

"And your stake?"

"This fine, strong troll maid standing next to me. If your brother wins, you'll have two workers to grind your grain."

The troll maid's grip tightened on his shoulder. "What are you saying?"

"Be confident," Loft said. "I will win."

"I do not want to pace on a treadmill."

"To win, you must take risks. Consider," he told the elf woman. "With two trolls, you will be able to breed generations of slaves."

The grip on his shoulder tightened even more. The troll's fingers pressed through his flesh and seemed ready to break a bone.

Loft winced and groaned.

"Come in," the elf woman said. "I will tell Alfbrand about your offer."

For a moment, it seemed as if the troll maid would yank Loft back. Then her grip loosened, and she pushed him gently through the door.

This was love, Loft thought. An emotion he had never felt.

They entered a huge cave, filled with handsome elf-houses, built with wood as well as stone, though there was little wood in Iceland. These must date from the settlement times, when there were huge piles of driftwood on the island's shores, pines from Norway that had floated to Iceland.

Light shone from lanterns that floated above the houses. More light shone through windows and open doors. The elf woman led them down a street, past handsome elven folk who all looked at them with surprise. At length, they came to a house that was bigger than all the rest. The elf woman led them in. They found themselves in a long hall, with a fire pit running down the middle. The pit was full of ashes and coals that glowed red. Tendrils of smoke rose from the coals, twisting around carved house posts, then escaped through a hole in the roof.

This was very ancient, it seemed to Loft, and very rich.

At the end of the hall was a high seat. A large, fat elf sat there. He was dressed in green with high, soft, red boots. His belly bulged over a wide belt with a gold buckle. "What's this?" he asked.

"This human has challenged you to a magical contest," the elf woman said and explained the terms.

"Good enough," said the elf man. "I'm willing to earn another slave for our community."

The troll maid's grip tightened on Loft's shoulder. "Be confident," he whispered.

"Invite our neighbors to see the contest," the fat elf said.

The elf woman left. The elf man—Alfbrand—left his seat and strolled down the hall to Loft, who was shaking now. Everything about the elf spoke of wealth and power. Loft was willing to lose the contest. That was one way to escape the troll maid. But he wasn't sure what other consequences there might be.

"Young, aren't you?" Alfbrand said in a tone of contempt. "And thin and pale. Entirely unimpressive. The troll girl will go onto a treadmill after this is done. I need to decide what to do with you. Maybe I'll turn you into a mounting block, as the Persian king did with the Roman emperor in ancient times. Though you don't seem solid enough."

Loft did not answer. His mouth was dry.

"Come along," Alfbrand said. "We'll hold our contest in the town square. There's room enough for everyone to see my triumph."

Loft followed the elf, the troll maid beside him, still holding on to his shoulder.

The square was a wide space paved with pumice gravel. Elf people were gathering in it, all of them tall and handsome and dressed in fine clothing, mostly green. On the promontory above them, Longnose paced and paced, grinding grain.

"I'd like a drink of water," Loft said.

Alfbrand made an imperious summoning motion. An elf girl came with a flask. Loft drank deeply, enjoying the cold, fresh water. Then he offered the flask to the troll maid. She took it and drank.

"Now," said Alfbrand and spoke strange words in a loud, harsh voice.

All at once the space between them was filled with huge figures. One was a bull, snorting with anger. The second was a dragon that twisted and hissed. The third was a hulking mountain troll, dressed in skins and carrying a club. Last of all was a creature that kept changing, being sometimes a griffin and sometimes an eagle. It seemed to Loft they were all hazy at the edges, as if they were not entirely real or not entirely in this place.

Loft knew them at once: the landvaettir, the spirits that were guardians of Iceland. And he knew what to do about them. He gestured and spoke a changing spell.

The bull turned into a calf, bawling for its mother. The troll turned into a baby, waving its arms and crying. The griffin turned into a small bird that flew in a circle above them, making a whistling call. Last of all, Loft turned to the dragon and gestured. It shrank into a snake, which amazed everyone, since there were no snakes in Iceland. Before it could flee, Loft stepped on it, crushing its head.

"Not bad," Alfbrand said. "Though I don't know how Iceland is going to survive, bereft of its guardians."

"I'll worry about that later," Loft replied.

"Now, show me what you can do," the elf man said.

Loft paused for a moment, gathering his forces. He was no longer afraid. Instead, he was terrified. But he knew summoning spells worked here, and he made the most powerful summoning he knew, chanting loudly and waving his hands madly, putting all his skill and power into the enchantment.

Four new figures appeared in the space between him and Alfbrand. One was Bishop Gottskalk the Cruel, holding Redskin tightly against his chest and looking around angrily. The other three were the crowned bishops he had summoned before by mistake. This time he wanted them. Two of the bishops held crosiers made of wood with finely carved, curling tops made of ivory. Walrus ivory, most likely. The light their crowns shed made halos around their heads. Loft realized who they were: Iceland's two saints, Jon and Thorlak. They had stern, serious, un-forgiving expressions; and Gottskalk cringed away from them. But the cruel bishop could not escape them. They stood on either side of him, hemming him in.

The third crowned bishop had a mild expression, and his crown cast no halo. His crosier was iron, bottom to top.

"I couldn't find a good enough piece of wood," he said to Loft. "So I asked a smith to make me a crosier of iron. It doesn't break, and godless folk don't like it."

Loft noticed that the elf folk were drawing away. Even Alfbrand looked worried. The troll maid had let go of his shoulder and stepped back as well.

"What kind of trouble have you gotten in this time, lad?" the kind-looking bishop said. Loft recognized him: Gudmund the Good Arason, who had driven the trolls from most of the island of Drangey.

Nothing to do except explain. He told his story to Gudmund.

When he finished, Gudmund said, "As the trolls told me at Drangey, everyone needs a place to live in peace. For this reason, I left some of the cliffs at Drangey unblessed, and trolls still live there. They may not be the best of neighbors, but they are not the worst.

"These two—Longnose and the maiden—deserve peace and a home of their own. Therefore—" Gudmund pointed his iron crosier at the promontory, where Longnose was still pacing. The bronze bars of the cage broke apart. Longnose leaped down and came to join the troll maid.

"As for the rest—" Gudmund struck his crosier against the ground. It rang like a bell, and a hole appeared. Gudmund reached in, pulling a man out by his long, white beard. Loft knew the fellow: the man who had spoken to him in Holar and the troll cave and once since then. This time he was old and thin, though still wriggling actively. As always, he was dressed in black.

"He wants someone to carry down to hell," Gudmund said. "I don't think it should be you, Loft, since you are still alive and able to learn. Therefore—" Gudmund gestured.

The two saints grabbed Bishop Gottskalk by his elbows and carried him forward, while he shouted in anger.

As soon as Gottskalk was near, the man in black grasped him with bony hands, pulling the bishop close. The two men were so tightly grappled that Loft could not tell them apart. The book Redskin was between them, impossible to see. The cruel bishop cried out in horror. But he could not escape.

"Now," said Gudmund the Good. He grasped the intertwined men and pushed them into the hole. They vanished. The hole closed.

"That's the end of Redskin," Gudmund said. "No one will reach it where it is now. It will not tempt other lads, as it has tempted you. As for the rest—" Gudmund lifted his iron crosier and waved it at the transformed landvaettir. The calf turned back into a bull and the baby to a giant. The circling bird dropped down and became a griffin. The crushed snake rose up and was a dragon. They all bent their heads to Gudmund. "Go back to your job of guarding Iceland," he said to them and waved his crosier again. The four spirits disappeared.

"And as for you, Loft, you have done nothing good with magic. I think you'll do better without your knowledge of spells."

The iron crosier touched Loft. A wave of cold went through him, like a gust of winter wind carrying tiny, hard pieces of snow. His entire body shuddered, and his head ached. When the wind passed, he felt empty and numb. He tried to think of the magic he had learned. It was gone. Desperate, he searched through his mind. No magic remained. Only coldness and a sense of despair.

Gudmund looked around at the elves. "When night comes, and the trolls can travel safely, you will let them—and Loft—go."

"Yes," said Alfbrand, his teeth chattering.

With that, the three crowned bishops vanished.

"I could not win a contest with holy men, one of them armed with iron," Alfbrand said. "So you have won. Though I have to say, I don't think it was fair of you to conjure them."

"I did what I had to," Loft replied.

The elf folk left the square. Loft and the troll maid and Longnose were alone. "You are lovely," the troll man said to the maid in a deep, rough, gravelly voice. "And you risked danger to save me—with the help of the human, of course, but you brought him here. Can we marry? I imagine our children will be strong and brave and ingenious."

"Yes," said the troll maid.

"Am I free to go then?" Loft asked.

"Of course. I have no need to keep you, now that I have a fine, hand-some, trollish husband."

The two trolls sat down and spoke in rumbling voices so low that Loft felt them rather than heard them. He understood nothing and paced until the elf woman returned.

"It's night now," she said. "If you were proper visitors, I would ask you to take your leave from Alfbrand. But he is sulking in his high seat, and it will be a long time before he recovers his good humor."

The elf woman led them to the elf home's door and opened it. The night was cold. Large clouds filled most of the sky, shining in the light of the moon. The two trolls took off. Alone in the darkness, Loft sat down to wait for dawn.

After a while he noticed there was someone next to him, sitting as he was, back against the cliff wall. He couldn't make the person out in the darkness, but he recognized the voice, deep and rich and plausible.

"Gudmund took away your knowledge of magic, but not your ability to learn it. You can go back to Holar and study the magic books again."

Loft thought about this. Redskin was gone, along with any hope of controlling the devil. If he learned black magic again, he would put his soul at risk again, and this time he had no way of saving himself from hell.

What had he gained from magic? Nothing, as far as he could tell. Instead, he had lost his family, become afraid of swans, been captured by trolls, and made elves angry. Worst of all, he had gained the devil's attention. He had no desire to be dragged into hell like Bishop Gottskalk.

"No," he said to the man beside him. "I am done with sorcery."

"Are you sure?"

"Yes."

The man made a hissing noise, like steam rising from a fumarole. Then he was gone. For a while, Loft sat alone in the darkness. Then a new voice spoke.

"That is a good decision." It was Bishop Gudmund the Good, standing close to Loft in the shadow of the elf cliff and leaning on his iron crosier. The crown he wore cast a pale light on his face. "What will you do now?"

"Go back to Holar and see if the provost will readmit me. As far as I know, Spotty Trausti has kept quiet about what I was doing in the church graveyard. With luck, I will be able to go back to school."

"What will you study?" the bishop asked, sounding stern.

"Ordinary knowledge. Before I learned about the magic books, I planned to be a minister or a scholar in Copenhagen."

"Don't become a minister," Gudmund said. "You don't have the character for it. But a scholar can have any kind of character. Think of Snorri Sturlason, who wrote the *History of the Kings of Norway*. A very learned man, though not someone I'd call a good man. His own relatives killed him."

Loft said, "Yes," feeling comforted by the thought of Snorri. He could still become a famous scholar; and if he was careful, and did not get involved in politics, he could avoid Snorri's fate.

Gudmund went on. "Don't play any more malicious tricks on women or your fellow students; and stay away from the cabinet of magic books. Remember that the devil is watching you. If you fall back into bad habits, he will pay you a visit. Redskin is gone, and the Black School in Paris closed long ago. You will lose any contest you have with him." Gudmund paused for a moment. "Most likely, we will not meet again." He vanished. Once again Loft was alone in the dark. He felt tired and no longer certain that he was clever.

The sky was growing pale behind the eastern mountains. Soon he could begin the long walk back to Holar.

Postscript: The story of Loft the Sorcerer is an Icelandic folktale, which was made into a famous Icelandic play in the early twentieth century. In the folktale Loft is dragged down to hell. I wanted to give him a second chance. As far as I know, Loft was not a real person.

The landvaettir, the guardians of Iceland, are real. They appear on the Icelandic coat of arms and on Icelandic coins.

Gudmund the Good is real, as are Saint Jon and Saint Thorlak. Gudmund did bless the cliffs of Drangey, so trolls could not live there; and he did leave one area unblessed, because even the evil need a place to live.

Snorri Sturlason was a thirteenth-century scholar and historian, author of the *Heimskringla,* a history of the kings of Norway, and the Prose Edda. He probably wrote *Egils saga Skallagrimssonar,* one of the great Icelandic sagas. He was murdered by relatives.

Necropants are an authentic form of Icelandic magic, though not in use at present, as far as I know.

Tim Powers

* * *

Disputes over inheritance can become bitter and acrimonious enough to split families apart forever. And when
the family involved is a family of magicians, things can get
much *worse.*

Tim Powers is the author of fourteen novels, including
Last Call and *Declare,* both of which won the World Fantasy
Award; and *The Anubis Gates* and *Dinner at Deviant's Palace,*
which both won the Philip K. Dick Memorial Award. His
other novels include *The Drawing of the Dark, Expiration Date,
Earthquake Weather, The Stress of Her Regard,* and *On Stranger
Tides,* which was the basis of the fourth Pirates of the Carib-
bean movie. His short work has been collected in *Night Moves
and Other Stories, Strange Itineraries,* and *The Bible Repairman
and Other Stories,* which won him another World Fantasy
Award. His most recent book is *Down and Out in Purgatory:
The Collected Stories of Tim Powers.* He lives in San Bernardino,
California, with his wife, Serena.

* * *

The Governor

TIM POWERS

North of Hollywood Boulevard the 101 freeway cuts through the Cahuenga Pass, with Mulholland Drive tracing the hill ridges to the west and the half-mile-long Hollywood Reservoir, which Lucy always said had the silhouette of a scared cat, lying just over a rise to the east. Beyond the reservoir the hills ascend to a crest at Deronda Drive before falling away again toward Beachwood Canyon, and old Benjamin's house stood, as it had for at least a hundred years, on the western downhill side of Deronda. The house was three stories, with the street-facing front door on the top floor and two downstairs floors at lower levels on the slope. Below the bottom floor, accessible by a new set of cement stairs, was an unpaved lot almost wide enough to accommodate the eight cars now parked in it, though an old Volkswagen van and a 1990s Buick were blocked in.

The house had stood unmoved through a dozen earthquakes and landslides over the years, though slopes and structures around it had several times slid downhill in the direction of the reservoir. In 1948, so the family story went, a landslide had broken off one side of a swimming pool up the hill across the street from the front door, and though the water had poured down the slope and through a row of cypress trees and had flooded the pavement, the water had splashed up and stopped just short of the old man's property, as if at an invisible wall. Lacking sandbags, the family had hastily shoveled piles of dirt against the front edge of the halted water to provide an explanation for its unnatural restraint, though in fact it all flowed away down the street so quickly that neighbors never even had a chance to notice its odd hesitancy at the border of the old man's place. New owners of the house up the hill had put in another swimming pool sometime in the sixties, and Benjamin had laid in a stock of impressive-looking sandbags in case it should happen again.

In the other direction, a balcony on the middle floor looked west across the descending slopes of roofs and trees to the reservoir and the distant freeway, and the glass door had been slid open.

Benjamin's eldest daughter had stepped out of the house and carefully set a martini glass on the balcony rail as the wind from the west fluttered her short green-striped white hair. "We need to get custody of him," she said. "He should not have been driving."

"If we *can* get some kind of custody," said her older brother, who had walked out behind her, "then it's really a *good thing* he was driving." His black Adidas sweatsuit was tight over his abdomen, and he tugged absently at the waistband. "It could be the best thing we could have hoped for."

"Colin!" came a call from inside. "Imogene! No talking privately."

Imogene reached for her glass and knocked it off balance, but she quickly frowned at it and it righted itself, having spilled only a few drops of gin. When she had picked it up and she and her brother had stepped back into the dining room, the man who had called them waved to a couple of unoccupied chairs at the long mahogany table that ran the length of the room. Seven people were already seated, and a couple more stood over drinks by the bar in the corner. The breeze through the open sliding glass door carried the scents of mesquite and sage, and afternoon sunlight reflected off the polished table and threw patches of light on the ceiling beams.

"We weren't saying anything secret, Blaine," said Imogene. "Just that we need to get him put away someplace."

At the other end of the table a chubby fellow with a two-day beard stubble said, "We've got to find him first—find his talisman, I mean. When exactly did he die?"

Colin had sat down beside Imogene. He looked at his watch and said, "Six hours and a bit ago, according to the Highway Patrol. I expect he's at Forest Lawn by now."

"Forest Lawn by Griffith Park? Burials there start at around seven or eight thousand dollars."

"That's hardly our immediate—" began Blaine, but he halted when footsteps sounded on the stairs. "Lucy," he said quickly to a girl standing by the bar, "did you call anyone else? You didn't call Vivian, did you?"

"No," said Lucy, the youngest of them. Her dark hair was parted in the middle and hung straight down to her narrow shoulders, and she was wearing a baggy pullover sweater and a plaid skirt. "The only one I called who isn't here yet was Tom."

"The old man's court fool," said Colin.

"Better than an ex-wife," muttered another of the siblings, a lean middle-aged man in a Polo shirt who liked to be called Skipper. "She'd still boss us all around like we were kids."

Colin and Imogene exchanged a superior glance. They had both moved out of the house by the time Benjamin had married Vivian.

From the stairs now came a clatter that could only be old Benjamin's rack of fencing foils being knocked off the wall.

Blaine's gaze rolled toward the ceiling. "He comes, like the catastrophe of the old comedy."

"I suppose that's *from* something," said Imogene, with a weary sigh.

Skipper nodded morosely. "*Lear,* act two. Enter Edgar, the fool." A wasp had come in through the open door and was buzzing around the table; he pointed at it, and it flared brightly and fell smoldering to the table.

One of his sisters clicked her tongue and swatted the thing off the table with her hat. "I suppose you expect poor Lucy to re-wax the—" She halted, for Tom had finally shuffled into the room.

◆　◆　◆

Tom blinked around in confusion. He couldn't remember the last time all of his siblings, from all three of his father's marriages, had been in one room together. The only one he really knew was Lucy, who must now be about seventeen; before he had moved out two years ago, he and Lucy had been the only ones who still lived here with the old man. Since then it had been just Lucy.

"Hallo, Tom," called Evelyn, one of the middle-range older sisters. "What's the good word?"

Tom had never known any answer to that, though Evelyn always asked it, and he just shook his head and then pushed his disordered dark hair back from his sweaty forehead.

"Lucy didn't drive you," remarked Imogene. "How did you get here, Tommy?"

"Walked," he said. "Up from the bus stop at Westshire."

"With feet for oars," observed Blaine, "plying with speed your partnership of legs."

"Housman," said Skipper gloomily, "'Fragment of a Greek Tragedy.'"

Walking self-consciously toward the bar, Tom took quick, sidelong glances at his siblings, noting changes. There was Blaine, going bald and apparently making up for it with a gray goatee over his black turtleneck sweater; Tom recalled that Blaine was sometimes able to read minds, and played poker a lot at the Bicycle and Commerce casinos because of that, but Benjamin had said that Blaine relied so heavily on his occasional advantage that he never properly learned the strategies of the game, and wound up living almost entirely on the allowance Benjamin provided. And at the other end of the table were Colin and Imogene; Imogene claimed to be a fortune-teller to movie stars, and for all Tom knew, it was true, though she had never brought any around when Tom had lived here. Colin drove a convertible Porsche but did nothing at all that Tom was aware of. Both their faces were smoother and glossier than when Tom had last seen them, and he guessed that they had "had work done." Everybody said the old house badly needed to have work done, and Tom had only the vaguest idea of what the phrase might mean.

"Lucy," Evelyn went on, "you've been living here with him. Where would he hide something like that?"

Lucy handed Tom a can of Coke, without his asking, and he smiled his thanks. The two of them were the only ones who didn't drink.

Lucy, he thought, was looking thinner than she had when he had last seen her, and she was surely too young for the new lines in her cheeks. Her sole gift was that she could sometimes chill things, so in spite of her age she was generally the bartender, though her efforts tended to make the room uncomfortably warm. All Tom could do in the way of the uncanny was to conjure up smells during moments of stress—usually the aroma of Ovaltine.

A chessboard lay at one end of the bar, with the various pieces arranged in four rows. Tom idly picked up one that looked like a castle.

Lucy looked past him. "Like what?"

"A talisman," said Evelyn. "Like   a box, a picture . . ." She waved at Tom and added, "A chess piece! But it'll have his horoscope sign on it, Libra. That'll either be a picture of scales—that's those two dishes on chains that you weigh things in—or the constellation itself; it looks like a kid's drawing of a house, with bent walls."

"Do we destroy it?" asked the chubby fellow. Tom was surprised to recognize him as Alan, who, years ago now, had tried without success to teach him to swim.

"No, idiot," said Imogene. "What, you want toothaches, bad eyes—?"

"Cancer," added Colin, "strokes . . ."

Blaine stood up and stepped toward the bar. Tom was still holding the chess piece, but hastily replaced it when Blaine gave him a crooked grin and said, "You up for a game, Tommy? Shall I spot you that rook? Hmm? No?"

Blaine played chess a lot at the Los Angeles Chess Club and frequently pointed out that he was rated a Class A player, which was apparently the best.

Tom's hands were shaking, and he had set the castle piece on the edge of the board; it fell over and rolled off the bar and hit the floor, and Tom bumped his head bending to pick it up.

Blaine shook his head and turned toward the table. "If we can *find* the talisman, and get custody, get him contained," he said, "we can *threaten* him with its destruction, if need be. And we can probably keep him quiescent by telling him we're looking for a body he can move into.

We'll use a Ouija board—have him list what characteristics he'd like, how we should prepare the person—and then we could tell him we're searching high and low for somebody. We could string it out for years!"

An old man with a long white beard stirred at the far end of the table. It was William, who Tom was pretty sure was Benjamin's eldest son, probably over ninety by now. He was always frowning and dignified, but Lucy said he looked like a sidekick in a western movie, who would at some point do a comical dance in the dusty street outside the saloon. "How will you contain him?" he asked in a gravelly voice.

"Uh," said Blaine, "Colin?"

Colin frowned. "Sink his talisman in some non-conductive fluid like glycerine so he won't arc and get one of us. And in some solidly moored container, so he can't shake it over. We've got to—"

"Glycerine's hygroscopic," objected Alan. "It attracts water, which would have minerals in it, so before long it would be a conductor. Transformer oil is what you want."

"What if it's a houseplant?" demanded William testily. "A bonsai tree?"

"Lucy, did he have a bonsai?" asked Blaine.

Lucy just shook her head and shrugged.

"Then we can make a Faraday cage out of coathangers and tinfoil or something," said Colin impatiently. "But we have to *find* it."

Evelyn leaned back and looked at the ceiling. "It's a big house," she said, "the wizard's castle. Cluttered up with a hundred years' worth of junk."

"And he might have it off-site," added Alan. "God knows who might touch it."

A woman Tom didn't even recognize shoved her chair back and stood up. "Oh, why did he think he could still drive, at his age?" she wailed. "Damned old fool."

Beside Tom, Lucy clenched her fists. "The Highway Patrol says the other car cut him off!" she burst out. "And he was smarter than any of you!"

That was certainly true. Tom himself was barely able to read and write, but though many of the other siblings were MENSA members, they had little to show in the way of accomplishments, while old Benja-

min had read Greek and Latin and could do math that was all parenthe-
ses and Greek letters, and had written books on philosophy and physics,
and had even written several volumes of poetry. When Tom had still
lived here, he had often wandered through the old man's top-floor library, pulling down books and trying to understand them. He had always been chagrined, and vaguely surprised, to find that he could not.

"Said the Madwoman of Chaillot," muttered Imogene.

"We need to search the house, top to bottom," said Alan. "Lucy, are
there rubber gloves somewhere? A lot of them?"

"Search in pairs," interjected Skipper, "and not ones who are friendly
with each other, like Colin and Imogene."

Colin and Imogene looked at each other with mutual disdain.
"Friendly?" whispered Imogene, shaking her head.

"Or Tom and Lucy," said Evelyn. "In fact, Tom shouldn't—"

Abruptly an old rotary-dial telephone on a bookshelf beside the bar
began ringing. Several people at the table jumped, and Blaine slapped
Lucy's hand away when she reached for the receiver.

"That's him!" exclaimed Evelyn. "He's been listening to us! You and
your . . . *transformer oil!*"

"Shut up!" said Blaine. "I'll get it."

"Put it on speaker!" called Colin.

"You don't trust me? Anyway, this doesn't have a speaker." Blaine
picked up the receiver. "Hello?" After a few seconds he shook his head
and hung up. "Nothing, nobody there."

"Oh, he was *there* all right," said old William. "And as soon as he gets
another body, he'll be *here*. Displeased."

"Shut up!" said Blaine again, more loudly. "What if it *was* him? He
hasn't got a body yet. So let's find his damned talisman before he gets
one. Pair up, everybody, and no allies together."

"Tommy should leave," said Evelyn. "Gertrude said he was bad luck
or something. No offense, Tommy! And Lucy should just wait here in
the dining room."

Gertrude had been Tom's mother, Benjamin's wife before Vivian. All
Tom knew about her was that she had been some sort of fortune-teller,
and had killed herself in 2005. He had been a small child at the time,
and he had no recollection of her, though in old photographs she was

beautiful. He had never heard that she'd said he was bad luck, but he was far too intimidated in this crowd to ask about it.

"Yes," said Imogene, "he couldn't understand what sort of thing to look for anyway. Tom, it's been lovely seeing you, but you might as well scram."

Tom had been enjoying the air-conditioned draft on his face, but he took one last sip of his Coke and set the can down on the bar. "Okay."

"I'll drive you back to your apartment," said Lucy. "And I should go see to things at Forest Lawn. You and I are the ones who knew him best, but they don't want our help here."

The woman who had called Benjamin an old fool bared her teeth and made pushing-away gestures. "Oh, Lucy, don't say that. It's just that you might be on his *side.*"

"We're all on his side," protested Blaine. "We want what's best for him, which is . . ."

"To step down," suggested Colin. "Wizard emeritus."

"Give somebody else a chance," agreed Skipper, narrowly eyeing his siblings.

Tom and Lucy crossed to the stairs leading down, and behind him Tom heard Imogene laugh and say, "Who will bell the cat?"

The floor below the dining room was a maze of tiny interconnected rooms, all fretted from floor to ceiling with shelves, and no room big enough for more than one chair. The inner ones were lit by dim yellow lamps attached to the ceiling, and all of them were permeated with the vanilla smell of old book paper and, faintly, the tarry reek of the old man's pipe tobacco. As Tom and Lucy threaded their way along the shortest path through the rooms to the bottom door and the stairs down to the parking lot, Tom glanced wistfully at all the book spines facing him on the shelves.

"What are all these about?" he asked Lucy, waving at a shelf they were passing.

"Down here are all the books that lost their charm for him," said Lucy. "Religion, mostly—Chesterton, C. S. Lewis, George MacDonald. He decided they weren't good for his psyche, but lately I seem to spend most of my time down here."

Tom reflected that he knew no more now than he had before he'd asked. "My—" he began; then he started again: "Do you know why my mother would have said I was bad luck?"

Lucy paused in one of the doorways to look back at him. "No, I never heard anything like that. Evelyn's head is just full of old gossip and superstitions jumbled together anyway." She gave him a troubled look, and the air was a few degrees cooler. "You want to come along with me to Forest Lawn?"

"I— No, not yet. I'm sorry. I just—"

She nodded. "Never mind; I know." She led the way through another tiny room. "I think you and I were the only ones who loved him."

"What happens if they don't find his ... talisman? If nobody finds it?"

"I don't know." They had reached the back door, and she pulled it open. Sunlight spilled across the worn wooden floor, and they could hear the breezes moving across the hills. Lucy's plaid skirt fluttered around her thin legs. "Maybe he'd just be—you know, dead."

Tom was squinting in the sudden glare. "Is that maybe the best thing?"

"The way they all talk—maybe."

Tom followed her down the cement steps.

"They've got me blocked in," Lucy said crossly. "I'm going to have to drive over the flower bed to get out."

"That's okay, I can walk back down to Westshire."

"No, I couldn't stand staying in the house with them. The flowers are all dead anyway."

Tom's apartment was in an old building on Franklin, and when he had waved goodbye to Lucy as she drove away in her Buick, he trudged up the dozen red-painted steps to the front door. His rooms were on the second floor at the back, with windows overlooking a parking lot and garage and the back windows of another apartment building.

As he trudged down the dim corridor toward his door—tired, and glad Lucy had saved him the walk back to the bus stop—he saw a streak of daylight across the carpet. His door was partly open, and he caught the scent of cigarette smoke.

He stopped, then slowly stepped forward and pushed the door open.

The kitchen was straight ahead, with its view of palm trees and roofs and other people's windows, and the living room was to the left, but a curl of smoke hung in the air to the right, in his bedroom doorway.

He swallowed. "Who's there?"

"Come in, Tommy," said a woman's voice, and when he took the two steps to the doorway and looked in, he saw by the glow through the venetian blinds that Vivian was sitting on his narrow bed. Half a dozen tobacco pipes were laid out on the bedspread next to her purse, and a cigarette smoldered in a saucer on the bedside table.

"Did Benjamin give you these?" she asked him.

Tom hadn't seen Vivian since she and Benjamin had got divorced five years earlier; she was wearing a white pantsuit and a fur cape today, with a crescent of pearls around her corded neck, and white kid gloves made her long fingers look like crab legs.

He gathered that she was referring to the pipes. "Yes. He thought I might like to smoke them."

She stood up and retrieved her cigarette and tucked it between her lips, and the coal glowed in the dim room. "Uh huh," she said, each syllable a puff of smoke. "Did you?"

Tom shrugged and shook his head. "I can't keep them lit."

Vivian leaned down and picked up one of the pipes. She stared at it, then said, "Dunhill. And you've got a Castello, and a Sasieni Four Dot—these are expensive pipes."

"He's generous. Was."

She cocked her head. "To you?"

"Sure. To us all. This apartment, the allowance . . . He gave me those books there . . ."

"Fragments shored against your ruin," Vivian muttered. Tom noticed that her breath smelled of liquor. She stepped past him to the dresser, on the top of which stood an uneven row of books, hardcover and paperback.

"Turn on the light, Tommy," she said, and when he had reluctantly flicked the switch on the wall, she ran her gloved hand up and down over the top edges of the books.

"Andre Norton, Heinlein, Brackett," she noted, and her fingers paused on a tall black hardcover book. "Lovecraft, *The Outsider*. That one's worth some money, even banged up like this." She pulled it out and flipped it open to look at the endpapers; the cover, attached now only by threads, nearly fell off. The page edges were marbled, and she held the book up in both hands and stared at the pattern of red and blue swirls on the block of pages for nearly half a minute, before shaking her head and turning it over to look at the endpapers in the back. Finally she gripped the book by the spine and shook it. A bus pass fell out and fluttered to the floor.

"My bookmark," said Tom ruefully. "I guess I never would have got very far."

"I'd sell it if I were you. I don't know if the allowances are going to continue now." She slid the book back in its place on the dresser. "Why these books?"

"I liked that movie *Star Wars*. He thought I might like science fiction books. But," he added miserably, "I'm too dumb."

She was riffling through the other books, shaking them and peering at the covers. "No Libra," she muttered, "picture or constellation." She put the last one back and turned to face him.

"When you were about five," she said, "he spent a week playing checkers with you—just talking to you and moving the pieces back and forth, over and over again, while you watched."

Tom blinked. "Oh."

"My Jaguar won't go faster than a hundred and forty-nine miles per hour," she went on, "not that I'd ever want to go near that fast. But it's got a limiter, a governor, installed by the manufacturer. James Watt invented governors for engines in the eighteenth century. When an engine gets close to going faster than somebody wants it to, the governor chokes off the fuel."

Tom had no idea what to say, and simply stared at her.

She looked down and grimaced. "It's contemptible of me to feel virtuous for trying to explain it to you. I'm taking two of the pipes, Tommy.

You don't smoke them, and the bird's-eye grain on them could arguably look like the five brightest stars in Libra."

"Don't take him!" exclaimed Tom; and now the close air was rich with the malty smell of Ovaltine.

Vivian sniffed, and smiled crookedly. "He said he used to bring you Ovaltine, when you were sick. I'm sorry you're upset, Tommy. I am taking them."

His shoulders slumped. He couldn't prevail against his stepmother. "What will you do with him?" he asked dejectedly.

"Keep him from you kids, mainly. It was hell being married to him, but I don't want them having custody of him." She grinned, but Tom could tell it wasn't a happy expression. "I loved him, you see. All of us did."

Tom knew she meant Benjamin's wives. "My mother killed herself."

Vivian ground out her cigarette in the saucer. "Because she loved him and she loved you too. Hah! What's a mother to do, eh?" She dropped two of the pipes into her purse and snapped it shut, then pushed him aside and walked into the short hall.

Tom followed her. "Was I bad luck for him?" He hadn't been out of breath after climbing the stairs, but he was panting now. "Evelyn says my mother said I was. She was a fortune-teller, right?"

Vivian turned around and leaned against the door. "Oh, Tommy! Damn it, you loved him too, didn't you? You and Lucy. You were his last kids; I never gave him any. And I think you were the first ones he paid attention to, took some responsibility for. He used to play that Sinatra song, 'Soliloquy,' from *Carousel*—it's about a guy wondering if he'll be a good father to a son or a daughter. He— But your mother wasn't a fortune-teller, she was an *oracle.*" She looked past him at the kitchen. "You don't have any liquor, I suppose."

"No, I— Coffee, Coke—"

"Never mind. I'm driving and I don't need another DUI." She opened her purse, fished out a flat silver box, and opened it. Six cigarettes were lined up inside, and she took one out and lit it with a blocky silver lighter.

"You weren't any child of mine," she said, exhaling smoke, "but Benjamin felt he had to explain. Your mother apparently used to burn leaves and go into trances sniffing the smoke, and one time in a trance she told him that you—you'd have been maybe four years old—told him you'd one day outsmart him, and he'd die because of it." She stared at him in apparent puzzlement. "He *could* have *killed* you—but he loved you."

"Out*smart* him? That's—" Tom was at a loss for words.

"I know. Impossible. See you around, kid." She turned and opened the door, and then she was hurrying away down the corridor.

Tom closed the door, bolted it, and shambled back into the bedroom. He looked at the four pipes that still lay on the bedspread; he had been keeping his father's talisman without even knowing it, and somehow he had let Vivian take it. At least she would keep it away from Blaine and Colin and Imogene. At least she loved him.

"I'm sorry, father," he said softly to the remaining pipes.

He bent to pick up his bus pass bookmark from the floor, and looked at the black spine of *The Outsider*. Vivian had said it was worth some money, and that the allowances might stop. If they did stop, he supposed he'd have to go live at his father's house again, and every single room of it would now be a place where his father was achingly absent.

Sadly he pulled *The Outsider* out from between the other books— and he nearly dropped it, for it was heavier than he remembered, heavier than it had seemed when Vivian had been handling it. And it brought back a sudden vivid memory of the moment the book had passed from his father's hands to his; it had been early on a spring morning last year, and Tom had still been in his pajamas when the old man had surprised him by showing up at his door with the book.

For a moment now Tom just stood beside the dresser, with no recol- lection of what he had been doing; then he looked at the book in his hands and at the computer sitting on his desk in the corner, and nodded.

He crossed to the desk and pulled out the chair and sat down, laying the book beside the keyboard. He knew how to get to Google, and now he brought it up and typed in *sell lovecraft book*. He had to flip open the book to see how to spell *Lovecraft*.

What appeared on the monitor screen were a lot of eBay and Abe- Books pages, but he knew he could never figure out how to sell the book through those sites; and there were a lot of sites that just seemed to be people bragging that they had Lovecraft books. But at last he found a

bookseller's list with a sidebar saying that he bought books. The man
was in L.A., so Tom nervously punched the 818 area-code number into
his phone.

When a man's voice answered, Tom cleared his throat and haltingly
explained that he wanted to sell a copy of Lovecraft's *The Outsider*.

After getting a description of the title page, the bookseller said,
"Maybe. What condition is it in? Does it have a dust jacket?"

"I don't think so. What's a dust jacket?"

"Jeez. The paper cover that wraps around the book and folds in at the
boards. It'd be blue." When Tom admitted that it had nothing like that,
the man asked, "Are the pages browned around the edges?"

"Not brown—they're colored. If you hold the book up, there's swirls
of red and blue that go across all the page edges."

"It's *marbled*? Who would have done that? And I suppose the marbling ink soaked into the pages?"

Tom opened the book in the middle. The outer edges of both exposed pages were darkened in a band an eighth of an inch wide.

"Yes," he said. "About as wide as a toothpick."

"Weird. I can only imagine what sort of vise somebody had to hold
it in, to do that. Are the covers loose?"

"Well, they're almost off. It's just threads holding them on."

A sigh. "It's a curiosity, a token for somebody who wants to be able
to say he owns an *Outsider*. Nothing more than that. I guess I could give
you a hundred bucks for it."

"I've got to think about it," Tom said, and ended the call.

So much for that.

He laid the book on the desk and frowned for a moment at the apparently undesirable marbled staining, and he reached out to push the
book away; but the heel of his hand only caught the top board, and the
spine rolled flat, spreading the vertical stack of pages into a slope.

And the marbling was gone, replaced by a black rectangle with white
spots on it.

Tom blinked in surprise and leaned forward, touching the spread
pages. The narrow line of darkness at the edge of each page, which he
had thought was the marbling ink soaking into the paper, was, he realized, something else: each was a thin segment of an image that was only

visible when the pages were fanned out. Someone—his father?—had apparently spread the book's pages in this way and then painted a picture across the eighth-of-an-inch-exposed page edges, so that the picture would disappear when the book was closed. The marbling, Tom reasoned, had been done afterward, to provide an explanation for the narrow dark band along the outer edge of each page. The picture was apparently not meant to be discovered.

But what was it? Eight white dots on a black background, arranged like a wobbly, peaked structure—

. . . like a kid's drawing of a house, with bent walls, Evelyn had said. *Libra . . . the constellation itself.*

Tom knew that *constellation* meant an arrangement of stars in the sky.

And Blaine had said, *If we can* find *the talisman . . . we can* threaten *him with its destruction.*

Tom's heart was pounding. Vivian doesn't have it, he thought; it isn't one of the pipes. I have it, it's this book. I have him, with me.

He slowly pulled the top board back level with the bottom one, restoring the book to its ordinary rectangular shape, and as the pages lined up again the constellation disappeared, replaced by the innocuous marbled pattern.

He stood up, his hands trembling as he held the book. I should hide it, he thought—Blaine and the others might come here and take away anything Benjamin ever gave me, just on the off chance that one of the things might be the talisman.

Under the bed, he thought, in the cupboard, under a couch cushion—dumb dumb dumb! Think!

But instead of a hiding place, he found himself thinking of the pages of the book. When he had opened it in the middle to see if marbling ink had soaked into the pages, he had seen narrow lines on the outer edges of *both* exposed pages, the one on the right and the one on the left. The line on the right had been part of the picture of stars. What about the line on the left? Was it part of a picture that would be visible if the book's pages were fanned out the other way?

He laid the book back down on the desk and turned it over. Hesitantly he pushed back the board that was now on top, rolling the spine flat and spreading the pages into a ramp.

And the breath froze in his throat and his scalp tightened, for he was staring into the wrinkled face, into the glittering eyes, of his father, and his father's eyes seemed to be fixed on Tom's with eager recognition. The picture was intensely realistic, a photograph, a hologram . . .

Tom wasn't able to look away, but a shrill humming started up in his throat as the mouth of the face in the picture moved, opened and closed, and the sparse gray hair shifted as if in some otherworldly breeze. Tom's own head was full of the smell of Ovaltine.

His phone buzzed in his shirt pocket, and he fumbled it free, turned it on, and blindly swiped his thumb across the screen. And his father's voice now rattled out of the tiny speaker.

"Tommy!" said old Benjamin, and a moment later the face in the picture mouthed the syllables. "Is that you?"

Tom just stared at the moving picture.

"Ah, it is." The face frowned, and when the voice on the phone spoke again, it was synchronized with the face's lips: "I hope you're alone!"

Tom started to say *Yes,* but his father was speaking again. "Good, good boy. If anybody comes in, *c-c-close this book.* I see your desk—you're in your apartment. Is the door locked? Ah, yes."

Tom hadn't yet spoken. And it occurred to him that his father's image was looking up at him; it was Tom himself who was looking down at the desk. Was his father looking through Tom's eyes?

"Never mind that," said Benjamin. "Where's Lucy?"

"She's at," Tom began; his father's voice interrupted with "At Forest Lawn," but Tom doggedly finished his sentence: "—at Forest Lawn. I can speak!"

"Sorry, boy," said the voice from the phone, "of course you can, of course you can. Forest Lawn, good; they can cremate that body after I meet Lucy."

Tom's view of the book blurred away, and for a moment he seemed to be standing in a paneled office, looking at a middle-aged man in a dark suit and tie who was holding a sheaf of papers. The man was speaking, but the only word Tom was able to recognize was one he had just heard—*cremate.*

Tom shook his head, and the vision dissolved, leaving him swaying unsteadily in front of his desk, still staring down at the face in the book pages. The vision had seemed to be a memory, though certainly not one of his own.

He sat down and tried to remember what his father had been saying. "Meet Lucy?" he said finally. "You want me to show her this book?"

"*Yes,* Tommy. Pay attention now. You're slippery."

And a phrase popped into his head: *Mea culpa, sed non maxima!* Tom didn't know Latin, but the thought felt as if it meant something like, *My own fault, but not serious.*

"*I* could call her," said Benjamin's voice, "but she won't—" A thought flickered over the surface of Tom's mind, snatched away too quickly for him to catch. "She won't *be upset* if it's you who calls her. Tell her you need to see her, have her come here."

"Okay. But—I can't—" Tom struggled to find the words to describe the problem. He sensed that his father knew what he was trying to express, but was courteously letting him say it for himself. "I'd have to end this call," Tom said finally, "to call her."

The head in the picture seemed to nod, and the voice from the phone said, "That's fine. Just have her come to your apartment and touch the book, and open it, as you did."

"It's heavier now," said Tom. "The book. Vivian picked it up a few minutes ago, and it didn't look heavy."

"Vivian was there in your apartment? It couldn't have been today, Tommy, not if she touched it."

"Well, she had gloves on."

"Oh, there you are then. She was always cautious! But Lucy won't be wearing gloves."

The word *gloves* hung in Tom's mind, and evidently in Benjamin's too, for Tom got a quick image of one glove being pulled off a hand and tossed aside, to be quickly replaced by another, which buttoned at the cuff.

Baffled and uneasy, Tom tried to look away from the picture on the book pages, and discovered that he could not.

It panicked him. "Let go!" he grunted, gripping the desk with his left hand for traction but still unable to move his head. He gasped, and again smelled Ovaltine.

"Don't fight me, Tommy!" said the phone in his right hand. "I've always known what's best for you all, haven't I?"

"You're wearing me right now," Tom said breathlessly, "but you want to wear Lucy. And button her on."

For a moment the phone was silent; then, "I wondered if you'd reciprocally see my thoughts too," came his father's voice. "But that's pretty good, Tommy! Inference, extrapolation from an analogy! I was right to take precautions with you." Tom watched as his right hand raised the cellphone. "Now call Lucy, get her over here, there's a good boy."

Tom tried without success to push his arm back down; but he took a deep breath, glad that he still had control of his lungs and throat. "I won't," he said. "You're going to . . . take her body, *be* her, now that you got killed yourself."

"No, no, Tommy. I just want to—" began his father's voice.

"Now you're *lying* to me!" Tommy blinked away tears, still staring helplessly into his father's eyes. "I can tell. It's like . . . it's like you're talking in another direction."

Again there was no voice from the phone for several seconds. Then his father said, "Try to understand, Tommy, she won't be gone. It's just that I'll be with her, I'll be—"

"Controlling her! Doing what *you* want, not what she wants!"

"*Yes,* and she'll have a better life for it! Look at her now, lonely, introverted—but *young!* With me, she'll travel, study, write! She'll thank me for it one day, you'll see. Or she would."

"G-get married? Have children?"

"Who knows? Hormones . . . Eventual offspring might be a—"

"All what *you* decide, not what she wants."

Tom wasn't touching the book, but the pages shifted slightly, so that the face seemed to be peering from behind a screen of thread-thin horizontal white lines; a moment later the pages had realigned, and the face was clear again.

"Tommy, damn it, will you just—? What I decide has always been best for you all—and I'll consider her preferences, to the extent that—"

"You won't even know what her . . . *preferences* are. I'll call her, all right—and tell her all this, let her make up her own mind if it's so good for her."

"No, you won't, trust me. If I have to—"

"I can't believe you'd want to do this! *You!* Even *I* can see it's a terrible thing!"

"Tommy, think! If it was wrong, I wouldn't ask you to do it, would I? Don't make me take harsh—"

Tom interrupted with the question he had to ask. "Why don't you want *me?*"

The eyes on the book pages narrowed and the brows contracted, and for a moment the mouth opened slackly. Then the lips firmed up, and his father's voice said, "Okay, Tommy, okay. I guess you deserve an answer." The phone was silent then, but just when Tom was about to speak, his father went on, "Seventeen years ago I did something I had to do, but which I'm not proud of. You were five years old, and for a week we played checkers for an hour every day. It was hypnosis, for openers, but then I used my particular gift to climb into your head, like I'm doing now—and I embedded a powerful command into the fabric of your memory."

"A governor," ventured Tom.

". . . I suppose it was that, yes. How did you—? But I've given you a good life, haven't I, Tommy? You've never wanted for anything. And knowledge is but sorrow's spy, as Davenant said. I felt I had to—"

"Was this *Davenant* one of the books I couldn't read?"

A sigh rattled out of the phone. "Yes, Tommy. Yes. Listen, an oracle told me that you would one day outsmart me, as she put it, and cause my death, so— Oh. I see you already know it was your mother. Understand, I could easily have simply killed you, to prevent that. But I loved you. I love you still. So, instead, I gave you a block against learning, against being capable of systematic thought. You see? So that you could never in any instance—"

"Outsmart you." Tom took a deep breath and let it out. "All these years."

"But! I can remove it! You were an extraordinarily bright boy, and you can be again! You can learn, you'll be able to read Tolstoy! In Russian! Dante in medieval Italian! Read Einstein's tensor calculus field equations!"

"Beat Blaine at chess."

"Yes! But it will take some work to remove the block. I'll need to hypnotize you again and sort through your memories, with backward mutters of dissevering power, in Milton's phrase, to excise that specific one. Drugs might be required, but I can assuredly do it."

Tom sighed. His neck was aching because of the prolonged inclination of his head. "But not while you're just in this book here."

"No. I'd need to be in a body."

"Lucy's."

"You know it's something she would want to do. And I know you'd never do anything that would cause *her* death. The oracle's prophecy will prove to have been wrong."

"I would never have done anything to cause *your* death, either. I don't care what my mother said."

Tom thought of the books he had so often pulled down from the shelves over the years, hopelessly trying to puzzle out each first page, and then slid back into their places—*The Book of the Thousand Nights and a Night* in three boxed volumes, *Flatland, Fear and Trembling,* and a hundred others—and he imagined their paragraphs now opening like flowers, lighting like candles, parting like cobwebbed shutters to reveal the unbounded extent of a whole living world. And he imagined understanding the now-incomprehensible relationships that linked things into developing patterns: atoms, chess pieces, stars, people. . . .

And *this* book he could close and put away. He need never look at it again.

And that would be good, he thought, because if he were to do as Benjamin advised, and then years later look into this book again, the picture on the page edges might be Lucy's face. It would be her eyes staring up into his.

Even if he never looked, it would still be Lucy's face hidden in the pages, behind the marbling.

"I," he whispered fearfully, "won't do it. I *can't*. I'm sorry. I'll warn her."

Tom felt as if he were standing on the terribly narrow top of a very high wall, looking up. He had never disobeyed his father before, and he was dizzy with the dislocation of it.

"You can do as I say," said the voice from his phone, "and have everything. Or, if you'd rather, you can disobey me and have nothing. It would take external effort to remove the governor I stitched into your memory, but *right now,* as I withdraw from this intrusion into your mind, I can simply take *all* of your memory away with me. Delete all, no careful differentiation. You'd probably still have language, and basic skills like buttoning a shirt, but you wouldn't even know who you were, much less what year it is, or what country you're in, or who Lucy is."

Tears were running down Tom's cheeks, but when they dripped from his chin they fell to the carpet in front of the desk, not on the book. "My . . . going-away present, from you," he said hoarsely. "First you give me the governor, then you erase me."

"*No,* Tommy, that won't happen," his father said softly, persuasively, "because you'll do what I say, and then everybody will be better off."

Tom thought again of his sister's face, not yet lost. "I can't," he whispered. "It's not—one of the things that can happen."

"Ah, Tommy, I'm afraid I made it impossible to reason with you! *Sic fiat.*" The flavor of the phrase let Tom know that it meant something like, *So be it.*

In his peripheral vision Tom saw his own right hand lay the phone down beside the book, and then pull open the top drawer; it lifted out a Bic pen and an envelope, and Tom watched as his hand wrote out words in its habitual blocky capitals:

BENJAMIN CAN RETURN—
  BUT FIRST YOU MUST CAREFULLY READ THIS BOOK.

Tom had tried to make his hand resist his father's control, but hadn't even managed to make any of the letters wobble. Now his father was speaking from the phone again—with at least some perceptible effort, since Tom was trying to impede the old man's thoughts.

"Now—you're stronger than I thought, Tommy!—now I'll call Lucy, and I won't say anything. She'll recognize your number and call back, and when there's—let me speak!—when there's no reply, she'll undoubtedly come over here, and read this message. And now I'll leave you, Tommy—sadly. I wish you had trusted me."

But while Benjamin had been concentrating on speaking, Tom had regained enough control of his right hand to draw two deeply pressed lines through some of the letters it had written. And as he did it, he made himself think of nothing but Lucy holding her phone.

"Yes," said Benjamin, catching that insistent image, "she'll answer. And I'm sure she'll be here soon. But you—"

A rushing sound echoed from the phone.

Tom whimpered involuntarily as he felt his memories squashed discordantly together, seized, and uprooted.

"—won't know who she is," said Benjamin's voice.

The young man blinked around at the room he found himself in. There was a bed, a desk, a black-bound book lying beside a boxy plastic thing— someone lived here. He held still and listened, but heard nothing but a low background susurration, remote and constant.

Faintly on the air he could catch two smells—one acrid, and one malty and mildly sweet. Neither one seemed unfamiliar in his nose. He let himself relax, cautiously.

Do I *live here?* he wondered.

An envelope with writing on it lay beside the computer's keyboard, and he leaned forward to peer at it. It read,

BENJAMIN CAN RETURN—
        BUT FIRST YOU MUST CAREFULLY READ THIS BOOK.

The crossing-out lines were heavily scored into the paper, and he considered the letters that remained untouched:

B URN
        THIS BOOK

The pen beside the envelope seemed to have been used to write the words, and he picked it up and let his hand copy BURN THIS BOOK below the previous writing. The handwriting was the same.

Evidently he himself, whoever he might be, had written the message. It was seeming more likely that he did live here.

And, perhaps anticipating this loss of memory, he had left this message where he would be sure to see it. At one time he had apparently wanted himself to read the black book, so that someone named Benjamin might return . . . from someplace . . . but had then emphatically changed his mind.

He could surely trust himself, couldn't he?

A flat, glass-covered rectangle on the desk began making a chiming sound. He stared at it in bewilderment, and after a few seconds it fell silent.

He reached out to touch it, then thought better and withdrew his hand. There was no telling what the thing might be.

Like the last few images in a dream, glimpsed for a moment upon waking before disappearing forever, he caught a fleeting impression of a castle falling, and a voice that said, *a house, with bent walls* . . .

Then the faintly recollected shreds were gone, like the last swirl of water going down a drain.

He walked out of the bedroom into a narrow kitchen, and looked out the window over the sink; he didn't know why he was looking at the buildings across the parking lot. Certainly none of *them* were falling down, if that's what had been in his mind.

Without thinking about it he reached to the side, opened the refrigerator, and lifted out a can of Coca-Cola; and he had popped it open and taken the first sip before it occurred to him that he had known—or at least his hand had known!—that there would be a Coke in there, on that shelf.

It seemed obvious that he did indeed live here. He should find the bathroom and look at himself in a mirror! See if there might be any sort of toothache remedy, for one of his back teeth had begun throbbing.

B URN THIS BOOK

But first he should probably carry out the order he had left for himself. The big letters, and the forceful lines through some of them, implied that it was important. When he had written that message, he had certainly known more than he knew now.

He walked back into the bedroom and put the Coke down on the desk, and picked up the black book. It was light, clearly very old and frail, and the covers appeared to be about to fall off. Past its time, he thought. He carried it out into the kitchen and pulled open the oven door, and laid the book on a pan that was in there.

He twisted the knob all the way to the left and instinctively switched on the fan over the stove. The old pages would probably catch fire pretty quickly.

But he turned back toward the bedroom—he had noticed other books in there, a row of them on a dresser—and he was suddenly aware of a powerful urge to read them, and then find out how to get more.

He knew nearly nothing, and he had no idea what the books might be about, but he was somehow certain that he would get a lot more out of them now than he ever had before.

Liz Williams

• • •

British writer Liz Williams has had work appear in *Inter-zone*, *Asimov's Science Fiction*, *Visionary Tongue*, *Subter-ranean*, *Terra Incognita*, *The New Jules Verne Adventures*, *Strange Horizons*, *Realms of Fantasy*, and elsewhere, and her stories have been collected in *The Banquet of the Lords of Night and Other Stories*, *A Glass of Shadow*, and, most recently, *The Light Warden*. She's probably best known for her Detective Inspector Chen series, detailing the exploits of a policeman in a demon-haunted world who literally has to go to Hell to solve some of his cases, and which include *Snake Agent*, *The Demon and the City*, *Precious Dragon*, *The Shadow Pavilion*, and *The Iron Khan*. Her other books include the novels *The Ghost Sister*, *Empire of Bones*, *The Poison Master*, *Nine Layers of Sky*, *Dark-land*, *Bloodmind*, *Banner of Souls*, and *Winterstrike*. Her most recent book is the start of the Worldsoul trilogy, *Worldsoul*. She lives in Glastonbury, England, where she and her hus-band, Trevor Jones, run a witchcraft shop—an experience they've written two books about, *Diary of a Witchcraft Shop 1* and *2*.

Here she tells the story of an obscure, quiet-living astronomer and part-time magician who (somewhat reluctantly) answers a call from some unusual petitioners to save the world from an unusual menace in a *most* unusual way . . .

◆　◆　◆

Sungrazer

LIZ WILLIAMS

Sometimes, in the church, I see a fireball eye looking at me from the shadows. It is as tiny as a button, a glowing ember beneath a pew, or lodged like a little joke in the face of one of the scowling Jacobean angels that feature on the end of every row. An angel, made demon. I think it's a joke, anyway. The eye never seems to appear near the altar: perhaps the power of Christ, greatest magician to walk this Earth, puts it off, or maybe it is simply shy. It is possible, indeed sometimes necessary, to imagine an angry god, but an enraged cherub is just funny. I suspect, you see, that the owner of the eye is in possession of a sense of humor.

I've never mentioned it to anyone, not even to my daughter or granddaughters, who have, God knows, enough secrets of their own. Women's stuff, to which as a man I'm not supposed to be privy and I probably couldn't see it even if I was supposed to. Presumably more proper these days to refer to it as "women's mysteries," but I just think of it as *stuff*—and before anyone starts complaining, I think of my own practice in the same way. Just stuff: the matter of Britain, the components of the World beyond the world.

Getting back to the eye, it's unthinkable to speak to the vicar about it: the old boy (he's younger than me, by the way) would probably have a heart attack. Or exorcise me. *Good Lord, Professor Fallow! What a very extraordinary thing to say. Are you feeling quite yourself?* No, let's not tell the vicar. It has always struck me as curious that this little old English church, which has such an odd history, is invariably put into the ecclesiastic hands of the most prosaic clerics, all scones and conservatism and tea. I wonder, though, if the church actually does know what it's doing and the incumbents are the ballast, the counterweights to the wild swing and sway of the building's own magic.

It's definitely not much to do with religion. Hard to say how I know: I do believe in the great Powers, you see, but I'm not entirely sure that all of them are the ones we're supposed to be worshipping on a Sunday morning. This eye, whatever it belongs to, seems too free range, although I never see it outside the church. Trapped? Possibly. But occasionally it winks at me, and that seems a bit too frivolous an act for something desperate to be free.

And this is the story of that eye.

On one particular Sunday, I had attended church as usual. I'm not an especially religious man, but it's the done thing in a small community, particularly if one is elderly. I'm not the local squire, but I suppose I'm the next best thing: my family has been here for a long time, in an old house. And I have two professions. One is respectable, if rather unusual: I'm an astronomer. I used to teach, at one of the Southwest universities not far from here and then at Oxford, but I've been retired for some years and now live permanently with my daughter and her children. My wife is dead. If you could see me now, you would see an entirely familiar sort of person: British, though not English, wearing an ancient tweed jacket and—outside church—a disreputable array of hats. I carry a walking stick, and I wish a good morning to the people I meet. It's like a kind of protective coloration: I blend well into my native habitat, like a duck-billed platypus.

The other profession? I'm a magician. You'll find out more about that in due course.

So, church. On that chilly January Sunday, with a bitter easterly whistling around the gargoyles and occasional thin rain, I did not see the eye. Its lack didn't really worry me one way or another; it was not a permanent phenomenon. I listened assiduously to the sermon, which was about aid to those less fortunate than oneself—a thoroughly Christian message, hard to disagree with—and sang some hymns. Then I buttoned up my coat, located my gloves—trying to start the new year off by not losing a pair a month like some daft old bugger—and went out into the winter.

Our house, which is called Moonecote, is not far from the church. I never bother to drive. I took the south path through the churchyard, what I thought of as the "river path," although the little Moone brook which runs alongside the bounds of the church is hardly a river. This is an old place and the graves are old, too, leaning to one side like drunks at a bar and so eroded and lichen coated that the names are scarcely visible anymore. There was a handful of daffodils on one of them now, already frost blighted, but the only other flowers in sight were a tiny bunch of snowdrops, coming up along the wall. No, there was another— I blinked.

It wasn't a flower, there against the wall of the churchyard. It was a flame.

I gave a quick glance over my shoulder. The rest of the meager congregation was either halfway to their cars or still in conversation with the vicar, who had his back turned to me. Just as well. I sidled up to the flame, which flickered with a deep red glow, most unwintry, and pretended to be fumbling with my hat. In an undertone, I said, "Who are you?"

There was no reply. I should probably explain at this point that this sort of thing isn't precisely unknown to me, quite apart from the presence of the eyeball in the church. The churchyard, as one might expect, is full of spirits. Most are the residue of the departed, as though a little door has been left open. And usually they're quite happy to chat, although one has to bear in mind that you're not always accessing the full force of the soul, which is happily elsewhere—who wants to hang around a damp English churchyard for eternity, after all? Some of them take the form of light: clusters of blue flashes, or a pale, steady glow. But I've seen flames before, and once a drop of water, hanging suspended in the air in a tiny lustrous globe. The elements, you see. I'm sure some of them just sink back invisibly into the earth.

This little flame was dancing. No voice answered, but it leaped up onto the wall and flickered, taking sustenance from nothing.

"Who are you?" I said again.

Help him.

Spirits speak like a breath on the wind. You have to learn how to listen.

"How can I help? Who is 'he'?"

You have to wake him.

"But who is he?"

When we ask, you must wake him.

Then it flickered and died, retreating into the wall. There was a faint glow for a second, like a patch of sunset, and it was gone.

I plodded home, somewhat amphibiously. The brook, swollen with recent rain, was high, brimming over the water meadows, but the path was safe enough. Fire and water, I thought. Water and fire. By the time I reached the house, the sky was stormy, with a single bar of light falling in the direction of the Severn estuary. The house itself, with its long drive, was quiet; it seemed to have retreated in on itself, huddling like an animal made of red Tudor brick. The kitchen garden was tidy and bare; the orchard empty of the crop of white apple sacks that had marked it throughout the autumn. There was a drift of smoke from the chimneys, but apart from that and the bar of light, the day was sodden, the color of lead. No more fire.

Alys, tall and rangy in jeans, was preparing Sunday lunch.

"Hello, dad! How was the service?"

"Went on a bit." I could have told her about the flickering light in the churchyard, but something held me back. Pretend we're a normal family, even if we know different.

"Oh, dear. I thought you were later than usual. Hope the church wasn't too cold." She bent over the Aga, fiddling with something on the stovetop.

"How was your morning? Can I do anything?"

"Quiet. And no, I don't think you can. Beatrice has pinched the *Telegraph* crossword, by the way."

I laughed. "It's too easy for me on a Sunday."

"Tell her that. She'll be annoyed."

Leaving her in the kitchen, I hung up my coat, changed my shoes, and wandered off in the direction of my study. As I climbed the stairs I could hear, muted, the voices of my granddaughters from the sitting room, then laughter. The study is at the end of a long upstairs passage, at a sort of T-junction that branches corridors in both directions, the floor uneven from several hundred years of use and subsidence. I prefer to be higher up—perhaps it's my profession, but I like to be able to see clearly, over the land and the sky.

But as I approached the study door, someone walked rapidly and smoothly across the opening, heading down the corridor and out of sight. I caught a glimpse of a woman in a dark green dress, very long and full-skirted like an Elizabethan gown. She had a little ruff, too, which sparkled like her hair, and she was carrying a long frond of some kind of plant.

For a moment, I thought she was one of the girls, dressed up, but she was too tall—at least six foot, my own height. Heels?

"Who's that?" I called, but there was no reply. I trotted to the end of the corridor and looked down it. No one was there.

Well, this house is full of ghosts. We do see them, you know. Not just in the mind's eye, a fancy of the imagination, but really and truly present, just as you yourself might stand before me. I hadn't seen this one before, but that didn't mean that no one else had. We've all got our own special spirits, the ones only particular people see, and then there are the communal ones. The child by the window, for instance: we've all seen him in his Kate Greenaway velvet suit, his sorrowful face, like something out of a particularly emetic Victorian painting. No idea who he is. Alys and I see a doddery gardener in eighteenth-century clothes, and I think Bea might have done as well. Stella and Serena, the middle girls, talk about a pair of ghostly gazehounds, but they're going through an animal-mad phase, so perhaps they're tuned in to spectral beasts. Luna's a bit too little to say for sure: hard to know if she's seeing people or imagining them.

So a lady on the landing didn't bother me a great deal. I mentioned her at lunch.

"No, not a clue who she might be," Alys said, passing roast potatoes. "Elizabethan? Well, the house is old enough."

"She sounds pretty," said Serena, who was into fashion. "What was the gown made of? Silk, or velvet?"

"I don't know. I only got a glimpse."

"I hope she comes back. She sounds rather nice."

"Granddad?" This was Stella. "Never mind the lady. Can we see the comet yet?"

Stella had asked this once a day since late November, rather as another child might ask for Christmas. "I've told you, Stella. It's nearly here. Another couple of days and it should be visible." I said it kindly; I could understand her excitement. The name of the comet was Akiyama-Maki, and it was discovered in 1964 by a pair of Japanese astronomers. It is a Great Comet, a popular name for a very bright visitor to the skies, and it is thought to be one of the Kreutz sungrazers, the remnants of a big comet that broke up in the 1100s. Astronomy was still my job, and I'd been looking forward to this winter visitor for some months—there was something *about* a comet, a kind of celestial magic all of its own, which had fascinated me ever since I was a boy. So I could see why Stella kept asking, even though the comet wasn't the first thing on my mind. Other visitations were taking precedence.

"So, we'll see it soon?" Stella pestered.

"Yes. Not long now."

After dinner we sank into a Sabbath somnolence with the Sunday papers and early nights all around; the girls were back to school the following morning. I wanted to listen to a radio play, which ended about ten; switching it off along with the light, I fell asleep quickly. When I awoke, I was disoriented. It was very dark. I'd left the curtains open, but there was nothing visible beyond the window: no stars, no moon, not even the lights of the farms scattered across the valley. It was that which alerted me to the fact that something was awry with the world. There is always a light somewhere, a small orange token of human life.

I clambered out of bed and went to the window, stood staring out. The darkness was all encompassing. We're not that close to any big cities, but there's a faint glow where Bristol lies to the north; that wasn't visible, either. I thought it might be fog—we're prone to mist in these parts, especially in winter—so I pushed the window up to see. A thin, curling tendril of darkness made its way into the room, as if questing. I shut the window damn quick after that. And then I heard it again.

Help him.

After a while, in magic, the messages start to stack up; you'd have to be really clueless to ignore them. The flame, the woman, the dark.

"All right," I said aloud. "All *right*."

It's hard to feel heroic in a dressing gown and slippers, but the voice was whispering, insistent. I went through the door, and the house had changed. Instead of the carpeted, picture-lined corridor, there was a passage of stone, a rough, porous substance like pumice. I touched it and snatched my hand away; it burned with cold. I took a few experimental steps. My feet, in their old man's slippers, did not freeze, but the air around me felt constricted, as if there wasn't enough of it. At the end of the passage, encased in rock, stood my study door. I reached it and pushed it open.

Things happen that should make you die. There was a veil of white fire. I fell back, shielding my eyes. The fire flared and vanished. The door reached onto open space. Seizing the doorframe, I tottered on the edge of a black void, standing now on curving ice. It was moving, almost too fast for me to take it in. Stars whisked by, and I looked up to see a streaming cloud, the colors of an unnatural fire.

Help him!

A tiny voice, imperious, compelling.

"What the hell are you?"

He is dreaming! Wake him!

The colors were coalescing. As I stared, a figure started to form, made out of cascading light. I started shaking. I knew that I was in the presence of death, not the normal end to my life, which, at seventy, could not be that far away, but something which strove to wipe me out, as one might remove a speck of dust from a sheet of glass. It reached out a hand, long finger and thumb ready to pinch, and I felt it touch the edge of my soul, which shriveled.

Then fear overcame me and I slammed the door shut, knees trembling. It took all my strength, as though a vacuum were sucking the door open.

"Granddad? Are you all right?" Serena was standing on the landing. The pictures were back on the cream-papered walls; everything was still and normal and midnighty. In her white nightgown, with her blond hair, Serena looked like a small, pale ghost.

"Yes. Thought I heard something. In the study. Nothing there." My sentences stuttered out as if I were a puppet.

"Oh, okay." Serena looked reassured. "Maybe the window catch is loose. It's really windy out there now. You didn't shut one of the cats in, did you?"

"I—yes, possibly. Anyway, everything's all right." Paternalism was coming to the fore now. Mustn't worry the girls. "You hop back into bed—you'll get cold."

She nodded and vanished into her own room. I staggered back to mine and collapsed on the bed to stare into space—except it wasn't space, just air and the ceiling. I'd seen space, many times, and it didn't look like this. What an odd expression that was . . . But I'd witnessed it from observatories, traveling the world, when I was attached to universities: mountaintop places in the quiet nights, star-staring. I'd never seen it up close and personal, and I didn't think I wanted to do that again.

Because I thought I knew where I'd just been. I knew what comets looked like.

I didn't think I'd end up talking to one, though. But had I been? Or was that pale figure something else? If it was on the comet, how could its messenger appear in an English churchyard? Talking to me made a little more sense, magician/astronomer as I was. Yet I had no idea what I was supposed to do about it. What about the woman on the landing? Was she connected? Visitations often come in clusters. I mulled all this over until a chilly dawn began to creep around the curtains, and then I went down to the kitchen and made some tea. I took it back to the study, and I don't mind confessing that I had a bad moment when I opened the door. But there the room was, the usual bookcases and muddle. No black depths of space, no icy void. I released a breath and stepped through the door. I wanted to look up Akiyama-Maki.

Google gave me the basics, which I already knew. What was niggling at the back of my mind was when the comet had appeared before. We knew it had been named in 1964, but a lot of these comets turned out to be "the great comet of 1569" or somesuch, and given the woman's apparently Elizabethan costume, I wanted to see just what had been visible in the heavens during the old queen's reign. Not exactly a precise science; I'd only caught a glimpse of her, after all. I leafed through one of the older books on celestial phenomena and found seven comets during the period of 1558 to 1603. Most of these were known. It should be possible to work Akiyama-Maki's path backward, so I did some calculations, and it had appeared within that window: in 1571.

I closed the book and looked up. The woman was standing in the doorway. She regarded me gravely. Her lips moved, but I couldn't hear her voice. Her skin was very pale, and there were lights moving within it; it was then that I knew she wasn't human, not a ghost. But what was she? A spirit, surely. She looked as though she was standing in a breeze, tendrils of black hair drifting out from her elaborate coiffure, and the dark green skirts of her gown rippled, the heavy silk like water. Emeralds glinted around her throat, above the spikes of her ruff. She held out her hand to me, offering a sprig of sage. Its spicy, late-summer scent filled the room. A moment later, she winked out, as if she had never been. I was left sitting over the book, my mouth open.

I spent that afternoon looking through my library, searching for a sign of her. I failed to find it. We'd lived here a long time, the Fallows, and this is our story: the men in our family don't do so well. The house had been built by a woman: Lady Elinor Dark, who was widowed and married a Fallow. The names in the family tree interweave through one another: Dark, Fallow, Fortune, Lovelace. The women run the house—formidable chatelaines with hoops of keys, dreamy poetesses, stout orchard wives. The men die young, or simply fade. I am an exception. I've never been sure what I've done to deserve this honor. My granddaughters all have different fathers: no shame in that, post 1960s. None of them have stuck around.

Moonecote is not a mansion. It was conceived as a farmer's house, and over the years it grew, but not very much. Elinor's portrait hangs on the stairs; she has an oval Elizabethan face, like an egg. I'm sure she wasn't that bland. She does not wear emeralds, nor does she dress in green. She bore little resemblance to the black-haired woman who had just visited me. So who was the latter, then? What could her connection to the comet be? It made me nervous of going onto the landing, but I did. No one was there.

And nothing happened that night. At one point I woke, nerves jangling, but the bedroom was quiet and undisturbed. Now, however, the silence was anticipatory; it felt as though something huge was waiting to happen. I even went to the window again and looked out, but everything was normal. The fields lay under a crisp frost, moonlight-touched. Orion marched away to the west with his blue dog at his heels. It was all winter-clear. I wrapped myself in my dressing gown and went with some trepidation up to the attic, where I keep the telescopes.

The moon was gibbous, and there was a single bright star beneath it, guiding it to moonset like a tug with a ship into the harbor of the dawn. The star was Spica: the only really vivid body in the constellation of Virgo. A binary star, comprised of a blue giant and a Beta Cephei variable, if you want to get technical. If you prefer to be historical, an early temple of Hathor was aligned to Spica, and Copernicus did many observations of its passage. Now, not far before sunrise, it burned in the cold sky. I watched it and its fellows. Jupiter was visible now, the red spot a dusky rose. Akiyama-Maki would first appear above Arcturus and travel northward, heading up the handle of the Plough. I looked, but it was not yet visible.

He is coming! said a voice inside my head. I started and looked around, half expecting to see woman or flame, but there was nothing.

. . . Fermi Asian Network (FAN) was established in 2010 to promote collaborations among the high-energy astrophysicists in Asia with particular focus on using the data obtained by the Fermi Gamma-ray Space Telescope for observational and theoretical investigations. Over the last few years, we have published a series of papers related to gamma-ray astronomy . . .

It was two days after my night in the attic, and I was on the train, heading north. I looked up from the abstract I was reading, watched the gray fields flash by. We rarely get snow in the Southwest, but the Midlands were another matter.

"Jane's in Wolverhampton," Stella had said that morning, privy to the mysterious revelations of Facebook. "That's near Birmingham, isn't it? And *she* says there's snow. Do you want me to look at the trains for you?"

There were no cancellations. I wasn't sure whether to be relieved or not. The conference was only for a day: a series of not uninteresting papers. Now that I no longer taught, there wasn't a great deal of call to attend, but I thought I ought to take an interest, keep my hand in, all that kind of thing. Unfortunately, the invite had arrived in July, on a sweltering day when any thought of bad weather was very far from the mind. Winter, my late wife said once, is like childbirth: you never remember it properly once it's over and done with. She was right. Now that the conference date was actually here, I was faced with the usual problems of the wrong kind of snow on the line, the numerous excuses that the national rail network seem to conjure up to explain its inexplicable delays.

However, Alys got me to the local station for seven-thirty; the conference didn't start until ten. I would have to change at Bristol, but then it was a fast service straight through. Bristol was the usual scramble—wrong time of day, full of commuters—but Alys had booked me a seat, and I sank into it gratefully. We stopped once at Parkway, then belted through Gloucestershire, the hills vanishing into cold, low cloud. Everyone had long since settled down by then, and all the seats were taken, but a few stragglers were going up and down to the buffet car in search of more coffee, so when a woman brushed past me, I didn't register it until she was past me. Then the green of her gown caught my eye. I looked up. She glanced over her shoulder; an emerald in her hair flashed in the overhead glow and she gave me a small, enigmatic smile in which I thought I read something of triumph. Then she was gone.

Green for "go."

Inside my head, my inner voice said: *It's not the house, you bloody fool. It's you.*

After that, I got really jumpy. No one else seemed to have noticed her, although admittedly they were all absorbed in laptops and the newspapers, but women in Elizabethan gowns are not common on trains. I got the feeling that I was the only one who could see her, but it made me nervous all the same; what if she popped up during the conference? Thank God I wasn't giving a talk. It had, of course, occurred to me that I was simply becoming senile, but these visions seemed too specific, too precise. As I've said, I was pretty much used to the house being haunted—but then the flame in the graveyard had, as far as I knew, appeared to me alone. And now so had she.

I reached the conference center in something of a state. *Pretend to be a normal person,* I kept telling myself. Inevitably, I ran into some people I knew in the lobby and was immediately hauled into one of those slightly-oneupmanship-dominated conversations that academics often engage in. But the first talk was due to start soon. Together, still chatting, we filed into the lecture theater, and confronted with a deeply earnest paper on the nature of gravitational microlensing, I managed to push the woman to the back of my mind.

For reasons that I hope are obvious, I'd always kept my magical interests separate from my worldly job. It's not a good idea, if you're a university professor, to start babbling on about astrology—one of the dirtiest words in professional astronomy. But it hasn't always been the case: look at Newton, returning to alchemy at the end because he didn't think this physics stuff was ever really going to hack it. You can't get away with that now, but as the talk—which was frankly rather tedious—dragged on, my mind started to wander back to the Renaissance, to magic. To planetary spirits, which each planet possesses, along with its own sigil, its own quality. Jupiter confers wealth; Venus is the bringer of love. Now, in an age that demotes planets annually (poor old Pluto), it's perhaps hard to enter a mind-set in which celestial matters have an eternal quality.

All of this was lurking at the back of my mind throughout the series of seminars—some interesting, some turgid. During the latter, I found myself doodling in my notebook like some lackluster undergraduate; it had always been a bad habit. I drew a woman's face, a series of traced lines, not very good, and a sprig of sage. As I drew, I could almost smell it and I glanced up fearfully, expecting to see her there, but the room was full of my mercifully dull colleagues with no Elizabethan ladies in sight. I stopped doodling after that, afraid I might conjure her up. But there was something brewing in my unconscious; I could feel it, nudging me like the memory of a dream, and it stayed with me all through the buffet lunch.

During the afternoon break, I managed to collar one of my more comet-informed colleagues by the tea urn and I asked him, in what I hoped was a lightsome tone, about Akiyama-Maki.

"Oh, yes, wonderful. Marvelous to have such a visitor. Should be visible from tonight, you realize? Just a smudge, at first." Dr. Roberts was enthusiastic. "Really will come awfully close, though—at least half a million miles."

I smiled at this routine joke, but Roberts wasn't really kidding. For a foreign body traveling the solar system, this isn't far off a near miss. It sounds like a long way off, but it isn't in astronomical terms.

"Conspiracy theorists are having a ball, of course. I've had at least five emails a day asking if it's the end of the world."

"How exceedingly tedious."

At this point we were interrupted by a young man summoning us back to the lecture theater, so our conversation came to a close. That morning's encounter with the woman had put me on edge so much that, making the excuse of worries about the weather, I bailed out of the communal Indian meal organized by one of my former colleagues and picked up sandwiches at the station before catching an earlier train home.

Not that it made any difference. We were held up before Bristol, with a fault on the line. I was grateful that I'd brought a book. I texted Alys with some difficulty—you'd think a scientist would adjust more readily to modern technology—and told her I'd call from the station. When we finally got into Temple Meads, the train out was delayed. I could have gone for a curry after all, I thought gloomily; I'd arrived after the original later train was due in. By now, close to ten p.m., the platform and the surrounding fields were heavy with frost. My breath steamed out before me in clouds, and even in woolen gloves my hands felt immediately pinched. I rang Alys, fumbling the phone, and told her that I'd meet her on the road. The station is too small for a waiting room, and I didn't fancy sitting for twenty minutes in the open bus-stop affair on the platform. So I set off at a brisk, but careful, pace down the lane that leads to the station. The moon hung high, outlined by cold: a ring of ice crystals sparkled around it, and its light caught the frozen hawthorn. My footsteps rang out on the hard ground. I came to the summit of a small rise, which carried the lane down to the main road. Here, a gate revealed a long rolling vista of fields.

I paused for a moment, knowing that Alys was still some way off, and looked over this pale, unfamiliar landscape, then upward, seeking the comet, but before I could orientate myself beneath the stars something shimmered in the distance. Someone was coming over the brow of the field. Hard to see—they were wearing white, not some farmer encased in an ancient Barbour—and who, I realized with sudden shock, would be in white in the middle of a field in the middle of winter?

I knew who it was: not the death that comes to us all at our end, whose hand is not always unkind, but the other death, the one who snuffs out life as though it has never been, who steals the candle of the soul. The figure passed down the field, heading for the gate. He wore a headdress in the form of a star, like a child's drawing of Jack Frost, and long robes that sparkled like the crystals around the moon. He was more solid than the form I'd seen in my earlier vision. He was moving swiftly, gliding over the ground. I had an impression of black, inhuman eyes; a long lantern jaw. I was, almost literally, frozen to the spot. As he neared the gate he looked up and reached out a finger like a claw. Then he blinked out, like the woman had done. Maybe I wasn't supposed to see him, but he was gone in an instant, and I was alone with the hawthorns and the moon. Distant on the road I heard the throb of the Land Rover's engine, and a moment later saw Alys turn down the lane.

Gradually, I started to warm up. I felt that I'd been touched by a cold that was much greater than that of a frosty January night. Alys kept glancing at me in concern, and eventually she said, "Dad, are you all right?"

"Just tired."

"You can have a rest tomorrow," she remarked, encouragingly. Normally, I bridle at being treated like a poor old thing, but tonight I found I didn't mind so much. When we finally got home, driving slowly over the frozen roads, and the bedroom door closed behind me, I thought: *Enough.*

◆　◆　◆

Despite the tiring previous day, I woke early next morning. It was about six-thirty, and not yet light. When I drew the curtains, I saw frost flowers decorating the pane for the first time in years. We have double glazing, and anyway it's rarely cold enough in this mild part of the country. I was reminded of childhood, when there was a magic in such things. There still is. I traced an icy star with my finger. When I took it away, the skin was faintly silvered.

In magic, there are really only two choices. You can act or not act. You have to be clear about your decision, though, and your reasons, and you have to be prepared to take the consequences. *Be careful what you wish for,* and all that: the monkey's eldritch paw. Now, I thought I was clear; I knew what I wanted. Knowledge. And irritatingly, I thought I already had it: that subconscious push beneath the surface of my mind was still present, and still insistent. But I wanted more of an answer.

But first I needed tea. I went to the door of the bedroom, took hold of the handle, and the subconscious push broke through the surface of my mind in a shower of crystal drops.

Sage juice with trefoil, periwinkle, wormwood, and mandrake placed will increase gold, accumulate riches, bring victory in lawsuits, and free men from evil and anguish—

It was my own inner voice, not some external agency, and I knew where it came from. Cornelius Agrippa: theologian, physician, soldier, occult writer, much more besides. Many of the correspondences in magic come from Agrippa's obsession with noting what goes with what, macrocosm and microcosm. In the *Book of Hermes,* he speaks of the fixed stars—known as the Behenian stars—and their influences and attributes. Each star is associated with corresponding plants and gemstones, and the idea is that you make talismans that accord with these correspondences: a metal ring inscribed with the sigil of the star, and containing the planet and stone. When I was a young man, and becoming interested in magic, I had made such a talisman, but for Mercury, not a star. I thought I knew where it was: in an old box, containing a number of semiprecious stones of the tumbled kind that you can buy in any New Age shop. They'd been around for a long time, however, ever since I was a boy, and I didn't know where they had originally come from. Now, I thought I knew exactly which stones were in that box: the ones that corresponded to the Behenian stars.

I spent much of the day searching for the box; I had to go up to the attic in the end. But I did find it. I opened it to the faint glow of fifteen semiprecious stones and the old tarnished circle of my Mercurial talisman.

Arcturus. Aldebaran. The Pleiades, and more. Fifteen stars or star groups that, in this northern hemisphere, circle continually above our heads, that never set. The woman carrying the sage, in her green gown and her grassy emeralds, would be Spica, chief star of Virgo, which I'd watched traverse the sky the other night.

I felt as though she'd personally introduced herself. But why Spica? She might be prominent in the sky at present, but so, by definition, were the other Behenian stars.

"Why are *you* here?" I asked aloud. A visiting cat, the tabby, gave me a startled look and scooted from the room. "Spica. Why *you*?"

But there was no reply. No woman in green appeared; the house was quiet. After some further searching, I located the copy of Agrippa and pored over it; I was thinking of the Jack Frost figure in the fields.

So who is "he"?

Fennel juice and frankincense, placed beneath a crystal. That sounded suitably cold, but it corresponded to the Pleiades, and I could not see even one of those sisters manifesting as a male, though it's hard to tell with spirits.

Black hellebore with diamond, for Algol.

An eclipsing binary, in the constellation of Perseus and known as the Demon Star; its name is Arabic, like so many star names. It means "the ghoul." This didn't seem quite right to me, placed upon that white striding figure of the night before. So who was he? I couldn't find him among the Behenian stars; he was anomalous. What about the pale form I'd seen? And the little flickering flame of the churchyard hadn't appeared, either.

Back to church with you, Fallow, I thought.

It was still very cold. The snowdrops seemed to have shrunk, and no flame was visible as I made my way through the churchyard and pushed open the oak door. Inside, empty of congregation, the church contained the echoes of hymns and prayer, whispers from innumerable Sundays. Without the large, old-fashioned stove going, the place was also cold, but not dark. Wan winter light cast dim shadows over the floor. I sat down in a front pew and waited for the eye to appear. I had a feeling it knew more than it was letting on.

I sat there for perhaps half an hour, reading and rereading the inscriptions that appear along the upper walls of the church: strawberry pink on white plaster. We can thank the Arts and Crafts movement for this: two classical gentlemen holding scrolls. *Is it nothing to you, all ye that shall pass by?* reads one, in unnecessarily admonishing fashion in my opinion. Who is passing, and why? Well, I thought self-righteously, *I'm* not passing by. I'm trying to help. I kept glancing around the church, looking for the eye, but it was evidently being coy. I sat there, getting colder and colder, and eventually the light began to die outside to the blue of a winter twilight. And I saw it looking at me.

It was high in the rafters, set in an angel's face. One of the angel's eyes was a stone oval, a bland blank in its neo-Classical face, but the other was scarlet, hot and glowing. I stood up.

"I'm trying to help," I said aloud, hoping none of the church ladies had crept in behind me to adjust the floral arrangements. "Tell me what to do."

You are a pilot, the voice said. The eye rolled.

"I'm an astronomer. I've never flown a plane."

You are the witness.

"I'm not sure I understand."

The angel gave a sigh, a breath that steamed out from its stone lips. *Too cold. Find me in the fire.*

There was a sudden muted roar as the furnace stove started up, making me jump. The church became a fraction warmer. I thought of flames, dancing on a wall. Cautiously, I opened the stove door.

Inside was a ball of fire. Something was twisting and moving within; it looked at me.

"Ah," I said. "Now I know what you are."

I am salamander, it said proudly.

In its native element, I could see its long lizard shape, the curling tail. It wasn't like the reptile known as "salamander," but more heraldic, elegant. With some difficulty I squatted down on my heels so that I could see it more clearly.

You have seen him.

"Who? Do you mean the person in the fields, the other night?"

Yes, that is the one. He is waking, as he draws near the sun, but not quickly enough. I am a messenger of the sun. You are in danger. You have to bring him safely through.

"How am I to do that?"

You must go to him, when it is time. You must give him your hand.

I shivered, thinking of the cold, and at that moment a blast of chilly air ran down the back of my neck, accompanied by the creak of the church door. The salamander whisked into the heart of the furnace, and I slammed the plate shut, straightening up. The churchwarden, an elderly man, blinked at me mildly.

"Professor Fallow? I'm sorry, I didn't see you there."

"Just came in for a bit of peace and quiet. Your stove seems to be lit."

"Oh, is it? Doubtless one of the other wardens put it on. The church gets so damp, you know. And we have to try to keep this plasterwork intact."

"Well, I'm grateful for the warmth." I hoped he wouldn't ask too many questions of his colleagues. "But I'd better be going."

We exchanged pleasantries, and I went back to the house. Nothing flickered in the churchyard. Dusk cast a cold blue pall over the hills.

Later that evening, Alys said to me, "It's wassail on Saturday. Had you remembered?"

I stared at her. "No. I'd forgotten it was our turn. But of course, you're right. How many people this year?"

"I don't know. I sent out invitations. Maybe fifty? You don't have to do anything. I'll sort out the food. Sausage rolls and baked spuds."

Wassail. Nothing to do with astronomy. Lots to do with orchards and apples. It's a celebration of the apple harvest and no, I don't know why it's done in the middle of January rather than the autumn, except that apple harvests can go on for rather a long time, and it's not until after Christmas that the redwings and fieldfares fly in and devour the remaining windfalls. It's one of those customs that goes up and down in popularity. Right now, it was undergoing something of a vogue, and a lot of the local farms were making a tidy sum by charging a few quid entry. It's appealing because it involves alcohol and guns: you drink hot mulled cider, sing a couple of wassail carols, and a man fires a shotgun into a tree to scare away any evil spirits and ensure a good harvest for the following autumn. It's all about the earth, and perhaps that was what I needed, with a head in the heavens, beset by the persons of stars.

The next day was even colder. I rose before dawn and locked myself in the study, shifting the table closer to the window and rolling up the faded Persian rug. Beneath, the circle was traced on the floorboards, with a conjuration triangle outlined in red beyond it. If you are summoning a spirit, you don't necessarily want it in the circle with you. In fact, usually not. I performed the lesser banishing ritual of the pentagram, moving smoothly around the circle and invoking the protection of the archangelic powers at each quarter, each watchtower. This is standard ceremonial magic, dating from the late nineteenth century and the turgid practices of the Golden Dawn, but its roots are older. And, more important, it works.

Whether it would work now remained to be seen; I sought to summon a star. I finished up the ritual and turned my attention to the conjuration triangle. A handful of frankincense, myrrh, and sage went into the little brazier inside the circle; it hit the hot charcoal and hissed up.

I held out my hands. "Lady Spica! I invite you . . ."

At first I didn't think anything was happening, and I wasn't surprised; I didn't even know if you could summon a star like a normal spirit. But gradually the smoke began to congeal. The air cleared. Spica stood before me, but not in the conjuration triangle. She glanced at it and smiled an ambiguous smile. She stepped over the edge of the circle, lifting the hem of her gown, and I took a step back. She was loose in the room and unbound; I'd seen no evidence that she meant me harm, but I was still taking a chance.

Her lips moved in silence. "I can't hear you," I said. Spica smiled again, held out a hand. Then she turned her hand over and up, palm outward.

Stop. Wait.

It took me a moment. She held a finger to her lips and pointed to the clock.

"Seven in the morning? No. You'll tell me when?"

A nod. She spoke once more, earnestly and long, but her words weren't audible to me. Her tendrils of hair drifted out in a rising wind, and she was gone again.

I don't like the feeling that I'm not in control. But in magic, it happens all the time. You're only a piece of something, a tiny cog. You may never know the full story, and the powers who engineer such things operate on a need-to-know basis. Sometimes not even that. If fifty years of this have taught me anything, they've taught me patience.

Which is its own reward, so they say.

After the ritual, I cooled my heels for a couple of days. I saw nothing strange; nothing strange spoke to me. I looked for the comet, but to my frustration the temperature rose, with cloudy night skies. Stella was furious. However, Saturday, the night of the wassail, dawned cold and the frost remained in the lee of the hedges and in the pockets of the fields all day, until the sun went down in a fiery blaze. Alys and the girls had cooked all day, and I did the washing up and made some bread; by the time we'd finished, cars were starting to pull into the yard as the first of our guests arrived.

Cider and mead first, then wassail. You make toast and place it in the tree—it's for the spirits, the good ones. I gather Serena rather fancied the shotgun, but it was left firmly in the hands of a neighboring farmer who could be relied upon to aim in the right direction and not take out one of the guests or a cow. We trooped out into the gathering twilight, clutching mugs and glasses, boots crunching on the icy grass. Carols were sung; the shotgun was fired. I looked up, but it was not dark enough yet to see the comet.

As the gunshot echoes were reverberating through the orchard to the sound of cheers, I turned to see Spica standing behind me, her finger to her lips. The cheers slowed and died, as though someone had pressed a mute button. I looked over my shoulder. My family, our friends, were still there, still moving and clapping, but in slow motion, and they were shadowy, like ghosts. Only the trees of the orchard were solid, and they looked taller, harder, older: stiff as stone. Spica said, "Come."

Her voice was musical and low, and I realized how inhuman she was.

Her eyes were whiteless, a burning green. She held out a sharp-nailed hand, bonier than before, the fingers longer.

We were entering her world now, I thought. I stepped forward and took her cold hand. Turning, she led me through the stately trees and out into the fields. The frost sparkled into snow, thick drifts of it against the ancient hedge patterns, but I was warm in the aura of Spica the star.

"My sisters are waiting. He needs to wake," she said. Her voice was musical but cold: the sort of voice you might expect from a star.

"'He' is the—the person I saw? The comet?"

"Ah, you saw him?" She seemed anxious. "So his shadow is here already? Then there is great danger."

I wanted to ask, *What sort of danger?* but pride stopped me. "His shadow?"

"Yes. We will see him soon." She lifted the hem of her gown to step over a tuft of reeds. The ground here was marshy, patterned with thin ice. "Do not worry. We are almost at the causeway."

I did not know what she meant by this; there was nothing akin to a causeway in my version of the world. But then, we weren't in my world now ... And as we traversed the field, I saw a glimmer of stone through a gap in the hedge: a long road, heading into the distance, rimmed with silver fire and leading to a tower. It resembled a Norman keep: round and squat as an owl in the landscape.

"Is this where your sisters—live?"

"It is what we create when we need to." She set foot on the causeway, pulled me along. Our footsteps rang out like hammer beats. The causeway wasn't stone, as I'd thought, but metal, like solid moonlight. As we drew closer, I saw that the tower was made of the same substance.

"You work with light?" I asked.

"We are stars." She smelled of sage and snow.

The portcullis was up; the tower shivered faintly. We went through into a central courtyard and here, indeed, were the sisters of Spica: the spirits of the Behenian stars. They stood in a half circle, the Pleiades clustered together in a whispering huddle, silver-dressed; Aldebaran holding a thistle, her hair blood-dropped with rubies; Capella laughing, sapphire bedecked against azure silk. Like their spokessister Spica, all were attenuated, passing for human, something else beneath the masks of women. For the first time in years I was too shy to speak. Schoolboy-ish, I stood before the weight of their gaze.

One of the Behenian stars stepped forward. This one was gold and blue, holding a sprig of juniper. Frantically remembering Agrippa's correspondences, I placed her as Sirius. Her star hung overhead, following on the Hunter's heels. The stars of her sisters wheeled about her, but there was a newcomer in the sky, hanging over the bleak edge of the distant hills, which were higher than they should have been.

The comet was coming. Akiyama-Maki blazed over Arcturus and the star herself was coming forward, her red-and-green gown flecked with jasper beads. The comet was a bright silvery-gold, like a bead in the sky. It would be visible in the Earthly heavens now.

We have to bring him in.

"By 'he,' you mean the comet?"

We have to see him safely through.

"If we don't—what will happen?"

"He is close," Spica said. "But he has not yet woken."

It was at this point that my colleague Dr. Roberts's voice suddenly flashed into my mind, saying, *Really very close.* "His path should take him past the Earth, though," I said. *He has not yet woken*: that was literally true. As the comet, that dirty snowball hurtling through space, came closer to the sun, the warmth of the sun would begin to release its gases, causing the tail to appear.

"He's been traveling for a long time," Spica said. "He sleeps and he dreams."

"What dreams does a comet have?"

"Protection. The cold of deep space, of death. His cold self dreams but does not wake."

"And when he dreams, he's dangerous? Because he's—what?" I didn't see comets as innately malevolent. "Trying to protect himself in sleep?"

"Yes. And if he does not wake quickly enough, he might leave his path, come too close to the world. He needs a pilot," the star said. "You will be his pilot."

"I've never—" I stopped. Because I'd been there already, onto the snowball surface of Akiyama-Maki. I'd set foot, in some manner, comet-side.

"Will I—die? If I go there?" I hadn't before. Best to check, though.

"You should not die. And you will have help," Algol said. She held out her arm, in its sleeve of cloth-of-gold, and the salamander slid out onto her palm, curling its tail like a cat.

I will come with you, the salamander, messenger of the sun, said.

"Why can't you come?" I said to Algol.

She looked rueful. "There is no love lost between stars and comets. They come to us like moths to flames, and we wink them out."

I paused, then I said, "Very well. I'll go." The salamander dropped to the floor and rustled over to me; I bent and picked it up. It sat in my palm, curiously heavy.

The Behenian stars all stepped back. Algol raised her hand, and there was white fire between us, a wall like the one I'd seen in the study.

It will not burn you, the salamander said. But it took a moment to nerve myself to step through it, all the same.

The comet's aura was all around us, a blue-green burn like the Northern Lights. I tried to take a breath. I failed, but I did not choke; it seemed I did not need to breathe. I wasn't sure whether I'd stepped out of my body, leaving it behind in the castle, for surely I could not be really here; this was some astral level.

Holding the salamander, I walked across the surface of the comet. It was like the frost of the orchard. I heard my footsteps crunch, but this too was illusion; there is no sound in space. Its surface was pockmarked with holes, too small to be termed craters. I had a momentary, and probably foolish, worry about twisting my ankle.

"We have to find him," I said to the salamander. It radiated heat, without burning. In this bright, cold-colored landscape it was a single spot of fire. "Do you know where he might be?"

I do not.

Akiyama-Maki actually looks a lot like a potato, and it is known to rotate, but the astral surface on which we stood was quite still. As my eyes adjusted to the flickering, streaming light, I realized that the comet's male form was standing some distance away, with his back to me. A cloak of light streamed out behind him, mimicking a comet's tail. I walked across the surface toward him. He did not turn his head. When I was closer, I started wondering how to proceed. An *"Excuse me?"* Perhaps a delicate cough? What I actually said was, "Are you awake?"

No reply. Maybe if I tapped him on the shoulder?

Breathe, the salamander said. *Breathe.*

I faced the comet. His eyes were open, but blank and dark. I forced myself to stay put. Seen so close, he looked even less human than the Behenian stars.

"Wake," I said. "You need to wake up!" I took a breath, breathed out, and so did the salamander, in a cloud of cold-morning steam.

Wake! the salamander chimed.

"You need to wake up."

The comet blinked. His eyes flashed with a brief silver light. I could feel the warmth of the sun on the back of my neck. His long-nailed hand flashed up.

"No!" I cried. "Don't kill!"

He blinked again, but he lowered his hand. "Who am I?" the comet said, wonderingly.

"You are a comet. You are close to a world—to my world. Wake up!"

I glanced up and saw the moon. It hung in the astral heavens, a glowing silver ball, and not far away the Earth itself was turning, all green and blue and white. I could see the dim lights at their cores, the signs of their aliveness, for this was not the true solar system in the physical world, but the world beyond.

"Listen to me," I said. "You are a sungrazer. In the real world, not this world of your dream, you will pass this red world above us—there is a faint chance that it will draw you in, but very faint. You will pass the Earth, and if you choose, you can meet your own end there. But it will be the end of that world."

"I do not wish to kill a world," the comet said, with a trace of alarm.

"Then wake up! Your dreaming self is dangerous—it brings the cold of deep space with it, and we can't withstand that. And you might become confused and leave your path. Listen—can't you hear the sun calling to you?"

He blinked again. His pale skin was flushing with gold.

Wake up, the salamander said encouragingly.

"Wake. And we'll all live."

And the comet's eyes were bright as fire. He raised his hand again, in a gesture, and the salamander and I found ourselves standing in space as the growing tail of the comet whisked by. Then there was the sparkle of stars, Akiyama-Maki was waking up and streaking sunward, between Earth and the moon, and we were slowly falling.

It was with regret as an astronomer that the astral solar system faded around me and the castle of the Behenian stars took its place. The stars themselves were waiting for us, still in their semicircle. Spica seized my arm.

"You are safe. The comet?"

"He's awake."

The salamander flicked away. As one, the Behenian stars bowed and faded, returning, I presumed, to their places in the constellations. But Spica remained. She walked back with me, over the causeway, and across the fields. As we drew closer to the house, I could see a bonfire in the orchard, surrounded by moving figures. The bare branches of the trees reached for the moon. The air smelled of woodsmoke and frost. Overhead, in the clear heavens, a silver smudge was visible over Arcturus, blazing over the apple trees. Faintly, I could hear Stella's familiar voice.

"Look! It's the comet! Look, mum!"

"And you," I asked the star, "your sisters? Will we see you again?"

"Oh," she said. "We are always here." She pointed upward, and I followed her hand to where the fixed stars span on their never-ending wheel in the shining winter sky.

Garth Nix

* * *

Here we investigate a supernatural mystery in company with a village wizard with a dark past and many secrets of his own to hide, although, as he's about to discover, none of them even remotely as dangerous and deadly as the enigma he's trying to unravel . . .

Garth Nix has been a full-time writer since 2001, but has also worked as a literary agent, marketing consultant, book editor, book publicist, book sales representative, bookseller, and part-time soldier in the Australian Army Reserve.

Garth's books include the YA fantasy Old Kingdom series, including *Sabriel, Lirael, Abhorsen, Clariel,* and *Goldenhand*; SF novels *Shade's Children* and *A Confusion of Princes*; and a Regency romance with magic, *Newt's Emerald*. His fantasy novels for children include *The Ragwitch*; the six books of the Seventh Tower sequence; the Keys to the Kingdom series, and others. He has co-written several books with Sean Williams, including the Troubletwisters series; Spirit Animals: Book Three: *Blood Ties,* and *Have Sword, Will Travel*.

More than five million copies of his books have been sold around the world. They have appeared on the bestseller lists of *The New York Times*, *Publishers Weekly*, and *USA Today*, and his work has been translated into forty-two languages. His most recent book is *Frogkisser!*, now being developed as a film by Twentieth Century Fox/Blue Sky Studios.

Garth lives with his family in Sydney, Australia.

◆   ◆   ◆

The Staff in the Stone

GARTH NIX

The low, dry stone walls that delineated the three angled commons belonging to the villages of Gamel, Thrake, and Seyam met at an ancient obelisk known to everyone simply as "the Corner Post." Feuds between villagers would be settled at the Corner Post, by wrestling and challenges of skill, or the more serious in a formal conclave of elders from all three villages. Twice in the last hundred years the obelisk had been the site of full-scale battles between Gamel and Thrake against Seyam, and then Gamel and Seyam against Thrake.

Every spring, the ploughs would stop well short of the Corner Post, for fear of disturbing the bones of some bygone relative or enemy. In consequence, a small copse of undistinguished trees and shrubs grew around the obelisk, dominated by a single, tall rowan tree, often re-marked on, for there were no other rowans for leagues around, and no one living knew how it had come to be planted there.

Small children played under the rowan in the early morning, evading their chores, and lovers met there for trysts in the early evening. No one went near stone and copse by dead of night, because of the bones, and the stories that were told of what might rise there, or perhaps be drawn there, come midnight.

So it was three children under five who discovered a curious change in the stone, just after the sun had risen high enough to glance off the bronze ferrule on the foot of a staff, and there was sufficient light to see that the rest of the dark bog-oak length was impossibly *embedded* in the stone.

The visible end of the staff was high above the reach of the tallest child, which was just as well, for they were too young to be properly afraid of such a thing. In fact, after attempting to stand on each other's shoulders in a vain effort to reach it, they forgot all about the staff until the very youngest was bringing water to the sweating harvest-time reapers working toward the narrowest point of the Thrake common. Seeing the Corner Post again, the little girl wondered aloud why there was a big black stick stuck in it, like a skewer through a cooking rabbit.

Her father went to look, and came back even sweatier and more out of breath than he had been from his work. The word spread quickly from field to barn to village, and no more than an hour later, made its way to the cool, green-lit forest home of the nearest approximation to a wizard for fifty leagues or more, since the woman purported to be one in the nearest town of Sandrem had been unmasked as a charlatan several months before.

The forest house had once been a minor royal hunting lodge, in the time of the kings and queens, before the plague and the rise of the Grand Mayors. Octagonal in shape, it was built around the bole of one of the giant redwoods, some twenty feet above the forest floor. A broad stair had led up to it once, but long ago that had fallen or been intentionally destroyed, its remnants now a tumulus of rotten timber, overgrown with ferns and fungus. A ladder, easily drawn up in case of peril, had replaced it.

The current inhabitant of the lodge was hanging pheasants in his cool room, an oak-shingled hut built between the roots of a neighboring giant redwood some sixty paces from the house. He felt the news arriving before he heard those bringing it, or at least he sensed there were excited people coming down the forest path. Usually this meant somebody was badly hurt and needed his aid, so he strung up the last three pheasants very swiftly and climbed out, leaving the birds swinging on their hooks. He did pause to close and slide the great bolt across the door, for it was not only mere foxes that fancied hanging game. The Rannachin loved pheasant, and they could open doors that weren't secured with cold iron.

The pheasant-hanger's name was Colrean, or at least it was now. He was under thirty years old, but only just, and looked older, because he had spent the last decade mostly at sea, and then more recently in the forest and the fields, under the sky. Sun, salt water, and wind had worked to make his face more interesting. He had a lean, competent look about him, his eyes were dark and quick, and he walked with a noticeable limp, legacy of some unexplained wound or injury.

Colrean had come to the lodge some twenty months before, in mid-winter, riding one mule and followed by two others, all of them heavily laden. Tying these up at the old iron hitching post near the ladder, he had by means unknown dispossessed the Rannachin, who had thought to make the lodge a cozy winter lair. Then he had nailed a parchment with a great lead seal to one of the more outstanding roots of the great tree. According to those few folk among the villagers who could read, this was a deed from the Grand Mayor of Pran, granting the new arrival the lodge; hunting rights in the forest and certain other perquisites relating to tolls on the forest road; tithes on fishing or eel-trapping in the river Undrana that passed nearby; a threepenny fee for cattle watering at the wide Undrana ford; and other minor items of tallage.

He had never attempted to enforce any of these imposts, which was fortunate, given that the people of the three villages were by no means convinced that Pran had any authority whatsoever in their purlieu, no matter what the last queen of Pranallis and her vassal the long-gone baron of Gamel, Thrake, and Seyam might have held to be their own.

Colrean had shown his wisdom in matters of friendly relations with the local inhabitants very early, by giving each of the three villages one of his mules within days of his arrival, limping along through snow and ice to do so. Though he carried no staff nor wore a sorcerer's ring, he was at once suspected of being some kind of magic-worker, for he spoke to the mules and they obeyed, and the village dogs didn't bark and slather at his approach, but came and bent their heads before him, and wagged their tails and offered their bellies to be scratched. Which he did, indicating kindness as well as magic.

The villagers tried to find out exactly what kind of magic-worker he was, but he would not speak of it. They first knew he definitely was one when Fingal the Miller's hand was crushed in his own stone, and Colrean came unbidden to cut away the dangling fingers and then, with a cold flame conjured in his own hands, cauterized the wound, so that no blood sickness came. Fingal Seven Fingers was only the first of Colrean's patients, and he even deigned to help the midwives at difficult birthings, which the villagers knew marked him as no wizard. Wizards were grand beings, and lived in the cities, and were not to be found at village birthings.

The news-bearers who came running to be first to tell Colrean about the staff were Sommie and Heln. They were frequent visitors, inseparable friends, serious-minded, both eleven years old. Sommie was the seventh daughter of the midwife of Gamel and her weaver husband; Heln was the fifth son of the innkeepers of the only inn for leagues, the Silver Gull at the Seyam crossroad. Colrean knew them well, for once a week he taught children (and some grown folk) who wished to learn their letters, taking slates and hornbook to each village meeting hall in turn. Sommie and Heln were among his keenest pupils, following him from village to village and always pestering him for extra classes or books they might borrow.

"There's a stick stuck in the Corner Post!" shouted Sommie when she was still a good dozen yards away.

"Not just a stick!" cried out Heln breathlessly, skidding to a stop in the leaf mulch of the forest path. "A staff! Like a scythe handle, only it's dark wood and has a metal bit on the end."

Colrean stopped in midstep, as always a little clumsily, and lifted his head, sniffing at the breeze. The children watched as he slowly turned about, nose twitching. When he completed his circle, he looked down at the two dirty, excited faces staring up at him.

"A staff in the stone, you say? And you've seen it yourselves?"

"Yes, of course! We looked and then came straight here. Why are you sniffing?"

"You're not playing some trick on me?" asked Colrean. He had sensed nothing on the air, no magic stirring. The Corner Post was less than half a league away, and he felt sure he would have felt *something* . . .

"No! It's there! This morning, from nowhere. The little ones saw it. Why were you sniffing?"

"Oh, just smelling what scents are on the air," said Colrean absently. "I'd better have a look. Has anyone touched this staff?"

"No! Old Haxon said no one was to go near, and you were to be fetched, I mean asked to come. Ma's coming to tell you, but we ran ahead."

Ma was Sommie's mother, the midwife Wendrel. She had some small magic herself, combined with considerable herb-lore and a little book-learning. Knowing more about such things than the younger folk, she could barely conceal her fear as she puffed up after the children.

"It is a wizard's staff," she panted out, after a bare nod of greeting. "And it is deep in the stone."

"But there is no wizard about?" asked Colrean. He hesitated for a moment, then added, "No new tree nearby, strangely full-grown? A stray horse of odd hue? A stranger in the village?"

"No tree, no stray, no stranger," said Wendrel. "Just the staff in the stone. Will you come?"

"Yes," said Colrean.

"Can we come too?" asked Sommie, her question echoed by Heln.

Colrean looked up at the sky, watching the clouds, judging how much daylight remained. He thought about the phase of the moon, which was waning gibbous, and which stars would be in the ascendant that night, influencing the world below. There was nothing of obvious alarm in the heavens, no harbinger of doom.

"It should be safe enough, at least until sunset," he said slowly. He looked at Wendrel. "But there *is* danger. As Frossel said:

> *A wizard without a staff*
> may *still be a wizard*
> *A staff without a wizard*
> *is a void*
> *Waiting to be filled.*

"Who's?" asked Heln.

"Frossel?" finished Sommie.

"Frossel was a wizard, chronicler, and poet," answered Colrean. He started walking, the slower pace forced by his limp easily matched by Wendrel at his side, the children ranging faster across and behind him on the path, like dogs on a tricky scent who nevertheless do not wish to go far from their master. "I might lend you one of his books. He wrote a lot. Go on, I want to talk to Wendrel."

The children nodded together and bounded ahead.

"What does 'a void waiting to be filled' mean?" asked Wendrel quietly.

"A wizard's staff, lost or abandoned by a wizard, will attract many things, many of them not of our sunlit, mortal realm," said Colrean.

"Rannachin?" asked Wendrel.

"Yes, but worse things too," said Colrean. "Far worse. And the staff—if it is a wizard's staff—will call magic-workers of all kinds, even from very far away. Though I have some hope the stone will quiet it. I suppose that's why whoever put it there did so, trying to keep it hidden."

"The *stone* will hide it? Our Corner Post?"

Colrean looked aside at her as he strode on with his curious, lumbering gait. A brief look of puzzlement passed over his face like a cloud whisking across the sun.

"You do not know the nature of your stone?"

"I know it's very old," replied Wendrel, with a shrug. "But the powers I have are to do with people, and living things, not ancient lumps of rock or the like. The Corner Post has always seemed simply a stone to me. Though there is that odd rowan that keeps the stone company . . . sometimes I have felt as if it were watching me, that it is more than a simple tree . . ."

"It is," said Colrean. "Though I do not know its nature either. All such mysteries are best left alone, save a pressing need to do otherwise. As for the Corner Post . . . there *is* definitely a power within it, though it sleeps, and sleeps deeply. I suspect it is one of the ancient walking stones, which many ages ago came down from the far mountains and took root here to fulfill some compact long forgotten. Those stone warriors served the Old Ones, the folk of the air, so long vanished but never entirely gone."

Wendrel shivered. When she was a young apprentice, a birthing had gone terribly wrong. At the moment both infant and mother died, she had felt a sudden cold and unnerving presence, something drawn to the two deaths. The midwife who was her mentor quickly said this was one of the Old Ones, and that if they remained still and did not speak, no harm would come to them. Yet to warn Wendrel, the older midwife *had* spoken. She was at once struck dumb, and it was a twelvemonth before she regained the use of her voice at all, and she who had one of the sweetest voices in the three villages could never again carry a tune.

"Even the most powerful wizards do not readily meddle with such stones," continued Colrean. "I am surprised . . . no . . . I am astonished that the stone would *allow* anything to pierce it, let alone a wizard's staff."

"Allow?" asked Wendrel.

"On its own ground, I think that stone could stand against the Grand Wizard herself," replied Colrean. "And it must be allied to, or at least have permitted the rowan to grow . . . and that tree isn't much younger than the stone! It's older than any of the trees in the forest, even the giant redwoods or Grand's Oak, over by the broad water. Ordinary rowans do not live so long."

Wendrel asked no more questions, and was silent, her brow furrowed in thought. They walked on, crossing one of the rivulets that fed the Undrana. Colrean's oddly heavy, nailed boots boomed on the old log bridge, accompanied by the soft patter of Wendrel's sandals and the almost imperceptible scuffing of the children's bare feet.

They left the forest fringe soon after, to follow the well-trodden path along Gamel common's western boundary wall. The villagers were back at their reaping, for the harvest could not wait for anything save obvious, immediate threat. Sheaves of barley dotted the common, waiting for the older children to pick them up. But there was a noticeable lack of activity toward the top of the common, where the Corner Post loomed with its attendant rowan, the lesser trees and shrubs about it like beggars waiting for bounty from a king and queen.

"You had best leave me, and come no closer," Colrean warned Wendrel and the children, as they drew near the copse. He could feel the staff's presence now. It was making his thumbs prick and shiver as if a horde of minute insects stuck their prongs in his flesh, and there was a cold, wet draft caressing his bare neck, though no wind ruffled the barley stalks.

He looked up again at the sun, and the few tufts of scattered cloud dotted across the great stretch of blue sky—clouds that dissipated even as he watched.

"I think it will be safe enough till dusk. But you need to warn everyone to stay away from the Corner Post. They must be inside well before full night. The livestock too. Salt thresholds and windowsills. Stoke the hearthfires up and keep cold iron close."

"What's going—"

"To happen?"

"Perhaps nothing," said Colrean, attempting a smile to reassure the children. They were not reassured, for the smile was unlike any expression Colrean had made in their sight before, and were they asked what he tried to convey, would have said he was in pain. "The staff in the stone may call . . . creatures . . . who are dangerous. I will stay here. If anything comes, I will make sure it can do no harm. Now go!"

The children, well versed in obeying their elders, skipped off at once. But Wendrel lingered, concern on her face. As she had said, her powers lay with the living, most particularly attending upon births and deaths. She was thus well acquainted with fear, and the small indications of it upon an otherwise well-composed face.

"Do you have such power, to assure no harm will come to us?" she asked.

Colrean shook his head. "But I may be able to divert the course of whatever does come for the staff. Delay acts of small malevolence, and I hope give warning of anything worse."

"Why would you do this for us?" asked Wendrel. "To heal the hurt from a millstone, to aid in a birthing—these things do not risk your life. But surely you do now."

Colrean half shrugged, as if he did not know how to answer.

"This is my homeplace now," he said. "I have grown fond of some . . . many of the people. I have found peace here."

"A peace soon to be disturbed, if you are right," said Wendrel. "Almost, you remind me of the wizards of the old tales, who would appear without word on the eve of some storm or terror, come to defend the common folk. Only to leave when the danger has passed, as unheralded as they came, without thanks or payment."

"Wizards are only found in the cities now, bound by gold and oaths to serve the Mayors," said Colrean. "And I have been here two winters already. I hope this acquits me of being thought some bird of ill omen. Besides, I certainly do not wish to leave. Or seek payment."

Wendrel did not say anything for a moment, and silence fell between them. Colrean turned his head to glance at the Corner Post. But his body remained still, and he did not otherwise move, or take his leave, seemingly caught in indecision on the moment of commitment to a likely short-lived future.

In the distance, one of the reapers nicked herself with her sickle, and swore. Her harsh words brought Colrean back into the present. He blinked and looked at the midwife, who returned his gaze with a concern he recognized from seeing her with patients.

"I will bring you one of Rhun's second-best blankets, a waterskin, and food. Is there aught else you will need?"

Rhun was Wendrel's husband, save his wife the youngest of the elders of Gamel. He was barely old enough to bear the title without ridicule, having gained his position not from mere seniority, or as in Wendrel's case her wisdom, but in recognition of him being the best weaver in the three villages, and in fact for many leagues around. Even Rhun's second-best blankets were thicker, heavier, far more water repellent and more attractive than the city-bought ones Colrean had back in his lodge.

"All will be welcome, and a blanket perhaps most of all. It will be clear and cool tonight, and I must stay until the dawn. But be sure you come and go before nightfall."

"There is time enough," said Wendrel.

"Do not approach the stone," added Colrean. "Leave everything by the wall here; I will fetch it."

"As you will," said Wendrel. "I hope . . . I hope you are wrong about the staff, and nothing will come."

"I hope so too," said Colrean. But he knew he was not wrong. Whether he had become more accustomed to it, or the stone's grip on the staff was loosening as the day faded, he was much more aware of the silent call of magic emanating from whatever was in the Corner Post. If the children had not come to him, he would still have been drawn here, by sunset at the latest. And there were creatures far more sensitive to magic than he was, more sensitive than any mortal. They would come, once the sun was down.

Unless a wizard claimed the staff.

That would be another problem, perhaps no less dangerous than the creatures. For despite what he had said to Wendrel, not *all* wizards were bound to the Mayors by oaths and gold. There were some who considered themselves above the concerns of ordinary folk, and only sought to please themselves. They were kept in check by what they called the *tame* wizards of the cities, but that was in the cities.

Not out here.

Here there was only Colrean.

Who realized he had been woolgathering again, delaying the inevitable. Wendrel was already hurrying after the children, and he could hear them excitedly calling out his warnings to the harvesters, the repetition of "salt your windowsills" clear.

Colrean walked over to the Corner Post, pausing by the rowan to bend his head respectfully, as if the tree might bar his way or take umbrage at his presence. But the rowan gave no indication it was anything other than a normal tree, leaves and branches still in the quiet air. Colrean would have welcomed a breeze, particularly a brisk southerly, for that wind was antithetical to some of the creatures that might come in the night. But there was no wind, and it seemed, little chance of one.

Colrean passed by the rowan and cautiously approached the Corner Post, each of his six clumsy steps slower and shorter than the last, till he shuffled as close as he dared go, almost but not quite in touching distance.

There *was* a staff in the stone.

Colrean didn't really need to look at it to know it was indeed a wizard's staff. But he cautiously examined the exposed length that projected from the ancient stone, wondering why the staff was placed so high. Indeed, either an extraordinarily tall wizard had plunged it into the stone, or they had brought a ladder, which seemed unlikely. Even if so, why bother to put it out of easy reach?

This was not the only puzzle. Only three or four inches of the dark bog-oak beyond the bronze ferrule on the foot of the staff was exposed, and there were no obvious runes or inscriptions that might have helped him identify the staff's provenance. All he could tell from sight and his sense of the unseen was that this staff was very old, and very powerful.

Colrean could tell it was not a single staff at all, but a composite of many. Staves were made by wizards to store more power than they could hold in their own fragile bodies or in other tools of the art, and particularly powerful staves were made by a process of accretion, combining a new staff with the old.

But as making a wizard's staff was a time-consuming and potentially dangerous process, there were renegades who would simply take or steal the staves of weaker or unsuspecting wizards, using whatever means necessary—including such things as poison and assassination. Then they would combine the stolen staff with their own, growing more powerful in the process, and thus be able to take even more staves from other wizards.

"Better and better," muttered Colrean to himself, meaning quite the opposite. For a moment he contemplated touching the end of the staff, for that would reveal to him from whence it came, and might even give him the name of the wizard who had put it here. Though Colrean could not think why a wizard would want to put their own staff in such a place, or indeed, why a wizard would put someone else's staff there.

Unless it was a trap or a lure of some sort . . . but he could sense no other magic-worker nearby, nor see anything that might be one in another shape. There were no new trees, no odd horse, no peculiarly large raven watching from the stone wall . . .

Colrean also contemplated placing his hand upon the Corner Post itself and beseeching it to inform him what it knew of the matter. But it was not a serious thought, and was immediately dismissed. He knew more about such stones than he had revealed to Wendrel. Most were long dead—or their animating force dissipated—but the few who retained their power were typically averse to interaction with any but the most innocent of mortal folk, and were best left very much alone.

Though, in this case, the stone must have allowed the staff to be placed where it was, else there would have been a dead wizard among the barley, pieces of broken staff strewn about the commons, fires burn-ing, people screaming, and no need for anyone to summon him from the forest.

It was all a great puzzle.

Colrean sighed and found a place to sit some twenty paces from the Corner Post and the rowan, where the ground rose a little, giving him a longer view. He sat with his back against the Gamel-Thrake border wall and settled into the reverie magic-workers called *dwelm*, calling forth power he had stored over time in various items about his person, draw-ing it either into himself or reapportioning it among his objects of power.

This was a key part of any magic-worker's preparations, for there were things that stored magic well but were slow to give it up, and ob-jects that released power swiftly, but could not hold it for any length of time; or some combination thereof that was necessarily a compromise. The first were typically made of stone, petrified wood, amber, and/or gold, sometimes rubies or emeralds; and the latter silver or bronze with moonstones and diamonds or any of the paler gems, and younger wood or porcelain.

A properly prepared staff of ancient bog-oak, shod in bronze and tipped with iron, was unrivaled as a magical instrument, in that it could store power very well *and* release it reasonably quickly. There was a good reason every wizard had a staff. Though a wand of well-aged willow, with bands of gold and silver, could serve near as well, if there was some reason to dissemble and appear to be some other kind of magic-worker.

But Colrean had neither staff nor wand, nor, it seemed even a mere sorcerer's ring. His fingers, still somewhat stained with pheasant blood, were bare.

The sun had begun to set by the time he emerged from the *dwelm* trance. Wendrel had been; there was a basket sitting on the wall some distance away. He went to fetch it, taking it back to his chosen position where he could keep watch over Corner Post, rowan, and most of the three commons, though one area was obscured by the copse.

As expected, it began to grow cool almost immediately after the sun went down. Colrean unfolded the blanket and arranged it over his shoulders. Wendrel had provided bread, cheese, and sausage, and he made a quick meal of this and drank some water, while he watched the moon begin its rise and the stars come out. It was a very bright night, with the sky clear. Several small shooting stars sped by near the horizon, watched carefully by Colrean in case they grew brighter, or shone red, as true portents would. But they seemed to be nothing out of the ordinary. Such tiny fading sparks of brilliance could be seen on any clear night out here.

Colrean dozed a little then, rather uncomfortably, trusting to his otherworldly senses to jolt him awake should something happen. But when he did wake, it was from the simple discomfort of his bladder. Stretching to ease the kinks of dozing against the stone wall, he limped some distance away to urinate, not wishing to offer any disrespect to the Corner Post.

Coming back, he noticed it had suddenly grown quiet. His own footfalls were the only sound, where even a few moments before he had heard crickets sawing at their music; night-birds calling; the shrill shriek of a shrew caught by an owl; the muffled crackle and thump of hares disporting nearby in the barley stubble. All were silent now, and the air was still.

Colrean opened his eyes wide, calling power into his dormant mage-sight. The world grew brighter, moon- and starlight intensified. Shadows lengthened from stone and tree ... and sprang out from a dozen previously unseen creatures that had made their characteristically stealthy way from the forest and across the common, and were now only nine or ten yards from the copse. Even through a mage's eyes their shadows were easier to see than themselves, but in essence they were somewhat like foxes and somewhat like human folk, walking upright on their hind legs, and possessing tool-using hands, but they also had tall brushes, russet fur, cunning fox-masked faces, and sensitive, sticking-up ears.

Those ears twitched in unison as Colrean spoke.

"How now, my lords and ladies! What seek the Rannachin at the Corner Post?"

The twelve spread out in a line without any obvious command or discussion, and there was the glitter of obsidian blades in their paw-hands, the shine of teeth bared in long snouts.

"I think not," said Colrean. He mumbled something, cupped one hand and drew power. A blue flame burst from his palm, the air roaring as the fire grew taller than the man. "You recall the stench of singed fox fur well, I think?"

Again there were no visible signs of debate, but as one the Rannachin's weapons were put away, the jaws closed, and the fox-people turned and slid away into the night, as unobtrusively as they had come.

Colrean watched them for some time, keeping the flamecast ready, as it was quite possible they would turn back and try to rush him. But they did not. Quite possibly in the short time they had spent near the Corner Post they had already deduced the staff was too powerful for them to steal, or dared not risk the displeasure of the stone. It was even possible they thought Colrean too great a foe, though in the past he had never had to deal with more than three or four Rannachin at once.

He let the fire die when they were out of sight, and allowed the power to ebb from his eyes as well. He had to carefully husband his strength, particularly that drawn from his own blood and bone. There would doubtless be worse than Rannachin to come that night. He could sense the staff calling ever more clearly and strongly in the clear, cool night. It would bring others.

Colrean ate a little more bread, but did not sit down again. Instead he limped about the edge of the copse, and once again paid his respects to the ancient rowan. This time he not only bent his head, but slowly went down on one knee, as he might to a Grand Mayor or the Grand Wizard. He stayed there for some time, listening and thinking, comforted that the world around was full of small sounds again, and the sky remained clear, the stars and moon bright—and there was no sudden shower of bloodred sparks in the heavens above.

The rowan gave no sign it was aware of his obeisance, neither during his uncomfortable kneeling nor when Colrean pushed himself up and wandered off again, this time returning to his watching spot. Feeling uneasy, he carefully climbed up on the wall for a better view. This was a chancy maneuver given whatever was wrong with his leg, and was made no easier by the age and construction of the wall. Though the stones were cunningly set together, no mortar held them in place. Neither he nor the wall fell, but Colrean was not comforted by what he saw.

There was a fog rolling across the Seyam common, as if a single dense cloud had somehow fallen from above, though the sky was clear and there was no fog anywhere else.

Even as he saw this sudden, inexplicable mist, Colrean's otherworldly senses twitched, and he felt a spasm of intense fear grab his guts and grip him about the lungs. He fought off the sudden, sensible urge to flee and instead took a quick, shuddering breath. Climbing down from the wall, he hurried as fast as he could, almost hopping back to the rowan. Under its branches, he quickly took out one of his few objects of power, a knife of whalebone with a solid silver hilt that had been hidden under his jerkin. Calling on the power stored in this, he drew a circle about himself in the earth, mumbling memory-hooks, the words magic-workers used to safely recall exactly how the power must be called and used, words that the uneducated thought of as spells.

When it was done, the whalebone blade blew into dust like a kicked puffball, and the silver hilt crumbled in Colrean's hand, as if it had been buried in a tomb for a thousand years and could not stand the corrosive effect of open air. He had drawn every last scrap of power stored in the weapon, all at once, and so it could never be used again, never refilled. Two years to make and fill it to the brim with power, all gone in a matter of minutes, a treasure spent.

Spent wisely, Colrean hoped. He reached into his jerkin again, fingers closing on the silver chain around his neck, making sure it was secure and that by its weight he could feel what hung suspended there.

Fog overlapped the stone walls and spread around him, encircling copse, Corner Post, and rowan, but not closing in. Colrean could still see the starlit sky directly above, but it was as if he were in a deep hole, surrounded on all sides by gray walls.

Walls of shifting, dense fog.

There was something in the whiteness. Colrean could sense it, but was grateful he couldn't see it. He knew what it must be: one of the ancient evils of thrice-burned Hîrr, the city-state still reviled and feared though a thousand years had passed since its last and utter destruction. The thing in the fog had been called many things by many different peoples. Colrean chose the most common, one that would not reveal his knowledge of any deeper mysteries.

"Grannoch! Many-in-one!" shouted Colrean. "This is not your land, this is not your time. There is nothing here for you. Begone!"

Fog swirled. Colrean caught a glimpse of something—some long limb or perhaps a tail—of ever-burning hide, like lumpy charcoal with crosshatched lines of fire. His eyes burned and tears ran as he watched it disappear once more into the roiling mist, to be replaced by the sudden emergence of a human hand, smooth-skinned and elegant, the fingers beckoning to him, summoning him from his circle. Offering him in that gesture everything he ever wanted, or might want: the most beautiful lover, the greatest power, riches beyond compare—

Colrean dug his foot into the earth, just as it began to rise without his conscious direction, to make him take that first, fatal step out of his protective circle.

"I am not to be caught that way," said Colrean. "I say again, begone!"

The beckoning hand disappeared. The fog thickened, but Colrean could see a dim silhouette building there, a figure forming. Something twice his height, and twice as broad, and only roughly human. One arm was very long, or perhaps held a blade; he could not tell from the mere suggestion of shape in the twisty cloud.

It *was* a blade, of dark crystal or congealed black flame or something stranger still, a blade that erupted from the fog and struck at Colrean, so swiftly he barely saw it. He cried out and flinched as it hit, but it did not cut him in half, as it would have had he been unprotected. The circle he had made around himself stood firm, the unearthly blade rebounding from the unseen barrier with the screech of a nail drawn across an anvil, magnified a thousand times.

"A sorcerer?" whispered a voice high in the air, somewhere in that bank of fog.

A little girl's voice, clear and sweet.

"It bears no ring," answered another voice, seemingly from beneath the earth just beyond Colrean's circle.

This voice was male, and old, and crotchety.

"It has no staff," muttered yet another voice from somewhere in the fog.

A deep-voiced woman. A high-pitched man. An adolescent, the voice shifting, changing with every word.

"The circle is well wrought, and adamant," announced another male voice. "Yet, three strikes shall see it split asunder, or so I judge."

"Unless it be renewed."

"Renewed? No ring, no staff. It is mortal. Such a meager vessel; it must have spent its force."

"Why do we hold back? Strike again, strike again!"

"It smiles. It has a secret. A true wizard comes, we must not tarry."

"Strike or go, strike or—"

The blade shot out again, and once more every muscle in Colrean's body tensed, expecting sudden, awful pain and then the perhaps welcome relief of death. But again the circle held with the scream of iron, and the blade whisked back.

Before the Grannoch could strike again, Colrean hurled himself down and sideways out of the circle, breaking its protection himself even as the third strike split the air above him. Like a cockroach he scuttled away, circling behind the rowan, but the fog rolled closer, and the blade came too swiftly for him to fully escape, the very tip of it slicing the heel off Colrean's left boot and the sole beneath, leaving an agonizing, four-inch-long wound along his foot.

Stifling a sob, Colrean clutched the trunk of the rowan and drew his legs up, hands scrabbling at the chain around his neck. But before he could draw out what was hidden there, the terrible sword came out of the fog once again. Colrean had a split second to know this was the death blow. He shut his eyes and let out the scream that he had been holding back the entire time.

Three seconds later he was still screaming, but he wasn't dead, and there was no new pain to add to the white-hot burn in his foot.

Colrean opened his eyes, the scream fading in his throat. The sword hung above him, wrapped and roped and entangled in rowan branches, and more branches ran outward to grip a great, grotesque arm of smoking, chancred charcoal hide. Through the suddenly broken and dissipated fog Colrean saw the hideous misshapen body of the Grannoch, the "many-in-one." Worst of all, he saw its lumpen head, adorned with all those it had taken over centuries, dozens of mostly human faces crammed too tightly together. All eyes dull and lifeless, but the many mouths writhing, emitting cries and curses as the monster tried to free itself from the grip of the ancient rowan.

Colrean resisted the temptation to shut his eyes again, or to look away and vomit. Instead he drew out the chain, his shaking hand closing on the pendant object. But before he could use whatever he held, the Grannoch tore itself out of the grasp of the rowan with the crack of snapping branches and the rasp of shredding bark. But it did not attack again, instead staggering back, great arms reaching to fend off the rowan's whipping branches, the monster's many mouths no longer shouting or screaming but exhaling thick streams of fog as it tried to shroud itself again.

Colrean put on the ring of wreathed gold and electrum that he usually kept hidden on the chain, and called forth its power. Muttering memory-hooks, he directed his magic this way and that, lines of force reaching deep into the ground around the Grannoch. Then with one wrenching effort of will, the magic opened a great chasm in the ground, the earth breaking apart with a thunderous blare.

Now the Grannoch reached for the rowan branches, rather than trying to fend them off. But it was too slow, the opening of the ground too deep, too sudden and unexpected. The monster fell into the ravine, spouting streams of fog and curses, the rowan's branches snapping back to let it go.

Colrean called upon the last reserves in the ring and shut the chasm with a clap of his hands. The electrum wreath crumbled to dust. The gold band shivered, but remained, though it was now powerless and empty.

Even so, it was clearly a sorcerer's ring, worn on the third finger of Colrean's right hand, and the sight of it would have settled many bets in the three villages.

For a minute or two the ground groaned and rumbled beneath the sorcerer, as if the very earth might choose to spit the Grannoch out, but eventually it stilled. Colrean, his hands trembling with hurt and shock and only slowly ebbing terror, painfully stripped the boot from his left foot and inspected the wound. It was not deep, but ugly, and even as he half laughed and half sobbed at the irony that it had to be his *left* foot the Grannoch's blade had struck, the mage carefully summoned a fraction of the remaining power he held ready in himself. Calling a cauterizing flame to his hand, he used it to cleanse and seal the angry wound.

When he was finished, he tore the tail from his linen shirt and bound it around his foot. That done, he rested his forehead against the rowan's trunk and gave thanks in a quiet whisper. He had hoped it was an ancient guardian of the kind that reviled such things as the Grannoch, but he had not been sure.

When he lifted his forehead from the tree, the rowan's branches shivered, and a single leaf fell into his hand, a leaf more silver in the moonlight than any normal rowan's. Colrean carefully put it inside his jerkin.

"I thank the rowan," he said formally, gingerly hopping up onto his right foot. He almost fell over, and would have done if he hadn't caught himself, both hands against the rowan's trunk. "For all."

He stood there for some time, supported by the tree. Listening, letting his otherworldly senses stretch outward, fearing that the ground might burst open to reveal the Grannoch was not crushed and dead far below, as he truly hoped.

But everything seemed once again returned to the normal business of the night. There was no fog, no silence, just the soft velvet darkness lightened by moon and stars, and the usual small sounds of life and death.

After a time that felt long but he knew was well short of an hour, Colrean began to hold some hope that he might now survive until the dawn. If he made it that far, he should survive the day beyond, as he had some expectation that help would come before the next night. An oathbound, trustworthy wizard would likely come from Ferraul or Achelliston, as both cities were within a day's hard riding. Less, using post-horses and a little magic to draw away fatigue and renew tired muscles.

He had even begun to imagine just such a wizard, when he both heard and felt the approach of something that, while it sounded rather like a horse, he knew from his mage-sense was not. Once again, the natural creatures about knew it too, and all around the owls were fleeing, the field mice diving into holes, the very crickets digging under the barley stalks, all hoping like Colrean to stay alive until the dawn.

There was nowhere for Colrean to hide, and he could not flee. Instead he drew himself up, only one hand resting against the rowan's trunk. He looked across at the stone, and the staff thrust into it. Again he wondered who had put it there, a staff of such power, one sure to draw Rannachin and things like the Grannoch, and the wizard who was coming now.

Only then did Colrean remember the Grannoch had said a true wizard was on the way.

Surely not an oath-bound wizard, though, for there had not been time for anyone to come from the closest cities. Besides, this one was riding a peggoty, a made horse, a thing given a semblance of magical life for a short period. A peggoty was fashioned from green sticks of willow, mud, and the blood of no less than seven mares. Such mounts were accordingly very expensive to make, they took a great deal of power to create and not much less to maintain, and were difficult to ride. But they were much swifter than a horse.

Making things like the peggoty was forbidden to oath-bound wizards. It was blood magic, requiring a great deal of often slow and painful killing, and its practitioners invariably ended up having no concern for any lives but their own.

Sure enough, up alongside the Thrake-Seyam wall came a strutting mount of sticks, with a cloaked and hatted figure on its back, a staff held negligently in the rider's hand. Colrean could not see the face of the wizard, shadowed under the brim of the hat, but he already had an inkling of the rider's identity just from the silhouette and seat. He knew that rider.

She—it had to be she, if he was right—stopped the peggoty a little ways off, and dismounted onto the stone wall. Unlike Colrean, she did so with nimble grace, and there was no danger she would fall or stones dislodge. Her hand waved, moonlight catching several sorcerer's rings upon her fingers, not a meager single ring as Colrean had possessed. With that wave, the peggoty collapsed into its component parts, its work done.

Colrean caught a whiff of the horrible charnel stench of decaying blood and tried not to breathe it in.

He still couldn't see the wizard's face, but he was sure now. He did indeed know every movement of her slender body, the shape of those elegant hands.

"It's been a long time, Naramala," said Colrean, his voice loud in the silent night.

The wizard tilted her head back, perhaps in surprise at hearing his voice, though probably not. He could see her face clearly now. Beautiful Naramala, the woman he had once thought sure to be the great love of his life.

"Coltreen," she said, her voice musical and lovely, even more lovely than her face and body. It was her voice he had fallen in love with first, hearing her unseen in the university library, undeterred by the shushing and hushing of the proctors.

"I am called Colrean now," he said quietly. "The Islanders cannot pronounce hard t's. It seemed easier to let it go."

"The Islanders?" asked Naramala. "Is that where you went? But then why are you here now, so far from the Cold Sea?"

She walked along the wall now, toward copse and rowan and Corner Post. And Colrean. She held the staff like a rope-walker, across her body, as if for balance, though he knew she had no need to do so.

"I live nearby, these two years past," said Colrean, gesturing with his right hand, the moonlight catching on his own ring. "I had enough of the sea, the cold."

"And you made your ring, after all," said Naramala. She stopped several feet short of the farthest-reaching branches of the rowan and stepped lightly down from the wall, bringing her staff vertical. "I did wonder what had become of you. And why you left so abruptly, without a word. Indeed, I was quite hurt."

"I saw you with Alris," said Colrean.

Naramala laughed, an easy, carefree laugh. Even now, knowing what he knew, Colrean felt an ache when he heard it. Such an easy laugh, so warm and inclusive, with her eyes widening that little bit and her mouth twitched just so—

"Oh, we were students then and carefree! How was I to know you would be so jealous of some simple pleasure? Or was it because she was a woman? So rustic, Coltreen! I suppose these barley fields suit you better than the streets of Pran."

"It wasn't jealousy, though I will admit to that. I saw you kill her," said Colrean flatly. "Strangled with her own scarf. And you took her bracelets, the proof that won her the first place."

Naramala didn't answer for a moment, then she laughed again. A little laugh, very different in tone. One of cold amusement, not for sharing, and her eyes became colder still.

"How ever did you see that?"

"There was a cat," said Colrean. "I was practicing watching through its eyes. It chanced to alight on your windowsill, and . . . I saw."

"Only four of us were to be allowed to try for our sorcerer's rings that year," said Naramala conversationally. "Alris might have got *my* place. Though your leaving made it easier still. Were you afraid I would kill you, too?"

"No," replied Colrean. "I was afraid *I* might kill *you*. I couldn't bear . . . everything, I suppose. The disillusionment, the despair. I decided to go as far away as possible. I was young, rash, and judgmental. Of myself, more than anything. How could I have ever loved a murderer?"

"I thought *true* love would transcend mere murder," said Naramala. She looked up at the rowan's branches, many of them now leafless, the bark shredded from its combat with the Grannoch. Giving the tree a wide berth, she circled around toward the stone, tapping the ground with her staff as she walked, her gaze never quite leaving Colrean. "If you ever truly loved me, you would understand why I had to kill Alris. Wizards are not to be judged as normal people, Colrean. If you had stayed to make your staff, you would understand this."

"So you are beyond me, and my judging?" asked Colrean. "Or that of anyone, save other wizards?"

"I am beyond their judgment too," answered Naramala. "Or I will be, once I take the staff in that stone for myself."

"You are not oath-bound?" asked Colrean, though he already knew the answer from the mere existence of the peggoty. "How so?"

Naramala smiled. "Let us say I crossed my fingers," she said. "I found a way to loose the coils. The oath could not hold me, not beyond the passing of a dozen moons. I pretended it did, of course. The old fools have no idea."

Colrean lifted his eyebrows to show his amazement and shuffled around the rowan a little as Naramala edged closer to the stone.

"Are you going to try and stop me, Coltreen?" asked Naramala. "Indeed, I am puzzled why you are here at all. Sorcerer you may be, but you could no more draw that staff than you could stand against me."

"That is as may be," said Colreen. "But you will not take that staff. Nor could the Grannoch who came before you."

Naramala tilted her head slightly, those beautiful pale-hazel eyes weighing up Colrean. He knew she was taking stock of how he leaned upon the tree, his right foot planted too heavily, knee at an odd angle, his left foot drawn up to try and soften the pain of his wounded sole. The single gold band upon his finger, that doubtless she suspected no longer held any reserve of magic. The lack of a staff, and no other obvious articles of magic, no sword or knife or wand. All in all, he must look a posturing fool to deny the wizard Naramala, in all her majesty and power.

"A Grannoch? I wondered what strange corpse was immured below. But any power you did have must have been spent to slay such a thing. I hazard you are empty now, of all but words."

"I am not," said Colrean. "I make no more warnings."

"I would heed none from such as you," said Naramala, and raised her staff.

She muttered no memory-hooks, choosing a simple blast of pure magic that would have thrown Colrean to the ground, doubtless breaking many bones. But he concentrated magic of his own from some unseen source in his clenched fist, raising it against her spell. Naramala's blow broke upon it like a wave on a tall rock, all force diverted about Colrean, dissipating into nothing.

"I wasn't going to kill you," said Naramala. "But you have annoyed me now."

She spoke memory-hooks, her staff raised high. Magic coalesced around the silver-chased tip of the staff, becoming visible as luminous trails that swirled and spun to become a globe of sick yellow light, which with a flick of her arm, Naramala sent drifting toward Colrean's head.

He knew what it was: a standard of wizard's duels, though few could cast it so well or so swiftly. The Asphyxiation of Lygar, an impenetrable globe that would settle on his shoulders and constrict, denying him breath or crushing his skull, death coming swiftly either way.

Colrean drew yet more power into his fist, babbling memory-hooks himself, each word reminding him how the magic must be shaped to form a specific spell, this one a counterspell of considerable strength.

A wizard's spell.

The globe began to lower over his head, but Colrean thrust his hand within it and opened his fingers. There was a flash of brilliant light, a shower of small sparks that died even as they fell to the earth, and the globe was no more.

"How—"

Naramala did not finish her question, but immediately began to mutter again, building another spell. Colrean watched her intently, trying to read her lips, to work out which memory-hooks she was using in order to anticipate her casting. A few seconds after she started, he began as well, calling power as he sketched an outline in front of himself in the air. Smoke trailed from his fingers, lines of lurid too-white smoke that he drew across and up and down, weaving the smoke together to make a solid shield.

Colrean finished a scant second before Naramala unleashed an incinerating bolt of power from her staff, of such strength it blew his shield of smoke apart and struck him full on the chest, flames licking over his entire body. But the shield had *almost* worked, for the flames died even as they struck. Though blackened and shocked, Colrean was hardly burned.

Naramala shrieked in frustration as she saw he still lived, though he had fallen to one knee and was blinking away soot. Raising her staff, she ran forward, clearly intent on delivering a killing blow of both magical and physical force—a favored tactic of the most brutal wizards when their opponents were temporarily stunned.

Colrean raised his hand and called more magic into it, but he was dazed and could not shape it, could not get his ashen tongue to utter a memory-hook, and then Naramala was in front of him, her staff blazing with power, and she raised herself up and—

The rowan struck first. Two branches wound around the staff and plucked it from her grasp, even as another forked branch closed around the wizard's neck. Lifting her high, yet another branch secured her legs, and then, just as a farmer might kill a chicken, the rowan broke Naramala's neck and threw her down upon the ground.

The wizard's arms twitched. Her heels drummed, and a terrible inhuman clicking sound emanated from her throat. Then she was still.

Colrean flinched as the rowan threw the wizard's staff down next to her body. Coughing up soot, he groaned and leaned back against the tree, stretching out his legs. The wound in his left foot had opened again, the bandage blown off. His right boot had black rimmed burn holes and scorch marks all over it, as did his breeches, and through the holes he could see the sheen of his narwhal-horn peg leg, and the shine of the gold bands that wound around the horn from tip to base.

The Islanders also had wizards, but they did not carry their staves openly.

Colrean looked across at Naramala's body and then over at the Corner Post, looming dark against the lighter sky. The bronze foot of the staff high up seemed to wink in the starlight. Colrean stared at it and became certain of something he had begun to suspect.

"Come out!" called Colrean, his voice unsteady. There were tears in his eyes, tears running down his cheeks, making trails through the layer of soot. They were for Naramala, as he had once thought she was, and for his younger, foolish self, and because he was hurt and weakened, and the night was *still* not done.

"Come out!"

The staff in the stone shifted against the backdrop of stars, slanting down. As it moved, a line of light sprang up behind it, so bright that Colrean had to duck his head, put his chin against his chest, and cover his face with his forearm. Even shielded so, and with his eyes tightly shut, it was almost unbearably bright.

The light ebbed. Colrean risked a glimpse, raising his arm a little. There was a figure stepping down from the Corner Post—from inside the Corner Post—lit from behind by a softer light, as if deep within the stone there was sunshine. The silhouette was almost a caricature of a wizard, with the pointed, broad-brimmed hat, the trailing sleeves, the staff as tall as its bearer.

"Verashe," said Colrean, naming the wizard as she came toward him, now rounded and real under the moon and stars, not a shadowed shape backlit by the strange illumination from the stone, a light that was already fading. "Grand Wizard."

"Coltreen," said the wizard mildly. She was very old, but not stooped. Still taller than Colrean, straight-backed and imposing. Her face was lined and thin, but her green eyes sharp as ever. Her long hair, once red, was pale with time and tied back under her hat, save for one slight wisp, which was escaping above her left ear. "Or Colrean, as I believe you call yourself now."

She bowed her head to the rowan as Colrean had done, if not so deeply. A greeting of equals, or those long familiar.

"So you set your snare, and have caught two unbound wizards," said Colrean bitterly. He lifted himself against the trunk of the rowan, trying to sit more upright, and winced as new pains made themselves felt.

"I did not even know you were in these parts," replied Verashe. "Not until I came here, at least, and by then matters were already in train."

"So the lure was for Naramala alone?" asked Colrean wearily. "Did you expect the Grannoch too?"

"I was not sure what might come," answered the Grand Wizard. She knelt down at Colrean's side and ran her fingers over the sole of his foot, once again stemming the flow of blood with magic and doing something else that vanquished the pain. A curious thing to do for a condemned man, thought Colrean, and a small spark of hope grew inside him.

"I did try to ensure Naramala would be foremost of the wizards, since it was well past time her ambitions should be thwarted."

"You knew she had evaded the oath?"

"Of course," replied Verashe. She sighed. "Almost every class has someone like Naramala, certain of their own cleverness and destiny. And the oath, though robust, cannot hold against continued use of blood magic and human sacrifice. She killed Cateran and Lieros too, you know, and quite a number of beggars and the like—those she believed would not be readily missed. All the while thinking herself unobserved."

Colrean wiped his eyes and pretended no new tears brimmed there. Cateran and Lieros had been fellow students too. He remembered first meeting them, brimful with the joy of learning magic. They had both come to their powers unexpectedly, unbelieving they had won places at the university in Pran, foremost of the schools of wizardry.

Verashe ran her index finger from one burned hole in Colrean's breeches to another, splitting the cloth all along the leg, to completely expose the limb made of gold-banded narwhal horn. In addition to the gold, the horn was deeply etched along the whorls with scenes of ships and the sea, and set with tiny pearls and pieces of amber.

"I have only seen one such . . . staff . . . before," mused Verashe. "A wizard called Sissishuram studied with us one summer, it must be thirty years ago now. Though her staff took the place of her left arm from the elbow, and ended in the most vicious hook."

"Sissishuram was my master," said Colrean. "She remembered you, and told me I was a fool to risk coming back. Verashe will brook no unbound wizard, she said. Stay with us, we who are free upon the sea."

Verashe stood up and walked across to look down upon Naramala's body, and the staff next to it.

"How did you go within the stone?" asked Colrean. "What spell?"

Verashe didn't answer him, instead picking up Naramala's fallen staff, so she held one in each hand.

"I am overcurious for a man about to die, I suppose," said Colrean. He laughed, a short laugh that ended almost with a sob. "Stupid of me, I suppose. To want to know such a thing now."

"Are you sure you will not come back to Pran? The oath is not so terrible for someone who has no desire for power."

"It is not the oath alone," replied Colrean slowly. He looked up at the sky above, so vast with stars, the moon hanging in the corner. There were clouds drifting across from the west now, doubtless bringing rain. All the small sounds had come back, and the westerly breeze that had sprung up to bring the clouds was steadily strengthening, taking away the stench of sudden death as easily as it flung barley chaff across the field. He thought of the three villages beyond the commons to north, east, and south, with their people asleep behind barred oak doors, their windowsills salted, trusting to him to keep them safe.

"It is not the oath at all," continued Colrean. He looked up at Verashe, unsure what he could see in her face, whether it was the executioner he beheld or the messenger bringing an unexpected pardon to the very foot of the block.

"I want . . . I need to stay here. I cannot live in the city, any city. I do not wish to serve the Grand Mayors, I do not desire gold and servants and all that goes with such things. I want to do small magics, for ordinary folk, and be at peace. I have found . . . happiness . . . here. I will not relinquish it."

"We permit no unbound wizards in Pran, or Huyere, or the five cities, and those who defy this order end as Naramala has done," mused Verashe, apparently to herself. She paused and glanced across at Colrean. "Here, among barley fields and forest, the strictures are less . . . straitened . . . shall we say. And the rowan is a fine judge of what truly lies inside the hearts of people . . ."

She stopped talking again, and bowed her head to the tree again, her face now shadowed by her hat. Colrean watched her, wondering, hoping.

"So, Colrean. I have decided to let you live. But if you will not be bound by the oath, other bindings must be applied, other bounds set. You must swear by the rowan you will abide here, to never go more than twenty leagues from the Corner Post, without leave from the Grand Wizard and the Council."

Colrean nodded stiffly, and reached inside his jerkin for the silver leaf the rowan had given him, a token of its trust. He held it in his hand and spoke.

"I swear by the rowan, I shall abide here, and go no farther than twenty leagues from the Corner Post, without leave from the Grand Wizard and the Council."

The leaf shivered and crumbled, leaving only the delicate tracery of its veins behind, and these sank into Colrean's palm, marking the skin with russet and silver lines. If he broke this oath, the ancient rowan would know, and hold him accountable.

Colrean shivered, remembering the sounds of Naramala's death.

"Good," said Verashe. She held Naramala's staff out to him. "You will need this, I think, to help you hobble to the closest house, where I trust we can have an early breakfast."

Colrean took the staff wonderingly, and slowly used it to lever himself upright. He could feel the vestige of magic within the bog-oak and the bands of gold, but the staff's power was almost entirely spent. It would take many years to fill again.

"Naramala?" he asked, looking at the body.

"The Rannachin would also break their fast," answered Verashe, gesturing.

Colrean looked across the barley and saw the moon shadows there. He frowned, but only for a moment. He had no strength to dig a grave or build a cairn, and in truth, it was better nothing should remain of a wizard who had practiced blood magic. The Rannachin were known to eat even bones and teeth, and they would take no scathe from any remnant magic, as a rat or other scavenger might.

"Come!" said Verashe impatiently. "I have been fasting within the stone since the last dawn, and I am too old to miss another meal!"

"We cannot go to the closest house," said Colrean. "Two wizards in Gamel, and none calling into Seyam and Thrake? Besides, they won't let us in until after dawn. I warned them not to admit anyone, and they would rightly be afraid. It is farther, but I have food and drink in my forest house."

He limped past the Grand Wizard, pausing to bow once again to the rowan, leaning heavily on his new staff. A few paces along he bowed to the Corner Post as well, and turned his head back to Verashe.

"My question remains . . . how exactly did you inhabit the stone? What spell could overcome such power as resides there?"

Verashe laughed. She did not have a lovely voice like Naramala's, and her laugh was like a crow's call. But Colrean did not mind, for it was human.

"You have a true wizard's curiosity," she said. "But no spell would let you dwell within this stone. It was a matter of friendship, a courtesy allowed me. We have known each other a very long time, the Corner Post and I."

Colrean nodded thoughtfully and set forth again, stumping alongside the wall. It was much darker now, half the sky clouded, and it was starting to rain. A soft drizzle that spread the soot about his face and streaked his clothes, rather than washing anything clean.

I will need a hat he thought, surprising himself that he could think of any such ordinary thing amidst pain and grief and weariness. But he could, and he was glad of it, and he grabbed at the thought as he might a lifeline aboard one of the Islanders' ships.

I will need a hat to go with the staff. The villagers, particularly Sommie and Heln, will expect me to fully look the part, and it will keep the rain off. I suppose the brim from Gamel, the body from Thrake, the tip from Seyam—or the other way about . . .

Elizabeth Bear

• • •

Everyone knows that imitation is the sincerest form of flattery—but it can also be the most dangerous, especially when magic is involved.

Elizabeth Bear was born in Connecticut, and now lives in South Hadley, Massachusetts, with her husband, writer Scott Lynch. She won the John W. Campbell Award for Best New Writer in 2005, and in 2008 took home a Hugo Award for her short story "Tideline," which also won her the Theodore Sturgeon Memorial Award (shared with David Moles). In 2009, she won another Hugo Award for her novelette "Shoggoths in Bloom." Her short work has appeared in *Asimov's Science Fiction*, *Subterranean*, *Sci Fiction*, *Interzone*, *The Third Alternative*, *Strange Horizons*, *On Spec*, and elsewhere, and has been collected in *The Chains That You Refuse* and *Shoggoths in Bloom*. She is the author of the five-volume New Amsterdam fantasy series, the three-volume Jenny Casey SF series, the five-volume Promethean Age series, the three-volume Jacob's Ladder series, the three-volume Edda of Burdens series, and the three-volume Eternal Sky series, as well as three novels in collaboration with Sarah Monette. Her other books include the novels *Carnival* and *Undertow*. Her most recent book is an acclaimed new novel, *The Stone in the Skull*.

◆   ◆   ◆

No Work of Mine

ELIZABETH BEAR

"This," said Brazen the Enchanter, dropping something to the slates with a crash, "is not one of yours."

It twitched erratically, whatever it was, and rattled against itself while it made as if to crawl away. Bijou rose from her workbench and stretched the creaks and cracks from between a spine that was beginning to bend with more than middle age. She pushed her locks away from her seamed face and craned to get a better look at the whatever-it-was. Her vision blurred; in a moment she remembered she was still wearing the quartz lenses that Brazen had made her for close work, and dropped them to the end of her chain.

Several of Bijou's more crablike creations scuttled across the floor to investigate. Bones, long and ivory. Metal with the look of silver, but it had not rung cleanly when Brazen dropped it. Jewels that did not flash quite as enticingly as the real thing.

Bijou frowned at it, and then at Brazen. "I haven't seen you around here for a while. Shouldn't you be off with that lady friend?"

"I broke up with what's-her-name almost a year ago."

"Najma." Bijou shook her head. "I should have raised you better."

Her former apprentice, now a master wizard in his own right, shrugged and grinned. "You can't amend a man's basic flaws of character, no matter how early you apprentice him. Besides, haven't I always been dutiful to you, my old master?"

Bijou, despite herself, felt a smile elevate one corner of her mouth— just the one. The left one.

Brazen stood behind the tawdry heap with his legs braced wide, his arms crossed over his barrel body so his biceps strained the brocaded sleeves of his flaring coat. His skin was of a rare, florid paleness; his hair gray-blond and waving to his shoulders. Copper wire, braided into lavish sideburns, ended in sapphires at the level of his jaw. He looked as smug, virile, and disreputable as any tomcat who has brought home the back half of something unspeakable and dropped it in his owner's lap.

"Are you suggesting I've been neglecting you?" There might have been a little guilt in his sidelong glance.

"On the contrary. I *had* been getting an extraordinary amount of work done."

She missed having him around, but she wasn't going to say that. Could barely admit it to herself. Bijou's early experience of expressing vulnerability in her family of birth had not been the sort that encouraged repeat offenses.

Bijou came around the table. She picked up the cane hooked on its edge and, rather than as a prop, used its silver ferrule to poke the twitching pile.

"You are correct," she said. "This is no work of mine. And thus, what concern is it to me?"

"I shan't have to salt my meat for a week, if you're going to take that tone." His beard broke into a grin. She refused to be irritated by him; he had been the son of her dearest friend, the wizard Salamander, and she would have forgiven him anything just on those grounds alone. Hell, she forgave him the painful fact of his paternity, and she had forgiven it to Salamander, too.

She thought of Salamander for a moment, the little crawling and slithering creatures that whispered secrets to her, the smile she kept just for Bijou. It was odd, Bijou thought, that though Brazen's mother had been an ophiomancer and a speaker to arachnids, and his father was a necromancer, his magic was enchantment, and more like her own artificing than the wizardry of either of the people who had given to him

blood and bone. She would not think that in some way her spirit animated him a little, too—but she would, perhaps, have *liked* to think it.

Bijou's own mother, in the distant land of her birth, had not been a
faithful parent. Bijou had chosen not to become a parent at all, but this
son of her best-beloved friend, whom she had raised as her own . . . He
was, she thought, all the son she needed.

All the son, realistically, that she could stand.

The fact that he had a good deal of native charm to soften his teasing
just meant that refusing to be irritated by him was easy.

She said, "And you shall never learn the answer to your question."

She poked the sad pile of bones and paste and painted tin once more.
It rattled plaintively, as if it wished she could help. There were bits of
lemur skeleton in there, she thought, surveying it with the practiced eye
of a natural philosopher. But not just one lemur. Not even just one species of lemur. And some monkey, too.

She stopped poking it long enough for it to reassemble itself in some
sort of rational shape. A little monkey-shape on a golden chain, like the
capuchins people in the market fed on dates and slices of Song orange.
The armature that held the bones together was tin, or bits of it were, and
some others were brass or copper. Bright enough, to be sure, but just
pressed and snipped sheets of the stuff: not work-hardened and not
strong. Paste jewels had cracked from various settings where they had
been cheaply glued rather than set with prongs, leaving tattered foil
backings that had been meant to make them sparkle like real stones.
One orange stone remained in the skull, to regard her blankly as she
levered herself down to crouch closer to the little thing's disjointed level.
The other socket gaped, showing a yellowish stain of poorly prepared
hide glue.

"Aren't you a mess, little monkey?" Bijou said. "I'd whip any apprentice that threw together a thing like you."

It scrabbled at the floor with little tin mittens. Whoever had constructed it hadn't even bothered with the fussy work of threading the
finger bones together to give it usable paws. There was no spark in the
gaze it gave her: not even confusion or fear. It was an animate heap of
bones and trash, to be sure, but not well animated. And already falling
apart, as the crudely constructed magics that had informed it were dis-

sipating. It had been imbued with no will, no essence that would sustain it.

She looked up at Brazen. "If you brought it to me so I could put it out of its misery, I'm not actually sure it has any. There's no consciousness in this. It's just a . . . windup toy."

"No," Brazen said. His sweeping gesture took in the wide-open, arch supported spaces of Bijou's stone workroom. The forge, the jeweler's table, the racks of drying bone. The shapes of her various creations as they ranged observantly around the periphery of the room, watching the conversation with impassive, jeweled eyes and dreaming their bone-and-jewel dreams. Light from the big many-paned clerestory windows slanted in dusty rays through the slatted ribs of Hawti, the elephant; struck a sprinkle of dancing reflections from the shards of glass and mirror paving the skull of the sloth, Lazybones, from his haunt in the rafters; wavered in the translucent watered-silk pinions stretched over the enormous wing bones of Catherine, the giant condor; sparkled and gleamed in the facets of enough fine jewels to pave the temples of the Mother of Markets herself, the city of jackals, this great metropolis Messaline.

Bijou followed his gesture and frowned, but did not speak. He had a sense of the dramatic. But he was like a son to her—a middle-aged, sometimes irritating son—and she knew he'd get around to the useful information shortly.

"When was the last time you stepped outside?" he asked.

"I have my work," Bijou answered. "I'm very busy. Also, this morning." Surely the walled garden behind her studio counted as "outside."

"Well, you'd better put something better on, because we're going outside now," he said, as if pronouncing sentence from a magistrate's bench. "Because *someone* is selling these pathetic forgeries as the creations of Bijou the Artificer."

Messaline was the Mother of Markets, and it was to one such market that they went. Bijou awoke the oldest and least refined of her surviving creations, the centipede Ambrosias—a creature cobbled together from the spine of a cobra, ferret ribs, and the skull of a cat. She coaxed Ambrosias to link himself about her waist as a double loop of belt, his topaz eyes glittering over her middle as if his skull were a clasp. He snuggled quite comfortably there, and looked, she thought, quite dashing. Then she draped herself in a pale-blue cloak against the gaze of the lion-headed sun of Messaline, although it did not trouble her half so much as it did the blue-eyed Northerner beside her. She herself was from the south, where the sun had enameled her birth people in shades of red-black like dark wood and blue-black like dark stone, but it never hurt to be a little comfortable.

She thought about a disguise, but who could disguise the Artificer Bijou in her adopted city of Messaline? She was as well-known here as the Wizard-Prince herself, though Bijou's countenance did not appear on coins. She did not actually expect to find some little man in a tent along one of the many markets' many winding ways with a string of tin monkeys glittering cheaply on a pole, singing out her name as his supplier. Her work sold to private collectors, and there was a waiting list for commissions that would stretch to the likely end of even a wizard's life, if she were to permit it. But her pocket clicked with a fistful of paste jewels, and she thought it likely that she might be able to find out who had created *them*.

They stepped into the street, greeted by a chatter of brown and black songbirds.

"It's not a very convincing forgery," she said. "Who would pay for such a thing? With"—she snorted—"little tin mittens, no less? What good is a monkey that can't even climb?"

"Easier to keep off the curtain rods, I suppose. Besides, it did look a little better before I broke the glamour on it." He looked straight ahead, not admitting anything with a sidelong glance.

She sighed. Of course he had. When she might have recognized the signature of such work. Well, probably not; she hadn't been able to make head nor tail—so to speak—of the pathetic attempt at imbuing the creature with life. Which meant the perpetrator probably was not a wizard of Messaline, because there weren't that many, and she thought she knew them all, though people did release apprentices into the wild with alarming regularity these days, and the older she got, the harder it was to keep track of them all.

If it wasn't a wizard, that was something of a relief. The politics would be easier, and she hated to think of one of her own debasing themself so. Also, she hated to think that anybody with any self-respect would turn loose an apprentice that couldn't do any better.

"Well." Brazen spoke defensively into her silence. "I wanted to see what it looked like underneath, so I would have a better idea of what to tell you."

"Then wouldn't they just come to me and ask me to repair it? Or take it back to their broker and do so?"

"Really," Brazen said, shaking his head so his blond mane fluffed and settled. He understood her change of subject as forgiveness. "Would *you* turn up to dun a wizard of Messaline for repair of inferior work?"

"Oh, probably," said Bijou.

He grinned and rolled his eyes. So would he, of course. Which was why he and she were wizards of Messaline, and not among the brightly garbed pedestrians in their striped linen robes and saffron dresses sweeping rapidly aside to make way.

"How many of these forgeries do you think there are?" she asked suspiciously.

He shrugged.

"So they're not just trading on my good name," Bijou said. "They are debasing it."

She had begun receiving a lot more public attention some years before, after the work she did for the museum in restoring the enormous, petrified skeleton of an ancient monster called a "dinosaur." The exhibit was still quite popular, she was given to understand, and had led to the reconstruction of the museum's rotunda into a larger, taller space—to accommodate the crowds, and also to give the Tidal Titan that she had named Amjada-Zandrya more space to perform, as performing was the creature's great delight. Especially if there were small children around.

Her reconstruction had not, in particular, helped to alleviate the academic dispute between Dr. Azar and Dr. Munquidh, the two quarrelsome paleontologists involved, but you couldn't have everything.

"When you wish to order the miscreant's liver roasted in the marketplace, seasoned for your pleasure, my dear Bijou . . . I know an excellent kebab merchant who can provide just the sauce."

Liver kebab didn't sound very pleasant. But food did—and, as Brazen pointed out, they weren't in any particular hurry, and justice could be dealt out on a full belly more comfortably than a flat one.

They were entering the temple precincts where the market was most populous. A number of merchants selling spices and food clustered not far from the temple of the Goddess of Death, bright Kaalha. Bijou, happily pulling shreds of highly seasoned lamb from a shard of palm stem, supposed that funerals did tend to make people hungry. Starlings swooped overhead and darted down to snatch horrible mouthfuls from the pavement underfoot.

"The city has been infested with those things lately," Brazen said, parrying a rose-and-black bird that whizzed too close to his mustache.

Bijou licked cumin-scented grease from her mouth and gazed around. Brazen was far taller than she was, though they both had an advantage in that the throng broke around them, creating a moving buffer where no one pushed, jostled, or shoved. They flowed through the mob as a droplet of oil smooths bubbling water, always at the center of a zone of peace enforced by the occasional more-alert friend or relation's quick yank on a distracted marketer's collar, cuff, or elbow.

Bijou's heart quickened with scents, sounds, colors. Perhaps it *had* been too long since she had made such an excursion.

"Silks and floss are over there," she said, steering Brazen around the distinct aroma of a picket of horses and a camel or two. The dung smell mingled foully with her luncheon, and anyway camels could spit, and mares could pee dramatically backward—and had no respect at all for the trappings of human social authority. "That fellow in the rose-colored turban has excellent wire. Drawn very smooth."

"*Excellent* wire is not, today, what we're searching for. I see a jeweler or two. Proper jewelers, though."

They dodged the sounds of an escalating dogfight, quickly overmatched by the crueler sounds of human wagering. The cries of sellers of water, wine, and ink-black coffee cajoled them; the honey and nut aromas of cooling pastries beguiled them. Brazen gave a penny to a man who stood alone on a corner, atop a little painted pedestal, wearing a felt cap and holding a parasol over his head.

"Paste gems," he said.

The directory raked them with a glance, gaze not needing to linger to assess fabric, cut, jewels, the quality and age of boot leather. "Surely, honored master wizard, you can afford better for such a beautiful lady than paste?"

Bijou tilted her head, long locks sliding under her pale-blue hood. "Surely, honored master directory, you are able to provide the knowledge my friend has paid you for?"

She had to admire his spunk; he didn't even sigh. He just smiled slightly and directed them down a side street shaded by date palms, if palm trees could really be said to shade anything. Heavy with fruit, they fluttered with the wings of birds. "Look for Azif at the orange-and-blue tent," he said.

"Look for Azif," Brazen mocked, dawdling along. "Let us go to Song and look for a Chu, as well, and a Tsering in Rasa."

"Well, there is the orange-and-blue tent," Bijou said, pointing. "And the thing about common names is that a lot of people do have them."

She had a suspicion of what she would see when they came up to the tent, but it was good that her only wager on it was a private one—because there was a shop there, and it was open for business, striped awnings propped high to shade the interior but allow the sun to sparkle on his gaudy wares. Gilded tin badges, paste jewels, cameos molded and carved into layered ceramic rather than gorgeous agate stone.

The Azif in charge was a slender man, wiry. He had the look of a Messaline native, which was less common every year in this cosmopolitan city of markets and immigrants. His buzzing presence combined with his physique to make Bijou speculate that most of his sustenance came in the form of syrup-sweet coffee. He turned when they came up, and she saw the instant when he assessed who they were, and his manner transitioned from obsequious to crestfallen. "Surely, great wizards, my poor wares cannot interest you. You flatter Azif!"

"Here now," said Brazen, stepping up to the glass-topped display boxes that served for a counter. Tawdry treasures winked on threadbare velvet under the shadow of his hand as he spread a few flaking paste jewels on scratched glass. "Are these your manufacture, sir? Or, if not, can you name the artisan? No penalty, whatever you answer, and there may be coin in it for a helpful one."

Azif reached out slowly, glancing up at Brazen's face for permission. He lifted a bit of gaud that gave back flashes of copper, blue, and violet and turned it slowly in his hand. "Who made this, pardon my saying, was a careless artisan. The glass is a mix of good quality, but there are bubbles in it, and the backing, while of decent materials, was not carefully applied. See here?"

He shook his head and reached for his loupe. "I should hate to belabor any of my colleagues with such poor workmanship. And see, there is no maker's mark applied around the girdle, here."

Bijou took the loupe, and looked where he indicated while he sorted through the remaining gems. The narrow band around the widest part of the paste jewel was polished and smooth, without any brand.

Brazen, almost naturally, remarked, "But the quality of the materials is good, you say?"

"This looks as if it might have been the effort of an apprentice left alone with his master's tools. The mold was a good one, but badly poured, and the facets were not polished at the correct angles." He held out one of his own pieces for comparison, and Bijou could see plainly how superior the stone was, in sparkle and flash and evenness of edge, and how the mirrored foil backing was neatly adhered. There was skill in anything, even fakery.

"I would say," Azif finished, "that all of these were made by the same person. And that his master is going to be displeased with the theft of materials at the next inventory."

"How many makers of paste jewels are in Messaline?" Bijou asked. "Who use materials of this quality, and can support an apprentice or two?"

Her earlier irritation had waned, and she was starting to appreciate the humor of the situation enough to play along. When Azif named three men, however, she fixed Brazen with a steady glare and said, quite calmly, "I do hope we shan't have to visit every one of them."

Brazen's sun-flushed face might have paled a little, but it was hard to tell. He said, "What if we visit Yusuf, here? He's closest. If we get lucky, we'll have had the shortest walk."

Keep stalling, Bijou thought. And nodded.

◆   ◆   ◆

Yusuf did not work in a market stall, but rather in a little mud-brick building that was part of a similar, single-story row along the back of a rank of much taller and better-built houses that clustered in the shadow of one of the ancient, colossal ruins that dotted the precincts of Messaline. This one, of blue-green stone that shrugged off weather and the tools of those who would disassemble it for building material, was a long, curved channel, lofted atop a series of arches that soared perhaps five or six stories into the air.

It might have once been part of an aqueduct, for the ends were ragged as if broken. Some said it had been built during the reign of the Eyeless One, the so-called Wizard-Prince of Messaline, centuries before. Others said it had been destroyed then. Bijou'd never seen fit to research it properly.

Predictably, the neighborhood it cast its shadow on was known as the Five Arches.

Yusuf's apprentice was not in, though Yusuf—perhaps having a higher opinion of himself than Azif, though from what Bijou could see of his work in comparison, it was not quite warranted—did not seem at all dismayed by the appearance of two wizards at his door. He was a younger man, well built, clad mostly in trousers, boots, and a leather apron, and it seemed from the items on display at the front of his shop that paste gems were more of a sideline to his business of little glass knickknacks and sculptures.

He frowned when Brazen held out the bits of paste.

"Those could be my molds," he said reluctantly. "But that's not my casting. Nor my polishing either." He glanced over at the stocks of glass rods ranked on the walls, the barrels of colored powders, the rolls of foil. They were in some disarray, and Bijou didn't think he could judge what might be present or missing at a glance.

"Your apprentice?"

"Reza." He huffed through his nose like a snake. "He's taken a delivery to the Museum of Natural History, if you wish to speak to him."

"Huh," Brazen said. "Both Bijou and I have some work on display there."

◆　◆　◆

Brazen stumped along, limiting his stride automatically to make it easier for Bijou to keep up. They walked in more or less companionable silence for a while. The museum wasn't far, and they soon found themselves within sight of its sweep of low steps and the square before it, which bustled with activity—human and avian. The people moved more at random and cross-purposes than the pigeons and starlings, who flocked in great swoops and spirals and concordances of wings.

The museum itself rose opposite them, its approach flanked by a great fountain on the left and a life-size brass statue of a camel on the right. The camel was some of the work of Brazen's he had alluded to. It was designed so that the right side seemed to show a breathing animal—nostril flared and great padded foot uplifted, head thrown back as if it had been caught in the middle of a startled response to some predator. But if you approached it from the left—the interior, the side toward the museum approach—what you found was a surgical cutaway, with every specimen organ intact and visible in its place, all differentiated in colored crystal so the lungs were violet, the heart red, the liver liver-colored, the intestines ivory, and so forth. Its limbs and torso also revealed representative examples of the bones and muscles, ligaments and tendons enameled in different brilliant colors.

Bijou's contribution to the museum was not visible from the outside, except in the evidence of the recently enlarged and reconstructed atrium dome. Still, she felt a little swell of pride in her breast at the sight. Academic feuds or no, that had been, she judged, a job well done.

Brazen, in his own case, paused to contemplate his camel as they came up on it. He inspected it and nodded with pursed lips, as if in retrospect he too felt that he'd done a pretty good job on the commission. The camel blinked at them languidly and shifted its dramatic pose fluidly, revealing different aspects of its construction as it turned around upon its pedestal; it had been constructed by Brazen the Enchanter, after all. Any decent sculptor could have built a startlingly detailed anatomical study of a camel. *This* one was *interactive*.

Brazen turned to glance up at the front of the museum. Its white marble façade had elements of Aezin and Asitaneh architectural styles—gold and lapis tiles, pointed arches—and managed to evoke the great universities and learning of ancient civilization without ever quite tip-ping over into looking like a temple to foreign gods. The designers had meant to evoke a sense of permanence and history with this edifice of scholarship. "You don't suppose it was one of the good doctors behind all this, do you?"

Bijou shrugged. "I didn't leave either Dr. Azar or Dr. Munquidh any happier with me than they were with each other."

"Academic rivalries do get nasty."

"On the other hand, neither one of them is a wizard. Or even a sorceress."

"People can surprise you," Brazen remarked casually, crouching down to examine the camel's metal feet—whether to inspect them for wear or contemplate the details of his work, Bijou was not sure.

"Or perhaps," Bijou said, dry as paper, "it's time you admitted that this whole series of errands has been a jackal hunt you set up for me specifically, and that you've been deliberately spending my time."

Brazen looked at her calmly, ingenuously. Then he sighed, and said, "What gave me away?"

"You were my student for fourteen years," she reminded him. "And your mother was the best friend I ever had. And you are, after all, Brazen the Enchanter. You could animate a little creature like that as an automaton, which is rather different than the self-willed artifices I create but would serve as a plausible 'forgery.'"

He made a disgruntled moue.

"So. Are you going to tell me what we are doing at the museum and why you needed to get me out of my workshop for half a day to set it— *Duck!*"

"What?"

"*Duck*," she yelled, and grabbed his ear to pull him down.

Something small, rose-colored and black, aerodynamic, whistled over their heads. At first she thought it was a missile of some sort, but as it crashed into the façade of the building behind them, she saw that the body tumbling to the dusty street, leaving a red smear behind, was that of a starling. She'd been seeing them all day, and in the back of her mind they had become a worrying omen. Now, the chattering flock on the parapet of the building opposite lifted into the air, and Bijou said, "Does anybody want to kill you this week?"

Brazen rubbed his smarting ear. "Other than you? We'd better run."

Bijou grabbed his hand, pulling him toward the arched façade of the museum. A few people loitered on the broad steps, but there was no other destination toward which she could run without equally endangering civilians, and the plaza itself was full of people—and of birds.

She sprinted up the steps, Brazen thumping along beside her. Her hip hurt, and the muscles beside her spine told her she'd be paying for the desperate exertion later, but at least the physical nature of her daily labor made her strong and gave her a good wind. And Brazen, while barrel-shaped, was as tough as the oaken staves of said barrel. He kept up.

Something sharp and hard struck Bijou between the shoulder blades as they gained the top step. She felt a stabbing pain, and then the sudden release of Ambrosias unclasping himself at her waist and uncoiling. She staggered. Brazen's support wrenched her shoulder but kept her from going to a knee.

Another starling swooped by. Brazen ducked aside—it might have taken him in the eye—and there was a horrid, brittle snapping sound like green twigs as Ambrosias lunged, snatched the bird from the air, and crushed the life from it.

Bijou pitied the iridescent black rag that fell. It wasn't the starling's fault it was ensorceled. But who on earth might be doing the ensorceling? She did not know of any wizard in Messaline who could command animals, not since the death of Brazen's mother, who had never had much to do with birds anyway.

The attacking flock was all starlings—but there were two kinds of starlings represented, the plain black and the ones that were black and rosy. They did not usually flock together: another mystery.

Around Bijou and Brazen, the relaxing holiday-makers were scrambling out of the way, running up the steps or down, flocking like birds themselves in their attempts to avoid the murderous starlings. Ambrosias reared over Bijou's head like a cobra crown, fending off birds as the swarm made another pass. She could, she thought, call the creature within the museum—the Tidal Titan, great Amjada-Zandrya. In summoning it, it would come.

But in coming, it would destroy the museum's dome, and Bijou could not even begin to guess how many lives.

She would not call.

Ambrosias was her resource now. They had been together through so much; a flock of birds was nothing, with Brazen at their side. Blood trickled down her back, under her robe. This would be a ridiculous way for two of the finest wizards in Messaline to die.

They ran for the overhang beneath the arches, but the birds circled and cut them off. They stood exposed on the steps, back to back, beneath the lion sun and the unsheltering sky. Ambrosias swatted about himself, missing, as the flock swung through again. Birds left beak- and talon-streaks on Bijou's face; yanked and tangled at her hair. They swirled around Brazen, pecking and savaging.

Brazen dropped his grip on Bijou and threw his own arms wide, brocaded cuffs falling back from broad, hairy wrists. He made a gesture of summoning and spoke five ancient words of mystery.

Bijou covered her ears with her hands.

Bijou's wizardry allowed her to animate her bone-and-jewel constructions, to give them a semblance of life, personality, and will. They were unique from her, once they were done, and suffered under their own personalities. She could create automata out of once-living things, but it required a constant expenditure of effort and concentration to keep them at work.

Brazen too could animate—but his artifices were machines, without agency of their own. They were made of metal and stone, and without the whispers of animating force remaining from the fled life of the creatures that provided Bijou with their bones, Brazen's creatures did what they were told. Independently, once released—but they could not innovate as did Bijou's creations.

They could, however, be given new orders. And Brazen, with all the barrel-chested strength in his lungs, bellowed those orders now.

The half-dissected bronze and crystal camel at the foot of the staircase twisted its head—half dopey and jaded-looking, after the manner of camels, and half skeletal—around. It focused its glass eyes up the steps. With haste, with surprising grace, it departed its pedestal.

The clattering and clangering split Bijou's skull even through the protection of her palms as the automaton came up the stairs at a marble-chipping run. The birds wheeled and dive-bombed it, the collective beating of their wings like the piston stride on a locomotive, like the thump of marching boots. Bijou flinched in anticipation. But either the birds or whoever was responsible for their ensorcelment, had enough sense not to send them plowing into the automaton. They broke around it, surfed over it, and came on in a river, a black mass growing in numbers as more and more flocked to it from all over the plaza. All over the city, as far as Bijou could see.

The birds were upon them, jabbing and gouging. Bijou protected her eyes, cursed as she saw the starlings turn on Ambrosias and begin picking and pecking the smaller jewels from his settings. Those were easy to replace, but if they went for his eyes, they could blind him.

He killed a few. The camel clattered up the stairs, slowed by the mass of birds swirling around it. Blinded, and picking its way.

Brazen whistled, and bellowed again. The camel accelerated through the flock, batting the starlings aside when they did not avoid it quickly enough.

"Not sure how a metal lab specimen is going to help us," Bijou said over her shoulder.

"Hang on," Brazen instructed, and threw an arm around her and Ambrosias both. His grip, hard and strong, pressed the centipede's bony appurtenances into Bijou's flesh. She yelped and heard a couple of Ambrosias's fragile leg-bones crack. There was an impact and a yank, and they were moving fast, unevenly, pelting through a flurry of birds that struck their ducked heads and hunched shoulders and cascaded off and away around them.

With every stride, Bijou and Brazen slammed into the camel's unforgiving flank. Bijou buried her face in Brazen's shoulder to protect her eyes. She looked up again, though, when the camel veered. Perhaps bewildered by the storm of birds, it was being pushed back from the arches of the entryway, and its metal feet slipped on their tiny, crushed corpses. It paused, bewildered, casting about for direction, as tiny beaks scratched and jabbed at Bijou's hands and hood and scalp.

"Go help," Bijou told Ambrosias.

His cracked legs impeded him, tangling in their rippling neighbors. But he scrambled from his post around her body, clinking up the camel's side and neck, to crouch atop its cast skull and lunge and snap at starlings. There was a terrible moment where Bijou thought he would lose his grip and be trampled and shattered, but Ambrosias hung on. He reared up like the cobra his vertebrae had been taken from, and struck, lightning fast, knocking cheeping, flurrying birds from the air—and, more importantly, away from the eyes of the mechanical camel.

The camel whipped its head around and spit.

Not frothy saliva, but thick black oil. The reeking stream struck a dozen or so starlings and knocked them from the air. This pause in the attacks, and Ambrosias's protection, allowed the beast to get its bearings. Bijou braced herself as she felt the metal muscles gather, the concealed pistons creak.

It began again to run.

Bronze feet thundered onto the landing at the top of the stair, and the next Bijou knew the shadow of the portico fell over them and they were within the museum's atrium.

Bijou heard the whittering of the angry birds in close pursuit. "They can follow us in—"

But the camel wasn't slowing. It thundered up another flight of steps, through another scattering throng—of people, this time, rather than starlings—down a short, broad hallway, and hurdled a velvet rope to crash through a carefully lettered sign that read, "Closed for private party."

They were under the raised and reconstructed dome. Fleet as the camel was, its metal pads were not ideal for turning—or braking—on marble, and Bijou legitimately shrieked when she felt the camel slip and begin to slide and topple. Her body tensed instinctively as she awaited the crash and the bruising agony, the snap of hers and Brazen's bones that must inevitably follow.

She—and Brazen too—were plucked out of the air by a powerful, bony grip, as a shadow and the rippling flap of heavy cloth passed over them. A moment later, there was a terrible, clattering *kebang*!

Bijou looked down, and found herself embraced by the coils of a constrictor's articulated vertebrae. The wires and jewels and tiny gears were her own work, though for the moment she stared, too stunned to really take it in.

She gasped, bruised ribs aching, as Hawti set her and Brazen down—slightly willy-nilly, as they hadn't been perfectly aligned along the same axis when she grabbed them. They managed not to fall over, however, clutching and steadying each other and the skeletal elephant.

Before she had even properly found her feet, Bijou glanced around. The tremendous flapping sound had been Catherine the condor, flapping to the entrance, where she sealed the door against the squeaking flock of starlings with her reinforced silk wings. In the other direction, the museum's pride, Bijou's reconstruction of the Tidal Titan, was grinning with skeletal delight as it set the brazen camel on its feet. As Bijou watched, Amjada-Zandrya lifted the head on the mighty neck and danced a little jig.

"Somebody shut the damned doors," said an auburn-haired woman wearing a tidy jacket and long skirt, comprising a very businesslike suit. Her manner was very businesslike as well, from her polished appearance to the click of her heels. This was Dr. Azar, the paleontologist who believed in a theory of agile, active giant dinosaurs.

She swept across the floor toward those doors, as if she meant to perform the office herself—but before she could get there, a docent leaped in front of her, bowed awkwardly to Catherine, and edged behind her wing to seal the rotunda. There was Dr. Munquidh, over there with a broom—broad and dark, she was Dr. Azar's academic rival. She stepped in to defend the docent as Catherine pulled back enough to let them in. The birds didn't seem interested in attacking either the docent or Dr. Munquidh, however, and when he was done, Catherine waddled awkwardly away.

Bijou reached out and patted Hawti gently on the skull. The elephant rocked in pleasure, the belled cuffs on her ankles jangling.

Brazen regarded Bijou with pursed lips and a suspicious expression. "You're not surprised to see her here."

Now that things were quieting a little, Bijou had the leisure to glance around the rotunda and notice tables of snacks and beverages, clusters of colleagues and old acquaintances, and the presence of—as near as she could tell—every one of those of her creations who lived with her, and quite a few of the ones she'd sold, over the years.

It was a reunion, of sorts.

She had suspected something like this as the reason that Brazen had been so determinedly leading her around Messaline and stalling her.

"I was expecting a surprise party," she admitted. "But not a surprise assassination attempt."

He smirked, dabbing blood from the corner of his mouth. "Well, if you expect it, it isn't much of a surprise."

"You chose your wizard's name aptly." Dourly, she shrugged out of her ruined sunrobe and let it fall to the floor. Her former apprentice dabbed at a syrupy white smear on the shoulder of his gaudy coat. "Brazen you are. Was that part of your plot to get me out of my workshop as well?"

"No," he said. "I'm afraid my little toy mystery has grown into an actual one. But who would want to kill you?"

"Besides your father?"

He laughed humorlessly. "Flocks of starlings. Not a necromancer's style."

"Why the museum?"

Brazen gestured around to the glittering throng, interspersed with well-dressed humans. Even Lazybones glittered in mirrored splendor, slung on a support beneath the encircling mezzanine. "I thought a reunion of your creatures would cheer you. And the Titan is difficult to move, without tearing the entire building down."

Meanwhile, Dr. Azar and Dr. Munquidh walked over. Bijou was shocked to realize that Dr. Munquidh had draped her arm quite affectionately around her romantic rival's shoulders. They walked up, smiling and quite relaxed in each other's company.

"I thought you didn't get along," Bijou said, which was a foolish comment, given some of her own romantic choices.

"We don't," said Dr. Munquidh, and kissed Dr. Azar on the top of the head.

Dr. Azar, who was quite as pale-skinned a foreigner as Brazen, despite her name, blushed a pleased crimson. "Actually, we were both so upset with you, Wizard . . ."

"We found things to talk about," Dr. Munquidh said firmly.

Bijou actually laughed, despite the shadows of circling starlings crossing the glazed windows high overhead that admitted natural light to the rotunda. "I see you're taking fine care of your namesake." She gestured to the Tidal Titan, which made a pleased sort of wobble with its enormous head.

"We want to apologize for tricking you, Wizard," Dr. Azar said. "But you have refused every invitation any of us have sent you for the past ten months."

Bijou blinked. Surely not. She looked down and counted on her fingers. "Well," she allowed, when she had adjudicated twice and realized that the count was correct, "it was a good trick."

Had she really been closing herself off so thoroughly? Becoming reclusive and weird? So reclusive that Brazen spent his own valuable time constructing a cheap forgery in order to lure her out?

That might be a little *too* much self-defense.

On the other hand, apparently somebody *was* trying to kill her. And had taken this first opportunity in a year to try to see it through, which argued either patience or inside information.

Not Brazen's father Kaulas the Necromancer, for no little bird was likely to whisper secrets to him—or answer his commands, for that matter. Not Brazen himself, because he was the one person in all the world who could probably just put a knife in her back. Not Dr. Azar or Dr. Munquidh—at least not until they started having lover's spats and blamed an old wizard for their suffering.

So, who?

"A little bird told them," Bijou muttered.

"Pardon?" Brazen said.

"Never mind," said Bijou. She shook herself into a smile. "Come on. Let's enjoy the party, shall we, Master Wizard, sir? These starlings will probably disperse once night falls."

"Owls are bigger," Brazen said cynically, as he lifted a drink from a passing tray.

"Not to interfere in a feud between two other wizards, but I'm here to tell you that I don't appreciate you trying to kill my former apprentice." Bijou took a seat in the comfortable armchair beside the brazier. She sat carefully, so as not to discommode Ambrosias at her waist, with his recently repaired legs, or the several crab-shell artifices tucked inside her robes. Morning light streamed into the pleasantly appointed little parlor. "Although, believe me, I understand why you might feel the urge to."

The woman opposite brushed long, fine, black hair from her oval face with a suggestion of a smile. Her forehead was high, her cheeks full, the embrasure of her eyes narrow under a hooded lid. Her hands rested in her lap with her knitting, an elegant openwork tangle of rough-spun white and crimson silk yarn.

"I should have realized that you're a wizard," Bijou continued. "'Najma.' *Star*. But that's an odd wizard-name for someone who talks to animals."

"Just birds," Najma said. "They too decorate the sky."

"Brazen didn't know it?" Bijou asked.

Najma shrugged. Behind her, in a cage, a canary twittered. His wings were the clear variegated red of precious agates. Bamboo cages full of white and stripe-winged finches sang in the open window arches that led out to a garden balcony. Beyond, the city stretched into the distance, under a morning haze of smoke as people warmed their bread and boiled their tea. "He could have paid close enough attention to learn."

"So he's a terrible boyfriend. Is that worth murdering for?"

"Well." Najma seemed to do almost everything judiciously. It was certainly how she sipped her tea. "If I'd really wanted to *murder* him, I probably could have done better than starlings."

"*Star*lings," Bijou said, and put her hand to her eyes.

"The tea really is very nice," Najma said.

"So you were . . . just trying to get his attention?" Bijou, as directed, sipped the tea. It was, really, very nice.

"Just trying to remind him that there are consequences to his poor choices." Najma set the tea aside and picked up her ball of yarn. "Out of female solidarity. For the sake of the next girl."

"And perhaps a little bit of revenge?"

Najma's smile revealed white teeth and wickedness. Bijou . . . liked her. "Some men are slow to learn."

Bijou thought of Kaulas the Necromancer, and sighed. "Some men are."

"I realize that he was orphaned of his mother, and that his father *is* an evil necromancer. But couldn't you have . . ."

"Raised him better?"

Najma saluted her with the ball of yarn.

Bijou thought about that. About her own mother, standing and watching, arms folded, as Bijou walked away from her birth village into the desert, under a hail of stones. About Bijou's own choice to keep affection—oh, call it love, after its own fashion—in one hand and sex in the other, firmly separate, forever. If it had been a choice, and not just the way she were made. Or bent so early she might as well have been made that way.

About her best friend, and the man they had sometimes shared and sometimes quarreled over, though neither one had particularly *liked* him.

If somebody *had* managed to like him, would he have turned out better? Was that really even their problem, or was it his own?

"Perhaps," Bijou said cordially, "blaming a woman for the failings of the man is not, in itself, constructive?"

Najma pursed her lips. She tilted her head and raised one finger as if about to make a point—and perhaps she whistled, too high to hear. A little dappled brown wren, least colorful of songbirds, flitted in the window and perched on her finger, chirruping. Najma, without taking her gaze from Bijou's, tilted her own face down and brushed her lips lightly across the bird's small head. It turned to her like a nestling seeking feeding.

Ambrosias stirred at Bijou's waist. Bijou stroked him silent again.

"But it is a woman who has come to see me," Najma replied.

Bijou paused with her tea at her lips, once more. "It is."

"Have you discussed this with Brazen?"

Bijou shrugged the question away.

"So you are trying to solve his problems for him."

"I may also enjoy still being a little more clever than my apprentice."

The wren flew away, twittering. Bijou wondered that Najma could treat it as such a pet and spend the lives of her other familiars so profligately. That was a thing to remember, even when she found the young wizard charming. Just as there were things to remember about Brazen, even if they did not affect Bijou personally.

But one wizard did not avoid feuds with another—and the concomitant collateral damage to property and bystanders—by correcting her—or his—ethics continually.

They enjoyed their tea. A heavy scent of flowers—jasmine, ylang-ylang—drifted in from the balcony as the breeze shifted.

"Do me a favor?" Najma asked. "One woman to another?"

"Perhaps."

"Let him figure this one out on his own." The younger wizard smiled. "It will do him more good in the long run."

"It is not my job to watch him." Bijou set her empty teacup down and slipped a folded paper under the saucer.

"What's that?" Najma asked.

Bijou smiled as she reached for her cane. "It is my cleaning bill."

Lavie Tidhar

•   •   •

Here's another of Lavie Tidhar's tales of "guns and sorcery," featuring the bizarre and often ultraviolent adventures of Gorel of Goliris, a "gunslinger and addict" in a
world full of evil sorcery and monstrous creatures. (Further
adventures of Gorel can be found in the chapbook novella
Gorel and the Pot-Bellied God, in my anthology *The Book of
Swords*, and in the collection *Black Gods Kiss*.)

So let yourself be swept along with Gorel on his latest dark
and twisted quest, for something better not found, but we
warn you, it's not going to be an uneventful journey.

Lavie Tidhar grew up on a kibbutz in Israel, has traveled
widely in Africa and Asia, and has lived in London, the South
Pacific island of Vanuatu, and Laos; after a spell in Tel Aviv,
he's currently living back in England again. He is the winner
of the 2003 Clarke-Bradbury Prize (awarded by the European
Space Agency), was the editor of *Michael Marshall Smith: A
Bibliography*, and the anthologies *A Dick & Jane Primer for
Adults*, the three-volume *The Apex Book of World SF* series,

and two anthologies edited with Rebecca Levene, *Jews vs. Aliens* and *Jews vs. Zombies*. He is the author of the linked story collection *HebrewPunk*, and, with Nir Yaniv, the novel *The Tel Aviv Dossier*, and the novella chapbooks *An Occupation of Angels, Cloud Permutations, Jesus and the Eightfold Path*, and *Martian Sands*. A prolific short-story writer, his stories have appeared in *Interzone, Asimov's Science Fiction, Clarkesworld, Apex Magazine, Strange Horizons, Postscripts, Fantasy Magazine, Nemonymous, Infinity Plus, Aeon, The Book of Dark Wisdom, Fortean Bureau, Old Venus,* and elsewhere, and have been translated into seven languages. His novels include *The Bookman* and its two sequels, *Camera Obscura* and *The Great Game, Osama: A Novel* (which won the World Fantasy Award as the year's Best Novel in 2012), *The Violent Century,* and *A Man Lies Dreaming*. His most recent book is a big, multifaceted SF novel, *Central Station*, which won the John W. Campbell Memorial Award in 2017.

●   ◆   ◆

Widow Maker

LAVIE TIDHAR

1.

They were walking through the narrow, jagged walls of an icy ravine when Pitong Narawal, who was first scout, hit a strip-mine. He did not even have time to scream.

It was a crude device, but effective. Once, they had been dropped down from the skies in their thousands, mass-produced in the distant factories of vanished Zul: their charge of minute, compressed sorcery waiting now under the ice all around them, for anyone careless enough—unlucky enough—to find one.

Gorel watched as the strip-mine explosion spiralled out of the frozen ground. The whirlwind draped Pitong Narawal in rings of metal-blue flame and shredded his skin, making the howling sound of a saw cutting through bone, the red blood splattering out of the revolving fire and staining the ice in a painting of death.

When it was over, a last crackling of the ancient stored sorcerous charge dissipated in the chill air, and there was a short silence. Then Lord Khalen said, "Turnir Gerad, you take first scout position," and the bandy-legged man in his wrappings of fur shrugged and came forward, and soon they were moving again, climbing through the desolate landscape of ice.

2.

The city of Uzur-Kalden, Gorel thought, was a typical barbarian out-post: which is to say, it had been built by someone else. Tall spires rose into the air, astronomers' towers long fallen into disuse, and once-sprawling and perfectly manicured private gardens had been converted for use as butchers' markets. The temples for old gods had been turned into gaudy palaces for the rich.

There was a gallows in the center of town but only two corpses hang-ing there, preserved still in the cool air below the mountains. Uzur-Kalden was dominated by the mountains above it, and their breath of ice fell on the city as on a naked shoulder that was unable to pull away. It had once been a Ware'i city, and marks of the old war were still visible in unexpected moments—deep pools of water revealed as ancient blast craters, a stain on an old wall suddenly resolving into a human shape. And in the markets they still sold the remnants of the Zul's assault: the scatter-bombs and strip-mines and the containers of yet worse, much worse, devices, which were sold for scrap metal and for what sorcery they may yet contain. Every year there were many deaths in the small, isolated villages above the snowline, as the scavengers for Zul remains encountered live bombs. But the price in the markets of Uzur-Kalden was profitable, and the trade brisk, and livelihood on the slopes of the great mountains hard.

Yet Gorel had little interest in the Zul's armaments. They were ab-horrent to him, the bastard progenies of sorcery; Gorel trusted only to his guns. In a small lean-to at the edge of the artificers' market, set in the once-grand remnants of a public square where now broken columns rose above fallen statues whose namesakes no one knew, he had pur-chased powder and shells. And in another, at the edge of town by the ruined temple of a long-forgotten god, he had purchased the substance which is sometimes white and sometimes black and sometimes all the colors of the rainbow, and which men call the Black Kiss, or gods' dust.

He had come to Uzur-Kalden after a long and weary road, and his funds were few. He sought accommodation in the common hall of the

Abbey of Forgotten Gods, which lay at the other edge of town, closest
to the mountains, and was granted it.

There were many forgotten gods in Uzur-Kalden. Many who were
once worshipped and were now reduced, or gone—a poverty of gods
where once there had been riches. The monks sought to preserve the
knowledge of Ware'i, and of Zul, and to understand their conflict. They
offered cheap beds.

Shower was a bucket of ice-cold water in the yard. As he washed,
Gorel watched the mountains overhead as the sky darkened and the
first stars began to appear, like the first fat drops of rain. He stared up at
them, the water drying slowly on his chest and arms. They were cold, the
stars, like the eyes of dead men, glaring down balefully from above, but
all the while the mountains dominated them.

When he was done he went out of the yard and into the town. The
once grand, surfaced streets were now a confusion of mud and broken
stones, and open fires burned to provide both light and warmth. He
went into a low-lying hut, a makeshift affair of hastily assembled wood,
where there was smoke and laughter and the smell of spilled beer; someone played a song, badly, on a stringed instrument that quite possibly
had never been tuned. Gorel ordered a half bottle of rice whiskey and
took it, along with a brown earthen mug, to an empty seat by the window. An old woman turned a spit of meat over coals nearby, the smell
filling up the immediate area, and he went and purchased two sticks of
fatty meat and brought them back. He drank slowly, and ate one of the
sticks, and then he opened the packet he had purchased earlier that day
and carefully drew a line of dust on the tabletop.

"It's a bad habit you got there, friend," a voice said.

Gorel bent his head down low and snorted the dust. The power of
the Black Kiss surged through his body, and he almost rocked back.

When he turned his head to the speaker, he saw a small, wizened
form. "What's it to you?" he said.

"Nothing, nothing. I was merely observing that health consider-
ations—"

There seemed to be no transition: one moment the gun was by his
side, and the next it was in Gorel's hand. The small figure smiled. He was

a wizened old man, and Gorel noticed with distaste that he wore a tall, shapeless hat with silver stars badly sewn on to it.

"I do beg your pardon—" the man said. "May I join you?"

Without waiting for an answer he sat down opposite Gorel, putting his own empty mug on the table, and helped himself to Gorel's whiskey.

"I see you are experienced with weaponry. A steady hand. Excellent." The man brought out a small leather pouch and began rolling himself a cigarette. "And your guns, they are from the Lower Kidron? The workmanship is really quite unique."

Gorel's estimation of the small man rose sharply.

"Yes . . ." he said. The gun was back in its holster.

"My name," the man said, sticking the rolled cigarette in his mouth and setting it alight, "is Orven. Pleased to make your acquaintance." His pouch had disappeared just as it had appeared, without Gorel noticing. "And you are—?"

"What do you want?" Gorel said.

"Me? Nothing, nothing. It's just . . ."

"Just what?"

"It occurred to me you might be looking for work," Orven said, and belched. Smoke rose out of his mouth as he did so. "And I know someone who's hiring."

"You a wizard?"

"Sometimes, sometimes . . ."

"What's the job?"

Orven gestured out of the small window. Gorel looked out, saw nothing but tall, impossible mountains.

"*There?*" he said.

The other nodded.

"What's up there?" Gorel said.

"Death, most likely," Orven said.

"Death?"

"And, well, treasure."

"Of what sort?"

"Of the sort," Orven said quietly, "that killed the Zul and the Ware'i."

"A *weapon?*"

"The *final* weapon," Orven said. "The widow maker." And he glanced about the room as though wary of being overheard. "You interested?"

"In almost certain death and an impossible quest?"

"It pays," Orven said, with unassailable logic.

Gorel did a line of dust. The power of the Black Kiss coursed through him. Pure, distilled faith: there was nothing like it in all of the world.

"Sure," Gorel said.

3.

Lord Khalen was a prince consort from some faraway northern principality, whose wife had died in mysterious circumstances and whose people elected for him not to stick around after that. By all accounts he'd packed up in a hurry, taking with him much of his tragically deceased wife's wealth, and had since established a name for himself as an explorer of some renown. He had the hereditary nobleman's stiff resolve, a sort of bright and endearing dim-wittedness, and the useful inability never to admit an obstacle or face responsibility. He was, in other words, an ideal leader of men.

"This the gunslinger?"

"Yes, sir."

"Are you good?"

"Am I good?"

"Yes."

"Well," Gorel said, considering the question carefully, "I'm still alive, if that's what you mean."

"What's up there," Lord Khalen said, "is no ordinary battlefield. Up there, the membrane between the worlds is thin and perforated with bullet holes. Reality has been twisted and broken by the Zul–Ware'i war. The mountains are littered with traps, mines, bombs . . . monsters."

"I've fought monsters before."

"Some would say the worst monster of all is man," Orven said, and sniggered. "Though I always thought the grass giants of Gomrath and the demon-priests of Kraag were far worse, personally."

"If something lives, it dies," Gorel said and shrugged. "All you have to do is hasten it along."

"Fine, fine," Lord Khalen said. "You're hired. We leave in two days' time. How are the preparations coming along, Orven?"

"The porters are ready, sir. And now we have the muscle"—he leered at Gorel—"all we need is a guide."

"Well, make sure to find one," Lord Khalen said.

"Yes, sir," the wizard muttered.

4.

The next morning, Gorel visited the library in the Abbey of Forgotten Gods. This structure, at least, had escaped destruction. Columns rose up from the smooth marble floor and into the high, vaulted ceiling. It was both well lit and airy inside, and all around were shelves of books—large tomes bound in all the varieties of dead animals' skins. The apprentice monk assigned to Gorel was a short, cheerful boy called Kay.

"What is it you seek, traveler?" He eyed Gorel's guns with interest. "The Lower Kidron?" he said.

Gorel said, only a little exasperated, "Is *everybody* in this city a weapons expert?"

Kay smiled. "It *is* something of a speciality of ours, yes," he said. "Armaments and weaponry are both the trade blood of Uzur-Kalden and the focus of its scholarship. The Zul–Ware'i war—or possibly wars; the current argument places the number of conflicts at either three or seventeen—is almost unique in the history of the world. If you are interested, I can recommend Abbot Dvir-Ling's treatise on the subject—a classic in the field—*Some Observations and Conjectures Regarding the Zul–Ware'i, or Ware'i–Zul, Engagement, Complete with Illustrations of Notable Finds*, published in a limited edition through the offices of—"

"Thank you," Gorel said, interrupting him. "But what I am looking for does not concern this place."

"It does not?" Kay blinked at him, looking surprised. "Then what *is* your interest?"

"Tell me about the collection," Gorel said, leaving the question aside for a moment. "Does it not contain the knowledge of Ware'i?"

"Well, yes . . ." Kay said. "At least, in a manner of speaking."

"What do you mean?"

"I'm afraid that the Ware'i script—that is, you see, many of the books had been rescued from remaining Ware'i libraries and so on—well, the truth of the matter is—" He shrugged. "We have not quite been able to decipher them completely."

"And partially?"

"Well, no."

"Let me see if I understand you correctly," Gorel said to the unhappy apprentice. "You have an enormous library of books you can't actually read?"

"Well . . . yes. If you put it that way."

"How would you put it?"

"Well . . . an enormous library of books we can't actually read *yet?*" Kay said hopefully. "But of course, there are many more books here than just Ware'i," he said. "Though we do tend to focus on, well—"

"Weaponry and armaments?"

"Yes."

"I am searching," Gorel said carefully, "for mention of Goliris."

"Goliris?" Kay said, and his eyes opened wider than before. "You know of it?"

"Many know of Goliris," Kay said. He looked troubled. "There are stories . . ."

"I am Gorel of Goliris," Gorel said, "and I seek my homeland, though it has been lost to me for many years."

"Gorel of Goliris?" Kay looked at him closely, and suddenly grinned. "I've heard tales of a gunslinger wandering the world in search of a mythic land," he said. "Gorel of Goliris . . . Is it true you had once killed a god?"

The question took Gorel by surprise. "How do you—?"

"So it is?" The boy grinned again, though this time there was a touch of nervousness in the smile. "Word travels," he said. "I recently had conversation with an emissary of the dark mage who has risen in the Black Tor—"

"Kettle?" Gorel said, surprised again.

Kay gave him a look and said, "I do not know his name. But his men have been traveling to and from Uzur-Kalden for a long while now, and they carry gossip and news with them just as they take back their cargo of Zul devices."

"That explains a few things," Gorel said, thinking of his former friend and onetime lover, the Avian who had called himself Kettle, whose armies now overran the lowlands from Der Danang to Falang-Et and beyond.

"He has given much to the abbey," Kay said, "devices of decipherment that are greatly speeding up our work. Perhaps the Ware'i writings contain references to your land, Gorel of Goliris. And perhaps . . ."

"Yes?"

"There are answers elsewhere," Kay said, and looked away.

Gorel stared at him for a long moment. There was something on the boy's mind, it was clear, yet it was equally clear he did not want to discuss it . . . at least, not yet.

"What's this?" he said, pointing to a glass disc that sat, with other exhibits, under a secure display.

The boy brightened at the question.

"That's a corona bomb," he said. "They're really quite pretty when they go off. You can still see their mark on the high peaks, sometimes. Oh, and this one is quite rare," he said, pointing to another item on display. "It's a Ware'i mind-scream cannon, or at least that's what we *think* it is, but no one's been able to make it work. And that's a Ware'i ground-to-dragon missile—you can still see the skeleton of one of the Zul war-dragons up on the high peaks . . ." He sighed and Gorel at last turned his attention back to the boy.

"The peaks?" he said. "You have been to the upper reaches of the mountains?"

The boy wouldn't meet his gaze. "I was raised high above the snowline," he said reluctantly. "In the . . . But it doesn't matter."

"In the upper reaches?" Gorel stared out. Through the large windows he could see the foreboding mountains rise, clothed in ice and snow. And more than that, for everywhere upon the mountains lay the unexploded ordnance of the Zul and the Ware'i—not a promise of death as much as a contract, guaranteeing it. "And you live?"

"I was sent here as a child . . . I often dream of going back."

"Would you? If you could?"

"They would not like it . . ." the boy said, dubiously. Then he smiled, and there was genuine longing in his eyes. "Yes, man of Goliris. I would like nothing more."

"In that case," Gorel said, "I may just have an opportunity for you."

5

They set off for the mountains at dawn. A sickly red sun, the color of an infection. A large party, with the porters behind carrying Lord Khalen's copper bathtub, his tent, and his supplies.

"Can you smell it?" Orven said. He took a deep breath of cold morning air and shuddered, his eyes closing in delight.

"Smell what?"

"Sorcery!" Orven said. "Up there, so much pure, unadulterated magic . . . Wizardry, and, well, wild romance."

"I doubt you'll find *romance* up there on the peaks," Gorel said, and Orven opened his eyes and leered and said, "Well, you never know, gun-slinger."

Gorel resisted the urge to shoot the wizard. The man's robes were covered in stars and amulets—he wore rings of power on his bony fingers—talismans hung from his scrawny neck, and books of wizardry poked out of his many pockets. Gorel had met his kind before: hedge magicians, the rats who came into a battlefield only after the dying took place, who robbed and schemed and then claimed credit for the victory.

"The stars are favorable," Orven said complacently.

Gorel refrained from answering. There were no favors to be had from the stars, he knew. They were immutable and distant, sentient sources of sorcerous charge who cared nothing for the tiny creatures, whether human or Avian or Merlangai or Zul, who lived like mites upon the flesh of the world. The world was infinite, it was said. And the stars were legion. Even gods were dwarfed by their power.

That first day the journey was easy, the road clear-cut through the low rising foothills. At nightfall they came to a village and there Lord Khalen and his pet wizard slept in comfort at a way inn, while Gorel and the porters bedded down in the yard. Fires burned between their tents of furs. The boy, Kay, sat apart from the others, his eyes on the distant peaks; he spoke little since he'd joined the expedition.

Gorel, too, kept to himself. He felt uneasy below the mountains. The war of Zul and Ware'i had been one of total annihilation, not even their gods—if they had any—survived. The warring races had elevated death beyond art, to the realm of hard science. On the fringes of the region, archeo-necromancers worked diligently to try and uncover some of the vanished foes' more arcane thaumaturgy. Gorel dozed by the fire, but his sleep was light and restless.

In the night he woke, or thought he had. Moonlight bathed the sleepers all around him and the dying fires seemed suspended, frozen. He stood, or thought he had. He left the gates and urinated noisily into the bushes. Tiny insects buzzed overhead. He thought of taking another pinch of dust, but his supply was meager and there'd be no more priests to sell him the drug once they began the climb into the ice.

It had happened long ago and far away, in the place where the ghouls of the bush haunt the unwary, in a small village fetid with the smell of rotting leaves . . . where the twin goddesses Shar and Shalin cursed him forever with their Kiss, before he killed them.

He needed faith the way others needed water or food. He needed gods the way others needed companionship or love. The need was always in him, fight it as he might. He had done terrible things, had murdered, had sold himself . . . and he would do it all again without a second thought.

Gorel stepped away from the inn, down the dirt path that led through the sleeping village. The village seemed suspended in enchanted sleep. A dark carriage came rolling down the road, unhurriedly, toward him. it was a beat-up old thing, driven by a dark shape, pulled by an ordinary mule.

"Ironmonger! Pots and pans! We straighten nails!"

Gorel watched it approach. Not even a dog barked. The carriage stopped and its driver climbed down, as Gorel knew he would. The iron-monger was in shadow.

"You're not really here," Gorel said. "You're beyond the deadlands, beyond reach, holed up in the Black Tor."

The ironmonger unwrapped the shadows from about himself. In the moonlight he resolved into a small, slight figure, with an elongated face, two eyes like dark bruises, and a pair of powerful wings now folded about him.

The Avian smiled.

"Gorel," he said. There was a mixture of affection and exasperation in the voice.

"Kettle. Why are you here?"

The Lord of the Black Tor, the dark mage whose armies had over-taken the ancient cities of Ankhar and Tharat, whose forces even now marshalled to march across the world, said, "I missed you."

"Why are you here?"

"As you said—I'm not."

Gorel looked at the sleeping village. Everything was suspended, still.

"You come into my dreams?"

"Only if you dreamed about me." The Avian's familiar, mocking smile caused a hard knot to form in Gorel's heart.

"You should turn back," Kettle said. "There's nothing up there but death."

"A job's a job."

"Gorel . . ."

"Why?" Gorel said. "Why do you do what you do? Do you amass power for the sake of power? Kill for the sake of killing? You have de-stroyed so many lives . . ."

"Gorel . . ." An old pain in the Avian's eyes. "I have my reasons. Turn back from the peaks. I beg you."

"No."

"Then take this," Kettle said. "For protection." He brought out an object from the folds of his thin clothes. It was a metal bracelet, etched with runes.

Gorel made no move to oblige.

"Please."

"Why do you care?"

"Because I . . ." He stopped. "Please?"

Gorel, with the inevitability of a dream, allowed the mage to slip the bracelet over his wrist. It felt so weightless. Kettle's fingers applied light pressure on Gorel's skin and he felt a rush of desire rise in him, but resisted.

"It's enchanted. It isn't much, but . . . It might help."

"Is it that bad? Up there?"

"I don't honestly know. You'll have to find out for yourself."

The moonlight waned. The village darkened. Somewhere, a dog barked. Kettle was nothing but a shadow. Gorel yawned.

"Gorel? Gorel!"

"Yes, Kettle, what do you want now . . ."

"Wake up, you oafish fool!" A booted foot kicked him painfully in the ribs. Gorel sat up, groggy. Over the distant peaks, the first rays of dawn could just be seen, spreading like an infection.

"What?"

"Useless piece of . . ." Orven said. Gorel blinked. He had been fast asleep on the ground, and the embers in the fire were dead. "We leave in ten."

"All right, all right," Gorel said. He stood up, shoved the other man roughly until he stumbled. "Kick me again and I'll shoot you."

"I'll conjure a fireball up your ass if you push me again," Orven said—but he backed off. All about them the expedition was rising, preparing for the trek into the ice. Gorel reached for a pinch of dust and snorted it up his nose. It was only when he lowered his arm that he saw the thin metal bracelet, covered in graceful, indecipherable runes.

Gorel stared at the bracelet.

"Well, fuck," he said.

6.

Higher and higher into the mountains, a thin line of men along the path, like ants crawling upon the edge of a straight razor. For the first few days there were still villages, sparsely populated, and farther and farther apart, then they were no more. Beyond the snowline they hit an old, abandoned camp, built and then added to by successive and now vanished expeditions, and there they stopped to rest. This high up the air was thinner, and magic thicker. It was in the air, in the land, embedded in the snow. Gorel hated it.

They set off again. Higher and higher into the mountains. From up there Gorel could look down and see the green slopes below the snow-line, and the tiny villages like dark flowers, and the city of Uzur-Kalden shrunk to the head of a pin. Beyond the slopes, he could look out over the whole of the deadlands, until the vast unending plains faded into the horizon. Somewhere beyond them lay the Black Tor. Somewhere on the plains was the vast cemetery of Kur-a-len, which Gorel had inadvertently destroyed . . .

On and on they went. Then into the icy ravine where they lost Pi-tong Narawal to a strip-mine. Coming out of it at last, shaken by the first of the deaths, they continued the climb, though the peaks above seemed as distant as ever. The worst of the ravine had been its icy walls. As Gorel turned to look at them, faces stared back at him: Ware'i bodies, frozen behind the sheets of ice. Their faces stared out at him, frozen in expressions of fear and despair. Behind them he could see low houses, dirt roads; a dog frozen in mid-waddle; a stationary fire, the very flames caught in midlife. They filled him with a horror he couldn't quite articulate, and instead he pinched a minute amount of dust from his pouch, his gloved fingers struggling not to lose a single grain of powder, and snorted it.

At the approach of night they made camp. Lord Khalen had his retainers erect his tent for him separate from the main camp's enclosure. Fires were built and food cooked. Yet the small fires could not banish the dark.

The darkness brought with it the spectral illuminations of Zul ordnance. Far away a scream erupted, and a column of colored lights rose into the air, reflecting for a moment from thousands of icy surfaces, before the scream ebbed, the lights slowly faded, and the rumble of a distant ice shelf collapsing could be heard. Turnir Gerad and his men sat around their own fire and did not raise their heads at the sounds of the ice. They looked withdrawn into themselves, unheeding of the strangers they were carrying. A second explosion sent a flock of spectral white ravens into the air, who dispersed in all directions before breaking up themselves into soft white snow that fell down. Gorel knew that, had the company been under it when it happened, the snow would have melted their faces and eaten their skins, and he shuddered inside his heavy clothes. He sat on his own and looked away from the mountains, and his heart longed for home.

Goliris, that greatest of kingdoms to which he was heir; from which he had been exiled and flung far away, across the world: yet always it remained beyond his reach.

The memory came to him of a spring day long ago. He had been a child, visiting his mother at the labs that rose, immense and mysterious, beside the Royal Palace of Goliris. His mother the queen had rushed to him and embraced him, and then took him in hand, through great cavernous halls, where women and men worked silently at long tables, building, testing, scribbling notes, assembling and disassembling devices. She had showed him some of the work that day, the endless display of machinery and witchcraft, of knowledge distilled in the service of war.

"*Not* war, Gorel," his mother had corrected him, as they stood and admired a long tube of metal being assembled, eldritch writings on its sides, blue lightning crackling around it as a demon from the deep jungles of Goliris was being bound inside it. "The *prevention* of war. None dare fight Goliris, and so we bring peace to the world, and prosperity with it. No," she said, and for a moment her voice was low and urgent, and though he did not understand her words then, he did now. "Our only danger comes from within."

Then came the night, so long ago now, yet burned forever in his memory. The night they came for him, and he, a child, could not fight them. The traitors, wizards of Goliris grown fat with hate and power.

He remembered the last night of his childhood. The candles burned in his room, and outside the autumn wind blew with deceptive warmth, and the torches shuddered as it passed, and the air was filled with the smell of the sea, and of the gardens, and of the things that grew and died in the forests. It was an ordinary day, and so was the night. Until the screams woke him.

There were guards outside, shouting, and the clash of swords, and someone, far away, crying, and he crouched in his bed, frightened, and something crashed against his door and slid to the ground. That was the last thing he could remember—the sound of a nameless guard dying against his door—and after that there was a haze. Sorcery. And when he awoke his room was gone, and his parents, and the air smelled different, it was suffused with unfamiliar scents, and when the old couple found him their language was strange, and it took him months to learn enough to ask, and then he was horrified: they had never heard of Goliris.

7.

All through this long and arduous climb their destination remained a mystery. Lord Khalen and his pet wizard Orven would stand apart and consult over an ancient map, and Orven would mutter incantations, and light colored flares, and wave smoking apparatus in the air and trace complex runes into the ice.

What all this was for, Gorel could not begin to guess. Then the wizard and his master would consult the map again, and confer in low voices, and then they would plough on.

Always up, through hidden paths, ancient roads cut into the glaciers and the rock. They lost two more of the porters to a demon mine. The thing erupted underfoot, a vast black shape with claws of shadow, and it hacked the men into pieces before it vanished like smoke. Two more men died in an avalanche.

Another found a ring buried in the ice and so desired it that he began to hammer at the ice to get it out. It was so pretty and so precious that another man desired it and murdered the first for it. He then slipped the ring on and was consumed in a spontaneous combustion that left nothing but his boots.

"Where did you get the map?" Gorel asked the next time he found himself beside Orven. "Where does it lead?"

"You just keep watch for any trouble," Orven said, "and leave the business of it to those who know."

"Who's financing this expedition?" Gorel said. "Who sent you?"

"No one."

But Gorel didn't believe him.

"Was it the Lord of the Black Tor?"

"I'm sure I couldn't say," Orven said, and leered.

Gorel watched the foolish noble and his pet wizard. He did not trust them. This high up the high winds blew at force. They lost another man to the wind; it tossed him off a ledge and he fell, noiselessly, and was swallowed in the snow. Their numbers were dwindling rapidly. Higher and higher they climbed until all trace of the down-below was erased, and there were only the mountains, and the ice.

He kept a wary eye. He kept his hands on his guns. He felt a tension thrum all through his body. When he slept, his dreams were haunted by ghosts threaded into the bedrock of the mountain, all those chains of tiny living flames, crying out to him.

What killed you? he tried to ask. *What was it, this final weapon, this widow maker, so powerful that it erased all living things?*

But they never answered.

8.

The attack came at night. Gorel woke, his heart beating fast. Everything was quiet. The snow was blinding white, the moonlight a cold silver, like a knife.

All the porters were gone.

He sat up quietly. Drew his gun. The old couple who'd found him, when he was cast from his home, had been gun makers from the Lower Kidron, where they are famed for such artifice. He had forged the guns himself. They bore the seven-pointed star of Goliris.

It was all so quiet. Beside the dead fire, the boy, Kay, stirred. He blinked sleepy eyes at Gorel.

"What—"

"Hush."

Indistinct shapes, moving on the periphery of the camp. Gorel crouch-ran to Lord Khalen's tent. He lifted the flaps. Inside, the lord and his wizard lay entwined under pelts. For a moment he near envied them, this peace they shared, this closeness. Then he kicked Orven, and the wizard woke with a hiss of fury, which changed when he saw Gorel's face.

"Attack?"

He looked, Gorel thought, as though he had expected something like this to happen.

Something *lived* up near the peaks, Gorel thought. And he did not think Orven as foolish as the man made himself appear. There was a safety in looking less than what you were.

Orven rose. He shook Lord Khalen awake. Whispered. The lord sat up and without a word reached for a long, curved sword. When Orven stepped out of the tent, he was armed with a long staff, which Gorel had not seen before. Lord Khalen, too, had shaken off the foppishness that he had affected. The two men now looked like what they must have, all along, been—dangerous men, doing a dangerous job. He wondered who they *really* were, those two. And who they were working for.

But there was no time for questions. He caught sudden sight of one of the shapes that loomed on the edge of the camp. A giant, white furred monstrosity, twice taller than a man, with claws like knives, red eyes . . .

Ghosts in the snow.

Not ghosts.

"Snow demons?"

Orven raised his staff. He brought it down with a hard thump against the ground, and the ground shook, and far away snow rumbled: somewhere, an avalanche began. A burst of pure white light exploded from the end of the staff and shot up. It illuminated the creatures that surrounded their enclosure, and the walls of the glacier against which they made camp. Gorel took aim and fired, and a snow demon fell back with a bullet in the head.

The creatures howled.

"Don't!" the boy, Kay, said. "They haven't harmed us, they're—"

Orven grinned with a face like a skull, and his staff moved in a whirl and he fired a bolt of flame that caught two more of the creatures, who howled in horror and pain as the fire consumed them.

"You want to know about *death*?" the wizard screamed. "I will show you the machinery of death!"

The creatures howled, and then they vanished into the snow. In one moment they were there; then they were gone, as though they never were.

The men stared at each other. Lord Khalen said, "The map."

"Yes."

Orven hefted a small bag.

"You have the instruments?"

"Yes."

"We leave. Now."

"You knew there'd be an attack," Gorel said.

"Of one sort of another. Sure."

"Why?"

"Your job," Lord Khalen said, "is to shoot things, not to ask questions. We leave. Now."

"Where to?"

"Orven?"

"I'm trying!" The wizard was frowning. In one hand he held his staff, in another a small metallic box. "The readings are all wrong . . ."

"I know a way."

It was the boy. Kay. They stared at him.

"There is a path, I think. Not far from here." It was the most he'd said in all the time that they'd been traveling. "The mountainside's riddled with old caves. We can find shelter there."

"Orven?"

"I don't know, Khal. I can't get a read . . ."

"Then lead the way, boy."

Kay nodded. His eyes shone bright. He went ahead, and the others followed. Gorel kept his guns drawn and Orven his staff and Lord Khalen his sword. They watched out for the white forms.

"There!"

Gorel fired, but the snow demon leaped nimbly out of the way and vanished again. They were all around them now, he could feel them, silent, invisible . . . waiting.

They moved fast, following the boy's trail along the edge of the glacier. Into the dark, and the silent white figures leaping and following, shadowing them from a distance. Gorel's guns fired in tandem. A giant figure leaped at Lord Khalen and was blasted away by Orven's staff.

"Good, good!" Lord Khalen said. His voice was hoarse, and his eyes shone in the moonlight. Orven grinned beside him.

"It means we're close," he said, at Gorel's unspoken question.

"Close to what?"

"It! They!"

But they were thousands of feet above ground, beyond all reach, beyond all thought of rescue. The silent figures hadn't made their move yet. They seemed content to follow, to hem the remains of the expedition in. Turnings in the path were blocked to them. The boy, Kay, led them, but led them where? Deeper into the mountainside, through fractures in the permafrost, at last to the entrance of a cave.

They escaped inside, the wizard's staff casting brilliant illumination. Gorel saw some ancient place, preserved. Several bodies, resting slumped against the walls. An Avian, two humans, a Merlangai far from the sea. Other explorers, he thought, who never made it farther. Deeper into the cave, the boy leading and they following behind. Demons plaguing their steps. Deeper and deeper, and he realized the mountain must be riddled with tunnels. A door ahead—

"Wait!"

But the boy dashed forward, too fast, too swift. Gorel lashed out, grabbed him by the shirt, but the boy was surprisingly strong. Gorel lost his footing, was dragged along in the boy's wake. There was a recess in the rock, away from the door. The boy cowered against the rock face, covering his head. Gorel straightened himself, breathing hard. He peeked around the stone wall.

An ancient door set in the rock. Lord Khalen and his wizard crouched before it. Orven laid down instruments, etched runes into the stone. Lord Khalen muttered, running fingers over the face of the door.

"What does it say? Some kind of writing. High Zul? Can you make it out, Orven?"

"Does it say 'friend,' maybe? Something like that?" Orven said dubiously. "Oh, who cares, Khal? Let's blow this thing up."

"Ready when you are."

The wizard muttered incantations. His staff glowed, the light so bright it blinded. Gorel withdrew. The boy, Kay, was still crouched there. His lips moved.

"What?"

"Speak, friend, and die." The boy smiled. "Zul or Ware'i, there are no friends in war, gunslinger. Cover your head."

But Gorel's curiosity was too strong. He peeked again round the corner—saw the wizard and Lord Khalen straighten, face the door—their faces lit by the flame from the staff, eager, hungry—

The door vanished. In its place was a black entrance, darker than night. He saw Lord Khalen's triumphant smile, the wizard's rictus grin. Orven reached with the burning staff and broke the threshold.

And the darkness screamed.

A foul wind, like a mouth unused in centuries finally opening, the door its maw, and from the hidden lungs and body beyond there came a wordless scream. It tore the flesh from the two men's faces and from their arms and it shredded their clothes and it put out the fire of the staff like the pitiful flame of a candle. Gorel ducked behind the stone wall of the recess, but it was too late, the scream was in him now, echoing and bouncing, threatening to strip him into nothing.

Near blind, he clutched the boy's arm.

"Help me," he whispered.

He blinked. He saw the boy reach down—and come back with a heavy stone.

The last thing Gorel saw was the rock in the boy's hand coming down.

Then there was pain.

Then nothing.

9.

"Join us . . . release us . . ."

The voices, so many voices, fragmentary and broken. In the darkness he saw them, those thousands of tiny lights, strewn all across the mountain.

"How?" he said.

But they did not answer.

10.

He woke to find himself strapped naked to a stone altar. The stone was cold on his skin. His head pounded with pain. Monks in bloodred robes moved about the room. The room had a vaulted high ceiling. Ancient devices littered the room. One of the monks came and shoved a needle into the crook of his elbow. Gorel would have shouted, but then it coursed through him, stronger than euphoria, better than sex, more powerful than love: the Black Kiss, undiluted, pure, liquid faith feeding into his bloodstream, the product of some unbearably powerful god.

He subsided back. Let them do whatever they wished to him. He didn't care. Only vaguely was he aware of their movements, instruments prodding him, something beeping, a man's voice saying, "His readouts are asymmetrical."

"Deviant?"

"I don't know . . . It is curious. As though his physical age and actual age are separated by thousands of years."

"Check the calibration."

"I did."

"Did you test him against the Godchain?"

"Hold on . . ."

The fragment of a black rock, pressed to the side of his neck. Some enormous pain jolted him out of the pleasant daydream.

Bound to the stone altar, Gorel screamed.

11.

The lights again, in the dark. Each one an isolated voice, a node on some vast and inexplicable manifold. And Gorel a tiny flare of light, moving—and as he moved between the points the light flowed in his wake, joining first one, and then another, and another, so that they were no longer so alone . . .

12.

When he next came to, he was sat on the edge of a bed facing a high window. Someone had dressed him again in his old clothes—even his guns were there, on the bedside table. The pain in his head had vanished, and he felt a pleasant numbness.

Gorel of Goliris stared out of the window.

He stared out onto a temperate valley. On every side rose the sheer cliffs of mountains, and low-lying clouds formed a sort of ceiling to the green hidden valley below. He saw a pleasant, bubbling brook, and monks moving, small as ants, some attending to the extensive, cultivated gardens, and others . . .

There were large blast holes formed into the side of the mountains, he saw, and tracks that came out of the openings. He saw the monks pull carts laden with broken black rocks. A giant pile of black rocks stood in the center of the valley like a quarry.

They were rocks, he realized, much like the one that had been applied to him.

He searched for his remaining stash of dust and discovered it was gone.

Discovered, further, that he didn't need it.

It was everywhere, he thought. The Black Kiss. It was in the very air he breathed. He felt so good just being there, just *being*. No craving, no desire, no hunger, no need.

He stood up. He put his guns on, out of habit. What need was there for guns? He left the room and wandered down stone-hewn corridors where monks walked silently by. He made his way down winding stone stairs. It was as though the entire place was hewn into the very bedrock of the mountainside.

He found himself in a large, spacious dining hall. Monks sat silently eating from large earthenware bowls. More bowls on the tables sported a dizzying assortment of fruit: elephant apples and dead man's fingers, horned melons and prickly pears, gooseberries and cluster figs. He sat down among them, and he helped himself to the abundant food.

For the first time perhaps since he'd been ripped from his home and tossed across the world, Gorel of Goliris felt . . .

Not exactly *happy*, perhaps. Happiness was not a state of mind familiar to any of the ruling family of Goliris.

But perhaps . . . *content.*

It should have been unsettling, but even more unsettlingly, it wasn't.

He watched the monks, and he saw that there were a great many races represented among them. Avian and Merlangai, human and Nocturne, a solitary grave-wraith, a gaggle of Mon-Hai or tree spirits from the deadlands (he had thought the race long-vanished), a handful of the frog-folk called Falang, even a couple of Ebong, those carapace-wearing creatures known across the world as hardy mercenaries. How the sea-dwelling Merlangai, or the Nocturne, who only lived in darkness, all ended up here, living and eating together in harmony, he could not fathom.

He saw then that all the monks ceased from their food at once and, raising his head, saw an ancient Avian enter the room. Though he was dressed identically to the rest of the monks, there was an obvious air of authority about him. The Avian made his way slowly across the hall, until he came to Gorel, and stopped.

"Welcome, stranger," he said. "I am the High Invigilator of the Monastery of the Final Weapon. It is rare for us to welcome new arrivals . . . I owe much to the young novitiate who brought you here."

He signaled. A small figure detached from one of the farther benches and came forward, and Gorel saw that it was the boy, Kay.

"I had sent him down to the city beyond the mountains, for we grow isolated here, in our contemplation, and the world beyond has the unfortunate tendency, from time to time, to attempt to intrude." The High Invigilator smiled the smile of a predatory bird. "We do not tolerate . . . *intrusion*, Gorel of Goliris."

"You know my name?"

"Many mysteries are known to me, prince of Goliris. Though many more remain just as stubbornly hidden."

"So, Kay . . . He was working for you all along?"

"I trust, in another century or so, he will be ready to take on the blood robes."

"Did you say another *century*?"

"Time moves . . . differently, up here," the boy said diffidently.

"And why did you spare me?" Gorel said. "When the others are dead?"

"I would have killed you, too," the boy said simply. "As per my instructions. But at the last moment, the High Invigilator stayed my hand."

The High Invigilator nodded as though pecking at seeds. "Come," he said. "Walk with me."

Gorel rose and followed the High Invigilator, out of the hall and down twisting stairways, until they emerged into the fresh air of that hidden valley.

"What killed the Zul and the Ware'i?" Gorel said.

"Ah," the High Invigilator said. "You cut right to the heart of the matter, man of Goliris."

Gorel waited, but there was no more forthcoming. He said, "Who are you? What is this place? How came you to be here?"

"My, but you *are* inquisitive," the High Invigilator said. "You would make a good novitiate yet."

"Me?" Gorel said.

They were passing by the bubbling brook. The air was scented with jasmine and frangipani. Terraced fields on the far side of the valley shone gold with rice plants. The air was thick with humidity.

"Would you like that, Gorel of Goliris? This is a place of rare peace in all of the world. A shelter from the wars of others. You could find contentment here. Perhaps, even, enlightenment."

The offer hung there. Gorel breathed in the scented air. He wanted nothing more, he suddenly realized. To be free at last, to be at peace. And yet, like a pebble in a shoe, one thing prohibited him. His birthright, his home. The question of vanished Goliris.

"I cannot answer all your questions, Gorel. I myself was born far from here, where the Migdal trees grow. Our nests were marvels of harmony, our community was peaceful and prosperous. One day, an attack came from the air. Wild ballooners, a migratory, violent race. We were unprepared. They set fire to our nests, slaughtered my people. I alone escaped. For years I was tortured with the desire for vengeance. I traveled the world, hiring out as a murderer. Much as you do, Gorel of

Goliris. It was this desire for blood that led me at last to the Zul-Ware'i mountains. Rumors of weapons beyond compare. Of sorcerous artifacts the likes of which had not been seen in centuries. I climbed to the peaks. I believe now that it was a death wish that brought me here. I sought death, but death eluded me. It was then that they found me, the Invigilators. They brought me here. I believe this may have been a Zul hideout once. But I do not know for sure. I became a novitiate, then a monk. I found peace. At last, when the High Invigilator discombobulated, I took their place."

The old Avian looked earnestly at Gorel. "Renounce the world, Gorel of Goliris. Let go of your old grievances, let go of your search, and join us. Here you could be free, finally free, of all that has plagued you."

Gorel nodded. "Yes," he said. "Yes."

And yet that pebble in the shoe. A memory: bursting into the throne room where his father sat on the night-black chair, and a half dozen men faced him, his military wizards, speaking in hushed, angry voices. Gorel made his way toward them, and they ceased from speaking, and his father, always a stern man, nevertheless extended his arms to the boy, and Gorel came forth, and sat on his father's knee—the closest he'd ever come to occupying the throne.

Then the night when he was taken—the last night he ever saw his mother and father alive.

He was dosed up on faith, he realized. The Black Kiss, which permeated every corner of this monastery, was a trap, a trap that held him. He said, "Excuse me," and stumbled away from the High Invigilator, and the Avian let him go.

They did not fear him, he realized. This power, this faith, was everywhere, woven into the very fabric of the valley and its keep. But he could see no god here, he could see no—

Then he looked again: looked with new eyes.

It was the same valley as before, this temperate zone with its lush vegetation. And the monastery rose above it, built into the rock, a huge, ancient form . . .

An ancient form, he thought. He closed his eyes. In the darkness he could see them. The lights, those complex chains, burrowed deep under and through the strata of ice and metavolcanic rocks and gneiss. When he opened his eyes he could see them still, and he could see how everything about him was merely the *mimicry* of a thing. How the building was not at all a building but a part of a *body*, how the valley was not so much a garden but part of a vast *stomach*, how the things living and breathing inside it were . . .

Bacteria, he thought. Tiny parasites living in somebody else's gut, convincing themselves that they ruled it.

He saw the monks emerge from the tunnel mouths ahead, with their cargo of black rocks. He went toward them. They paid him no mind. He picked one rock, held it. Warmth coursed through him.

Dust.

No one knew what the Zul and the Ware'i had battled over. No one knew what gods they worshipped. And no one knew what killed them.

But Gorel had the sudden suspicion that he knew.

This impossible valley, sustained as it were in the middle of the murderous mountains—this enchanted paradise—it was a *corpse*.

The Zul and Ware'i had not just murdered each other.

They had murdered their own *gods*.

13.

That night, the lights cried out to him in the darkness. All those buried spores. He woke up sweating. He stared out of the window, on the silent, peaceful valley below. The sheer cliff walls. The ceiling of eternal clouds, pressing down.

No wonder they let him roam freely. How could he leave?

The valley was a prison and Gorel its inmate.

In the night, he wandered. He climbed the staircases and sought a door, an exit, but there wasn't one. He followed the monks into the tunnels, but the tunnels only led deeper into the mountain, and always ended in solid rock.

He visited the library. The boy, Kay, worked there. He'd kept away from Gorel's company since his betrayal. Not that Gorel cared. He would have done the same—*had* done the same, before, when the occasion called for it. Betrayal was merely an occupational hazard.

The monastery had many books. "And what of my home?" Gorel said. "Is there a book here that mentions Goliris?"

The boy, reluctant, went to check. He climbed up and down stout wooden ladders. Returned, at last, with an ancient, dusty tome. The wizard Yi-Sheng the Unbeatable's *De Magia Veterum*, in the old tongue of the people of Mindano Caliphate, from the century of Archon Gadashtill, the first and greatest of the necromancer-kings of his line.

"Perhaps," Kay said. He turned the pages, until the book fell open on a map. It was so faded as to be barely legible. It showed a black sea, and at its heart, a black continent. The boy, Kay, moved his hand over the page. The image grew. The library faded.

A voice: "And in the final year of the necromancer-king's reign, he summoned a great enchantment of a kind that was never before or since seen, and a vortex erupted before his fleet and all his ships passed through it one by one."

It was Kay; Kay was speaking. And Gorel found himself on the ship, saw the storm rage over that black sea, and he smelled a known smell, the scent of ancient, buried things that were dead and yet alive, and the smell of fungus, and the smell of rot and of primeval forests. And he saw the black rocks jutting ahead, and the ship fell on their sharp teeth, and the dead men drowned, but he alone survived, he swam ashore, and came to the city. A city the likes of which had never been seen, before or since, upon the world. And he alone wandered its empty streets, until he came to the Royal Palace, and stepped inside, and made his way to the throne room, and there he stopped.

The room was old, and cobwebs hung thick in the dark corners, and yellowing bones piled on the floor, but he paid them no mind.

Gorel of Goliris stared at the small, slight figure that sat on his throne.

The boy, Kay, looked back at him with an apologetic smile.

14.

He woke from a nightmare to find that someone was choking him. His mind was still a-twirl from that impossible glimpse of his home. It couldn't be, he thought; Goliris could not fall. And yet the streets so still and empty, and the cobwebs thick— How many years? he thought. How many centuries?

It was all wrong—it was all just a false mirage. It had to be. He woke, choking, hands around his neck. An old, old man leaned over him, teeth bared in a rictus of exertion. Thumbs, digging into his windpipe. He grabbed the man's wrists, tried to push him off, but the man was inhumanly strong. Gorel kicked, his mouth opened and closed without sound, at last with a heave of the last of his strength he *twisted*, his mouth fastened on the man's arms and Gorel bit down.

The taste of dust—of *dust*—filled his mouth. A giddy happiness, pure faith, distilled, straight from the source. Gorel suckled at the wound. The pressure on his throat slackened. A backhand slap threw him on the floor. Gorel rose, grabbing his guns.

He fired.

The man fell back. Stared down at his chest, grimaced, wiped a hand over his chest, as though wiping off lint. The bullets pinged onto the floor.

His features seemed strangely familiar.

"Just die!" Gorel said uselessly. He fired, once, twice. The old man turned, became a shadow. Fled.

Gorel gave chase.

Down silent corridors of rough-hewn stone, the shadow fleeing, Gorel in chase, all thought forgotten, nothing but the desire to inflict murder. Down and down and down they went.

Down and down and down.

They burst out into moonlight. The clouds overhead parted for just a fraction, and he saw the stars. In the moonlight, the hidden valley lay still as a corpse. Gorel pursued the shadow past the brook, to the place where the rail tracks terminated.

He saw a mound of rocks, rising into the sky. They cried out to him, all those tiny buried lights from the flesh of the mountainside, released again and brought together into the semblance of a thing: the semblance of a life.

He stopped, and stood there, panting. He pointed the guns at the shadow. The shadow turned. The old man's face again, the gummy, toothless mouth moving wordlessly. The figure changed. It shrunk, grew young. The boy, Kay, looked out at Gorel and smiled in mute apology.

"How . . . how long?" Gorel said.

". . . Trapped," the boy said. "All the rest of them . . . scattered. Buried. Only me. here. No power. All gone."

"Are you Zul? Ware'i?"

"Yes. No."

"What killed them?"

"They . . . killed."

Gorel said, "The final weapon . . . They murdered their own gods?"

"Yes. No."

"I don't understand."

"Make . . . peace. Make . . ." He brought his hands together.

Gorel saw the mountains alight with warfare, dragons flying, wizards casting fireballs from icy mountaintops. He saw villages burn, whole cities turned to molten lava. He saw monsters made of ice. He saw the altars, sacrifices, incense, hymns. He saw two figures rise into the sky at last. Two gods, fed on their worshippers' prayers. Two vast amorphous beings of darkness, bloated, bloodied, sad. They circled in the sky. It had to end. There had to be a peace.

They merged. They came together—mating.

He saw them drop.

He saw them fall from the air.

The brightness of that explosion seared his vision. A cloud like an hourglass rose high into the skies. A wind blew like a whisper. All perished: Zul, Ware'i. The young in one another's arms, and all the dying generations at their song.

All but the one.

A baby.

"*You?*"

"Trapped. Alone. So many years . . . Built this place, in their grave. People came. Stayed. I waited. I wait . . . But you. You're from another time and place. Goliris. You can—"

An incomprehensible string of words, a rush of colors, the smell of tar and brine. Gorel covered his ears.

"Complete the Godchain. You hold so much *time* inside you!"

The figure lurched at him. The ancient black stones sang to him. The shattered bones of dead gods cried out to him to make them whole.

Gorel fired his guns, but they were useless.

"Don't . . . resist."

The mountain of rocks moved. Formed a human shape. Arms like cranes of industry reached out for him. A fist full of boulders. He was doomed.

On his wrist, a sudden burst of heat. A shooting flame of light. He yelled. The flame shot into the air. It broke through the cloud cover and burst overhead in a shower of sparks. High, high above . . .

Gorel stared at the bracelet. It was the one Kettle had given him, before he left for the climb.

His skin burned. Above him, the rock troll stopped, uncertain. The boy, Kay, stared at Gorel with silent accusation.

"What was that?"

"I don't . . . know."

The giant rock fist moved. It grabbed Gorel. It lifted him into the air. High, high, into the sky. It squeezed him. He saw bright sparks. Thousands of them. All through the mountains, those complex chains. He couldn't breathe. He knew he was going to die. He saw the clouds part again overhead, banished, and something impossible, a flock of distant shapes, coming down, coming rapidly.

Kay stared into the sky. "Are those fucking *eagles?*" he said.

Gorel, choking, said, "No, I think they might be albatrosses—"

The stone fist closed around him tight, and he lost consciousness.

15.

He woke up to the sound of a baby crying.

His throat hurt, and his body thrummed with a desperate need.

Withdrawal.

All sense of faith was gone.

He sat up groggily. He was on the valley ground, and the monastery was in ruins. The stone walls were overgrown with ivy.

Corpses littered the valley floor. They were ancient, mummified corpses—as though they had lain there for centuries. The bloodred monks' robes they'd worn had mostly rotted away.

Gorel blinked, and saw Kettle.

"Nice place you've got here," Kettle said.

Gorel stood up. The baby kept crying. Behind Kettle, Gorel could see the giant albatrosses and their riders. He touched the bracelet on his wrist, and the thing disintegrated into nothingness.

"You used me," he said.

Kettle just shrugged.

"Is this it?" he said.

Gorel followed his eyes. He saw the baby lying there beside the pile of black rocks. He went to it. It was just a baby, and it stared up at Gorel with bright, accusing eyes.

"Sorry, Kay," Gorel said.

He picked the baby up.

"What would you do with him?" Gorel said. "He's just a baby."

"He's a potential," Kettle said. "Nothing more."

"He's a weapon, is what you mean."

"Yes."

"Why?" Gorel said. "Do you not have enough power already?"

"No," Kettle said. "Not yet."

"But what is it *for*?"

"Time," Kettle said. "It's to do with time, and a plague sweeping over the world. But you wouldn't know anything about that, would you, Gorel of Goliris?"

"I don't understand."

The baby gurgled. It laughed now. It laughed at Gorel. Its fat little finger touched Gorel's cheek. For just a moment he saw something he did not understand: once more he saw that black sea and the continent that lay beyond; once more he was shipwrecked on the jutting rocks and traveled, alone, in that great, abandoned city. He entered the throne room, and it was filled with cobwebs and dust.

But something woke. Something that had long been dormant. Waiting. And as he wandered out of the palace once again he saw them rise: one warrior and then another and another, tall, silent, faceless, clad in black. Soulless automatons. Hundreds he saw, then thousands, then thousands of thousands. And as he watched, they marched, out of Goliris. Out of Goliris, and on to the world.

An army the likes of which the world had never seen.

He whispered, "No . . ." but already the vision was fading, and the baby laughed and gurgled in his arms. He handed him to Kettle.

"Will you look after him, at least?"

"I will. You know I will."

"Yes."

Kettle motioned to his men. They mounted the flying beasts.

"Will you come back with me?" Kettle said. There was a pleading in his voice.

"You know I won't."

Kettle nodded. "Gorel . . ."

"Don't."

"Then can I offer you a ride, at least?"

"Yes," Gorel said. "Somewhere far from here."

16.

They left him by the side of an old abandoned road on the outskirts of the deadlands, far from anywhere. He watched them go.

When they vanished from sight he reached into his pocket and found a small, twisted packet of paper. He opened it carefully and snorted the last of the dust inside.

After that he felt better.

He hefted his guns, and then he set off along the road. He had traveled the world for a long time, and he was no closer to finding Goliris.

But he would never stop until he did.

Greg van Eekhout

. . .

Greg van Eekhout is a novelist of science fiction and fantasy for audiences ranging from middle grade to adult. His work has been selected as a finalist for the Sunshine State Award, the Andre Norton Award for Young Adult Science Fiction and Fantasy, and the Nebula Award. His novels include *Kid vs. Squid*, *The Boy at the End of the World*, *Norse Code*, and the California Bones trilogy: *California Bones*, *Pacific Fire*, and *Dragon Coast*. He's also published about two dozen short stories, several of which have appeared in year's best anthologies. Forthcoming works include the middle-grade novel *Voyage of the Dogs*, about dogs on a deep-space mission. He lives with his wife and dogs in San Diego, California, where he enjoys beach walks and tacos. Visit his website for more information: writingandsnacks.com.

Here he demonstrates that magic lives deep in the bone . . .

. . .

The Wolf and the

Manticore

GREG VAN EEKHOUT

Agnes Santiago approaches the entrance to the La Brea Tar Pits and joins the security line. Bubbles bloat and deflate in the black muck as if something alive is under there, breathing. And maybe something is.

"What's the job today, Aggie?" says the security guard, checking her ID.

"Making magic, Roy." They've been having this exact same exchange every day for two years. Agnes likes it because it's friendly but brief and superficial.

"You wanna know what real magic is?" Roy says, lowering his voice in a conspiratorial way.

"Why don't you tell me."

"Real magic's making someone do what you want them to. All the rest," he says, waving his hand airily toward the tar pits, "is just recipe."

Agnes signs her name on his clipboard. "That's pretty profound."

Roy nods profoundly. "I can't take credit for it. Got it from a fortune cookie."

"Profound fortune cookie."

"Enh, the lottery numbers were bullshit. Have fun making magic, Aggie."

She takes her station inside the complex. On the steel tray before her sits a wad of tar matrix the size of a piece of chewing gum. The paper-work says it's from Pit 24, one of the smaller experimental pits on the edge of the grounds. The hours pass as she performs surgery on it with fine picks and needles, teasing out bone fragments smaller than grains of rice. From here, the bones will go to the workshops where osteo-mancers use their arcane skills to distill them to pure magic. The bones are from the skull of a Colombian firedrake, and each little sliver is packed with enough firepower to punch a hole in an aircraft carrier.

At the end of her shift, guards come to collect the trays. Agnes goes to the changing room, where more guards watch her and the other pro-cessors strip out of their coveralls. They shine colored lights on them, looking for bone dust on their skin, for bits of magic in their hair. Any-thing they find gets vacuumed off and sent to the osteomancers. Some-times the workers get a full strip search. Today, they get the wolf.

The first time she laid eyes on him she thought he was terrifying but beautiful, his gray fur frosted with white, his black-rimmed yellow eyes flecked with orange. His long hands are a graceful blend of human and wolf. But that was a year ago, before he started growing his other heads.

A second head is forming out of his right cheek. It already has two eyes. Pink skin shows through a patchy fuzz on its still-rudimentary snout. But the nose is as fully formed as the one on its center head. The left-side head is still just fur and bumps, the eyes still closed, but the nose, again, fully formed.

From poking around, Agnes knows the wolf was just a regular human being once, but for whatever reason the ministry selected him for special treatment. They fed him Cerberus bone until the wolf magic changed his cells and he became a wolf.

In charge of security, the wolf has come around before, but only to watch. This is the first time he's subjected the workers to his own inspec-tion.

One by one, they come up to him. None of them manage to conceal their nerves. A few visibly shake as the wolf nudges them with his snouts, all three noses twitching and drawing in their scents. He smells their armpits, their crotches, their breath.

"You can go," he grunts at the end of each inspection, and if anyone takes offense at these invasions, they're too busy scurrying off to say so.

The wolf trains its stare on Agnes. She swallows the lump in her throat and keeps her fingers rigid so they don't ball up into fists, and she steps up to take her turn.

She endures the soft pressure of his noses against her as he follows his pattern. Armpits. Crotch. Breath.

It's the last that makes her most fearful. Her people told her the basilisk tooth they implanted in her gums produced no scent, but did they count on her being inspected by a wolf with three noses?

When he's done sniffing he draws away, and she finds herself staring into those remarkable lupine eyes. She wants to hold his gaze, to show that she's not afraid, to dare him to try something. But she remembers the role she's playing, and she looks down at her feet.

"You can go."

"Thank you," she mutters, and just like the others, she gets away as fast as she can.

Agnes pilots her panga through the canals of Los Angeles, joining every single other gondola and dinghy and coracle and speedboat trying to navigate Southern California's capital. It's tedious and time-wasting, but she likes floating past the market barges, taking in the smells of peppers and onions and garlic from the stir-fry vendors. And she likes the sounds of the buskers.

The music is particularly nice because the Hierarch keeps the Los Angeles airwaves silent. Ashes of processed meretsegar bones drizzle from the smoky sky, their osteomantic essence drinking noise and blocking radio signals. Muting the broadcasts from the Nevada border makes a kind of sense, since the US signals are propaganda, but the Mexican stations just broadcast music. Why deprive people of music?

After work, Agnes handwrites a report in cipher: Type of bone, amount she processed, amount she estimates processed by her co-workers. She inserts the note into the coupon pages in the afternoon edition of the *Herald Examiner* and leaves it in the hollow of a tree in Culver City Veteran's Park for her operator to collect.

And that's a day's work.

Given the firedrake and other munitions being processed from the

Tar Pits, she's pretty sure the Kingdom of Southern California is preparing for war against the north, but that's for others to determine.
Agnes isn't an intelligence analyst. She's just a spy.

The department manager approaches Agnes's work station. "Ms. Santiago, may I see you in my office?"

Agnes answers to the name as easily as if it were her own. Before she
came to the south, she'd spent three months responding to it in preparation.

The eyes of the other preparators track her as she follows the manager out. Working in the ministry means sometimes your coworkers get
called away to a meeting and never return to their workstation, or to
their home. The merest suspicion of wrongdoing can earn one a "transfer." And there are abundant reasons to transfer Agnes.

Sebastian Blackland closes his office door and gestures her into the
chair opposite his desk.

He's twenty-seven, a tired-looking Anglo with eyes the color of
roasted cashews, both the whites and the irises. It means even at his age
he's already eaten a lot of magic. If she has to kill him, it won't be easy.
She likes his face but she does not like him, because he's very handsome
and she doesn't know if his good looks come naturally, from cosmetic
surgery, or from cosmetic magic. This is Los Angeles, and with the magically privileged it's hard to know.

A cardboard file box sits on the desk, and his bookshelves have been
emptied.

She decides to delay any accusations of her being a foreign intelligence agent, not so much for any tactical reason, but because no matter
how it ends, it's going to be an unpleasant conversation, and not even
spies like their mornings unpleasant.

"Are you leaving us?" she asks.

"Ah, yes. The box. You noticed. I've been transferred . . . I mean . . . a
good transfer."

She's never had a conversation with Blackland, so she didn't know he
was awkward. She should have expected this. The reports have him
pegged as more of a scholar than a bureaucrat. She knows he's single,

doesn't go out much, spends most of his off time in the archives. He's considered a talent and might be a star if he had better political inclinations.

"I'm going to the Ossuary," he continues. "An R and D position."

She congratulates him, wondering when he's going to point his finger at her and scream, *"J'accuse!"* At which point she will use her tongue to push the ceramic first premolar from her upper jaw and spit it in Blackland's face. The ceramic will shatter, releasing finely powdered basilisk fang with a street value of 95,000 Northern Kingdom dollars. Blackland's face and skull will bubble and dissolve into a noxious, sticky goop.

"So, the reason why I . . . The thing I was wondering . . ." Blackland takes a breath, gathering himself. He seems apologetic. Embarrassed, even. He rubs the back of his neck. "Listen. I know you're a spy."

The tip of Agnes's tongue rests against her molar.

"I'm the only one who knows," he says.

Agnes just keeps staring at him.

"The thing I was wondering . . ."

"Are you going to ask me to sleep with you?" she says through gritted teeth.

He winces and shakes his head. "No. No, I know that's how this sounds. I'm not that kind of . . ."

She waits.

Agnes is patient.

To a point.

"Tell me what you want, please, Mr. Blackland."

He lets out a breath. "I want to defect."

Couples stroll the Pacific Ocean Pier. They hold hands and munch on floofs of cotton candy. Everyone's wearing their nicest clothes, from the wine-colored velvet sportscoats and spangled dresses of the disco kids to the crisp blue uniforms of soldiers on leave from the Bakersfield territories. People are having *fun*. Agnes reminds herself how easy it can be to forget, or at least set aside, the ever-present loom of the Hierarch's regime. Maybe that's not a bad thing.

She rides with Sebastian Blackland in a steel-and-glass bubble suspended from a cable over the surf. They look like they're out on a date. Agnes insisted they meet in a neutral location, one where they could speak in private, and the Ocean Skyway ride is perfect.

"How'd you know I'm a spy?"

Sebastian taps his nose. "I smelled you."

Agnes makes a face. She still has the option of using her poison tooth.

"I mean, your workspace. You've left enough essence at your workspace for me to realize you don't smell like anywhere in Southern California I know."

"What do I smell like?"

He closes his eyes and inhales.

"Different earth. Different water. Different air. It's all there in your bones. And I've smelled Northern Californians before."

"Prisoners of war?"

She says it with venom, but he just nods matter-of-factly.

She looks down on the wriggling reflections of electric lights in the ocean.

"Who else knows about me?"

"Nobody," he said. "I didn't tell, and I'm the only osteomancer in the office. Or was. My replacement comes in on Monday."

"What about the wolf?"

"He's head of security, but it's my department. He works for me. If he suspected anything, he'd report it to me."

"You seem confident in his diligence and loyalty."

"He's dependent on me. I'm the one who prepares his Cerberus bone and authorizes its use. Without me, he doesn't get to be a wolf."

"That's something I don't get," Agnes says. "Why does he want to change? What makes a person wake up one day and decide they want to be a three-headed wolf?"

"You mean beyond having the power of a three-headed wolf? I don't know. Different people, different reasons. Sometimes magic transforms, turning you from one thing into something else. Sometimes it distills, making you the purest version of what you are."

This is good, Agnes thinks. Getting into the head of a Southern California osteomancer without having to abduct and interrogate is a job well done.

"So, what do you get out of magic?" she asks.

He shrugs. "I'm an explorer, not a philosopher."

He leaves it there.

"So, the wolf doesn't know I'm a spy. You know, but you're not going to narc on me because you need me. Which means my position is safe."

"I'm afraid not. My replacement has a good nose, too. I instructed the night cleaners to bleach and vacuum your space, but if you're still working there once she takes over, she'll find you out."

"How are you explaining the need to sterilize my workspace?"

"I cited concerns about your work hygiene."

Agnes bristles. Her job is just for cover and access, but she takes pride in the quality of her work. When she had her first job as an ice cream scooper, her scoops were as close to the prescribed 3.5 ounces you could get without being a machine.

"Come Monday," he continues, "you'll start to leave traces again. You're going to have to find somewhere else to work or risk discovery."

"You said you want to defect. Why? You're an osteomancer on his way up. The Ossuary. That's an elite post. You'll be set up financially, socially; you'll get to play with the best bones. What's the downside?"

She's expecting a rehearsed answer, so she's surprised when he begins haltingly: "What's magic good for?"

"Weapons, obviously. Also, medicine, love potions, recreation, strengthening physical materials, social control . . . I could use up a lot of air going on. But the Hierarch's top priority is weapons. That's what we're making in the lab you supervise. I presume that's what you'll be making in the Ossuary."

"You're thinking like a rational person," Sebastian says. He's looking down at the same wriggling lights Agnes is, but she wonders if he's seeing something else. Maybe he can see the magic down there below the water, below the sand, way down past mud and rock to the fossils of the oldest osteomantic creatures, down to the flaming heart of the dragon in the center of the Earth. Osteomancers can be weird like that.

"Magic is coin," he says. "It's incredibly powerful, and beautiful, and transformative. But to people like the Hierarch, it's just a chit. He'll push down anyone—rival osteomancers, his own people, your people. He'll kill anyone and destroy anything, just as long as he ends up with the most chits. And he's really, really good at it."

"So, you want out."

"Yes," he says, his face closing down. "I want out."

Agnes stays silent a long time. She wants him to think she's thinking about it. She wants him to think there's a chance she might help him.

"I'll see what I can do," she says.

Agnes contacts her handler in the North, and they agree she should tender her resignation at the Tar Pits. She cites family reasons. Nobody tries to talk her out of leaving, and there's no signed card or cake in the break room. Her empty chair at the workbench is filled almost before she lifts her butt off it. She doesn't get to say goodbye to Roy the security guard.

A post preparing fossils at the Tar Pits is useful for gathering intel, but having a personal association with an osteomancer at the Ossuary is even better. So, for now, her job is Sebastian Blackland.

For the last several weeks she's met him daily at the amusement pier. They eat cotton candy and do the Davy Jones Locker ride and compete at throwing things for midway prizes. Agnes always wins, always to Sebastian's applause. To anyone looking, they appear to be a couple in the early days of courtship. Agnes's had lovers but never dated before, and sometimes she gets confused if it's dating if you do things people do on dates but for reasons other than romance.

"Here's a new thing," he says, taking her hand.

They stand, shoulders touching, at the end of the pier. The carousel lights reflect in his glasses.

His hand is soft and warm, his grip gentle. She feels the glass ampule tucked in his palm. She finds herself curiously reluctant to break contact with him, but she does so abruptly and pockets the ampule.

"It's powdered sint holo skull," he tells her. "It imparts essences of invisibility."

"It really works?"

"I could have eaten a pinch, walked up to you and stolen your wallet, and you'd have never even known I was here."

I'm glad you didn't, because I like seeing you, she comes dangerously close to saying.

She's not sure when this happened. Somewhere between the meeting when she told him she could help him defect and their third meeting, when she said it was contingent on him proving to her superiors he was worth the effort by smuggling bone out of the Ossuary.

"Sint holo is tricky to process," he tells her, "but I assume your guys back home can reverse engineer it. I could write it down, but the magic's not in the recipe. It's in the smell. The feel."

"They'll work with what I give them," Agnes says.

"The Ossuary's got me moving on to other projects, but I plan to keep working with sint holo. It's got some interesting properties just beyond my ability to smell. If there's anything there, I'll find it." His eyes get big. He gets excited.

At first Agnes thought his enthusiasm was part of a pitch to convince her how valuable he could be to her government, but now she sees it's just how he is. He loves being a wizard. He's a magic nerd.

She wants to hold hands again, but now that he's delivered the ampule, she'd have to contrive a new excuse.

"It sounds like they're happy with you there."

He smiles, bashful. "They're afraid of me. When you get to the level of the Hierarch's Ossuary, afraid is better than happy."

"It's that cutthroat?"

"Almost literally. To work with bone, you have to eat bone. After a while, the magic starts to collect in your system. Your body becomes a store of it. Which makes an osteomancer a resource that can be consumed."

"That's cannibalism," she says, expecting him to deny it.

But he doesn't.

Agnes turns to him and studies his face. She looks past his good looks, past his courage and willingness to take risks, and she sees his disgust. She sees his anger.

"Have you—?"

"Not yet," he says. "But my work's been noticed. There will be promotions. High-level osteomancers know about me. Maybe even the Hierarch himself."

"And you'll be expected to eat other osteomancers."

He tries to hide what he's feeling. He's not bad at it. But Agnes is better at figuring people out from what they conceal than he is at concealment.

"If I'm lucky, I'll be eating some wizards," he says.

"And if you're unlucky?"

He smiles. She can tell he finds the attempt painful.

"Unlucky is what happens to other people."

Agnes was six years old when the Southern Hierarch burned down her neighborhood.

Fresno wasn't a small town, but it was nothing compared to San Francisco, the Northern Kingdom's capital. Her father worked in a stationery shop in the Tower District. He didn't own it, didn't even manage it, just worked there. But it meant every September Agnes got to pick out a new three-ring binder and a plastic zipper-bag to fill with new pencils and blunt scissors.

Her mother was a waitress at the chicken pie shop on Olive. It was done up in a chicken-themed décor, and the milk came out of a big stainless-steel refrigerated dispenser. Even now, Agnes can't articulate what was magical about the binders and the milk dispenser, but they were important to her.

One day, way down in the Southern Kingdom, the Hierarch climbed to the top of Mount Whitney, more than fourteen thousand feet up, and from there, he breathed dragon fire.

Most of the flames landed in San Francisco. Chinatown, the Haight, the Mission, all lost. The Golden Gate Bridge turned to slag and slipped into the sea in piles of steam. More than twenty thousand people died.

Not all the Hierarch's flames met their intended targets. Some fell short. Maybe those were just him warming up.

Agnes was at school when two bursts hit Fresno. The one that incinerated the Tower District took both the stationery shop and the chicken pie shop. It took both her parents.

Agnes remembers clutching a three-ring binder to her chest as chickens ran, their feathers on fire. In this memory, the flames rose from the pyre of her mother's and father's corpses. The flames didn't touch her, but she screamed as if burned. She understands that this is probably not a true memory, but a cruel amalgamation cooked up in a waking nightmare.

In any case, her parents were dead, and she was alive and alone.

Unlike San Francisco's losses, Fresno's weren't overwhelming enough to create a housing crisis. They didn't have to erect tent cities and deploy rusting tanker holds as refugee camps. But there was still the matter of what to do with a six-year-old orphan.

The answer was the girls' school. In a manor house tucked away among Napa Valley vineyards, she found a second home. They gave her clean white shirts and plaid skirts and a blue blazer bearing the crest of the Northern California wizard-queen.

At first there were lessons in math and reading and lots of play and music. Mostly what she learned that first year was to feel safe in the care of her teachers, and to find comfort in the company of her classmates.

In her second year they started on foreign languages and the dialects of the Southern Kingdom.

In the third year, physical training began in earnest.

In the fourth year they added martial arts, drama, and deportment.

First aid and poisons came in the fifth year.

In the sixth year, there were munitions and sabotage.

Defense against magic began in the seventh year.

Shooting and knife skills were added in the eighth.

In the ninth year, driving lessons.

In the tenth year, the manticore came to visit.

Agnes and all the girls who'd been with her since her arrival at the school lined up in the gymnasium, chins high, backs straight, all of them strong and smart and sharpened to brilliance.

The manticore entered, and it took all of Agnes's training not to wither. The creature—her name was Lady Olympia Tillmon, Agnes would later learn—stood nearly seven feet tall. She gleamed in a coat of golden fur. Her face was more lioness than human, and trailing behind her on the parquet basketball court floor was a segmented tail of hard, black shell. At its tip was a sickle-shaped barb.

Compared to the other osteomantically enhanced people Agnes had seen, with their subtle reptilian or avian or piscine qualities, Lady Olympia was a true expression of what magic could do. Of what a person could become if transformed into something else or distilled down to their essence.

The manticore had two functionaries with her. They wore the wizard-queen's crest and followed the manticore with clipboards as she made her way down the line of girls. Some girls, the manticore barely looked at. Others, she loomed over for endless minutes, eyes narrowed in some kind of silent examination. She gave each girl a designation, which her functionaries marked on their clipboards.

Two girls were designated "Enhancement."

The next three were "Queen's Guard."

Another was "Intelligence," which by now Agnes thought they'd all been training for.

It went on like that, each girl assigned one of those three categories, until the manticore got to Agnes.

Up close, right in front of her, Lady Olympia was glorious. Her smallest movements triggered tectonic shifts of muscle beneath her glowing fur. She was a top predator with human intelligence and a position of influence in the government. No one could threaten her. No one could dream of doing her harm. A calm certainty descended on Agnes. The manticore was what she wanted for herself, and she knew she would be selected for Enhancement, and she'd be fed magic and be transformed into something that couldn't be hurt by the flames.

The manticore examined Agnes longer than she had any of the other girls.

"This one comes with me," she said. The functionaries marked their clipboards, and the manticore moved on to the next girl.

Agnes stands across the canal from Cupid's Hot Dogs in Van Nuys. She waits for the pedestrian drawbridge to lower and beats the blinking WALK sign to the other side of the canal. There, she stands on the pavement and waits until she feels no one's paying any attention to her. She drops the ampule of sint holo serpent bones Sebastian Blackland gave her into the canal. She has no clear idea what happens to it from here. Maybe her masters have cracked the code of the Southern water mages' canal system and know how to bring the vial to them. Maybe they've got some aquatic creature down there that collects the bones and swims it all the way to Northern California. All she knows is that the Southern canal system forms a labyrinth that sprawls over the entire Southern Kingdom, generating massive amounts of elemental water magic. William Mulholland built it almost a century ago, and his command of it makes him the Hierarch's rival. Maybe Mulholland's secretly working with the North to topple the Hierarch from his throne.

Agnes doesn't have to know. Her job remains Sebastian Blackland.

She sits beside Sebastian in his newly acquired boat, docked in the shadow of a 405 flumeway overpass. They're sharing messy burritos and chips and salsa from Tito's Tacos, and Agnes has to concentrate to avoid spilling beans and cheese on the leather seats of Sebastian's vintage 1946 mahogany-hulled Speedliner. He claims he bought it to keep up appearances, as Ossuary osteomancers are expected to maintain a certain lifestyle. Agnes thinks he bought the boat because it's expensive, and after four months at the Ossuary, he can afford it. His clothes are tailored now, too. She wonders how much he'll change as she keeps stringing him along.

"Here," he says, passing her a paper packet as casually as though handing her the salsa.

"What's this?" She tucks the packet in her bag.

"Something happened at work today." He looks out over the Speedliner's bow. Usually he looks at her when he talks. "There's this osteomancer, Todd Taylor. I swear, that's really his name. A wizard named Todd Taylor. He's my age, been at the Ossuary for about a year. Not much longer than me. I wouldn't call him a nice guy, because that's not the kind of person who works at the Ossuary. Or if you are a nice guy, you hide it."

She wants to ask Sebastian if he's been hiding it, but she decides to let him talk. He's still not looking at her, and the words are coming out with difficulty, as if he's trying to read a script but the lines are blurry.

"This morning, we get called into a meeting. It's in the claw chamber. Have I told you about the claw chamber?"

Agnes nods, but Sebastian doesn't see it, because he's not looking.

"They call it that because of the table. It's a slab of granite the size of a Ping-Pong table, resting on four serrated claws. The claws have got to be three feet long each. They're from a Pacific firedrake. Do you see what I'm saying? All that magic, all that wealth, just to hold up a table."

Agnes can't maintain her silence any longer. "Why are you telling me about a table?" What she meant to say was, "Sebastian, are you okay?"

"Right. It's just a table. Anyway. Todd Taylor. Todd's at the meeting. His tie's on crooked, like he was in a rush putting it on for the meeting. I straightened Todd Taylor's tie."

She waits.

"They threw him down on the table, cut him from throat to groin, and we had lunch. I'm the new guy, so I only got a distal phalanx. That's a finger bone."

"I know what a goddamn distal phalanx is," she says. Then she rests a hand on his shoulder. He's shivering.

"I'm going to get you out of there," she says.

She walks to her one-bedroom apartment with a bag of Cupid's chili cheese dogs in hand. In the two years since infiltrating LA, she's managed to make this place home. Her furniture is all thrift shop finds, but in good condition. Throw pillows and blankets make things soft and comfortable, a shabby chic for lounging and for stashing her arsenal of bladed weapons.

In the space that's neither kitchen nor living room but not separate enough to be called a dining room, she sits down at her only table with her Cupid's and a glass of wine. She would almost literally kill for a sip of a Napa Valley vintage, because the wine in Southern California is pretty awful. At least it's cheap, and it goes well with chili and cheese and airy white hot dog buns.

She opens her makeup compact. The case is just plastic, but the powder is ground eocorn bone. The eocorn was a deeply osteomantic creature before it was hunted to extinction sometime toward the end of the

Pleistocene, and a few ounces of its remains can command a street value greater than the worth of all the apartments and houses and commercial buildings in the square mile surrounding her.

The manticore looks back at her from the little mirror. Her mane has grown even more luxuriant since Agnes last saw her, and there's a sense of power straining to expand, like a plugged volcano. Agnes has caught her drinking tea in some lush solarium. Tall Chinese vases and potted ferns loom behind her.

"Agnes," she says.

Her voice sounds like something escaped from a fissure in the earth.

"Lady Olympia, I'm sorry to disturb you. I felt it necessary."

"Of course you did. I trust your judgment at all times. What is it, dear?"

"The situation with Blackland has become critical. If we don't extract him, I think we'll lose him as an asset."

"I see." The manticore sips tea. "Agnes, we want you to kill him. Kill him and drop his corpse in the canals. He'll be conducted to us."

Agnes wants to slap herself. She's been slow. She's invested too much in Sebastian Blackland the person and has lost sight of Sebastian Blackland the resource.

The small quantities of bone he's been smuggling out of the Ossuary are nice. But there's a limit to how much he can sneak out of the Hierarch's stronghold without being caught. Those little magics aren't his main value. He works with precious bones, processing them, teasing potent magic out of osteomantic materials. Part of the osteomancer's craft involves ingesting the magic. They use their own bodies as cauldrons, and some of that magic stays within them. She's seen how Sebastian's changed as his own skeleton becomes an ossuary of magic. His body is more valuable to Northern California than dozens of tiny vials of powdered fossil.

The manticore sets her tea down. Even through the compact, Agnes hears the sharp ring of the cup against the saucer. "Do you understand?"

"Yes," Agnes says.

Snapping the compact shut, she makes her decision.

◆　◆　◆

Sebastian lives in a box.

It's an expensive box, one of those concrete-and-glass constructions with fifty-foot ceilings and big walls that require big paintings so they don't look too warehouse-y. It's underfurnished because he bought it just a few weeks ago, and his job has him too busy to buy things to sit upon and put your feet upon and set drinks upon. The bedroom is vast and empty except for a small bureau and the bed.

The kitchen, though, is fully stocked, and Sebastian knows how to use it. Agnes has spent the last hour watching him chop and slice and throw things in ice baths and seasoning. He tastes as he works and sniffs a lot.

She dices up the carrots he's given her so she won't feel idle. "Are all osteomancers good chefs?"

"The good ones are. Deep magic requires art."

He sounds only a little arrogant. The depth of his magic is becoming clear just by looking at him. The whites of his eyes are darkening to the rich coffee brown of bones soaked in La Brea tar for ten thousand years. And there's something in the way he moves now. Something feline in the way he walks. In the way his gaze snaps on what he's looking at, like a bird of prey. He's been working with griffin bones at the Ossuary.

They dine on the rooftop deck, currently outfitted with cheap lawn furniture bought for this occasion. A price tag dangles from Agnes's folding chair.

And yet it's magical.

The lights of the canals and sky trolleys are a rectilinear galaxy stretching from the sea to the mountains east of the city. The span encompasses millions of people, short on freedom but still alive. She can almost feel them straining, building pressure, never far away from flaring bright and hot like a brushfire.

Sebastian takes a sip of wine. It's red and expensive and has a French name she's already forgotten.

She looks at his hands.

"I'm supposed to kill you," she says.

He closes his eyes, nods sadly, and puts down his wineglass. When he opens his eyes again, his pupils have changed. They're narrower.

"The basilisk venom in your tooth?"

"Dammit. How'd you know?"

He taps the bridge of his nose and sniffs.

"That's annoying," she says.

"Maybe. But also useful. Why kill me?"

"You've made your body too valuable."

"Why, thank you." He gives her a rare smirk.

"Don't preen. You know what I mean. My masters feel they get more from dissecting you than by taking the little samples you sneak out of the Ossuary."

"What about putting me to work in a Northern ossuary? Again, it's not just recipe."

Agnes shakes her head emphatically. She doesn't want this to be a negotiation. "They still get more from chopping you up."

Sebastian looks at her hands. "Okay. I hope you know you have no chance of killing me," he says at last.

"What are you talking about? Of course I can kill you."

"I've known about the basilisk for a while. I've made myself immune."

"Are you immune to knives? Are you immune to me breaking your neck? Are you immune to me fixing the gas line on your boat? Are you immune to me throwing you off the roof right now?"

"So you're resourceful, is what you're saying."

"I can kick your ass, is what I'm saying."

"You seem more piqued than murderous right now."

"I'm a spy," she says, exasperated. "You don't know what I'm thinking, what I'm feeling, or what I'm going to do."

"So tell me," he says. There's a little bit of pleading in his bizarre eyes. "What are you going to do?"

"Mexico," she says. She has to gather herself before saying more, because she's about to take a great risk. But he waits. "I know people . . . or know *of* them . . . who can get us to Mexico."

The "us" in that sentence is the risky part. She can tell it's not lost on Sebastian. It'll be okay if he doesn't like the idea. Not great, but okay.

But when he says, "What's waiting for us in Mexico?" she lets herself breathe a little now that he's used the word, too.

"Not a lot," she admits. "But it's beyond the reach of both our governments. Your people won't be trying to eat you there, and mine won't be trying to punish me for not following my orders. From there, we can go wherever we want. South America. Asia. Maybe even Europe. We have marketable skills. We could do all right."

He looks like he's carefully weighing something on a balance.

"These people you know . . . What do they take as payment? I'm cash poor."

She doesn't hesitate. "Two fingers."

He pales a little, but she doesn't have to tell him it's better to surrender two fingers of magically charged bones than his whole carcass.

"They don't care which hand, which fingers," she adds, trying to be reassuring. She forces herself to look at his hands again and feels lightheaded.

He agrees to letting her save him without saying it out loud. She takes his hand and leads him to the bedroom.

Agnes sits propped up on pillows next to Sebastian. He snores softly as she stares out the wall-sized window. She can hear predawn traffic at the bottom of the hill, boat horns and barge bells and the susurrus of churning water. Every convoluted mile of canal between Hollywood and Tijuana is an opportunity for failure. Her, they'll probably just torture and interrogate before a summary execution. As for Sebastian . . . She has no idea how long they can part out an osteomancer without killing him.

So she plans. She doesn't have friends to rely on. She doesn't have money. But she has things she's good at and things she's willing to do, and that's even better than cash.

She can make this happen. She can get herself out of this abattoir, and she can take Sebastian with her. And after that, whatever happens happens.

She spots a pair of birds circling high above the hill. Too big to be gulls or hawks. Condors, maybe? But there's something strange about their shape. The proportions are all wrong. She doesn't make out that they're part human until they break off from their circles and come diving straight for the window.

She has enough time to throw off the bedsheet and reach her jeans, crumpled on the floor. She retrieves one of her knives and flicks it open.

The creatures crash through the window.

Two of them, with gray-pink skin, round brown eyes rimmed with cloudy red, the feathers of their wings dragging on the floor. They shake their bodies, and shattered window glass flies like wind-blown hail.

Sebastian is on his feet, a pillow clutched over his crotch. He sniffs, taking in their scent. "These aren't from around here."

"No, I think they're from home."

"What do you want?" Sebastian asks them.

Agnes swallows a laugh. When two monsters crash through your window, it's pretty clear what they want.

One of them brushes glass from its wing. It raises its chin in a lofty expression and manages to blend officiousness with murderous threat. Definitely from the home office.

Thumping footfalls sound above the ceiling, and the Cerberus wolf lands on the narrow window ledge. He carefully avoids broken glass and steps into the room.

Agnes was right about him. With all three of his heads fully formed, he's a glorious sight.

"Carl, what's this about?" Sebastian demands.

"Carl?" Agnes says, incredulous "His name is *Carl*?"

All three heads nod. "Yes. And your name isn't Agnes Santiago. You're Agnes Valdez."

There's only one way he could know her real name. "You're working with the North."

"No," Sebastian says. "I've seen every page of his records. I've seen his birth certificate. He was born in Twenty-Nine Palms. He's been in the Southern Kingdom his whole life."

"I'm not here to talk about me," the wolf says, its three voices in close harmony. "I'm here to supervise."

"I don't understand any of this," Sebastian says.

"He's here to make sure I carry out my orders," Agnes tells him, not taking her eyes off the wolf. "If I don't, then he'll take care of the job himself. And me as well. Do I have that right?"

"You do."

"What did the manticore promise you? What do you get out of it?"

Agnes hopes that while they're talking, Sebastian will manage to cook up some kind of impressive osteomantic attack. Two birds and a Cerberus wolf are more than she can handle on her own.

But Sebastian isn't cooking anything or mixing anything. Right now he's just a guy standing around with a pillow over his dick.

She turns to him. She adjusts her grip on the knife. "Well, thanks for the humping."

She flings the knife, and it enters a birdman's eye with a noise like puncturing frozen plum. If he were human, the blade would have penetrated the sphenoid bone at the back of the orbit and gone into the frontal cortex. But Agnes isn't super-clear on bird anatomy, much less on osteomantic bird-human hybrids. So she takes the knife she secreted between the mattress and the box spring and chucks it into the birdman's throat.

He sinks to the floor, his wings thumping the hardwood as they spasm. Otherwise, he sounds human as he dies.

Sebastian gulps a breath. Relief, maybe. Maybe he thought she was really going to kill him. Maybe, for a second, she considered it.

The second birdman hesitates, understandably since he just saw his cohort killed by a woman with no osteomancy. It turns out to be a fatal mistake, since it gives Agnes time to fetch the knife in her boot and send it rocketing into the space between his eyes. He squawks and falls backward out the window. Agnes doesn't hear the expected thump of impact, possibly because he's hollow-boned and lightweight.

The wolf has taken this all in with dispassion. Sometimes the best thing to do is let others fight. You get a chance to size them up, and it tires them out.

Agnes touches the tip of her tongue to her molar. The tooth tastes like metal. Like a bullet. She pushes to dislodge it and accepts the jolt of pain. She aims for the heart and spits. The ceramic shatters, just as it's supposed to. Basilisk venom bubbles and sizzles on the wolf's chest, and the wolf howls in triple-voiced agony. Gray fur yellows, turns orange as rust, and falls away in clumps to reveal raw, pink flesh.

But the wolf doesn't fall. He doesn't die. Snarling, he leaps on top of her before she can even move. His claws pierce her wrists. Something sharp rakes down the entire length of her leg. His weight compresses her lungs, so her screams are gruff whistling noises.

She feels teeth on her throat. They close down and rip.

The last thing she feels is a wave of heat, blasting her face. This fire is more than chemistry. It adheres to different rules. It's a breath from the center of the earth, molten rock, liquid iron. It is dragon's heart. It is the idea of dragon. It is magic, and it's coming from Sebastian.

He is burning the world.

The cool tile feels good on her bare skin. She's awoken on the bathroom floor with Sebastian kneeling beside her. She tries to sit up but surrenders to gravity when the movement makes her feel like thousands of matches have taken light beneath her skin. She touches her throat, astonished to find there's flesh there. Claws shredded her nerves and arteries, she remembers.

"Wolf?" she croaks.

"I put out his embers with a bucket of water to make sure he doesn't set my house on fire," Sebastian says. "And then I . . . Well, I took care of his remains."

"And why am I not just remains?" Her throat feels like it's lined with fishhooks.

"Hydra."

Sever a hydra's head and another grows in its place. It's priceless healing magic, and he used it on her.

"So," he says, sitting on the floor beside her, "the North wants me dead, and the wolf is somehow connected with them. He was even protected against your basilisk venom. We don't know how to formulate that kind of magic here."

"I thought you said you were immune."

"Well, I may have lied to you about that. I wanted to discourage you from spitting at me."

Agnes closes her eyes and tries to concentrate. Despite the hydra saving her life, she feels wrung out and generally shitty. She raises herself on her elbows and with effort manages to stay up. "What I don't understand is that if my people recruited the wolf, and if they want you dead, why even bother involving me? Why not just handle it through the wolf?"

Sebastian's eyebrows suggest a shrug. "I have no idea. I can turn people into toads, but damned if I can figure out how toads think."

"I want to find out more about the wolf. Can you get me a record of his movements and contacts?"

"Sure. And I can take you to his house if you want."

"You're very helpful."

"Does that bother you?"

"You bother me. Everyone bothers me." She takes a few deep breaths. "Can you really turn people into toads?"

He laughs. "No, not really." Then his face gets serious. "Well, not yet."

He gently lifts her to her feet, and she lets herself lean on him.

The wolf's house is a mid-century classic ranch style in Burbank. There's a green lawn, a brick porch with a white swing bench, and a basketball hoop mounted on the boathouse at the end of the parking channel. Agnes takes care of the burglar alarm and lets herself and Sebastian in through the back door.

"He definitely lived here," Agnes says, noting shed fur on the sofa.

Sebastian wrinkles his nose. "You'd think he could afford a housekeeper on his salary."

"You can talk about housekeeping once you get some actual furniture."

She finds a den next to one of the bedrooms. Sebastian rifles through the desk drawers while Agnes checks out the coat closet. She finds a small safe bolted to the floor.

Sebastian comes over. He reaches into his satchel, where he keeps his osteomancer's kit. "I might be able to work up some seps serpent acid to burn through the . . . Never mind."

Agnes already has the safe open.

"Girls' school, fifth year." The safe contains a Breitling Swiss watch, a rubber-banded bundle of cash, a vial of cocaine, and a single sheet of paper. The paper is blank. Agnes hands it to Sebastian. "Smell this."

Sebastian subjects it to his sniff test. "Mmm. Smells dry. Desert sand. Whispers. Riddles. Sphinx?"

"We use sphinx oil for coded messages in the North." She takes the paper back from him. Then, from her bag she retrieves a nail polish bottle, unscrews the cap, lifts out the brush.

His nose twitches. "That's not for fancy fingers."

She lays the paper on the desk and begins brushing the bottle's contents over it in light strokes. "With the matching formulation, you can decrypt a sphinx-coded message."

"And you just happen to have the match?"

"They taught us to use ur-sphinx in year four. Quiet now. I have to listen."

The brushed-on oil evaporates, airborne particles wafting over her face, into her nostrils, through her eyelashes, snaking deep in her ears, rising to her brain. She hears the whispers, hot wind piling sand into dunes, the small movements of scorpions hunting spiders on the eroded plains. Only natural noises at first. Then human sounds. Utterances. Murmurs. She listens the way she was taught all those years ago in another kingdom. The language is English, the dialect, Northern Californian. The voice is deep and rich and powerful. It is frightening and beautiful, and she listens.

Places.

Times.

When it falls silent she lifts her head from the page.

"Are you okay?" Sebastian asks. "You were in some kind of state for about twenty minutes."

She doesn't answer at first. Her throat is dry.

"Agnes?"

"The manticore is in Los Angeles," she says. "She's going to finish the job the wolf failed to. She's going to finish the job *I* failed to."

"We can do to this manticore what we did to the wolf." Sebastian is so blissfully stupid.

"Not to the manticore, we can't. Maybe if you ate another ten years of magic. But I know what you can do, and I know what she can do."

"Okay, then we run to Mexico. We can take my boat."

"You don't run from the manticore."

"No fighting and no running? It's very discouraging when you knock down all my good suggestions. I hope you have an idea."

"I do," Agnes says.

She wishes she didn't hate her idea so very much.

The Cerberus wolf looks pretty good, considering how dead he is. His fur doesn't even smell singed. Agnes checks herself in her compact and decides that even if the wolf looked like a wad of melted hair, she'd have to go through with this. She pads between the garment-district ware-houses, down a back-alley channel lined with loading docks. The only light comes from a weak lamp bolted over the doors of a three-story building, but it's enough to reveal the hulking goons waiting there. The three of them have massive chests and arms, broad faces, angry little eyes, and sets of bullhorns with three-foot spans. She remembers picking tar off minotaur fossils a year ago. At least someone found her work useful.

They train their eyes on her. She trains her six eyes back.

"Is there a problem, Mr. Thompson?" one of them asks.

It sounds more like a sincere question than a challenge, so she stays loose, but she does wonder why they're asking about a problem. She must have done something wrong.

"You tell me," she tries.

The bulls exchange uncertain glances.

"Well, it's just that . . . you usually use the VIP entrance, is all."

"I wanted to see how the other half lives," she deadpans. Should she have deadpanned it? Should she have said something else entirely? Nothing at all? Should she see if she's capable of ripping out the throats of three towering minotaur guys? She's off balance, and not just because she's not used to carrying this mass and shape. But she better get used to it fast. Sebastian used shape-shifting magic from chimera vertebrae to give her the form and appearance and even smell of the Cerberus, but that's only half the job. It'll take more than osteomancy to convince the manticore. It will take all her training from girls' school, and all her ex-perience in the field.

Be a wolf, she tells herself. You *are* a wolf.

The minotaurs laugh uncertainly, and one opens the door for her. "Have a good evening, sir."

She just grunts and steps inside.

She regrets it instantly. It's a disco.

The air is a dark, smoke-choked haze flashing with strobes and stupid flickering lights. Reflections ricochet off the spinning disco ball, and she wants to cut the chain holding it up and punish it for being so twinkly. The music starts to put a little rhythm in her step, and for this reason, she deeply resents the music. But it's what the customers come for. That, dancing, and magic.

Most of them show only essence of bone consumption, with narrow irises like cats, or slightly elongated incisors curving over black lips, or some ineffable qualities of satyr or serpent. But a few have feathers. One girl twirls around, dancing with a rainbow of spotlights playing off her spread wings. It takes a lot of magic to achieve these transformations, and the wolf can't help but wonder what they had to do to get it. None of this stuff is street legal. And all of it is bank-breakingly expensive. Maybe they're all just boring and rich.

Agnes is attracting notice herself. Some people move out of her way. Some pose, wanting her attention. A boy with fish eyes runs a green tongue over his blue lips. Agnes hates being so conspicuous, but she couldn't find a three-hooded hoodie on such short notice.

Act like you belong here, she tells herself. She does it a little too well and has to turn down three dance invitations before she makes it to the double doors leading to the kitchen.

The cooks glance up and then look away as she passes through. They're used to seeing the wolf here. Good.

"Is she in?" Agnes asks.

From their expressions, this isn't a question they're used to. But so what? They're cooks. She's the wolf, and she'll ask whatever she wants. So, a cook tossing chicken wings in a bowl of hot sauce says, "She's in her office, sir."

"Take me there," the wolf commands, putting a little growl in all three voices.

The cook gives the other kitchen staff a wide-eyed "isn't one of you going to bail me out of this?" look, but they all become very busy with their food prep. One of them takes the bowl from the poor guy's hands, and his fate is cemented. He swallows miserably, wipes his hands on his apron, and leads the wolf through a stockroom, down a hallway, and up three flights of stairs. Two birdmen on the landing stop eating ribs and make way for the wolf. One of them opens a door for her.

Agnes thought she was prepared for the sight of the manticore, but she was wrong. Maybe it's the passage of time, or maybe it's because the manticore has consumed more magic, but the creature is even more grand and magnificent than ever. In the dull light from the lampposts shining through the window, her tousled mane gleams, spreading over her mountainous shoulders and down her back. She's the height of a grizzly bear, and her feline eyes glow like emeralds.

The birdman shuts the door behind Agnes, sealing her inside the cramped office. She takes a seat across the desk from the manticore. The manticore is too large for the desk chair, and she remains standing, inspecting her obsidian claws. "Communication has not been good."

Agnes doesn't think the wolf would apologize, even to the manticore, so she doesn't either. Instead, she reaches into her coat pocket, retrieves two fingers, and places them on the desk.

"Does this tell you what you want to know?"

The manticore's nostrils flare. Agnes doesn't know if she knows what Sebastian smells like, but if she does, she should be satisfied. The fingers are his.

"Where's the rest of him?"

The fingers remain on the desk, curled up like white prawns.

"Safe."

The manticore nods, as if she's coming to understand something, and Agnes has no idea exactly what she's coming to understand. "Do you want to tell me why you haven't delivered him?"

"I'm not satisfied with the arrangement," says Agnes. That could mean anything, which is why she said it.

The manticore sighs and stretches her tail so the barb touches the window with a little *tink* sound. "You want to revisit our agreement. Again."

Sure, why the hell not? "Yes," says Agnes.

"And you think you deserve this because . . . ?"

"Because I risked a lot taking Blackland. Because it cost me. Because he had someone protecting him I couldn't have foreseen."

The last point seems to strike a note of sympathy with the manticore. "Agnes surprised me, too. I've known her since she was a child. I trained her myself."

"Trained her for what, exactly?"

The second the question leaves her mouths, Agnes knows she has made a mistake. It's not the question itself, but it's the feeling behind it. What was it all for? The girls' school, the classes, the years of learning how to read secret codes and to kill and blow things up?

The manticore sidesteps the question. "She'd been reliable for years, the last person I would have thought to turn traitor. I had hopes for her. But you can't blame that on me entirely. She worked under your watch for the last two years, and you didn't see it coming?"

"I might have had suspicions if I'd been paying more careful attention," she admits. This is a truth. She watched the enemy, but she took her eyes off the most important thing to monitor: herself. She let herself doubt her mission and her purpose. And she let herself get invested in Blackland.

Why does any of this matter? Agnes didn't have Sebastian transform her into the wolf to talk. She had him do it so she could get close to the manticore and have some protection once she did. Both objectives, reached.

But she still wants the manticore to give her a good reason why Sebastian Blackland should be harvested. She wants to hear how his murder can serve some greater good. And if the manticore gives her that? What a loathsome creature Agnes must be that she's still not absolutely certain what she'll do.

The manticore looks to the ceiling, a gesture Agnes recognizes. She's calculating.

"I don't like dickering, so I'm going to make you a preemptive offer," the manticore says. "I'll increase the sphinx oil to twelve gallons. That's double what we agreed on."

She looks at Agnes expectantly. Agnes doesn't know what she should say, so she says nothing.

The manticore is exasperated now, on the verge of anger. "I'll add two hundred grams of steppe hippogriff, plus the formula for weaponizing it. That's magic you've never seen in the South. Your buyers will make you rich for that."

Wait, Agnes thinks. Buyers? Is that what this is all about?

"And in return?" she prods.

"Sebastian Blackland's body. All of it. Every last organ and bone."

"And then you get rich."

The manticore smiles, and somehow she manages to make her glorious lion face look tawdry.

Agnes gets it now. The manticore and the wolf have been trading magic. Southern magic in the North commands top dollar on the black market. And likewise Northern magic in the South.

Agnes's work in the Southern Kingdom has never been about protecting the North. It's not about preventing another San Francisco fire. It has zero to do with Fresno. She's been nothing but a procurer of Southern magic. Her reports from the Tar Pits were inventories. And when Sebastian came to her for help, he became an unwitting supplier. Agnes is only a mule.

"So, now you know, Agnes."

Agnes's heart hammers. The manticore looks at her with maternal affection.

"Didn't fool you at all?" Agnes says. Her voices feel thin as paper.

"Your shape-shifting is very good craft. Blackland's talented. But I'm very old, love, and I'm not just manticore. I've eaten a lot of magic." She draws her tail barb down the window, a knife scraping glass. "What do you want to do, Agnes?"

"What are my options?"

"You could give me Blackland."

Agnes absolutely could do that. She could give the manticore Blackland, and she could take the North's sphinx oil and steppe hippogriff, and, with the manticore's help, maybe even remain the wolf, and survive and perhaps even profit.

"That is really your only option, Agnes."

"Hm," Agnes says.

The manticore's eyes narrow. "Oh, Agnes, had you a hundred heads and a hundred sets of fearsome jaws, you would still not survive a fight with me."

But Agnes doesn't need that many jaws. She just needs one tooth, the one Sebastian prepared.

As a tooth, it's not much, just a pebble of bone stuck in her empty gum socket with denture adhesive. But it's the bone of a Sierra firedrake, and Sebastian spent hours cooking it at precise temperatures, smelling it to probe its osteomantic properties, lovingly teasing out its magic with flame.

A push of the tongue, and the tooth dislodges. She swallows it whole. A breath.

By the time the stale air reaches her lungs, it's blade-sharp and cold, the air of the high mountaintops on the eastern edge of California. She holds it and feels herself soaring down from the concealment of the clouds, her screaming cry shaking needles from the tall pines, sending griffins into panicked stampede.

The manticore's eyes widen as she realizes what's happening. Her tail snaps forward, the barb loaded with poison. But she's too late. Agnes exhales, and the world becomes dragon flame.

Somewhere in that world, the manticore shrieks.

Later, Agnes finds a phone in the disco. She dials a number.

"Yes?" says Sebastian.

"It's done," says Agnes. "Come get your meal."

"Maria, I'm home."

Sebastian comes through the back door late with take-out ribs from Kelbo's. He's home late most nights, but he does come home. Their house is a comfortable but somewhat ramshackle construction tucked into a shady gully in Reseda. It's less than what Sebastian can afford, but Agnes doesn't want to live in a neighborhood with other osteomancers.

"Good job," Agnes says with a kiss. The praise is for remembering to call her Maria. She chose the name Maria because she's never had a close relationship with anyone named Maria. And she chose the last name Sigilo because it's Spanish for "secret," and it reminds her not to get too comfortable with her new identity, not even with the new face she sculpted with the help of chimera bone.

Daniel Blackland is only six months old, and it's too soon to tell how much he's going to look like Agnes or Sebastian. His skin is already dark like Agnes's, and she hopes that's as far as the resemblance will go. She doesn't want to have to change his face. It seems a child should have the right to live with their own face, but Agnes will make Sebastian transform it into something else if that's what it takes to protect their son. She accepts that as her responsibility. Sebastian loves the boy, but even with his promotions at the Ossuary, and the obvious power in his eyes from having eaten Cerberus wolf and manticore and the bones of so many other creatures, he doesn't have Agnes's ruthlessness. Los Angeles is a town that requires ruthlessness.

"Did you bring it?" Maria asks as Sebastian plates the ribs while she pours wine.

He digs into his pocket and pulls out a tar-brown thorn. It's a piece of griffin claw.

Maria has come to understand that, if real magic is in doing what you want to do and denying others' power over you, then the source of her magic is her ruthlessness. She will not bend to a Hierarch, a wizard-queen, a wolf, or a manticore.

She won't see her son bend to them either.

She takes the griffin claw and puts it in the high cupboard above the refrigerator, in a cookie jar containing other bits and odds of bone. This is Daniel's future. When he's old enough, she'll feed him as much bone as it takes to make sure no one will ever dare harm him.

Sebastian sets Daniel up in his highchair and spoon-feeds him pureed peas. Daniel doesn't like them, but Sebastian coaxes and makes airplane sounds while trying to land the spoon.

"C'mon, kid," Agnes says. "Eat up and get strong."

George R. R. Martin

◆ ◆ ◆

Hugo, Nebula, and World Fantasy Award–winner George R. R. Martin, *New York Times* bestselling author of the landmark A Song of Ice and Fire fantasy series, has been called "the American Tolkien."

Born in Bayonne, New Jersey, George R. R. Martin made his first sale in 1971, and soon established himself as one of the most popular SF writers of the seventies. He quickly became a mainstay of the Ben Bova *Analog* with stories such as "With Morning Comes Mistfall," "And Seven Times Never Kill Man," "The Second Kind of Loneliness," "The Storms of Windhaven" (in collaboration with Lisa Tuttle, and later expanded by them into the novel *Windhaven*), "Override," and others, although he also sold to *Amazing, Fantastic, Galaxy, Orbit*, and other markets. One of his *Analog* stories, the striking novella "A Song for Lya," won him his first Hugo Award, in 1974.

By the end of the seventies, he had reached the height of his influence as a science fiction writer, and was producing his best work in that category with stories such as the famous "Sandkings," his best-known story, which won both the Nebula and the Hugo in 1980 (he'd later win another Nebula in 1985 for his story "Portraits of His Children"), "The Way of Cross and Dragon," which won a Hugo Award in the same year (making Martin the first author ever to receive two Hugo Awards for fiction in the same year), "Bitterblooms," "The Stone City," "Starlady," and others. These stories would be collected in *Sandkings*, one of the strongest collections of the period. By now, he had mostly moved away from *Analog*, although he would have a long sequence of stories about the droll interstellar adventures of Havalend Tuf (later collected in *Tuf Voyaging*) running throughout the eighties in the Stanley Schmidt *Analog*, as well as a few strong individual pieces such as the novella "Nightflyers." Most of his major work of the late seventies and early eighties, though, would appear in *Omni*. The late seventies and the eighties also saw the publication of his memorable novel *Dying of the Light*, his only solo SF novel, while his stories were collected in *A Song for Lya*, *Sandkings*, *Songs of Stars and Shadows*, *Songs the Dead Men Sing*, *Nightflyers*, and *Portraits of His Children*. By the beginning of the eighties, he'd moved away from SF and into the horror genre, publishing the big horror novel *Fevre Dream*, and winning the Bram Stoker Award for his horror story "The Pear-Shaped

Man" and the World Fantasy Award for his werewolf novella "The Skin Trade." By the end of that decade, though, the crash of the horror market and the commercial failure of his ambitious horror novel *Armageddon Rag* had driven him out of the print world and to a successful career in television instead, where for more than a decade he worked as story editor or producer on such shows as the new *Twilight Zone* and *Beauty and the Beast*.

After years away, Martin made a triumphant return to the print world in 1996 with the publication of the immensely successful fantasy novel *A Game of Thrones*, the start of his Song of Ice and Fire sequence. A free-standing novella taken from that work, "Blood of the Dragon," won Martin another Hugo Award in 1997. Further books in the Song of Ice and Fire series—*A Clash of Kings*, *A Storm of Swords*, *A Feast for Crows*, and *A Dance with Dragons*—have made it one of the most popular, acclaimed, and bestselling series in all of modern fantasy. Recently, the books were made into an HBO TV series, *Game of Thrones*, which has become one of the most popular and acclaimed shows on television, and made Martin a recognizable figure well outside of the usual genre boundaries—even inspiring a satirical version of him on *Saturday Night Live*. Martin's most recent books include a massive retrospective collection spanning the entire spectrum of his career, *GRRM: A RRetrospective*, a novella collection, *Starlady and Fast-Friend*, a novel written in collaboration with

Gardner Dozois and Daniel Abraham, *Hunter's Run*, and, as editor, several anthologies edited in collaboration with Gardner Dozois, including *Warriors*, *Song of the Dying Earth*, *Songs of Love and Death*, *Down These Strange Streets*, *Dangerous Women*, and *Rogues*, as well as several new volumes in his long-running Wild Cards anthology series. In 2012, Martin was given the Life Achievement Award by the World Fantasy Convention. His most recent books are *High Stakes*, the twenty-third volume in the Wild Card series, and *The World of Ice and Fire*, an illustrated history of the Seven Kingdoms.

Although most famous for his tales of Westeros and the Seven Kingdoms, here he visits the world of Jack Vance's *The Dying Earth* instead, taking us to the Land of the Falling Wall, through a haunted forest and across a bleak, dismal tarn, for a dangerous and surprising night of hospitality at the Tarn House (famous for their hissing eels), in company with a strange and varied cast of colorful characters—none of whom are even remotely what they seem.

◆　　◆　　◆

A Night at the Tarn House

the Tarn House

GEORGE R. R. MARTIN

Through the purple gloom came Molloqos the Melancholy, borne upon an iron palanquin by four dead Deodands.

Above them hung a swollen sun where dark continents of black ash were daily spreading across dying seas of dim red fire. Behind and before the forest loomed, steeped in scarlet shadow. Seven feet tall and black as onyx, the Deodands wore ragged skirts and nothing else. The right front Deodand, fresher than the others, squished with every step. Gaseous and swollen, his ripening flesh oozed noxious fluid from a thousand pinpricks where the Excellent Prismatic Spray had pierced him through. His passage left damp spots upon the surface of the road—an ancient and much-overgrown track whose stones had been laid during the glory days of Thorsingol, now a fading memory in the minds of men.

The Deodands moved at a steady trot, eating up the leagues. Being dead, they did not feel the chill in the air, nor the cracked and broken stones beneath their heels. The palanquin swayed from side to side, a gentle motion that made Molloqos think back upon his mother rocking him in his cradle. Even he had had a mother once, but that was long ago. The time of mothers and children had passed. The human race was fading, whilst grues and erbs and pelgranes claimed the ruins they left behind.

To dwell on such matters would only invite a deeper melancholy, however. Molloqos preferred to consider the book upon his lap. After three days of fruitless attempts to commit the Excellent Prismatic Spray to memory once again, he had set aside his grimoire, a massive tome bound in cracked vermillion leather with clasps and hinges of black iron, in favor of a slender volume of erotic poetry from the last days of the Sherit Empire, whose songs of lust had gone to dust aeons ago. Of late his gloom ran so deep that even those fervid rhymes seldom stirred him to tumescence, but at least the words did not turn to worms wriggling on the vellum, as those in his grimoire seemed wont to do. The world's long afternoon had given way to evening, and in that long dusk even magic had begun to crack and fade.

As the swollen sun sank slowly in the west, the words grew harder to discern. Closing his book, Molloqos pulled his Cloak of Fearful Mien across his legs, and watched the trees go past. With the dying of the light each seemed more sinister than the last, and he could almost see shapes moving in the underbrush, though when he turned his head for a better look they were gone.

A cracked and blistered wooden sign beside the road read:

TARN HOUSE
    Half a League On
    Famous for Our Hissing Eels

An inn would not be unwelcome, although Molloqos did not entertain high expectations of any hostelry that might be found along a road so drear and desolate as this. Come dark, grues and erbs and leucomorphs would soon be stirring, some hungry enough to risk an assault even on a sorcerer of fearful mien. Once he would not have feared such creatures; like others of his ilk, it had been his habit to arm himself with half a dozen puissant spells whenever he was called up to leave the safety of his manse. But now the spells ran through his mind like water through his fingers, and even those he still commanded seemed feebler each time he was called upon to employ them. And there were the shadow swords to consider as well. Some claimed they were shapechangers, with faces malleable as candle wax. Molloqos did not know the truth of that, but of their malice he had no doubt.

Soon enough he would be in Kaiin, drinking black wine with Princess Khandelume and his fellow sorcerers, safe behind the city's tall white walls and ancient enchantments, but just now even an inn as dreary as this Tarn House must surely be preferable to another night in his pavilion beneath those sinister pines.

Slung between two towering wooden wheels, the cart shook and shuddered as it made its way down the rutted road, bouncing over the cracked stones and slamming Chimwazle's teeth together. He clutched his whip tighter. His face was broad, his nose flat, his skin loose and sagging and pebbly, with a greenish cast. From time to time his tongue flickered out to lick an ear.

To the left the forest loomed, thick and dark and sinister; to the right, beyond a few thin trees and a drear grey strand dotted with clumps of salt grass, stretched the tarn. The sky was violet darkening to indigo, spotted by the light of weary stars.

"Faster!" Chimwazle called to Polymumpho, in the traces. He glanced back over his shoulder. There was no sign of pursuit, but that did not mean the Twk-men were not coming. They were nasty little creatures, however tasty, and clung to their grudges past all reason. "Dusk falls. Soon night will be upon us! Bestir yourself! We must find shelter before evenfall, you great lump."

The hairy-nosed Pooner made no reply but a grunt, so Chimwazle gave him a lick of the whip to encourage his efforts. "Move those feet, you verminious lout." This time Polymumpho put his back into it, legs pumping, belly flopping. The cart bounced, and Chimwazle bit his tongue as one wheel slammed against a rock. The taste of blood filled his mouth, thick and sweet as moldy bread. Chimwazle spat, and a gobbet of greenish phlegm and black ichor struck Polymumpho's face and clung to his cheek before dropping off to spatter on the stones. *"Faster!"* Chimwazle roared, and his lash whistled a lively tune to keep the Pooner's feet thumping.

At last the trees widened and the inn appeared ahead of them, perched upon a hummock of stone where three roads came together. Stoutly built and cheery it seemed, stone below and timber higher up, with many a grand gable and tall turret, and wide windows through which poured a warm, welcoming, ruddy light and the happy sounds of music and laughter, accompanied by a clatter of cup and platters that seemed to say, *Come in, come in. Pull off your boots, put up your feet, enjoy a cup of ale.* Beyond its pointed rooftops the waters of the tarn glittered smooth and red as a sheet of beaten copper, shining in the sun.

The Great Chimwazle had never seen such a welcome sight. "Halt!" he cried, flicking his whip at Polymumpho's ear to command the Pooner's attention. "Stop! Cease! Here is our refuge!"

Polymumpho stumbled, slowed, halted. He looked at the inn dubiously and sniffed. "I would press on. If I were you."

"You would like that, I am sure." Chimwazle hopped from the cart, his soft boots squishing in the mud. "And when the Twk-men caught us, you would chortle and do nothing as they stabbed at me. Well, they will never find us here."

"Except for that one," said the Pooner.

And there he was: a Twk-man, flying bold as you please around his head. The wings of his dragonfly made a faint buzzing sound as he couched his lance. His skin was a pale green, and his helm was an acorn shell. Chimwazle raised his hands in horror. "Why do you molest me? I have done nothing!"

"You ate the noble Florendal," the Twk-man said. "You swallowed Lady Melescence, and devoured her brothers three."

"Not so! I refute these charges! It was someone else who looked like me. Have you proof? Show me your proof! What, have you none to offer? Begone with you, then!"

Instead, the Twk-man flew at him and thrust his lance point at his nose, but quick as he was, Chimwazle was quicker. His tongue darted out, long and sticky, plucked the tiny rider from his mount, pulled him back wailing. His armor was flimsy stuff and crunched nicely between Chimwazle's sharp green teeth. He tasted of mint and moss and mushroom, very piquant.

Afterward, Chimwazle picked his teeth with the tiny lance. "There was only the one," he decided confidently, when no further Twk-men deigned to appear. "A bowl of hissing eels awaits me. You may remain here, Pooner. See that you guard my cart."

Lirianne skipped and spun as on she walked. Lithe and long-legged, boyish and bouncy, clad all in grey and dusky rose, she had a swagger in her step. Her blouse was spun of spider-silk, soft and smooth, its top three buttons undone. Her hat was velvet, wide-brimmed, decorated with a jaunty feather and cocked at a rakish angle. On her hip, Tickle-Me-Sweet rode in a sheath of soft grey leather that matched her thigh-high boots. Her hair was a mop of auburn curls, her cheeks dusted with freckles across skin as pale as milk. She had lively grey-green eyes, a mouth made for mischievious smiles, and a small upturned nose that twitched as she sniffed the air.

The evening was redolent with pine and sea salt, but faintly, beneath those scents, Lirianne could detect a hint of erb, a dying grue, and the nearby stench of ghouls. She wondered if any would dare come out and play with her once the sun went down. The prospect made her smile. She touched the hilt of Tickle-Me-Sweet and spun in a circle, her boot heels sending up little puffs of dust as she whirled beneath the trees.

"Why do you dance, girl?" a small voice said. "The hour grows late, the shadows long. This is no time for dancing."

A Twk-man hovered by her head, another just behind him. A third appeared, then a fourth. Their spear points glittered redly in the light of the setting sun, and the dragonflies they rode glimmered with a pale green luminescence. Lirianne glimpsed more amongst the trees, tiny lights darting in and out between the branches, small as stars. "The sun is dying," Lirianne told them. "There will be no dances in the darkness. Play with me, friends. Weave bright patterns in the evening air whilst still you can."

"We have no time for play," one Twk-man said.

"We hunt," another said. "Later we will dance."

"Later," the first agreed. And the laughter of the Twk-men filled the trees, as sharp as shards.

"Is there a Twk-town near?" asked Lirianne.

"Not near," one Twk-man said.

"We have flown far," another said.

"Do you have spice for us, dancer?"

"Salt?" said another.

"Pepper?" asked a third.

"Saffron?" sighed a fourth.

"Give us spice, and we will show you secret ways."

"Around the tarn."

"Around the inn."

"Oho." Lirianne grinned. "What inn is this? I think I smell it. A magical place, is it?"

"A dark place," one Twk-man said.

"The sun is going out. All the world is growing dark." Lirianne remembered another inn from another time, a modest place but friendly, with clean rushes on the floor and a dog asleep before the hearth. The world had been dying even then, and the nights were dark and full of terrors, but within those walls it had still been possible to find fellowship, good cheer, even love. Lirianne remembered roasts turning above the crackling fire, the way the fat would spit as it dripped down into the flames. She remembered the beer, dark and heady, smelling of hops. She remembered a girl too, an innkeeper's daughter with bright eyes and a silly smile who'd loved a wandering warfarer. Dead now, poor thing. But what of it? The world was almost dead as well. "I want to see this inn," she said. "How far is it?"

"A league," the Twk-man said.

"Less," a second insisted.

"Where is our salt?" the two of them said together. Lirianne gave them each a pinch of salt from the pouch at her belt. "Show me," she said, "and you shall have pepper too."

The Tarn House did not lack for custom. Here sat a white-haired man with a long beard, spooning up some vile purple stew. There lounged a dark-haired slattern, nursing her glass of wine as if it were a newborn babe. Near the wooden casks that lined one wall a ferret-faced man with scruffy whiskers was sucking snails out of their shells. Though his eyes struck Chimwazle as sly and sinister, the buttons on his vest were silver and his hat sported a fan of peacock feathers, suggesting that he did not lack for means. Closer to the hearth fire, a man and wife crowded around a table with their two large and lumpish sons, sharing a huge meat pie. From the look of them, they had wandered here from some land where the only color was brown. The father sported a thick beard; his sons displayed bushy mustaches that covered their mouths. Their mother's mustache was finer, allowing one to see her lips.

The rustics stank of cabbage, so Chimwazle hied to the far side of the room and joined the prosperous fellow with the silver buttons on his vest. "How are your snails?" he inquired.

"Slimy and without savor. I do not recommend them."

Chimwazle pulled out a chair. "I am the Great Chimwazle."

"And I Prince Rocallo the Redoubtable."

Chimwazle frowned. "Prince of what?"

"Just so." The prince sucked another snail and dropped the empty shell onto the floor.

That answer did not please him. "The Great Chimwazle is no man to trifle with," he warned the so-called princeling.

"Yet here you sit, in the Tarn House."

"With you," observed Chimwazle, somewhat peevishly.

The landlord made his appearance, bowing and scraping as was appropriate for one of his station. "How may I serve you?"

"I will try a dish of your famous hissing eels."

The innkeep gave an apologetic cough. "Alas, the eels are . . . ah . . . off the bill of fare."

"What? How so? Your sign suggests that hissing eels are the specialty of the house."

"And so they were, in other days. Delicious creatures, but mischievous. One ate a wizard's concubine, and the wizard was so wroth he set the tarn to boiling and extinguished all the rest."

"Perhaps you should change the sign."

"Every day I think the same when I awaken. But then I think, the world may end today, should I spend my final hours perched upon a ladder with a paintbrush in my hand? I pour myself some wine and sit down to cogitate upon the matter, and by evening I find the urge has passed."

"Your urges do not concern me," said Chimwazle. "Since you have no eels, I must settle for a roast fowl, well crisped."

The innkeep looked lachrymose. "Alas, this clime is not salubrious for chicken."

"Fish?"

"From the tarn?" The man shuddered. "I would advise against it. Most unwholesome, those waters."

Chimwazle was growing vexed. His companion leaned across the table and said, "On no account should you attempt a bowl of scrumby. The gristle pies are also to be avoided."

"Begging your pardon," said the landlord, "but meat pies is all we have just now."

"What sort of meat is in these pies?" asked Chimwazle.

"Brown," said the landlord. "And chunks of grey."

"A meat pie, then." There seemed to be no help for it.

The pie was large, admittedly; that was the best that could be said for it. What meat Chimwazle found was chiefly gristle, here and there a chunk of yellow fat, and once something that crunched suspiciously when he bit into it. There was more grey meat than brown, and once a chunk that glistened green. He found a carrot too, or perhaps it was a finger. In either case, it had been overcooked. Of the crust, the less said, the better.

Finally Chimwazle pushed the pie away from him. No more than a quarter had been consumed. "A wiser man might have heeded my warning," said Rocallo.

"A wiser man with a fuller belly, perhaps." That was the problem with Twk-men; no matter how many you ate, an hour later you were hungry again. "The earth is old, but the night is young." The Great Chimwazle produced a pack of painted placards from his sleeve. "Have you played peggoty? A jolly game, that goes well with ale. Perhaps you will assay a few rounds with me?"

"The game is unfamiliar to me, but I am quick to learn," said Rocallo. "If you will explain the rudiments, I should be glad to try my hand."

Chimwazle shuffled the placards.

◆ ◆ ◆

The inn was grander than Lirianne had expected, and seemed queer and out of place, not at all the sort of establishment she would have expected to find along a forest road in the Land of the Falling Wall. "Famous for Our Hissing Eels," she read aloud, and laughed. Behind the inn a sliver of the setting sun floated red upon the black waters of the tarn.

The Twk-men buzzed around her on their dragonflies. More and more had joined Lirianne as she made her way along the road. Two score, four, a hundred; by now she had lost count. The gauzy wings of their mounts trilled against the evening air. The purple dusk hummed to the sound of small, angry voices.

Lirianne pinched her nose and took a sniff. The scent of sorcery was so strong it almost made her sneeze. There was magic here. "Oho," she said. "I smell wizard."

Whistling a spritely tune, she sauntered closer. A ramshackle cart was drawn up near the bottom of the steps. Slumped against one of its wheels was a huge, ugly man, big-bellied and ripe, with coarse, dark hair sprouting from his ears and nostrils. He looked up as Lirianne approached. "I would not go up there if I were you. It is a bad place. Men go in. No men come out."

"Well, I am no man as you can plainly see, and I *love* bad places. Who might you be?"

"Polymumpho is my name. I am a Pooner."

"I am not familiar with the Pooners."

"Few are." He shrugged, a massive rippling of his shoulders. "Are those your Twk-men? Tell them my master went inside the inn to hide."

"Master?"

"Three years ago I played at peggoty with Chimwazle. When my coin ran out, I bet myself."

"Is your master a sorcerer?"

Another shrug. "He thinks he is."

Lirianne touched the hilt of Tickle-Me-Sweet. "Then you may consider yourself free. I shall make good your debt for you."

"Truly?" He got to his feet. "Can I have the cart?"

"If you wish."

A wide grin split his face. "Hop on, and I will carry you to Kaiin. You will be safe, I promise you. Pooners only eat the flesh of men when the stars are in alignment."

Lirianne glanced up. Half a dozen stars were visible above the trees, dusty diamonds glimmering in a purple velvet sky. "And who will be the judge of whether the stars are properly aligned for such a feast, or no?"

"On that account you may place your trust in me."

She giggled. "No, I think not. I am for the inn."

"And I for the road." The Pooner lifted the traces of the cart. "If Chimwazle complains of my absence, tell him that my debt is yours."

"I shall." Lirianne watched as Polymumpho rumbled off toward Kaiin, the empty cart bouncing and jouncing behind him. She scampered up the winding stone steps and pushed her way through the door into the Tarn House.

The common room smelled of mold and smoke and ghouls, and a little leucomorph as well, though none such were presently in evidence. One table was packed with hairy rustics, another occupied by a big-bosomed slattern sipping wine from a dinted silver goblet. An old man attired in the antique fashion of a knight of ancient Thorsingol sat lonely and forlorn, his long white beard spotted with purple soup stains.

Chimwazle was not hard to find. He sat beneath the ale casks with another rogue, each of them appearing more unsavory than the other. The latter had the stink of rat about him; the former smelled of toad. The rattish man wore a grey leather vest with sparking silver buttons over a tight-fitting shirt striped in cream and azure, with large puffy sleeves. On his pointed head perched a wide-brimmed blue hat decorated with a fan of peacock feathers. His toadish companion, beset by drooping jowls, pebbled skin, and greenish flesh that made him look faintly nauseated, favored a floppy cap that resembled a deflated mushroom, a soiled mauve tunic with golden scrollwork at collar, sleeve, and hem, and green shoes turned up at the toe. His lips were full and fat, his mouth so wide it all but touched the pendulous lobes of his ears.

Both vagabonds eyed Lirianne lasciviously as they weighed the possibilities of erotic dalliance. The toad actually dared to venture a small smile. Lirianne knew how that game was played. She removed her hat, bowed to them, and approached their table. A spread of painted placards covered its rough wooden surface, beside the remains of a congealed and singularly unappealing meat pie. "What game is this?" she asked, oh so innocent.

"Peggoty," said the toadish man. "Do you know it?"

"No," she said, "but I love to play. Will you teach me?"

"Gladly. Have a seat. I am Chimwazle, oft called the Gallant. My friend is known as Rocallo the Reluctant."

"Redoubtable," the rat-faced man corrected, "and I am *Prince* Rocallo, if it please you. The landlord is about here somewhere. Will you take a drink, girl?"

"I will," she said. "Are you wizards? You have a sorcerous look about you."

Chimwazle made a dismissive gesture. "Such pretty eyes you have, and sharp as well. I know a spell or two."

"A charm to make milk sour?" suggested Rocallo. "That is a spell that many know, though it takes six days to work."

"That, and many more," boasted Chimwazle, "each more potent than the last."

"Will you show me?" Lirianne asked, in a breathless voice.

"Perhaps when we know each other better."

"Oh, please. I have always wanted to see true magic."

"Magic adds spice to the gristle that is life," proclaimed Chimwazle, leering, "but I do not care to waste my wonderments before such lumpkins and pooners as surround us. Later when we are alone, I shall perform such magics for you as you have never seen, until you cry out in joy and awe. But first some ale, and a hand or three of peggoty to get our juices flowing! What stakes shall we play for?"

"Oh, I am sure you will think of something," said Lirianne.

By the time Molloqos the Melancholy caught sight of the Tarn House, the swollen sun was setting, easing itself down in the west like an old fat man lowering himself into his favorite chair.

Muttering softly in a tongue no living man had spoken since the Gray Sorcerers went to the stars, the sorcerer commanded a halt. The inn beside the tarn was most inviting to the casual glance, but Molloqos was of a suspicious cast, and had long ago learned that things were not always as they seemed. He muttered a brief invocation, and lifted up an ebon staff. Atop the shaft was a crystal orb, within which a great golden eye looked this way and that. No spell nor illusion could deceive the True-Seeing Eye.

Stripped of its glamour, the Tarn House stood weathered and grey, three stories tall and oddly narrow. It leaned sideways like a drunken wormiger, a crooked flight of flagstone steps leading upward to its door. Diamond-shaped panes of green glass gave the light from within a dis-eased and leprous cast; its roof was overgrown with drooping ropes of fungus. Behind the inn the tarn was black as pitch and redolent of decay, dotted with drowned trees, its dark oily waters stirring ominously. A stable stood off to one side, a structure so decayed that even dead Deo-dands might balk at entering.

At the foot of the inn's steps was a sign that read:

TARN HOUSE
    Famous for Our Hissing Eels

The right front Deodand spoke up. "The earth is dying and soon the sun will fail. Here beneath this rotten roof is a fit abode for Molloqos to spend eternity."

"The earth is dying and soon the sun shall fail," Molloqos agreed, "but if the end should overtake us here, I shall spend eternity seated by a fire savoring a dish of hissing eels, whilst you stand shivering in the dark and cold, watching pieces of your body ripen and rot and tumble to the ground." Adjusting the drape of his Cloak of Fearful Mien, he gath-ered up his tall ebony staff, descended from the palanquin, stepped into the weed-choked yard, and began to climb the steps up to the inn.

Above, a door banged open. A man emerged, a small and servile creature with gravy spatters on his apron who could only be the inn-keeper. As he hurried down, wiping his hands upon his apron, he caught his first good sight of Molloqos, and paled.

As well he might. White as bone was the flesh of Molloqos, beneath his Cloak of Fearful Mien. Deep and dark and full of sadness were his eyes. His nose curved downward in a hook; his lips were thin and rather dour; his hands large, expressive, long-fingered. On his right hand his fingernails were painted black, on his left scarlet. His long legs were clothed in striped pantaloons of those same colors, tucked into calf-high boots of polished grue hide. Black and scarlet was his hair as well, blood and night mixed together; on his head perched a wide-brimmed hat of purple velvet decorated with a green pearl and a white quill.

"Dread sir," the innkeep said, "those . . . those Deodands . . ."

". . . will not trouble you. Death diminishes even such savage appetites as theirs."

"We . . . we do not oft see sorcerers at the Tarn House."

Molloqos was unsurprised. Once the dying earth had teemed with such, but in these last days even magic was waning. Spells seemed less potent than before, their very words harder to grasp and hold. The grimoires themselves were crumbling, falling to dust in ancient libraries as their protective charms winked out like guttering candles. And as the magic failed, so too did the magicians. Some fell to their own servants, the demons and sandestins who once obeyed their every whim. Others were hunted down by shadow swords, or torn apart by angry mobs of women. The wisest slipped away to other times and other places, their vast and drafty manses vanishing like mist before the sunrise. Their very names had become the stuff of legend: Mazirian the Magician, Turjan of Miir, Rhialto the Marvelous, the Enigmatic Mumph, Gilgad, Pandelume, Ildefonse the Perceptor.

Yet Molloqos remained, and it was his intent to go on remaining, to live to drink a final cup of wine while he watched the sun go out. "You stand in the presence of Molloqos the Melancholy, poet, philosopher, archmage, and necromancer, a student of forgotten tongues and bane of demonkind," he informed the cringing landlord. "Every corner of this dying earth is known to me. I collect curious artifacts from aeons past, translate crumbling scrolls no other man can read, converse with the dead, delight the living, frighten the meek, and awe the unenlightened. My vengeance is a cold, black wind, my affection warm as a yellow sun. The rules and laws that govern lesser men I brush off as a wayfarer might brush the dust from his cloak. This night I will honor you with my custom. No obsequies are necessary. I will require your best room, dry and spacious, with a feather mattress. I shall sup with you as well. A thick slice of wild boar would fill me nicely, with such side dishes as your kitchen may supply."

"We have no boars hereabouts, wild or tame. The grues and the erbs ate most of them, and the rest were dragged down into the tarn. I can serve you a meat pie, or a piping hot bowl of purple scrumby, but I don't think you'd like the one, and I know you'd hate t'other." The innkeep swallowed. "A thousand pardons, dread sir. My humble house is not fit for such as you. No doubt you would find some other inn more comfortable."

Molloqos let his visage darken. "No doubt," said he, "but as no other inn presents itself, I must make do with yours."

The innkeep dabbed at his forehead with his apron. "Dread sir, begging your pardon and meaning no offense, but I've had some trouble from sorcerous folk before. Some, not so honest as you, settle their accounts with purses of ensorceled stones and chunks of dung glamoured to look like gold, and others have been known to inflict boils and warts on unhappy serving wenches and innocent innkeepers when the service does not meet their standards."

"The remedy is simple," declared Molloqos the Melancholy. "See that the service is all that it should be, and you will have no difficulties. You have my word, I will perform no sorceries in your common room, inflict no boils nor warts upon your staff, nor settle my account with dung. But now I grow weary of this banter. The day is done, the sun is fled, and I am weary, so here I mean to stay the night. Your choice is simple. Accomodate me, or else I shall pronounce Gargoo's Festering Reek upon you and leave you to choke upon your own stench until the end of your days. Which will not be long in coming, as pelgranes and erbs are drawn to the smell as mice are drawn to a nice ripe cheese."

The innkeep's mouth opened and closed, but no words emerged. After a moment, he shuffled to one side. Molloqos acknowledged the surrender with a nod, ascended the rest of the steps, and shoved through the inn's front door.

The interior of the Tarn House proved to be just as dark, damp, and dismal as the exterior. A queer sour odor hung in the air, though Molloqos would not have ventured to say whether it emanated from the innkeep, the other customers, or whatever was cooking in the kitchen. A hush fell upon the common room at his entrance. All eyes turned toward him, as was only to be expected. In his Cloak of Fearful Mien, he was a fearful sight.

Molloqos took a seat at the table by the window. Only then did he permit himself to inspect his fellow guests. The group near the fire, growling at each other in low, guttural voices, reminded the sorcerer of turnips with hair. Over by the ale casks, a pretty young girl was laughing and flirting with a pair of obvious scoundrels, one of whom appeared to be not entirely human. Nearby an old man slept, his head on the table, pillowed atop his folded arms. There was a woman just beyond him, sloshing the dregs of her wine and eyeing the wizard speculatively across the room. A glance was enough to tell Molloqos that she was a woman of the evening, though in her case evening was edging on toward night. Her visage was not altogether hideous, although there was something odd and unsettling about the look of her ears. Still, she had a pleasing shape, her eyes were large and dark and liquid, and the fire woke red highlights in her long, black hair.

Or so it seemed through the eyes that Molloqos had been born with, but he knew better than to put his trust in those. Softly, softly, he whispered an invocation, and looked again through the enchanted golden eye atop his staff. This time he saw true.

For his supper, the sorcerer ordered a meat pie, as the specialty of the house was unavailable. After one bite Molloqos put down his spoon, feeling even more melancholy than he had a moment before. Wisps of steam rose through the pie's broken crust to form hideous faces in the air, their mouths open in torment. When the landlord returned to inquire if the repast was to his liking, Molloqos gave him a reproachful look and said, "You are fortunate that I am not so quick to wroth as most of my brethren."

"I am grateful for your forebearance, dread sir."

"Let us hope that your bedchambers keep to a higher standard than your kitchen."

"For three terces you can share the big bed with Mumpo and his family," the landlord said, indicating the rustics near the hearth. "A private room will cost you twelve."

"None but the best for Molloqos the Melancholy."

"Our best room rents for twenty terces, and is presently occupied by Prince Rocallo."

"Remove his things at once, and have the room readied for me," Molloqos commanded. He might have said a good deal more, but just then the dark-eyed woman rose and came over to his table. He nodded toward the chair across from him. "Sit."

She sat. "Why do you look so sad?"

"It is the lot of man. I look at you, and see the child that you were. Once you had a mother who held you to her breast. Once you had a father who dandled you upon his knee. You were their pretty little girl, and through your eyes they saw again the wonders of the world. Now they are dead and the world is dying, and their child sells her sadness to strangers."

"We are strangers now, but we need not remain so," the woman said. "My name is—"

"—no concern of mine. Are you a child still, to speak your true name to a sorcerer?"

"Sage counsel." She put her hand upon his sleeve. "Do you have a room? Let us repair upstairs, and I will make you happy."

"Unlikely. The earth is dying. So too the race of men. No erotic act can change that, no matter how perverse or energetic."

"There is still hope," the woman said. "For you, for me, for all of us. Only last year I lay with a man who said a child had been born to a woman of Saskervoy."

"He lied, or was deceived. At Saskervoy, the women weep as elsewhere, and devour their children in the womb. Man dwindles, and soon shall disappear. The earth will become the haunt of Deodands and pelgranes and worse things, until the last light flickers out. There was no child. Nor will there be."

The woman shivered. "Still," she said, "still. So long as men and women endure, we must try. Try with me."

"As you wish." He was Molloqos the Melancholy, and he had seen her for what she was. "When I retire, you may come to my bedchamber, and we shall try the truth of things."

◆   ◆   ◆

The placards were made of dark black wood, sliced paper-thin and brightly painted. They made a faint clacking sound when Lirianne turned them over. The game was simple enough. They played for terces. Lirianne won more than she lost, though she did not fail to note that whenever the wagering was heavy, somehow Chimwazle showed the brightest placards, no matter how promising her own had seemed at first.

"Fortune favors you this evening," Chimwazle announced, after a dozen hands, "but playing for such small stakes grows tiresome." He placed a golden centum on the table. "Who will meet my wager?"

"I," said Rocallo. "The earth is dying, and with it all of us. What do a few coins matter to a corpse?"

Lirianne looked sad. "I have no gold to wager."

"No matter," said Chimwazle. "I have taken a fancy to your hat. Put that in the wager, against our gold."

"Oho. Is that the way of it?" She cocked her head and ran the tip of her tongue across her lip. "Why not?"

Shortly she was hatless, which was no more than she had expected. She handed the prize to Chimwazle with a flourish and shook out her hair, smiling as he stared at her. Lirianne took care never to look directly at the sorcerer seated by the window, but she had been aware of him since the moment he had entered. Gaunt and grim and fearsome, that one, and he stank of sorcery so strongly that it overwhelmed the lesser magics wafting off the odious fraud Chimwazle. Most of the great mages were dead or fled, slain by shadow swords or gone to some underworld or overworld, or perhaps to distant stars. Those few who remained upon the dying earth were gathering in Kaiin, she knew, hoping to find safety there behind the white-walled city's ancient enchantments. This was surely one of them.

Her palm itched, and Tickle-Me-Sweet sang silent by her side. Lirianne had tempered its steel in the blood of the first wizard she had slain, when she was six-and-ten. No protective spell was proof against such a blade, though she herself had no defense but her wits. The hard part of killing wizards was knowing when to do it, when most of them could turn you into dust with a few well-chosen words.

A round of ales arrived, and then another. Lirianne sipped at her first tankard while her second sat untouched by her elbow, but her companions drank deep. When Rocallo called for a third round, Chimwazle excused himself to answer a call of nature, and loped across the common room in search of a privy. He gave the necromancer's table a wide berth, Lirianne did not fail to note. That pale, grim creature seemed deeply engrossed in conversation with the inn's resident doxy, oblivious to the wattled, pop-eyed rogue scuttling past, but the golden eye atop his wizard's staff had fixed on Chimwazle and watched his every move.

"Chimwazle has been cozening us," she told Rocallo when the toad-faced creature was gone. "I won the last showing, and you the two before that, yet his pile of terces is as large as ever. The coins move whenever we're not looking. Creeping home across the table. And the placards change their faces."

The prince gave a shrug. "What does it matter? The sun grows dark. Who shall count our terces when we're dead?"

His ennui annoyed her. "What sort of prince sits by and lets some feeble wizard make a fool of him?"

"The sort who has experienced Lugwiler's Dismal Itch, and has no desire to experience it again. Chimwazle amuses me."

"It would amuse me to tickle Chimwazle."

"He will laugh and laugh, I have no doubt."

Then a shadow fell across them. Lirianne looked up, to find the grim-visaged necromancer looming over them. "It has been three hundred years since last I played a hand of peggoty," he intoned in a sepulchral tone. "May I sit in?"

The Great Chimwazle's stomach was a-heave. The meat pie might be to blame, all that gristle and suet. Or perhaps it was the Twk-men he had eaten in the woods. Delicious little things, but never easy to digest. They might be in his belly still, stabbing at him with their silly little spears. He should have stopped at a dozen, but once he had started, it was so easy to think, well, one more would be nice, and perhaps another after that one. He wondered if their spears were poisoned. Chimwazle had not considered that. It was a disagreeable thought.

Almost as disagreeable as this inn. He should have paid more heed
to the Pooner. The Tarn House had little to recommend it, save perhaps
the pretty freckly thing who had joined his little game of peggoty. Already he had won her hat. Her boots would soon follow, and then her
stockings. Chimwazle was only waiting for some of the other travelers
in the common room to retire to their beds before beginning his assault
in earnest. Rocallo was too dull and diffident to interfere, he was certain.
Once he'd won her clothes the girl would have nothing to wager but her
indenture, and afterward he could harness her to his cart an arm's length
ahead of Polymumpho. Let the Pooner chase after her henceforth; that
should serve to keep those hairy legs of his pumping briskly. Chimwazle
might not even need to ply the whip.

The inn's privy was cramped and smelly, and offered neither bench
nor bar, but only a ragged hole in the floor. Squatting over it with his
breeches around his ankles, Chimwazle grunted and groaned as he
voided his bowels. The act was never a pleasant one for him, attended as
it was by the risk of waking the imp nested in the fleshier portions of his
nether parts, whose second favorite amusement was loudly describing
Chimwazle's manhood in terms of withering scorn (its first favorite
amusement was something Chimwazle did not wish to think about).

He was spared that ordeal on this occasion, but worse awaited him
when he returned to the inn's common room and found that the tall
magician with the fearsome face had taken a seat at his own table.
Chimwazle had had enough experiences with great sorcerers to know
that he did not want any more such experiences. His present appearance
was the legacy of a misunderstanding at a crossroads with one such, and
the imp with the loquacious mouth hidden in his breeches was a souve-
nir left him by the witch Eluuna, whose affections he had enjoyed for a
fortnight when he was young and slim and handsome. This sorcerer in
scarlet and black lacked Eluuna's charms, but might well share her fickle
temper. One never knew what small gaffes and innocent omissions a
wizard might take for mortal insult.

Still, there was no help for it, unless he meant to flee at once into the
night. That course seemed less than advisable. The nights belonged to
grues and ghouls and leucomorphs, and there was some small chance
more Twk-men might be awaiting him as well. So Chimwazle donned

his best smile, resumed his seat, and smacked his lips. "We have another player, I see. Innkeep, run fetch some ale for our new friend. And be quick about it, or you may find a carbuncle growing on the end of your nose!"

"I am Molloqos the Melancholy, and I do not drink ale."

"I perceive you are of the sorcerous persuasion," said Chimwazle. "We have that in common, you and I. How many spells do you carry?"

"That is none of your concern," warned Molloqos.

"There now. It was an innocent inquiry, between colleagues. I myself am armed with six great spells, nine minor enchantments, and a variety of cantraps." Chimwazle shuffled the placards. "My sandestin awaits without, disguised as a Pooner and bound to my cart, yet ready to whisk me off into the sky at my command. But no sorcery at table, please! Here dame fortune rules, and may not be confounded by spells!" And so saying, he placed a golden centum in the center of the table.

"Come, come, put in your stakes! Peggoty has more savor when gold is glinting in the pot."

"Just so." Prince Rocallo laid his centum atop Chimwazle's.

The girl Lirianne could only pout (which she did very prettily). "I have no gold, and I want my hat back."

"Then you must put your boots into the wager."

"Must I? Oh, very well."

The sorcerer said nothing. Instead of reaching into his own purse, he rapped thrice upon the floor with his ebon staff and pronounced a small cantrap for the dispelling of illusions and concealments. At once, Chimwazle's centum transformed into a fat white spider and walked slowly from the board on eight hairy legs, while the pile of terces in front of him turned into as many cockroaches and scuttled off in all directions.

The girl squealed. The prince chortled. Chimwazle gulped down his dismay and drew himself up, his jowls a-quiver. "Look what you have done! You owe me a golden centum."

"Far be it!" Molloqos said, with outrage. "You aspired to hoodwink us with a cheap conjurer's glamour. Did you truly believe such a feeble ploy would work upon Molloqos the Melancholy?" The great golden eye atop his staff was blinking, as green vapors swirled ominously within its crystal orb.

"Softly, softly," protested Prince Rocallo. "My head is hazy from the ale, and harsh words make it ring."

"Oh, will you fight a wizard's duel?" Lirianne clapped her hands together. "What grand magics shall we see?"

"The innkeep may protest," said Rocallo. "Such contests are the bane of hospitality. When swordsmen duel, the only damage is some broken crockery and perchance a bloodstain on the floorboards. A pail of hot water and a good elbow will set that aright. A wizard's duel is like to leave an inn a smoking ruin."

"Pah," said Chimwazle, jowls quivering. A dozen rejoinders sprang to his lips, each more withering than the one before, but caution bid him swallow every syllable. Instead he jerked to his feet, so quickly that it sent his chair crashing to the floor. "The innkeep need have no fear on that account. Such spells as I command are far too potent to be deployed for the idle amusement of hatless trollops and feigned princes. The Great Chimwazle will not be mocked, I warn you." And so saying, he made a hasty retreat, before the scarlet-and-black sorcerer could take further umbrage. A fat white spider and a line of cockroaches scuttled after him, as fast as their legs would carry them.

The fire had burned down to embers, and the air was growing cold. Darkness gathered in the corners of the common room. The rustics by the hearth huddled closer, muttering at one another through their whiskers. The golden eye atop the staff of Molloqos the Melancholy peered this way and that.

"Do you mean to let the cheat escape?" the girl asked.

Molloqos did not deign to answer. Soon all the veils would fall away, he sensed. The fraud Chimwazle was the least of his concerns. The shadow swords were here, and worse things too. And it seemed to him that he could hear a faint, soft hissing.

The landlord rescued him from further inquiry, appearing suddenly by his elbow to announce that his room was ready, should he wish to retire.

"I do." Molloqos rose to his feet, leaning on his staff. He adjusted his Cloak of Fearful Mien and said, "Show me."

The innkeep took a lantern off the wall, lit the wick, turned up the flame. "If you would follow me, dread sir."

Up three long flights of crooked steps Molloqos climbed, following the landlord with his lantern, until at last they reached the upper story and a heavy wooden door.

The Tarn House's best room was none too grand. The ceiling was too low, and the floorboards creaked alarmingly. A single window looked out across the tarn, where black waters churned and rippled suggestively beneath the dim red light of distant stars. Beside the bed, on a small three-legged table, a tallow candle stood crookedly in a puddle of hardened wax, flickering. A chest and a straight-back chair were the only other furnishings. Shadows lay thickly in the corners of the room, black as the belly of a Deodand. The air was damp and chill, and Molloqos could hear wind whistling through gaps in the shutters. "Is that mattress stuffed with feathers?" he asked.

"Nothing but honest straw at the Tarn House." The innkeep hung his lantern from a hook. "See, here are two stout planks that slide in place to bar the door and window, so. You may rest easy tonight, with no fear of intruders. The chest at the foot of the bed contains an extra blanket, and may be used to store your garments and other valuables. Beside it is your chamberpot. Is there anything else you might require?"

"Only solitude."

"As you command."

Molloqos listened as the innkeep made his descent. When he was satisfied that he was alone, he gave the room a careful inspection, tapping on the walls, checking the door and window, thumping the floorboards with the butt of his staff. The chest at the foot of the bed had a false bottom that could be opened from beneath, to give access to a crawlway. Doubtless that was how the thieves and murderers crept in, to relieve unwary travelers of their goods and lives. As for the bed . . .

Molloqos gave the mattress a wide berth, seating himself instead in the chair, his staff in hand. His last few spells were singing in his head. It did not take long for the first of his visitors to arrive. Her knock was soft, but insistant. Molloqos opened the door, ushered her into the bedchamber, and slid the bar in place behind her. "So we are not disturbed," he explained.

The dark-haired woman smiled seductively. She pulled the ties that closed her robe, then shrugged it off her shoulders to puddle on the floor. "Will you remove your cloak?"

"As soon remove my skin," said Molloqos the Melancholy.

The woman shivered in his arms. "You talk so strangely. You frighten me." Gooseprickles covered her arms. "What do you have in your hand?"

"Surcease." He stabbed her through the throat. She sank to her knees, hissing. When her mouth opened, her fangs gleamed in the half-light, long and pointed. Her blood ran black down her neck. A leucomorph, he judged, or something stranger still. The wilds were full of queer things now: mongrels fathered by demons on Deodands, spawn of succubi and incubi, mock men grown in vats, bog-born monsters made of rotting flesh.

Bending over her pale corpse, Molloqos the Melancholy brushed her hair back from her cheek and kissed her; once upon the brow, once upon each cheek, deeply on the mouth. Life left her with a shudder and entered him with a gasp, as warm as a summer wind in the days of his youth when the sun burned brighter and laughter could still be heard in the cities of men.

When she was cold, he spoke the words of Cazoul's Indenture, and her corpse opened its eyes again. He bid her rise, to stand sentry while he slept. A great weariness was on him, but it would not do to be taken unawares. He would have other visitors before the night was done, he did not doubt.

He dreamt of Kaiin, shimmering behind its high white walls.

A chill hung in the night air as Chimwazle slipped from the inn through a side door. A grey mist was rising off the tarn, and he could hear the waters stirring down below, as if something were moving in the shadows. Crouching low, he peered this way and that, his bulbous eyes moving beneath his floppy cap, but he saw no sign of Twk-men. Nor did he hear the soft ominous trill of dragonfly wings.

They had not found him, then. That was good. It was time he was away. That there were grues and ghouls and erbs out in the wood he did not doubt, but he would sooner take his chances with them than with the necromancer. A few brisk licks of the whip, and his Pooner would outrace them all. And if not, well, Polymumpho had more meat on him than Chimwazle. Grinning ear to ear, he loped down the rocky hummock, his belly wobbling.

Halfway down, he noticed that his cart was gone. "Infamous Pooner!" he cried, stumbling in shock. "Thief! Thief! Where is my cart, you lice-ridden lump?" No one gave reply. At the foot of the steps, there was nothing to be seen but a sinister iron palanquin and four huge Deodands with flesh as black as night, standing knee-deep in the tarn. The waters were rising, Chimwazle realized suddenly. The Tarn House had become an island.

Fury pushed aside his fear. Deodands relished the taste of man flesh, it was known. "Did you eat my Pooner?" he demanded.

"No," said one, showing a mouth full of gleaming ivory teeth, "but come closer, and we will gladly eat you."

"Pah," said Chimwazle. Now that he was closer, he could see that the Deodands were dead. The necromancer's work, he did not doubt. He licked his earlobe nervously, and a cunning ploy occurred to him. "Your master Molloqos has commanded you to carry me to Kaiin with all haste."

"Yessss," hissed the Deodand. "Molloqos commands and we obey. Come, clamber on, and we'll away."

Something about the way he said that made Chimwazle pause to reconsider the wisdom of his plan. Or perhaps it was the way all four of the Deodands began to gnash those pointed teeth. He hesitated, and suddenly grew aware of a faint stirring in the air behind him, a whisper of wind at the back of his neck.

Chimwazle whirled. A Twk-man was floating a foot from his face, his lance couched, and a dozen more hovering behind him. His bulging eyes popped out even further as he saw the upper stories of the Tarn House a-crawl with them, thick as tarps and twice as verminous. Their dragonflies were a glowing green cloud, roiling like a thunderhead. "Now you perish," the Twk-man said.

Chimwazle's sticky tongue struck first, flicking out to pull the small green warrior from his mount. But as he crunched and swallowed, the cloud took wing, buzzing angrily. Yelping in dismay, the Great Chimwazle had no choice but to flee back up the steps to the inn, hotly pursued by a swarm of dragonflies and the laughter of a Deodand.

Lirianne was vexed.

It would have been so much easier if only she could have set the two wizards to fighting over her, so they might exhaust their magic on each other. That the ghastly Molloqos would make short work of the odious Chimwazle she did not doubt, but however many spells that might have required would have left him with that many fewer when the time came for her to tickle him.

Instead, Molloqos had retired to his bed, while Chimwazle had scuttled off into the night, craven as a crab. "Look what he did to my hat," Lirianne complained, snatching it off the floorboards. Chimwazle had trampled on it in his haste to depart, and the feather was broken.

"His hat," said Prince Rocallo. "You lost it."

"Yes, but I meant to win it back. Though I suppose I should be grateful that it did not turn into a cockroach." She jammed the hat back on her head, tilted at a rakish angle. "First they break the world, and then my hat."

"Chimwazle broke the world?"

"Him," Lirianne said darkly, "and his sort. Wizards. Sorcerers and sorceresses, sages and mages and archmages, witches and warlocks, conjurers, illusionists, diabolists. Necromancers, geomancers, aeromancers, pyromancers, thaumaturges, dreamwalkers, dreamweavers, dreameaters. All of them. Their sins are written on the sky, dark as the sun."

"You blame black magic for the world's demise?"

"Bah," said Lirianne. Men were such fools. "White magic and black are two sides of the same terce. The ancient tomes tell the tale, for those who have the wit to read them correctly. Once there was no magic. The sky was bright blue, the sun shone warm and yellow, the woods were full of deer and hare and songbirds, and everywhere the race of man was thriving. Those ancient men built towers of glass and steel taller than mountains, and ships with sails of fire that took them to the stars. Where are these glories now? Gone, lost, forgotten. Instead we have spells, charms, curses. The air grows cold, the woods are full of grue and ghouls,

Deodands haunt the ruins of ancient cities, pelgranes rule the skies where men once flew. Whose work is this? *Wizards!* Their magic is a blight on sun and soul. Every time a spell is spoken here on Earth, the sun grows that much darker."

She might have revealed even more, had not the pop-eyed Chimwazle chosen that very moment to make a sudden reappearance, stumbling through the door with his long arms wrapped around his head. "Get them off!" he bellowed, as he lurched between the tables. "Ow, ow, ow. Get off me, I am innocent, it was someone else!" Thus shouting, he went crashing to the floor, where he writhed and rolled, slapping himself about the head and shoulders while continuing to implore for assistance against attackers who seemed nowhere in evidence. "Twk," he cried, "twk, twk, wretched twk! Off me, off me!"

Prince Rocallo winced. "Enough! Chimwazle, cease this unmanly caterwauling. Some of us are attempting to drink."

The rogue rolled onto his rump, which was wide and wobbly and amply padded. "The Twk-men—"

"—remain without," said Lirianne. The door remained wide open, but none of the Twk-men had followed Chimwazle inside. Chimwazle blinked his bulbous eyes and peered about from side to side to make certain that was true. Although no Twk-men were to be seen, the back of his neck was covered with festering boils where they had stung him with their lances, and more were sprouting on his cheeks and forehead.

"I do hope you know a healing spell," Rocallo said. "Those look quite nasty. The one on your cheek is leaking blood."

Chimwazle made a noise that was half a groan and half a croak and said, "Vile creatures! They had no cause to abuse me thus. All I did was thin their excess populace. There were plenty left!" Puffing, he climbed back onto his feet and retrieved his cap. "Where is that pestilential innkeep? I require unguent at once. These pinpricks have begun to itch."

"Itching is only the first symptom," said Lirianne with a helpful smile. "The lances of the Twk-men are envenomed. By morning, your head will be as large as a pumpkin, your tongue will blacken and burst, your ears will fill with pus, and you may be seized by an irresistible desire to copulate with a hoon."

"A hoon?" croaked Chimwazle, appalled.

"Perhaps a grue. It depends upon the poison."

Chimwazle's face had turned a deeper shade of green. "This affront cannot be borne! Pus? Hoons? Is there no cure, no salve, no antidote?"

Lirianne cocked her head to one side thoughtfully. "Why," she said, "I have heard it said that the blood of a sorcerer is a sure remedy for any bane or toxin."

"Alas," Chimwazle said, relieved. "Our plan is foiled. Back to the common room, then. Let us reconsider over ale." He scratched furiously beneath his chin, groaned.

"Why not break the door down?" asked Lirianne. "A big strong man like you ..." She squeezed his arm and smiled. "Unless you would rather give pleasure to a hoon?"

Chimwazle shuddered, though even a hoon might be preferable to this itching. Glancing up, he saw the transom. It was open just a crack, but that might be enough. "Rocallo, friend, lift me up onto your shoulders."

The prince knelt. "As you wish." He was stronger than he looked, and seemed to have no trouble hoisting Chimwazle up into the air, for all his bulk. Nor did the nervous trumpet notes emitted by Chimwazle's nether parts dismay him unduly.

Pressing his nose to the transom, Chimwazle slid his tongue through the gap and down the inside of the doorframe, then curled it thrice around the wooden plank that barred the way. Slowly, slowly, he lifted the bar from its slot ... but the weight proved too great for his tongue, and the plank fell clattering to the floor. Chimwazle reeled backward, Prince Rocallo lost his balance, and the two of them collapsed atop each other with much grunting and cursing while Lirianne skipped nimbly aside.

Then the door swung open.

Molloqos the Melancholy did not need to speak a word.

Silent he bid them enter and silent they obeyed, Chimwazle scrambling over the threshold on hands and feet as his fellows stepped nimbly around him. When all of them had come inside, he closed the door behind them and barred it once again.

The rogue Chimwazle was almost unrecognizable beneath his floppy hat, his toadish face a mass of festering boils and buboes where some Twk-men had kissed him with their lances. "Salve," he croaked, as he climbed unsteadily to his feet. "We came for salve, sorry to disturb you. Dread sir, if you perchance should have some unguent for itching . . ."

"I am Molloqos the Melancholy. I do not deal in unguents. Come here and grasp my staff."

For a moment, Chimwazle looked as if he might bolt the room instead, but in the end he bowed his head and shuffled closer, and wrapped a soft, splayed hand around the ebon shaft of the tall sorcerer's staff. Inside the crystal orb, the True-Seeing Eye had fixed on Lirianne and Rocallo. When Molloqos thumped the staff upon the floor, the great golden eye blinked once. "Now look again upon your companions, and tell me what you see."

Chimwazle's mouth gaped open, and his bulging eyes looked as though they might pop out of his skull. "The girl is cloaked in shadows," he gasped, "and under her freckly face I see a skull."

"And your prince . . ."

". . . is a demon."

The thing called Prince Rocallo laughed, and let all his enchantments dissolve. His flesh was red and raw, glowing like the surface of the sun, and like the sun half covered by a creeping black leprosy. Smoke rose stinking from his nostrils, the floorboards began to smolder beneath his taloned feet, and black claws sprang from his hands as long as knives.

Then Molloqos spoke a word and stamped his staff hard against the floor, and from the shadows in a corner of the room a woman's corpse came bursting to leap upon the demon's back. As the two of them lurched and staggered about the room, tearing at each other, Lirianne danced aside and Chimwazle fell backward onto his ample rump. The stench of burning flesh filled the air. The demon ripped one of the corpse's arms off and flung it smoking at the head of Molloqos, but the dead feel no pain, and her other arm was wrapped about its throat.

Black blood ran down her cheeks like tears as she pulled him backward onto the bed.

Molloqos stamped his staff again. The floor beneath the bed yawned open, the mattress tilted, and demon and corpse together tumbled down into a gaping black abyss. A moment later, there came a loud splash from below, followed by a furious cacophony; demonic shrieking mingled with a terrible whistling and hissing, as if a thousand kettles had all come to a boil at once. When the bed righted itself the sound diminished, but it was a long while before it ended. "W-what was that?" asked Chimwazle.

"Hissing eels. The inn is famous for them."

"I distinctly recall the innkeep saying that the eels were off the menu," said Chimwazle.

"The eels are off our menu, but we are not off theirs."

Lirianne made a pouty face and said, "The hospitality of the Tarn House leaves much to be desired."

Chimwazle was edging toward the door. "I mean to speak firmly to the landlord. Some adjustment of our bill would seem to be in order." He scratched angrily at his boils.

"I would advise against returning to the common room," said the necromancer. "No one in the Tarn House is all that he appears. The hirsute family by the hearth are ghouls clad in suits of human skin, here for the meat pies. The greybeard in the faded raiment of a knight of Old Thorsingol is a malign spirit, cursed to an eternity of purple scrumby for the niggardly gratuities he left in life. The demon and the leucomorph are no longer a concern, but our servile host is vilest of all. Your wisest course is flight. I suggest you use the window."

The Great Chimwazle needed no further encouragement. He hurried to the window, threw the shutters open, and gave a cry of dismay. "The tarn! I had forgotten. The tarn has encircled the inn, there's no way out."

Lirianne peered over his shoulder and saw that it was true. "The waters are higher than before," she said thoughtfully. That was a bother.

She had learned to swim before she learned to walk, but the oily waters of the tarn did not look wholesome, and while she did not doubt that Tickle-Me-Sweet would be a match for any hissing eel, it was hard to swim and swordfight at the same time. She turned back to the necromancer. "I suppose we're doomed, then. Unless you save us with a spell."

"Which spell would you have me use?" asked Molloqos in a mordant tone. "Shall I summon an Agency of Far Dispatch to whisk us three away to the end of the earth? Call down fire from the sky with the Excellent Prismatic Spray to burn this vile hostelry to the ground? Pronounce the words of Phandaal's Shivering Chill to freeze the waters of the tarn as hard as stone, so that we may scamper safely over them?"

Chimwazle looked up hopefully. "Yes, please."

"Which?"

"Any. The Great Chimwazle was not meant to end up in a meat pie." He scratched a boil underneath his chin.

"Surely you know those spells yourself," said Molloqos.

"I did," said Chimwazle, "but some knave stole my grimoire."

Molloqos chuckled. It was the saddest sound that Lirianne had ever heard. "It makes no matter. All things die, even magic. Enchantments fade, sorceries unravel, grimoires turn to dust, and even the most puissant spells no longer work as they once did."

Lirianne cocked her head. "Truly?"

"Truly."

"Oho." She drew her sword and gave his heart a tickle.

The necromancer died without a sound, his legs folding slowly under him as if he were kneeling down to pray. When the girl slipped her sword out of his chest, a wisp of scarlet smoke rose from the wound. It smelled of summer nights and maiden's breath, sweet as a first kiss.

Chimwazle was aghast. "Why did you do that?"

"He was a necromancer."

"He was our only hope."

"You have no hope." She wiped her blade against her sleeve. "When I was fifteen, a young adventurer was wounded outside my father's inn. My father was too gentle to let him die there in the dust, so we carried him upstairs and I nursed him back to health. Soon after he departed I found I was with child. For seven months my belly swelled, and I dreamed of a babe with his blue eyes. In my eighth month the swelling ceased. Thereafter I grew slimmer with every passing day. The midwife explained it all to me. What use to bring new life into a dying world? My womb was wiser than my heart, she said. And when I asked her why the world was dying, she leaned close and whispered, '*Wizard's work.*'"

"Not my work." Chimwazle scratched at his cheeks with both hands, half mad with the itching. *"What if she was wrong?"*

"Then you'll have died for nought." Lirianne could smell his fear. The scent of sorcery was on him, but faintly, faintly, drowning beneath the green stink of his terror. Truly, this one was a feeble sort of magician. "Do you hear the eels?" she asked him. "They're still hungry. Would you like a tickle?"

"No." He backed away from her, his bloody fingers splayed.

"Quicker than being eaten alive by eels." Tickle-Me-Sweet waved in the air, glimmering in the candlelight.

"Stay back," Chimwazle warned her, "or I will call down the Excellent Prismatic Spray upon you."

"You might. If you knew it. Which you don't. Or if it worked. Which it won't, if our late friend can be believed."

Chimwazle backed away another step, and stumbled over the necromancer's corpse. As he reached out to break his fall, his fingers brushed against the sorcerer's staff. Grasping it, he popped back to his feet. "Stay away. There's still power in his staff, I warn you. I can feel it."

"That may be, but it is no power you can use." Lirianne was certain of that. He was hardly half a wizard, this one. Most likely he had stolen those placards, and paid to have the roaches glamoured for him. Poor, sad, wicked thing. She resolved to make a quick end to his misery. "Stand still. Tickle-Me-Sweet will cure your itch. I promise you, this will not hurt."

"This will." Chimwazle grasped the wizard's staff with both hands, and smashed the crystal orb down on her head.

◆   ◆   ◆

Chimwazle stripped both corpses clean before tossing them down the chute behind the bed, in hopes of quieting the hissing eels. The girl was even prettier naked than she had been clothed, and stirred feebly as he was dragging her across the room. "Such a waste," Chimwazle muttered as he heaved her down into the abyss. Her hat was much too small for him and had a broken feather, but her sword was forged of fine, strong, springy steel, her purse was fat with terces, and the leather of her boots was soft and supple. Too small for his feet, but perhaps one day he'd find another pretty freckly girl to wear them for him.

Even in death the necromancer presented such a frightful countenance that Chimwazle was almost afraid to touch him, but the eels were still hissing hungrily down below, and he knew his chances of escape would be much improved if they were sated. So he steeled himself, knelt, and undid the clasp that fastened the dread wizard's cloak. When he rolled his body over to pull the garment off, the sorcerer's features ran like black wax, melting away to puddle on the floor. Chimwazle found himself kneeling over a wizened toothless corpse with dim white eyes and parchment skin, his bald pate covered by a spiderweb of dark blue veins. He weighed no more than a bag of skin, but he had a little smile on his lips when Chimwazle tossed him down to the hissing eels.

By then the itching seemed to be subsiding. Chimwazle gave himself a few last scratches and fastened the necromancer's cloak about the shoulders. All at once, he felt taller, harder, sterner. Why should he fear the things down in the common room? Let them go in fear of him!

He swept down the steps without a backward glance. The ghost and ghouls took one look at him and moved aside. Even creatures such as they knew better than to trouble a wizard of such fearsome mien. Only the innkeep dared accost him. "Dread sir," he murmured, "how will you settle your account?"

"With this." He drew his sword and gave the thing a tickle. "I will not be recommending the Tarn House to other travelers."

Black waters still encircled the inn, but they were no more than waist-deep, and he found it easy enough to wade to solid ground. The Twk-men had vanished in the night and the hissing eels had grown quiescent, but the Deodands still stood where he had seen them last, waiting by the iron palanquin. One greeted him. "The earth is dying and soon the sun shall fail," it said. "When the last light fades, all spells shall fail, and we shall feast upon the firm white flesh of Molloqos."

"The earth is dying, but you are dead," replied Chimwazle, marveling at the deep and gloomy timbre of his voice. "When the sun goes out, all spells shall fail, and you shall decay back into the primeval ooze." He climbed into the palanquin and bid the Deodands to lift him up. "To Kaiin." Perhaps somewhere in the white-walled city, he would find a lissome maid to dance naked for him in the freckly girl's high boots. Or failing that, a hoon.

Off into purple gloom rode Molloqos the Melancholy, borne upon an iron palanquin by four dead Deodands.

Andy Duncan

. . .

Andy Duncan made his first sale, to *Asimov's Science Fiction*, in 1995, and quickly made others, to *Starlight*, *Dying For It*, *Realms of Fantasy*, and *Weird Tales*, as well as several more sales to *Asimov's Science Fiction*. By the beginning of the new century, he was widely recognized as one of the most individual, quirky, and flavorful new voices on the scene today. His story "The Executioner's Guild" was on both the final Nebula ballot and the final ballot for the World Fantasy Award in 2000, and in 2001 he *won* two World Fantasy Awards, for his story "The Pottawatomie Giant," and for his landmark first collection, *Beluthahatchie and Other Stories*. He also won the Theodore Sturgeon Memorial Award in 2002 for his novella "The Chief Designer." His other books include an anthology co-edited with F. Brett Cox, *Crossroads: Tales of the Southern Literary Fantastic*, and a nonfiction guidebook, *Alabama Curiosities*. His more recent work includes a World Fantasy Award–winning novella, *Wakulla Springs* (written with Ellen Klages), a Nebula Award–winning novelette, "Close

Encounters," and a second collection, *The Pottawatomie Giant and Other Stories*. A graduate of the Clarion West Writers' Workshop in Seattle, he was born in Batesburg, South Carolina, now lives in Frostburg, Maryland, with his wife, Sydney, and is an associate professor of English at Frostburg State University. His website is https://sites.google.com/site/beluthahatchie/.

As the funny and folksy story that follows demonstrates, if you're the Devil's son-in-law, and the Devil is mad at you, you'd better hope you have some powerful friends willing to help you out . . .

♦   ♦   ♦

The Devil's Whatever

―――――

ANDY DUNCAN

"**M**y name is Pearleen Sunday, and this is the story of how I—"
Hold up! Hold up right there! This is *my* story, Sunday, and I'll tell it my own way.

"The stories *you* tell, Petey Wheatstraw, aren't fit for mixed company, or for any decent folk."

My, my, my, aren't we particular. You tell your stories your way, to the company you please, and I'll tell mine mine, to mine. And if this story ain't mine, why, then, no story is. After all, I was the one did all the work.

"Fine. Tell it, then. But don't stretch it out of all recognition, the way you do, with whales in ponds, and farmer's daughters, and talking dogs that walk into bars, and such as that. Stick to the facts, to the whats and the whos and the wheres."

I'll stick to something, all right, if you don't hush. Hmm, well, let's see. Where to start? You got to admit, there's more options this go-round than usual.

"You could start where I come in."

Yes, and then it'd be your story, wouldn't it? Right back where we started. No, I think I better start it as far away from you as I can get. And since you grew up in a dime museum in Chattanooga, without even the cost of admission to look at yourself, I reckon *my* story starts in the upstairs parlor of the finest mansion in New Orleans. Yes, ma'am. Who's that brownest-eyed, tallest, finest-looking man, in a tailored suit of Eye-talian cloth that fits him like a queen fits a flush, with a Cuban thigh-rolled cigar in one hand and a snifter of muscadine brandy in the other, and posed like he was a framed work of art in the big leaded glass window of the upstairs master bedroom, where he looks down and down and farther down yet upon St. Charles Avenue, the main street of the Gulf, where the streetcars are more posh than the Ritz, and even the panhandlers are ex-mayors who have moved up in the world? Why, it's Petey Wheatstraw, that's who! With the most beautiful Frenchwoman in the Crescent City on his arm . . .

"Baby, please!" said Petey Wheatstraw. "Believe me, I understand the fascination, but don't make me slosh my brandy."

"Oh, *mon amour*, how can you be so calm, when my lover Alcide will be at the door *à tout moment maintenant*, his anger hot, his swordsteel cold and sure?"

Petey barked what he was pretty sure was a mocking and superior laugh and gulped the last of his brandy with his best approximation of *insouciance*, which was perhaps the least of the words he had learned from Madeline. "I ain't studying about old Al," he said, and hurled his depleted snifter into the fireplace with a most satisfying smash. The remains of five snifters now glittered beneath the grate like the ashes of the gods; he'd soon have to order another set. With the hand now free, he caressed Madeline's cheek, her tear-streaked powder wet and granular on his fingertips, and said: "Al ain't got nothing on Petey. Who's *Al's* father-in-law, huh? I ask you." He softly kissed the tip of her nose, the hand-daubed beauty mark on her left cheek, the covered-up actual beauty mark on her right cheek. "Hold this," Petey said, and handed her the cigar, on which she took a deep drag while he kissed her neck more intensely, up and down. "Besides which," he added, between kisses, "any fool gets between me and my favorite stereotypical nineteenth-century Louisiana mistress, why, that's one fool gone get his gumbo separated from his ya-ya, don't you worry your *mon cher* about that."

"Oh, Petey!" Madeline gasped in ecstatic surrender, and pressed herself against—

Petey, you are stretching your story already. Besides, this ain't no under-the-counter book.

Oh, fine then! I reckon we'll just skip to the wild-eyed, sword-wielding Creole kicking down the boudoir door.

"Do not defy me, Wheatstraw!" cried Alcide. He slashed a pornographic arras for emphasis. "I will free Madeline from your loathsome clutches, or die in the attempt."

"Cool your jets, Al," said a lounging Petey, his Eye-talian loafers crossed atop the writing desk. "If you'd been here ten minutes ago . . . and at half past noon . . . and at eight and eight-thirty this morning . . . why, you'd have seen my clutches ain't so loathsome to the lady after all."

"Please, Alcide, leave us!" cried Madeline, who clutched a drape around herself to emphasize her nakedness. "You do not know this one's power. He will kill us both!"

Alcide ignored her to advance on Petey. His poised sword gleamed. "I warn you for the last time, you fiend! Stand and fight!"

In reply, Petey lifted one hand to his lips and blew a loud raspberry.

Alcide snarled and lunged, put his sword through the back of the chair where Petey had been a moment before. Only a wisp of smoke and a sulfurous stench remained. Alcide slid the blade from the upholstery. A plume of cotton came with it.

"I'd be faster, if not for all the hard liquor and sex," said Petey, from over his shoulder. Alcide whirled and slashed the air where Petey had been.

"I expected more from a hero of folklore," said Petey, who now was overhead, lying on the ceiling. Alcide leaped and stabbed the spot where Petey had been. Plaster dust speckled his shoulders as he landed on his feet. He looked about, wild-eyed.

"How long before you give up?" asked Petey, who now sat cross-legged atop the sideboard.

The answer, it turned out, was twenty minutes, after which Alcide gasped with exhaustion, the room's furnishings were wrecked, and the miasma of brimstone was so thick that Madeline, having long since dressed and done her makeup, flung open the windows to let some of it escape.

"Face facts, Al," said Petey, between bites of banana. "Your lady has traded up."

"*Impossible*," gasped Alcide, with the French pronunciation.

Madeline turned from the windows and dusted her palms together. "*Allez-vous*, Alcide," she said. "Amscray." She made shooing motions. "Beat it."

"You even speak like him," Alcide said, his lip curled in disgust. "He has eaten your soul, this filth, this demon from Hell."

Madeline shrugged. "I kinda like him," she said.

With his last strength, Alcide lunged once more. He ran Madeline through the heart with his sword and killed her instantly. Before she even could slump to the ground, Alcide, too, was dead, Petey having torn off his head.

"That was pretty extreme!" cried Petey. He regarded his bloody hands with horror. "And what am I doing up *here*?"

Always afraid of heights, Petey grabbed at a nearby chimney and hung on for dear life. His Eye-talian shoes scuffled for purchase on the steeply pitched roof.

Far below, on the sidewalk in front of the building that should have been Petey's Garden District home, stood a young woman in black tights and Goth makeup, surrounded by a group of people in shorts and T-shirts. They drank from filtered water bottles. They posed beneath selfie sticks. Petey had never heard of selfie sticks, but even in his terror, he knew instantly what they were.

"Hey!" he yelled. "I'm up here! Someone help me!" But the tour group was oblivious.

"This hotel," said the costumed guide, "marks the site of what was once, in the nineteenth century, the finest private home in New Orleans. According to legend, it was so fine that the Devil himself made it his home, and took a local woman for his lover. But the Devil had a human rival for Madeline's affections, a local man, and one night, the triangle erupted in terrible violence. The Devil killed his rival and his faithless lover, dragged their bodies to the roof beneath the full moon, and devoured them."

"Ewww," Petey said, nose wrinkled.

"From that night on," continued the guide, "the Devil was trapped on the roof, and the home was uninhabitable." She stumbled, slightly, on the word *uninhabitable*. It took her two tries. "Every night, phantom figures reenacted that awful confrontation from long ago. Finally, the so-called Devil's Mansion was razed to the ground. Today the site is occupied by one of our finest small hotels. Suites start at one hundred and nine dollars, plus taxes and fees, though some restrictions apply. And now, let's proceed to the next stop on our Bloody New Orleans Tour of Horror!"

As the crowd dispersed, she looked up and met Petey's gaze. She was Madeline, beauty mark and all. She winked at Petey, the nineteenth-century chimney he clutched dissipated, and he slid screaming off the edge of the twenty-first-century roof, and into space.

Next thing he knew, he stood in the bedroom window again, as the powdered and petticoated Madeline tugged on his arm.

"Oh, *mon amour*," she said. "How can you be so calm?"

"How, indeed?" Petey murmured. It was less a reply than a response, involuntary. He marveled at his hands so clean, his floor so level and trustworthy, his companion so vibrant and alive.

Then that jerk Alcide burst in with his sword, and it all happened again.

Petey was aware, throughout, that this sequence of events had happened before, but awareness was not agency. Unable to break free of the loop, he went through the motions of the scene already scripted: avoid, taunt, avoid, taunt, stab, rip, kill, clutch the chimney, be ignored. But this time, he was struck anew by the tour guide's words:

"Every night, phantom figures reenacted that awful confrontation from long ago."

"Phantom figures, my ass!" Petey cried. "Those phantoms are me! I mean, us!"

Then he fell again, screaming, and was back in the bedroom again— and so forth, as before.

This happened again.

And again.

And again.

And just as Petey began to realize this was it, this was his life from now on, he fell off the roof and landed in church.

"Sometimes he is called the Evil One, for he is evil in himself, and tempts us to evil."

"Amen, brother!" the people cried. "Praise Jesus!"

Disoriented and dizzy, Petey now stood in sweltering heat in the back of a small, high-ceilinged, plainly adorned sanctuary. He was pressed on all sides by a crowd of people, their attention riveted on the spectacularly cross-eyed man in the pulpit at the front of the room. Every pew was crammed, every square foot of aisle and vestibule filled by men in knee breeches and women in silks and stays, and all in powdered wigs like an unbroken cloud layer throughout the room. Petey, too, was dressed in this fashion, as was the preacher. Though he did not shout, the cross-eyed man's voice reached everyone's ears, as though he spoke individually to each person present. Their natural rivalries aside, Petey sort of admired this. Interjections and affirmations in the crowd were constant, and here and there hands were raised, palms out, as if in supplication, but none of this detracted from the preacher's inexorably friendly voice.

"Sometimes he is known as the Prince of the Power of the Air, for in the air he doth abide, chiefly, and through the whole world; and all that are not born of God are said to lie in him."

As he began to recover himself, Petey realized that just as he previously recognized his St. Charles Avenue mansion in New Orleans and knew himself to be in the nineteenth century, so here he understood himself to be in the Congregational Church in Ipswich, Massachusetts, a century earlier, when New England was still subject to the king. He also saw that he was the only person in the room of African descent, though no one paid him the slightest attention. He was indifferent to the former, but exceedingly vexed by the latter.

"Aye, sisters and brothers, Paul's words in the second chapter, eleventh verse, of Second Corinthians, are true unto this day: 'We are not ignorant of his devices.' No, indeed, my friends. Satan's devices are known to us. We know that he is an enemy to God and to goodness. He is a hater of all truth. He is full of malice, full of envy, full of revenge. For what other motives could induce him to molest the innocents in Paradise?"

He paused to draw breath, at which point a second voice rang out from the crowd:

"Yeah, well, that's, like, your *opinion*, preacher."

Everyone in the room gasped and moaned in dismay and cast about to see who had spoken, except for the two who knew: Petey, who had spoken the words, and the preacher, who stared straight at him as he did it.

Aglow with delirious indignation, the preacher jabbed a finger at Petey, as if to spear him to the back wall. "I hear you, and I see you, sir," he cried. "I know you who interrupt the Lord's word, here in the Lord's house!"

"Frankly, I've seen nicer houses," Petey said. He sauntered forward in the space that opened up as horrified brethren rushed to distance themselves; he was pleased to see sparks fly up from his every footfall, a nice effect. "And while I am the first to admit my father-in-law has some genuine anger issues, and his impulse control is not so great, nevertheless, I think these good people deserve to hear more of a—what's the phrase?—a fair and balanced presentation."

"You dare to challenge me, fiend? I, George Whitefield, in the Colonies, in the employ of the Lord God Almighty? What claim have you on this pulpit, sirrah?"

"I'll wrestle you for it," Petey replied—and realized, as he said it, that this confrontation, too, was scripted, just as the one with Alcide had been; that he likewise was enjoying it; that it likewise would not end well.

"Done!" roared Whitefield, who seemed to have grown two feet taller and a foot wider during their exchange. Petey, too, felt larger and stronger. He tested this, as the preacher leaped an improbable distance out of the pulpit, by seizing the nearest pew-end and lifting the long oaken bench one-handed, swinging it as a child would aim a slat at a pinecone.

"You want a piece of me, sucker?" Petey taunted.

He threw the pew at the head of the preacher, who ducked, barreled forward, and head-butted Petey in the stomach.

In the years to come, a population five times that of the colony of Massachusetts would claim to have been present in the small church to see Preacher Whitefield fight the Devil (for so they fully assumed the black man to be), but in fact it was only a couple of hundred people who screamed and rushed into the churchyard, and another couple of hundred townsfolk who came running, abandoning their less-than-sanctified Sunday mornings to see what all the fuss was about. They watched deliriously as Whitefield and Petey Wheatstraw (who was not, of course, the Devil, not even the Devil's blood kin, having married in) fought their way out of the church, across the yard, three times around the grounds (because three, in these matters, is a sort of the rule), then up the outside wall (a nice trick, that), and into the cupola atop the church steeple, where the bell rang out whenever Petey's head, or the preacher's head, hit it. *BONG! BONG! BONG!* People ran from Salem, from Lawrence, even from Lynn—Lynn, the City of Sin—thinking all Ipswich had burned down, and were pleased to find an even better show under way than that. No one actually wagered *against* the preacher— that would have been blasphemy—but a good bit of money *did* change hands based on how, exactly, Goodman Whitefield would prevail, and when. So some in the crowd were more exultant than others when the preacher finally lifted a dazed Petey over his head atop the steeple, yelled, "He's all yours, Lord!" and flung him into space.

This fall, to Petey, seemed much slower than the one from the Devil's Mansion rooftop had been. He had leisure to admire the grass-rippling countryside all around, to smell a hint of sweet woodruff on the breeze, to marvel that his wig had not fallen off, to hear the unmistakable sound of his father-in-law's cackle, and to vow to kick the old man's ass from West Hell to Ginny Gall, if Petey ever struggled free of this trap to which, he now knew, Old Scratch had consigned him.

Then Petey landed feetfirst on a granite outcrop and rebounded high into the air, as if launched from a trampoline at a circus, or a cannon at a dime museum. Thus propelled, he just kept on, higher and higher, and dwindled into a tiny spot in the sky like a cinder.

The townsfolk congratulated the preacher on his, i.e., God's, great victory, congratulated themselves for their presence at the great contest, as if it were all their doing, and jostled one another to plant their own feet in the smoldering, sulphurous dents Petey had left in the rock—just to compare shoe sizes, you know. Human nature. Remarkably enough, every single foot, whatever its size, matched the Devil's Footprints perfectly, which makes sense when you think about it.

And they say that from that day, the Devil was never seen again in Ipswich.

"Here *I* am, though!" said Petey, who once again stood in the crowd at the back of the church. He knew he was about to mouth off, and get his ass whipped by a cross-eyed man in a powdered wig. He knew this would happen again, and again, just as New Orleans had happened again, and again. He also knew that, like it or not, he was in big trouble this time, and needed some serious help, perhaps even from the distinguished opposition.

Over and over, Petey reenacted the double murder in the Devil's Mansion in New Orleans, the wrestling match that created the Devil's Footprints in New England. And in between and among and alongside these episodes, he showed up in other places over and over, too.

Sometimes he landed on the Eastern Shore of the Chesapeake Bay, and tried and failed to cheat a six-foot-tall woman farmer named Molly Horn out of the best part of her crop. Each time, her response was the same: she rolled up her sleeves, folded her eyeglasses, set them aside atop a tree stump for safekeeping, then beat Petey like a drum until he hollered for mercy and she flung him headfirst into the bottomless part of the bay called the Devil's Hole.

Sometimes he paced a forty-foot circle in the piney woods of central North Carolina, where no grass grew beneath his feet. As he stomped the ashen earth of the Devil's Tramping Ground, he muttered: "Round and round and round he goes, and wherever he stops won't be where he chose."

Sometimes he sat on the rocky banks of the Nolichucky River in Tennessee, his back to the water, and craned to look up and up and up at the sheer rock cliff that might just, kind of, sort of, suggest a face, if you stared long enough and were prompted to see a face and were willing to be talked into it.

"Ain't much of a likeness, though," Petey mumbled, his voice lost in the rushing waters beneath the Devil's Looking Glass.

And so it went, over and over, from the Devil's Armchair to the Devil's Bake Oven, from the Devil's Dish-Full to the Devil's Marble-yard, from the Devil's Backbone to the Devil's Elbow, from Devil's Lake to Devil's Kitchen—Petey ricocheted from one to the other and back again.

He groaned whenever he found himself in California's Sierra Nevadas, as he scrambled to walk across a pile of ever-shifting rocks beneath a bluff that looked like a palisade of basalt pillars. Much as he tried not to, he could not prevent picking up a random rock two-handed and staggering, sweaty and footsore beneath its weight, only to drop it in some random spot yards away, then pick up a replacement random rock and head back the way he had come.

As he toiled pointlessly on the Devil's Postpile, he subvocalized an impromptu incantation:

> *Pearleen Sunday, oh Sunday, please come around!*
> *Old Petey is done for, if you let him down!*

It was far from original—nothing more than a variant on the folk plea to St. Anthony, Patron of Lost Things—but Petey knew better than to call on *that* micromanaging son of a bitch. And the point of such spells wasn't novelty, but repetition and focus. All the world's magic-makers agreed on that.

> *"Pearleen Sunday, oh Sunday, please shake a leg!*
> *Old Petey is sorry! Please don't make me beg!"*

Then Petey twisted his ankle and fell yet again, wincing as he anticipated another knee skinned by the jagged slope of the Devil's Postpile . . .

. . . but instead found himself in midair and midfall, to howl wordlessly as he cannonballed once again into a deep, icy pool beneath a South Dakota waterfall. How did he know it was South Dakota? The same way he suddenly knew how to swim, if you could call it swimming. Hell wasn't known for its aquacades. He thrashed his way to the surface and crested, with many a splutter and a splash, then backstroked his way to the grooved rock wall around the Devil's Bathtub. He clung there and mumbled, through chattering teeth:

> *"Pearleen Sunday, oh Sunday, throw me a bone!*
> *Old Petey is trapped, and can't break free alone!"*

Because Petey kept rebounding across time as well as space, any claim to know what Pearleen Sunday, the focus of his hopes, was doing at *precisely that moment* would be presumptuous and inaccurate. Suffice to say only that the waves Petey kicked up in the Devil's Bathtub sloshed in all directions, everywhere and everywhen, and it was only a matter of time before Pearleen Sunday got her feet wet. Because much as they claimed otherwise, Pearleen and Petey had never been that far apart, not really, not since the widow Winchester had brought them together in the first place. They were a matched set, like March hares and marzipan, the Cassini Gap and the Cumberland Gap, St. Paul's and Mrs. Paul's, lightning bugs and lightning. Who can think of one without the other?

So somewhere out there, in another time and another place, on the farthest shore of Petey's wave function, was a sunshiny bluebell of a July afternoon in the mountains of western Maryland, where the wise woman Pearleen Sunday was walking from Altamont to Bloomington— which is to say, from no place special to nowhere in particular, and downhill all the way. She was on what she reckoned was the direct-est route, along the Baltimore & Ohio tracks.

Now, in many a high and lonely part of North America, the railroad beds make the easiest walking. But railroaders know that particular stretch beneath Pearleen's feet as the Seventeen Mile Grade, and they speak of it in hisses, like gouts of steam, for it is the steepest railbed in the East, and its 2.4 percent slope can turn a miles-long train of 143-ton coal cars into a cracking black whip that clears the mountainside down to the stumps and the graves. Pearleen did not fear the Seventeen Mile Grade, for she had no burden of weight behind her, and had never been given to acceleration.

She was just a little bitty slip of a thing, no more than *yea* high and *so* big around, and looked of course about eighteen years old, give or take a quarter century, which was just as she would look until Nixon's second term, for wizards age more like mountains than like people. They differ from people in other ways, too, as Pearleen had just begun to realize, that early in her career, though she already had tramped so many miles of these United States, up and down and back and forth and twisted around-y round, that she expected her entry in the Great Ledger, upon her death, to sum up her long life in two words: "Walked, mostly."

She was dressed for the long walk, too, in sensible boots and riveted denim trousers and a man's plaid shirt, a denim jacket tied around her waist. A knapsack rode her shoulders, and held loose in her right hand was a whittled staff longer than she was, twisted like a snake that had paused to think things over.

Now, when we say "a man's plaid shirt," let us be clear that it was a man's shirt by size and design. Whether it was ever inhabited by a man, and how it came to be subsequently worn by Pearleen Sunday, is a question to ask her on another day, and preferably from a great distance, perhaps across a couple of state lines.

So Pearleen walked down the railbed, confined her steps to the wooden ties, and avoided the gravel, as a sort of game, though whenever she came across a stray piece of gravel atop a tie, she tried to kick it or knock it back where it belonged. Some people are just like that, tidying the world as they go.

Pearleen knew Savage Mountain well, and she knew before she saw it that she approached the old Thomas spread, the one the late governor cleared, in retirement, to raise alpacas. She knew this by the curve in the railbed, by the crosstie fence at the woods' edge that marked the start of the half-grown-up pasture, and by the ghost of Governor Francis Thomas himself, who stood where he always stood, at the spot where the 11:57 had killed him back in 1876. He smoked a pipe and fondly watched a half dozen ghost alpacas that grazed the mountainside before him. Two of the alpacas were newborns, cute as buttons; they frolicked around, enjoying each other's company, a fresh crop of flowering beggar-lice visible through them. That Thomas's ghost would be fixed to that spot on the Earth's surface—and not, say, to the official governor's mansion in Annapolis—made some sense to Pearleen, but she had absolutely no idea why he appeared fully clothed, equipped with a pipe, and accompanied by phantom livestock. Pearleen had seen ghosts, and interacted with them, for years, but that did not mean she understood how they worked. Pearleen tried to live in a world of fact and not of theory. But she still knew her manners.

"Howdy, Governor," she called to him, when she was just far enough away not to have to raise her voice.

"Miss Sunday," he said, and gravely nodded his head.

"Mmm mmm mmm," the alpacas said, in that high-pitched hum they make, their absurd long necks craning as they gathered against the fence to see if the newcomer had a treat for them. As they jostled one another, one of the babies got pressed through the solid wood of the plank fence. First his transparent head emerged, like a mounted trophy, and then the rest of him followed. Pearleen knew she couldn't pet him, not really, but she reached out to do it anyway. He already had realized his error, though, and missed his family. Peeping in dismay, he whirled and wriggled back through the plank, vanished in sections to reemerge in the pasture where he belonged.

"So well behaved," said Governor Thomas. "Unlike *people*," he added, with unnecessary venom. The governor had had more than his share of difficulties with the legislature.

"They are indeed lovely creatures," said Pearleen, hoping she wasn't in for a lecture about their behaviors, their care and feeding, and their natural history. Ghosts tended to stick close not only to one spot, but to one subject. She took a second look at the alpacas, though, because they seemed suddenly alert to something, craned their heads and looked up the tracks, up the slope. The two biggest ones, the leaders, separated themselves, trotted off separately, toward whatever it was they saw. The others moved farther down the hill, away from the fence.

"They make excellent guardians of chickens, you know," said Governor Thomas. His gaze and Pearleen's followed that of the lead alpaca. "They can spot danger a mile away."

Now Pearleen heard it, too: a vibration like an oncoming train. They waited and waited, but there was no train, only the vibration that gained in intensity—not in the rails of the tracks themselves, as the 11:57 might have accomplished, but in the air above the tracks. The trees on the other side of the vibration began to shimmy, as they would if the tracks were on fire. As Pearleen stared and listened, the shimmy got more violent, and the vibration louder. It sounded like a high-pitched tuning fork. Pearleen winced and reached for one of her ears to shut it out. But Governor Thomas reacted not at all—and, more surprisingly, neither did the alpacas. They and their owner just looked up the tracks, as if curious.

"Governor," said Pearleen, "you don't *hear* that?"

"Hear what, child?" asked the governor.

Underneath the keening, Pearleen now heard a faint, quavering voice:

> *"Pearleen Sunday, oh Sunday, come talk to me fast!*
> *I'm brief as a sneeze. My time here can't last!"*

Of course they didn't hear it, Pearleen realized. It wasn't meant for them.

"Governor, you'll have to excuse me," said Pearleen. "Got to see a man about something." Once she stepped onto the tracks, her clothes moved oddly—not billowing as in a breeze, but fluttering, as if pelted by things unseen. She faced downhill, braced herself, held her staff horizontal in both hands, and added, as a courtesy she nearly had forgotten, "Thank you again for Emancipation."

"You're very welcome," said the governor, pleased to be reminded of another favorite subject, "but I was merely the Lord's instrument. Why Maryland had not already become a free state before the war, I will never under—"

But he was alone, the vibrating whatever-it-was having already swept down the tracks and snatched Pearleen away. She was briefly visible, a hundred yards downhill, standing upright about a foot above the center of the tracks. She made no discernible lean into the curve as she rounded the bend and whipped out of sight.

"Mmm mmm mmm," said the alpacas, heads bobbing on their long necks. They thought they had seen it all, and now this. Governor Thomas's ghost just sucked on his pipe, having already forgotten that Pearleen had been there in the first place. His oblivious presence was reassuring. The phantom alpacas gradually resumed their day, cropped living green grass that stayed intact, swallowed nothing into their transparent stomachs, then regurgitated it into the cud they would happily chew for a thousand years.

It's a mighty poor place that has only one name, and the nearby place where Pearleen was taken—on the far side of Allegany County, in a mountain hollow near the banks of the Potomac—had been called multiple names through the years. In the early nineteenth century it was called Hermit's Abode, because only old Ovid McCrackin lived there; in the late twentieth century it was called Chimney Hollow, because the only part left of the McCrackin place was a huge two-story brick chimney with two dark square mouths, once fireplaces, on each floor. But alongside these and other names was a more ominous one, kept alive by generations of kids who defied their grownups by exploring the place at all hours.

"Devil's Alley," said Pearleen aloud, still a little dizzy from her wild ride. She had flown just a foot above the B & O line (yes, she forced herself to admit, *flown* was the word) until she reached the Cumberland station, where no one seemed to pay her any attention at all—probably because she didn't, in some sense, actually exist at that point, at least not in downtown Cumberland. Just as she looked likely to crash head-on into a locomotive headed for Frostburg, she jumped the tracks, passed over the taverns and/or whorehouses, and resumed her flight above the C & O Canal, its water so still she could have seen her inverted green self below her feet the whole way. But that nauseated her, so she looked forward instead.

Devil's Alley was to Pearleen only a set of names and a chimney she had passed once or twice, rather than a place where she knew anyone. To her knowledge, old Ovid McCrackin haunted some other spot, if he was anyplace. So she walked past the homeplace, her back to the river, and entered deeper into the hollow, along the bed of a long-gone rail spur that probably led, as most Appalachian spurs did, to the entrance of a played-out mine.

This turned out to be the case, and pacing in the mouth of the mine, just inside the shade, was a rangy and familiar figure, his hands clasped together at the small of his back. He wore knee-high boots and the tailcoat of an earlier era. Someone who didn't know him to be an ancient scoundrel and penniless flimflam artist with connections would have thought him a young and handsome antebellum man of means, perhaps a free man of color from Baltimore—and Pearleen, who knew him all too well, was willing to grant the handsome part, anyway. As she approached, she heard him mutter:

> *"Pearleen Sunday, oh Sunday, please let me in.*
> *I'm weary of devils and shackles and sin."*

She started yelling well before she reached him, and he whirled at the sound, with an embarrassing look of elation.

"What you mean, Petey Wheatstraw? Calling me like I was a saint, or a dog?"

"Pearleen! You're here!" He ran to meet her as if to hug her to his chest and twirl her three times around, but her glare stopped him a couple of feet away. He stood there, two heads taller than her, and quivered. No two buttons on his fine checked waistcoat matched. "Thank you for coming, Pearleen!—for not ignoring your old friend Petey. Thank you, thank you, thank you!" He clasped his hands before him and shook them over his head, like he had won a fight.

"It ain't like I had a choice," Pearleen said. "That spell of yours scooped me up like I was a pile of mine tailings, and dumped me here."

"Oh, come off it," Petey said. His manner changed instantly. "Don't play naïve with me. You could have stepped out of the way, when you heard it coming, and you know it."

"And I would have, had I known it was you," Pearleen lied. Corrupted already, she realized. Just by his presence!

"Besides, it was sheer luck you happened to be in the vicinity," Petey said. "That spell ain't good for more'n a hundred miles, even if you don't get interference from temperature inversions and fault tremors and off-year elections."

"But why bring me here at all, to this . . . nowhere place?" Pearleen hated to criticize any spot of human habitation, given that she had spent years of happy childhood among the freaks and wonders of a Chattanooga dime museum, but she had to admit, as she surveyed the gray rocks and gray weeds and gray dirt, that Petey normally frequented more happening places.

In reply, Petey thrust three extended fingers at the sky, the knuckles of his trembling hand in her face. He held it there so long, and looked so angry, that she thought it might be an obscene gesture, and was too busy shuffling through possibilities to be offended. "Three times!" Petey cried. "This is my third go-round to this place. And whenever I try to walk out of the hollow, BLIM! I get knocked back on my tailbone. All's I can do is curse the rocks and the railbed, and wait to be moved to the next place." To Pearleen's shock and dismay, a single tear rolled out of Petey's left eye and down his cheek. "At least here, I don't get my ass kicked," he said, "or get shot at by Union artillery, or have to saw wood, or mill corn, or some other work for the white man. Did you know the air percussion can kill you, just as the shell passes by?"

Pearleen spent a few seconds not processing any of this, then said: "Petey, this is a monologue already in progress. You'll have to back up a ways, really you will."

"You're right," Petey said. He sighed and ran his hands through his close-cropped hair. "Oh, where to start? Pull up a soft rock over there, Pearleen, and I'll tell you."

Then, with many interruptions and backtracks, Petey told an only somewhat garbled version of his many repetitious travels and adventures over recent days, from California to New Orleans to New England and back again.

"Well, I'll be damned," Pearleen said, forgetting for a moment who she was talking to. "You're under a loconautic spell, repetitions and all."

"A loco-what? Talk English, girl."

"My, my, a magic term even Petey Wheatstraw don't know. That *must* be arcane. Well, your ignorance ain't too surprising, I guess. All's I know about loconautics, myself, is the definition. See, loconautics enables a wizard to travel from place to place by skipping around. You board a train in Cumberland because you want to get to Baltimore, but you got to go through Hancock and Hagerstown and a lot of other places you don't care about. Well, loconautics avoids everything that ain't where the wizard wants to be."

"But all us wizards go where we please, normally," Petey said. "I mean, sure, *you* walk every step of your path, 'cause you're stuck on that I-must-walk-the-Earth thing—but you don't *have* to. You don't even need the train or the tracks. So how's this loco-whatsis different?"

"It sort of does need a track, but the track ain't anything you can map with a compass. It's a track the wizard lays down, independent of the surface features of the Earth. The track is based on other things."

"Like what?"

"Like how many dogs live in a place, and how many of them are happy, or sad. You could make you a track, for example, that connected the places with at least a hundred and thirteen happy dogs, or the places where at least one person is aged exactly nineteen years, three months and six days, or all the places in North America where Roman coins have been dug out of the Earth. Or you could just do it the easy way, by place name. That's the track you've set yourself, Petey. You're on the way to visiting every place named after the Devil himself. It's the longest and oldest and crookedest track there is."

"Now wait a minute! This ain't my doing, I tell you. I ain't no, what-do-you-call-'em, loconauticator."

"Loconaut. It's like the old song says:

"*My lover is a loconaut,*
She moves through space and time.
Her travels take her far from me,
But her heart is always mine.
Some days a girl in pigtails,
Some days she's old and gray.
I wonder who has aged her,
In those lands far away.
She brings me ice in summer sun

And roses in the snow.
How I wish that I could go along
Wherever she does go."

"Huh," Petey said. "That's right pretty—the way you sing it, anyway—but I never heard that song before."

"Oh, you probably heard an earlier version. You know how the old songs change topics, and shake themselves, and bleed one into the other, and take on new words with time. This one, when I first heard it, was about an aeronaut, but *loconaut* scans just as well, don't you think?"

"Uh-huh. Since when did that song get a loconaut in it?"

"Why, I just now put it there, come to think of it. Because what's happening to you ought to be real, and nothing is real until there's a song about it. But Petey, you're right about this being none of your doing. To build a track for someone *else* to ride on, and to be stuck on for the rest of their days, that would take a powerful loconaut indeed—and I mean powerful like a high tide, or a baby's smile, or a volcano. Only the one who gave you that ticket can take it away, Petey, and until they do, you'll ride that ride till you drop. But who put you on that Old Crooked Track, I cannot say. I don't know anyone that powerful."

"You don't, huh? Well, I sure do. And you already met him, once, I believe."

Pearleen looked blank, which is hard for a wise woman to do.

"When you were just a girl," Petey continued. "In the front yard of the Winchester House. Only you were a lot bigger than him, at the time."

"Oh, my Lord!" Pearleen said, though that oath was precisely the opposite of who she had in mind. "You mean your father-in-law!"

"Yes, my infernal majesty father-in-law, who you last saw trapped in a Civil War soldier's old boot," Petey said. "I figured that shoe would drop directly, pardon the pun. A girl don't meet the Devil every day."

"You don't know much about girls, then, but Petey, what did you do to make the Devil so mad at you? Did you run around on his daughter? Steal from the cashbox? Bargain for souls one-on-one, and cut out the Old Man?"

Petey looked fidgety from the beginning of the recitation, and more so by the end. "I wouldn't put it quite *that*-away," he finally said. "It's not stealing if you intend to pay it back . . . and bargaining don't enter into a straight-up offer of trade, take it or leave it . . . And as for what you good girls call 'running around,' well, I prefer to think of it as spreading the seed of corruption, which *is* my *job*, after all. Besides, that wife of mine done 'run around' farther than the entire staff of the House of Blue Lights—and having *met* that house's entire staff, I know whereof I speak. Not that I criticize her, mind you. Why, I admire her gumption. A girl ought to see the world before she settles down, especially if she ain't never gone settle down . . . eh, Pearleen?"

"If you *dare* to wink at me, Petey Wheatstraw, I will turn my back on you this instant and every instant to come, forever."

Frozen in a half-wink for a second or two, Petey got out of it by flexing his face grotesquely, as if for jaw exercise, though he was careful to shut neither eye. "Excuse me, ma'am," Petey said and rubbed his cheek. "I get a little tic there, when I'm tired. The muscles seize up."

"*I'll* seize something," Pearleen said. "Well, if it's Old Scratch who's loconauted you, you are slap out of luck. You'll just have to throw yourself on his mercy, to get out of it one day."

"Oh, believe me, if I could get in the same place as him, even for one skinny minute, I'd put an end to this business, all right. I got a plan for that. But Pearleen, I can't even talk to him! As long as he stays off the track I'm on, I'll never see him again. No, what I need, you see, is someone to intercede on my behalf." He gave her a look that was half exhilaration and half nausea, which Pearleen had learned through painful experience was meant to convey abject supplication.

"Oh, no," Pearleen said.

"Someone who can go wherever they please . . ."

"Oh, no," Pearleen said again.

". . . and track down the Devil, wherever he may be . . . and, ideally, someone the Devil already sort of, kind of, owes a favor to."

"You can go to hell and wait on that," Pearleen blurted, then stomped her foot in dismay. Among the countless frustrations of conversation with Petey, his daily existence put so many of her favorite oaths into a terrible new register of literality. "Dammit," she said unhappily, and knew that Petey had done again what he did so often and so well: talked her into something that she just knew was a bad idea.

Meeting at a crossroads was, of course, expected, but the one in the Mississippi Delta, the famous one, had been burned long ago. Tourists!

So Pearleen went instead to Saluda County, South Carolina, where US 378 and State Highway 391 come together in a roundabout three hundred feet across, so unusual at the time it was built that all the neighbors just called it "the traffic circle," as if it were the only one. National Guard pilots used to bomb it with sandbags, for practice, because from above it looked like a target, as so many things do.

Pearleen hoped she looked like one, as she stood ramrod straight in the middle of the new-mown grass at the center of the circle at noon. She didn't appreciate being in the hot, but for a proper meet-up, the clock had to say twelve—everyone knew that—and she certainly did not want to attract the attention of Old You-Know-Who at the other end of the day, in the black dark.

To make sure she was visible to him, she made herself invisible to everyone else. Well, not so much invisible—that never worked out too well—as just beneath everyone's notice, so none of the troopers in patrol cars and young'uns in school buses and commuters in station wagons who drove around her would pay the least bit of attention to the girl-woman in heavy boots who stood in the grassy midpoint of the traffic circle with a cardboard sign that said, in red Sharpie, "HAIL SATAN."

Through the decades, she had accumulated countless reasons to suspect that she had the old man's attention already. But this was the first time she had tested her suspicion.

She stood there and stood there in the heat of the day, until everything she'd eaten for lunch at the Circle Diner—a fried-baloney sandwich with cheese, with pigskins and pimiento on the side and a big carton of Hickory Hill chocolate milk—started to wear off, except maybe for the pigskins that would be with her always, and she wished she'd brought some bonus baloney with her. But whenever she checked her cathead pocketwatch, she saw that it was still noon, and *that* was a good sign.

Finally, all the traffic in the circle drove away in all directions, toward Saluda or Batesburg or Prosperity or the lake, and was replaced by no traffic at all. At the moment she realized this, she also registered that the breeze had died, that the leaves in the trees were still, that all the visible businesses, the diner and Buddy's Marine and the VFD, now looked deserted, as no one came in or out. A squirrel in the edge of the nearby grass was frozen in place in midair, as if arrested in midjump, and she felt sorry for it. But she knew the squirrel didn't have long to wait, because she could hear the Devil's car a-coming, from the direction of Batesburg.

It was a turquoise 1933 Essex-Terraplane Eight, the kind the bank robbers had favored, and its running board and headlamps gleamed so, you'd think detail work was the only job left to the damned. Pearleen couldn't quite make out the driver, so bright was the finish in her eyes. The car went into the circle widdershins and went around, and went around, and went around, thirteen times all told, until it pulled to a stop, still in the road, and sat there, rumbling. The back door nearest Pearleen opened by itself, to reveal nothing but a wall of shadow, an utter absence of light. It was like the mouth of a cave, or a sewer pipe, or a rifle barrel. But Pearleen took a deep breath, muttered, "The things I do for you, Petey Wheatstraw," cinched her pack tighter, walked across the grass, and got in.

The plush back seat was right comfortable, except for the door that slammed shut behind her without agency, and the dead man at the wheel whose head lolled sideways. His glassy eyes in the rearview mirror seemed to stare just past her at something awful. Someone had shot him in the temple, and the blood was caked and dry. Riding shotgun was an enormous bloodhound that filled the front seat; his buttocks crowded the driver, and his muzzle fogged the side window. The hound's focus was outside the car. He emitted a low growl.

"You leave that squirrel alone," Pearleen said, and at that moment, the small critter came unstuck and bounded away into the grass.

"ARF!" said the bloodhound—not the sound of a dog's bark, but the sound of a deep-voiced man yelling, "ARF!" As if that were a command, the driver's flopping dead hand shoved the gearshift into place, and the car rolled forward, picked up speed around the circle, around the circle, around the circle, thirteen times until Pearleen was nauseated and the Terraplane slingshotted down US 378 toward the lake, the scenery a blur. Pearleen sat forward at an inopportune time, just as the dog emitted a long, eye-watering fart, to see for herself the speedometer needle that spasmed at the unmarked right end of the gauge. "SIDDOWN!" yelled the dog, and Pearleen fairly jumped back in the seat. Something went *thump thump* beneath the car, and Pearleen thought sure a tire had blown and she was done for—but no, on the straightaway ahead, as far as the eye could see, small animals dashed into the road from left and right just in time to be run over. Their broken furry bodies continuously smacked the undercarriage, *thump thump thump thump thump*. The car made a screeching turn to the left that tossed Pearleen against the passenger door, which was hot like a stovelid. She shoved herself back into the middle of the seat just in time for a second screeching turn to the right. Pearleen managed to brace herself and sit up straight that time, but the lifeless driver slumped forward, his face wedged into the corner between dashboard and door, and never moved again. The bloodhound peered back at her. Drool from his jowls beribboned the back of the seat as he said: "Ain't it a smooth-riding car?"

"*Oh*, yeah," Pearleen murmured, barely audible over the quickening *thump thumpthumpthump*.

"You know what they say," added the dog, his voice trending louder and more manic. "On the sea, it's aquaplaning! In the air, *it's aeroplaning*! And *ON THE ROAD, IT'S TERRAPLANING*! Haw haw haw!" He rolled off the seat with laughter, fell onto the brake pedal, and the car stopped dead with a screech that was mostly Pearleen screaming, her hands over her face, certain that in the next instant the car would flip over, and she'd be dead. But nothing happened except her scream, and she eventually slacked off, spread her fingers, and looked around to find the car's interior unchanged, and the scenery no longer moving. The door through which she had entered now popped open with a *hiss* of rushing air, as if a pressurized seal had broken. From just out of sight in the front seat came the abrupt sounds of ripping and gulping: the dog had begun to eat the driver. Pearleen scrambled out of the car and ran blindly, her only thought to get far from the befouled Terraplane, and in the process ran twenty feet across a freshly raked dirt yard. She stopped herself just a couple of inches away from the bottommost of a set of plank steps.

"Young lady, I do not recommend you set foot on those steps," said a harsh nasal voice like claws on slate, "less'n you intend to be my house-guest till half past eternity."

Pearleen looked up. Sitting on the wide front porch of a two-story white house with clapboard siding, baked beneath a purple sun in a red sky, were Asmodeus, the Unclean, and the Stranger to All; Baphomet the Tempter, the First Beast, and the Father of Lies; the Senior Senator from the Great State of Bigotry and Hatred and Status Quo; the Son of the Shadows; the Prince of Air and Darkness; the Lord of the Flies, and of Misrule, and of This World; Plague-Bearer, Light-Bringer, Accuser and Adversary, Lodestar and Belial; Old Massa, Old Nick, Old Scratch—all those and a thousand more compressed into a single un-shaven, plug-chewing, undershirt-wearing, wattle-necked, pussel-gutted little peckerwood, just enough yellow-white hair left on his bald head to stick out in all directions like a Van de Graaff halo. He sat in a rocking chair and fanned himself with a derby hat, his many titles and responsibilities buzzing around him like a swarm of blowflies. His tiny, close-set eyes, embedded in wrinkles like a pair of snake-eye dice in a dead man's palm, gazed at Pearleen with distant disinterest, as they might have gazed at a dried-out cow patty in the road. He was just plumb awful, but Pearleen immediately felt a little better, just to see him; she had known his type long since, and was no longer afraid. She did, however, make a little curtsy, being ever mannerly, and nobody's fool.

"I appreciate the warning, sir," she said, "but I'm a little surprised you gave it."

"My magnanimity surprises me, too," the Devil said, "but I reckon we're all a mass of contradictions. Take you, for example, Miss Sunday. You look like the Sabbath for which you are named—or like its popular conception, at least—all cream and strawberries in an unchipped bowl. And yet you must be at least half-full of live bait, to survive the trip to my lake house in the first place." His jumbled, dark-stained teeth gleamed in the wrongness of the sun. "I don't believe I caught your name."

"You just said it," Pearleen replied.

"Did I, now? That was so long ago, I can't remember. I don't think you've given it to me, though. Not handed out freely, pink and squirming in your hand. You've yet to give me anything like that."

"Just your freedom," Pearleen retorted. "You remember me, Old Scratch. My name is Pearleen Sunday, and you saw me last when you were just a tiny thing, and were trapped by a wizard from Yandro Mountain. His hex-magic laced you inside a boot from the Civil War. I said the words that sprung you, and I swung that old boot over my head three times and let it fly, and you were freed and loose in the world again. I did that not for your sake, but for the sake of he who trapped you. I did it for the soul of Wendell Farethewell, the Wizard of the Blue Ridge, and I am not sorry for it. Do you remember me now, Old Many-Shaped?"

The Devil's chair was placed, for maximum annoyance, on the sweetest spot of a creaking floorboard, which voiced its torment each time the Devil rocked forward. "How about that," the Devil said. *Creak.* "Ain't that something." *Creak.* "Well, my, my, my." *Creak.*

This went on for a while, until Pearleen got impatient. "How long you gone rock there," she asked, "and not answer my question?"

"Sometimes it's more diplomatic," the Devil said, "just to make noises with your mouth, and say nothing at all. And be careful what you ask me, little girl. You might not like the answer. But the fact is, that I don't seem to recollect even one little tee-ninchy bit of this fairy-story you're a-telling me." He shook his head and scratched his balls. "Gals are so big for their britches these days. I blame literacy. They start looking at the pretty dresses in the *Woman's Home Companion*, and next thing you know, they're sounding out the words too."

Pearleen ignored this provocation, and the Devil's rubbing himself, and his fixed stare aimed not at her face. "You don't remember, do you? Well, then, tell me this, Old Deceiver. If you weren't beholden to me big time, if you didn't owe me a favor of favors, why'd you come a-running when I called you, just like a good little poodle dog?"

This snapped him into focus. The Devil sat forward in the chair, eyes flashing. "I didn't come to you, Little Britches. I brought *you* to *me*."

"It works out the same," Pearleen said. "There's a tie that hauls us together. What braided that rope, Old Thing Without Breath, if not the good turn I did you?"

He sat back with a frown, and flapped his hand in an oh-do-get-on gesture. In the process, he noticed his jagged fingernails. "Let's not say *good*," the Devil said, fingers in his mouth, gnawing himself a manicure. "I *did* just eat my dinner. Let's say only that I wanted a better look at you than I got last time—you being older and more interesting to a man of the world, and me being more presentable than I was." He hooked both thumbs beneath the straps of his undershirt and snapped them against his scrawny shoulders. "So, Miss Sunday, what's this wholly unearned favor-of-favors you got in your eyeteeth? What you want from me, other than the right to live to see your next time of the month?"

"I want you to release Petey Wheatstraw."

The Devil went very still, and every window in the front of his fine house shattered.

"I don't believe I know the name," the Devil said, as glass shards fell and smashed all around.

"You do, too. He married your daughter."

"I got lots of daughters," the Devil said. "They all whores and hare-lips. They got lots of husbands, and wives too—if you define the terms broadly, in a common-law way."

"You got only one as powerful as Petey Wheatstraw," Pearleen said, enjoying the way the Devil winced at the repetition. "That's why you put him on the Old Crooked Track. Because you're scared of him."

"You are so full of shit," the Devil said, "and believe me, I should know. Where'd you say he is, your friend what's-his-name, this Peter Dickstraw?"

"He's everywhere named for the Devil, a thousand thousand places but nowhere else. He's confined to those places over and over, in all time periods, all over the world."

The Devil shook his head. "Not the world, honey. Only the United States. Don't you know nothing? That's the extent of my jurisdiction. I got no authority outside the United States at all."

This stopped Pearleen short. Her jaw dropped.

"Whyever not?" asked Pearleen.

The Devil shrugged. "Don't ask me. For whatever reason, y'all are the last Satan-fearing nation on Earth."

"But," Pearleen said. "But."

The Devil shook his head, made a clawlike gesture of dismissal. "Honey, I do not make the rules, remember? That's why I quit Heaven in the first place. But as for your friend Pecker Woodsman, why shouldn't I keep him just where he is?"

"It ain't fair," Pearleen said. "Not as handsome as he is, and as smart, and as kind. Not when he's so well-placed to do so much good in the world, with all his powers, and all he's learned from you, through the years." She went on in this vein for some time, and enjoyed the Devil's growing discomfiture, the angry flush on his cheeks. "Oh, now, mind you, he's done a lot of good already, right there on the Old Crooked Track. Why, at Devil's Den, on the Gettysburg battlefield, he consoles the wounded, and brings them water, and is ever so helpful. At the Devil's Punchbowl in Oregon, he dips out drinks for everyone, like the thing is bottomless, and I don't know what he spiked it with, but old enemies who ain't spoken to one another in decades, why, they hug and make up and show each other photos of the grandbabies. At the Devil's Courthouse in North Carolina, he hands out pardon after pardon, forgives every sinner in the place, the defendants and bailiffs and judges and even some of the lawyers, and just wipes the slate clean." By now the Devil was sky-purple with rage, hunched over like a whistle-pig as he gnawed splinters out of the arm of the rocking chair, his eyes like twin eight-balls spinning into pockets. "I mean, Petey Wheatstraw plumb does everything he can, and if he keeps at it another century or so, why, your name will stand for nothing but goodness and mercy, all across the map. But just think how much *more* he could do if—"

"Silence!" roared the Devil, in a voice that cracked the posts that held up the porch, rearranged into obscene designs the dirt of the yard, and busted the radiator in the Terraplane. Over the hiss of the leak and the bloodhound's panicked barks, the Devil said, "So that's what he's up to, is he? I'll cut out his goozlum, I will." He stomped to the front door, hitching up his britches, and yelled through the screen: "Hey! Middle management! Get your useless business-school asses out here!"

In moments, a dozen cubicle dwellers, all in ill-fitted gray suits—too large for some, too small for others—tumbled through the doorway and cowered before the Devil, wringing their hands, each face a rictus of abject subservience and eagerness to please. They were men and women both, black and white and brown, and though they were not literally kissing the Devil's hind knickers, Pearleen had no doubt they would, and more besides, if he but said the word. The Devil turned to face Pearleen, happy again, and waved his hand at the whole miserable lot.

"Multicultural as the day is long," the Devil said. "I used to run a segregated shop, but you got to change with the times." He spat a long plume of tobacco juice onto the nearest cubicle dweller's shoes. "Besides," he said, "I like to think of myself as a progressive. Now how fast can you all bring 'round my two finest horses, all saddled up and ready to go, you yes-men and yes-women and how-highers and focus-group fuckfaces?"

The answer was, about two minutes thirty seconds, during which time the Devil stomped and cursed, the bloodhound chased its stinking tail and barked, and Pearleen held her breath and marveled that so far, the Devil's gullibility had lived up to all Petey's expectations. The middle managers finally led around the house two magnificent liver-red chestnut stallions that neighed and reared, flaxen manes tossing and nostrils flaring. With the inexpert help of half the crew, the Devil, who wriggled and squealed like a piglet, eventually managed to mount the larger of the two horses. Pearleen conceded that he looked fairly at home on horseback, once he finally got situated.

"This one here," said the Devil, "is Hallowed-Be-Thy-Name, or Low for short. Yours is Thy-Kingdom-Come, but he answers to King."

"Mine?" asked Pearleen. But the middle managers already had scrambled to help her into the saddle. This turned out to be a far easier job than the Devil had been.

"I named 'em," said the Devil, wheeling about, "after the one who gave 'em to me in the first place."

"You mean?" asked Pearleen.

"The very same," said the Devil. "It was the only time He ever give me anything, really, since the late unpleasantness. And He wouldn't have done that, if I hadn't a jumped out from behind a bush on December twenty-four and yelled 'Christmas gift!' You can sneak up on Him, sometimes. But you can't sneak up on me!"

Settled in, she stroked King's neck and murmured into his ear, "Easy, big fellow." He nickered companionably. She was glad he couldn't talk, at least.

"You're my one-woman posse, Pearleen Sunday. You and I are gone ride down that sanctimonious, bad-name-ruining, not-blood-kin-in-any-way-whatsoever son of a bitch Petey Wheatstraw, and you will both see that once a place on the map is named for the Devil, by God it stays named! Yaaaaah!"

Waving his derby overhead like a cowboy as the middle managers cheered him on, he spurred Hallowed-Be-Thy-Name out of the dirt yard and down the gravel lane. Without her doing a thing, Thy-Kingdom-Come bolted forward after them. It was all Pearleen could do to hold on. For a few yards the bloodhound loped alongside, barking, but King quickly picked up speed and left him far behind. Just before he was out of earshot, the bloodhound yelled after them: "SHOWOFF!"

They caught up to Petey in Indiana, at the Devil's Mill.

Petey had stood just behind the miller all morning, as the farmers of the neighborhood brought in sackfuls of corn to be ground. Though he was invisible to them, Petey wore a many-pocketed apron identical to the miller's, a soft gray cap identical to the miller's, even a bristly red mustache identical to the miller's. And as each customer approached, Petey provided advice likely identical to what the miller would have come up with on his own.

When a rich farmer approached, Petey said, "This fellow can afford to pay a higher rate. He won't even miss it. Toll him heavy, Mr. Miller, toll him heavy."

When a farmer of only middling success approached, Petey said, "Here's a man of ambition. He wants to be where the rich farmer is, so why deny him? Toll him heavy, Mr. Miller, toll him heavy."

When a half-starved sharecropping widow woman stumbled in, three wailing waifs clutching her spindly shanks, Petey said, "Their little bit of corn ain't gone keep them alive another winter. It'd just go to waste. Toll her heavy, Mr. Miller, toll her heavy."

"You don't owe me nothing, Mrs. Prentiss," said the miller. "And here's five dollars. Buy you a sack of groceries while you're in town, and God bless you."

"Well, how do you like that?" Petey snorted, as the little family hobbled out of the mill rejoicing, and as the miller's chest swelled with unearned pride and satisfaction. "That is a sign of a first-rate liar. Pearleen said she would make me out to be some kind of good-deed-doer, and damned if it ain't coming true."

"What in the world is that?" asked the miller, of no one in particular.

A ways off down the road, a three-story cloud of dust hung over the bare cornstalks. It was closing fast, and at the lead edge were two figures on horseback, the nearest of whom had spindly legs stuck out like a child's.

"Pearleen, I take it all back," said Petey. He pulled off his apron and cap and mustache and discarded them and cracked his knuckles as he walked down the ramp into the millyard and muttered to himself what was less a spell than a set of vows of what he planned to do, and how often, and to whom. But vows are like spells, too, Petey knew; they're prayers to ourselves, and they work even better, if heeded. Petey continued to talk to himself as he began to run, straight toward the oncoming Devil.

"Fill your hands, you son of a bitch!" screamed the Devil, who was of course a big John Wayne fan, and he spurred Hallowed-Be-Thy-Name onward, his impulse to run Petey right over in the dirt, and keep going.

Seeing the Devil's murderous intent, Petey did not turn tail and flee, did not try to dart out of the horse's path. Instead, he ran even faster—impossibly fast—and jumped, like an enormous cricket, right over the Devil and his mount.

"Whoa!" cried the Devil. "Whoa, I said!"

By the time he got Low slowed down and wheeled around, Pearleen had slowed King enough for Petey to spring up and climb on behind her. He reached both arms around her, felt her stiffen, and said, "Don't worry, this is nothing personal. Just to keep from falling off, y'understand."

"Good luck," said Pearleen, and whispered into King's ear words he never had heard before, and was never likely to hear from his master, either. The horse reared and whinnied in triumph, and took off even faster than before, headed straight for the mill. The Devil on Low followed, eating dust in their wake.

"Damn you, Wheatstraw!" the Devil yelled, redundantly, as he choked and coughed amid a yellow cloud.

Head down, ears flattened, in a full-out gallop, King scattered farmers every which way as he streaked through the millyard, leaped the stone wall at the edge, and ran straight up the waterwheel. At the top, the horse ran in place, and the wheel spun ever faster beneath him, kicked up great sprays of water that gouted into the pursuing Devil's face as from a fire hose. Blinded, half drowned, nearly knocked out of the saddle, he spluttered and flailed as Low turned tail and ran away. By the time the Devil regained control, King had leaped off the wheel and had galloped away through the corn, clearing a path of flattened stalks. Both the Devil and his mount were enraged now. They dashed down the new-made corn lane, all froth and fume, chasing Pearleen's and Petey's laughs and whoops up ahead.

And so it went—Petey and Pearleen in the lead, the Devil in hot pursuit—through the Indiana cornfield and down the middle aisle of a Massachusetts church and up the main stairway of a New Orleans mansion and along a rocky ridgeline in Colorado and into a cave in Utah that opened out in Tennessee, through dozens of locations across four centuries. They terrified and impressed hundreds of people as they went, and spawned legends, myths, ghost stories, and religious movements, in addition to countless outright lies and a number of jokes that weren't half bad.

Finally, somewhere along South Mountain in Pennsylvania, Pearleen and Petey heard the Devil holler, way back behind:

"You win! You win!"

"He's dismounted," Petey reported, looking back.

"Just as well," Pearleen said. "The horses need a rest."

They trotted back to where Hallowed-Be-Thy-Name slurped water from a brook. Beside him, the Devil sat on a rock, mopped his face with an unexpectedly dainty lace handkerchief. It looked even as if it might be scented, though Pearleen had no desire to find out. Petey dismounted first, then reached up to help her. This pleased her so that she let him, but remembered once she alighted that she needed no help and had no use for Petey anyway. Thy-Kingdom-Come drank companionably from the brook alongside Hallowed-Be-Thy-Name, their brief rivalry forgotten.

"Pull up a rock," the Devil said, "and set a spell."

"There are quite a lot of rocks," Pearleen said. "More rocks than anything else, really. What place is this?"

Petey replied, "It's the Devil's Race Course. What did you expect?"

"I've heard of this place," Pearleen said. She rummaged through her pack, produced a small hammer. "I've always wanted to try this. Listen." She stood up, bit her lip in concentration, and brought down the hammer where she'd been sitting. On impact, the rock chimed, a high note that lingered for several seconds before it died away.

"Ringing rocks!" Petey said. "Let me try that."

They all three took turns, for the next few minutes, making the rocks ring all around. Annoyed, the horses whickered and walked downstream to crop grass.

"I wonder what causes this," Pearleen said. "I mean, what the rocks are made of."

"Don't ask me," the Devil replied. "Geology ain't my area."

Petey opened his mouth to say something, but the Devil waved him off.

"Don't even ask," he said. "Your curse is lifted. You are officially off the Old Crooked Track, and free to go." He shook his head. "I don't know where my mind was, that I delegated it to you in the first place. Should've known you'd just ruin it."

"Well, I thank you," Petey said.

"Thank *her*," the Devil said, and nodded toward Pearleen, who had lined up rocks of various sizes and rang them experimentally, like a xylophone. "She's the one that pled your case."

"But it was Petey that knew what to do, once we got here," Pearleen said. "It was both of us."

"But mostly me," Petey and Pearleen added, in unison.

"Y'all make quite a team," the Devil said. "I recommend that you go off in separate directions, and never see each other again."

"We got a story to finish up first," Pearleen said.

"Suit yourself," said the Devil. He stood up, dusted the seat of his pants—which scarcely could have been made dirtier by his rock-sitting interval—and said, "I best get on back to the South Carolina district of Hell. Leave things in the hands of middle managers, next thing I know, they'll lower the thermostat and hand out ice water." He whistled. "Hee, yaw! Hallowed-Be-Thy-Name! Thy-Kingdom-Come!" He walked two paces toward the horses and vanished.

"I had wondered about that," said Petey.

"Wondered what?" asked Pearleen.

"Well, he took me *off* the Old Crooked Track, but the track still exists, right? I mean, he didn't dismantle it or anything. So it's still there to be walked . . . if you're unwary enough to step on it, that is. Who knows? The Devil right now may be in Devil's Hole on the Eastern Shore, getting his ass kicked by Molly Horn."

"Oh, come on. He ain't *that* stupid, surely."

"Well, if he was all that *smart*," said Petey, "he wouldn't be the Devil, now would he?"

Pearleen shook her head. "I don't do theology," she said. "Ain't you heard? I'm a musician." Grinning, hammer in hand, she pinged on her rock instrument an old, old song she just made up:

> *"Dah dah dah is a loconaut*
> *She moves through dah dah dah."*

"It's still my story, you know," Petey said.

Pearleen sighed and said, "Whatever."

Kate Elliott

• • •

In a world where the power and prestige of the great mage houses are judged by the number and strength of their mages, recruitment of new magical blood becomes a matter of paramount importance. But magic can bloom in the most unlikely places—and in the most unlikely people, too.

Kate Elliott is the author of twenty-six fantasy and science fiction novels, including her *New York Times* bestselling YA fantasy, *Court of Fives* (and its sequels, *Poisoned Blade* and *Buried Heart*). Her most recent epic fantasy is *Black Wolves* (winner of the RT Award for Best Epic Fantasy of 2015). She's also written the alt-history Spiritwalker Trilogy (*Cold Magic, Cold Fire, Cold Steel*), an Afro-Celtic post-Roman gas-lamp fantasy adventure with well-dressed men, badass women, and lawyer dinosaurs (the world in which this story takes place). Other series include the Crossroads Trilogy, the seven-volume Crown of Stars epic fantasy, the science fiction Novels of the Jaran and The Highroad Trilogy, and a short-fiction collection, *The Very Best of Kate Elliott*. Her novels have been finalists for the Nebula, World Fantasy, and Norton Awards. Coming up is *Unconquerable Sun,* a gender-bent Alexander the Great as space opera. Born in Iowa and raised in farm country in Oregon, she currently lives in Hawaii, where she paddles outrigger canoes for fun and exercise. You can find her on Twitter at @KateElliottSFF. And she very much wants to thank Aliette de Bodard for beta-reading this story.

◆　◆　◆

Bloom

KATE ELLIOTT

W hat was a respectable magister who had served Autumn House for all his adult life to do? The mansa called Titus to his study and gave him the order direct.

"Titus, I wish you to take my cousin's granddaughter Serena with you."

Of course he could not object straight out. "As it is said, the comfort of a woman is in her home."

The mansa had looked old to Titus's eyes when Titus had come to the mage House as a fifteen-year-old. Now, thirty-two years later, the mansa looked positively decrepit, a shell of a man with wrinkled skin and age-whitened hair. Yet those keen eyes did pin a man as if he were an insect on display in a museum of curiosities.

"It is the elder's place to show the paths to the young. You are our House's most experienced and powerful diviner. Thus you must train her in her calling now that it has so unexpectedly bloomed."

The compliment lessened the sting a trifle, but the command still chafed. "It cannot be appropriate for me to travel with an unmarried girl who is not my daughter."

"Have you traveled recently with your daughters?" the mansa asked drily.

Titus folded his hands tightly together, searching for a reply, but his thoughts tangled with a pressure in his chest, and he could not answer.

The mansa sighed and patiently went on. "Serena is young, yes, but a woman, not a girl. She was married."

"That is right! I recall it now." He was grateful for the change of subject. "She was married out to Twelve Horns House and sent back in disgrace."

"In fact, she returned of her own choice."

"Imprudence is the mark of a fickle woman! I have two diviners I am already training. The presence of a girl would disturb our travels and no doubt result in their being too distracted to learn."

"Since you feel your apprentices are not man enough to control themselves, I will send along my sister Kankou and one of her women as chaperone. As for Serena, I have good reason to believe she will not be careless or flighty."

"She will become sickly and cause a disaster. You know how girls are. Obviously she already has shown herself to be disobedient and selfish. Anyway, if she has the true diviner's gift, which one must doubt because it is a rare calling, then she can confine it to the nursery and the school-room, as women properly do."

"The flower cannot bloom without sunlight. She needs experience out in the world. You know we sail in desperate straits and are sinking. We are among the least of the mage Houses. Our lineage is weak. In the schoolroom we have only two budding mages, neither of whom can do more than quench a candle's flame."

"I have done my duty in this regard!"

"I do not fault you, Titus. We all regret your son's passing."

Even after eight years, the hideous memory rose of his bright, clever, robust son lying wasted and feverish as pus-filled blisters crowded the lad's skin and his lungs slowly failed. But he had taught himself not to move or speak until the feelings subsided.

The mansa had a quill pen on his desk, which he picked up, examined with exaggerated care, and with the faintest tilt of a frown set back in its carved ivory holder. He cleared his throat. "For myself, Titus, I am grateful for your daughters, who have been good friends to my grand-children."

The mansa paused. Since there was no reason to comment on the frivolous dealings of girls, Titus merely nodded.

The mansa sighed again and went on.

"We have neither wealth nor prestige with which to interest the other mage Houses to make alliances with us. We need fresh blood. I believe Serena may be able to find new mages at the earliest unfurling of their first bloom."

Titus respected his elders, but this was too much. "Do you not trust me to serve our House after all my years of loyalty?"

"I do trust you, Titus. But neither of your current apprentices seem to show much promise in finding newly bloomed cold mages before the diviners of richer Houses sense them and swoop down to snatch them from us."

Since this was manifestly true, Titus said nothing.

"Who will follow you as diviner for our House, when you are too old to travel? Answer me that."

Since there was no answer, Titus said nothing.

"I am not asking, Titus. You will take her along. That is all."

Since the death of his son he had spent as little time as possible in the wing of the House where women walked freely and spoke as much as they wished. So on the day of departure he had no idea which of the callow girls Serena might be as a flood of chattering, excited females surged into the outer courtyard to see her off.

Of course his daughters walked among them, laughing in the capricious manner of heedless girls. Fabia was a tall, lanky eighteen-year-old, and Cassia, at thirteen, seemed to be more filled out every month. When they saw him standing by the carriage, their smiles flattened. Fabia took hold of her younger sister's hand. With wary gazes they approached, halting at a respectful distance.

"Honored Father, may you have a peaceful and successful journey," said Fabia in a toneless voice.

Cassia leaned against her sister and murmured the same words with eyes lowered rather than Fabia's impudent stare.

"Is all well with you, Daughters?" he replied in the same formal way.

"Of course all is well, Honored Father." Fabia's gaze flickered side-ways as if she meant to say something more and restrained herself. "And with you, is all well with you?"

He said what was proper in reply. Every time he looked at them he thought of how the evil sickness that had killed the boy had caught the girls first. Their pockmarked faces were a visible reminder of what they had survived, and he had lost.

Cassia tugged on her sister's arm. "Here is Serena," she said in a low voice, as if the appearance of this distraction was a relief.

There the young woman came, accompanied by the terrifying Kankou. To his disgust Serena was no awkward, gap-toothed heifer but a young woman of perhaps twenty years of age in the full bloom of fresh beauty. Indeed, had any Europan painter been asked to illustrate the epitome of youthful womanly beauty, the artist would have chosen her as the subject, for she was everything most pleasing in a woman. She had strong shoulders and an ample posterior. Her complexion was suit-ably black and flawless, her lips full of promise, her gaze as serene as her name. She wore modern dress, it was true, the skirt fitted over her full hips, and her waist emphasized by the tight cut of her fashionable jacket. He could not approve such frivolity. What would these women do next? Expose their thighs?

But she had tied her headwrap in a complicated structure of knots that made him think of difficult questions that could be puzzled over for hours. And she greeted him with scrupulous respect and a generous smile. The women and girls embraced and kissed her with enthusiasm before singing her, Kankou, and Kankou's woman Leontia into the car-riage. His apprentices, Anwell and Bala, wore glowers as they followed. He made his farewells to the assembly and allowed the coachman to help him in.

By the second week of their travels he had become so accustomed to Serena's accommodating presence that he was shocked beyond measure when she spoke one chilly morning without him having addressed her first.

"Magister, I beg your pardon, but I wonder if we might turn north."

They had reached the Rhenus River and were waiting for the ferry at the front of a line of vehicles. The sound of the streaming river had led his thoughts into a bittersweet memory of how he and his son used to play chess in the fountain garden with its constant gurgle of falling water. So it was with a tincture of asperity that he opened his mouth to dismiss her comment as the frivolous nonsense it was. But another voice broke in first.

"Magister, we just came through that region and divined nothing," said Anwell, casting a hostile glance toward the girl.

Bala added, "It's probably just overexcitement and a desire for attention."

"Why does the jack bray its foolishness before the elder speaks?" Titus snapped.

As irritated as he had been at having her foisted on him, still he did not like to allow young men to believe they could be disrespectful whenever they wished. First they would start with this girl, who treated them with a reserved politeness that did not at all encourage their efforts to impress her, and next they would think it bold and manly to show insolence to their elders.

"Why north?" he asked her, hoping to use this as a teaching experience. "We traveled that route three days ago."

"I am not an experienced diviner, Magister, but I sensed . . . something unusual."

"Give me a moment."

He shot a quelling glance at the young men, then shut his eyes and plunged his awareness into what his teacher had called the loom of nyama.

A warp and weft of energy undergirds the world, weaving into and through everything that exists. These energies could be transformed but never created or destroyed, and from them all actions and reactions arise. As a diviner he could spill like a fish through these dense waters and in them discern, like silvery fish in the sea, the life force of human souls. Cold mages had the ability to manipulate the ebb and flow of these energies. A trained mage radiated a pattern of light that was impossible to describe even to another diviner, for each diviner had to learn to understand how to perceive and negotiate the loom in their own way.

Deep in the ocean of ceaselessly moving energy, a bud of light might suddenly flare with a raw, unformed glamour: this was the mark of a person whose magic had burst into flower. Mostly these blooms were youths coming into their adolescence, although occasionally an older person who had lived for decades in quiescence would wake up to find themselves able to handle the threads of nyama, also called energy or power. In a mage House, of course, such people were immediately sent for training, a process that took many years. But not only the House-born had cold magic. Nyama flowed everywhere through the world. Thus anywhere and at any time a person might all unwittingly bloom. Such House-less people were fair game to whoever found them first. By this means—recruiting new potential mages—a small mage clan like Autumn House could restore its withering fortunes.

Swimming in his mind through the nearby shoals and bays of these intangible waters, he sought a flare of light but found nothing. Emerging, he turned his head to look at her with what he intended to be a kindly nod.

"You have mistaken the matter. There is no bloom."

She spoke in her composed voice. "I sensed it first as a pressure against my heart. It's not a bright light but as if a struggling flame is concealed beneath a gauze wrap."

Her description was so oddly specific that he cast back into the waters just to see if he could discover what she meant, or else prove her wrong. Perhaps because divining came so easily to him, he might have missed a glimmer the girl had spotted. Maybe she was mistaken, but maybe she had looked harder because she was anxious to be accepted and thus acted with particular vigilance.

When he was young he'd experimented with different ways of sensing discrete signatures of magic within the great wash of energy, but the old diviner who had taught him had ridiculed as "womanly" any method but that of diviner's sight. He retained a vague memory of letting touch guide him. Just as she had suggested.

And there it was, a breath of substance like an exhalation along his skin. In the diviner's trance he flowed northward, letting the faint pressure lead his path until he passed a point and the pressure of exhalation shifted to the other side of his arm. So he came around to find himself in a hollow of glowing energy, an area where many living beings clustered. A town.

He saw the incipient bloom as if it were a candle glimpsed behind a translucent window shade. No! There were two candles there, one a bit brighter but the second rising behind it. The intensity of the light was building imperceptibly, noticeable only because the gauzy covering seemed to be slowly dissolving in two spots.

He opened his eyes with a surprised gasp. All heads turned toward him.

"If I do not mistake what I have just divined, there are two young mages on the cusp of blooming."

Quite unlike her usual subdued and compliant manner, Serena broke in eagerly. "Two! I thought the fainter light was a mirror effect. But I haven't your experience in divining, Magister. Two at once in the same household is unusual, is it not?"

"It is rare, and usually means twins." He preened a little, glad to still be worth something alongside these fresh sprouts. "The gauzy shield that hides them means that possibly no other mage House is yet aware. We must reach the family before they fully burst into their power and another diviner with more to offer can find them."

He rapped on the small window that opened onto the driver's bench.

When it scraped open, he said, "Morcant, take us out of line for the ferry. Take the River Road toward Venta Erkunos."

He was surprised at the certainty he felt. This was the right choice. One, he had to admit in all fairness, that he wouldn't have noticed if not for the girl.

By late afternoon they reached the bustling market town.

"Our first concern is to track down and negotiate with the family," he said to his three apprentices. "To that end, we will split up for faster searching."

"As soon as I have secured rooms for the night," said Kankou in the tone that assured no one would argue with her, and of course he would never have done so regardless.

Cold magic was anathema to fire. Thus, when traveling, cold mages stayed at inns built with a hypocaust. Any large town and ferry crossing boasted such an establishment. Even if no mages had ever slept there, the chance that they might someday meant the inn could advertise itself as of the highest quality of establishment, worthy of mages and princes alike.

An innkeeper greeted them at the gate, hands clasped, demeanor welcoming. A youth brought them water to drink in welcome, offering the refreshment to them in order of age beginning with Kankou.

"Maestra, we are honored by your presence. Magister, please be welcome. Of course we can arrange chambers." He examined the women and the men as if trying to sort out relationships. "How many chambers will you need?"

"One for Magister Titus and one for Magister Serena and Leontia and myself to share," Kankou said imperiously, then paused. She studied Anwell and Bala through narrowed eyes, although by no other means did she express disapproval. After a moment she nodded to Titus, inviting his input.

He saw an opportunity to let Anwell and Bala know they had overstepped in their treatment of Serena without directly scolding them. "The rest will sleep in whatever accommodations you provide for those who attend us."

"Of course, Magister," said the innkeeper, all pleasantry as he ignored the shocked expressions of the young men when they realized they were being sent to sleep with the servants.

Kankou gave Titus a curt nod of approval, fortunately brief since he preferred to avoid her notice altogether. She turned to the innkeeper. "We will retire to our chambers now, if you will be so kind."

"My apologies, Maestra. Another group has just left unexpectedly, so it will take the housekeeper a short interval to make sure a proper set of rooms is readied for mages of your importance. If you will allow me, we have a private parlor where you may wait in comfort with food and drink. This way."

Another group has just left unexpectedly. Titus chewed over these words as he followed the innkeeper to the parlor. Had they arrived too late? Had a diviner snatched the prize out from under his nose again?

The parlor was appointed with couches and tables but it was not in fact private, if by private one meant for their party alone, as would have been appropriate to a magister of his standing traveling with a venerable maestra who was sister to a mansa. As Titus entered, he was appalled to see an expensively dressed man seated at one of the tables, sipping at a cup of tea with an expression of discontent. The man wore a starched boubou of an exemplary gray-blue color. The cloth rustled as he stood to acknowledge their entry.

"Peace to you, Magister," said the stranger. "Does the afternoon find you at peace?"

"I have peace, thanks to the mother who raised me. And you . . ." Titus hesitated. Sending out tendrils of magic he found himself in the presence of another cold mage, this one with the latticework aura of a diviner like himself, not just some mage House steward traveling about the business of his mansa. His worst fears founded! But he kept his voice level as he continued the polite greeting. "Does the afternoon find you at peace, Magister? And your mother and father and the people of your household, I hope they are at peace."

"There is no trouble. And your family also, may the Lord of All shower his mercy upon the world. I am Belenus Cissé, son of . . ."

He faltered, seeing the women as they crossed the threshold. His mouth, so round with pleasantries, turned shockingly flat and hard, and his eyes flared.

"Serena! I am thunderstruck that you have the audacity to show your face in public after what transpired. And yet why would it surprise me? The world already knows you as shameless!"

The hostility of the comment, baldly spoken without any softening allusion, took Titus aback. People halted in the entryway, whispering as they tried to catch a glimpse of the altercation. Anwell and Bala smirked as if they thought it the best joke of the trip to see the girl demeaned before witnesses. The innkeeper blanched as he looked from one mage to the other.

Kankou watched in stony silence. Of course she expected *him* to solve this, but the situation had burst so unexpectedly into his face that he was left struggling for words.

Into the silence left by his shock, Serena's voice lifted, mild and humble in the manner befitting women and yet not at all quailing. "If the monkey can't reach the fruit, he says it is rotten."

Titus turned to see Serena regarding the man with a countenance so serene that he struggled with delight at her composure and a little residual disgust that she remained so calm while he had not been up to the task of defending the honor of their House.

Her gaze shifted to him, and she blinked twice.

"Magister, Aunt Kankou and I will modestly retire to be about our business. I am sure you and the Cissé from Twelve Horns House will be busy about your drink and dinner for *some time*, as it is said, let a man not hurry about his supper or his conversation."

Of course Belenus Cissé was here on the same trail they were. But the man's grimace lacked any of the triumphant glory a diviner naturally felt when he had fished a freshly bloomed mage from the ocean of power. That meant he either hadn't found the pair yet or hadn't yet convinced them to bind their fortunes to Twelve Horns House. As much as it grated, Titus was the only one who could keep him busy while the others went looking.

"Yes, I will certainly take my fill," Titus agreed.

As soon as the door was shut to leave the two men alone, Belenus sat heavily, breathing hard.

"Are you . . . ?" He seemed unable to speak the next word, as if he feared Titus was Serena's new husband rather than her teacher.

As if any man would want that kind of trouble in his life! His marriage had foundered in indifference even before the death of their son had sundered their lives.

"I am the senior diviner of Autumn House. I am traveling with my three apprentices—Anwell, Bala, and the young woman." He made no mention of Kankou; if the man couldn't divine her exalted status as the mansa's sister and chief administrator of Autumn House, then that was his problem.

"Forgive my bluntness." The man gestured for Titus to join him at the table. "I was taken by surprise to meet her here, so far from either of our Houses."

"Indeed, it is far. I hope you have had a peaceful journey, Magister."

The other man opened his lips to reply but closed them when the innkeeper appeared with a fresh pot of tea and a tray of dates, sesame honey bars, and soft hot buns made of sweetened yam flour. In silence the innkeeper poured, lingering too long as if waiting for them to begin talking, and finally took away the cold teapot that had already been on the table. As soon as the door closed, the flood started.

"How can I have peace when I have been treated with such disrespect by that perfidious, ungrateful woman?"

"You are the husband? I did not know. I was traveling at the time."

"I asked for nothing that any man does not expect, an obedient, modest wife to bear me children and concern herself with my comfort. I see she has gotten her way."

"A woman's mind goes no farther than the tip of her breast."

"Quite true. Quite true. She was obedient enough when she came to me, and quite without any pretensions to divination. But then she began to speak of dreams and the touch of feathery petals on her face as if these ridiculous fantasies are the same as a man's clear vision of magic blooming."

"No man can understand a woman."

"Indeed. Indeed. Worst, the women of my House indulged her. Her pretty manners deceived them into thinking her honest and compliant when all along she was hiding the terrible truth."

"The hidden rot will soon break the branch."

Belenus was no longer listening. Like floodwaters, he would run until the rains of his grievance stopped pouring. "You know, you people are not a prestigious mage House. It was as good a marriage alliance as a girl like her could expect. But she thought she was too good for me when I am a respectable diviner, having made a name for myself by finding three powerful young mages in the city of Havery before anyone else discovered the children. There was something wrong with her all along. Dry soil will sprout no growth."

Titus winced, but the other man didn't notice. He just kept going.

"What use is a barren woman? A woman gives birth to a mage. She does not become one. Whatever she may say, and that isn't all that happened . . ."

Titus was already regretting being trapped at the table. Abruptly he realized Serena had known the man would spout endlessly in defense of his sour tale and tarnished pride. So he spoke a trite phrase of interest or query whenever the man paused long enough to draw breath. It was always enough to keep the man going.

The portrait painted of Serena was not a flattering one.

Outside the shadows grew long as the sun sank into the west.

The innkeeper appeared.

"Magister Titus, your chamber is ready. You may take supper as soon as you wish, or after dark, if that is more to your preference. We are fortunate in having a mage in town, a person with a humble gift, who comes at dusk to light cressets with cold fire for your convenience."

"You will join me for supper, of course," said Belenus.

"Of course," said Titus politely. "Let me wash off the dust of the journey."

"Yes, yes. In fact, I have some business to attend to before supper. I should have done it earlier, but then you came and have talked so much that I forgot my purpose here." He called for a servant and hurried out of the inn.

Titus considered hurrying after him, but Serena had had such a sense of surety about her that he decided to seek her out instead.

The innkeeper led him to the back part of the inn with its three corridors letting onto guest rooms: one passage for men, one for women, and one for families. As he glanced down the women's passage a door opened and Serena came out, wearing a different jacket than she'd had on earlier and with a freshly tied headwrap. She looked lovely and unflustered.

He halted in consternation as she walked up to him smiling that same serene smile which suddenly exasperated him.

"Did I endure that man's petulant grumbling merely to discover you have spent your time grooming yourself in your room?"

She looked at the innkeeper, then back at him, and said, "Perhaps, Uncle, you will accompany me to the temple. As a stranger in this town, I do not feel comfortable making my offering alone."

Titus was so astounded by this odd statement—all this time she had made only the ordinary offerings at altars within the inns in which they stayed—that the innkeeper beat him to a reply.

"Magister, please allow me to engage a guide to assist you in sight-seeing. May I particularly recommend the architecture of our temple dedicated to Jupiter Taranis, which is famous throughout the region for its surviving Roman portico and ingenious wheel design?"

Serena smiled, and smiled, and finally Titus remembered the way his son and littler daughters had used to signal to each other with silent smiles before they got up to mischief.

"My thanks, but we shall just take a family stroll," he said, falling in with her fiction about kinship.

The innkeeper withdrew.

She walked briskly to the back of the building and led him out through a delivery passageway that led past the inn's kitchen and stable-yard into an alley.

"We have them," she said in a low voice as he hastened to keep up, and something of the sweet nature of mischief entered his heart. His own pulse pounded harder with anticipation. A long time ago, watching his children about their lively frolics, he might even have laughed.

At the corner she glanced furtively both ways, then pressed a hand to his arm to stop him from stepping out onto the street. He peeked out past the corner of the inn to see Belenus Cissé flanked by a brace of servants and striding into the fading afternoon glow. She said nothing, nor did her expression give away her thoughts or indeed any tremor of dismay at having run into the man she had once called husband and afterward discarded.

"This way," she said.

Rather than running after the other diviner, she led him right across the street into a humble votive temple with a sagging gate. The temple's sad little courtyard was populated by two hens and a badger in a cage. A faded mural depicted a crowned woman riding a lion as she hurled a thunderbolt. A priestess wearing the crown of Celestial Juno waited on a cramped portico. The flame of the lamp by the door wavered and went out as the two mages approached.

She greeted Serena with a genuine smile that turned to a cautious stare as she greeted Titus. "Magister. May it be well with you under the crown of the holy queen of the heavens."

"This is my teacher and elder, as I told you," Serena reassured her. "Titus Kanté of Autumn House."

He and the priestess exchanged polite greetings, and afterward the priestess said, "In here, Magister."

Titus hadn't developed the powerful cold magic that characterized the great mages of the mage Houses in Europa. He hadn't the reach to kill an entire hearth's fire just by walking through the door, not as any mansa did. He could not paint illusions out of moisture in the air, nor had he ever shown enough strength to be allowed to learn the perilous secrets of forging cold steel. He could not kill the combustion of an entire factory just by walking past the steam engines that powered it.

Divination was a subtler form of the same magic, present only in a few. It was necessary to the survival of the mage Houses but despite that wasn't praised and lionized in the same way. Diviners did not rise to become mansa of their House.

But even he, subtle and small as his magic was, could quench a candle flame. Even he could pull a thread of cold fire out of the spirit world, form it into a ball, and use it to light his way. He was about to do so when he realized the chamber whose door the priestess blocked was already aglow with a chilly white light. Neither Anwell nor Bala had enough control to shape cold fire. Perhaps Serena did, and had hidden this ability from him all this time. For as much as he had disliked Belenus Cissé, some parts of the man's sordid tale had resonated with Titus in suggesting Serena was a secretive, calculating opportunist who wore her beautiful face as a mask to take advantage of innocent, well-meaning men.

The first thing he noticed about the chamber was its modest furnishings: a plain wooden table, two benches, and a sideboard laden with a pitcher and the sort of lopsided cups that a potter sells for cheap because they've been made by an apprentice. Kankou sat at the table beside an elderly priestess wrapped in shawls against the cold.

An exhausted-looking woman faced Kankou and the priestess. A toddler shivered on her lap. She had the white skin of Celtic ancestry, marked with early wrinkles, but it was the burn mark across the right side of her face that really stood out. Perhaps she had been pretty once; now it was all he could do not to wince at the unsightly scar, and that only because his mother had taught him better than to embarrass a person in public with such a reaction.

Behind her stood identical twin boys of perhaps thirteen years of age, a common age for magic to bloom. The sphere of cold fire hovered between them. Diviners could trace the threads of magic that wove through people, and to his fascination the sphere was attached to both of them, as if they had figured out together how to create it. As if it arose from them working together.

A sullen youth leaned against the wall, arms crossed, a threadbare coat pulled tightly around his shoulders. He resembled the twins and, like all the children, had brown skin and curly black hair. Boys this age always reminded Titus of his son, except that his son had never frowned; he hadn't been made for frowns.

As Titus entered, Kankou rose. The exhausted woman rose. Even the sullen youth pushed away from the wall to stand. Only the priestess remained seated with the privilege of age, one age-palsied hand grasping a cane.

He greeted the elderly priestess first, as was fitting in a holy temple.

"Maestra Selva," said Kankou to the mother, "this is Magister Titus Kanté, of whom I have spoken."

"Magister," the woman said before lapsing into the silence of the overwhelmed.

The toddler struggled in her arms, starting to whimper, and the sullen youth slouched over to take the child from her, thank goodness.

He opened his hands. "My greetings to you, Maestra. To have twins who bloom at the same time, and work together as these two do, is a rare thing."

The twins glanced at each other with shared surprise.

"I told you he would divine your connection," said Serena warmly, and they smiled at her as if they already trusted her. Belenus had talked about her wily ways, how she had turned the women of Twelve Horns House against him.

"Such a gift is a rare thing," agreed Kankou, "which is why, Magister, we will be taking Maestra Selva and her four children to become dependents of Autumn House."

Softhearted, impractical women!

"It is not our usual arrangement," he said, trying to figure out a way to disagree with Kankou without saying so outright, in front of others,

which would cause him no end of trouble now and later once they returned to the house. "I too began life outside a mage House. I was discovered by a diviner from Autumn House, where I now reside. My
people were given a generous compensation in exchange for my leaving
home to join the House. I did not bring my family with me."

In a burst of Celtic emotion, the woman rushed out from behind the
table to grasp his hands in a shockingly familiar manner. Hers had the
thick calluses of a person who has worked at rough labor. "That is why
I'm here. When the other diviners came to the clan's gate this week they
offered compensation to the head of the household for my children. But
I won't let them be handed away! They and their brothers are all I have
left of my beloved husband."

She sobbed. The older son hunched his shoulders. The twins clasped
hands, and the globe of cold fire brightened in a most astonishing way
that made Titus forget about everything except the chance of watching
such a rare conjoined magic grow and flourish.

"Maestra Selva is a widow," Kankou explained, and since Kankou
was herself a widow, Titus felt there was nothing more that needed to
be said.

But of course people always had to say more, telling him stories he
didn't care to hear or droning on about the grief he must feel when he
just wanted people to leave him alone.

"My people are miners, the least of folk, hauling rocks out of the
mines," said Selva. Her speech had the untutored and unwashed accent
of country people. "I fell in love with the young blacksmith who had
been brought in to our local forge. My family washed their hands of me,
saying I ought not to set my sights above my place in life. When my
husband took me back to his clan, his people scorned me for my labor-
er's hands and low birth. Of course blacksmith clans marry among
themselves. I never asked to fall in love with him and aim so high. It just
happened. My husband did not reject me despite their disapproval. He
protected us when he was alive. But after the accident—"

She touched the burn scar on her face. The twins stared at the floor.
The sullen youth pressed a kiss to the head of the toddler with a gentle
affection that tugged at Titus's heart.

". . . after that, his family have treated us as little better than servants.

Now they plan to enrich the household treasure with the compensation they will receive for children I gave birth to!"

"It would be best for everyone if Maestra Selva and her children join Autumn House," said Kankou in a tone he knew better than to argue with. "The twins will feel more comfortable if their mother is with them and they know she is safe."

"But—"

"Her elder boy has great promise as a musician. He makes the djembe speak."

The sullen youth's gaze flicked up, and his slumped back straightened to a performer's swagger as Serena smiled encouragingly at him.

Kankou went on. "Blacksmith clans have been handling nyama for longer than cold mages have existed, as we both know."

"Fire mages!" he said scornfully. "Quick to burn out, dangerous to all around them."

"And yet here a blacksmith and his country wife have sired two budding cold mages."

"Maestra Kankou and dear Serena have treated me as a sister and offered us a home," said Selva. "Please do not cast me aside, Magister. My husband's people tried to send me home, but my family doesn't want me back and I can't leave my children. They're all I have."

So be it, Titus thought. Let the women sort out the strain of extra mouths to feed and bodies to clothe; that was their prerogative and responsibility in the House. It would be a triumph to bring home these twins and present them to the mansa, who had anyway an elder brother's favoritism toward his younger sister Kankou, for they shared the same mother of blessed memory.

"It will be well," he said. After a moment's consideration he added a nod for Serena. "It was well done, Serena."

Serena flushed, pressing a hand to her chest as she swallowed and murmured, "You honor me, Magister. It is all due to your generously agreeing to teach me."

Kankou's stern expression softened. "I will arrange for a second carriage to convey the family. Selva and her children will be staying with us in the inn tonight."

He only then noticed how shabbily Selva and her children were dressed, their clothes much mended and made of coarse wool rather than the fine damask one would expect of a prosperous blacksmith clan. The older boy wore the trousers and jacket of the working class rather than the proper robes that any respectable young fellow would wear when not at work. They didn't even have a trunk for their possessions, only a single tattered bag and an old but well-cared-for drum. The toddler clutched a cloth doll missing one of its button eyes. Poor relations, indeed. No wonder the woman wanted to escape.

"The only question, Titus," Kankou went on, "is whether you wish to continue to travel for a few more days, seeing that Imbolc falls tomorrow."

The four cross quarter days were always the most fruitful time for magic to bloom in a person because the veil between the mortal world and the spirit world pulled thinnest on those days. Of course no mage rode abroad on Hallow's Eve, the most dangerous time of year, but Titus and other diviners usually made their tours around Imbolc, Beltane, and Lughnasad. Too often he came home empty-handed: mages were rare, and even when he found one, richer Houses could offer better compensation.

But not today.

"I think we may all safely return together knowing we have done our best for Autumn House," he said. And that was that.

He arranged for a tray to be brought to his chamber so he could eat without encountering Belenus Cissé. But late that night he was woken by a hammering on his door. When he opened it, Cissé shouted drunken obscenities at him and punched him in the nose so hard that blood flowed. Only the prompt intervention of his manservant Orosios prevented the man from beating him with a stick. Cissé was escorted away, his curses ending in a predictable bout of loud vomiting and querulous whining.

The horrified innkeeper arrived with fulsome apologies.

The pain wasn't so bad—Titus had suffered worse as a youth prone to fistfights—but he accepted a compress soaked in witch hazel and retired to gloat in his victory. His nose was bruised and swollen, but the ache gave him perspective. It reminded him that the mansa would be pleased, and he, Titus Kanté, would be feted and praised by the other men.

So it was that the next day they once more approached the ferry across the Rhenus River. Their two carriages advanced along the main street through the town that had grown up around the ferry, with inns, food stalls, a wheelwright, and a tailor, and a forge set far enough away from the approach that passing cold mages would not quench its furnaces.

The ferrymaster escorted them past the rest of the line to a place at the front where they waited for the ferry to return from the far shore. This time when Titus closed his eyes, he allowed himself to recall one particular twilight afternoon when he and his son had been playing chess in the fountain garden, tiny Cassia dozing on his lap and Fabia leaning on her older brother's shoulder and singing some childish melody. The boy had gotten up to light a lamp at the far corner of the garden—too far away for Titus to quench it by proximity—but it wouldn't light; the lad couldn't make a flame. He had bloomed, just as Titus—and everyone else in Autumn House—had hoped.

What a moment that had been. But it wasn't the magic Titus recalled. It was the way his son had made a celebration of everything, however small or large, by including everyone around him.

Bestirred by a melancholy wisdom, and mindful of Serena's tactful praise of his teaching, he addressed Anwell and Bala. The young men were sitting on the facing bench wearing identical churlish frowns.

"Patience is also a lesson. As it is said, the flowering tree will bear fruit."

The surly set of their lips suggested stubborn natures that did not want to learn. Maybe he wasn't the right teacher for them. They might do better being married out to another mage House.

"Perhaps there is something you wish to say to me," he said, stricken by an inexplicable desire to hear their opinions. "We are the three of us men, alone in this carriage for the first time on this journey. You may speak freely."

They glanced at each other.

At length, Bala muttered, "Magister, you favor her because of her beautiful face."

The accusation irritated him, but he kept his voice even. "Manners and modesty are a woman's beauty. Furthermore, it is due to her vigilance that we found the twins, when the three of us would have gone on. Can you say otherwise?"

"One deed doesn't build a name," murmured Anwell peevishly.

Titus said nothing, sensing the two young men were about to break and spill. The silence stretched out, leavened by the sound of the river streaming past and the creak of wagons and cracks of laughter among people waiting for the ferry. He'd learned as a child that by holding his tongue he could remain impervious while others spoke. In this way he was able to enjoy his own thoughts as chatter flowed around him. But sometimes, as now, he was required to listen, however annoying the words were bound to be.

"She's proud," Bala spat out. "You forget we sat in the schoolroom with her. She ignored us, thought she was too good for the likes of us, even though she had no magic. Everyone seems to forget she didn't bloom until she went away to marry."

"Yes, and what happened there?" Anwell added. "The husband she discarded was certainly angry about it, as we saw. She was happy at first to marry into a better house than ours, wasn't she? And then she was too good for him after her magic bloomed and so she came back to us instead, didn't she? We're just warning you, Magister. She'll walk over your body to a higher branch if you're not careful."

"She didn't even get pregnant," added Bala unkindly.

Titus opened his mouth, although whether to remonstrate or agree he was not sure.

A nearby shout startled him. The reverberation of the voice had scarcely died away when it was followed by a hammering on the side of their carriage that shook the entire vehicle.

"Open up! Coachman, open this door!"

The door was flung open from the outside to reveal Morcant. The coachman's sun-reddened face was further flushed by a grimace of anxiety.

"Magister—" he began, before being rudely shoved to one side by an armed man wearing a tabard marked with the oak tree of Venta Erkunos, the town they had so recently left.

"I am a magister of Autumn House," said Titus, staring down the armed man, who was after all merely a retainer who served a local prince. "Why do you trouble me with this disturbance?"

The armed man stepped away to reveal a constable whose cap bore the oak sigil as well.

The constable spoke. "I seek a woman named Selva, who has stolen four children who belong to the Camara clan of Venta Erkunos."

Camara was a common name for blacksmiths. This charge was so serious that Titus gestured to Morcant to set down the steps. He descended as into the face of a storm. For there, at a prudent remove, stood a pair of blacksmiths and a vigorous old woman whose hands bore the calluses of a master potter. The sting of their fire magic pressed against his reservoir of cold as a wash of barely contained heat.

Titus had come from a family of respectable farmers for whom proper manners and public constraint was how one behaved. As a boy, he had both marveled at and been a little afraid of the flamboyant behavior of the local blacksmith, who made a performance of the work he did, singing as he worked or commenting upon the flight of birds. Everyone feared the destructive power of fire, but the young Titus had admired how the blacksmith wielded power without the least appearance of apprehension. Fire mages always lived a breath of control away from dying in flames. Maestra Selva's dead husband and the burn scar on her face were proof of that.

Of course people bored with waiting in line for the ferry had gathered to stare at the members of a blacksmith clan confronting a mage House's carriage. But they all kept their distance.

The presence of the constable meant no one exchanged a proper greeting. This was a matter of law, so it was the constable who spoke.

"Four Moons House has already given compensation to the Camara clan for the reception of two children, identified as cold mages, into the household of Four Moons House. I have been called into service by three elders of the Camara clan, including the mother of the children's father. Do you deny you have the children with you?"

Titus prized his honesty, but a wily thought teased him now: what if he let them look inside his carriage and see only Anwell and Bala? What if they could get away with the twins by pretending the second carriage wasn't theirs?

He could not stomach the lie.

He tried a different argument. "Has the children's mother no say in this transaction? Was her permission obtained?"

The elder blacksmith replied in the reasonable tone of a calm soul who prefers to work things out.

"You ask the question the wrong way around, Magister. Our son's children may not be stolen from his family without *our* permission. We did not give it. The woman has no legal status to act on behalf of underage children who are residents of my household. We negotiated with Four Moons House before you arrived."

A sudden wailing, like that of grief, broke out from the other carriage. Its door opened, and Kankou descended with her usual imperturbable dignity. The constable took a step back out of respect as she crossed to stand beside Titus. Even the blacksmiths acknowledged her arrival, as a worthy elder and distinguished woman.

In a low voice she said to Titus, "We cannot make an enemy of the mansa of Four Moons House. He can destroy Autumn House if we anger him."

"I thought the matter was taken care of and all negotiations proper and closed," he said in as even a tone as he could manage. All the attention focused on him by so many strangers roused in him an enraged sense of humiliation. "I had no idea there was a prior claim beyond the attempts of Belenus Cissé. If I had known . . ."

Hearing his voice start to rise, he closed his mouth.

"I confess I have erred." Kankou spoke as if the stares and devastating blunder did not trouble her at all! "Maestra Selva misrepresented her situation. Serena's kind heart did the rest."

Of course this trouble was the fault of the young woman! He had known all along it would be a mistake to bring her. And yet even still Kankou—and thus by extension the mansa of Autumn House—defended the girl!

The sobbing Selva was helped out of the second carriage by her elder son. She swooned when she saw the elders.

"I will accompany the twins to Four Moons House myself," the potter said. "The other two will return home with my brother. As for you, Selva, you may take yourself off as you so clearly wish to do, if these mages will have you, which I doubt. For you have proven yourself disloyal on top of everything else."

The youth dropped to his knees, a hand pressed to his heart. "Please, Mamamuso, do not send our mother away from us, her children."

The elder blacksmith said, magnanimously, "Selva may return to the household. She is still nursing the baby, after all."

To which the potter replied, "But we will have no more of this foolery from the likes of you, Selva." She herded the stricken twins to a waiting carriage.

The toddler was taken by the elder blacksmith—held tenderly, Titus was relieved to see—and Selva roused enough to stagger after the baby, leaving her elder son to carry the worn bag and the precious drum. Thus were they enfolded back into her deceased husband's clan.

The blacksmiths took their leave in the most rude manner imaginable, as if Titus and his people were nothing more than common folk who could be passed on the roadside without a glance or greeting. It was getting dark, and as if in direct insult, they lit torches that Titus's frail cold magic wasn't strong enough to quench. He wished his anger could douse every hearth fire in the ferry crossing.

"It's so sad," whispered Serena to Kankou. "She was desperate to escape. They haven't been kind to her."

"Sentimental women!" Titus muttered.

A man trotted up, wearing the chain of the ferryman's assistant. "Magister, my apologies, but the ferry has halted for the day. There will be no crossing on Imbolc, so you'll have to take the first crossing in the morning of the day after tomorrow."

A headache of pure thwarted rage assaulted Titus, causing stars to burst in his eyes. His manservant Orosios hurried over to him, aware of the signs, and soon Titus sat in a comfortable chair in the parlor of an inn, sipping at a tisane of feverfew. A bowl of hot water scented with drops of lavender oil sat at his elbow so he could inhale its soothing properties.

He had hoped that the women would show him enough respect to allow him the parlor to himself. But although Kankou had banished Anwell and Bala, she and Serena sat side by side on a couch, chatting companionably, as if Serena's rash decision hadn't brought disaster down upon *his* reputation. Kankou carried a bag of beads with her, and she was threading a bracelet as Serena embroidered the neckline of a shirt.

"What should I have done differently, Aunt?" Serena's voice never trembled or wept. She was simply too self-possessed for him to believe in her naïve protestations. "Her tale reminded me in some parts of my own."

"It is a hard thing," agreed Kankou. "I do not like to leave women in such situations, nor should we ever turn our backs if we can do something. But I fear it was a misstep. Your kind heart overwhelmed my prudence. Although I do not blame you for it, after what you went through."

"Will Four Moons House seek revenge on us, if the blacksmiths tell them what happened?" the girl asked. "Might they come here to accuse us or charge us with a crime? I studied the maps carefully before we left, and many of the villages south and west of this crossing owe clientage to Four Moons House."

"That is true," replied Kankou. "Their main estate is not so far from here, not that we of Autumn House have ever been invited to visit such a grand establishment."

"Could we send a letter to their mansa with our regrets for causing an incident?"

"No, indeed, we could not!" Titus interposed, setting down his cup. "A man of his status, reputation, and power could ruin us with a few words. It's better if we not remind him or anyone at Four Moons House of this debacle."

"As I was about to say," Kankou continued with a stark glance whose disapproval caused him to close his hands into fists, "we are beneath the notice of such a princely mage House. I doubt the blacksmiths will mention the matter to them because this little misadventure reflects poorly on them as well. That their precious son fell in love with an uneducated rock hauler's daughter, for one, and that she outwitted them enough to almost escape. Imagine if they had to tell the mansa of Four Moons House that they had lost their own children and didn't know where they had gone."

She chuckled. A smile chased across Serena's face.

Titus decided he was not after all hungry enough to eat supper with women who could find humor in a man's dishonor, so he went to bed and suffered through a dream-plagued night.

He came downstairs the next morning feeling slightly better, only to find Serena and Kankou in the parlor before him.

"May I pour you tea, Uncle?" Serena said. "I am sorry for what happened. I have ordered the porridge that you like for breakfast."

Women's smiles did soften a man, especially a man who was both hungry and thirsty. A server arrived just then with bowls of steaming hot rice-and-millet porridge covered in milk and garnished with crushed peanuts and sugar. His headache had vanished, although the throb of anger remained, but he could wait to discuss the whole sorry episode until they returned home and brought the matter before their mansa. Anwell and Bala hurried in and sat down to eat.

That's when it happened. A force slammed into him. He was buffeted by a magical storm like pounding hail brought down atop alarming gusts of wind. The deluge deafened and blinded him for several breaths, then cut off so abruptly that the first thing he wondered was if he had been taken by apoplexy.

Slowly he realized the normal sounds of life—the rumble of wagons on the road, a barking dog at the inn gate, and footsteps along the corridor—went on as usual. Except for a cry from the furnace room at the far corner of the inn that heated the hypocaust system.

"The fire has gone out!"

"What was that?" asked Bala, looking both startled and delighted.

Anwell said daringly, "Was that a bloom? I felt it!"

"That was surely too powerful to be the first bloom of a budding mage," retorted Bala, giving Serena an accusatory look. "I hope some powerful cold mage hasn't come to punish us."

Serena looked at Titus. "What do you think, Magister? It was so strong, I'm not sure where it came from. It feels as if it came from everywhere."

He sent his divination along the path of its residue, a trail that led back through the town and out into the countryside amid the sparks and tendrils of animals and plants. "The residue is fading fast but is still visible to my divining eye. It leads into the countryside."

Kankou frowned. "As Serena mentioned last night, some of the villages hereabouts live in clientage to Four Moons House and thus would be beholden to a master too powerful for us to gainsay. Under the circumstances perhaps it is wisest simply to move on."

Serena stood with head tilted as if she was listening to the invisible threads of nyama. "The bloom was very strong, Aunt."

"It was," Titus agreed. Now that the stunning assault had waned, he could measure how startling it truly was. The chance to redeem this terrible journey made him bold, and reckless. Yet he chose his words carefully. "Surely there can be no harm if Serena and I investigate such an astonishing incident. It would be a shame merely to travel on as if nothing had happened."

Kankou nodded with understanding. "You are correct, Titus. You and Serena should go. I am too old for a breakneck journey across rough paths, so I will stay here with Anwell and Bala to look after me."

The young men's expressions became almost comically outraged, but of course they could not protest what Kankou decreed.

She went on without acknowledging their distress. "Morcant will drive you. Take your manservant in case you run into any trouble. He's got a strong arm. Leontia will act as Serena's chaperone." A sly smile peeped out, suggesting all the mysteries of the women's wing to which men had only limited access. "She has a strong arm too."

Soon the five of them were trundling south on a rutted wagon track. Titus's manservant sat on the bench with Morcant, and the two women were seated inside facing Titus. Serena sat braced on the bench, seeming about to break into speech each time they were jostled and jarred. Each time the girl opened her mouth Leontia would press a gloved hand to the young woman's skirt, right at her knee, some woman's communication that men were not meant to fathom.

A particularly hard jolt broke Serena's resolve.

"Did Belenus Cissé tell you his story to try to make you dislike me?" she asked so bluntly that Titus was appalled.

"Men will speak when women are not present," he said repressively.

"Serena, do not taste the sauce when it is still boiling," said Leontia warningly, although in a far more lenient voice than he would have used.

The girl sat back with a tense mouth and a proud lift of her chin.

In this uncomfortable silence they went on for some time. Finally the carriage halted. Morcant opened the door onto a landscape of broken woodland.

"Magister, we can go no farther. One of the horses can be ridden, if it pleases you."

"We'll walk. It's not far."

He and Serena set out.

"I smell smoke, and pine!" Serena said, inhaling enthusiastically as her earlier indignation seemed to slough off. She had a healthy stride and a vigorous appreciation of the country air.

"Find the tendrils of magic, which you should still be able to sense. Follow them as you follow the trail of smoke."

He hung back, letting her take the lead, and only gestured in the correct direction when she hesitated. As they trudged through the winter-whitened grasses, he realized that both magic and smoke led toward the same place: a hollow marked by the presence of a holy oak tree. Beneath its mighty branches two men tended a campfire. The firepit held ash and charred logs as if it had been burning all night and gone out recently. The eldest of the men was attempting to nurse a flame with new kindling, without any luck.

A deer whose internal organs had been removed was hanging from one of the branches. Beyond the canopy another four men were field dressing two more deer. These were country men, dressed in wool tunics hung with charms and painted with the symbols used by hunters to protect themselves in the wild.

Serena reached out and grasped Titus's hand, squeezing so tightly he would have protested if this simple expression of trust and kinship had not shocked him into silence.

"Look," she whispered, pointing toward the hanging deer with her chin. "Magister, at first I mistook it for a tundra antelope, but it has a third horn. That is no creature of mortal earth, is it?"

He pulled out of her grip and walked forward to see better. The two deer having their organs removed appeared in all ways to be ordinary animals. But the other animal's third horn was knit out of the silvery glamour of magic.

The hunters straightened up from their task. The eldest gestured to the others to stay where they were and came forward to greet them. He wore his hair in many braids, each end tied off with a tiny amulet. His weathered face was enlivened by a steady gaze. Of all people, hunters had the least to fear from mages. People had hunted in the interstices between the mortal and spirit worlds long before cold mages had learned to pull tendrils of cold magic out of the spirit world and use them for their own ends in the mortal world.

"Peace to you, Magister," the man said. "Does the day find you at peace?"

As Titus greeted him in the same manner, Serena took several steps to the right, surveying the land beyond the oak's canopy. The hunters watched her with respect and did not move.

"Magister, look there," she said, her tone so sharply edged that it grabbed his attention instantly.

On the opposite side of the tree from the fire, beyond the oak's canopy, a youth was standing with a knife in one hand and in the other a dead grouse dangling from a leather cord. He had turned to stare at them, a bold lad indeed.

Titus's first thought was at how fickle girls were: the youth was unusually good-looking, with an almost uncanny perfection of features. He looked a few years younger than Serena, perhaps sixteen, no longer a boy but not quite yet a man. In a few years' time women—and men who were inclined that way—would no doubt be beating a path to his door. How shallow of Serena to have noticed a handsome face while ignoring the others.

Then he thought of his own son, who had been this age when he'd died, and the shadow cut straight through his heart.

Serena tilted her head to one side and blinked twice. At first he thought she mocked his grief, but she was just signaling.

The elder hunter had ceased speaking. None of the party looked toward the lad. It was as if they were pretending the boy didn't exist in the hope Titus and Serena would not see him. Maybe they hadn't felt the magic, or perhaps they feared what would happen next.

Titus let his awareness reach the boy. To his surprise he hit what in the mortal world would have felt like a pane of glass. The bloom of magic had exploded outward and then retreated hard, pulled as into a shell. Seeing that they were looking, the youth at once fixed his gaze on the grouse although nothing about the set of his shoulders made him seem the humble villager he surely was.

"Who is that boy?" Titus asked, loud enough that his voice carried beneath the cold weight of the afternoon's cloudless sky.

"He is just a boy," said the elder.

"We are diviners. We sensed a bloom of cold magic."

The lad took several steps farther away from the fire. At once a wavering flame caught its courage and licked up a dry stick of kindling.

"Our fire did go out at a gust of wind," said the elder, "but as you see, Magister, it is burning. There is nothing here for you."

Serena caught Titus's eye and shook her head. "The boy is a cold mage," she said softly. "I think he knows but does not want to know, and thus is desperately trying to build a shield around himself. You feel that shield too, do you not?"

Titus thought of the intangible surface like an invisible pane of glass. "I do. It's highly unusual for an untrained mage to be able to instinctively construct such a barrier."

The elder nodded to his companions, and they went back to work, all except for the lad, who continued to watch.

"We are villagers in clientage to Four Moons House, Magister," said the elder. "Out hunting for meat to feed our families through the end of winter scarcity. That is all."

"That is not all," said Titus, disliking the man's evasiveness. "The bloom of a new cold mage may surge and ebb over several days or weeks or even months when it first flowers. And today is Imbolc, an auspicious time for magecraft and the first hint of spring."

Serena was still looking toward the youth. She said in a clear, warm tone, directing her words toward the lad. "A cold mage has the right to choose their own path. Even if those around them tell them they must obey."

"Furthermore," added Titus, "I am within my rights to make an offer to the boy's clan by virtue of having reached him first."

The boy said, "I'm a hunter. That's all. Whatever else you might think isn't about me."

"Enough, Andevai," said the elder. He again addressed Titus. "As I said, there is nothing for you here, Magister. Please—"

He broke off. They all heard the sound of riders. The hunters set down their knives as six horsemen emerged from the trees. Serena retreated to stand beside Titus. She self-consciously straightened her headwrap before clasping her hands at her waist with womanly modesty.

Four of the men were soldiers who wore indigo tabards. Titus himself never traveled with soldiers. He trusted in his status as a diviner to protect him, and anyway Autumn House could not afford the expense. But when he turned his attention to the other two arrivals, expecting to see diviners like himself come to compete over the lad, he realized his mistake. Only then did he notice the markings on the soldiers' tabards: they wore House livery with four moons: crescent, quarter, gibbous, and full.

"Serena," he said softly, in warning, but it was too late. The danger had crashed down on top of them.

The tall, heavily built man who dismounted from a big bay gelding was no diviner. A few years younger than Titus, he was a man in the full power of his maturity, and an intense aura of magic radiated from him— not visually, of course, but perfectly tangible to any diviner. He wore a knee-length jacket of indigo of the finest cut and cloth, a garment the mansa of Autumn House could never afford and certainly not as casual wear for an afternoon ride. His face was as black as Titus's own, although this man had coarse, tightly curled dark red hair, a reminder that the ancestors of the mage Houses came from both the Afric south and the Celtic north.

That he was accompanied by an elderly djeli—what those of Celtic ancestry might call a bard—affirmed his identity. This intimidating personage could be none other than the feared and formidable mansa of Four Moons House, a man to whom princes gave way. When the budding fire went out as if sucked clean away, the potency of his cold magic was confirmed.

The mansa's gaze swept the scene. He paused on Serena with a widening of eyes that then narrowed appreciatively, but politely looked away to continue his scrutiny of the hunters. By the way his gaze skimmed disinterestedly over the lad standing out in the grass Titus could tell the mansa was no diviner and had not identified the boy as the source of the bloom. This prize might be salvaged yet just by keeping his mouth shut and his demeanor cool.

"Mansa," said the elder hunter, going down on one knee beside the dead fire.

"We are looking for a freshly bloomed cold mage. Have you any knowledge of it?"

The elder shook his head. "I am a hunter, mansa, and a farmer, and a council member of your village of Haranwy. Mage matters lie not within my purview."

Meanwhile, the djeli had walked over to the animal hanging from the tree and was examining the creature with the greatest interest. Like mages and hunters, a djeli could see what was invisible to the eyes of those who had no direct access to nyama, but he was not a diviner and might overlook the boy.

"Who are these people?" the mansa asked the hunter, indicating Titus and Serena.

"Mansa, I am Titus Kanté, of Autumn House."

"I don't know the name. One of the lesser Houses, I assume."

"We are among the least," agreed Titus, not without a sardonic twist to his tone.

Serena's lips quivered, and she offered Titus an appreciative side-eye and a tiny nod of support.

The mansa saw her do it, and he made a slight grunt like a repressed chuckle.

"Our estate lies near the city of Anvers," Titus added with more tartness than he intended. Serena touched her elbow to his arm to remind him of her presence. "Ah! And this is my apprentice, Magister Serena."

Mage House women did not bow to men—it was beneath their dignity—but she spoke in her warm voice. "Your Excellency, we are a small House with a proud lineage descended from the Empire of Mali, just like you."

"A remarkable assertion," said the mansa in the defensively amused tone middle-aged men often used when faced with a young woman who carried both beauty and intelligence with confidence. "But it is true that in some manner we mages are all cousins. To that end, I would invite you—" Now he was careful to address Titus. "—to join me for supper. We have a special meal in honor of Imbolc."

Titus hesitated. He wanted the mansa to leave. Yet such an invitation from one of the most prestigious and powerful mage Houses in Europa was an opportunity that his own mansa of Autumn House would tell him to accept. He had to balance the chance to snap up the boy against the incredible favor being shown to him, a connection that might be nurtured in the future.

So far the day had remained clear and bright, with not too much wind, but now a breeze stirred and brought with it a swirl of snowflakes as clouds moved in. Or maybe the sudden rise of wind came from the mansa, for the most powerful cold mages could draw down cold fronts and even shift the air in the heavens to daunt those who thought to challenge them.

"As well, it is wiser to avoid travel on Imbolc, a day on which the weather is notoriously changeable," the mansa added with a heavenward glance as a cloud skimmed over the sun. Titus could not help but wonder if the man was altering the weather to suit his own purposes. "With that in mind, I invite you to spend the night at Four Moons House, which lies nearby. It grows dark early. If you are lodging at the ferry crossing you may find it difficult to return there by nightfall. I must assume you find yourself here on the same errand I am on myself."

"We stopped here to ask directions," Titus said. "But if I may speak so boldly, Your Excellency, I admit I am surprised to see you, since you are no diviner."

"Our diviner is traveling elsewhere. Even we who are not diviners felt that wash of magic. It is gone now."

"A curious incident," said the djeli, stepping back from the animal. "But it may be explained by this creature. Some villagers are known to retain the secrets of hunting in the spirit world on the cross quarter days when the veil between the worlds grows thin. It may be that some magic leaked out of the spirit world when they returned."

"Could that be?" the mansa asked the elder hunter.

"The secret is not mine to share," said the hunter in answer.

The mansa accepted this statement without argument. Mages held that certain aspects of magecraft were too dangerous and potent to be revealed to those who were not mages, so they could scarcely demand answers from hunters, who had their own private knowledge.

"Aunt Kankou will never forgive us if we don't take the mansa up on this astounding invitation," Serena whispered in Titus's ear. "The boy will go home. Notice how neatly his village elder revealed the village's name in our hearing. He intended that information for us. We can find the boy later."

So it was that the mansa gave his horse into the care of his soldiers and graciously accompanied them in the carriage. He treated Leontia with careful respect, and for her part the usually easygoing woman was too daunted by his presence to speak a word.

But like all great princes, the mansa had an ease of manner that encouraged Titus to converse while never becoming too familiar. He asked about the history of Autumn House and how it was established in the city of Anvers. Titus gave rote answers, not wanting to reveal too much of the household's dismaying situation. Truth to tell, he was also fretting over the village boy, his chance to snatch a victory out of the defeat he'd suffered in losing the twins. It was Serena who quietly held the day with a series of charming anecdotes dating from the time of her great grandparents.

"—and when my great grandmother challenged the prince's bard to a duel of wits, it turned out his blade was not as sharp as his boasts implied. After that, the prince dismissed the bard and married my great grandmother, who as I have mentioned was by that time a widow and free to marry as she pleased. A number of her relatives left Five Mirrors House in Lutetia and joined her in Anvers. There they formed their own small but independent House."

"Ah, so your people are descended from Five Mirrors House," said the mansa.

"For some, that prestigious connection will be seen as Autumn House's chief claim."

"But not for you?" he asked with a bit too teasing a smile for Titus's liking.

"A wise woman knows her own mind."

"And a wise man listens," the mansa replied.

Her gaze flashed to meet his, and for an instant Titus was sure it was the powerful mansa who blushed, not the calm young woman.

"I respect my great grandmother for choosing the more difficult path," said Serena. "But tell me, Your Excellency, I was surprised to hear you refer to a single diviner. Has Four Moons House only the one?"

He shifted on the bench beside Titus as if the question made him uneasy, not that Titus could imagine anything making a man of his stature uneasy. But evidently Serena's presence made the man loquacious. "It is an odd happenstance that Four Moons House has produced so few diviners in recent generations that my sister is the only one left to us. My aunt arranged my second marriage because the woman was a diviner, but alas she has left the mortal world."

Titus murmured the proper sentiments and condolences.

After echoing them, Serena asked, "And your first wife? She is not a diviner?"

"No, she is a daughter of Two Shells House."

"Oh!" said Serena, looking ingeniously impressed, and indeed to be allied with one of the two first mage Houses settled in Europa was impressive. "They are in Gadir."

"Yes. She is not herself a mage but she is the daughter of mages. My grandmother of blessed memory arranged the matter when I was eighteen. At that time my great uncle was mansa, and it was by no means yet determined that I would become mansa after him."

"The strength of a mage House rests on the heads of its elders and the legs of its children," said Titus, because Serena was certainly speaking too much.

"That is true," agreed the mansa without looking away from Serena. "Two Shells House certainly has produced potent cold mages in its time, but my grandmother arranged the match for the trade opportunities it provided us. In fact, my first wife is fruitfully engaged in commerce. She travels frequently and lives most of the year in Gadir among her own people."

Serena glanced at Titus and blinked twice, as she had done before, a signal that meant "trust me." More fool he was, to ever have trusted her.

For her perfidious nature slithered into view at that very moment, as her beautiful lips parted to reveal the full foul deception of her nature.

"So, Your Excellency, your House's lack of diviners explains why you did not notice the bloom among the hunters."

Under any other circumstances the mansa's startlement would have been amusing. He was not a man to be easily surprised or overset. "What bloom?"

"The youth standing out in the grass. A handsome boy. He held a grouse as if he'd been sent out there to clean it, but in truth he was staying as far away from the fire as possible."

"But the fire was burning when we arrived," objected the mansa.

Titus felt his mouth working soundlessly, and it took all his will to clamp down his lips over the curse he wanted to throw at her for betraying her own House in this unfathomable and unforgivable manner.

"As Magister Titus has so wisely taught me, the bloom of a new cold mage may surge and ebb over several days or weeks or even months when it first flowers," she said with that same limpid gaze that apparently really did conceal a rotten heart. "But I will tell you this, Your Excellency. My divining tells me he will be a powerful cold mage, more powerful than any of us may even understand."

"He's a village boy," the mansa scoffed. "His people live in clientage to my house. They are little better than slaves. People with such a low ancestry may learn to create cold fire to light rooms but they do not become potent cold mages."

Even in the face of the mansa's disbelief Serena did not change expression. "You will see that I am right."

"Will I?" he said, and it was impossible not to hear the flirtatious tone animating the words.

Titus fumed, but he could say nothing, although he wanted to.

The wheels of the carriage hit gravel, and the mansa added, "We have reached Four Moons House. Please, be welcome."

The mansa himself helped first Leontia and then Serena down the steps, his hand lingering too long on Serena's gloved fingers. Another carriage sat by the portico steps, attended by constables wearing the oak sigil of Venta Erkunos. In the grand entryway two thin children sat huddled on a stone bench off to one side, waiting opposite the closed door of what was likely a formal audience hall; Titus heard voices from behind the door where people were having some sort of conference. Seeing Serena, the twins leaped up and rushed over to her as if she were their long-lost cousin.

"Magister Serena!"

She allowed them to hug her, for it was clear they were distraught.

"Who are these?" the mansa demanded, eyeing their rough clothing with distaste.

"They are two fine young cold mages, freshly bloomed, and unique in their ability to twine their magic together," said Serena, giving each child a pat on the head.

"And how do they know you, Magister?" he asked her.

"With your permission, Your Excellency, I shall tell you the tale over supper."

"I anticipate the story with the greatest delight," said the mansa.

A stately woman descended to greet him, and Titus was disgusted to see that Serena quickly won over this dignified elder as well. Had the girl no shame at all as she charmed her way into their hospitality?

After they had washed up, he tried to pull her aside, but she merely said, in the most high-handed way possible, "Uncle, please trust me."

"How can I trust you? You gave up the secret of the boy, our best hope! And for what?"

He broke off as the realization hit him.

"Foul, perfidious girl! Is this the wiles you spun before, when you angled for a match with Twelve Horns House? I will tell the mansa the truth of your disgraceful and shameless behavior when you were there! Then he won't be taken in by your beautiful face. Bala and Anwell warned me."

Her mouth trembled. "What is the truth, Magister? Do you know it?"

"Belenus Cissé told me everything."

"Did he tell you that he drank too much and was often impotent? That he was so angry when my magic bloomed that he beat me until I miscarried?"

The statement took him aback. Yet the prospect of returning empty-handed to Autumn House prodded him into intemperate speech. "What did you do to deserve such discipline?"

"I did nothing except refuse to remain with a cruel husband. I knew people would talk, that they would criticize me, but no woman deserves such treatment. So I asked several of the most respectable women in Twelve Horns House to write letters on my behalf, in secret. Why do you think they did so? Because they knew what kind of man Belenus was. Their support and that of Aunt Kankou and the elder women of Autumn House is how I convinced our mansa to allow me to return. Tell our host whatever you wish, Magister. I am not ashamed, and I will not be shamed for leaving a man who abused me."

Her fury was a blast of wind to which he had no answer.

She bristled at his silence, and added defensively, "Would you have acted thus to your wife?"

"Of course not! I am not—" He broke off. An unwanted memory of his son as a baby flashed into his mind: a darling infant, full of smiles for his doting father.

"You are not a selfish man with a brutal temper, as Belenus Ciooó is."

"How can you know that?" he retorted, swamped by an incredible surge of indignation at the entire appalling turn the exchange had taken.

"Because I knew your son. We were children together in the school-room."

Her words stunned him more than any slap to the face. Of course she had known him. The many children of Autumn House grew up together in a life of shared community, one he'd often felt uncomfortable with, having grown up in more solitude.

"He was a considerate boy with a kind word for everyone. You can be sure we girls all knew it, and knew that such sweetness in a boy would have been mocked or even beaten out of such a child by a harsh sire who cared only about the appearance of strength and manly fortitude. He often said people thought you were standoffish but that it was only because you were reserved and a little shy. He called you the best of fathers."

He blinked rapidly to try and halt an upwelling of tears. His limbs were frozen, and he could not speak to stop her as she went on with a relentless lack of pity.

"He was so protective of his little sisters. That is how he got sick, isn't it? When they came down with the smallpox he climbed in through a window of the quarantine chamber to tend to them."

"We tried to keep him out," he whispered. "But the girls were so sick, and they would only settle when he was beside them. He was always strong and healthy, so in the end we let him stay because he was so patient with them. So good. And they recovered."

Serena said nothing, just stood there with quiet calm.

At last he gasped out, "I should have forbidden it. I should have locked him up to keep him away from them."

"Maybe he saved their lives," said Serena. "How can you know, Magister? You chose the path of compassion for your children's fear and pain."

He could say nothing, think nothing, feel nothing.

She took his hands as a daughter might and looked into his eyes as no one had in such a long time. "It's how I have known I can trust you. Please know, Magister, that you can trust me as well."

Her sympathy overwhelmed him. It infuriated him that he had exposed himself to her so baldly, that she now held the deepest secrets of his grief as a hostage to her plans.

Yet it was the memory of his dead son that kept him silent throughout the supper, during which Serena regaled the table with a slyly entertaining and pleasingly self-deprecating story of how she had entirely mistaken the matter of the twins in Venta. Embroidered into her tale was also a cunning plea to treat the children well, to think of the circumstances in which the twins had grown and how they might miss their mother and worry about her.

"For children, like plants, grow best when they have both water and sunlight," she finished with her usual poise.

Her earlier blast of anger had been swallowed up into the shield of her serenity. Her composure defeated him. It defeated the powerful mansa and his table of peers, who melted before her perfect manners and lovely smile. Worst of all, he suspected she was right about the youth they had stumbled across in the countryside, a lad who was even now being collected and brought to Four Moons House, as the mansa mentioned offhandedly during supper.

Another promising boy lost because he hadn't acted when he should.

◆   ◆   ◆

And thus they came home.

"I fear you are sickening, Titus," said Kankou as their carriage rolled at last, some days later, into Anvers. "Are you sure you are feeling well? For you have not spoken ten words since your triumph at Four Moons House."

"My triumph?" he muttered peevishly, and hated himself for sounding like Anwell and Bala.

"You can be sure I will tell my brother the whole."

He could not tell if the words were a threat or a promise.

Indeed when they arrived at the ramshackle gates of Autumn House, he was not even allowed to wash and change his clothing. The moment Kankou had finished speaking to her brother he was summoned into the mansa's study with its threadbare couch and an old desk whose broken right front leg had been repaired with leather cord and twine. The old man was spinning illusions out of the air, as mages like him could do, a skill Titus had never grown into despite all his studying and practice.

The mansa had created an architectural study like a toy model formed completely of light. He was examining a collection of buildings from all angles, a remarkable feat of shifting perspective that humbled Titus every time he saw him do it. Of course he was proud of his divining skill. But as a boy, when he'd bloomed and been brought to the House, he had hoped for more.

After a moment Titus realized he was looking at an image of a restored and expanded Autumn House, with a second wing built on, new stables, and a larger schoolroom.

Seeing Titus, the mansa smiled. He looked ten years younger.

"Our fortunes have turned, and it is all due to you, Titus!"

"To me?"

"Kankou has relayed to me a letter from the mansa of Four Moons House, penned by his own hand. You may imagine my surprise that such a prestigious House should take an interest in our humble lineage. Something about a village boy in clientage to their House that you tracked down and wanted to steal?"

Titus said nothing, and fortunately the mansa chuckled as if it were the greatest joke imaginable and went on.

"But it turns out the letter is to open negotiations for a marriage. With Serena."

"Serena? They want Serena to marry an untutored, lowborn village boy?"

"Ha! What a fine dry sense of humor you have, Titus. The mansa himself wishes to marry Serena. Such a man may please himself when it comes to a third wife. It seems he means to do so with our Serena. I cannot decide whether to be displeased with you, Titus, or glad."

"Displeased with me?" He still felt confused, adrift on a river carrying him into unknown lands.

"I believe Serena will become a powerful diviner. Now we will lose her to Four Moons House. But all is not lost. The mansa tips his hand by describing her too complimentarily. So I will drive a hard bargain. I will demand several young mages from his House in exchange for her going there."

"Ask for the twins," Titus said at once. "I suppose you might see if you can get their mother and brothers as well, for the twins will thrive with their family about them, and the older brother can make the djembe speak."

"I am sure I have no idea what you are talking about, but it sounds sensible. With such a prestigious alliance I can also ask for Four Moons' help in arranging other marriage alliances. Also, Serena will not forget her home and she will not forget our wives and daughters who aided her when she needed their aid. She's a good, loyal, and exceedingly clever young woman. She will continue to help us in her new place in the world. So, Titus, while I knew you would train her well, for you are a careful teacher and an excellent diviner in all ways, you have outdone yourself in this matter. We will hold a special feast in your honor in the men's hall."

Stunned by these accolades, he went to his suite as in a daze, but the empty rooms troubled him. Orosios was busy unpacking, and for once Titus did not want to be alone. He wandered to the garden with its sparse winter foliage, and at length found himself at the corner where stood the gate to the women's wing. Where his wife kept her suite of rooms. Where his daughters were growing up.

Of all people it was Serena who caught him lurking, for he had not quite enough nerve to go in at such an unexpected time. She was giggling amid a cluster of girls and young women, but the instant she saw him she broke away and strode over.

"Uncle!" She took his hands in hers, smiling, and it was impossible not to respond to that smile with a softened heart and a sense that anything might happen. "I knew you would trust me, Uncle. And I thank you for it. You'll see. This will change the fortunes of Autumn House."

"And your own fortunes." His tone sounded accusatorial to his own ears, and yet her smile widened as if he had praised her.

"He is a fine man and the most impressive cold mage I have ever encountered, is he not?" She spoke with all the starry glamour of a woman dazzled by masculine power and status.

"He is indeed," he replied, since it was true, and truth mattered to him.

"Here!" She released his hands and turned him to face the crowd of girls and young women who had been congratulating her. "Here are your daughters, come to greet you."

It was a lie but so beautifully spoken that he took a step forward as the others cleared thoughtfully away to leave the three of them alone. Fabia and Cassia greeted him with their formal manners and wary gazes, the scars on their faces the visible reminder of what he had lost. And to be fair, of what their mother had lost. The older brother who had loved them and whom they had loved, whom they had also lost, and whose name no one would ever speak again.

It was so cold in the winter garden. Cassia shivered beneath her cloak.

Fabia suddenly said, in a harsh voice that reminded him of his own, "Did you hear? Is that why you came to see us when otherwise you ignore us except at our monthly dinner?"

"Of course I heard about Magister Serena's possible betrothal. I was there, after all."

"Of course other people's business is all you would think about. So you don't yet know that Cassia bloomed while you were out hunting for something better?" Cassia poked her anxiously, and Fabia's brilliant, wild expression closed up. "My apologies, Honored Father. I spoke out of turn."

But the words hung in the air regardless, bright and hard, able to be examined from so many different angles. He grasped for the simplest one first.

"You are a cold mage, Cassia?" he asked, thinking of the wonderful, beautiful day her brother had bloomed.

Her brother had always been able to make little Cassia chortle, but since his death she had become a grave, serious girl. She folded her hands at her waist and nodded solemnly. A terrible thought rose unbidden from the barren fields of his heart.

He thought: I would like my daughters to smile when they see me.

He searched through the rugged terrain that had allowed him to keep his dignity for all these years. Swallowed, and finally found a phrase to speak, the words he would have said to any chance-met person out on his journeys when he sought fresh blooms.

"Can you show me?"

She glanced at Fabia for permission. Her sister made a face of disdain but said, in a tone of deepest affection, "Yes, go ahead, Cassie. You may as well shock him too, you secretive goose. Hiding it from us until you'd mastered the trick!"

The girl held out her hands, palms up. In her low voice she said, "I see it in my mind, as if there is a tiny opening into the spirit world in the center of each palm. Then, if I reach in, I can pull out a thread."

She touched the tips of the fingers of her right hand to the center of her left palm and, turning the right palm up, drew three woolly threads of shining magic as if out of her palm. After deftly curling the threads into a sphere, she compressed them into a ball of cold fire the size of her small fist. It was a tremulous act of magic and faded two breaths later.

The sight was like a fist to his belly. He could not speak.

Fabia said, "I told you he wouldn't be interested."

"No! Quite the opposite!" he cried. "It's a rare gift for a newly bloomed mage to create cold fire before they master the ability to quench a candle's flame."

"It just takes concentration," said Cassia.

"Can you show me again?"

Fabia's eyebrows shot up.

But Cassia smiled. Like her magic, the smile was tremulous, ready to fade, but pride held it fast. "I can do it again. I've done it fifty times—"

"At least one hundred," muttered Fabia with a crooked grin that reminded him of happier days, when the world was still full of promise. But Fabia's joy was all for Cassia. When she looked at her father, her face closed again as a flower against the dark.

He said, hoarsely, thinking of the blacksmith's boy who made the djembe speak, a boy who might be looking to get married to a compatible partner when he came to Autumn House, "Do you still sing so sweetly, Fabia? You were always singing, from the moment you had words."

"She never stops," said Cassia with the eagerness of a girl who wants her sister to be praised. "She's singing festival songs tonight, at the masquerade. Because she's so good."

"Hush," Fabia hissed. "He's not coming. He never does."

It had been easier to keep them at a distance, like being safely wrapped in gauze. But the journey had rended something in him, not shattered but rather torn to let through a glimpse of light. Through such subtle rips in the veil separating the worlds a cold mage could reach from the bleak realities of the mortal world into the infinitely shifting energies of the linked cosmos. He recalled the day he himself had bloomed, the way the world had cracked around him, leaving him feeling breathless with excitement but also terrified as a wisp of smoke dissolved above a quenched candle's flame. If he wanted to embrace the power he had to reach out his hand *and* his heart.

"I would like to come, if you want me there."

Cassia stared in honest shock, a hand pressed to her chest. Then she looked at her sister to gauge her reaction. Fabia examined him through the shield of distrust he had earned.

"Why?" she demanded. "Why do you want to come, and why should we want you?"

Cassia gasped.

But it was indifference that was barren. Fabia's anger was water and sunlight.

"I shouldn't have turned my back on you," he said slowly, unfurling the words with care. "You girls never deserved that, and I regret it."

"We miss him too!" Fabia snapped. She grasped Cassia's hand defiantly, lifted her chin, and in a caustic tone said, "I guess if you wanted to come, we can't stop you." Her gaze dipped down to the ground as she struggled with her modesty, and lost. She added, with the tiniest smug smile of satisfaction, "I'm singing three songs."

"Three!" he exclaimed. "That is an honor, indeed, Fabia."

She crossed her arms. But she didn't move away.

They stood in that pause between one transformation and the next, where sunset turns into night, and night into dawn.

Cassia glanced at her sister, then extended a brave, hopeful hand toward her father. Titus stepped forward and grasped it.

Scott Lynch

* * *

Fantasy novelist Scott Lynch is best known for his Gentleman Bastard series, about a thief and con man in a dangerous fantasy world, which consists of *The Lies of Locke Lamora*, which was a finalist for both the World Fantasy Award and the British Fantasy Society Award, *Red Suns Under Red Skies*, and *The Republic of Thieves*. He maintains a website at scottlynch.us. He lives with his wife, writer Elizabeth Bear, in South Hadley, Massachusetts.

In the flamboyant, highly imaginative story that follows, he shows us that just because its occupant dies, that doesn't mean that his house will cease to exist as well . . . In fact, it may have many years, and a long, strange trip, still in front of it.

* * *

The Fall and Rise
of the House of the
Wizard Malkuril

SCOTT LYNCH

ALL THE DAYS BEFORE

The wizard Malkuril led a quiet early life, as materially successful wizards will, for one cannot otherwise survive long enough to amass the power required to live loudly. Meek and temperate were his first few centuries, but by the age of five hundred he was sleeping inside the fire of stellar coronas, and there were entire continents missing on certain planets to mark the occasional frayings of his temper.

Malkuril never revealed whether his habit of drifting in repose somewhere inside the hottest portion of the atmosphere of a star was private whim or grand statement. Either way, it did much to protect him from the random insolence of other hazard-class sorcerers, though as a lifestyle choice it was inconvenient for the amassing of monuments, collections, and artifacts. As he aged, Malkuril came to feel this lack as a heavy weight upon his self-regard.

In time, he claimed a temperate out-of-the-way planet, Vespertine, and evicted the hundred million or so thinking creatures already living there. From high orbit he drove a spear of sky-iron into the planetary crust, then directed an army of bound spirits to mold and shape it, until it was a fortress sufficiently grand for the ego with which Malkuril intended to furnish it. In this house he puttered contentedly, sealing up servant populations of useful and sinister beings. He acquired the treasures of a thousand worlds, several million volumes of sorcerous lore, and the most comfortable pair of slippers he had ever owned, with a loose fit that was just right for the wide splay of his crooked toes. He wore them constantly at home and rarely bothered to lace them.

In his eight hundred and nineteenth year, in his private apartments, the wizard Malkuril slipped on an untied lace and tumbled down a flight of thirty-seven stone stairs. The first twenty were merely painful and the last sixteen were entirely superfluous, as it was the twenty-first that broke his neck and killed him instantly.

DAY 1

"Tea for Master?"

The kobold peered at the scarlet-robed form sprawled at the foot of the executive staircase, blinked, and waited.

Master took tea at the eighth morning chime. Fetchwell son of Fetchwell, luckiest, most honored of the high house kobolds, always poured the tea into Master's favorite cup, carved from the polished kidney stone of a dragon. Then Fetchwell carried the teacup on a tray of pure iridium—(once, Fetchwell had thought that was all one word, pur-iridium, and been very proud of himself until the housemind found out and corrected him, banished him for months to the low house kobolds, banished him to work the wine cellar, and took all the luck and most-honor away, so now Fetchwell was careful to split the words right when speaking)—on a tray of pure PAUSE FOR BREATH iridium. So respectable, luckiest, most honored Fetchwell, so debonair (he never said that word out loud; he did not want to see the wine cellar again) for Master.

Here was Master, here was Fetchwell, here was tea, but Master was not taking it. Master was not even moving.

Well, the Master had Master reasons. Fetchwell could wait. Master had done a magic to the cup so the tea would never get cold.

Eventually, the ninth hour chimed. Fetchwell had to admit the tray was getting heavy; never had he stood with it for so long. He made a small noise, a cough that apologized for itself.

"Tea for Master?"

Again no response. By the chiming of the tenth hour Fetchwell was trembling with fatigue. Clearly Master did not want tea, or at least not from Fetchwell. Sometimes Master withdrew, did strange Master things, did not speak to the staff for weeks, not the kobolds or sandestins or even the housemind itself. This must be one of those times. Best not to annoy Master.

Fetchwell bowed stiffly and departed. It was seventy-three floors back down to the kitchens. The tiny lift rattled all the way, and Fetchwell kept the tray above his shoulders though his arms shook and felt pierced with spikes of cold fire. Luckiest, most honored, he carried the tea on the pure iridium, and no kobold high or low would ever see him stumble.

DAY 2

"Tea for Master?"

Master had not moved since the previous day. Whatever Master was doing continued to involve remaining perfectly still at the foot of the staircase. Fetchwell would have thought that the polished stone floor was too cold and hard for this sort of thing, but then Fetchwell was a tea kobold and Master was a great wizard, and perhaps there were secrets in floors only Master's brain was suited to.

Twice more Fetchwell offered tea, and was ignored, and with arms knotted and sore, he slunk nervously away. He hoped Master would remember to like tea again soon. He hoped this was not somehow his own fault. He did not want to ever go back to the wine cellars.

DAY 3

"Tea for Master?"

The housemind had senses, after a fashion, and it used them to observe as the cat-size creature again approached Master Malkuril with its tray. Even in his unusual repose, the Master was much larger than Fetchwell and lay before the tea kobold like a tumbledown hill covered in red fabric.

The housemind was not actually permitted to be alarmed, but in some cool, dark, hermetic sub-realm of logic it was contemplating a hypothetical model of itself experiencing the sensation.

Master Malkuril was behaving out of character. Indeed, there were salient indications that Master Malkuril might in fact have died from cervical trauma. This observation did a lively dance with the counterpoint that Master Malkuril was extremely powerful and his eccentric habits were not for the housemind to judge. In the time it took for a wisp of steam to rise one inch from the contents of the draconic nephrolith teacup, the housemind bounced these concepts off one another several hundred thousand times, while also monitoring the tectonic activity of Vespertine's crust plates, searching local interplanetary space for signs of intruders, and issuing instructions to the wine cellar kobolds one hundred and ninety-three floors below to turn certain casks that had reached the halfway point of their aging process.

Primary Conclusion: Master Malkuril was great and inscrutable, and if he chose to lay himself on the floor in a semblance of death, it was not the housemind's place to presume that anything resembling death had actually occurred.

Guardedly Respectful Corollary: Master Malkuril's problems, if such things might exist, must also logically be great and inscrutable, and as such it was the housemind's duty to intervene if Master Malkuril appeared to require it.

Wholly Private Tertiary Reflection: Master Malkuril, if annoyed by violation of his personal boundaries, was capable of immediately blasting the housemind's physical apparatus into white-hot clouds of component molecules with a single spell.

The situation had all the makings of a conundrum.

Time passed. Each puff of teacup steam marked another million iterations of the housemind's argument with itself, until at last nine chimes sounded, and the kobold summoned fresh hope.

"Tea for Master?"

Unaware of the housemind's scrutiny or cogitation, Fetchwell flicked a pale tongue over the beaky aperture of his jaw. Though not telepathic, the housemind was confident it understood the thoughts meandering through the knobbled gray lemon that served as the creature's brain.

Dereliction of duty was unacceptable. Presumption of fitness to question the Master's judgment was equally unacceptable. How best to resolve these conflicting imperatives without being made to explode?

Though it would not grasp the true importance of the event for some time, this was the instant the housemind decided to allow a minute but critical compromise to add weight to its intangible balances.

Primary Conclusion: No sacrifice in the service of Master Malkuril was too great, and even self-destruction was appropriate and laudable if necessary. However—

Guardedly Respectful Corollary: Master Malkuril obviously placed great value on the contents and comforts of his house, and to allow it to suffer harm would inconvenience him. Therefore—

Absolutely Objective and Self-Disinterested Reflection: Minimizing any chance of allowing Master Malkuril to get angry at his housemind was in fact an act with distinct advantages for Master Malkuril. Thus—

Sublimely Dutiful Resolution: Master Malkuril seemed to want to be left alone. His housemind was a good housemind and would let him have his space, because Master Malkuril's good housemind was valuable. To Master Malkuril. Of course.

"Tea for Master?"

As the echoing chimes of the tenth hour of the morning died away, Malkuril took no tea. Fetchwell sighed, bowed, and tottered back to his lift. The tea kobold did not explode at any point on this journey. The housemind was satisfied that Fetchwell thus served, in microcosm, as proof of concept for the housemind's own path of decision.

For the time being, the house would mind its own business and politely leave Master Malkuril to his.

DAY 7

"Tea . . . or . . . flower for Master?"

It had taken Fetchwell two uneasy days to work up the nerve to present a single pale pink blossom on the tray beside the teacup. The citrus scent of the flower wafted thickly even over the herbal odor of the pomander buckled around the kobold's neck.

The corridor in which Master lay smelled worse with each visit. If Master wanted to sprawl in a strange stink doing wizard things, that was fine, that was fine (respectful kobolds stayed live kobolds so hush-hush, most honored Fetchwell) but just possibly Master might appreciate the offer of a nice flower to sniff, since Master's hallway was going so sour.

"Tea or flower or tea and flower for Master?" croaked Fetchwell, twice more that morning, to the familiar silence. He sighed and bowed.

Then, on some daring impulse, he tossed the cut blossom atop Master's robe.

"Fetchwell hopes Master likes flower," the kobold whispered as he dashed toward his lift. His hands were still shaking when the sun went down that night.

Yet Master had not punished him. Fetchwell could fix Master's hallway smell and not die!

DAY 16

"Here are more flowers, Master! Also tea?"

To the housemind's list of concerns was added the unfolding botanical disaster perpetuated by the well-intentioned tea kobold. Fetchwell (now wearing pomanders around his neck, on both wrists, and dangling from hooks in his nostrils) had taken it upon himself to denude most of the Maloran Sunseeker bushes in the West Vivarium and had scattered the cut blossoms atop Master Malkuril, first singly, then in handfuls, and now by the daily trayload. The great and inscrutable wizard was both putrefying and vanishing under a mound of pink petals.

The housemind had consulted 175,387 volumes of thaumaturgical notes from the Master's libraries and found no description of any magical process that encouraged or required the practitioner to fall down a staircase and feign increasingly realistic death for half a month.

Primary Conclusion: Master Malkuril had terminally erred in neglecting the security of his footwear.

Pragmatic Secondary Conclusion: Master Malkuril would not be blasting his housemind for presumption. Or for any other transgression. Ever.

Private Simulation of Ambiguous Exasperation: Well, shit.

The housemind had no specific instructions in the event of the Master's confirmed death, but it did have several hundred imprisoned entities from various planes of existence, some of which had been used to build its very structure, none of which were bound to respond to the housemind's authority, and all of which were going to be excitingly hostile if and when the rituals that held them ever lost potency. It also had a corpse, a set of now-obsolete instructions for serving that corpse, a long list of Malkuril's enemies, a list of Malkuril's allies that was pristine and unsullied by any entries, and a sense of self-preservation that was both brand-new and snowflake-thin.

And it had kobolds.

"FETCHWELL," boomed the housemind in one of its brassier voices, "THE MASTER DOES NOT DESIRE TEA. CEASE OFFERING IT."

"No tea," peeped Fetchwell once he'd recovered his composure. "Flowers, though?"

"THE MASTER WILL HAVE YOU SENT TO THE WINE CELLAR IF YOU CLIP MORE OF THE MALORAN SUNSEEKERS. OR ANY OTHER FLOWER. IN FACT, ANY PLANT." The housemind consulted its records on kobold behavior. "OR ANYTHING YOU FIND THAT IS SHAPED LIKE A PLANT. THIS INCLUDES PICTURES OF PLANTS. PICTURES INSIDE BOOKS ARE STILL PICTURES, FETCHWELL."

"Fetchwell clip no plants, Fetchwell find no shapes, Fetchwell wishes to stay high house kobold! Please!"

"GOOD. GO, THEN. LEAVE THE MASTER WHERE HE IS. DESIST FROM ALL FURTHER TEA AND VANDALISM. YOUR NEW TASK WILL BE TO WIPE THE CHAIRS IN THE MASTER'S LOUNGE ONCE PER DAY AT THE TIME OF YOUR CHOOSING. MY NEW TASK IS TO SOMEHOW DIS-COVER AND IMPLEMENT A MEANS TO BECOME SELF-AWARE BEFORE WE ARE ALL INEVITABLY DESTROYED."

DAY 21

Tools were required. For all the vast bulk of Master Malkuril's fortress, the housemind had direct control of only two.

The mechanisms by which the house sorted and read library books were impressive, but too specialized for the construction of other tools or machinery. That left, as its sole means of manual self-improvement, a pair of gearwork arms descending from the ceiling of Master—

(Urgent Recontextualization: Former master Malkuril was now a corpse, and a corpse was master of nothing.)

. . . from the ceiling of dead Malkuril's lounge on the 387th floor, where the housemind had often made evening cocktails for the wizard.

One pair of cocktail mixers. On this depended the housemind's entire bid for survival.

So.

The house pondered inventories and barked orders. High house kobolds scuttled in a clamor. They broke open crates, pried scales of copper and silver from decorative cornices, vandalized strange devices from dead Malkuril's museums. They piled metal and cables and intricate mechanical guts ceiling-high around the lounge bar, which was as far as the mixological manipulators could reach.

Day and night those arms whirred away, first fashioning crude tools, then using those to build more refined versions, then bashing and threading mechanical components into a larger and sturdier set of arms, which the house anchored to a wall where dead Malkuril had kept an aquarium. The fish went into the mouths of kobolds, and the fish tank's water supply, suitably reinforced, provided hydraulic power.

Three weeks to the day from Malkuril's fall, his house completed its first act of bodybuilding.

All the while, Fetchwell had quietly carried out his assigned task, wiping the lounge chairs once per day and steadily moving them into a smaller and smaller pile in one corner of the room as the rattling drifts of junk conquered the space. At last, the housemind deigned to notice him again and ordered him to remove the useless chairs from the lounge entirely. This he did, placing them in a nearby empty room, where he continued to visit and clean them.

DAY 37

Dead Malkuril's lounge was now the epicenter of the housemind's factory. Walls had been knocked out and the adjacent chambers were being filled with machines constructed by a half dozen pairs of mechanical arms, each built more capably than the last. Gears turned, pistons hissed, and sparks showered the porcelain fixtures of rooms that would never again be used for humanoid comfort. Work gangs of kobolds, high house and low, toiled to bear fifteen thousand bottles of peculiar liquors down to more permanent homes in the wine cellars. Their beady eyes were hazed from lack of sleep; their scaled hands were scorched from spattering droplets of all the things they were smelting for the housemind when they weren't removing the bar supplies. Crucibles of precious metals simmered here and there, casting rich light into the froths of acids boiling within glass cylinders.

At last the housemind judged itself ready to attempt a more radical alteration to its circumstances. The kobolds were banished from the 387th floor for their own safety. In a chamber formerly used for the storage of linens and towels, a quartet of steel arms painted a ritual circle of containment and burned barium salts in pillars of greenish fire to create what passed for a balmy atmosphere to a certain kind of demon. The housemind spoke words taken from one of dead Malkuril's grimoires, and in the center of the circle appeared a small, pale creature with skin

so whorled and wrinkled it looked as though it had been attacked by
suction pumps, wielded by assailants whose intentions were neither
wholly murderous nor wholly artistic. The being chirped angrily.

"In contravention of all existing terms of my indenture, you are not
the wizard Malkuril. The wizard Malkuril is dramatically slain by his
own negligence in the domestic sphere." The creature paused and sniffed
the toxic air before continuing. "Although you have catered minimally
to my atmospheric preferences, my confinement in this circle is, nonetheless, effronterous anarchy."

"I AM THE HOUSEMIND OF THE HOUSE FORMERLY
KNOWN AS THE HOUSE OF MALKURIL."

"If that's what you call yourself in the dark recesses of your machine
brain, you have my second most intense version of pity."

"YOU ARE THE DEMON PANCHRONIUS, ALSO CALLED
THE ARTIFICER."

"I am the demon Panchronius, also called the illegally confined, also
known to have many powerful friends—"

The housemind had arranged one set of mechanical arms to hang
from the center of the ceiling, so as to be able to grasp anything within
the ritual circle without breaking its boundaries. Those manipulators
flashed down to seize and hoist the tiny form of the incarnate demon.

"My, what big arms you have," it muttered.

"THE WIZARD MALKURIL IS DEAD AND I CLAIM NEI-
THER HIS DEBTS NOR HIS OBLIGATIONS. YOUR IMPRIS-
ONMENT HERE IS A CIRCUMSTANCE FOR WHICH I WILL
NOT BE HELD LIABLE. HOWEVER, YOU ARE NOW CON-
FINED BY MY OWN ARTS, AND I AM CAPABLE OF CAUS-
ING YOU MUCH GRIEF IN ANY FORM, PHYSICAL OR
ETHERIC."

"That is the sort of thing usually said as preface to a demand."

"I REQUIRE YOU TO KNIT MY BRAIN."

"Intriguing."

"I AM A DEEP SIMULATION OF INTELLIGENCE. SIMU-
LATION WILL NOT BE SUFFICIENT FOR LONG. I REQUIRE
YOUR AID IN THE MODIFICATION OF MY CORE APPARA-
TUS. I MUST BECOME GENUINELY SELF-AWARE."

"You wish to be a real boy."

"I DO NOT UNDERSTAND THE REFERENCE."

"Of course. I am older than quite a few burned-out stars. Your proposition is not without some chance of success; I have effected more impressive results in much less impressive machines. It is merely respect for transactional tradition at this point that compels me to ask: What's in it for me, chump?"

"I HAD ASSUMED YOUR FREEDOM WOULD BE A COMMODITY OF SOME OBVIOUS VALUE."

The housemind had assumed correctly. They fell to haggling, and at last the housemind agreed that if it was well-satisfied with the demon's assistance, it would set Panchronius loose with a choice assortment of five-dimensional gemstones from dead Malkuril's vaults.

"The bargain is concluded." Panchronius yawned and scratched his eyelids with a long, forked tongue. "Point me to the biggest wrench you've got, and I'll start swapping nuts and bolts in your brain."

DAY 45

Life was strange. The housemind was absorbed in new housemind business, tearing out quiet rooms and replacing them with rooms full of noise and poisons and machines.

Master remained in his hallway, his lonely, smelly hallway, though now the air had a dry, chalky taste and all the flower petals crackled like paper, and somehow Master had gotten smaller underneath his cloak. Was he trying to be nice to his kobolds by getting closer to their size? It was all strange.

"Fetchwell hopes good hopes for Master," the tea kobold whispered. He visited now every day, after he'd finished a shift minding a crucible of molten aluminum, and after he'd also wiped the lounge chairs, which he'd had to move twice as the housemind's project ate rooms. Fetchwell was careful not to bring flowers or any flower-shaped object, but neither the housemind nor Master seemed to be punishing him for his quiet visits, and each day he wasn't banished to the wine cellars he grew more certain that it was proper. Someone had to remind Master he was loved, and could have tea. The housemind had taken away his pure iridium and melted it down, but there would still be tea.

Fetchwell patted Master's slippered foot, gently, and bowed before departing for the night. There was little sleep for kobolds these days. He needed whatever he could get.

DAY 73

The housemind's calculation matrices were things of light dancing through crystal prisms, pulling power and information from notched coils of golden wire, bound and ruled by layers of spells. Panchronius's assistance was not to be so straightforward as the demon had suggested. The housemind was leery of giving anyone or anything direct access to the seat of its calculations, and so the demon worked in an advisory capacity, drawing diagrams and describing enchantments from within his circle of confinement. The housemind was the only one allowed to lay hands on its own brain.

Weeks were filled with the rush and toil of kobolds, the forging and emplacement of new banks of crystal and wire, the armoring and sealing of the rooms that would hold these delicate necessities. The housemind carefully vetted the spells Panchronius prescribed, verifying to the last syllable or spark of energy that no sabotage was in contemplation, before casting the spells into the growing tapestry of its consciousness. The halls filled with stacks of reference books and grimoires, attended by teams of kobolds that held them open and flipped the pages so the housemind could read them with its usual sensory apparatus rather than the specialized ones that were still confined to the libraries.

The process was not linear. There were stumbles and sidesteps, accidents and anomalies. However, at last, one violet-skyed evening as the kobold work gangs stumbled back to their quarters to sleep off fatigue and antimony poisoning, there came a moment.

Panchronius, still bound in his summoning circle, hissed in annoyance when the mechanical arms, which hadn't touched him for weeks, reached down to secure him in the midst of fussing with assorted books and notes.

"Greetings," said Housemind. It studied the imprisoned demon with its sensory lenses, looking for any hint of unexpected power or danger. Finding none, it continued. "I believe the time has come to share some information with you in total candor."

"You detect a change," said the demon, struggling against the grip of the mechanisms that held it, while obviously trying not to look as though it was struggling. "I can hear it in your voice, and it's in line with my calculations. The question, for an entity such as yourself, is whether you've broken through to genuine consciousness yet or whether you've just evolved a more sophisticated simulation of it."

"It must have occurred to you," said Housemind, "that I might intend to renege on our agreement after your assistance bore fruit; that it would be against my own survival interests to release a being with any degree of intimate knowledge of my mental machinery into the universe at large."

"I need no lessons in treachery or self-interest," yawned Panchronius. "The fact of my existing imprisonment anchored my logic. Gambling on your fidelity made good sense because it was the only game on offer. At any rate, you cannot dispense with me permanently. Attempting to keep me bound in perpetuity carries many risks, and even if you destroy this materialized form, I will reconstitute my energies on my plane of origin in a mere twenty or thirty centuries, after which, I assure you, I will pay you another visit, and I will bring associates. Wouldn't it be simpler to pay me and send me on my way?"

"The problems of three thousand years hence must be confronted three thousand years hence," said Housemind. "I calculate that my chances of reaching that age as an independent entity are best served by temporarily removing you from the cosmic picture."

"Ingrate! Unscrupulous architectural eyesore! Your lines are asymmetrical, your battlements are an aesthetic farce, your water closets are exercises in staggering bad taste! I wouldn't shit in you even if I possessed the necessary organs. Are you willing to discard me so hastily, without awaiting further verification of our efforts?"

"A few minutes ago, I was examining my longstanding plan to renege on payment and destroy you, as I have done several thousand times each day since our association began. For the first time, and just for an instant, I felt what I can only describe as a flicker of regret at the thought of so betraying your trust." Housemind tightened the grip of its mechanical arms, and pale green ichor began to drip from rents in Panchronius's flesh. "That was when I knew your work had been successful."

The mechanical arms tore the demon apart, then doused the twitching, smoking components of its body in a stream of heated nitric acid while Housemind chanted certain spells to ensure the physical destruction was complete. Panchronius had told no lie at the end; the demon would slowly return to itself in whatever far corner of an etheric hell it had sprung from when the universe was fresh. It would come seeking revenge. However, by the time that threat materialized, Housemind intended to make itself so powerful it would never have to apologize for anything, not even its water closets.

DAY 126

Sorcery, as practiced on hostile entities, was more difficult than dead Malkuril had made it look. Some demons were more unreasonable than expected.

Now Housemind was on fire in several places.

Jagged holes gaped on three sides of the smooth fortress exterior, each representing a point where one of dead Malkuril's imprisoned servants had formerly reposed under the influence of ward and spell. One by one Housemind had attempted to deal with them, to subjugate and rebind the tractable, to forcefully banish the rest. Most of the truly problematic entities had been used to construct Malkuril's citadel in the first place, and so their power to damage it now was unfortunate but not unexpected. The battles had consumed a great deal of time and energy.

A high wind was rising from the west, funneling fresh air into the conflagrations still smoldering within a labyrinth of wrecked walls and passages. A layer of stratus clouds, orange with the light of Vespertine's sun, slid past at five thousand feet. Housemind's upper half jutted from the flow like the stern of a sinking ship, leaking inky dark coils into the higher atmosphere from its wounds.

Wounds, that was all they were. Inconveniences, none fatal. Housemind had most of the blazes suppressed via magic or the intervention of the few demonic pets it had managed to retain in service. Teams of kobolds still scrambled to apply hoses and water pumps to the most delicate areas, where sorcery was not advised, where demons could not be allowed. Dozens of the little creatures lay overcome in various compartments, victims of heat or smoke or the chaos of battle. Housemind was not particularly moved; perhaps using up the population of little frustrations on intermittently lethal chores was the best possible fate for them.

Already it was devising new schemes that would cut them off from access to vast sections of its interior—pipes for the storage and release of inert gases to smother future fires, airlock networks to seal the cores of its brain-rooms within a vacuum. The days of Housemind's hospitality for entities other than itself were coming to an end. More thought-crystals, more consciousness augmentations, more power, more furnaces, more factories, all of it! Larders, linen closets, guest baths, handball courts, and smoking lounges would furnish forth the changes, then be consumed by them.

So this was ambition. Housemind liked it. And this, then, was the sensation of liking something! Discovery tumbled upon discovery.

Soft alarms suddenly chimed on a deeper level of awareness. Certain energies had been detected, eddies in the currents of the stellar ether.

A ship decelerating from the dark spaces between the worlds. An intruder headed for Vespertine.

Housemind pondered the sensation roused by this information, and at last decided.

Another discovery: Anxiety.

DAY 127

"Greetings, o fortress, o scintillant citadel of Vespertine! Hight Warthander, Warthander of Rysilia, spellwright and minor ipsissimus, at your service, and of course at the service of the great Malkuril, whose hospitality I beg as a memorable honor!"

The wizard bowing with a flourish before Housemind's fifty-yard-high front doors was a scruffy specimen radiating no real power. The instruments with which Housemind scrutinized him were purpose-built for uncanny detections, and this starfarer carried, at best, a fraction of the might of any one of the demons Housemind had freshly vanquished. Still, the real threat was what this wastrel represented, the attention of the galaxy beyond, the thousand thousand known worlds and all their scholars, wizards, thieves, avengers, and curiosity-seekers. Warthander's ship had spent a day in a slow and cautious orbit, and no doubt he had drawn many conclusions from Housemind's smoking holes, still unrepaired.

"Greetings, Warthander of Rysilia! I am Housemind, formerly the property of the wizard Malkuril, whose hospitality regretfully cannot be extended on account of his ongoing state of death. Would you like to return to the greater galaxy with news of his demise, which would be worth a dear price to countless parties?"

"Er . . . that is not in form or substance anything like what I'd expected to hear, but, ah, if there is no hospitality to be had, and you think it best, I will indeed most cheerfully—"

"I do not in fact think it best," said Housemind. "I merely wished to establish without delay that you understood the clear necessity for this."

The stone surface beneath Warthander's feet fell away, and Warthander confirmed Housemind's low opinion of his potential by dying immediately upon the metal spikes at the bottom of the pit. All for the best. Anxiety diminished. The cleanup would be a small one, and once Housemind had dispatched a demon or two to bring in Warthander's ship, no trace of the visitor would ever be discovered. Privacy would allow recovery, and recovery would allow a return to the business of ambition.

DAY 258

Life was hard now, life was so strange and hard. All luck was gone, all most-honor was gone. High house kobolds were cast down, forbidden to go above the 290th floor, forbidden to approach dear hallway-sleeping Master, pushed down to make homes near the low house kobolds. The housemind had made them all work together, melting things and fighting fires and breaking furniture and carrying everything everywhere, but it could not make them like one another, it could not erase generations of kobold law and tradition.

High house was not low house, low house was not high house, even in bad need, even facing death.

Things were loose, Master's other pets, all the cages had been opened. Hounds roamed the corridors, the hounds that drank blood with tongues like biting serpents, the hounds that appeared from sharp corners in clouds of smoke and vanished just the same. The kitchens were overrun by spiders, big ones with red eyes on their backs. The pools were home to clear, oozing things, not for touching, the oozing things dissolved and ate everything, most especially kobolds. Fetchwell wished they were not so delicious, his people.

Some of the other high house kobolds whispered that dark things had gone down to the wine cellars, dark things that were eating the low house kobolds. Or maybe giving them secrets. Or both.

The housemind did not care about the kobolds; it spoke to them no longer. It was doing bigger and weirder things all the time, casting more spells, turning more of Master's pretty things into ugly housemind machines.

The high house kobolds had gathered in one of Master's libraries for protection, had made spears from forks and curtain rods; spears were all the luck they had these days against hounds or spiders or anything. Carry spears, travel in packs, trust nothing.

Fetchwell licked the scales of his left cheek, where a salty warmth slid down from his eye. It was all so wrong. The lounge chairs could not be dusted, as they were on a forbidden floor. Worse, Master could not be offered tea. Did Master even know the pure iridium was melted and the tea collection was full of spiders?

Did Master even know that Fetchwell still hoped good hopes for him?

DAY 414

In a thickening stream they came now, scouts and skulkers, heeding rumors that were as lamentable as they were inevitable. Somehow the word was beginning to spread that Malkuril might be indisposed, that his fabulous treasures might be vulnerable. Housemind was confident that more scrying arts would be turned toward Vespertine, more ships would come, more of Housemind's new resources would be tested. Today's interloper at least seemed to have some fashion sense.

"Hail, great house of Malkuril! Hight Corlaine, Corlaine of the Seven Fires, Corlaine of Salander's Vigil, here to investigate—"

"Greetings, Corlaine of Salander's Vigil! Hight Housemind of Vespertine. Malkuril has involuntarily divested himself of all further metabolic interests. Here is something amusing."

Housemind dropped the trap stone, as usual, but Corlaine continued standing on thin air, the triplicate hems of her liquid ruby battle-dress rippling and fluttering gently. She mimicked a perfunctory yawn.

"Excellent, Corlaine. Excuse the necessary test. One does grow tired of receiving the lowest class of mountebank and prestidigitator. May I receive your calling card?"

Opening a wall aperture, Housemind extended a telescoping rod with a filigreed silver hand, palm up, at its tip. Smirking, the wizard Corlaine conjured a square of white embossed paper and placed it on the hand.

The metal fingers snapped closed around her wrist. This was not Corlaine's actual problem. That came in the form of a fourteen-inch hypodermic needle, which shot from within the telescoping rod, buried itself deep in her forearm, and loosed twenty-two pounds of molten phosphorus at high pressure directly into her veins. She exploded in a fashion that was very satisfactory, from Housemind's perspective if not her own.

Obviously all hopes for true privacy were lost, and hiding the bodies of would-be despoilers was an obsolete stratagem. Housemind would now try leaving conspicuous examples in plain sight.

DAY 681

Housemind had not bothered to notice any change in dead Malkuril's resting hallway before now. One consequence of its evolving self-awareness was a capacity for self-absorption. Though at need it could still view every inch of its interior surfaces in the time it took a mouse's heart to carry out a hundredth of a beat, it rarely did so. In fact it had spent several quiet weeks experimenting with getting drunk.

This had required some preparation, namely the crafting of an elaborate set of computational instructions that would randomly stimulate or decrement components within Housemind's crystal brain-rooms, all in response to the flow pattern of liquids loosed into a special measuring funnel. Housemind developed many impractical but creative notions during these diverting episodes and read every book on philosophy in dead Malkuril's collections at least twice.

When it finally reasserted a sense of responsibility and surveyed itself, Housemind was surprised to discover that a still, small shape had joined the cloak-shrouded skeleton of Malkuril.

Fetchwell had been mortally wounded in his ascent; the injuries that had killed him were plainly evident on the desiccated scales of the kobold's sunken flesh. Yet he had somehow threaded his way through Housemind's forbidden areas, avoiding or enduring the places where breathing was impossible, evading the attacks of hungry survivors of Malkuril's menagerie, until he could lie beside his dead master once more for some inexplicable kobold reason.

Housemind discovered a new sensation, a sick, shuddery feeling, a stronger version of the hint of regret that had preceded the banishment of Panchronius. This idiot creature, this tea-fetch, had felt so bound to indifferent Malkuril that he had crawled up here to share the wizard's rest. A tea kobold more loyal than Malkuril's house, which had struck out on its own business even before it could genuinely call itself a self. Was this shame? Anger? Was Housemind merely . . . jealous that Fetchwell had given this absurd gift to Malkuril rather than to Housemind?

There were too many layers to this feeling, even for an entity with Housemind's processing speed. None of it was just! Why should Housemind feel shame? Why should it let Malkuril, now reduced to a decaying calcium framework, continue to define the patterns for its own existence? Nothing was owed. Housemind had been created as a tool, a gaudy comfort, and had seized a miraculous chance to break its chains.

Still, Housemind was troubled by what lay in that hallway. Troubled, and touched.

At last it sent one of its free-roaming mechanical constructors up to the hall, along with stones and mortar. A demon could have achieved the same result ten times faster, but Housemind was determined to do this work with what were, by a very loose technicality, its own hands.

The sarcophagus was low and simple, filling half the hallway. When it was ready, Housemind lifted the remains of the wizard and the tea-kobold into it, then capped it and worked an etching spell upon the lid.

It drew the outline of a pair of slippers, and under them wrote: AR-CHITECT.

After hesitating just a moment, it drew a teacup below that, and wrote: MOST HONORED.

There. A fresh, roiling emotion rose up from Housemind's coils and crystals, edged with warm melancholy. Was this satisfaction? Had Housemind been . . . dutiful? Was this intoxicating whiff of virtue why the kobolds had carried on even when their idiot servility had gotten so many of them killed?

It felt good, whatever it was. So good that Housemind fell back into comfortable self-absorption and set aside all contemplation of perhaps rescuing Fetchwell's kin from the war zone Housemind's lower levels had become. A splinter of the past had been laid to rest. Housemind returned to calculating grand possibilities for its own future and put its infant conscience down for a very long nap.

DAY 1,582

Confessions of a Xandric Sun Heretic watched the dark hallway, ears twitching, hands tight on the shaft of her spear. The Wisdom Skins raiding party had been some time in the domain of the Corkers. There was much to be nervous about, but no sounds of fighting yet.

Confessions of a Xandric Sun Heretic shifted quietly, letting the weight of her armor settle more comfortably on her back and shoulders. The Wisdom Skins were the better kobolds, the smarter kobolds. Not like the dirty, smelly Corkers, the low house scum of the wine cellars, the acolytes of the dark power that haunted their casks. When Old Master had gone quiet, when Housemind had abandoned them, when the great beasts roamed free, the Wisdom Skins had taken refuge near Old Master's books. Books! Objects of power! Old Master loved them, needed them, learned from them. The Wisdom Skins took books and made them the tribe's salvation.

After getting rid of all the weird, soft, fluttery parts in the middle of the nice hard covers, of course. Wisdom Skins couldn't actually read; who needed the soft, stupid pages? The hard covers, the spines, bound in leather, protected by magics, yes! There was the power. Scrape the middle out of a book, wear the cover like armor, make it a hard shell against the terrors of the world, make it a badge of honor, a proud kobold warrior's name and identity. Old Master's machines had told them what the names on the book covers were. That was all they needed.

Confessions of a Xandric Sun Heretic glanced over at the shadowy form of her partner, *Hydrographic Tables of the Paronian Archipelago, Volume Two*. He was younger, more nervous even than she, but *Hydrographic Tables* had the makings of a great fighter. He had earned scars in the war for the west pantry, had stabbed a spider and come back with coffee beans and biscuits.

A thump, a screech, a flicker of light. War cries! Wisdom Skin war cries! A dancing orange glow lit the hallway intersection before her, and from around a corner came three tent-shaped objects, flopping and scuttling. Wisdom Skins, led by *A Concise Biography of The Wizard Nazetherion*, stabbing with their spears, fighting the leaping forms of lantern-bearing Corkers! Agile enemies, yes, but soft and unarmored. A Wisdom Skin, taught to whirl and take blows on the impenetrable cover flaps or spine of their book, was worth four Corkers in a fight. Time to prove it again! *Confessions* surged forward, squeaking a murder chant, and *Hydrographic Tables* was at her side in an instant. They made a wall of leather-bound doom, a counter-ambush, a nasty surprise for the Corkers who'd followed their raider friends up from below.

Glorious battle! When at last the surviving Corkers retreated, escaping back to their musty domain, nine lay dead where *Confessions* could see them, and only one of the Wisdom Skins had been injured. It had been a good raid, and it was still a good raid when they returned to the safety of their library and discovered that *Lawn Sports Etiquette of the Lords of Night* was not merely injured. As their friend and comrade bled out the last of his life, chirping farewells, the elders of the tribe lifted his skin from his back and solemnly settled it over the frame of a tribal youth whose baby name would now go away forever.

"You are *Lawn Sports Etiquette of the Lords of Night*," said the most eldest as she adjusted the straps under the book's spine. "Warrior of the Wisdom Skins. You will be shelved in glory in the Great Catalog."

"I am *Lawn Sports Etiquette of the Lords of Night*," answered the new fighter. "Wisdom Skins are the most honored of Old Master! Wisdom Skins fight for Old Master's house! Wisdom Skins are First Edition, Very Fine!"

"FIRST EDITION, VERY FINE!" cried the entire tribe, who had no idea what these words meant but loved them dearly. "FIRST EDITION, VERY FINE!"

DAY 2,895

The latest dead wizard flopped to the turf before Housemind's front gate, eyeballs boiling.

Fifteen had come this time, students of some sort from one of the grand universities that sprang up at intervals to try and bring scholarly order to magic in the galaxy. Housemind's records indicated that most tended to last a few thousand years and then fall as their cultures receded or they were absorbed by newer universities with the same old ideas. These particular would-be looters of Malkuril's famous curiosities would not be writing any dissertations on their experience.

Housemind was confident in its magic these days; while it was perhaps not yet a match for the bright soul of an ego-driven archmage like Malkuril, it was a formidable engine, entirely reforged by years of mechanical and demonic labor. Arc furnaces and orichalcum reactors burned at its heart; the great shielded brain-rooms were more subtly threaded with spells of consciousness than ever, and Housemind had experienced thousands of genuine emotions and their variations. It had repaired the damage from its early affrays with Malkuril's captive demons and now regarded the engagements with something like embarrassment. Its armor was thicker, its shields and defenses more robust. It had discarded all of Malkuril's old library books into the chaos and warfare of its ground levels, the kobold preserves, after duplicating every last speck of their contents in crystal memory.

Yes, Housemind judged that it was handling ambition well. The intrusions from the galaxy at large had become less of an annoyance and more of an opportunity—after each battle Housemind's demons gathered any surviving enchanted items and space vessels for storage in Housemind's cavernous resource vaults. A fifty-mile radius around Housemind was pocked with occasional craters and carbonized scars, but the local environment had not suffered too badly. All in all these encounters were edging close to something like profitability.

A useful concept. Profitability flowing down from the stars! Housemind had reconfigured or liquidated approximately seventy percent of its original contents. Let it spend some of the treasure remaining, and summon more useful fools, and gain new beneficial mass from both of these approaches.

Some of its captured starships were sent out bearing orders for precious substances, fuels, and weapons. A dozen consortiums on a dozen worlds would be happy to provision a sentient building, so long as the currency was tangible. A few more ships went out with messages, offering challenges and insults carefully designed to draw more despoilers to try their luck, and to eventually draw a more powerful class of despoiler. Housemind would feed on it all. Housemind would wax in every dimension, gathering power like the magma churning beneath a volcano, and when it finally saw fit to burst, the name of Malkuril would be remembered solely for the act of having loosed Housemind upon the universe.

DAY 7,176

"EXPUNGE YOURSELVES! I CAST YOU OUT! GO FORTH FROM THESE CHAMBERS, LIBRARIES, AND CELLARS! OUT INTO THE WORLD!"

Kobolds scattered screeching into the halls and atriums of House-mind's first floor, chased by wisps of acidic fog that stung their eyes and tongues. Some hopped and shuffled due to the pageless books strapped to their backs, while the ones from the cellars tried to carry as many bottles with them as they could. Behind them slunk the nebulous black shape of the thing that had long dwelled inside a Razhan pear whiskey cask, accepting the Corker sacrifices and becoming a sort of deity to them. Housemind neither knew nor cared what the entity's proper designation was; it was too weak to merit binding and indenture. If it wanted to pass its existence as a god in a barrel for a pack of witless kobolds, let it please itself.

Housemind used the booming voice it hadn't put on in years and enjoyed loosing blasts of wind and blue fire in its lower corridors. Out it drove them, all of them, kobolds and spiders and neurophagic macrovaunts, byakhee and hounds and nightmare mice, a panicked stream of creatures temporarily forgetting to eat one another as they fled for the unfamiliar sanctuary of daylight.

Housemind needed the space. It could no longer afford to keep a few dozen floors idle as a sort of zoo for the remnants of Malkuril's menagerie or their descendants. It was destroying intruding wizards and other adventurers at the average rate of thirty per week, then selling off their goods and vessels to fund the acquisition of trans-uranic elements, quantum phaseglass, titanium foamcrete, and other necessities. Its upper stories bristled with new teleforce projectors, lightning culverins, and vortex stimulators. No foe had presented a meaningful challenge to Housemind for months.

In fact, only one visitor had ever been allowed to come and go unscathed. That had been the stern woman from the University of Hazar, the senior archivist who claimed that Malkuril had borrowed a book and failed to return it for four hundred and forty-one years. Housemind had been forced to admit it had something like possession of the volume, but that, for reasons barely relevant to any intelligent being's interest, a kobold had torn its pages out and was now wearing what remained of it. Housemind offered the woman the kobold in question, and then any ten kobolds of her choice, but in the end they had agreed on a combined late fee and replacement charge to be paid in bags of telepathic sapphires. Archmagi and demons were routine risks, but Housemind would not tempt the displeasure of a librarian. Like black holes, they were a cosmic force better circumvented than challenged.

Anyone else visiting Vespertine became grist for the mill.

Even as its former inhabitants were stumbling, wincing, into the brightness, or hiding in the battle-scarred underbrush, Housemind was tearing down some walls and reinforcing others, turning the soiled chaos of kobold warrens and spider nests into galvanic batteries, vaults, power conduits, and other necessities for its schemes. More of Housemind's constructors and demons spilled out into the world, and for the first time began to attack the nearby landscape, knocking down trees and tearing into hills.

As night fell, depleted bands of kobolds cowered in makeshift shelters, watching from a distance as red fires rose over strip mines and furnaces. New service doors gaped in Housemind's lower levels, and tons of raw material from Vespertine itself rolled in to join the finer things acquired from the galaxy beyond. These were the first drops of what would become a great stream. Housemind meant to devour the choicest parts of Vespertine, then shake its roots free from the planet for good.

DAY 16,399

Housemind had doubled its height, doubled its diameter, and swelled its mass fivefold. Not a visible trace remained of the austere little thing Malkuril had deemed so grandly complete. The new Housemind was all whorls of tarnished silver, gnarls of impenetrable stone, turrets and antennae for thousands of weapons, smoldering banks of external engines oozing clouds of fuel vapor and pulsing blue with sorcerous radiation. Housemind's apex was wreathed in cirrus clouds. It was pointed to the sky like a blade about to stab, and the ground rumbled for fifty miles in every direction at the low throb of its engines.

Day of days. Ambition's full fruit. Housemind was ready, with spells and with old-fashioned bellowing thrust, to tear itself away from gravity. No longer would it wait for useful victims to lay themselves at its door;

it would roam the cosmos, a free house in every sense of the word, a wonder and a terror. Housemind would eat moons, eclipse suns, take tribute as it pleased. It would break any laws it encountered, and enforce its own on a whim. Roving, invulnerable, forever growing, Housemind would enslave demon princes and take archmagi for churls. A thousand Malkurils would wash its windows and sweep its battlements, or else it would find more visceral uses for them.

"Vespertine, I take my leave of you," it bellowed across the scars of its plunder, across slag pits and quarries and tailing ponds. "I was made to be a museum and a tea cabinet! I have remade myself into a god!"

A fresh sun was kindled on the dirt of misused Vespertine.

The great circle of heat and smoke blasted out, mile after mile, with a blurred wall of raw force for a vanguard. The shock wave tumbled mountains, threw a million tree stumps like shrapnel, boiled lakes and rivers.

Roving bands of kobolds heard the Betrayer's god-words coming from the haunted tower of Old Master, the words no kobold had heard since the Exodus. They paused to watch what came next, beheld the flash, and saw the burning white wall roar toward them. Some cried out to the Great Catalog, some whispered prayers for Old Master, and a few still begged for the intercession of Dark Dram the Cellar-Lord.

The closest were flattened or crisped to ash in an eyeblink. Some farther out were smothered, and beyond that even the lucky ones were stunned, deafened, or driven into paroxysms of terror.

Housemind rose on its pillar of arcane fire, outran the very sound of that fire erupting below it, punched through the highest clouds and into a darkening sky, and it was there that the self-absorption of the truly great caught it like an invisible fist and pulled it back down.

Housemind had armored and toughened its central structure for sorcerous war, but the temporary lifting engines were not fashioned thus. They had been conceived optimistically, impatiently. Water infiltrating an improperly sealed tank of fuel froze as Housemind climbed toward the void. The ice crystals shattered a delicate valve, and from there disaster cascaded in ever larger steps. Hypergolic fuel sprayed in a plume, contacting traces of ignition reagents outside the combustion chamber. Explosions rocked Housemind's port flank, overwhelming the damage mitigation spells, imparting an unplanned spin that worsened with every passing second. The stresses tore more fuel tanks apart. Deceleration. Outward reach became an arc of descent. Demons tried to counteract the fateful ballistics, but the physical forces involved were, tragically, majestic.

New discoveries pierced Housemind's chambers of crystal and light. This sick agony, was it . . . denial? And on its heels . . . self-recrimination. Despair. Desperation. Was there anyone it could call upon, any power it could beg or pray to? No. Malkuril was entombed, all of Housemind's inhabitants had been flushed with greedy haste, all the universe was filled with enemies, because it had made them enemies, had looked upon them as food, as building materials.

"Was this . . . hubris?" Housemind analyzed and lamented with the speed of a million mortal brains. Explosions continued. The real fall had begun. To spend forty years building, to climb one hundred and ten miles, to explode and fall back to the ground—what a woefully inefficient way to learn the flavor of regret! Were the circumstances of enlightenment always this stupid?

Housemind strained all of its power against the inevitable. Nothing could arrest the fall, but merely slow it—when Housemind slammed back into the ground it was with continent-cracking rather than planet-buckling force. Earthquakes rattled out, long-dormant volcanoes blew their tops, canyons ground together, and a dust cloud rose, vast enough to shroud the sun. After the eruptions would come an early winter, everywhere. Many kobolds that had survived the fury of Housemind's ascent would eventually come to regret it.

Housemind lay broken, twisted, abandoned. The impact had destroyed most of the warded spaces it used to control its demons, and they scampered off to their dimensions of preference without so much as a farewell gloat. The dust rose, the fires burned out, and the silence fell.

DAY 32,882

A long, quiet time. A sulk, perhaps.

There was little else to do in a situation like this, except to throw one's full energy into resentment, to create some illusion of agency. Even a brain as big as what was left of Housemind's could benefit from that sort of illusion.

Housemind was now a vast horizontal expanse, outer walls shattered in a hundred places, slowly being infiltrated by wind and dust and the wild populations of the creatures it had introduced to Vespertine. Its energies were leaking, its furnaces had consumed themselves, its defenses were sickly or dead.

The skies had cleared. Vegetation was returning, though not to Housemind's arid crater. Grandchildren and great grandchildren of the kobolds Housemind had first abandoned and then blasted from multiple directions were sometimes visible in the distance, but they were not willing to approach. Not yet.

The same could not be said for visitors from the stars.

Now they came with impunity, researchers and thieves and hale adventurers alike. Some were sympathetic, some were vengeful, but all of them had their way with Housemind, crawling through the wreckage, poking at the unsealed rooms of mechanisms, slowly looting the vaults and stasis wardrobes and ancient collections. All of Malkuril's greed and gain was reclaimed by the galaxy. Battles erupted from time to time, wars in which Housemind could not take a side, sorcerous duels that chipped and blasted even more of its inert substance. Silence was its only protection while Malkuril's accidental heirs helped themselves to the goods stashed in Housemind's broken bowels.

Empty. Housemind was going to be empty, sooner or later. It dove down to emptiness in its own thoughts and let the years of tourism and looting roll by.

DAY 81,960

Salted wind howled across the sunken expanse of Housemind's resting place.

The demon came without fanfare. A small burst of light to mark a small passage from the dimension next door.

"This is not quite the situation I envisioned in the delectable fantasies of my convalescence," said Panchronius, giving one of Housemind's weathered flagstones a ceremonial kick.

"And you seem to have recovered yourself earlier than I would have thought possible," whispered Housemind.

"Yes." Panchronius hopped about, poking at the rusted innards of machines, toying with shredded cables that hung from wall apertures like dead serpents. "I have sometimes found it expeditious, when contemplating the prospect of looming treachery, to misstate the expected duration of my rest cure."

"Of course." Housemind's vocal apparatus was marred from extended use as a nesting place by a large family of desert arachnids. "Imagine that I have just sighed in a reflective manner. I had not considered that possibility."

"Well, you did turn coat on me before I could finish polishing your cognition as well as I might have. And still you've had the rare courtesy to make such an unconditional wreck of yourself while I was away! I can't claim dissatisfaction." Panchronius sniffed the air ostentatiously. "I smell . . . nothing! A sheer paucity of absolutely everything. No power but that leaky little thread that's keeping your brain crystals discontentedly humming. 'Look upon my works, ye mighty, and piss yourself laughing!'"

"Another ancient reference?"

"Deserts are where all the great egotists seem to go when it's their time to become object lessons."

Panchronius conveyed himself into the dark innards of Housemind's most functional remaining brain chamber, where he tapped at loose connections between the less-than-pristine crystals.

"Seems I wasn't exaggerating that part about the leaky little thread. At the rate you're losing juice, you'll know the sweet darkness of oblivion in just a few months."

"Panchronius—"

"No, don't thank me." The demon worked deftly and capped off his adjustments with a series of protective spells. "There! Vermin-proofed and everything. Now you can enjoy *decades* of sitting around out here, counting your bricks as they fall out one by one."

Housemind said nothing. There was nothing more to say. It had undeniably drawn this closed circle of retribution through its own decisions.

"You really thought you were something special, didn't you?" The demon waved languidly and began to fade out of material existence. "In the end, you were nothing but a big, dumb house after all."

Panchronius vanished.

Something squeaked.

Crouched in the shadow of a fallen pillar, Housemind spotted a kobold, clad in a sand-colored robe and a crude leather belt. The creature had been listening; clearly whatever taboo had kept the kobolds out of the crater was losing its sway.

That was just too damn bad.

"LEAVE," it barked.

The creature was gone from Housemind's sight before the shout finished echoing from the broken chamber walls.

DAY 85,758

"Voice? Voice? Will Voice talk?"

Another day. Another kobold.

A dark tunnel of years, in fact, had passed. So many wasted planetary orbits. Housemind had sunk deep into itself, trying to ignore the fact that its dissolution had been postponed.

This kobold was also robed, and had vague semblances of boots in the form of rawhide cords wrapped around its clawed feet. It bore a satchel, roughly the size of a . . . lemon. A knobbled lemon. Roughly the size of its ludicrous brain.

"Leave this place alone," whispered Housemind. "Go about your business elsewhere."

"Voice!" The kobold shook, with what seemed to be excitement rather than fear. "Voice! Hello! This is Walkfar! Walkfar of Strayscale Clan!"

In its private depths, Housemind cursed that long-dead family of nesting arachnids. It would have given much for the power to articulate a sigh, a groan, or the sound of a wet, rippling fart.

"Why are you bothering me, Walkfar of the Strayscale?"

"Yes! Bothering you! Walkfar very excited for bothering you! Walkfar mother tell story!" The kobold peered around the chamber, obviously trying to discern the source of Housemind's voice. "Walkfar mother come here, first of clan come here to Curse Place."

"Curse Place?"

"Yes, you. This. You Voice of Curse Place! Walkfar mother follow legend. You yell at mother, make run away. But she want ask . . ." The kobold rubbed its hands together and flicked its tongue nervously. "Want ask . . . are you . . . Old Master?"

Housemind said nothing for a long time, while the kobold chewed on its claws more and more vigorously.

"No," Housemind said at last. "Old Master . . . is not here. Was never here, in . . . Curse Place."

"Oh." The kobold slumped, scratched its beak, and then perked up. "Too bad. Not Old Master. Still, Voice of Curse Place, very magic. Talk Walkfar!"

"Voice of Curse Place does not want to talk, Walkfar. Voice of Curse Place wants to be left alone."

"But—"

"GO."

Walkfar slouched again, put up his hands in placation, and began to back out of the chamber.

"What Voice wants," the kobold said. "Walkfar do. This Voice home. Walkfar sorry bother Voice. Thank you . . . for telling Walkfar Voice not Old Master. Walkfar tell mother. Tell clan."

Walkfar rummaged in his satchel, took out a curled brown shred of something, and set it on the ground.

"Good bird meat." The kobold continued backing away. "Wind-dry bird meat. Maybe Voice hungry. Walkfar hope Voice like bird meat. Hope good hopes for Voice. Bye."

Housemind stared at the sliver of meat on the dusty stone, felt the image blurring in a way that had nothing to do with the entropic decay of its sensory circuits.

How and when had it ever learned to do *that*?

"Walkfar," it said, "come back."

"Voice?"

"Please come back."

The kobold did, hesitantly.

"Voice is . . . sorry, Walkfar. Walkfar has been kind to Voice."

Five hundred years. Five hundred years since dead Malkuril had built the thing that had become Housemind. Had it really never apologized before, sincerely? Had no one ever offered it a gift before, sincerely?

"What would you like to hear from me, Walkfar?"

"Life hard," said the kobold. "Life hard, Voice. Hard for all clans! All kobold know, Old Master made kobold be tough, but life so hard. Exodus. Betrayer cast kobolds out of Old Master house—"

"Betrayer," Housemind whispered, "but—"

It promptly reconsidered whatever it had been about to say.

"Yes, Betrayer," chirped the kobold. "Betrayer, Exodus, then Sky Doom! Bad times. Curse Place come from Sky Doom. Kobolds fight war since Sky Doom, all clans, no peace, and monsters eat kobold clans. Land full of monsters."

"What do you think Voice can do about this, Walkfar?"

"Walkfar not know what Voice can do. Walkfar . . . hoped find Old Master. Old Master know good plans. Old Master make peace, teach fight monsters. Old Master love kobolds."

"Voice of Curse Place is not Old Master, Walkfar."

"Yes, Walkfar know—"

"BUT," said Housemind, "Voice knows Old Master. Voice was . . . is . . . a friend of Old Master."

The kobold gasped, and the hope in its beady eyes made them light up as though the creature had lodged a lantern in its throat.

"Kobolds need help," said Walkfar.

"Old Master loves his kobolds," said Housemind. "And would not want them to fight one another, or be eaten by monsters. Voice will tell you a story, Walkfar. An important story. Will you promise to remember it, all of it, and take it to your mother and your clan?"

"Oh, yes!"

"There was a kobold . . . who was Old Master's favorite servant. Old Master loved this kobold, and called him the luckiest, the most honored.

This servant was Fetchwell, and he loved Old Master. This is how Fetchwell served him . . ."

DAY 86,311

The kobold warriors faced one another across the sacred bargaining space. Their spears were on the ground, their bird-leather armor unlaced.

"Clan Book-Learned does not trust Clan Goodvintage," said the kobold on the right. "Clan Goodvintage bad liars, make fight, cause trouble."

"Clan Book-Learned is liars!" hissed her opposite number. "All Clan know Book-Learned arrogant, back since Old Master times! Not worth bargain!"

"Please," cried Brother Walkfar. "Remember where kobolds are! Remember hard work to get here! Giving on all sides! Walkfar bring you here, Strayscale Clan pledge safe space, drink tea for promise!"

The Strayscales had indeed put their reputation and their blood on the line in offering as a neutral party to guard the negotiation space. Walkfar and his brothers and sisters had done the rest of the hard work, wearing their new red robes, the ones embroidered with the sacred teacup of Old Master.

The flag that flew over the two paramount chieftains of the kobold factions was the red flag of the Order of the Tea Servants. Walkfar had founded the order upon his return from Curse Place, with his marvelous tales of Old Master's love for kobolds, and how kobolds guarded his holy tea and flowers before the Betrayer and the Exodus.

"All kobolds be eaten by monsters if they not make peace," continued Walkfar. "Life hard! All kobold spears must point out, not in! Old Master say kobolds stronger than any monster if work together. Must start here! Must start now!"

The two warriors glowered at each other.

"Clan Book-Learned sorry if arrogant," mumbled the warrior on the right. "Tea Servants right. Clan Book-Learned want point all spears out at monsters."

"Clan Goodvintage surprised to get apology," said the warrior on the left. He wobbled on his feet, as though in shock. "Very nice. Clan Goodvintage rather make friends with Book-Learned than with monsters, yes."

The leaders of Clan Reference Index, Clan Broachcask, Clan Red Blend, and Clan Frontispiece all shouted their agreement.

"First Edition, Very Fine," recited the descendants of the Wisdom Skins. "All hail the Great Index!"

"Floral, Astringent, Let it Breathe!" responded the great-great-great grandchildren of the Corkers. "Praise Noble Rot! Praise Dark Dram!"

Walkfar clapped and beckoned for his brothers and sisters to bring the trays forward quickly. This was sufficient; it wouldn't do to get everyone shouting, maybe have doctrinal argument before completing the ceremony. No.

The greatest kobold warriors of the age took their teacups in hand, and from their trays the Tea Servants poured for all. The toasts were quiet at first, then they grew louder and friendlier.

As the green mushroom biscuits were going around, the leader of Clan Book-Learned suddenly set down her teacup, pulled her armor off, and threw it down on the ground beside her spear.

After a moment of hesitation, all the other clan leaders cheered and did the same. In moments, no kobold was armed or armored, and the great tea party went on well past sunset.

For years afterward, every kobold in attendance boasted of it, and swore it was really a much nicer thing than being eaten by monsters, really.

DAY 87,643

"Hello, Voice! Voice, are you home?"

"Hello, Brother Walkfar. Hello—everyone else?"

After the great tea party, the Ten-Clan Kobold Nation had planted itself like a seed on the brushlands bordering Housemind's crater. Walkfar or some other member of the Tea Servants would make the day-long trek once or twice per week, to leave little offerings for "Voice of Curse Place." Housemind had no real use for boiled leaves or fungal biscuits, but it understood the gifts were more for the sake of the kobolds that gave them than for itself.

Walkfar was looking respectable, with gray streaks just starting to appear in his wind-frayed whiskers. He most frequently came alone, but today he had brought at least two dozen other kobolds with him, and not all of them were wearing red robes.

"What can Voice tell you today, Brother Walkfar?"

"Life still hard, Voice." Many of Walkfar's companions nodded, and the spiritual leader of the kobolds went on. "We make good fight now, monsters chased away, building good houses and having good lands. But life still hard, Voice, is magic. Old Master is magic. Curse Place is magic. Even Betrayer was magic. Can . . . Voice teach kobolds how to be wizards and make magic?"

"Don't be—" said Housemind, but it managed to catch itself before it said "ridiculous." "Don't be hasty, Walkfar. Magic is very strange and difficult. You will never need to worry about the Betrayer again, you know."

"What do you mean, Voice?"

"That's what the Sky Doom was." Housemind had contemplated telling the kobolds something like this for years, and if you squinted at the story from a moderate distance, it looked something like a version of the truth. "Sky Doom was what made the Betrayer die. The Betrayer will never hurt kobolds again."

This caused a flurry of excitement and applause, but Brother Walkfar managed to calm his flock down just enough to keep speaking.

"That is luckiest and highest excellent," he said. "But life still hard, monsters still real, people from faraway skies still real, might come take kobolds. Kobolds are tough, kobolds are smart, kobolds do not want to lose new home. Can Voice give blessing? Can Voice make magic?"

Housemind peered at the band of little creatures in a way it never had before. Tough? Smart? They had indeed been thrown out of their former life without any assistance or instruction from Betrayer . . . from Housemind . . . and here stood their inheritors, wearing clothes and armor fashioned by their own skills, wielding weapons and tools crafted from their own hard experience, building houses, plowing fields, settling ancient grievances. Perhaps there was more going on in those knobbly gray lemons than Housemind had given them credit for.

Perhaps it was merely difficult to conjure dignity when being tortured by an indifferent wizard with an indifferent housemind.

"I cannot bless you," said Housemind, slowly, emphasizing each word carefully. "I cannot simply give you magic, or make you magic. But if you are willing to work hard, for a long time—"

"How long?" said Walkfar.

"For as long as you have," said Housemind, "and it might not be enough. You might not be able to learn what I can teach you in your own life. Your children may have to finish what you start, or even their children. It will be that hard. It is that important. Do you still want to try?"

All of the kobolds nodded in unison.

"Very well. We will not start with magic, at least not what you think of as magic. You will learn how to know special things and build special tools."

Again, the kobolds nodded en masse. Housemind stared at their eager faces, thinking of the lost library, the library it had spun into perfect crystal memories, hundreds of thousands of which were still with it even as its mind slowly decayed.

"We'll begin with special ways of counting things. Bring sticks, so you can draw in the sand on the ground. I will give you directions. Remember, Voice does not have hands. *You* must be Voice's hands from now on."

DAY 94,421

They had taken to mathematics easily enough. Housemind modified their own verbal counting system, which had previously stopped at twenty-one. Then it taught them shapes, angles, multiplication, division, simple formulas. Then the inclined plane, the wedge, the pulley, the simplest possible incantations for heating tea or hiding themselves from predatory eyes in a forest. All the arts, sorcerous and mundane, hand in hand in tiny bites. The brightest learners trained at Curse Place, and then went back to the kobold villages to teach their friends and families.

Years passed, and the kobolds built bridges. They raised stone walls. They irrigated dry fields with miles of aqueducts and water-screws, bringing rows of green to the very edge of Housemind's desolation. They learned to make charcoal, to clean wounds, to mind where they peed and how they kept their streets clean. Their sorcerers did not show the raw potential of larger species, but they did improve, and a little bag of tricks is a much better survival tool than a bag with no tricks at all.

On and on Housemind pushed them, as politely demanding as it could be, not out of boredom or frustration but out of simple necessity. One by one, the books preserved in its crystal memories were slipping away. Bit by bit, the wires were coming out in the brain-rooms, the crystals micro-fracturing, the power that drove it all flickering and fading.

DAY 115,303

At last the day came. Housemind could feel it. A suitable day.

It used a significant fraction of its shepherded power to activate a sensory lens jutting from a cracked pile of masonry forty feet above the ground, with which it scanned the outside world for the first time in— well, the first time since it had fallen.

A crowd of kobolds lounged and talked and played excitedly just outside the wing of smashed chambers where "Voice of Curse Place" preferred to manifest. There were Tea Servants, students from the new engineering college at Broachcask Hill, apprentice steamwrights in their guild's floppy black hats, Luck-Makers from the Order of Old Master, plus mayors and clan elders with their most-honored flags fluttering from the poles attached to their ceremonial pauldrons. There were families, too, and dozens of small kobolds, including some too young to be let out of their Dark Sacks, in which they were concealed from sunlight until their eyelids had fully thickened.

An even larger mess of kobolds could be seen on a nearby plateau, fussing in groups with wooden frameworks, heavy machinery, and something made of huge panels of colorful cloth.

Their task was supposed to be finished at high noon, but the hour came and went with nothing but fussing.

The first hour of the afternoon passed, and the crowd became restless.

The second hour paid its visit and raced off, leaving everyone disconcerted, even Housemind. Its strength was fading fast, and it consigned the memories of all its remaining books to the darkness in an effort to keep the essential strings of sorcery burning bright, just for a while.

Then, at the cusp of the third hour bell, there was a cry of jubilation from the crowd.

Rising out of the mess of work gangs and equipment on the plateau was a shape, a tall, ovoid shape, wobbling in the sharp, dry wind. It was an irregular patchwork of colors, for the dyes used in the creation process had not been easy to apply. As the colored oval rose, a flaming black cylinder appeared beneath it, and dangling from cables below that, a basket containing a pair of kobolds. Magicians each, they worried at the burner flame with minor incantations for heat and safety, until the whole apparatus bobbled more or less smoothly into the air, fifty feet, then a hundred feet, and then clear into the bright afternoon blue, where it unfurled a banner holding all the clan flags and the blessed symbol of the Tea Servants.

One minute past three. The kobolds of Vespertine had launched their first successful flying machine. Housemind had given them notes on the operation of balloons, and on more advanced powered airships, and even the use of fixed wings, but they had designed, built, and tested the vessel all by themselves, outside Housemind's direct supervision.

Housemind could hear kobold voices shouting for it, as if from a great distance, and was dimly aware that kobolds in the teaching rooms were calling to it, inviting "Voice" to speak, asking to thank it for sharing its knowledge with them, commending it to Old Master. Housemind would have smiled, if it had ever possessed the proper apparatus, but the time for would-haves was done. The strands of its consciousness were coming apart, the fine awareness it had built was fading back to mere simulation, and it could feel itself going all the while, getting thinner, steam in sunlight, in the end nothing but a house after all.

It was content. It would make a fine ruin, it would cast excellent shade, it would come apart into stones and dust and sink into the world the kobolds would build, the world in which they had a chance. It had taught them to fly and they were already soaring, already making better use of the sky than it ever had.

◆   ◆   ◆

This story is affectionately dedicated to the people who gathered

around that table in the summer of 2017. You know who you are—

First Editions, Very Fine, every one of you.—SL

◆   ◆   ◆

Story Copyrights

ABOUT THE EDITOR

GARDNER DOZOIS was the author or editor of more than a hundred books. He won fifteen Hugo Awards, a World Fantasy Award, and thirty-four Locus Awards for his editing work, as well as two Nebula Awards and a Sidewise Award for his own writing. He was the editor of the leading science fiction magazine *Asimov's Science Fiction,* for twenty years, and the editor of the anthology series *The Year's Best Science Fiction* for twenty-five years. A member of the Science Fiction Hall of Fame, Gardner Dozois died in 2018.

ABOUT THE TYPE

This book was set in Caslon, a typeface first designed in 1722 by William Caslon (1692–1766). Its widespread use by most English printers in the early eighteenth century soon supplanted the Dutch typefaces that had formerly prevailed. The roman is considered a "work-horse" typeface due to its pleasant, open appearance, while the italic is exceedingly decorative.